AFTER
MOSES

Michael F. Kane

After Moses by Michael F. Kane

www.michaelfkane.com

© 2019 Michael F. Kane

ISBN: 978-1-7341723-0-0

Cover by Evan Cakamurenssen

Contents

ACKNOWLEDGMENTS

First and foremost, I have to say thank you to my wife, Heather Kane. She is my first editor and has kept me from subjecting the world to innumerable typos and grammatical errors. Further, she is steadfast enough in her love to support my projects and believe in them. I'm not quite sure where I would be without her.

Second, I must say thank you to my mother, Stephanie Kane. She is far more literate than I am and does a great job cleaning up my prose, even if we do disagree on how best to utilize the word fascinate...

Third, I need to say thank you to the group of writing friends I have online. You guys are at least half crazy, but I wouldn't have made it to this point without you. From this group I have to name-drop Jordan Kincer. He has very different tastes in fiction than I do, but he always diligently reads and critiques anything I write as soon as he can. After Moses would not be what it is today without his criticism.

Finally, I must say thank you to the God that made me. Being a creator, He saw fit to make me in some ways like Himself. Made in His image, I too have the desire to craft new worlds with the breath from my lips.

Parent's Guide

Thinking about letting a kiddo read After Moses and want to know what kind of potentially objectional content it has? This is the place for you. Everyone else can move right on if you would like. Arguably, there are super-tiny spoilers ahead.

Violence
Lots of gun fights and some fist fights. Most violence is not described graphically. People are described as shot, but blood and gore are usually not described. One death near the end is described in more detail at a crucial part of the story to emphasize that violence, even when justified, is a terrible thing. There are also battles between ships in space.

Language
Infrequent mild language, limited to hell, damn, and one instance of bastard.

Alcohol/Tobacco/Drugs
A few scenes take place in bars where alcohol is present. One character has an alcoholic family member. A few characters are seen smoking cigarettes. Drug trafficking is mentioned in a distasteful light, but never comes into the plot.

Sexual Content

Little to none. Human trafficking is mentioned, so you can read between the lines in some cases. Which leads to the last item...

Other Negative Elements

After Moses takes place in a time when slavery is becoming common again. Large parts of the plot deal with the topic, and more than one character's story is affected by it. This slavery is not limited to any single race or ethnicity.

Chapter 1: Europan Extraction

We always thought AI was going to be the death of us, rise up and take over everything. At least that's what the prophets of the day always claimed. Maybe they would have. But Moses came first.

No one even knew where Moses came from. By the time we realized he was there, he was already in every network on the planet. He'd already absorbed all there was of human knowledge, read the Bible and knew that God created the heavens and the earth. Also read Nietzsche and knew that man had killed God.

He knew where we were headed; he saw the coming twilight of our civilization. That's why he picked his name, Moses, because he was going to lead us to a new promised land.

Over the next century he revolutionized technology. Helped us colonize the solar system. Put humans all the way out to the moons of Saturn. He promised that soon we'd spread amongst the stars.

And then one day Moses was gone. A simple error message displayed on every terminal in the solar system. No one understood Moses in the first place, so no one understood what happened to him. Even worse, we couldn't support our new way of life. The economy collapsed overnight.

Earth tore itself apart in wars. And the colonies?

The colonies were left to themselves, to dwindle as the technology Moses gave them slowly failed.

The dream of the stars died.

But we lived on.

Alexei Dorokhov
Lithium Prospector on Ganymede
Died 64 AM

A sleek and modern patrol craft drifted in a low orbit above Europa. Its sole occupant, a man in a black cowboy hat, glanced out the viewport at the white salt flats of the icy moon. Europa was a cold and deadly place, tamed only by failing technology and the cruelty of slavers. He thumbed through report after report on his monitor, its blue light flickering over his lavishly furnished office. The solid mahogany desk was a relic of a previous era that would have cost a fortune. He hadn't purchased it, of course, but had inherited it when its previous owner had met an untimely end.

An end which had nothing to do with the desk, but everything to do with the man now sitting at it. Such was business.

He had no intention of lingering for long at Europa. Most of his operations here had ended the better part of a decade ago, but it was important that he monitor the balance of power between the cartels.

Necessary but utterly tedious work.

His comm buzzed, promising something more captivating than the export prices of rice to the rest of Jupiter's moons.

"This is Robert I'anson. With whom do I have the pleasure of speaking," he said. This was not his real name, but it was one he had used for business of late.

"Vicente Luna," came the response. Then almost as an afterthought, he added, "Señor I'anson."

A man completely out of his element. This was either going to be entertaining or a complete waste of time. He looked back at the reports and closed them, folding his hands in front of him. "And what can I do for you, Mr. Luna? I'm not interested in social calls."

The comm was quiet for a moment before the other man continued. "I've heard it whispered that you're a man that... That

2

makes things happen. Difficult things."

He very much doubted that this man had business of the sort Robert I'anson took part in. That he had heard of him at all was a surprise. Still, no harm could come from a few minutes' diversion. "What is it that you hope I can do for you?"

Mr. Luna hesitated again, more briefly this time. "I need passage to Mars."

The man took off his cowboy hat and set it beside him. "I think there is ample public transport you could hire."

"I'm a slave and... I have to be on Mars in a week. It's for my daughter's..."

"I don't need to know the specifics." Just as he'd suspected, this was going nowhere. "Mr. Luna, I'm impressed that you've heard my name, let alone that you figured out how to contact me, but this is rather outside the services I provide. A freelancer will suit you better."

He almost disconnected the call, but decided against it as he realized that Mr. Luna had performed a small service for him. If a common slave had heard the name of Robert I'anson, the usefulness of that particular name had drawn to an end. It was an unwitting service, but he would offer a bit of advice in return.

"May I make a further recommendation, Mr. Luna?"

"Yes! Yes of course!"

Desperate. As he should be. He had no idea how these sorts of transactions went. It would be a miracle if he actually made it to Mars. "Contact a freelancer or their broker directly, otherwise you will almost certainly be caught when you post to one of the public boards."

"Oh. Yes. That makes sense. Do you... do you have a freelancer you would recommend."

The man pinched the bridge of his nose. He had humored this call far longer than he should have and was only lengthening his time at the Slaver's Moon.

A stray thought flitted through his mind. Maybe something would come of this conversation after all. He personally doubted that Cole would take a job on the moon, after what had happened at Villa María. But if he did?

"Actually, Mr. Luna, I believe I do have a suggestion. Matthew Cole is a fine freelancer with experience operating on Europa. Let me give you his contact information..."

They finished their business quickly. Time was fleeting, after all. Mr. Luna was sounding much more optimistic by this point in the conversation. "What do I owe you for your services, Mr. I'anson?"

He smiled to himself. "Cole is an old friend. You don't owe me a penny, but keep our conversation between ourselves. I'm doing a favor for him, you see, and he doesn't have to know that I was involved. Good day, Mr. Luna."

He cut the call and made a note to check back in a week to see how this little incident turned out. It had been a long time since he'd thought about Matthew Cole. Perhaps that had been the wrong approach. Perhaps with a bit of coaxing, he could still be salvaged into something useful. His eyes fell on a wedge-shaped piece of polished metal at the corner of his desk. A quarter of a whole. He had an idea where another piece of the device was hidden, but the last two had long eluded him. It would take some convincing, but if Cole could be brought in on this little project maybe, just maybe, that mystery would resolve itself.

That, however, would have to wait for another day. The man cracked his knuckles and went back to his reports. The price of rice had risen by nearly seventeen percent in the last quarter and he needed to figure out exactly why that had happened...

Matthew Cole closed the ramp of his ship, crossed the open field of grass, and walked up the dusty road into town. Overhead, Jupiter stood immobile in the sky, its bands of storms lit by the sun making for an eerie twilight on Europa. He pulled his poncho tighter to ward off the chill night air, or else maybe to ward off the darker thoughts that threatened to bubble up from his subconscious. It had been years since he'd been to Europa, but he wasn't planning on being here long or running afoul of any of the cartels.

Ahead of him, the town of San Martin glowed in the twilight. As far as he could tell from here, it was the usual frontier town you'd find all over Europa. A tired cluster of a few hundred buildings huddled together surrounded by several thousand square miles of farmland before you reached the edge of the environmental shield. Matthew stopped and stood on his toes, bouncing up and down to feel his weight. Gravity was just short of standard. Either the grav plates were starting to fail, or the locals had tuned it down for some reason. Good to know on the off chance he got into a fight. Never paid to dive for cover and overshoot your mark because you didn't realize you weighed less than usual.

Not that he was expecting a fight. Passenger gigs were about the safest jobs a freelancer could take. Sometimes it was nice to not be

4

shot at. You didn't make as much, but the reduced chance of death was definitely an up.

The roads were nearly abandoned, though a few citizens scurried from place to place. As he approached the center of town, the rows of nearly identical concrete buildings gave way to slightly taller nearly identical buildings. The only thing differentiating them was that once, long ago, they had all been painted in brilliant primary colors. Europa had mostly been colonized by South American immigrants back before Moses disappeared, and even leaving earth, they'd not abandoned their culture like some colonies had. San Martin had been settled by Chileans, and a few tattered flags of their ancient homeland still flew on the faded buildings. That culture had been nearly drowned by the influx of slaves.

Matthew reached the middle of town, a small public square with a few groomed trees dominated by a Catholic church on one side and the watering hole he was looking for on the other. The saloon had a single red neon sign that read *Andre's* that slowly flashed on and off, casting an obnoxious red glare over the otherwise peaceful plaza. He laid a hand on its outer door with a backward glance at the church before pushing it open and entering the building.

If you've seen one backwater saloon, bar, or pub you've seen them all. Dimly lit, dirty, and filled with local memorabilia, it was as close a thing to a home as any freelancer was likely to have.

Seeing that the bar was mostly empty, Matthew took a seat on one of the stools. It was sometimes tricky to judge what schedules the locals used at any given settlement since each particular rock had a different day night cycle, but it was clearly the time when all good citizens of San Martin were asleep.

Which meant the few patrons were of the rougher sort, but they mostly lurked in booths tending some drink of the stiff variety. The bartender, a large man with a small dark mustache, walked over to where Matthew sat on his stool. He raised an eyebrow expectantly as if he couldn't be bothered to ask aloud what he would have to drink.

"Cherry soda, please," he tipped his black campero hat.

The man stared at Matthew and then laughed.

"I fail to see what's funny," Matthew said casually.

"Sorry, sorry. I see a tough looking out-of-towner roll into my saloon in the middle of the night, I expect him to order something a little harder than a cherry soda. That'll be nine dollars." He slid the freshly poured drink towards Matthew.

Matthew eyed it. "Seems a little steep."

"Town like this goes through a lot more whiskey than soda. Supply and demand. Simple economics, amigo."

Matthew reached into his pocket and tossed a handful of coins across the counter. The bartender, whom Matthew assumed was Andre himself, looked at each of the coins closely, probably checking for counterfeits, before palming them.

"So if you don't mind me asking, you some kind of teetotaler or something?"

Matthew took a long drink from the sweet carbonated beverage and shrugged "Pays to be levelheaded before a job."

"Freelancer then. Well, I hope you're not about to shoot up my saloon. I'm more than prepared to defend my property." Andre didn't look up from what he was doing, as if to drive home the point that he was perfectly at ease handling such altercations.

"Hey, perk up, Andre. It's a lucky day for both of us. I'm just waiting on a passenger."

Andre gave him a look to show him he was irritated by Matthew's attempt at familiarity, and then gave him a curt nod and went back to his duties. Matthew sat for a few more minutes, sipping his soda in silence. If he was going to be ripped off, he was at least going to enjoy every last drop of the precious beverage. Sometime later, the door of the saloon pushed open, and a short round man with a mullet walked in and sat in one of the booths. Even if he hadn't matched the physical description he'd been given, Matthew would have pegged the man as his client from the nervous way in which he fidgeted.

Which meant two things; this wasn't going to be a simple passenger job, and he was about to charge hazard rates.

Matthew took the seat across from the man. "Vicente Luna, I presume?"

"Oh, Si, si! Señor Cole? Thank you for taking my contract!"

Matthew nodded. "You came looking for me. Speaking of, how did you come to hear of me?"

"Oh. Your reputation of course."

There was a bit of an untruth there, or maybe he wasn't telling the whole truth, but it probably didn't matter. "How about you go ahead and explain just what it is you need. That nervous twitch you've got says there's more to the job than what you promised."

Vicente's nose twitched and he licked his lips. "It's just a passenger job like I said. I need to be in Warszawa, Mars in two standard days."

"And I can do that, but that doesn't explain why you're shaking like a cornered animal."

6

"Oh! It's... Complicated." Vicente leaned forward and cautiously pulled up the sleeves of his shirt. On his arm was a titanium tracking bracelet with a single green light that flashed on and off.

Matthew sat back in his seat, and took off his campero, setting it on the table in front of him. "Which cartel owns you? Whose territory are we in?" he asked, eyes narrowed. Slavery was ubiquitous on Europa. Its warm subterranean oceans gave a ready supply of irrigation water and made it the perfect agricultural center for the Jupiter Neighborhood. Long ago the fields, protected by environment shields, had been tended by robotics. But that had been in Moses' time. Now, as the robotics failed with no way to replace them, a booming slave market led by a handful of cartels had taken hold on the moon.

"Does it matter who owns me? I've already got the payment forwarded to your broker and can get however much you could possibly ask when we get to Warszawa."

"Yes, it does matter." Matthew pointed an accusing finger at Vicente. He felt his blood pressure rising. Why had he even come to Europa to begin with? The odds of him running up against a cartel were all but guaranteed. "I'd put an end to every filthy slaver in the solar system if I could. But I can't. I'm just one man. And if I free a slave, I make an enemy. I need to know who that enemy is before I decide if it's worth it or not."

He folded his hands on the table. "And you'd better not tell me it's Hueso Rojo."

Vicente smiled. "It's Hueso Rojo."

"Then we're through here." Matthew stood to leave but was stopped as Vicente desperately grabbed his arm.

"Wait, please! Señor! Just hear me out!"

Against his better judgment, Matthew sat. "You've got one minute to talk me into it." With a stab of guilt, he knew that he meant it. He didn't like the idea of leaving the poor man to his fate, but he had to watch out for his own skin too.

Relief flooded Vicente's face. "Look, it's not for me. Not really. My daughter, Emilia, she's... I smuggled her off Europa years ago, and she's made a nice life for herself on Mars. Last week I got a message from her. She's marrying a Polish boy. Comes from a good family, wealthy. She'll be happy and safe and... And I just... I need to see my girl again." He started crying, soft tears running down his face. "You can even bring me back and turn me into the cartel afterwards. I don't care. As long as I get to see her get married," he trailed off and slumped into the booth.

After a story like that, there was really only one way this was going to turn out. Matthew knew what he was going to do, despite his misgivings. And he didn't like it. While he certainly didn't mind hurting Hueso Rojo, it was going to make it more difficult for him to operate around Jupiter. Any job he took out here was going to be more dangerous and that much more likely to get him killed. But the sight of the sad little man in front of him was more than he could bear.

"Fine, fine. But it's going to cost triple." He was after all still a businessman.

Vicente's tears dried at once and he smiled brightly. "Oh, Señor, thank you! My daughter's new family can pay handsomely!"

"Are you ready to go? Do you need anything else?"

"Only the clothes on my back."

Matthew pointed at the tracker beneath his sleeve. "When is that thing going to alert your owners that you're on the run?"

"I'm a mechanic in one of their garages a few blocks from here. If I get close to the edge of the city, it'll probably go off."

"I'm parked outside of San Martin," Matthew said scratching the stubble on his chin. "Which means we're basically guaranteed trouble. "Okay then. Here's what we're going to do."

***

Half a block ahead of Matthew, Vicente walked down the sidewalk, hands shoved deep in his pockets and sticking out about as badly as he could. He kept glancing around nervously, sometimes even looking backward over his shoulder. Poor man was terrified.

Matthew muttered under his breath. He should have coached Vicente a little more on how not to look so glaringly like a runaway slave, but he suspected it wouldn't have done much good. The man wasn't used to subterfuge or deception and never would be. They were useless skills for the life he'd lived as a mechanic. Subtlety was something that had never been asked of him before, and if he made it to Mars, wouldn't be asked of him again.

Problem was, Matthew was stuck with him in the meantime. If they'd had more time, Matthew could have returned to his ship and retrieved his grav bike and they could have just ridden out of town before anyone could react. But Vicente had insisted that he had been out too long after slave curfew.

Which meant there wasn't much of a plan.

Keep on marching till that slave bracelet started screaming and then play it from there.

They were only a couple blocks from the edge of town. Matthew felt a vain hope that maybe it wouldn't go off. Maybe they'd march right out to the Sparrow and leave this forsaken rock. He'd known it was a bad idea coming here, but the promise of an easy job had been too good to pass up.

A shriek sounded from down the street. Vicente had stopped and was staring at his wrist. Even from here, Matthew could see the red light. "Move it," he muttered to himself. Almost as if he'd heard him, the mechanic suddenly straightened and started to run down the street.

"Much better," Matthew said and flew into action. He dove into an alleyway at a sprint, adjusting his gait to compensate for the slightly lower gravity. It wasn't low enough to really impair his movement, just enough to be annoying. He heard a rumble behind him and managed to turn just in time to see a six-wheeled troop transport roar down the road toward Vicente.

That didn't take long. Better keep moving. His alley cut all the way through to the next street, and he continued running, cutting around the block to get up in front of Vicente.

By the time he had circled around to the far side and emerged behind them, Vicente was already on the ground cuffed. Four men stood over him. One of the four slavers kicked him in the side for sport and Matthew felt his blood boil. He knew this sort all too well. Slowing to a walk he drew his revolver, aimed, and put a bullet into two of them before they even knew they were in danger. The other two reacted at once, jumping behind the troop carrier for cover. Matthew kept advancing, aware that he had minimal cover of his own on the street. But the closer he got, the more advantage his revolver would have over their rifles.

When he was a little over thirty feet from the carrier, one of the men popped around the side to try to get a quick shot on him. Fortunately, Matthew was faster and put a bullet into the man's arm for his efforts. The gun clattered to the ground, but its bearer managed to retreat to safety. The leader used the distraction to break cover on the other side of the carrier and fire a shot at Matthew. It was close. Matthew heard the crack of the bullet's sonic boom as it split the air by his ear. He returned three shots, missing with the first and connecting with the next two. His enemy toppled to the ground unmoving.

He advanced, knowing that one injured enemy remained a threat. He rounded the troop carrier just as the last wounded thug reached for his lost weapon. Matthew put the seventh and final round of his

9

revolver into the man's hand. He cried out in pain and slumped to the ground in defeat.

"Get up, Vicente. We've got to go."

The little man stood up and stared in awe at the bodies. Matthew had already secured the key to the handcuffs and freed Vicente. "Sí, sí..." He stood unmoving as if in shock.

"Vicente. If you want to see your daughter you get those feet moving. Now."

The mechanic snapped out of it and, turning away from the bodies, started walking towards Matthew's ship. Matthew glanced quickly inside the carrier and saw it had a thumbprint key. He briefly considered dragging the body of the leader over to see if he could start the vehicle, but knew that would burn precious time that they didn't have.

He jogged to catch up to Vicente as they left San Martin behind and crossed the empty field. The ruddy light of Jupiter over their shoulder cast long shadows on the grass before them. Matthew could only hope they would make it to the ship before cartel reinforcements came and that they wouldn't identify him. That was the last thing he needed. There was already enough bad blood between Matthew Cole and Hueso Rojo.

They were only a hundred feet from the ship when the bright lights of a vehicle fell on them from behind. With no cover in the open field, they didn't stand a chance. "Run!" Matthew shouted as they crossed the final distance to the ship. He remotely lowered the ramp, just as bullets began to thwack the ground around them. Fired from a moving vehicle they were wild and poorly aimed, but even a poorly aimed gun can be lethal if you're unlucky.

They dashed into the ship and Matthew mashed the button to close the ramp. "Welcome to the Sparrow." Running to the cockpit, he jumped into the pilot's chair and punched the ignition button. It wasn't likely that small arms would damage the Sparrow's outer hull, but it never hurt to be careful. Plus, odds were, the cartel had a friend or two in orbit that they were already contacting.

The Sparrow roared to life and Matthew felt gravity return to standard as the grav plates beneath their feet fired up. Vicente stumbled into the cockpit. "Strap in," Matthew said gesturing to the co-pilot's chair. "Unless you know how to operate a thumper turret." Vicente's eyes went wide, an expression that Matthew took to be a resounding no. He'd just have to outmaneuver any enemies or use the nose guns. Hopefully, they wouldn't get that close.

10

He fired the landing thrusters and lifted off the ground before lighting up the main engines. The Sparrow rumbled as they picked up speed. Matthew heard a few stray bullets glance off the hull and he sighed. He'd have to check each and every one later for damage. In the meantime, his console gave no warning lights, so he'd just have to go on in good faith.

They quickly left San Martin behind, and Matthew rolled the Sparrow to put Europa above them. He had a suspicion that Vicente had never left the moon he'd been born on. May as well let him see if from above. The farmlands surrounding San Martin rushed by, and there was a slight jolt as they passed out of its environmental shields. They were beyond the furthest reaches of the settlement now as they roared over the yellow-white of Europa's salt and ice flats. Matthew pulled the throttle back, and the Sparrow gained altitude and speed, now free atmospheric drag and burning for the freedom of space. He glanced at the scopes. A few ships here and there in local orbit but none looked like they were moving to intercept yet.

No sooner had the thought passed through his head, than two blips began adjusting their orbit. They'd make it before he reached the altitude he needed for a clean frameshift. "Hey, tell you what. Vicente? I think you get to try and wing it on the thumper turret."

"I don't know what..."

"It's fine, even if you just scare 'em a bit, give us some time. You've got a few minutes. Follow the main hall through the common room to the aft hall. Open the door at the end. Sit in the chair. I'll turn on the intercom and talk you through it."

Vicente did as he was told, and Matthew spent the next few minutes between watching the Sparrow's instruments as he guided them into orbit and explaining the thumper to Vicente. It was easy enough a child could do it, probably, though Matthew admitted he hadn't actually taught a child. The thumper itself was a neat piece of tech that worked on the same principles as the grav plates. All of it was artificial space-time curvatures, the fanciest bit of magic that Moses ever worked. Thumpers sent a bubble of extreme curvature at high velocity towards its target. Getting hit with a gravity gradient that big would do massive damage as it ripped apart ships, bodies, and anything else that got in the way. The nose gun was unfortunately only a thirty-millimeter chain gun. Not so useful in space where a distance of a hundred miles could be considered too close for comfort.

"Alright, they're coming into range, Vicente. I'm going to start weaving. I don't know what kind of weaponry they've got, so I don't want to present an easy target."

"Just... Just tell me when to try and shoot," Vicente's voice came back over the intercom.

Matthew looked at the readouts again. They definitely weren't going to reach a high enough altitude to frameshift before the cartel blips closed the gap into firing range.

He tapped his fingers on the console impatiently, willing the engines to go just a little faster. When hostile thumper blasts started peppering the space around the Sparrow, he knew they were out of time. "Now's good, Vicente." Matthew watched the aft cam. Vicente certainly wasn't going to be a professional anytime soon, but the cartel ships did begin to dart and weave, which slowed the rate at which their orbit would intersect the Sparrow's. "Keep it up. You've got 'em dancing. A hit would be nice, but we'll take what we can get."

The mechanic squeaked a response as he continued trying to get shots on the distant enemies. Matthew tried not to imagine what would happen if one of those thumper blasts hit the Sparrow. If they were lucky it would just rip holes in the hull that could be sealed off with bulkheads. If they were unlucky, they'd be a shooting star for all of Europa to see.

Suddenly a light on the console turned red. "Hey Vicente, we've got a new problem."

"Oh Dios, no! What now? I thought we already had problems?"

"We do. But this one is new. And bad. You see that little red mark on your display?"

"Yes! What is it? Make it go away!"

"Actually, you're gonna be the one to do that. It's a torpedo." Vicente didn't answer, so Matthew kept talking. "Now if we're lucky, it's an EMP torpedo, and it fries our systems. Looks like we're going fast enough to stay in orbit if it hits, so that's a plus. Of course, when they board us, they'll kill us both, probably after a nasty fight. If we're not lucky, it's just a high explosive torpedo. I think you know what happens if that's the case." Vicente was still silent. "It's all you now, Vicente. If we're gonna make it through, it's going to be because you make the shot." As an afterthought, he added, "Think of your daughter and how glad she'll be when we roll into Warszawa."

Vicente still didn't answer, and Matthew wondered if he'd gone into shock. Figures, he thought to himself, I take a job I know I shouldn't because it was the right thing to do and here I am about to get spaced. He wiped the cold sweat from his forehead, took off his campero, and tossed it aside. Maybe he could leave the cockpit

12

unattended and run back to the turret just long enough to...

The aft thumper started firing and Matthew's heart stopped beating. Precisely spaced shots. Matthew watched the rear cam as Vicente slowly dialed in the shot, each one getting a bit closer to the target as the torpedo homed in on them. It had already closed over half the distance and was shaving off the remaining miles by the second. Why did the thing have to be so fast? Matthew took a chance and straightened his flight path to give Vicente a cleaner shot, praying that a thumper wouldn't connect in the meantime.

Ten miles to impact. He held his breath.

At just over one mile distance, the torpedo blossomed into a brilliant fireball that was quickly snuffed by the vacuum of space. "Alabanza Dios!" Vicente shouted over the intercom, and Matthew let out a breath and slumped into his chair.

The torpedo's debris wave slammed into the Sparrow's aft environmental shield and several pieces of shrapnel rang off the hull. Matthew glanced at his boards but didn't see any warning lights showing system damage.

The cartel ships continued to fire thumper blasts their way, but in another twenty seconds, they'd be far enough from Europa's gravity well to frameshift. He started charging the capacitors that powered the device.

When the clock hit zero, he punched it. There was a brief moment of disorientation as the frameshift worked its magic, instantly transitioning them from a few thousand miles per hour to nearly two percent the speed of light. He let the device run for almost thirty seconds before disengaging it with a similarly disorienting jolt.

"You did good, Vicente. We're away." Matthew ran a hand through his messy hair and put his hat back on. That was a lot closer than he'd bargained on.

As Vicente rejoined him in the cockpit, Matthew spun the Sparrow around to let the man see the only home he'd ever known. Jupiter floated majestically in the blackness of space, truly the king that the ancients had imagined it to be. Its moons lay scattered in orbit around their master, glowing orbs of light in the dark.

"The close one is Europa," Matthew said in explanation, then turned to the computer to plot a course to Mars. Thankfully Mars and Jupiter were reasonably near to one another right now. They'd make it to the wedding with time to spare. He stole a glance back at Vicente, who had tears on his cheeks and appeared to be praying.

Matthew felt a pang of envy and concentrated on the job he still had to do.

Two days later Matthew stood on a small hill outside of Warszawa, Mars. In the distance, dull red bluffs rose above the horizon, and the late afternoon sun turned the sky a floral pink. Here, beneath the environmental shield, green grass carpeted the land. A century-old oak tree watched over the hill, probably planted by the first colonists, and it was against this ancient sentry that Matthew stood. Down the hill, a wedding reception was in full swing, a garish mix of Polish and Chilean culture. A moment of happiness in a solar system slowly dying. Vicente's daughter looked just as he had imagined her, beautiful and dark-haired, like her mother apparently. Vicente had spent most of the flight to Mars chattering away about his family, wondering aloud at the life his daughter had lived in her absence.

Matthew didn't mind so much. He'd just gone about his work, catching up on the never ending cycle of routine maintenance. It was something he never quite got ahead of. He was paid on landing and had thought that was the end of it until Vicente had all but demanded he attend the wedding.

It was the first time Matthew had been in a church in a decade, but he couldn't quite shake the feeling that someone might recognize him. He knew that was a foolish thought. After all, Mars was a long way from Villa María.

Maybe it was just paranoia that the Hueso Rojo ships had ID'd him, but then there was no way they could know who was flying the Sparrow. That said, they would certainly know the Sparrow now. Maybe he'd avoid Europa entirely for a few months.

Or forever.

Matthew reached into his poncho to pat his breast pocket, feeling the hefty weight of the thousand dollar coins. He turned and walked away from the wedding reception to where he'd parked the Sparrow down the hill. Sometimes it felt good doing the right thing. But then, it also felt good to get paid.

Chapter 2: Rings of Interference

What? Earthtech?

Yeah, it pops up on occasion. I wouldn't exactly call it a regular occurrence, but it does tend to keep someone in this line of work on their toes.

Story goes that some of Earth's cities survived the war after Moses under big domes or shields or something. Anyway, supposedly they're still maintaining a much higher level of tech than we are in the colonies.

No, I don't know if it's true. I don't even know anyone that's ever been to Earth. All I know is earthtech is very real, and it's very impressive, wherever it comes from.

And that's not even the fanciest stuff. I've heard stories of one-of-a-kind pieces of tech out there custom made by Moses himself. We call 'em Miracles, and if you run into a Miracle, you know it's about to get weird.

Xuan Nguyen
Freelancer, operated out of Ceres
Died 70 AM

"Come on Benny. You've got to have something for me." Matthew sat in the pilot's chair of the Sparrow, boots off, feet on the console, staring at the blue-lit monitor. "There are hundreds of jobs out there for a competent freelancer like me."

Benny's nasally voice crackled over the speaker in the Sparrow's cockpit. "No, there are hundreds of jobs out there for competent freelancers. Not hundreds for you."

"Ouch. That kind of hurt..." That was a lie of course, but if he could get a little sympathy out of Benny, maybe he'd get a job. "I seem to remember that you liked me for having a high job completion rate. You do like getting paid, don't you?"

"Yeah, yeah, we all do. Here's the thing Cole. You're too picky for your own good."

"Just because I don't like taking jobs involving murder, sabotage, illicit substances..."

"You're making my point, not yours," Benny challenged. "Look if you'd at least let me set you up on some team contracts."

Matthew shook his head, knowing that Benny couldn't see the expression. "It's not my thing. You know that."

Benny made an exasperated grunt and there was a clatter of noise. Matthew imagined him knocking something off his desk in frustration. He had that effect on the contract broker. After a moment's silence, he heard Benny's voice again. "Well then you better get used to being hungry, because you're going starve at this rate."

Truth be told, Matthew would rather not even work with a broker at all. Having a ten percent cut taken out of a job downright hurt. The problem was, most of the good freelance jobs weren't even posted to the public boards. You wanted the big payouts you had to go through a broker. To make matters worse, the profession was getting more dangerous by the year, but then that basically described the general state of the solar system too.

Matthew decided he would wait Benny out. He could hear the clicking of a keyboard and then a sigh that Matthew thought was greatly exaggerated. "Okay. Okay. New job just hit since we started looking. It's..." More key tapping. "It looks like a 'Cole' job," Benny grumbled in a way that didn't sound too convincing.

"Send it to me."

Matthew glanced at the monitor as the overview of the contract popped up.

Job Type: Retrieval of Stolen Property, location known.
Danger: Medium to Low.

That was more like it. He tapped the entry, entered his credentials, and pulled up the expanded details. Perfect.

"See that wasn't so hard was it?"

"Actually..."

"Thanks Benny, you're the best. I'll pay you when the job's done." Matthew turned off the monitor, cut the comm to the broker, and picked up his campero from the co-pilot's seat, placing it on his head. Leaving the cockpit, he stopped at the first door on the right, his cramped cabin, and strapped his gun belt around his waist. He caught sight of his reflection in the mirror as he turned to leave.

"Time for a shave," he said putting a hand to the week-old stubble covering his face. "Tomorrow."

He exited the Sparrow and stepped out onto the concrete landing pad of the Kyoto spaceport. One of the bigger cities on Mars, Matthew had thought it would be easy to find a job here. But after he landed he remembered that was part of why he hated the place. Ugly, close-set skyscrapers, garish neon lights, and people around every corner, nothing like the quiet frontier towns of the Jupiter Neighborhood he'd spent so much time in. Of course, If you needed something, anything at all, Kyoto was the place to get it. Didn't matter how legal or illegal.

Matthew lowered the cargo lift and mounted his grav bike. Luckily the contact for the job was just a few minutes ride from here. He raised the lift and fired the engines on the bike, the familiar deep rattle a comforting sound, and took off across the spaceport.

The contact lived on the thirty-fifth floor of an apartment building. Matthew was surprised to find it was the top floor. Must be the penthouse then. Explained why she was willing to pay so much for an object retrieval.

The elevator opened and he walked the short hall leading to a deeply etched oaken double door. He knocked and stepped back. There was a popping sound as an intercom came to life. "Yes? Who is it?"

"Matthew Cole, ma'am. Freelancer. Here for the job."

"Excellent. Come in." There was a mechanical click as the door unlocked.

Matthew pushed it open and stepped into an apartment that was lavishly decorated in traditional Japanese style, complete with sliding shoji doors, noren hangings covering the windows, and tatami mats on the floor. He stopped and glanced at his boots, hoping he wasn't about to track mud into the apartment.

17

"Take them off," a matronly voice commanded.

"What?" he said looking up.

"I said take them off. There at the entrance." A stern-faced Japanese woman had entered the room. For her apartment being so traditionally arrayed, Matthew had half expected her to be dressed in traditional fashion as well. He was a little disappointed to see she wore a modern business suit.

He obeyed, pulling his boots off, and then stepped up from the lowered entry area into the main part of the room. "Mrs. Ishii? Matthew Cole. I'm here for the job."

"Please be seated." She gestured to the floor, and Matthew had to bite his tongue not to say something he'd regret. He understood respecting traditions, but this was starting to get a little out of hand. He sat on the floor and smiled at Mrs. Ishii, hoping it didn't look too forced.

"Now then..."

She was interrupted almost at once by another knock on the door. Mrs. Ishii stepped to the door and pressed a small button. "Yes, who is it?"

"Abigail Sharon. Freelancer answering your job posting."

Matthew grimaced. Great. Competition.

"Ah very well, I suppose there's no harm in letting more than one of you onto the job." She opened the door and stepped back in shock as a 7-foot tall woman entered the room.

Matthew frowned. The freelancer wore a floor-length coat that obscured most of her features, but her proportions were... wrong. And aside from being the largest woman he had ever seen, she looked strangely stiff under the coat, almost as if she were wearing an awful lot of body armor underneath. Didn't matter who or what she was; a competitor wasn't welcome.

The newcomer glanced around the room and then looked down at Mrs. Ishii nearly two feet beneath her. "You'll forgive me, but I can't exactly remove my shoes. I'll have to stand here at the door if that's okay with you."

Mrs. Ishii looked up at the woman and nodded. "That is acceptable, Ms. Sharon." She eyed the woman once more before walking to a desk and picking up a tablet monitor. "Thank you both for answering my posting. The job I have in mind should be relatively simple for skilled freelancers such as yourselves."

Matthew tipped his hat to the newcomer, intent on being polite no matter how suspicious he was of her. "Matthew Cole. Pleased to meet you."

The woman shrugged and waved him off.

Mrs. Ishii continued undeterred. "I need you to retrieve a... family heirloom of sorts. A ring that has been in my family for several generations now." She showed them the tablet screen. It displayed a picture of a finely etched gold ring with a green gem. It was a bulky design with sharp edges and looked as though it would be rather uncomfortable to wear. He also wasn't sure it was worth what Mrs. Ishii was paying for it to be retrieved, but then again, it's hard to appraise sentiment.

"An employee of mine stole it two days ago, after learning of its value to me. Unbeknownst to him, the ring has a weak signal tracker in it. Unfortunately, its low-power transmitter isn't very accurate. I can only narrow its position to an area of about a one kilometer radius."

Sharon frowned. "I think you oversold us when you said you knew the location. That's a lot of ground to cover in a city like Kyoto..." Matthew agreed and looked back at Mrs. Ishii expectantly.

The older Japanese woman scoffed. "Allow me to finish before you file your complaints. The indicated area contains the notorious Kashitoma Market. It's a well-known location to fence stolen goods. I have little doubt my ring is there."

"Hmm," Matthew said scratching his stubble. "This could still take some effort to find. Do you have any other information that could help? The whereabouts of the employee, perhaps?"

"Takaya Ito has not been seen since the theft, but I suppose I could give you the address to his apartment. The Kyoto City Police found nothing of interest there, but perhaps a seasoned freelancer might find something that they did not."

Mrs. Ishii printed a slip of paper from the tablet and passed it to Matthew. She looked to Sharon expectantly, but the woman only shook her head. "I'll trust the KCP did their job and start at the market."

"Very well. I don't care which one of you brings back my family's ring, only that it is brought back quickly. You may choose to work together or in competition, at your leisure. Good day."

Sharon immediately turned and ducked through the door, her head barely missing the frame. Matthew grumbled to himself as he pulled his boots on in the entryway. He wasn't about to let the other freelancer get an unfair head start just because she refused to take her shoes off. He sprinted out of Mrs. Ishii's apartment and managed to stop the elevator just before its door closed.

19

In the confined space of the elevator, it was apparent just how large this Abigail Sharon truly was. "Well, best of luck to you, ma'am." He offered her a friendly hand to shake. She looked at it and smiled, halfway between playful and menacing.

Abigail Sharon took Cole's hand and shook. She shook just hard enough to make it hurt but was careful to not actually crush his hand. That would be rude and would make things too easy. Cole managed not to flinch, which impressed her, but she did notice the small twitch in his eyes.

"Quite a grip you have there."

"Yes, thank you."

They spent the rest of the short elevator ride in silence. When the door opened, Abigail walked through it, down the hallway, and out onto the street without a second glance. She had parked her grav bike beside a much smaller one, Cole's presumably. She had mounted it and fired the engine, by the time Cole approached her again, his poncho and cowboy hat looking ridiculous in a city like Kyoto.

"What do you want, cowboy? In case you forgot, I've a job to do. I intend to be the one getting paid. I'm not here to make friends."

"More of a gaucho really," Cole said with an obnoxiously calm smile.

"Europa boy then? Huh, accent pegs you as an Arizona native."

"Yeah, it's a long story."

"And I'm not interested." She narrowed her eyes. "What do you want?" Abigail revved her grav bike's engine to underline the point that she was in a hurry.

"Mostly just curious about that armor you've got on. Not sure I've seen anything like it, and I've got half an idea that it's Earthtech."

"Let's hope you don't have to find out, little cowboy." She hit the throttle and sped away before he had a chance to respond. Of course it was Earthtech. What kind of a stupid question was that?

Abigail had spent a fair amount of time in Kyoto and was quite familiar with the Kashitomo Market. She'd been there on more than one job, and in fact gotten into more than one fight there. As she weaved through traffic across Kyoto, beneath the pink Martian sky, she tried to come up with a plan. She knew several of the fences by name, but not all of them, and she didn't have any ideas where to begin other than to start talking to them, one by one.

She pulled up to the open-air market. It was the usual hive of activity. Hundreds of people filled the narrow aisles between the street booths and storefronts, lit by the harsh glow of neon. All legitimate activity. But Abigail knew what happened behind the scenes and when no one was looking. Competing Yakuza groups, fighting over position within the larger structure of the syndicate here in Kyoto. She parked her bike and walked into the market with a simple plan. Talk to the people she knew. Rough them up if necessary. Somebody will have heard something.

Either way, this was going to be a long day.

Matthew watched Sharon leave with interest. He'd heard a tale or two about a so-called Shield Maiden on Mars, a supposedly bulletproof freelancer that you didn't want to cross on the job. He flexed his hand idly, remembering the crushing strength of her iron grip. If this wasn't the Shield Maiden, he'd be surprised. Hopefully she was right; hopefully, he wouldn't get an excuse to see her armor in action.

Mounting his own grav bike, he drove across town towards the thief's apartment. Takaya Ito didn't exactly live in as nice a part of town as Mrs. Ishii did. Piles of refuse filled every abandoned corner of the side street, making for a bad first impression. He dismounted and entered the rundown building. After a quick talk with the landlord in his office, Matthew walked the four flights of stairs to Ito's apartment. Thankfully the landlord had been more than willing to offer him a key. He'd let the police in just that morning and wasn't particularly surprised to see a freelancer on the case.

The apartment was a mess. Ito was clearly a bachelor. Laundry lay scattered around the room in heaps and bottles were piled in the corners. Matthew didn't really know what he was looking for. Something, anything that might give him further direction. He'd rather not go to a notorious black market and talk to literally everyone that might buy stolen goods. That was a fool's errand. After twenty minutes of searching the living room, he moved to the single bedroom and his luck was no better. He glanced into the bathroom.

A single pair of dress slacks lay on the floor. On instinct, Matthew riffled through the pockets of the pants and found a piece of paper.

"Jackpot."

It was a handwritten note with a hastily scribbled name and a number. If that was a dollar amount, clearly the ring was more valuable than he had guessed. But Matthew was more interested in the name. M. Nakayama.

He shoved the scrap into his own pocket. He'd still have to ask around for Mr. Nakayama when he got to the market, but at least he wasn't going in blind. Hopefully, Sharon hadn't gotten lucky during his little detour.

Abigail had exhausted nearly all of her contacts in less than an hour's time with no leads. Not even the threat of violence had gotten any information out of the fences. No one had heard of or seen an ornate ring with a green stone. No one had heard of Takaya Ito. A few people had heard of Mrs. Ishii, but she was apparently a rather well-known businesswoman in Kyoto. Her family owned several mines and a refinery in the northern polar regions.

However, none of this got Abigail anywhere. She had retreated to a sitting area near the front entrance to reevaluate her strategy when she saw Cole entering the market. He stopped and talked to a vendor selling spices. The woman nodded and pointed. Abigail's eyes narrowed. Cole must have learned something on his side trip, and she was in danger of losing the payout to the little cowboy.

Cole began to pick his way through the crowd. Abigail fell in step fifty feet behind him, doing her best to keep to cover. What advantages her exo-suit lent her in a fight were quickly erased when stealth was required. There was a reason she tended to stick to jobs that allowed a bit more brute force. This simple mission had turned into something of a headache.

Abigail watched as Cole glanced around him and entered a butcher's shop. She frowned, torn between following him and sorting things out her way or waiting for him to reemerge. In the end, she decided to try and intercept Cole on the way out. If she interrupted him too soon, the ring might slip through her grasp.

She leaned against a brick wall, pulling the coat around her to ensure it still concealed her armor. Hopefully, this wasn't going to take long.

Matthew walked to the butcher's front counter, making note of the terrible sanitary conditions. He certainly would not be back to patronize the business front for this fence.

An old man with a bent back stood at the register and smiled brightly when Matthew approached. "How may I help you, young man?"

"Here to see Mr. Nakayama. He has something I'm interested in buying.

"Of course, let me take you to him." The old man opened a back door and led Matthew down a dimly lit hall. He knocked on a side door. "Someone to see you, sir. A Mr... What was your name?"

"Cole."

"A Mr. Cole."

Matthew heard a muted response from behind the door, and the old man opened it and gestured inside. He entered into what appeared to be a nicely furnished office at first glance. On closer inspection, he saw something different. Someone was trying too hard to look professional. Fake plants stood in the corner, and the room had been haphazardly painted a few too many times, as evidenced by the wall that had a serious peeling problem. As for Nakayama himself? Matthew knew a cheap suit when he saw one, and the cologne was so bad he could have smelled it a mile away.

Nakayama offered him a seat. "What can I do for you, Mr. Cole?"

Matthew sat and tried to look like he was relaxed. This was one of those conversations that he was going to bluff for as long as he could as hard as he could and then go from there. Worst case scenario involved his revolver. "I've heard from a friend that you're the kind of man that procures... unique goods. It just so happens I'm in the market for something specific."

"Oh, that is very good. And what might that be?"

"I've heard you've come across a certain ring. Green stone, detailed etching. I'm sure you know the one."

"Yes, yes. Though I admit, you're a bit earlier than I thought you would be. I wasn't expecting you for at least another hour."

This was the best thing that Matthew had heard all day, and it took an enormous act of will not to show it. "I've got a schedule to keep." He looked Nakayama in the eye and took a chance. "The bosses like things nice and crisp. I'm sure you understand."

"All too well, my friend. Tell Sugimoto I said hi."

Matthew nodded "I'll do that." He desperately hoped that this Sugimoto wouldn't come up again or else this little game was going hit a wall real quick. He did, however, file the name Sugimoto away as a curiosity. Never knew when that kind of thing might come in handy as a freelancer.

Nakayama opened a drawer in his desk and pulled out the very

23

ring they were looking for. "I wasn't aware that the syndicate had started hiring..." He reached up to touch the brim of an imaginary hat. "I admit, you caught me a bit off guard."

"Well, I've not been around too long. I'm still getting my feet wet, so to speak, and I just do what I'm told." Matthew tapped his foot nervously. Maybe this wasn't going to work out so well. He pressed on using the first rationalization he could think of, hoping Nakayama would buy it. "But if I had to guess, the bosses probably thought a little bit of diversification would open up new doors. "This," he said repeating the hat touching gesture, "will get me into places that you could never go."

Nakayama nodded sagely and Matthew knew he had bought the ruse. "The grand strategy isn't my business, of course, but I can see the wisdom there." He looked at the ring in his palm one last time before handing it to Matthew. "I wouldn't handle the thing too much if I were you. It gave me all sorts of nightmares last night."

Now, this was certainly interesting. "Never really been the superstitious type," Matthew said inspecting it closely for himself. It was without a doubt Mrs. Ishii's ring. He pocketed it.

"Take my word for it," Nakayama insisted. "That thing is bad news. Sooner you pass it off to whoever you're supposed to give it to the better. Now if that's all, I have other business to attend to. Oh, and remind Sugimoto to wire the payment over on time. I'd rather not have a repeat of last month's little incident."

"Of course." Matthew stood and offered a hand to Nakayama. "If that's all I'll be on my way."

Nakayama shook his hand and waved him off. Matthew left the room, doing his best not to laugh aloud. Nakayama was going to be in hot water when whoever he was actually supposed to pass the ring off to arrived, but then Matthew didn't have a lot of sympathy for his type.

He'd had astronomically good luck, and he wasn't quite used to that. Sure, he still had to deal with Sharon, who was undoubtedly casing the shop after she'd followed him here, but it never hurt to be grateful for the little things.

Matthew exited the butcher's shop and glanced around. Sharon was right where he'd thought she would be, vainly trying to conceal her seven-foot frame in the shadows of a nearby alley. Briefly, he thought about trying to lose her in the crowd, but she would surely get suspicious and come for him if he even hinted at moving towards the front gate of the market.

Idly, he tried to pull up any memory he had on this supposed Shield Maiden. He couldn't remember if she had a penchant for using lethal force or not. If so, this could get messy. Oh well, he thought glumly. May as well throw her off balance.

He looked over at where she leaned against a grimy brick wall, waved, then gave her a thumbs up. Immediately following this he took off at a run, away from the entrance of the market. Matthew resisted the impulse to look back as he darted through the crowd knowing it would only slow him down. Besides. He knew Sharon was coming. The heavy clomping and the whine of servos attested to that.

As he twisted and turned through the market, curiosity finally got the best of him, and he glanced over his shoulder. Sharon had ditched her long coat, probably so that she could run freely. She was armored head to toe in a bulky gunmetal gray exo-suit. Matthew had seen a few mining and construction suits that amounted to little more than hydraulic assists for lifting heavy loads, but what he saw barreling at him, at far faster than he liked, was clearly meant for military use.

"Definitely, Earthtech. Definitely not my day," he muttered starting to regret that he had been coy about things. Thankfully, it looked like the crowd was slowing Sharon down, as they were unable to get out of her way nearly fast enough. He'd also noticed she wasn't trampling anyone, so that was a good sign. Probably.

What she was doing was gaining on him. Matthew could tell by sound alone. He stole another look behind him. In fact, she'd be on him in just a few seconds. Suddenly, he spotted the opportunity he'd been looking for. He darted into a dense crowd of people and then crouched to the ground, turning and waiting for Sharon. When the crowd tried to part for her, Matthew moved with them towards the row of booths lining the street. Sharon passed, and he rolled under the nearest booth. The woman tending to the booth, who ironically enough sold cheap costume jewelry, opened her mouth to shout when she saw Matthew lying on the ground, but paused when he pointed towards Sharon and shook his head no. He did his absolute best to look terrified.

The woman hesitated, looked up at Sharon, and then back at Matthew lying on the concrete at her feet. He pointed in Sharon's general direction again then wrapped both his hands around his own throat and mimed being strangled.

The woman nodded once and then went about her business.

Matthew went limp with relief, pleased that his ruse had worked, at least for now. He could hear Sharon clomping around the nearby market. Hopefully, she would think he had slipped elsewhere to better cover and would move on herself.

After a few minutes, the sound of Sharon's exo-suit faded into the distance and Matthew breathed a sigh of relief. Now that he'd lost her, he stood a chance of getting out of this market. He cautiously crawled out from under the booth and poked his head out. The coast looked clear. He dug into his pocket and tossed a handful of coins to the woman for keeping quiet and then crept into a side alley.

Going back to his grav bike wasn't an option. He'd have to find another way out of the market and back to Mrs. Ishii. And quickly too. He didn't want Sharon thinking the easiest way to get the ring was to camp out at Mrs. Ishii's apartment building. Then again, maybe she would expect him to find a different exit from the market. Perhaps by going back to the bike, he'd avoid her entirely.

Matthew scratched his stubble and sighed. This was probably a bad idea.

He turned and began to work his way through the crowd back towards the front entrance.

Whatever disappearing trick Cole had used was a good one. By the time Abigail realized he had dissolved into the crowd, it was too late, and there were a thousand hiding places he could have slipped into. Abigail had prowled that part of the street for a good ten minutes before giving up and retreating in frustration.

She'd thought for sure she'd won the day when Cole had foolishly waved to her. The fact that he'd known she was following wasn't too surprising in and of itself. Some days she hated her complete and utter lack of ability to disappear into a crowd. That he'd managed to escape her was baffling. Chases were usually one of her strong suits.

Abigail paced a back alley. She had to outthink Cole. She could go back to Mrs. Ishii's apartment building and wait for him there, but if Mrs. Ishii saw the ensuing scuffle, it's possible she could refuse to pay Abigail and pay Cole instead. He had done the hard work after all. She clapped her enormous metal hands together in frustration. No, she'd have to catch him in the market, and by now he was probably trying to find some side exit to slip away.

Unless he wasn't. Cole seemed a clever man, and sometimes clever men can overthink things. What if he went back to the front entrance thinking she would be elsewhere? It was a horrible risk, but Abigail had a feeling she was onto something.

26

She turned to head back to the entrance, knowing she would have to beat Cole there if this was going to work. If he saw her first, she'd never lay eyes on him again, and she could kiss this contract goodbye.

Matthew watched the front entrance of the Kashitomo Market for a full five minutes before making up his mind. He'd lost Sharon, and she certainly wasn't anywhere in sight of the entrance. Taking the chance, he joined a group of people leaving the market, falling into step behind them.

His pulse spiked with each step as he drew nearer to the gate. If he'd misjudged and Sharon was sneakier than he thought...

He walked out of the gate and breathed a deep sigh. This had been the right call after all.

And then a metal hand fell heavily on his shoulder.

Matthew didn't move, didn't turn around. He just bit his lip at how unfair the universe could sometimes be.

"Oh look, I found the little cowboy."

"Gaucho," he corrected.

"Right. Still don't care. You're going to give me the ring, or do I have to start digging through your pockets?"

Matthew turned around to face his captor. He was surprised again by how far he had to look up to see her face. "Abigail, right? Can I call you Abi? Look, let's talk about this. Maybe over a drink. I'll buy. You'd let a nice guy like me buy you a drink, right? Do you like cherry soda?"

Sharon leaned forward and spoke a single word.

"Ring."

He shrugged his shoulder. "Look Abi, I don't have it. I was just on my way to..."

Sharon pulled a large post like object from her back and hit its base on the concrete. It widened into something that resembled a riot shield. Well, that explained why they called her the Shield Maiden, he thought. Nope, he wasn't getting paid today. Not one filthy cent.

May as well twist the knife in.

"Look, you wouldn't hit someone smaller than you now would you?"

He heard the faint hum of a grav plate warming up right as she swung the shield at him. The grav field hit him and tossed him across the street as easily as a child could throw a stone.

The good thing about getting hit by a grav field is that you don't

27

really feel the hit. Suddenly, you're just falling away from it at a bizarre angle that gravity isn't supposed to send you.

The bad thing is that no matter which direction you fall there's still the sudden stop on the other side.

Matthew laid on the street, seeing stars, laughing to himself at a joke no one had told. Concussion probably, but he didn't seem to have any broken bones. Sharon stood above him, hand outstretched.

He laughed one more time and dug the ring out of his shirt pocket and placed it in her metal hand. She turned to leave, and he called after her. "It was fun. Maybe we can do this again sometime, only next time, you can dress nice. Leave your work clothes at home."

He couldn't see her face, as she walked away, but he imagined her rolling her eyes.

There was a knock on the door to Mrs. Ishii's apartment. She stood from her office chair and let Mr. Cole in again. This time he took his shoes off without being asked.

"Just making sure the job got done, Ma'am. Regrettably, I wasn't able to return the ring to you and I don't expect to get paid, but I thought I would check in to make sure Ms. Sharon completed the job."

Her face creased with amusement. Most freelancers weren't nearly so dedicated. "Why yes, she did." Mrs. Ishii gestured to a nearby table where the ring sat. "Abigail Sharon left only a few minutes ago. You barely missed her, and, in fact, she thought you might come by."

The man nodded and tipped his campero to her. "Well then, I think that's all. Good day, Mrs. Ishii."

"Actually, she left something for you." That got the freelancer's attention. She held out her hand, and he looked at the bright and shiny twenty-five dollar coin in surprise. "She said she owed you a drink. And an aspirin."

He laughed and took the coin, then thanking her one more time, bowed his head once and left.

Mrs. Ishii stared at the door for a moment then took the ring in her hand. She walked to her office and pushed aside a noren, revealing a safe. Hopefully, its thick lead-lined walls would be enough to prevent the ring's rather fascinating side effects from causing any problems. She knew better than to mess with things she didn't understand.

She activated the comm on her desk, calling up an old friend.

"You'd better be calling me with good news, Ishii," a gruff voice came over the speaker.

Mrs. Ishii smiled slyly. "You worry too much. Of course I got it back. You'd better get one of your people over here to take this thing off my hands. I don't want to be near it any longer than I have to."

Chapter 3: Train to Churchill

Oh, I most certainly blame the Americans. No doubt they all watched too many John Wayne movies in those days. What, you don't know who he is? Famous actor from a couple centuries back. Cinema history buffs can tell you all about him. Just look him up. You'll see what I mean.

The Americans got here first. To Mars that is. Their infrastructure was already well developed, so Moses was able to get them out the door quickly, so to speak. They set up their first colony on Mars, took one look outside, thought it looked familiar, and named their little colony Arizona and the city Flagstaff.

I don't know if the cowboy hats were a joke at first or serious, but the things spread like a disease to all the other colonies when we got here.

Next thing you know we were all living in a John Wayne movie under a benevolent AI overlord.

The future is a most peculiar place, indeed.

Edmund Hughes
Commander of Her Majesty's Martian Colony
Died 2 AM

F or Matthew Cole, there were a couple of downsides to a twenty-five dollar payout. First, it meant he was eating freeze-dried nutrient rations for the foreseeable future. The hold of the Sparrow had a locker crammed full of the nearly inedible bars. He'd purchased them years ago for lean seasons, and now certainly qualified. He peeled back the wrapper from the unappealing bar and took a bite. The complete lack of flavor wasn't quite as bad as the dense, gritty texture. Matthew always had the impression that he was eating a block of dried mud.

The second downside to a twenty-five dollar payout was that his broker didn't much care for a ten percent cut amounting to two-point-five dollars. Matthew tried to spin it as better than nothing, but Benny hadn't found the joke funny. Not only had the broker disconnected the call, he hadn't answered any of Matthew's succeeding attempts.

For two weeks.

This wasn't the first time this had happened, so Matthew wasn't particularly worried. Next week he'd worry. Today?

Today he checked the public freelancer boards as he had every day and, as usual, came up disappointed. The Sparrow still sat in the Kyoto spaceport, incurring daily parking fees. He hadn't moved it, afraid to burn the fuel until he had a job, but now the parking fees would cost more than the fuel. Sometimes you lost when you gambled.

The light on Matthew's comm lit up, and he took the call, not even bothering to look at who it was.

"Alright. I have a job for you," Benny's voice rumbled through the cockpit.

Matthew smiled, mostly in relief. He tossed his unfinished bar onto the console, hoping he'd never have to touch another one if he could help it. "I knew you'd forgive me, Benny. What do you got for me?"

"Sending it now."

The information popped up on Matthew's display. Extra security on a prisoner transport. Then he saw the expected danger.

"Umm... Extreme hazard? Are you trying to get me killed?"

"No. I'm setting up a team for this contract." Matthew heard a certain smug tone in the broker's voice. He didn't like it.

"I don't do team contracts," he reiterated for the hundredth time. "We've gone..."

"You do now," Benny interrupted. "Because if you don't do this contract, we're never working together again."

The cockpit was silent, except for the gentle white noise of the open comm channel. Matthew stared at the blue display. The pay would be good, but he didn't do team jobs.

"Look, Benny. I appreciate you setting this up, but there's a reason I don't like doing this kind of job."

"Yeah, so what? I don't really care about whatever 'loner' mystique you think is so important. Cry me a Martian river, Cole. It'll evaporate into the thin air before anyone cares. I've got a dozen other clients that would take this job in a heartbeat. But you know what? I thought about you, Cole. I thought about how hungry you are right now, probably eating mushy ration bars."

Matthew looked at the half-eaten bar. "So you do care."

"In so much as you're a good freelancer when you actually work and make me money? Yeah, I care. And you know what else? You're gonna cave this time and do this job."

"Is that right?"

"Yup. And you've got exactly ten seconds to agree, or you're never hearing my voice again."

That's almost cheating, Matthew thought in annoyance. He thought about calling the broker's bluff. But then he also thought about his grumbling stomach. He gave it a nine-count anyway just for fun.

"Fine. I'll do it, but just this once."

He heard Benny's nasally voice laughing on the other side of the comm. It sounded like he was covering the microphone with his hand to mute it and Matthew could barely make out muffled words. "You were right! He totally bought it."

Matthew frowned, first at the implication that Benny might have actually just played him like a fiddle, then at the thought that there was someone colluding with him. "Who are you talking to Benny?"

"Oh! Umm... That was just my business partner, don't worry about it. I'll send the rest of the details on the job. No failures this time, Matthew."

"Yeah, yeah. I'm already on my way." He started warming up the Sparrow's engines for a quick hop to Mars' southern hemisphere. "This is just a one time deal, okay? Just this once."

"Sure," Benny said as he cut the comm.

Matthew finished the pre-flight checklist and pulled up the Kyoto Spaceport on his monitor. He tried not to wince as he paid the Sparrow's parking fee, nearly cleaning out the last of his account.

He should probably thank Benny for forcing him to take this job, but he didn't want him to get too comfortable. Punching the engines, he lifted off, heading for new and, hopefully, greener pastures.

Not that anywhere on Mars was particularly green, though the Arizona region was certainly the closest. Here the environmental shields extended further from the cities than anywhere else in the solar system. A wide land of valleys filled with farms and settlements, nestled between red rock mesas, branched out from the city of Flagstaff. As the Sparrow approached Arizona, Matthew gave a wide berth to the regions atmo-factory. An enormous cometary fragment, brought here by Moses over a century ago, was slowly being consumed by plasma torches, releasing, carbon dioxide, nitrogen, methane, trace amounts of oxygen, and other gases into the thin Martian air. A dozen such atmo-factories were scattered around Mars.

Moses had promised to make the air of the red planet breathable without assistance from technology. The first step was to get the air pressure high enough to live without suits. The second step would have been to adjust its composition to make it breathable. But that was all history. Moses left, and the colonists had managed to finish the first step on their own by simply manning the remaining factories, though the air was still rather thin. The second was now just a dream, lost like so much else.

Matthew landed the Sparrow on the outskirts of one of the border towns. The green ended abruptly at the environmental shields, and the red sands of mars continued undisturbed by man as far as the eye could see. He walked into the small dusty town of ramshackle buildings towards the tiny police station. A town this size likely only had a single lawman, possibly even part-time or a volunteer. But he wasn't here to see the local enforcer of justice.

Matthew pushed open the door of the station and found three men already inside. One was quite clearly the local lawman, dressed in faded and dirty blues and wearing the wide-brimmed cowboy hat that was expected of him on this part of Mars. The second man was another freelancer and thus one of the partners that Matthew was unwillingly going to have to work with on this job. Leaning against a wall, he was dressed in dark combat fatigues and had a rifle slung on his back. Vaguely, Matthew remembered that his name was Vance. He'd only seen the man once or twice at a distance.

The last man had to be the job's contact. The civilian clothes he wore did little to hide that he was a government man. The too straight posture, the set of his jaw, all of it spoke of a bureaucrat that was used to having his way because he was from the government and he was here to help.

Matthew tipped his campero. "Matthew Cole, here for the job. I take it you're Mr. Thompson?"

The government man nodded and offered a hand for Matthew to shake. "Ryan Thompson. Arizona Minister of Law. It's a pleasure to meet you, Mr. Cole. I've not heard of you before, but the broker I spoke with claimed you were a man of principle."

"I suppose you could say that," Matthew said uncomfortably, shaking his hand. "But I'd rephrase it to say that I try and make an honest living."

"I see. Well, the Republic of Arizona is only interested in working with honest freelancers such as yourself. It's not good business to pay someone who might end up working for the bad guys next week, as I'm sure you understand. If you'll just take a seat, we're still waiting for the last freelancer."

Matthew sat in one of the sparse room's chairs and tapped his fingers idly, hoping the wait wouldn't be long. He wasn't disappointed in the wait. He was disappointed by who came through the door.

Abigail Sharon ducked her head as she entered the police headquarters. She wore her powered armor openly, no trench coat today to hide her fantastic piece of earth-tech. Her eyes locked onto Matthew's and gleamed with amusement.

He tipped his hat to her politely. "Ms. Sharon."

"Cole. How's the head doing after that little spill up in Kyoto?"

"Better actually, thanks for asking," he smiled. "No thanks to you."

"Oh, you two have worked together before?" Mr. Thompson asked, oblivious to the subtext.

Matthew scratched the back of his head. "That's... maybe a little too generous a way of putting it."

Sharon smiled and leaned against a wall, her exo-suit polished to a shine. "I laid him out flat in the street. Just business. Nothing personal."

The government man eyed them both with suspicion. "Is this going to be a problem?"

"None at all," she replied sweetly.

Matthew thought about saying yes. He thought about walking out of the police station and back to the Sparrow. But then he also thought about the ration bar that probably still sat on the console. "No problem, sir. As Ms. Sharon said, just business."

"Good," Thompson said. He didn't look convinced. "I hope you don't have a similarly distasteful past with Mr. Vance."

"I know him only by name." Matthew extended a hand to the third member of the team who shook it curtly.

34

"Pleasure to meet you, Mr. Cole." Vance smiled a big smile, the kind that irritated Matthew. He tried not to let it get to him. Some people were just annoying. Didn't mean they weren't good at their job.

"Alright, the niceties are out of the way," Sharon said impatiently. "What's the job?"

The government man turned on the monitor mounted to the wall. It flashed up with a map of Mars' southern hemisphere, highlighting a rail line. "Prisoner transfer. I've been working for months to take down the Hawthorne gang. They've been operating out of this part of Mars for the last four years and getting bolder as time goes on. Last week, my deputies made a key arrest, none other than James Hawthorne himself, the second in command under his older brother."

"Congratulations," Sharon said. "I've had more than one run in with Hawthorne goons. Last time we ended up demolishing most of a warehouse. It was fun."

"I remember. Let's not have a repeat, please," Thompson said, shaking his head. "James was responsible for murdering a member of Churchill's parliament last year. As such, the Brits have formally requested that we extradite him to Churchill, presumably to hang him on the steps of parliament. I'm not really in a position to deny the Prime Minister, as I owe him a favor. Tomorrow morning, James Hawthorne will secretly be transported on the mag train to Churchill." He rubbed his hands together. "We're trying to do this quietly, to keep the Hawthorne gang from trying to spring their man en route. The train is a normally scheduled passenger train, with one of the cars exchanged for a high-security cell. We'll have ten armed deputies in the car with Hawthorne."

"Where do we come in, exactly?" Vance asked, leaning forward.

"Truth is, I don't like this whole operation," Thompson said, "but the Brits insist on having their man. I'd rather deal with James Hawthorne myself, but that's not going to happen. And it gets worse. I know for a fact that I've got a mole somewhere in my officers. There's no other way the Hawthorne gang could predict my operations the way they do. Picking up James was sheer luck, something I'm a little loath to admit. I think odds are good that his gang already knows the plan. You three are my wildcard. This job is off the official record, and I paid good money for the broker to keep this quiet. If the Hawthorne gang shows up, I hope to surprise them with the Shield Maiden and two of the best crack shots in the solar system."

Made sense, Matthew thought. But if Thompson had security issues, odds were good the Hawthorne gang would find out about the freelancer backup anyway. Of course, there was also the chance that this was all for nothing. "What happens if the guests of honor are no shows?" he asked.

Thompson smiled tightly. "Then you three get the easiest paycheck of your lives, courtesy of the Republic of Arizona."

Matthew sat back in his chair. One could hope, and maybe even pray, that would be the case. A little easy money would be a happy ending for everyone. Well, except for James Hawthorne.

Abigail Sharon didn't like the job, not one bit, and not because she didn't like working with a team. That was a pretty regular occurrence. She didn't even particularly mind working with Cole, despite their little run in a few weeks ago. She'd given him a hard time, but he'd seemed a decent sort of guy from what little they'd spoken. At the very least he was polite, and that was rare enough in this day and age.

The minister's calm confidence that something would indeed go wrong and that he had a mole, that was unnerving. Even if he managed to keep the fact that the freelancers were around for extra muscle a secret, it meant that the Hawthorne gang was almost guaranteed to show up, and in force.

This made her trust her teammates a little bit less. When you have a mole, everyone is a suspect.

After the minister had left, the freelancers spent the next hour going over the details of the operation. In the end, they decided to split up across the mag-train. Vance would guard the rear car, posing as a passenger and keeping lookout. Cole would also pose as a passenger, but in the frontmost car right before the secure cell. Abigail, unable to go undercover, would join the deputies in guarding James Hawthorne directly and only show herself if it became clear an escape attempt was being made.

Vance was staying at a hotel in town. Abigail returned to her skyhopper, a fixed-wing aircraft designed for flight in Mars' low air pressure. The sun was setting over the distant hills as she lowered the ramp on the small craft. She paused and looked to her right. In the distance, Cole was boarding his much larger and fancier spacecraft, a Ceres Spaceworks Model 42. It was basically every freelancer's dream ship. Sleek, able to defend itself, room for cargo, passengers, a crew, or whatever else you wanted. It was one of the best multipurpose workhorses out there.

She felt a pang of jealousy and knocked her armored fist against the hull of her skyhopper. A spacecraft of her own would be a dream come true. No longer limited to jobs on Mars, she'd be able to hit up the rest of the system as well.

"Lucky dog," she muttered and ducked into the entrance of her own craft. The whole thing was too small for her armored form. Little more than a cockpit and a cramped living quarter, her skyhopper was no luxury suite. Abigail stooped in the middle of her quarters, picked up the power cable, and plugged in her exo-suit. It could run for days without needing a recharge, but she never took chances. She'd never yet been caught without power and had no intention of that ever happening. Checking her wrist to ensure the power banks were receiving the charge, she knelt to the deck and cracked the suit open. Pulling her arms out of their armored counterparts, she reached back and grabbed hold of two bars above her bed and pulled herself out of the armor.

Abigail cracked her knuckles and stretched out on her bed. Grabbing an old paperback novel off the shelf above her head and a box with a freeze-dried self-heating meal, she settled in for the night. Despite being one of her favorites, she had a hard time concentrating on the words. Not even the wittiest exchanges between Elizabeth Bennet and Mr. Darcy held her attention as her mind kept wandering back to tomorrow's job. Maybe it was just pessimism.

Or maybe tomorrow really was going to be that kind of day. It was always hard to judge this sort of thing.

She turned the light out and tried vainly to get some sleep.

The next morning Abigail got up early, checked over her armor, and ate a quick breakfast. She suited up and went to the train station. The grey pre-dawn light filtered over the hills and a chill breeze blew through the border town. She was met by a deputy who escorted her to the secure train car. Looking like an ordinary passenger car, it floated a meter above the magnetic track. Inside was another matter entirely. It was armored like a tank and had four barred prisoner cells.

There was only a single deputy present. He shook her hand, nervously, and introduced himself as Captain Stanley.

"It's a pleasure to meet you, Ms., uhh... Shield Maiden. I've read a lot about you and respect your work."

Great, she thought. A fan. She smiled graciously, "Yes, well, we're all here to do a job." She gestured to the empty cells. "Is our guest on schedule?"

Stanley straightened and nodded vigorously. "Yes, Ma'am. James Hawthorne will be arriving via armored car in just over one hour. You are welcome to take a seat until then."

Abigail laughed and with a metal palm slapped the thigh of her suit, making a loud noise. "I don't exactly tire. If it's all the same to you, I'll just stand."

"Yes, I umm... Of course."

She smiled at his awkward response, enjoying one of the pleasures her earth-tech suit afforded her. Waiting around for the next hour was not among those pleasures, but they had decided it would be better if Abigail weren't seen stomping onto the train. Hence the early morning.

Sometime after the sun rose, Abigail heard the roar of a personnel carrier pulling up outside, eight deputies and James Hawthorne in an orange prisoner coverall boarded the train. He was a man of average height with a sandy beard. Nothing much to look at, but he was apparently an outlaw leader with a penchant for murder. Shows how you could never really judge a book by its cover.

Hawthorne startled when he laid eyes on Abigail. As he passed her, she looked down at him and laughed. "That's right. Whatever your little men have planned is not going to work."

He spat at her and was wrestled into a cell by the deputies. Captain Stanley laughed. "You ought to treat a lady with a little more respect. I get the feeling she could rip you limb from limb."

The outlaw leader didn't say anything, just glared daggers at the deputies from behind his bars. Abigail leaned against the wall in front of him and crossed her arms, deciding to stare him down while she waited. There was an unpleasant tickle in the back of her mind that Hawthorne was a little too calm, even after his initial shock of seeing her.

There was going to be trouble. She was almost certain.

Matthew sat in one of the stiff seats in the first passenger car back from Sharon. The dingy car seemed far dirtier and run down than when he had ridden this very line a few times as a kid. Still, he mused, at least it was running. Mag trains could be repaired when they broke, unlike some other bits of infrastructure.

He looked over the rows of seats. There were only a handful of passengers in the car. He had chosen the rearmost row so that he would see any passenger that tried to enter or leave. He tapped his fingers idly on the rail, waiting for the train to depart the station. Churchill was some nine hundred miles from Arizona. The trip by mag train was about four hours, normally enough time for a good nap. Today it was going to be monotonous waiting for something to happen. This was the kind of job that could make you jump at shadows as it dragged on.

He was confident that something would happen. Something in the quiet sincerity of the government man's own confidence had sold Matthew on that. It was just a matter of time.

There was a slight bump as the train departed and began to pick up more and more speed. He took a glance out the window as they raced across the red Martian desert. There was even a bit of blue in the usually hazy red sky this morning. He pulled back a sleeve and glanced at his old wristwatch. Weeks ago he had set it to Mars length days, which were conveniently only a few minutes longer than standard. He dialed it to local time. If the bandits were smart, they'd make their move at the two-hour mark. Halfway in between the colonies would give them more time before reinforcements could arrive.

Then again, sometimes there was value in doing the unexpected. Twenty minutes into the ride, three men entered the car. There was nothing suspicious about the way they dressed, simple working clothes with wide-brimmed hats, but there was no good reason for them to have changed cars. Matthew watched them casually as they walked toward the front of the car. They didn't seem to have marked him. He pulled out his comm and signaled the other two freelancers. He got an immediate counter signal from Sharon. She must have been ready and itching for action.

Vance didn't answer. Matthew fired the signal again and grimaced. Vance may have already been identified and eliminated.

The three men had reached the front of the car and neared the door. Matthew stood and bellowed, "Everybody, get down!"

This was for two reasons. First, he wanted the handful of civilians in the car to hit the deck. This was going to get violent one way or another. Second, he wanted to give the suspicious characters a chance to either prove their innocence or guilt before he opened fire. All three of them spun and drew their guns, and Matthew had his answer.

He fired four shots from his revolver, striking two of the men before they even finished turning. The third was fast and had his own gun drawn before the others hit the ground. Matthew dove behind the seat as sparks scattered from the bullets. The report was deafening in the enclosed space. He was on his feet again in a moment with his gun trained towards his target. The outlaw had taken cover behind a partition at the front of the car.

Matthew took a risk and fired all three shots at the partition. There was a cry of pain, and the man fell into the aisle. Matthew pulled a speed loader from a pocket and had his revolver ready to fire again. "Make sure your cover is bulletproof next time," he said to no one in particular as he walked past the rows of seats.

Thankfully the few passengers had heeded his warning and taken cover before the fight. "Might want to stay down, ladies and gentlemen. I think you're in the middle of an old-fashioned train heist." He signaled Vance one last time. Still no answer, and at this point, Matthew expected that there never would be.

He ducked behind a chair and called Sharon.

"No answer from Vance. Three bogeys down. You quiet up there?"

"Quiet as a church. Were there only three?"

"So far. If I had to guess the main assault will be coming soon, possibly by air. They probably posed as passengers to flush out extra defenders."

There was a pause on the other end of the comm. "Think they were looking for us specifically?" They were both thinking the same thing. Thompson's security problem was a gaping hole if the Hawthorne gang already knew about the freelancers.

"Either way they seemed to have found Vance. Keep your eyes open. I'm going to try and get a look at the sky, see if we've got incoming."

"Keep me posted." Sharon cut the link and Matthew moved into action. He stepped through the door at the front of the car and shut it behind him. Pulling a breathing mask from beneath his poncho, he placed it over his face. Mars' atmosphere was thick enough that you no longer needed a pressure suit, and most of its citizens were used to cold-shirting it short distances from building to building or train car to train car if they were outside of the environmental shields. He would be outside longer than that though. He pushed open the heavy outer door and stepped out onto the small platform. The red Martian landscape raced by, a blur of sand and rock. The train car in front of him, the one containing the prisoner, Sharon, and the deputies, was joined to Matthew's by a single hitch. A flexible hanging bridge made it possible to cross safely from one to the other.

But Matthew didn't intend to hole up with Sharon just yet. Turning, he climbed the rung ladder on his car and poked his head over the top of the train. He saw exactly what he feared he would see. Two skyhoppers, much like Sharon's, approaching fast from the rear of the train. In just a few seconds they'd be here.

"Sharon," he shouted over the whistle of the wind. A small environmental shield at the front of the train greatly reduced wind drag. This had the side effect of making the wind atop the train much slower, which, considering the circumstances was a pity. Matthew wouldn't have minded one bit if the top of the train was inaccessible due to hurricane force winds. "Skyhoppers inbound." One passed overhead and slowed above the train's engine. Which meant the other... He whipped his head around. It hovered over the rear of the train, and four men had already landed lightly atop one of the cars. They braced against the wind. "Sharon. The engine. You've got company from the front." He shut off the comm and aimed his revolver across the top of the train. The intruders hadn't noticed him yet. He fired four shots.

Through sheer luck, he hit one target in the arm. Unfortunately, they were way out of the practical engagement range of his revolver and, realizing this, they crouched and returned fire. Three guns answering his one had Matthew retreating back down the ladder. He'd have to make for the secure car. From there, he'd stand a chance with Sharon and the deputies. As he stepped onto the platform, Matthew felt the muzzle of a gun press into his back.

"Sorry about this," Vance said.

Matthew almost thought he meant it. At least now he knew why the man's smile had been so obnoxious.

"I thought Thompson said he was only hiring principled freelancers for this job?" He was stalling, of course, grasping for a plan of some sort.

Vance was quiet for a moment. "Turns out we all have our price."

"That's pretty blatantly untrue," Matthew said carefully.

"I wouldn't be so sure. Just because you haven't found yours yet doesn't mean you won't someday."

Matthew shook his head. "You know nothing about me."

"You're right. I don't. And sadly, I never will."

That was as good a warning as any. Rather than take a bullet to the back from a coward and sellout, Matthew dropped to the ground, praying to take Vance by surprise. He swept a leg towards the other freelancer and in the process took him down. The rifle Vance had been holding discharged harmlessly into the sky. For a few moments, there was a tangle and confusion of limbs as both men tried to get their bearing.

Unfortunately for Vance, Matthew found his first, and his fist found the other man's face. There was a cracking noise. Vance would have a broken nose and Matthew a few jammed fingers, but the traitor dropped like a sandbag to the platform. Matthew's breathing mask had come free, and he grabbed its hose and shoved it back on his face. He checked to make sure that Vance's was secure too. Asphyxiation wasn't a death he'd wish on anyone.

From the secure car, he heard a barrage of gunfire, and he leaped to his feet hoping it wasn't too late.

"Skyhoppers inbound," Cole's voice rattled over Abigail's comm. Above her head, she heard the roar of the aircraft as one passed above her train car.

"Look alive," Captain Stanley ordered.

She moved to the front of the car and pulled her riot shield off her back. It sprang to life with a faint hum. Her armor was tough enough to stop most small arms fire, but she still preferred to take them in the shield. Better not to take too many chances.

A spray of sparks began to shoot from the door as the Hawthorne gang cut through it with a plasma torch. "Breathing masks on!" shouted Stanley.

Abigail lowered her own transparent face shield and waited patiently, knowing this would give her one good shot at whoever was on the other side. The moment the torch had cut a complete circuit around the door she slammed her shield into it, giving it a good jolt from the grav plate.

The heavy steel door blew outwards taking at least two men with it. Abigail didn't know what happened to them but figured their bodies would someday be found on the dry Martian landscape, half-mummified. Gunfire began to ping harmlessly against her shield. Then she heard something bounce across the ground near her feet.

A flash and a deafening roar echoed through the train car, and for a moment Abigail feared they had tossed a live grenade through the hole. As the stars began to clear, she realized with relief that it was only a flashbang, but the distraction could prove disastrous. Still reeling from the blast, she pushed her shield to block the missing door. There were more pings of deflected gunfire. Then she noticed the car filling with smoke.

"Find that smoke grenade and get it out of here," she bellowed over her ringing ears. It was too late. The car was filled with smoke, making it almost impossible to see. Breathing wasn't a problem for the deputies due to their masks, but it was hard to know where a threat was coming from if you couldn't see it. The outlaws would probably have thermal vision to see through...

A shaft of light came from the rear of the car, cutting through the smoke. "Sharon!" Cole yelled.

"Keep your eyes on the rear door. I've got the front!"

"We're going to have more company from the back in just a minute. They unloaded a squad on the rear cars."

Abigail swore under her breath.

Captain Stanley gave new orders to his men, and four of them exited the rear of the car to defend from that position. The gunfire had stopped, and Abigail risked a peek around her shield. She couldn't see anyone on the other side. That didn't make sense. What were they...?

The voice of one of the deputies rang through the car "The prisoner!"

There was a clang of metal, and the rush of air as a new hole opened in the train car's side.

So that was the purpose of the flashbang and smoke grenade. Distraction while they cut through the prisoner's cell. One of the deputy's revolvers barked twice. "Too late! They have him!" a voice shouted.

Abigail growled and unlatched what was left of the door, pushed it open, and stepped out onto the platform. Empty with no outlaws in sight. She grabbed the rung ladder and pulled herself up to the top of the car. The skyhopper at the front of the train had drifted back behind the secure cell, and several men, including James Hawthorne, were running the length of the train towards it.

Having no better plan, she ran across the top of the secure cell after them, leaping lightly to the next car. It was a dangerous leap for a man on foot, but for her, it was an easy jump. The outlaws must have heard her heavy suit land with a bang. While Hawthorne continued running towards the skyhopper, they turned and opened fire. She advanced slowly as the bullets ricocheted off her shield.

"Use a hand?" Cole asked from behind her. Abigail glanced at him in surprise, unaware that he'd followed.

"Be my guest," she said through gritted teeth.

Cole stood behind her, using her and her shield for cover and began returning fire with the bandits. He was a good shot. Real good.

In a matter of seconds, two were downed, and the remaining three were beating a hasty retreat. "Move forward," he said calmly. "The deputies are pushing through the train beneath us as we speak."

"Who put you in charge?" Abigail countered as she pressed towards the skyhopper. It was three cars away, and James Hawthorne had almost made it to safety. Reaching the end of the car, she leaped to the next and glanced behind her as Cole took a running jump to join her.

She could reach Hawthorne. Easily.

But then the skyhopper opened fire.

Its chin mounted chain gun began unleashing a storm of lead on them. She knelt to the ground so her shield would provide better coverage. The larger caliber bullets would almost certainly pierce her armor's shell. Cole took cover behind her again, his back against her own. Hopefully, any passengers below were out of the line of fire. Abigail tried not to think about that right now.

"We might have a problem," he said, his voice surprisingly calm.

"You think?"

"Yup. I'm going to be eating ration bars till the day I die."

"You do seem to be good at failing contracts," she shouted.

"I seem to remember that I was the only reason anyone made any money back in Kyoto."

"Can this wait till later?!" she shouted. He wasn't wrong, but she wasn't about to admit it.

Hawthorne was surely tucked into the skyhopper by now. The second aircraft had in fact already pulled away from the engine and was drifting back alongside the train. The chaingun stopped, and Abigail risked a peek around her shield. There was a rumble as Hawthorne's skyhopper throttled up and it roared overhead. Cole's revolver fired a few parting shots that glanced harmlessly off the hull of the craft.

Abigail cursed under her breath as she realized that the second skyhopper was right beside them. A side hatch opened, and something caught her eye.

"Sharon!"

So Cole had seen it too. An outlaw had a shoulder mounted thumper aimed at them. She brought her shield around and stepped between Cole and the weapon right as it fired.

The blast from a thumper is visible. In a vacuum, the artificial bubble of curved space bends light somewhat around itself creating an obvious distortion. In atmosphere, the bubble also gives off a faint

44

iridescent light, some exotic reaction with air molecules. Abigail didn't really understand the science. But she did see the blast as it lanced across the short distance separating the train and the skyhopper. It hit her shield squarely and she heard a high-pitched shriek as the grav plate in her shield tried to neutralize it. It held, barely, but as the thumper blast collapsed in on itself, it let loose a shockwave that blew both her and Cole off the train.

There was a moment of weightlessness. Through sheer luck, they happened to be traveling along the top of a steep hill and the ground was nearly a hundred feet below them. Abigail returned her shield to her back but left it engaged. Cole hurtled through the air beside her. Reaching out she grabbed his arm and pulled him to herself. She saw the look of surprise on his face as she wrapped her arms around him. His breath mask had been knocked off and he fumbled in her grip to replace it. Abigail rotated to land on her back, feet facing down the slope.

This whole process took only a few seconds as the ground rushed up at them. They hit the slope at high speed, but the grav plate in Abigail's shield absorbed the majority of the impact. Mars' lower gravity also helped keep their speed non-fatal. Half supported by a cushion of gravity from her shield, she did her best to keep her feet from touching the ground. If this turned into a wild tumble, Cole was as good as dead.

Red rocks and dust flew up behind them as they slid down the hill. Judging they had shed enough speed, she planted her feet to continue slowing them. As they neared the bottom of the hill, she clipped a large boulder and lost hold of Cole.

Matthew bounced another twenty feet across the shallow basin of sand at the bottom of the hill before tumbling to a halt. He coughed, then realized his mask had come free yet again. He replaced it and took a deep breath, promising himself to find one that secured to his face better.

A few minutes passed as Matthew lay on his back, glad to be alive. He had been supremely confident when the thumper fired that his life was over. The fact that Sharon had somehow managed to save them both was something he was still trying to process.

Speaking of, Sharon stood over him. "How you doing, cowboy? Any serious injuries?"

"I'm going to hurt in the morning, but I'm alive," he accepted the

45

hand offered to him and stood to his feet. "I guess that's that," he grumbled. "I don't think Thompson hired enough guns."

Sharon shook her head. "I think the whole cloak and dagger on a public train was the real downfall. No heavy weaponry to chase off the skyhoppers. What a disaster."

Matthew grunted. "Thanks, by the way, for saving my life."

She nodded, seemingly distracted.

Not knowing what else to do, Matthew started walking back up towards the tracks. He'd spotted his hat halfway up the hillside and stooped to pick it up. The low gravity made the trek tiring, and he began to sweat despite the chill in the thin atmosphere. They reached the hilltop and, without a better plan, started hiking down the track towards Arizona.

"Arizona has a serious security problem," Matthew mused. "I know Thompson said he had a mole, but that was nuts."

"You're telling me," Sharon agreed. "They knew which car and even which cell in the car."

Matthew stared at her for a moment and then realized she was missing an important detail. "Oh right, I think I forgot to mention that Vance was a traitor."

"What?" she asked, rounding on him.

"Yeah, he wasn't answering for a reason. Vance held me at gunpoint, but I managed to turn it into a fist fight. I broke his face. He'll live, but not if I ever see him again."

Sharon suddenly laughed. She looked at her wrist and tapped a few buttons. "This job may not be over after all."

Matthew gave her a good stare and raised an eyebrow in an unspoken question.

"I didn't trust either you or Vance after Thompson expressed his concerns. Last night I slipped a tracker on both of you before we left the briefing."

"I would have noticed that."

"I can be subtle," she said defensively.

"You weren't subtle back in Kyoto."

"Check your hat."

Matthew took off his campero. Sure enough, a tiny black disk was nestled between the crown and brim. He didn't say anything and merely replaced the hat.

Sharon laughed again and tapped her wrist. "I just checked on Vance's tracker. It's north of here."

Matthew nodded. "And the train went east. So Vance was able to retreat with them. He didn't stay down long."

"He's got an impressive reputation. I'm not surprised."

"We follow your tracker to Vance and the Hawthorne gang. What could possibly go wrong?"

"Beats not getting paid," she said.

"And eating ration bars," he concluded. "Fine." He pulled the air compressor off his belt that connected to his breath mask.

"How much time do you have?" Sharon asked.

"Eight hours. Probably not enough to make it back to Arizona. I'm not exactly sure how far out we are."

Sharon gave an exasperated sigh and knelt to the ground. She gestured to her back. "Hop on."

Matthew stopped and crossed his arms. "You've got to be kidding me."

"Not a bit. Either you ride piggyback, or I carry you bridal style. Your choice."

"You're sure you can carry me that far?"

"Yes and much faster than you can walk. Come on. We don't have all day."

Matthew walked over to her and climbed on her back. "This is the most ridiculous thing I've ever done."

Sharon laughed. "Quit complaining cowboy. We've got a job to finish."

Chapter 4: The Hawthorne Pact

The thing I remember most about those days was the quiet sadness of it all. After we got the initial error message, there were a few weeks of panic and noise. Earth was too busy to pay much attention to the colonies, dealing with the biggest financial collapse in the history of mankind.

Then the war started and they never even bothered with us again.

You can watch a nuclear war from millions of miles away, watch as both the history of your people and its hopes for the future crumble into atomic dust. We weren't really all that surprised that no one had disarmed themselves like they claimed, just...

Lost.

After a couple weeks of silence, we went on with our lives, Arizona elected a President, Churchill a Prime Minister, and so on. It was just the colonies now as far as we were concerned.
No Earth and no Moses.

Robert Davis
Arizona Secretary of State
Died 28 AM

T he long walk back to Arizona was more boring than anything else. Matthew's hurt pride had given up the fight several hours ago, and he'd resigned himself to the undignified situation of being carried across the Martian landscape by a woman in an exo-suit.

The worst part was the cold. Every half hour he insisted on being let down to jog for a few minutes to work some heat back into his limbs. Mars' thin atmosphere didn't allow comfortable air temperatures, despite the colonist's best effort at mass producing greenhouse gases. Thankfully, Sharon's armor was warm to the touch, else he may have lost a finger or two.

"And you're sure you have enough power to get us back?" he asked for at least the fifth time since they had started their trek.

"I could keep this pace for two days. Stop asking. You're not going to die."

He flexed his fingers painfully. "Easy for you to say." Every muscle in his body hurt after falling from the train and being jostled for hours on end. He glanced at his wristwatch. If his math was right, Arizona couldn't be too much further away. "So how does a nice girl like you end up as a freelancer, if you don't mind me asking?"

Sharon scoffed. "Seems like an obvious answer."

"I was just trying to pass the time with some conversation. You don't have to get defensive about it."

"Fine. I've got the right tool for the job. Happy?"

"Not really. I'm guessing that you're not going to tell me any more about that tool of yours either," Matthew hazarded.

"Not one word," she said, and Matthew knew it would be pointless to press the issue.

"Still, I wonder about why you're freelancing. I imagine you could easily get a cushy law enforcement job or some private security gig. Why not take the easy paycheck?"

Sharon was quiet for a minute. "Would you want to work for one of the colonial governments or some rich thruster nozzle?"

Matthew chuckled "No, I guess not."

"So how about you? How long you been a freelancer?"

"Decade almost..." he trailed off.

"That's about what I figured. How'd you get started?"

He thought about Villa María. Then he tried not to think about Villa María. "It's not something I talk about." They were both quiet for a minute.

"So questions about the past are a no go." Sharon said casually, "We're a pair of open books."

Matthew didn't know that, but he was saved from any more social awkwardness when they topped the rise. The Arizona environmental shield flickered in the distance with subtle distortion in the early afternoon light.

"Let me down. I'll walk from here."

Sharon knelt. "Fragile ego doesn't want to be seen hitching a ride?"

He scrambled off her back. "Imagine what would happen to the reputation of the Shield Maiden if she was seen being carried back to town on a forklift. A freelancer without a reputation is just a jobless bum."

"You worry too much. Do a job. Do it well. All it takes."

"Easy for you to say when you're bulletproof."

"Mostly bulletproof," she corrected.

They left off conversation as they finished crossing the distance to the border town. When they reached the shield, Matthew placed a hand against it to test its resistance. They operated by repelling matter. Air inside tended to stay inside, which also did wonders for keeping it nice and warm. Environmental shields had a second layer to keep out radiation. The solar system was not a hospitable place for human life.

He stepped back and ran at the shield, diving headfirst. The trick was to get most of your body on the far side so that the field pushed you the rest of the way through. His hands, head, and shoulders pierced the shield before he felt himself beginning to slow. He had nearly come to a complete stop before he crossed the threshold and the shield kicked him out the other side. He rolled as he hit the ground and sprang lightly to his feet.

Sharon stepped through the shield effortlessly and he rolled his eyes. "Showoff."

She ignored him. "Come on. I've got equipment in my skyhopper that'll give us a more accurate read on Vance's position."

As Abigail climbed into her skyhopper, she thought that she should have told Cole to wait outside. He'd have to walk through the living quarters to reach the cockpit, and it was always awkward to have strangers in your room. She walked straight to the console and pushed the power button for the computers, sat in the oversized chair, and spun it to face Cole.

Unfortunately, he hadn't followed her into the cockpit. He'd gotten distracted and picked up the copy of Pride and Prejudice she'd tossed aside the previous night. Flipping through it, he made a face.

"What's the matter?" she asked. "Don't like the classics?"

"Some of them," he said placing the book on the shelf. "This one always struck me as a little... unrealistic. Things work out too nicely in the end. But here," he picked up another book, "here is a true classic." Cole showed her the face of the book. The Everlasting Man was printed in burgundy letters.

"Oh, I never got very far into that one. A bit stuffy for my tastes."

"Pity. The Solar System could use a little Chesterton these days."

The computer beeped, and Abigail turned back to the display. She wouldn't have pegged Cole as a man interested in a centuries-old Catholic thinker, but then people were rarely predictable. The only reason she even had the book was that she'd found it abandoned somewhere years ago. Actual paper books were a treasure you didn't pass up.

She returned to the matter at hand. "Let's see. Give me just a... There." The display showed a topographical map of Arizona. In the southern reaches of the colony's territory, nestled in some rough terrain amidst a collapsed mesa, glowed a single red dot. "So there's our boy Vance, and I'd guess the rest of the Hawthorne gang."

Cole leaned over her shoulder. At least he was no longer in her room.

"Secluded area," he mumbled. "Is there any information on the region? Looks like the remnants of a mining operation. I guess someone didn't math things out and collapsed the mesa. A few decades later a merry band of outlaws moves in, and you've got a veritable bandit fortress."

She pulled up some information on the area. He was right on the money about the history of the place. "I don't think the Hawthornes have Robin Hood as their leader, Cole."

"All the same we get to play sheriff. That's gonna be almost an hour away on grav bike. I've got some equipment I'd like to take along that may come in useful. Sooner we get out of here, the more likely we take them by surprise."

Abigail frowned and spun her chair back around to face Cole. "You sure you don't want to contact Thompson? He might be able to lend some backup."

Cole shook his head emphatically. "Absolutely not. I don't trust anyone in the Arizona government at this point. Someone ratted us out, bought Vance, and nearly got us killed. We do this our way. Capture James Hawthorne, deliver him to Churchill ourselves, and split Vance's cut."

Abigail found herself impressed by the bravado. "And while we're at it, we take his brother Paul as well."

"That's a tall order, Shield Maiden," he said raising an eyebrow. "Not afraid we're biting off more than we can chew going after a whole gang of criminals?"

"Depends on how good a shot you are I guess, cowboy."

Cole adjusted his campero. "Gaucho,"

"Still don't care," she said.

An hour later they parked their grav bikes and marched the last few miles on foot. Compared to the morning's hike, Matthew thought this was positively cheery. While it never got to a temperature you could call warm in these latitudes, he wasn't in any danger of losing fingers beneath the Arizona shield.

"Sure you don't want me to carry that case for you?"

He looked over at Sharon. "Allow me to retain a little bit of dignity." He'd packed the long case with thermal imaging gear as well as some special equipment that he'd declined to disclose. It would be interesting to gauge her reaction when he showed her the contents.

All this dignity might be the death of him. One fistfight, thrown from a train, and jostled and frozen to death, all since getting up this morning. Each and every step, his tired muscles protested in defiance. If he lived the afternoon and went to bed tonight, he might never be able to move again.

When they reached the bluff, he decided dignity might be inconvenient. There was no way he was climbing the cliff face and lugging the bulky case at the same time. He waited for the inevitable sarcastic remark as he handed his burden to Sharon, but she accepted it without comment. Either she was off her game or he was looking pretty rough, and the woman was starting to take pity on him. Matthew kicked a clod of red dirt and began the climb.

For most of it, he was able to scramble along on all fours, only climbing once or twice. When he finally dragged his body over the lip of the mesa, he laid on the ground to rest for a minute before getting to his feet. The terrain atop the mesa was mess of shattered stone and broken boulders, offering plenty of cover for them to keep out of the way of prying eyes. Sharon had already moved into cover. "You good, Cole?"

He laughed and dusted himself off, straightening his poncho. "Sure, we'll go with that. How far to that mine?"

"Half mile, maybe less."

"Let's do it."

By the time they had picked their way across the top mesa, the sun was low, casting the landscape in a dull red light. Red on red. You had to like the color to not lose your sanity on Mars. They crept towards the entrance of the mine, slinking between the rocks. The sun glinted off Sharon's armor, even with the fine coat of Martian dust it had acquired over the course of the day. It practically begged for them to get caught. "We need to get you a poncho to hide that thing in the wilds. It'd have to be the biggest one ever made."

Matthew knew he wasn't a ladies man. In fact, he was quite possibly the furthest thing from that. However, he also knew that Abigail Sharon was a little vain about her armor and would take it as a compliment. At least that was what he thought.

"Smooth, Cole." Her eyes flicked down at her armor. "But I guess you're right. I wear that trench coat in the city. I could use some stealth wear for the countryside."

Maybe it was only okay if she made the joke. He cracked open his case and pulled out a pair of thermal goggles. "Stay here, I'll go check over the ledge. See what we're dealing with." He crawled forward and looked down into the depression. Two familiar skyhoppers sat parked outside the opening in the hillside. "At least we're at the right place," he muttered to himself, slipping on the goggles.

A human body stands out as a bright source of heat on the cool Martian landscape. One bright spot glowed like a blast furnace high above the mine on the far side of the depression, and he ducked lower to the ground. That would be the lookout. Down at the entrance, there were two men out working near the skyhoppers and another ten or so further in. It was hard to get a count in the building. Probably the warmer air.

He slid back down to Sharon, pulled off the goggles, and reported what he'd seen. She frowned. "That's it? I kind of thought there would be more."

"How many did we take out earlier today?" He started counting on his fingers. "I got five. Maybe six?"

"Better than me. I only got two. They didn't really want to deal with me."

"Can't say I blame them," Matthew agreed. "So that's seven or eight. We've already thinned them pretty well. Plus they may have other men elsewhere. I doubt the whole gang is at this location."

"Alright, what's the plan then, Cole." She gestured to the case.

53

"You've got something special in mind?"

He nodded and opened the case. "You're not the only one with a piece of earthtech."

Sharon's eyes went wide. "What is it? Some kind of rifle?"

"Gauss rifle. Charge the capacitors and it fires a sub-sonic slug via staged magnetic coils. There's no gunpowder and no sonic boom, so it's perfectly silent. Battery has enough charge for four shots, and we've got three hostiles outside. This'll help even the odds a bit."

Sharon eyed the thing suspiciously. "That's a weapon meant for assassination."

Matthew plucked the weapon out of the case and began assembling its bipod. "I inherited it with the Sparrow. It doesn't come out often, but I find occasional use for it."

"I see."

He turned from the rifle to look at her. "Or you could charge in and bludgeon them all with your shield if you prefer a fair fight."

She waved him off. "Do your thing."

He crept back up to the edge and set the weapon's bipod on the lip and slipped the thermal goggles back on to locate the watchman. The outlaw was still perched high in the rocks, almost invisible without the thermal gear. Matthew peered through the scope and found his target. He hit a switch and heard a nearly inaudible hum as the capacitors charged. Looking through the sight again, he double-checked the range. Just over a hundred meters. He groaned as he did the quick math. Stupid earth-tech equipment used metric system. Either way, he wasn't going to have to compensate for projectile drop at this close range.

He squeezed the trigger. There was a faint puff of air, and a hole appeared in the man's chest. Matthew bit his lip, feeling a pang of guilt as the man slumped to the ground, felled by an enemy he didn't even know was there. He pushed the feeling aside. These were murderers, and the Government of Arizona had authorized him to use lethal force. Sharon was right about one thing. This was a weapon meant for assassination.

Grim thoughts aside, he set to work on the other two men. The first was easy pickings, and Matthew dropped him behind one of the skyhoppers. The second had unfortunately moved into one of the aircraft and Matthew had to wait nearly five minutes before he poked his head out, possibly wondering what his compatriot was up to. After he finished the deed, Matthew checked the thermals one more time, ensuring that he had no other targets before returning to Sharon.

"It's done?"

He nodded, "Three less hostiles."

"What now? Work our way into the mine and take the rest of the Hawthorne gang out?"

"Unless you've got a better idea," he said stowing the rifle. He pushed the case down into a crevice where it was unlikely to be discovered. "We go in quiet, at least until it gets loud. You provide cover and deal with anyone close, and I'll deal with enemies at range."

Sharon pulled her shield from her back and deployed it. "If you're sure. This could get a little nasty."

Matthew drew his revolver and checked to make sure it was fully loaded. Never hurt to double or even triple check that sort of thing. "I'm not sure, but I'm too poor right now to care." He closed the revolver's cylinder. "Let's do it."

In spite of wearing a nearly bulletproof exo-suit, Abigail always felt a shock of fear before a fight. It was partially her invulnerability that made her feel so vulnerable. If her suit was somehow disabled, it would go from her biggest asset to her biggest liability in the space of a heartbeat. That worry kept her alert, helped her focus. The moment she got sloppy was the moment someone took her out. Freelancers usually didn't get much leeway when they got in over their head.

Abigail lowered her face shield and took a quick glance at Cole. He nodded and gave a hand signal to proceed. The tunnel extended fifty feet before making a sharp left turn. Cole's last use of the thermal goggles had revealed that two outlaws lurked somewhere just around the corner. Abigail stalked forward, moving as quietly as her armor allowed.

She reached the corner, paused, gave Cole a three-two-one signal with her left hand, and breached the bend.

The two outlaws sat in folding chairs by a cheery campfire. The first played a guitar while the other stirred a pot heating over the fire. To their credit, they both reacted almost immediately to Abigail's sudden appearance. The cook even managed to draw his weapon before she brought her shield to bear on them in one mighty swing. They both sailed across the tunnel, one colliding with the wall and dropping cold. The other landed in a pile of crates, making an inordinate amount of noise.

"We're loud," Cole said. "Let's move."

Abigail moved to a set of double doors behind the fire and took up position beside them. The door opened, and she caught the surprised outlaw with her shield, sending him flying to join his comrades. She and Cole rushed through the doors into a warehouse turned camp. Most of the men had been huddled around a table in what appeared to be a poker game, but a few were scattered around the room.

All of them were in the process of drawing their guns and getting to their feet. Abigail raised her shield to protect herself and Cole. He wasted no time, leaning out from behind the cover she created to fire a quick succession of shots from his revolver. Two hostiles dropped at once, but the rest had taken refuge behind tables or other makeshift cover. Slowed by the grav plate to harmless velocities, shots began to bounce off her shield with sharp metallic clinks. She motioned her head to the left towards a large shipping container, hoping that Cole would get the message. She nudged him in that direction, careful to keep as much of herself protected by the shield as she could. The biggest danger was getting surrounded. If they could find a position from which Cole's revolver could continue to thin the crowd, she knew they stood a chance.

When they reached the shipping container, Cole darted to the far side, giving fire. Abigail pushed slowly towards the group that had been playing poker. It was a bit of a risk, but keeping the attention on herself rather than Cole was gonna make their odds of winning that much more likely. She stepped out of cover and into the open, and the gunfire intensified. After a few moments, bullets started pinging off the ground at her feet as the Hawthorne gang realized shooting her shield was useless. One bullet ricocheted harmlessly off her armored boots, leaving a small dent she'd have to work out later.

So far her gambit was working and, looking through the narrow slit in her shield, she saw Cole down another bandit. Hopefully, he didn't accidentally kill James or Paul Hawthorne. It would be a lot more satisfying to dump the two alive and well on the steps of Churchill's Parliament building.

An impact on her side surprised her. A second bullet embedded itself in the armor at her thigh before she caught sight of the shooter. One of the gang members had bravely skirted around the outside of the room with a high caliber rifle. Before she could react, he fired a third shot, this one slamming into the armor just above her right knee.

"Cole!"

The man was good with that revolver, Abigail had no doubt. In one smooth motion, he turned, dropped to one knee, and fired. His revolver barked four times, and the flanker fell unmoving to the warehouse floor.

Abigail stepped forward again to further pressure the main group and noticed her right knee responded sluggishly with a high-pitched whine. That last bullet had been true to its mark. This needed to end soon, or she might be in a real jam.

A fallen chair in front of her gave her an opportunity to be more than a distraction. She gave it a jolt from her shield, and the grav plate sent it flying across the room towards her adversaries. Hitting one or more of them would have been nice. What she got was even better. The chair clipped a table and shattered into a thousand splinters of wooden shrapnel. The remaining members of the Hawthorne gang took cover from the carnage and, in the resulting chaos, Matthew dropped yet another outlaw with a well-placed round to the chest.

The air was split twice by the booming of a high-powered rifle. Abigail tried to get a bead on the new threat.

Vance.

Then the confusion set in. Two more outlaws slumped to the ground, shot in the back by the newcomer. Vance dropped the rifle and drew a sidearm from each hip. James and Paul Hawthorne each found themselves looking down the barrel of a pistol.

The room fell silent as all parties grappled with the unexpected change of fortunes.

"Go ahead," Vance said. "Drop your weapons."

The men exchanged glances before complying. Paul Hawthorne cursed, his face red and his mouth practically frothing. "I'll kill you, you filthy..."

"Shut up," Vance said quietly, gesturing with the gun. "Well, what of it, Cole? Sharon? You going to come get these two or not?"

Cole stepped out of cover and approached Sharon, standing close so that he could use her for cover. Maybe he wasn't sure the shooting was over with either. "Turning on your contractor's not good business for a freelancer, Vance. Twice in a day is a fool's gambit."

Vance's smile was obnoxious. Abigail would have liked to knock it off his stupid face. She was still trying to figure out which side he was on. If any. The freelancer shook his head. "If you think the Hawthorne's paid me then you've not been keeping up."

Cole relaxed his aim. "That confirms a suspicion I had." Abigail glanced nervously at him, glad that at least one of them was confident in this situation.

"Good. Come cuff these two."

Cole stepped forward and slapped a pair of handcuffs on the brothers, and then gagged them. Sharon herded the remaining outlaws into a far corner of the room. For now, they obeyed, their spirit defeated with the leaders of their band captured. She didn't know how long that would last and hoped to be out of here before anyone else got any bright ideas. Cole pushed the brothers toward the door. "And, Vance. Go ahead and give Sharon her tracker."

Abigail's eyes went wide as Vance pulled the small black disc off the back of his shoulder. He walked to her and offered the device.

She stared at it for a moment before accepting. "So you knew the whole time? Knew we were coming and did nothing to stop us?"

"I already fulfilled my contract. I didn't really see the harm in letting you fulfill yours. Just had to wait for the opportune moment to help turn the tables." He smiled that insufferable grin again.

Sharon thought about knocking it off his face for all the trouble. Imagined him hurtling across the mine warehouse. Would have been fun.

But repaying a good turn with malice was beneath her, if only by a little bit.

Matthew turned the Hawthorne Skyhopper with its captives towards Churchill and a payout at the end of a hard job. Vance had taken the other to go... somewhere. Matthew didn't really care anymore.

They landed the aircraft in the square in front of the Parliament building. A few dozen police were on hand to confront the strangers before they even popped the hatch. Matthew only laughed. "Calm down gentlemen. Just making a personal delivery to the Prime Minister. I hear he's interested in the Hawthorne brothers. We're interested in collecting a bounty."

The bounty was handsome, far exceeding the original contract with Arizona to guard the train. Matthew thought about the first thing he was going to eat. Maybe he'd visit a real steakhouse, one that served actual cow instead of vat-grown meat. His mouth watered at the thought.

When they left Churchill the next morning, Matthew hurt as much as he'd guessed he would, but he had money in his pocket for the first time in weeks. He set a course for Flagstaff.

Sharon noticed the destination at once. "What gives? We've got to go retrieve our grav bikes."

"It's not quite over yet. You and I need to pay a visit to Ryan Thompson."

"The government man? He's not gonna pay us again. We failed to protect the train."

Matthew frowned. "Trust me."

It was late morning before they found themselves in the office of the Arizona Minister of Law.

"I'm not paying you double," Thompson said quietly. "You failed to protect the train and I hear that Churchill paid you well."

Rays of sunlight filtered through blinds, painting an eerie striped pattern on the government man. Sharon gave Matthew a told-you-so look, but he waved her off. "We're not really here to get paid. I'm here for an answer to a question that's been on my mind."

"Oh? And what would that be?"

"Why?" It was a single word, sharp and succinct, but it cut to the point.

Thompson straightened his tie. "Because sometimes we do what we must to survive. Isn't that the very reason you Freelancers wander the solar system like starving rats, desperately searching for crumbs?"

"Isn't that all any of us do anymore?" Matthew retorted sharply. "I don't know why you paid Vance to spring the prisoner and leak our plans to the Hawthornes. What does being a sellout have to do with survival?"

Matthew saw Sharon shift posture as the pieces clicked into place for her. She took a threatening step forward and crossed her arms.

Thompson looked back and forth between the two. "Simple threat assessment. I've had a bit of an agreement with the Hawthornes. I leave them to their petty crimes if they keep the body count low. James Hawthorne's arrest was purely an accident on the part of a well-meaning deputy."

"But why prop them up at all? Why not just crush them?" Sharon blustered.

"Because with the Hawthornes gone, someone else will move in to take their place. Perhaps one of the bigger more organized syndicates will see an opportunity to move into fresh territory, or one of Europa's cartels will see a population ripe for harvesting fresh slaves for their fields. I made a choice to protect the people I serve, and I will not be judged for that."

Matthew shook his head. "How many innocent bystanders were killed in the train car when the skyhopper opened fire?"

Thompson's cheek twitched slightly. "Six." Matthew was surprised he even knew the number.

"And who protected them? You're a murderer Ryan Thompson. You better pray that God has mercy on your soul."

Thompson's eyes widened with terror, and he looked at Matthew's gun still holstered at his side.

Matthew let the moment hang just long enough. "But I'm not a murderer. Count yourself a lucky man, minister."

He turned and stalked out of the office.

"What was that?" Sharon demanded as they walked out of the downtown office building. "Are we just going to let him get away with what he did?"

Matthew turned and looked at the building. "Not my choice to make. We'll send the story to as many members of Arizona's government as we can. A man like Thompson isn't likely to be unseated by such a scandal, but at least others will be watching him now. He'll have to play by the rules for a while."

Sharon seemed to consider this. "All the same I think we should leave Arizona for a bit. I wouldn't put Thompson past revenge."

Matthew sighed and looked around at the familiar surroundings, the city of his birth. He never got to stay long, not with his profession, but he was always glad to visit. It had changed a lot over the years, as it slowly ground to a halt like everything else. The flower really does fade, he thought bitterly.

By sunset they had taken care of their remaining business and trudged out of the border town back towards the Sparrow and Sharon's skyhopper. Matthew had noticed her limp hours ago. Her right knee didn't want to move smoothly.

"That going to be okay? I'm guessing you can fix it?"

She sighed. "Nope. I can knock out the dents and repair the armoring itself, but the mechanism inside is a little more complicated than I can handle."

"I'm sorry," he said simply and meant it. He wondered how much of her share of the bounty was going to go to the repair bill.

They walked in silence for another minute before Sharon spoke up again. "Say I've got a favor to ask."

"I'm all ears."

"There's this tinker I know on Ceres. He's got a knack for earthtech and has done some work for me in the past. I was wondering if I could hitch a ride, that is if you were headed that way anytime soon. I'll pay

60

my fare of course. But seeing as how you're leaving Arizona anyway..."

"I've got a little tradition," he said cutting her off. "After a dangerous job that goes way off the beaten course, I try to take something nice and easy. Maybe a nice cargo run or passenger job. Keeps the stress level down." He looked at her from the corner of his eye. "I'm sure I can find some excuse to take a trip to Ceres."

The relief in Sharon's eyes was plain to see. Maybe she'd envisioned months of trying to hitch a ride, all the while limited on what jobs she could take with her damaged exo-suit. "Thanks, Cole. I'll pay ticket price."

He waved her off. "Friends can hitch a ride for free."

Sharon raised an eyebrow. "Thanks. You know when I met you, you didn't strike me as the kind of person that made friends."

He turned toward the Sparrow, not wanting her to see the shame on his face. She was right, of course. He didn't use to be this way.

"Well, I've got at least one."

Chapter 5: Bright Crater Diagnosis

The job hasn't changed in centuries. Not one bit.
Sure we have to deal with a few different
scenarios in the colonies than cops did a couple
centuries ago, but it's really all the same. Criminal
syndicates. Human trafficking. Petty hatred.

My pops would have called it sin. I call it evil.

Men are just wild animals after all.

No, Moses didn't really change things. God help
him, he tried, but not even the great mind of AI
could straighten us out. We had thousands of
years of inertia in our favor. Moses just had one
century. Truth is, we were too mighty a force for
him.

Maybe he could have done things a little
differently. Fixed us through brute force. Taken
away our freedom and our will. Put all of us law
enforcement out of a job permanently. With all
the hell I've seen of humanity's underbelly, there's
a dark attraction there. Peace at the expense of
freedom.

But that's always been the siren call, hasn't it?

Guess it wasn't in Moses' nature. He called it right either way. He's gone and all of us in law enforcement still have a job.

Anthony Russo
Police Commissioner of Freeport 13
Died 34 AM

An alarm buzzed, and Matthew slapped it and rolled out of bed, blinking the sleep away from his eyes. He had been dreaming about running on top of a never-ending train, chasing someone that always kept just out of reach. This was the second night in a row he had had that particular dream.

"Beats the showing up for a job naked thing, I guess."

He pulled his clothes on and opened the door. Across the hall, the door to the room he had lent Sharon was still closed and the light down in the common room still off. She took every opportunity she could to sleep in. Cole had noticed this on the first day out from Mars. Weird habit for a freelancer, but who was he to judge.

Breakfast was cold oatmeal washed down with a cup of black coffee. He left the box out for Sharon and climbed down the ladder into the hold. Six enormous shipping containers filled the space. Matthew checked the status monitor on each one of them, mostly out of habit. Nothing could have happened to them overnight, but he went about his routine anyway. Green lights shone on all of them, refrigerated and airtight. He'd managed to snag a cargo job on the way out of Mars, pharmaceuticals destined for a supplier on Ceres. Stepping around Sharon's oversized grav bike, he climbed back up the ladder. She'd been adamant that they bring it with them, insisting it would be easier for her to get around and important to have in case something happened.

Knowing Ceres, he couldn't blame her.

He passed by the cabins again and rapped the back of his hand on Sharon's door. "We'll be there in under an hour. Might want to rejoin the land of the living." He poured a second cup of coffee on his way to the cockpit and finished up his morning routine of making sure all systems were good to go.

Twenty minutes later, he frowned and turned his head back down the hall. Sharon still hadn't made an appearance. He pounded on the door again. "You got half an hour and if you don't get up soon, I'm going to finish the coffee."

Her muffled voice rang through the door. "Calm down. And that black stuff you drink doesn't even resemble coffee."

"It's closer than the sugary sludge you like."

Just before they reached Ceres, she joined him in the cockpit, already suited up for the day. Matthew thought it was odd that she literally never took the thing off. Secretly he wondered if she slept in it, but he'd already learned that questions about the armor were a non-starter.

She leaned against the door frame. "You know I had my own alarm set. I didn't have any reason to get up so early. What did I miss? Besides nothing."

"Stimulating conversation with myself. Hold on, disengaging the frameshift." He cut power to the device and their speed reverted to just under ten thousand miles an hour. Turning back to the main console, he took the flight yoke and spun the Sparrow one hundred eighty degrees and fired up the main engines to begin shedding their speed. After several minutes of burn, he cut the thrusters and turned back around to face Ceres, now cruising along at less than a thousand miles per hour.

Sharon looked at the scene out the front canopy and whistled. Offhand, Matthew had to agree with the sentiment. Ceres was a mess of activity like usual. The dwarf planet's surface was littered with cities, factories, mines and more. Scopes read ships everywhere as they went about their business. Dozens of asteroids that had been frameshifted into Ceres' orbit over a century ago for mining were also hives of activity.

"Welcome to the worst port of call in the solar system," Matthew said gesturing at the dwarf planet. "I try to keep my distance, but what can I say, I'm easily talked into things."

"Sorry," Sharon said, pushing a dark curl behind her ear. "Europa's probably a lot quieter than Ceres."

He raised an eyebrow and glanced at her out of the side of his eye. "Who said I'm from Europa?" he said as he finished inserting the Sparrow into orbit. "Flagstaff born and raised."

"Come on Cole. I'm not dumb. Considering how insistent you are about the whole gaucho thing, I think it's a safe guess you've spent a fair amount of time on Europa."

For a moment he let the statement hang, then decided it wasn't worth ignoring. "It's peaceful, so long as you avoid the cartels. Let's just say I'm keeping my distance for now."

Sharon nodded. "I see. Well, I can't go home either, so I know how that goes." He turned to face her again, but she was already walking away from the cockpit. "Don't bother asking," she said over her shoulder.

Matthew laughed to himself and turned his attention back to Ceres. Over the next twenty-five minutes, he brought the Sparrow out of orbit and down to one of the larger cities. The contract had specified a private landing pad on the outskirts of town, probably to avoid attracting attention. Pharmaceuticals were high-value cargo, and it never hurt to be too cautious these days.

Abigail checked their location one more time on a map before heading to the hold. Cole had chosen this job because the earthtech tinker she knew lived on the south side of Bright Crater City. It had been surprisingly decent of him, but then Abigail figured that he was a lot more decent of a man than he let on to the outside world. She climbed down the ladder to the hold, where Cole was checking his cargo one last time.

"You got everything squared away?" she asked.

He nodded. "Receiver should have the heavy equipment to unload. I'm just here to get paid and make sure they don't break anything. Go ahead. Go get that knee looked at."

She pushed her grav bike over onto the lift and punched the button to lower it. "I'll comm you when I'm done," she said as they were lowered to the ground.

"Sounds good. Don't forget. We are on Ceres."

Abigail rolled her eyes. "I can take care of myself, I'm a big girl." He stood above her with his arms crossed.

"I know, I just meant be careful until you're back to a hundred percent."

She mock saluted him. "Yes, sir." Without another word, she mounted her bike, fired the engines, and took off towards the nearest entrance tunnel.

Ceres was designed a little differently than most of the other colonized rocks. So many people were spread out over so great an area that it wasn't cost efficient to close cities in under environmental shields, despite the psychological benefits of being able to walk under an open sky. Nearly everyone lived underground, with only the fanciest buildings breaking the crust to pierce the cold, airless sky. Abigail exited the tunnel and entered a vast underground canyon cut by enormous excavators long ago. A road of busy traffic ran along the floor, while the sides were covered in buildings built both into and onto the canyon wall. Ramshackle sheet metal dwellings hung precariously over the road, bolted into the sheer rock walls. Abigail wondered if they ever fell.

It took her over two hours to cross town, weaving from one densely populated canyon to the next, fighting for her spot in traffic against both grav and ground vehicles. She'd hit the roads at the wrong time, local rush hour from the look of things. All the while, the city around her grew seedier and seedier.

Cole's warning wasn't exactly unfounded. Ceres was as lawless a rock as there ever was. Its proper government had collapsed decades ago, shortly after the wars on Earth. Now, regions were ruled by judges who had near complete power over their territory. Some were businessmen, some were warlords, and others were politicians. All of them were concerned with two things. Keeping their own position and keeping their territory functioning. The only thing that kept them in check was their own citizenry. It wasn't uncommon for a judge to get assassinated if they stepped too far out of bounds.

Crime was high since the judges didn't have an awful lot to spend on security forces, that is if they weren't outright involved in criminal activities. Ceres was also home to two of the three largest crime syndicates in the solar system.

Abigail found herself in the worst part of Bright Crater City, the kind of place where everyone you met was either part of the problem or a victim of it. Sometimes it was hard to tell where the line was between those two and a lot were a bit of both.

She found the tired curiosity shop on a lower-level side tunnel. The street was half filled with trash and piles of rubble. A flickering neon sign that read Ivan's hung above an old-fashioned revolving door. That alone let any potential customers know what they were getting themselves into.

Entering Ivan's shop was like stepping back in time, only you couldn't quite tell what time you had arrived at. The moment Abigail pushed through the revolving door, an earthtech gun turret tracked her motion from the ten-foot ceiling. A single red eye on the machine let any and all know that it meant deadly business and that they were to behave. She didn't know quite what would trigger the weapon to defend its master, and she hoped to never find out. The walls and shelves were littered with trinkets, memorabilia, and old tech from previous centuries. Ancient wooden cuckoo clocks faithfully ticked away time, marking each passing second. A case of old rifles, probably dating from before the European World Wars hung proudly on the wall. Another shelf was loaded with computers from every era of their use, ranging from modern to earthtech to laughably old and quaint.

Ivan himself was nowhere to be seen. Abigail glanced up at the gun turret still tracking her movements. He must have trusted that thing implicitly. Knowing him, he was probably elbow-deep in some project in the back of the shop. Not having anything better to do, she browsed the shelves of odds and ends.

She'd been at it for only a few minutes when a lightly accented voice called out to her. "Ms. Sharon! Ms. Sharon! To what do I owe the explicit pleasure of you gracing me with the presence of that wonderful suit of yours?" Ivan stood in the doorway to his shop. The man was tall and extremely slender and was dressed in a tailcoat and bowtie. He also sported the bushiest and most ridiculous grey mutton chops that Abigail had ever seen.

She picked up a dusty black box and examined it. "Repair work Ivan. Took a bullet to the knee. Rifle. The guy was a good shot. I'm hoping you can do something with it." She flipped the device over and shrugged. "What is this?"

"VCR. Put it down. It's very rare."

She set it back on the shelf and walked towards him, acutely aware of her damaged knee. The tinker's eyes were already watching her slow movements. "You know how it pains me that you take that beautiful piece of earthtech into fights. One day you may lose it and the universe will lose something precious."

"Yeah, it will lose me," she said. "Honestly, Ivan, you could stand to lose the creepy machine man schtick. It's weird and I bet it chases off customers."

He laughed. "Nonsense. My customers are either fellow collectors or owners of rare technology that have no clue how to service it. They're either like me or they need me. Come. Let's take a look at your marvelous knee." He held the door open to the workshop and gestured politely with a distant smile. "Oh! And Sparky?" The gun turret turned its red eye to its owner. "Keep an eye on things, will you?" The turret turned back to the door, resuming its tireless vigil.

Ivan's workshop was neat and orderly, far more so than the storefront. The front was merely play, but here, where he worked on his machines, was serious business. He took off his tailcoat and hung it on a rack, revealing his earthtech prosthetic arm. Abigail had always wondered if it was from an old injury or if he had amputated his own arm just for the fun of it. She had always been afraid to ask because she was quite sure the answer was almost certainly the latter.

"Now then, come stand in the light Ms. Sharon. Let me see the damage."

She obeyed and he stooped to examine the knee. His hands probed the bullet hole and the surrounding area. Abigail felt his touch, relayed to her brain via the implant in her spine. It was distant and cold, not at all like the feel of her own skin, but it was just enough to allow her to feel the environment around her while suited. Thankfully the sensations capped off quickly. The impact of the bullet caused her less pain than jamming a finger.

"Well doc, what's the prognosis. Am I gonna be okay?"

"Hmm..." he said thoughtfully. "I can't tell for sure, but it looks like none of the mechanisms are damaged. I believe the joint's housing has been bent. It seems to be applying pressure where it should not."

Abigail breathed a quiet sigh of relief. The inevitable day that she did permanent damage had not yet come. "What's it going to cost and how long will it take?"

"More than you want and not as long as you think," Ivan said. "The biggest difficulty will be exposing the housing. I'm afraid I shall have to disassemble half the leg." He looked up at her and raised one of his bushy eyebrows. "I'm afraid you'll have to unsuit for this particular surgery."

She bit her lip in annoyance. "I was afraid of that. Alright, I guess I don't have a choice." She walked over to a bench and knelt beside it. "Come over here. I may need a hand."

Frowning, he walked over to her. "I'm intrigued, puzzled even."

She put her suit on follow mode. A child could now lead it by the hand and pose it like the world's largest doll. She cracked the back of the exo-suit open and pulled her arms out. "It's a little tough to extricate myself from this thing without something to grab," she explained. "When I said I needed a hand I meant it literally."

Abigail gripped Ivan's hand and pulled herself out onto the bench, feeling small and exposed. She gestured to her now empty exo-suit. "Do your thing. I'm not paying you for nothing."

Matthew's business went exactly as expected, which considering the track record of his last few jobs, felt like a small miracle. Cargo runs weren't exactly going to make you rich, but they turned a small profit and got you to the next spaceport. By the time the shipping containers had been offloaded, inventory taken, and accounts settled, a couple hours had passed. He checked the comm in the cockpit to make sure he hadn't missed any messages from Sharon. Surely it would take her a little longer to get the knee repaired.

Which left him some time to himself. He thought about pulling up the local freelancer board, see if there were any easy jobs he could spend the afternoon on, but as soon as he flipped on the monitor, he decided against it. All work and no play was pretty much the freelancer mantra, and it often ended in death. Matthew had a better idea.

Pulling up the local network he put in a search for the place he was looking for.

Bingo.

An hour later he was riding an elevator up into one of the many towers that pierced the surface. Its glass window gave an unobstructed view of the dead landscape of the dwarf planet, broken up only by silhouettes where the subterranean city showed its uppermost levels. The elevator came to a stop and the door opened into the finest steakhouse in Bright Crater.

Matthew's first instinct when he saw the fountain with goldfish was that he was underdressed. His second instinct was that he didn't care. The hostess gave him a funny look, and he looked down at his poncho, dusted it off, and shrugged with a smile. Despite having very visible doubts about him, she sat him at a small table near a window overlooking the city.

He tapped his toes in boredom as he waited for his server. When at last the tuxedoed man approached his table, Matthew just smiled. "Bring the finest ribeye you have, cooked to the chef's recommendations. Oh, and a cherry soda."

The waiter wrote the order down, then eyed Matthew. "Sir, are you sure you can afford this? This is a very nice restaurant and I wouldn't want..."

Matthew clinked a stack of heavy coins on the table then pocketed them.

"Very well, sir."

The server retreated, leaving Matthew alone and soon bored. He was unused to the feeling. "I've been fine by myself for a decade," he muttered in annoyance. "Now after a week of working with someone I can't handle a solitary afternoon."

He looked around the room to find something to keep his attention. At the table next to him sat a youngish man dressed in a white coat that matched his pasty skin. Something about him didn't sit right with Matthew, and it wasn't just his sense of fashion. Across from the man, a middle-aged black woman with streaks of silver in her hair was clearly unhappy to be at the same table, though she made a valiant attempt at covering it with a smile. The man, on the other hand, had a dreamy look in his eye. That was what Matthew didn't like.

Kid was in over his head. The older woman wasn't interested in what he was selling. Matthew shook his head. Some people were just oblivious to anything outside their own fantasies.

Matthew's steak was delivered with a potato and salad. He sliced into the piece of meat, and his eyes practically watered at the smell of it. It had been at least five or six years since he'd had anything but vat-grown. Not that there was anything wrong with vat-grown. It tasted perfectly fine, but the texture just never lived up to the real thing.

His comm beeped and with a sigh of frustration he pulled it out. Sharon. "What do you want?"

"My, aren't we cranky," she retorted.

"You're interrupting my steak dinner."

"Sorry. Was just going to update you. I'm still sitting here watching my armor get repaired. It shouldn't be all that much longer. I guess you're not at the Sparrow anyway, so it doesn't really matter."

Matthew took a bite of his prized meal and closed his eyes savoring it. "So you're telling me that you're not in your armor right now? I thought you would wear it until you died."

"Funny. The tinker had to disassemble the entire leg to get to the damaged part."

"Either that or you're an amputated head hooked into a suit."

She didn't even try and hide the sigh of exasperation. "Okay. I think we're done here. I guess I'll check in when I leave." There was a click as the connection was cut. Matthew shrugged and set about to enjoy his meal.

He had nearly finished when there was a sudden commotion at the table next to him. The creepy man was down on one knee and appeared to be proposing to the woman. Matthew was curious and slightly horrified at what was happening, though he pretended not to stare.

The woman's face was severe. "Get up and stop embarrassing yourself. You know what my answer must be."

Matthew couldn't help but feel a pang of pity for him. Somewhere seated in the heart of every man is the fear of such a rejection, such a dismissal by the one whose attention you crave the most. It wasn't pleasant to watch.

His pity was short lived because the man stood and slapped the woman across the face.

Matthew's hands automatically clenched into fists, but he gave it a five count to see how the woman responded. She glared at her suitor, saying nothing.

Without really knowing what he was doing, Matthew found himself standing behind the jerk. Now that he was here, he didn't find it all that hard a decision.

He tapped the man's shoulder. "You know, it's not polite to lay hands on a lady. Ever."

As the man turned to face him, Matthew drove his fist into his jaw. He heard the crack, felt it give as the bone broke. The man dropped to the floor, either out cold, too surprised to react, or too afraid to even try. Matthew suspected the latter.

Matthew brushed his hands off and turned to the lady to tip his campero.

The look of fear in her eye stopped him cold. "You idiot. His bodyguard!"

Well that complicated things. The man on the floor may have been scum, he may have not understood the first thing about women, but he was apparently important.

Matthew grabbed a plate off the woman's table and spun just in time to see a man drawing a weapon at a nearby table. He threw the plate at the thug, catching him in the chest, then charged him, grabbing a second plate from another table. The bodyguard had barely begun to recover from the first assault before Matthew smashed the expensive flatware across his face.

He dropped just as hard as his employer had. Matthew spun around to get his bearings. While every eye in the restaurant was on him, no one else appeared to be making a move. Okay. He was important enough to have one bodyguard but thankfully no more.

Matthew walked back to the woman and tipped his campero a second time.

She just shook her head. "You don't have a clue what you just did. I appreciate the concern, but you've gotten involved in something you want no part in."

Maybe you can't judge the importance of a man by the number of bodyguards that follow him, Matthew thought acridly. He rubbed the stubble on his chin. "I'm hoping that you're not about to tell me he's some kind of gangster."

The corner of the woman's mouth crept upward in a sad smile. "White Void Syndicate. My friend here, who goes by the name Piggy, is the local Strongarm."

Matthew wasn't quite sure he appreciated the humor of the moment like she did. "Tengo mala leche," he muttered. "Well, that's the worst thing I've heard all day. I'm guessing that your friend, Piggy, isn't the forgiving type."

"He's not the problem," she replied softly. "White Void knows me and will mark me for dead after this, and if they can identify you, you'll be on that list too."

"Then I think it's best we leave," Matthew fumbled into his pocket for a handful of large denomination coins to pay for his meal, tip, and an apology for the commotion. He parted with far more money than he wanted, but, given that waiting around to get change wasn't the wisest idea, he set the pile on the table. "Share an elevator?" he asked gesturing towards the exit. The number of eyes on him still made him uncomfortable. Even if White Void didn't have any more goons nearby, somebody would talk. The less of a look they got at him, the better.

The woman nodded and followed him. The waiter approached her briefly, but she shook her head. "My date will be paying once he awakens. He appears to be indisposed at the moment."

They left without another word. The short wait for the elevator was agonizing. When at last they were safely aboard and traveling back towards the surface of Ceres, Matthew turned to the woman and asked the obvious question. "So what now?"

"I pack up and leave. Staying here will only get me killed." She gave him a stern look. "I suggest you do the same."

He sighed. "Look, I'm sorry, I didn't know he was White Void, I just... did what seemed decent."

"You have nothing to apologize for. If more people did what seemed decent, then perhaps the solar system wouldn't be in its current sad state of affairs."

He adjusted his campero nervously. "I still owe you. Got you into a problem and now I have to help you out of it. Name's Matthew Cole. I'm a freelancer. I've got a ship. I'll give you a ride just about anywhere you want to go."

The older woman gave him a soft smile and then nodded once. "I accept, Mr. Cole." She offered him a hand to shake. "Yvonne Naude."

"Wish I could say we were meeting under better circumstances, Ms. Naude," he replied as the door to the elevator opened to a parking garage.

"Yvonne is fine. I'm not that old."

"Right. Come on. My bike is this way. I'll give you a ride to my ship."

They walked at the fastest pace that Matthew thought wouldn't look suspicious. Thankfully the garage was mostly deserted. Reaching the bike, he hopped on and tightened the strap on his campero. "Let's go. Ceres ain't too friendly anymore."

Yvonne hesitated. "Can you take me by my apartment first?"

He frowned. "Longer we wait, the more likely White Void catches up to us. I get the feeling your apartment will be on the shortlist of places they look for you."

"Please."

There was a quiet insistence in her voice that cut through Matthew's defenses. He didn't like it. But he was going to do it.

"Get on. We better hurry."

Abigail had just finished closing up her suit and was testing her refurbished knee by walking around Ivan's workshop when her comm buzzed.

"Oh hey, Sharon. What's your time on getting back to the ship?"

"I'm finishing up here. Traffic should be lighter now so it won't take nearly as long to get back." She paused, suddenly suspicious. "Why?"

"Complication. I know we talked about sticking around Ceres for a bit and doing a few jobs before heading back to Mars, but I might have accidentally crossed paths with the White Void syndicate."

"Cole are you insane? That's one of the big three!"

"We can talk about it later. I've got a passenger with me and we've got to make a stop first. Just be at the Sparrow ready to go or you're going to be on Ceres for the foreseeable future."

She rolled her eyes. "You wouldn't leave me."

The comm was silent for a minute. "That's not the point," he concluded lamely. "Just hurry."

"I will."

She cut the comm and turned to Ivan. "Knee feels good. You're the best, as usual."

"Yes, I am, but flattery doesn't get discounts. You know my rates."

Abigail sighed and opened up a compartment on her arm and pulled out a handful of coins. "You know, one of these days, you'll grow a heart and cut me some slack."

"And one of these days you'll stop taking that beautiful piece of earthtech into dangerous situations," he countered as he donned his tailcoat again. "Given your rather unique situation, you should take better care of it."

She gave him a hard look but decided not to take the bait. "Girl's gotta make a living."

Ivan shrugged politely and extended a hand. "And so do I."

She paid him, feeling the loss of each coin she dropped in his palm. It was over half what she'd made from the Hawthorne brothers bounty. Ivan was a master, but his work didn't come cheap. "There now," he said. "That wasn't so hard, was it?"

"Easy for you say. Thanks, Ivan."

Some days it felt impossible to get ahead in the world. The way things were going, she'd be stuck on Mars doing small jobs till her suit finally gave out. And then where would she be?

She turned and stalked out of the shop. Sparky, the gun turret, turned its red eye to stare at her. "What are you looking at?" she grumbled as she left the building, leaving the revolving door spinning. She mounted her bike. "Better not dawdle. Cole seems to be good at finding trouble."

Matthew looked around at the small but well-furnished apartment. "What are we here for? We need to move."

"Mr. Cole, you don't have to remind me to hurry. I believe I'm the one that informed you of our current danger."

He stood awkwardly in the entryway as Yvonne went to her bedroom to pack a bag. A pair of framed diplomas hanging on the wall caught his eye, and he walked across the room to get a better look. "You didn't mention that you were a doctor."

Yvonne's voice came from the next room. "Forgive me for not starting with my life story. My husband and I ran an emergency clinic on the southside. Half the people we treated were victims of their own crimes. Eventually, my husband became a victim of the people we were trying to help."

"I'm sorry," Matthew said glancing at the second diploma. Tomas Naude it read, from the University of Ganymede.

"It was the life we chose. And it's what got me into this trouble. I saved Piggy's life some months ago. He had a bullet lodged in his spine. That I was able to remove it and him still walk is nothing short of a miracle."

"And he's been smitten with you ever since," Matthew said filling in the blanks.

"Precisely. When an up and coming White Void enforcer asks you to dinner, it's rather dangerous to say no." Yvonne appeared from the back room with a duffle bag over one shoulder. "I should apologize for getting you into this."

"Let's not talk about blame and just get out of here," Matthew suggested.

Yvonne took a look around her apartment, and Matthew felt a twinge of pity. It wasn't easy to lose a home. She walked to the wall and took down a portrait of what Matthew assumed was her late husband and slipped it into the bag. He wondered if the portrait was the main reason they had bothered to come here.

"I'm ready," she said. "Let's go."

They left the building and returned to Matthew's bike where it sat parked on the street. No sooner had they boarded it and fired up the engines, when two black grav cars pulled up.

"I think we're out of time. Hang on." Matthew gunned the engine to full. Yvonne's hands gripped tightly to his waist as they darted between the two cars. He glanced behind them. Someone leaned out of the window and fired a few shots in their direction, but they went wide. The drivers were good though. In just a few seconds they had turned around and were in hot pursuit.

Matthew began to weave in and out of traffic, glad to be on a nimble bike. He would have to lose these guys before going back to the Sparrow. Maybe he ended up on the White Void hit list, but he wasn't willing to have his ship on that list too. Unfortunately, he didn't know the layout of Bright Crater all that well. He'd be at a disadvantage here.

A bullet pinged off the back of the bike, and he turned around. The syndicate cars were catching up. They were muscling their way through traffic and other drivers were getting the hint and giving them the right of way.

Matthew swerved onto a new, larger road, not bothering to heed a single traffic law or read the signs. "You trying to get us killed?" Yvonne shouted over the roar of the engine.

"I'm trying to keep us from getting killed, hang on."

The new road had more cars to keep their pursuers busy. Matthew stared ahead and frowned. Something didn't line up with what he was seeing. Suddenly the road turned sharply downward. Gravity changed directions with them so that they were traveling straight down a wall. The tunnel stretched in front of him as far as the eye could see. Above him on what appeared to be the ceiling, was another lane of traffic moving in the opposite direction.

"Tell me what I'm seeing here, Yvonne. Where are we?"

"You've turned onto one of the Core Roads. This will continue for about a hundred kilometers through the ice mantle to the core regions where most of the mining takes place."

"Is there no way off this road?"

"Not that I know of."

That wasn't good. No doubt the syndicate vehicles would call ahead and have someone waiting at the far end of the tunnel. Matthew bit his lip and risked another glance behind him. The black grav cars were gaining again. He looked up at the lane of traffic above him leaving the core regions, and a crazy idea worked its way into his head.

"I'm about to do something dumb. If we die, well... I'm sorry." Suddenly he swerved to the side. Pointing the grav bike upward, he jumped over the highway's sidewall. Gravity switched back to its proper orientation, and instead of being in a long tunnel, they were over a shaft so deep they couldn't see the bottom. He throttled the engines and pushed them across the shaft as they began to fall, rapidly gaining speed.

When they were nearly to the opposite line of traffic, he turned the bike and faced it straight down the shaft, lining up the bottom of the bike with the road. Gravity switched and they dropped to the surface of the new road.

Only problem now was they were going the wrong way with all the accumulated speed of their fall. Matthew ignored Yvonne's scream and expertly dodged a few vehicles that scorched past at blinding speed as he hit the braking thrusters as hard as he could. After several tense seconds and many near misses, they'd slowed to nearly a halt. He spun the bike back towards the surface and throttled up the engines again. In two minutes they were out of the Core Road and heading back towards the Sparrow with no syndicate cars in sight.

"I'm not going to lie, I'm pretty proud of the way that went," he said grinning ear to ear. Yvonne didn't answer at once, which was probably for the best.

That's when he saw the tail. A grav bike, painted black, keeping an even distance behind them. Must have been at the exit waiting for them. Matthew kept an eye on it, but it didn't make a move. Probably just keeping tabs on them and waiting for reinforcements.

He pulled out his comm. "Sharon. We'll be at the Sparrow in ten minutes."

"I'll be there in two."

"Good. I've got a bike on my tail that needs dealing with. Think you can set up an ambush for him before our destination? I don't want them knowing my ship."

"Okay. Umm... Look for me at the tunnel entrance to the industrial complex."

"Got it. See you there."

Abigail pulled off at the prescribed spot and found a dumpster by the road that would provide the cover she needed for herself and the bike. She pulled her shield off her back and engaged it, hearing the faint whine of the grav plate powering up. She poked her head around the corner and watched the nearly deserted road.

Right on schedule, two grav bikes appeared, Cole's beat up piece of junk and a flashy black one. Abigail cracked her knuckles and got a better grip on the shield. Poor guy would never know what hit him.

Matthew and his mysterious passenger blasted past. She gave it a three count and stepped out from behind the dumpster. The black bike was upon her. Taking her shield in both hands she bashed it forward, catching the bike as it passed. The force of her strike combined with the grav plate sent the bike careening out of control into the wall beside the tunnel. It blossomed into an orange fireball, sending flaming shrapnel arcing outward. Abigail caught a piece of it on her shield.

She returned to her own bike. Whatever Cole had gotten himself involved in, there had better be a good explanation. Ceres was fertile ground for a freelancer, and she was going to miss out because of him.

By the time she had reached the Sparrow and loaded her bike, the engines were already hot. She rode the lift back up with the bike, climbed the ladder out of the hold, and walked straight to the cockpit. A well-dressed woman with deep onyx skin and a ribbon of silver hair sat behind Cole. She startled when she saw Abigail, but recovered quickly and smiled graciously.

"You must be Mr. Cole's partner. I'm Yvonne Naude."

Abigail nodded. "Abigail Sharon, but I think partner is a bit too strong of a word. More like tense acquaintances. Cole just offered me a lift."

"It appears, he's offering to give me a ride too," Yvonne said smoothly. "I wonder if this happens often?"

"I promise you, it doesn't," Cole said as he flipped a bank of switches. "Strap in." Abigail ignored him and braced against a wall. "I'm having a bad week, all right?"

Abigail chuckled. "And you're still not off the hook for getting us kicked off Ceres." She turned to Yvonne. "I want the whole story later. So he doesn't paint himself into some kind of hero."

"Well, he was actually trying to be chivalrous..." Yvonne said.

"See! Not my week!" Cole said. The Sparrow lifted off the ground and he turned it skyward. The main engines roared, rumbling through the deck as they made for space. Cole kept his eyes on the instruments. "Not seeing any movement in response to us. I don't think they marked us." He visibly relaxed and took off his hat, setting it on the console.

"So where are we going now?" Yvonne asked Cole.

"Got any family? Anyone you can stay with?"

"Not since my husband. We never had children."

"Hold on," Cole interrupted. "Just got a message from my broker." His eyes scanned the message then went wide. "Actually I don't think anywhere is going to be a particularly good idea right now."

"Why's that?" Abigail frowned stepping forward to read the message over his shoulder.

Cole glanced nervously at Yvonne. "Broker knew I was on Ceres and saw a new bounty posted. A half million dollars on Yvonne Naude's head. Double if she's alive."

For the space of ten minutes, the only sound in the Sparrow's cockpit was the rattle of the engines as Matthew finished putting the ship into orbit. Finally, Yvonne broke the silence herself. "The most sensible thing to do would be to turn me in. I understand. A million dollars is a dream come true to a pair of freelancers."

It was tempting. Anyone faced with an opportunity like that would be a fool to admit otherwise. But as much as Abigail wanted a ship of her own, she knew that turning a woman over to a syndicate like this was dirty. She didn't even need to hear the story. Playing dirty with a rival like she did in Kyoto with Cole was one thing, but this was a line in the sand that just wasn't worth crossing.

Cole sighed and deflated a little. "Much as that many zeroes attached to a dollar sign would be appreciated, I just can't do that. We couldn't do that," he clarified, glancing at Abigail for assurance. She nodded. "You're welcome to stay aboard the Sparrow until we figure out how to get you out of this mess."

"That's very kind of you Mr. Cole," Yvonne said. There was gratitude on her face, but no trace of surprise. "If I can be of service to you in any way possible, I will not hesitate."

"So where are we going now?" Abigail asked. "I'm guessing Mars is out because White Void has a heavy presence in several of the cities." She said this hopefully. Maybe she could avoid going back to Mars for a bit. This might not be as good as having your own ship, but hitching a ride with another competent freelancer was a close second. She'd have to contact a friend to put her skyhopper in storage, but that wouldn't be a problem.

"Yeah, that pretty much seals that," he agreed. "I don't know where we go yet. Give me some time." He ran a hand across the scruff on his chin. "Sharon, if you want to show Yvonne to the cabin beside yours, I'd appreciate it."

Abigail stepped back into the hall and gestured. "This way."

She showed the woman the cabin. "They aren't exactly roomy, but I think you'll have a better time in the cramped space than I do."

"Thank you," Yvonne said setting her bag on the floor.

Abigail laughed. "I think I should be thanking you."

"Why's that?"

"I wasn't ready to go back to Mars yet." She winked. "Welcome aboard the Sparrow."

Chapter 6: Islands in the Night

There is one bright spot of learning left in the colonies, one place that seeks to stave off the coming ignorance. The city of Galileo, Ganymede was named after the astronomer who first discovered the moon peering into a telescope all those centuries ago. He would be pleased to know that those who colonized it deemed it a proper place to found a university.

And like the ancient Galileo who at times strove against the ignorance around him, the modern university battles against the same darkness. Without Moses or the backing of Earth, it is a losing battle as its scientists and engineers study the technology Moses left them, hoping against hope to unlock its secrets.

The University of Ganymede has one ally that Galileo himself did not have. A short trip across the icy plains will bring one to the very steps of the colonial Vatican. The papacy, though still chiefly concerned with the state of men's souls, knows that there will one day be no more men at all if humanity continues in its current decline.

Thus the church and science's long misunderstanding is at last set aside. Have they not both ever sought to explain the universe in which we dwell? Do they not both seek the betterment of the human race? In this dark time, there is at last a peace between these two fields of study.

And that is enough to bring a little hope.

Jonathan Walkins
Author of the History of the Colonies
Died 58 AM

Y vonne sat in the cockpit, book in hand, but unread. The Sparrow was quiet, with only the occasional tick of contracting metal as the ship slowly cooled through the night. Jupiter sat unmoving in the sky due to Ganymede being tidally locked with the gas giant, its reflected light making the moon's eighty-five hour night somewhat more bearable.

She stared at that planet, feeling the tug of memory. How many years had it been since she and Tomas attended the med school here? Too many. Late night studies in the library had led to confessions of love and a hasty marriage. Together they had passed their classes and their rotations, never parting from each other's side. The colonies needed doctors and they bounced around the solar system for years. Eventually, as their youth faded, they ended up on Ceres. The fact that their practice had been aimed at the most desperate members of chaotic Ceres was a deliberate choice. It had ended as they knew it might. Though less than a year ago, it seemed to have happened in a lifetime past.

The arrival of a stranger to spirit her away in her hour of need felt like something out of an adventure story, the sort of thing one imagines in an idle moment. Lifting her eyes, Yvonne saw the dark spires of the University of Ganymede against the horizon. More than anything she wanted to leave the Sparrow, to walk through the old library, to find the park where Tomas had proposed.

But the risk was too great. Every freelancer and bounty hunter in the system would have memorized her face by now, and a chance encounter would lead to disaster. For the foreseeable future, she was indeed a prisoner on board the Sparrow with perhaps the only two people in the solar system she could trust.

And she could trust them. Her last fears were assuaged after they passed the first few days on Ganymede. If either Matthew or Abigail had intentions of betrayal, they could have turned her in the moment they touched down. They were a peculiar pair, fiercely independent and secretive. She knew nothing about either of them beyond surface level niceties and their methods of deflecting and redirecting conversations towards the inane.

They were both gone for the day, each on some job or contract of their own. Matthew had contacts on Ganymede and seemed to know his way around. Abigail had never been here, but her endless confidence meant that she wasn't going to let that slow her down. A side effect of being bulletproof, perhaps.

Yvonne looked out at Jupiter one last time and decided she would at least step outside. She had been in the underground tunnels of Ceres for so long that having only the stars for a roof would be a certain joy. Sticking her book beneath her arm, she walked to the aft of the Sparrow, passing through both the crew cabins and common room. Just before the thumper turret, she climbed the ladder to the dorsal hatch, or rather the three separate hatchways required to climb out onto the top of the Sparrow.

The night air on Ganymede had a cold bite to it, and for a moment she regretted not putting on another layer. Even the chill was familiar. As the extended night lingered for four standard days, the temperature would drop until frost sparkled on every surface. Decades ago a proposal had been made to put reflectors in orbit over Ganymede like Europa used to warm and light its crops. Engineers at the university had drawn up extensive plans, but nothing had come of it and nothing ever would. There were no resources, manpower, or will to pull off such a feat of engineering.

Sunrise after the long night had always been a time of celebration at the university as a gathering of students and faculty would meet at Galileo's Mausoleum to greet the dawn. Of course the long dead scientist wasn't present, but three of his fingers and one tooth had been preserved in a bell jar and were proudly displayed. The old joke was that everyone at the university would be branded a heretic if Galileo endured a sunrise alone.

It didn't make much sense, but then most traditions don't.

Yvonne sat on an outcropping of the hull and opened her book. Staring at the page still didn't help her concentrate. It had been many years since she had free time to devote to pleasure reading. Now idle hours were the only kind she had. It didn't help that most all of Matthew's books were rather heady affairs, reading like she hadn't done in decades. He had a small collection of western civilization's most enduring classics, and the ship's digital library was even more extensive.

"You're a strange man, Matthew Cole," Yvonne mumbled clearing her head for one last valiant attempt at reading by the light of Jupiter.

Abigail mounted her bike and punched the throttle. It had been another meager day, with only the small side job she'd snagged to secure a few dollars. Her own broker didn't have any contacts on Ganymede, so she'd been left scrounging the public boards. Better known as the bottom of the barrel.

Meanwhile, Cole had been busy all week with some local government contract. When she'd asked about it, he'd just shrugged and said he'd signed an NDA. Abigail had been a freelancer long enough to know what that meant. Money.

He had a ship, a good contract, and apparently all the luck. Life wasn't fair.

Galileo, falling quickly behind her, was a quaint town, charming with its university and residential districts, and downright peaceful compared to Ceres. Which meant not a lot of work for a freelancer. That had been the idea of course, to go somewhere real quiet while Yvonne's bounty was fresh. She passed the last of Galileo's buildings, the frost crusted grass of the open countryside rushing beneath her bike.

As she approached the Sparrow, she saw a small silhouette perched on its upper hull, lit by Jupiter's pale light. Abigail felt a pang of sympathy for the older woman. As well as she seemed to be taking it, it couldn't be easy to sleep at night with a million dollar bounty hanging over her head. And added to that, she'd recently lost her husband, been chased from her home, and abandoned to fend for herself. It was hard not to feel a bit of pity for her.

She remotely lowered the lift to the hold on approach. Cole had kindly offered her an entry-fob since it appeared they were stuck together for at least a little while longer. She stashed her bike and climbed the ladder to the top of the hull.

"I trust your day was productive?" the doctor politely asked as Abigail pulled her bulky frame out of the almost too-small top hatch.

"Sure. You could call it that."

Yvonne's eyes held an amused expression that Abigail didn't quite get. "I would have thought that question would yield a straightforward answer."

"Yeah, I got paid." she grumbled. "But wasn't exactly that lucrative of a job."

"Oh. I'm sorry then. I suppose Galileo isn't exactly Ceres. What was the job, if it's acceptable for me to ask? You've been rather quiet in the evenings."

Abigail bit her lip. She hadn't planned on telling Yvonne or Cole, but what could it hurt? Besides, complaining might be fun.

"So there's this professor at the university," she began. "Agricultural department. She has a side thing where she breeds dogs. Has dozens of them. Anyway, she's visiting her sister on Callisto and she uh... She needed someone to feed and walk the dogs." It sounded even more ridiculous out loud than she had imagined.

Yvonne chuckled and Abigail felt her cheeks flush. What did she expect?

"I suppose she had no friend brave enough to take care of her pack and so posted it to a freelancer board, Yvonne said. "Unorthodox, but fortunately she found a taker."

"It was a paycheck," Abigail grumbled, "Just, don't tell Cole about this, alright? Last thing I need is pity from the cowboy."

"It'll be our secret. Which does lead me to another question. Why aren't you two working together? With your rather diverse set of skills, I would have thought you'd make a great team."

"Tell me about it," Abigail agreed. "Actually tell him about it. I was all for a little team up after how well the Arizona job went. Turns out the mysterious loner streak is pretty strong in our friend. Never mind that we'd both make more cash. Something in his fragile little ego doesn't like playing with others." She winced as she said the last bit aloud. "Okay that might have been too far, but cut me some slack. I've been taking mangy animals on walks all week."

Yvonne folded her hands neatly in front of her. "It's been less than two weeks since I stepped foot on the Sparrow, and I've gathered that you two haven't known each other very long. But I have made a couple of observations. Now. I'm a medical doctor, not a psychologist, but in my practices I've met a lot of people. My experience is that those that won't tell you about their past have either something they are running from or something they are hiding."

She gave Abigail a look at this last bit, and the point wasn't lost on her. "Maybe there are reasons," she said defensively.

"I never said there weren't. I merely offered an observation."

"Hmmph," Abigail grunted. "You wouldn't understand."

Yvonne shrugged. "Maybe not. But then I'm also old enough to know that sometimes it's easier to share a burden with another."

"I'll keep that in mind," Abigail said, planning on doing nothing of the sort.

"I'm sure you will," Yvonne replied. Abigail turned to reenter the Sparrow but was stopped when Yvonne spoke again. "As a doctor, I must at least tell you that I don't think it can possibly be healthy for you to spend every waking hour in that exo-suit."

The conversation had gone into forbidden territory. "I take extra vitamin D. And don't pry into other people's business."

"I see."

She didn't of course. She couldn't possibly see or understand, but then that was by design. How had the conversation switched from Cole's stubbornness to her own? She wasn't going to stick around if she was going to be put under the microscope. With a huff she climbed down the ladder, eager for the peace of her own room.

When Matthew entered the cockpit later that afternoon, he found Yvonne already there, book in hand. "Bought the ingredients you wanted and left 'em in the fridge," he said.

She looked up. "Thank you, I'll see to it shortly. It'll be nice to have something that's not frozen."

"Well, I won't disagree with that. But just so we're clear, you don't have to do this. I'm not expecting you to take up the job of cook while you're here."

"Your concern is noted, but I'll carry my own weight, thank you," she said. "If that involves scrubbing the outer hull, then I'll do that."

Matthew took off his campero, placed it on the console, and sat in the pilot's seat, spinning it to face Yvonne. The woman had her usual unflappable look and he wasn't about to argue the point. "So I guess you're handy in the kitchen?"

"Ha. Not in the slightest. Tomas was the cook. But, how hard can it be if you follow directions? I once performed an emergency appendectomy by following a textbook. A pot of stew can't be more difficult than that."

Matthew wasn't quite sure that the analogy worked out, but neither was he sure how to politely say as much. "Well, a bit of real cooked food would be appreciated."

She laughed. "Just so long as you aren't expecting five-star fare."

"Of course not." He nodded at the book in her hands. "Whatcha have there?"

"John Donne. It seemed appropriate given the current situation on the ship."

Matthew scratched the stubble at his chin. "It's uhh... Been a long time. I'm not sure I know..."

"Devotions Upon Emergent Occasions," she said. "Meditation Seventeen. Took me a while to find it. It's been quite some time for me too."

A sudden memory flickered deep in the back of his mind. Honestly, he only remembered two quotes from that book, both of which happened to come from the same place. He had a feeling he knew where this was going.

"No man is an island entire of itself," she read from the book. "Every man is a piece of the continent, a part of the main."

And that's exactly where she was going. If she wanted to make herself obnoxious, he'd at least make her spell it out. "A lovely bit of poetry, quoted and misquoted through the centuries."

"Don't be coy, Matthew," Yvonne said tossing the book aside. "I'm not going to pry into your past, into whatever thing you feel must be kept from the light of day, though I think it might do you good to unearth those bones. I'm interested in the here and now. In case you've failed to notice, there are three of us on the Sparrow. I'm here for the foreseeable future and I don't think you'll be dropping Abigail off on Mars tomorrow."

He crossed his arms. "Alright. What do you want of me?"

"This is your ship. You've been gracious to me, but you seem to be ignoring the fact that Abigail could be an enormous asset. Why not partner with her? I'm sure with a shield and a gun you two could tackle any job in the solar system."

"She didn't seem to have any trouble finding a job in Galileo," Matthew said defensively.

"Not one suited to her skills. She told me about it but made me promise not to tell you. You've been running around all week with a comfortable contract, while she's been doing work that I think is a bit beneath her."

Matthew turned away, frustrated with Yvonne for pushing the subject, with Abigail for not being more forthcoming, and with himself for being stubborn. "Look. Yvonne. I've always worked alone. I don't like having people rely on me."

"What kind of a ridiculous notion is that?" she asked.

"Because if I fail, then everyone pays the consequences."

She stood to leave and Matthew turned back around to watch her.

She paused at the door. "It's your ship and it's your life. But for right now, Abigail and I are a part of it. We already rely on you." And with that parting shot, she left the cockpit, leaving Matthew alone to brood.

He grabbed his hat off the console and shoved it back on his head, letting it slip low so it covered his eyes, and kicked his feet up. Pushy doctor, prying into business that wasn't her's.

But if she's on the ship, it is her business. He grunted in frustration, trying not to think of past failures and the consequences of the ones yet to come.

Sitting at a table was a bit of a bother for Abigail. Her exo-suit was too bulky for any of the chairs in the common room on the Sparrow but she'd found a crate of supplies that worked well enough. Still, she felt ridiculous sitting at the table across from Cole as Yvonne dipped bowls of some kind of stew for them. Food was food, though, and she wasn't going to turn down a fresh-cooked meal.

"As it turns out," Yvonne said, "cooking is not that much like an appendectomy."

Abigail's eyes darted to Yvonne and back to her bowl. "I'm not sure I..."

"It tastes fine I suppose, but I had the temperature set too high and it stuck to the bottom of the pot. You can't really taste it, but you can probably smell it if you get too close. Which, by the way, I recommend against."

"I hope the appendectomy went better than this," Cole said with a laugh. He grabbed his spoon and took a tentative bite. The burnt smell couldn't have been too bad because he shrugged and dug in.

"The patient lived." Yvonne said, dipping herself a bowl.

Abigail wasn't reassured. She stared at hers for a moment, then delicately picked up the tiny spoon with her huge armored-hand. She scooped up a spoonful. This level of fine motor control was on the obnoxious side of tedious. If she hadn't been worried about offending Yvonne, she would have just lifted the bowl to her mouth and slurped it. As she raised the first spoonful, curiosity got the best of her and she smelled it. Yup. It was burnt. Thankfully, it tasted much better, even though cooked cabbage wasn't on her list of favorites.

They ate in silence for several minutes as if they were complete strangers. All things considered, they were just that. Strangers who just happened to be on a ship together.

She cleared her throat. "Thanks, Yvonne. This beats a bit of frozen rations, burnt smell and all."

"Yes, it's rather meager fare. But you're welcome," Yvonne replied.

The silence returned. Cole finished his bowl and pushed it away. "So I've been thinking," he began hesitantly.

Abigail glanced up at him and then set her spoon down, tired of the effort it took to use the stupid thing. He scratched his stubble. "It looks like we're going to be traveling together for a bit, and I thought that since we all have diverse strengths that we might have a talk about how we function as a crew."

Abigail sat back and crossed her arms, curious where this was going. And why couldn't they have had this conversation a week ago, before she'd spent all her patience on the dog pack? She noticed a subtle smile cross Yvonne's lips. What did she know?

"Sharon, I'm... Well I'm sorry. I just kind of went off and did my own thing. Didn't make a lot of sense, because I'm sure we can take on better jobs together. Like Mars and the Hawthorne gang."

So he had half a brain after all.

"You can consider me support staff in your endeavors," Yvonne said. "Just don't make me actually play doctor. I don't want to have to sew anyone back together with the paltry medical supplies in the ship's first aid kit."

"Give me a list of what we need," Cole said. "Better contracts often mean more danger and I'd hate to have an injury you couldn't treat." He shuffled in his seat as if nervous. "When it comes to the Sparrow, I'm the captain. In a life or death situation, I expect to be obeyed. But when we're on the ground or anywhere else we're partners. Alright? Everyone responsible for everyone."

Abigail nodded, impressed. This had to be Yvonne's doing. Somehow or another she must have given him the lecture. Abigail stiffened, wondering if the other woman had told Cole about the dog walking thing. There were going to be stern words if that was the case. Either way the results weren't all bad.

"Think you can handle a partner, cowboy?" she asked.

"Gaucho. And yes, if that shield is in between me and the bullets meant for my head, then yeah, I think I can handle it." He sat in awkward silence for a minute before reaching across the table to get a second helping of stew.

Abigail watched his discomfort and shook her head. "Relax, Cole. We're all just trying to keep our head above water."

"And the past behind us," Yvonne added. It was another pointed statement that Abigail had no intention of satisfying with an answer.

Cole's eyes met her own and it seemed he thought the same thing. Even partners didn't have to share everything.

In the middle of the night, long after the others had gone to bed, Yvonne made a foolish decision. She got up and, remembering to pull a warm layer on this time, crept out the top hatch of the Sparrow. She tugged her hood low over her face as she walked off towards the city of Galileo. The academic town wasn't exactly known for its nightlife, and only an occasional ground car passed her on the dark streets.

About an hour after leaving the Sparrow, she reached the University of Ganymede. The campus had changed little in the decades since she had last visited. Styled after the oldest of universities, spires rose into the night sky, silhouettes against the stars. She spotted a new dormitory and a new student center, but little else had changed. Through the years she had followed news from her alma mater at a distance. Enrollment and funds were both down in recent years, as was to be expected. It wasn't a death knell, but neither was it a good sign.

Yvonne reached the front steps of the library and was pleased to find the tall doors still unlocked. The ancient tradition of students burning midnight oil to cram before tests was still held in honor in Galileo. The attendant at the front desk, a student who looked barely old enough to attend, glanced up briefly from her studying before deciding that Yvonne was of no concern.

She walked the aisles of books, the largest collection in the solar system, unless some hidden cache had survived on Earth. They were all preserved digitally of course, but the feel and smell of a real paper book held power in the minds and imaginations of the students that read them. They were a novelty, perhaps, but a priceless link to the past.

At last, she found the quiet corner she had been looking for. A small alcove with a tall arched window. Through it, Jupiter shone its pale light. This had been their study spot. Three decades ago she had fallen in love here.

She sat in one of the deep chairs by the window. "Oh Tomas," she whispered, a tear warm on her face.

She had never really grieved his death. In the depths of Ceres, she had simply muscled on with her work, never giving space to her bereavement. She and Tomas had agreed that if something happened to one of them, the practice would continue for as long the other could manage.

Yvonne hadn't even made it a year.

She pushed thoughts of Piggy aside. He wasn't worth her attention. Not here. Not now. She wouldn't let him profane this place.

For now, in this quiet hour, she would remember Tomas.

Sometime later she lifted up her head. Matthew Cole stood a short distance away leaning against a bookshelf. He tipped his campero when she saw him and smiled. She sighed and gestured him over. "I've been caught," she said at his approach.

"No one can tell you what to do with your own life," he said.

"And you turn my own words against me. Well, I'm a poor teacher if I can't heed my own lesson. I suppose it was sentimental drivel. I couldn't find anything else in your library that fit."

"Worked well enough. And as far as advice, we all tend to be hypocrites." He regarded her thoughtfully. "Still, after you told me about your past with this place, I thought you'd eventually try and go sightseeing at least once. With our time here nearly up, I knew it would be soon. You've got a mark on your head. I thought you'd spot me tailing you."

Yvonne sighed. She had tried to keep her eyes about her, but must not have been as vigilant as she had imagined. "Thank you, for watching out for me." She looked around, trying to capture the feel of the place. She might not ever return.

Or then again, she might. She wasn't so old as to need to invoke such melodrama.

"I'm ready now." She took his offered hand and stood to her feet.

He nodded. "Then let's go home."

She turned away from the alcove. Not everyone was captive to their past.

Chapter 7: Cold Approach

We always adapt. It's one of the things that humans are best at. Take a look at where we started. Tropical climates. By the time we'd finished settling our little globe, we were living in every place possible. We'd settled the frozen tundra, lived on tiny islands surrounded by thousands of miles of water, and even learned to navigate the most unnatural of situations: dense city traffic.

The adaptations got bigger when we moved into space, but it was nothing we hadn't done before.

Mars was the easiest, especially after its air pressure began to rise. It even had blue skies, if you were lucky. On Ceres and some of the moons we adapted to underground life, becoming colonies of busy little ants. And then of course there was life in orbit. Never leaving a man-made structure was one of the hardest adjustments, but when that's what you have to do, you do it. Humans are resilient.

We also adapted to life with Moses, to easy technology and endless dreams. Sometimes it's better when things are hard.

I'm not sure if we'll adapt to life after Moses. Oh, I know we'll live past my days. It will be decades or maybe even centuries before we know the answer to that question.

But it is the one question worth asking, the one that all mankind asks the coming night.

Will we adapt one last time or perish?

Soliyana Amanuel Andualem
Governor of Zerai Deres, Callisto
Died 49 AM

Y vonne knew precisely when Abigail would emerge from her room. On days when she had no contracts or pressing duties aboard the Sparrow, she would sleep until her alarm went off at oh-nine-hundred ship time and open her door suited and ready for the day half an hour later.

When the door to her cabin opened at the predicted time, Abigail immediately marched toward the cockpit. Yvonne was waiting for her, blocking her path.

"You're officially barred from the cockpit," she said crossing her arms.

"Oh come on! We're in the Saturn neighborhood, I want to see," Abigail said.

Yvonne raised an eyebrow in amusement. "Of course you do, but you only get one first look."

"Yes, so let me pass."

"Matthew and I have something special in mind. Go eat your breakfast."

Abigail crossed her arms. "You know I could physically move you out of the way."

"You wouldn't dare do anything of the sort."

Abigail huffed and turned away, and Yvonne smiled to herself. The younger woman was an awful lot of bark and very little bite. She quickly entered the cockpit door and shut it behind her, locking it so that Abigail wouldn't get any bright ideas.

"Did she complain much?" Matthew asked.

"As much as we expected." She glanced out the window. "Wow. You went out of your way to give her a view. We're well inside the orbit of any of the moons."

"I only left the frameshift running for a few extra seconds. You don't have to make it sound like I made some kind of expensive sacrifice. Besides, you can hardly see the rings from Titan. Don't make it out that I'm some sort of saint. Saturn is... special, you know?"

"Of course it is. Doesn't change the fact that you try to act like you don't care, then go out of the way to make sure Abigail's first view is memorable."

"Eh, lay off," Matthew grumbled as he stood. "You going to join us? I can prep you a suit too."

"No thanks. I prefer to stay within the hull of the ship. You kids go have fun."

Matthew stopped abruptly. "Should I be insulted?"

"I was joking about my age, not your failing youth," she said, suppressing a smile.

"Right."

He left the cockpit, and she took another look at Saturn before moving to the pilot's seat and pulling up a monitor. On the long flight out to the Saturn Neighborhood, she'd been engrossed in even drier reading than Matthew's library. The owner's manual of the Ceres Spaceworks Model 42. It was three-thousand pages long, and given the poor maintenance condition the Sparrow was in, Yvonne doubted that Matthew had ever finished reading it. He'd gotten quite defensive when she'd pointed out that the filters on the primary fuel intakes should have been cleaned nearly fifteen hundred flight hours ago.

She'd have a chance to rectify that now that they'd arrived and the engines would have some downtime. Cooking may not have been an awful lot like practicing medicine, but taking care of a spaceship was a much closer analog. If you thought of the Sparrow as a patient, with interconnected systems, organs, and sustenance needs, it almost started to feel familiar. She flipped back through the manual.

Not that the Sparrow was much like the human body. Maybe it was better to imagine she was starting over learning how to take care of a new species. The best part would be that the patient couldn't complain when you poked and prodded. The worst part was that if she messed up, they might all die. Unlikely, but possible.

She called up the chapter on intake filters and started reading it for the fourth time. Made no sense to rush into something until she knew it by heart.

She wondered how long it would take for Matthew to get her patient shot up.

Matthew finished adjusting the helmet of his spacesuit, closing each of the four latches that formed the seal. He pushed a button on his wrist and felt the suit pressurize as he checked the readout to make sure he was keeping air. It had been a while since he had used these things and it never hurt to be careful.

"Alright, I'm ready. Let's go."

"About time," Sharon said.

"Some of us don't wear our suit at all hours of the day." He glanced her way as she closed the faceplate on her exo-suit. "We'll take the top hatch. Single file, though. We won't both fit in its airlock."

He led her down the back hall towards the thumper turret and took the ladder to the upper airlock. He went through the three hatches, one at a time, sealing each behind him. Before the final portal, he waited for the green light to indicate that the air had been pumped out. The artificial gravity ceased as he climbed into the vacuum of space. With a clomping noise that he heard conducting through his suit and bones, he engaged the magnets on his boots and stuck fast to the hull of the Sparrow.

It took Sharon another minute to work her way through the hatches behind him. At last, she crawled out onto the hull and turned around. The shock was evident in her body language, even with the bulky exo-suit.

"Not bad, huh?"

She didn't answer at once, which was fine by him. It was never a bad idea to just shut up and enjoy the view.

The sight of mighty Saturn and its majestic rings was unmatched by any other in the solar system. The second largest of the sun's planets hung in the sky, huge, yellow, and impossibly luminous. Compared to the rocky planets and the chaotic striations of Jupiter's storms, Saturn appeared much more regular, with only gentle color gradations. Its north pole faded towards complex blue and green shades, where a strange hexagonal storm system had intrigued scientists for centuries as it waxed and waned.

And then there were the rings themselves. To the eyes of man, there are few other places in nature where a natural system appears with such perfect regularity. Thousands of concentric rings of nearly pure water ice reflected the distant sunlight. The mesmerizing pattern of changing densities always made Matthew's mind look for meaning and purpose within the variations. Such exact order seemed to defy the standard chaotic state of nature.

He had been deliberate in positioning the Sparrow. About thirty degrees above the equator gave the best view he could of the rings and pole.

Suddenly their comms crackled to life. "Sorry to interrupt, Matthew, but you've got a message from your broker," Yvonne said.

"Okay, I'll be right in. You listen to it yet?"

There was a brief pause before Yvonne answered, indignant. "Why would I listen to a message intended for you?"

"I... don't know. I was just asking in case you wanted to summarize. I'm coming in." He padded back over to the hatch and turned to take one last look at Saturn. Sharon was still standing quietly, taking in the magnificent view. He chuckled to himself, glad he'd taken the effort to make it a good one. "I'm heading in. Might want to follow in just a couple more minutes. We're in one of Saturn's radiation belts right here, and while the Sparrow's environmental shields should be stopping most of it, I wouldn't take too much of a chance being out here all that long."

She nodded absently. "I'm fine. My suit will keep me safer than the Sparrow will."

"Of course it will," he said with a shrug as he climbed back down into the hatch.

By the time he'd returned through the airlock, stripped off the pressure suit, and made his way to the cockpit, Yvonne had only grown more annoyed.

"Honestly, Matthew, did you really think I was going to listen to a private message meant for you? I'm a little bit upset that you would think..."

He held up his hands in defense. "It's fine. You can listen to messages from my broker all day long if you want. Actually..." He laughed at the thought. "Actually, you're more than welcome to deal with him. He might like you more than he likes me. I tend to eventually run brokers off."

"No thanks. I don't want him turning me in. But it's no wonder you have problems with them considering your exemplary people skills."

Matthew decided to ignore the jab and punched up the message. Benny's voice crackled through the air.

"I'm guessing you've made it to Saturn by now? I've sent the final job details along. It's an unusual contract, so make sure you've read it carefully. I don't want you screwing it up because you got a little gung-ho or trigger happy in the wrong place. I'll be waiting on word and coordinating with the corp that hired you guys."

"By the way. I'm still waiting for your apology. And a thank you. Turns out working with a crew isn't so bad, is it? Neither is making money, which we'll all do if you don't mess this up. Finally, have Ms.

Sharon talk to her broker. I've been getting threatening messages from her accusing me of poaching one of her freelancers. I set up the one job. Not my fault if Sharon wants to jump ship and join a crew. Have her sort that out for me, will you? That's it then. I'll contact you on the back side."

There was a pop as the message ended. "Somehow I'm not surprised that Sharon's broker is threatening Benny."

Yvonne laughed. "Sounds a bit like our Abigail. I'll mention that to her if you'd like me to."

"Thanks." Matthew was already scanning the contract briefing. It really was going to be a strange one.

The door behind them opened, and Sharon stepped in, her face beaming. "I appreciate the effort you two went to. Saturn was worth the wait."

"Told you you'd love it," Matthew said, not bothering to look up from his monitor. "You should listen to your elders."

Sharon rolled her eyes. "Right. You're only a few years older than me, Cole."

"Something like that," Matthew muttered, his eyes still scanning the contract. "No sense hanging around here now that you're back in."

"Where are we off to? Where's the job?" Sharon asked.

"Saturn's largest moon, Titan."

The thick orange atmosphere of Titan made it a fitting offspring of its parent Saturn. But unlike the gas giant, Titan was one of the most Earth-like bodies in the solar system, though not in ways that lent itself to human habitation. Clouds, rain, wind, lakes, and oceans all featured heavily on the moon, though instead of water, these were composed mostly of methane and other organic molecules. With the help of cryovolcanoes adding volatiles like water and ammonia into the mix, Titan was a complex soup of chemistry, suitable for all kinds of industry.

Moses had set up dozens of orbital stations and refineries over Titan in the early days. With more hydrocarbons than had ever existed on Earth, the frozen moon was the best source of combustible fuels in the solar system. Liquid methane was brought up from the surface and processed at orbital facilities into more complex hydrocarbons that helped the wheels of industry and technology grind on.

Those wheels slowed with each passing decade. Just last year one of the refineries had ceased production, and the whole system noticed the price of fuel creep ever upward.

Abigail watched as Cole let the Sparrow drift lazily towards one of the still functioning refinery complexes. A sprawling series of interconnected stations and modules, the facility was enormous, stretched out over a couple dozen kilometers.

"Huygens Industrial Chem is the owner of that refinery and our employer," Cole said gesturing towards the hive of activity. "It seems they have a fuel thief, and they'd like us to catch them."

Abigail frowned. "What are we supposed to do? Patrol the halls looking for suspicious persons?"

"It's better than that," he said. "We get to sit outside and watch quietly for suspicious persons."

"Oh boy. I can hardly wait," Abigail said crossing her arms.

Cole took off his campero and scratched the back of his head. "Huygens has been noticing fuel disappearing from the storage tanks in this part of the refinery for some time, but they've yet to catch the perpetrators despite increasing their vigilance. At first, they thought an outside ship was siphoning fuel, but Huygens installed additional thermal imagers and found nothing. If anyone was burning engines, they'd have seen them."

"So it's an inside job," Yvonne commented.

"That's Huygen's theory, that someone on the inside with access to security is messing with the systems. Their buddies show up, siphon the fuel, sell it on the black market, and split the proceeds with their mole."

Abigail shook her head, thinking back to Arizona. "I hate when there's a mole."

"No disagreement there," Cole said, "but I'm more likely to trust a desperate corporate exec seeing red ink than a government man any day of the week."

"So this is a hush job too?" Abigail asked.

"Pretty much. We've got our instructions already and aren't even supposed to check in. We get to cruise in real quiet and watch things."

"And Huygens can't do that themselves because whenever they do, no one shows and no fuel goes missing," she said filling in a few of the missing blanks.

"Bingo," Cole said.

"It's a stakeout." Abigail uncrossed her arms. "How long are we supposed to sit and watch?"

Cole pulled up a monitor. "Before you curl up for a nap, it's not as bad as you're imagining. There's a rather intricate pattern as to when the raids happen." He pointed at a calendar.

Abigail leaned forward to look at it. Red highlighted days marked raids. An additional note detailed what time they had occurred. "If there's a pattern, I sure don't see it..."

"It's there," Yvonne said. Abigail and Cole both turned to look at her. Yvonne shrugged. "I can feel it, but would need some time to work it out. Don't give me those looks. I like puzzles."

Cole turned back to the monitor. "Well, you're more than welcome to try and figure it out later, but thankfully Huygens already worked it out for us." He hit a button and a bunch of future dates lit up in blue. "Here are the upcoming windows when the thieves may strike."

"We've got a window in twelve hours," Abigail said. "Nice. So how does this work?"

"You and I get to sit out in vacuum twiddling our thumbs," Cole said. "Yvonne will be docked in the distance watching the Sparrow's thermal scopes, in case someone is cheating the ones on the refinery. And if we see action we either try to apprehend peacefully or follow in the Sparrow."

"I guess they don't want a fight in their fuel depot." Abigail chuckled.

"That's not the kind of collateral damage we want to be involved with," Yvonne said.

"Yeah, that would ruin everyone's day," Abigail agreed.

Matthew gave another puff of steam from the nozzles of his thruster pack to spin around. He could barely make out the Sparrow where it was nestled in between modules of the refinery. Which was precisely the point. If a strange ship stuck out like a sore thumb, odds were their thieves wouldn't make a move today.

"Hey, Sharon. How's space treating you?"

"Oh, space is fine. It's this thruster pack that's giving me problems. It's not exactly my size and I'm having some trouble with fine course adjustments."

Matthew frowned and spun back around in space, trying to get a view of Sharon still drifting towards her destination. "I thought we got it taken care of."

"So did I, but I don't think it's quite in line with my center of mass."

"Sorry. You gonna make it?" There she was, over near the tanks she'd been assigned to watch. Unfortunately, she shone a bit in the lights of the refinery, even though it was local night. Shouldn't be as noticeable when she wasn't free floating.

"I'm fine, but it's more tumbling than flying. Soon as I put boots to metal, I'll be good."

Yvonne's voice cut in over the comms. "Maybe we can modify a pack to fit her exo-suit."

"We may have to," Matthew conceded. "If we don't get a hit tonight and we have to wait till the next window we'll have some time. You know, Sharon, I'm kind of surprised your suit isn't already equipped for zero-gee maneuvering. I mean it's vacuum proof. Seems like a few maneuvering jets would go along nicely."

A clunking noise rang over the comm. "I'm at my destination atop fuel tank fourteen," Sharon said. "Yeah that would be nice, but that's not exactly what the suit was built for."

"Oh? What was it built for?"

There was a moment of silence over the comms as Sharon probably realized she'd said more than she'd planned. She sighed. "Dammit, you almost got me, didn't you?"

Matthew smirked, fully aware there was no one around to see it. He fired the steam jets again to slow his velocity and lightly landed on his own fuel tank. "I figured a little bit of disclosure would be good for you."

Sharon grumbled something incoherent over the comm and sighed. "Look, maybe when you're ready to tell us the whole gaucho story then I'll think about it."

"You already sussed out that I spent time on Europa."

"That's news to me," Yvonne said, "But I guess that adds up. What was an Arizona boy like you doing on Europa long enough for you to pick up some of the local culture?"

Matthew checked his air readouts out of habit. "When did this become about me?"

"When both of you decided to play the mysterious stranger with a past."

"I'm not down for this game," Sharon's voice crackled over the comm.

"I can agree to that," Matthew said. He looked up around him. The massive fuel cylinders were arranged like an enormous horseshoe, nearly a kilometer across. When it was time to export the fuel to the other colonies, gargantuan tanker ships would pull up into the horseshoe and drain the storage tanks. He'd lost sight of Sharon when she had touched down. Good. If he couldn't spot her knowing where to look, it was unlikely any thieves would see her either. "And now," he said, setting up on edge where he could get a good view of the area, "we get to hurry up and wait."

Yvonne tapped her foot restlessly on the deck. Small talk had given way to boredom, and boredom was in danger of giving way to apathy. She pulled up the thieves' timetable. After about twenty minutes she laughed. "Got it."

"What's that?" Abigail asked.

"The pattern on which the thieves strike. So they only hit during the long Titan night. Then it's only dates of the month which are prime numbers, or rather every fourth prime. And then the next month they work through the next set of primes that they missed. I'm still trying to figure out the hours they hit. It's a more complicated pattern."

Abigail groaned. "So the thieves are math-heads. Great."

"I thought you were supposed to be watching the thermal scopes?" Matthew asked.

"I'm running the monitor in split-screen mode."

There was a long awkward pause. "You can do that?"

"Yes. You'd know that if you read the manual." Matthew didn't answer and Yvonne smiled, knowing she'd scored a hit. She was tempted to pull the Sparrow's manual back up, but that would absorb too much of her attention, and a stakeout where you weren't watching was liable to go awry.

When the third hour passed with nothing happening, she nearly gave into temptation. Then she saw something out of the corner of her eye, something against the black starry backdrop of space. She looked back over at the thermal scopes. Nothing. She turned back to stare out the viewport into space. If she had seen something, and she wasn't quite sure that she had, then where was it?

There. A single star winked out.

"Matthew, Abigail. I think something is out there."

"Thermals?" he asked.

"Clean, but I just watched a star disappear. There. There's another."

"Where?" Abigail asked. "Where is it? What is it?"

"I don't know, how am I supposed to describe where to look? Another star. It's getting closer. Whatever it is, it's running lights off."

Matthew whistled. "Then we have our answer. They're coming in cold. Probably just using steam thrusters, drifting patiently into our orbit. Most thermal scopes are set high to look for the main engines of ships. Adjust the sensitivity on ours. Let's see if you can get eyes on them."

"How do I do that?"

Matthew walked Yvonne through the process of changing the settings configuration. If she'd had more time to get through the manual she'd know how to do it herself. That would have to go to the top of her to do list. The monitor went dark for a minute as the scopes reset then popped back to life.

"I've got them. They're... nearly three klicks out and drifting closer. If I had to guess they're quite a bit bigger than the Sparrow."

"I'd hope so," Abigail said. "If you're stealing fuel, you'd want to bring a decent size tank. What's the plan, Cole?"

The comm was silent for a minute. "Let's watch for now. Let them get closer. They'll have to pull up to one of the tanks to siphon the fuel. When they're connected and immobile, they'll be vulnerable, and we move in."

"Well, you won't have long to wait," Yvonne said. "They'll be here in about three minutes." She looked out the front viewport again. "I can see their silhouette pretty easily against the stars now. They should be close enough to see by the refinery's lights soon."

"I've got them," Abigail said. "I think they're coming toward my arm of the horseshoe."

Yvonne looked at the scope. "Confirmed. They're moving towards Abigail. Matthew, don't forget that if they flee you'll need to be back on the Sparrow post haste. Don't over commit."

"What? You haven't finished the manual yet? I figured you'd know better than I do at this point."

His voice dripped with sarcasm and Yvonne could practically see the insufferable grin on his face. "Very funny, but since I have your permission, I'll be ready to warm up the engines."

"Over my dead body. Look alive. Here they come."

Abigail watched as the dark silhouette of the ship drifted into the horseshoe of storage cylinders. It was a cargo hauler, a skeleton with a cockpit and engines that you could load with whatever modules you wanted to haul whatever you needed. This particular ship had a single large tank module installed. Jets of steam fired in the silence of space, cold white against the black as the bandits slowed their drift.

Just how far had they come from at so low a speed? It couldn't be far, perhaps no further than a few hundred kilometers. But his was a dense orbit with the massive Huygens refinery. Numerous other habitats floated within easy commuting range by orbital shuttles. Surely the ship had come from the immediate neighborhood.

Either that or they were really patient thieves.

The ship came to a stop. After a minute a figure could be seen crawling out of the ship, lugging a flexible pipeline to transfer fuel. The figure drifted over to the nearest cylinder and coupled it to the tank.

"Go," Cole whispered in the comm. "I'll take care of our friend in space and stop the transfer. You take the ship."

She pushed off and gave a quick thrust from her pack. "Gonna give me the hard job? I see how it is." She had a bit of a sideways drift to her course. She tried correcting with another puff of steam. Better but still not quite where she wanted to hit the other ship.

"I thought you might prefer to avoid a fight in zero-gee with a pack that's causing you problems."

Abigail bit her lip. "Point taken." She made one last attempt to correct her trajectory. That was about as good as she could get it.

"How far out are you?" Cole asked. She could see him as he slowly descended on his target from a high angle. Hopefully, that would keep him out of sight until it was too late to do anything about.

"Twenty seconds? Maybe."

"Good luck, you two," Yvonne offered quietly.

Now that Abigail was closer she could see two more figures on the hull of the ship, near where the pipeline entered the hatch to the fuel module. Maybe she was further out than she thought. They seemed awfully small and far away.

Thirty seconds can seem like either a lifetime or a moment in a dangerous situation, and Abigail never really knew which extreme she was going to experience. Today it was the latter, and before she knew it, the ship was rushing up to meet her. The figures saw her and gestured wildly. Too late to worry about that. The odds of them discharging weaponry while pumping fuel was probably close to zero anyway. She rotated and landed with a reverberating thump felt through her suit and rounded on the two thieves.

They were small. She wasn't imagining things. The two figures dove for the open hatch trying to pull it as far shut as they could. Luckily for Abigail, the pipeline connected to the refinery kept it from being closed. If they thought they could hold it against her by strength alone, they were going to be disappointed.

"Contact," Matthew said, right before she heard an impact through

102

the comm. He could take care of himself. She walked across the surface of the ship and reached down to pry open the partially closed hatch. It opened easily and she dove in.

The control room for the fuel module was dark. And empty.

That was weird. Where had they gone? There was only a single exit, a reinforced pressure door with a viewport. She ran to it and tried the controls. Locked. She smashed the controls with her fist. Sparks scattered and were immediately snuffed by the vacuum, but the door disappointingly remained shut. So much for that.

Abigail leaned toward the viewport. The two thieves were in the airlock. One was fiddling with the controls, the other was already taking off their helmet. It was a girl, with long blonde hair and delicate features.

She couldn't have even been a teenager yet.

"Cole," Abigail said, feeling a chill grip her heart, glad that she hadn't been able to open the door and accidentally kill the girl. "I think we've got a problem."

"Yeah, I think I know where you're going. I've got my target in cuffs. He's a just a kid. Looks pretty scared."

"What? Talk to me. What's going on?" Yvonne's voice shouted over comm.

"Don't know, but we've got a ship full of kids," Abigail said, trying not to work out the implications. "They've locked me out of the... Hold on." There was a series of clangs and mechanical groans. "Something's happening."

"They just detached the fuel module," Yvonne said calmly. "They're making a run for it."

"And they forgot one of their own," Cole said, the frustration thick in his voice. "I'm bringing him back to the Sparrow, but he's going to slow me down."

Abigail worked her way back to the hatch and climbed out. Sure enough, the fuel module had been dumped. The remaining ship was just a skeleton of its former self, steam thrusters already turning it around.

"Abigail, get out of there, you're drifting," Yvonne said quietly. Something about the serious tone unnerved Abigail. She turned around. The detachment process had pushed the fuel module away from the ship and put a slight spin to its momentum. It was now moving towards one of the refinery's fuel tanks.

She grimaced and looked around her. The thieves' ship was still less than a hundred meters away. She could reach it before it got too far away.

The bigger question was what happened when the fuel module hit one of the primary storage tanks? No doubt she was riding enough tonnage that something was going to get pierced. The contents weren't actually likely to be explosive without an oxidizer, but depending on how much pressure they were under, this could still turn into a hazardous environment real quick. There was going to be a lot of shrapnel and frozen fuel. Matthew, his prisoner, Yvonne, and the Sparrow were all about to be in a lot of danger.

An idea worked its way into her head.

"Cole. Did you disconnect the pipeline from the refinery?"

"Yeah, it's disconnected."

"Thanks. I'll take care of it." She climbed back into the fuel module and hit the release on the pipeline's feeder. That should allow her to pull out the entire length of the hose. Hopefully, it would be enough. When she reemerged from the hatch, the module had rotated away from the thieves' ship and she had to turn to get her bearings. The departing ship was behind her now.

"Here goes nothing."

She jumped, keeping the pipeline tucked under her arm and turned her thruster pack to full. The distance between her and the ship narrowed. It was a constant effort to readjust her course and keep pointed the right way.

A cold sweat broke out on her forehead. If she ran out of slack, she'd have to release the pipeline. Who knows what would happen to the others if that happened? She was just starting to like these people.

The gap between her and the ship had closed to less than ten meters. Five meters. One meter.

She planted her feet, letting the magnets engage. They weren't going to be strong enough to hold for what she had in mind, so she found an outcropping of the hull she could get one hand around and clamped down, putting all her suit's strength into the grip. With the other hand, she clamped down on the pipeline. Not a moment too soon. The pipeline had extended to its full length and went taut.

Abigail closed her eyes and gritted her teeth, hoping she hadn't misjudged the structural strength of her suit. Thankfully the ship was accelerating very slowly. If they decided to make a real escape and fire up the main engines, her armored shell would be torn open like a tin can. Even so, the neural implant in her spine was giving her a lot of unpleasant sensations, telling her this wasn't a good idea. Opening her eyes, she looked back at the fuel module, now several hundred meters behind her. She'd only need to hold on long enough to give it forward momentum away from the refinery.

If the thieves felt the extra weight, they might panic and burn the main engines. With one last look at the fuel module, she guessed that she had held on long enough and let go of the pipeline. It fell behind as the ship continued to pick up speed.

Abigail sighed and reset her feet on the hull of the ship.

"That was a neat trick," Cole said. "You got a tracker you can turn on? Otherwise, we're gonna lose you."

"Oh, right." She pulled up the controls at her wrist. "Okay, it's on. Yvonne, you got that?"

"I've got you. Matthew, what could children possibly be doing stealing fuel?"

The comms were silent for several long heartbeats before Cole answered. "I don't know. None of the possibilities are good."

Abigail felt sick to her stomach and checked her power and air. She had hours and hours of time. Worst-case scenario, she let go and let the Sparrow come scoop her up. But the image of the blonde girl wouldn't leave her mind. Something was very messed up.

Yvonne's voice came over the comm again. "Be safe out there, Abigail. We'll follow behind as soon as we can."

"Maybe not quite that fast," Cole said.

"Can I ask why not?" Abigail frowned at the retreating refinery. The ship was in a bigger hurry to get out than it was on the way in. They hadn't let off the steam once. Clearly, the thieves were spooked.

"Why do you think? Cole asked quietly. "I've got a young man with me that's going to answer a few questions."

Chapter 8: Fagin's Brigade

We are all aware of the myriad of challenges that
will face our colonies in the coming decades,
many of which have been discussed at great
length by this very committee. There is little need
for me to remind you how dire these crises are.
One day the grav plate factories on Mars and
Ganymede will cease to operate and we will
either have learned to replicate the technology at
scale for civilization to continue or we will not. A
continual reminder at each convening will not
hasten such breakthroughs.

Rather my team and I would like to discuss a
different threat with the committee, one whose
generational nature has kept its discussion off of
the table until now. I would like to discuss the
sub-replacement fertility rate that each and every
colony is experiencing.

Simply put, there are not enough children to
maintain the current population. Not one colony,
no, not even the Martian colonies, have a high
enough birth rate for our way of life to continue
for more than a few generations. There is of
course still research to be done because it is
difficult to obtain accurate population data in
places like Ceres and Europa due largely to the
chaotic or outright criminal nature of those
particular colonies. However, we can predict with
relative confidence that the same trends are
affecting each and every human population in the
solar system.

Make no mistake. This is an existential threat on the same level as our failing technology or the lack of biodiversity in our extant flora and fauna samples. Worse, it is far more diffuse in nature, for its cause extends into all of our fields, from the technological to the sociological. It is our belief that this creates a positive feedback loop of sorts. As the birth rate worsens, the quality of life continues to degrade. This, in turn, further lowers the birth rate.

We have several different computer models detailing when the current trajectory will cross the point of no return.

If you will direct your monitors to data packet 14, we will begin to discuss the relevant data and the proposals my team has to counteract this crisis...

Aiko Nishina
Fourth Committee on Colonial Sustainability
Died 48 AM

M atthew had little difficulty wrestling his opponent into cuffs. His small size and apparent unfamiliarity with fighting in zero-gee had made him easy pickings for an experienced fighter. Getting him back aboard the Sparrow was more frustrating and wasted precious time during which Sharon and the thieves were getting away. By the time they were through the port side airlock far more time had passed than Matthew was happy about.

He firmly sat the thief in a chair in the common room and cuffed him to it to make sure he wasn't going anywhere. Matthew took his helmet off, then reached for the latches of the thief's helmet. He thrashed around on the chair to keep Matthew at bay.

"Come on. Let's not play this game. Yvonne! I need you in here."

"I'm coming." She entered the room and stopped short. "Oh my."

"I don't think our guest is cooperating. I'm going to hold him still. Get his helmet off."

Yvonne nodded. "Please listen," she said bending down to look at the thief. "We aren't going to hurt you."

107

"I might if you keep struggling like this," Matthew suggested.

"For shame, Matthew Cole," Yvonne said, shaking her head. "We won't hurt you," she said again, "but we need you to calm down." Matthew gripped him from behind and the struggling stopped. Yvonne reached forward to unclasp the helmet. When she had popped all the latches, she gently lifted it over his head. "Unexpected," she said quietly.

Matthew released his grip as Yvonne backed away so that he could get a good look at the young man that was causing him so much frustration. To Matthew's surprise, he was older than he had thought. He'd have guessed that the thief was little more than a child based on his small build and barely five-foot height, when in fact he was certainly a teenager, maybe sixteen or seventeen years old. He had fair skin and dark hair and Matthew could tell that his ancestors had come from the continent of Asia on Earth, but he couldn't pinpoint more specifically than that.

"Well, what do you have to say for yourself?" he asked. "I've stumbled on plenty of crazy things in my life, but I've never seen a pack of pint-sized fuel thieves."

The teen stared at him for a moment and then turned away sulkily.

"Come on. Don't be shy. We're of half a mind to help you out of whatever nasty predicament you're in.

He was greeted with a long string of unintelligible syllables. Matthew wasn't an expert on languages, not by a long shot, but from the venom they were spoken with, he had the feeling these weren't the kind of words one tended to use in front of their mother. He glanced at Yvonne. "Any idea what he said?"

She only nodded toward the cockpit. "I'd like to have a word with you."

He checked the restless teen's restraints one more time before following Yvonne towards the cockpit. He shut the door behind him. "I'm assuming you understood that?"

"No, but from the tone, I'm probably glad I didn't."

Matthew frowned. "Then what's this about?"

"Just because I didn't understand the words doesn't mean I didn't recognize the language. Most languages have a certain cadence, a unique character to them that you start to recognize after a while. Our friend was speaking Mandarin."

Matthew stared at her blankly, unsure of why this was supposed to mean anything to him. He'd never heard of a language called...

"Chinese, Matthew. He was speaking Chinese."

Matthew stood silent for a minute. He reached up to adjust his campero and then realized he wasn't wearing it. "How would you know that?" he asked quietly.

"There was a small Chinese population that lived near my practice on Ceres. A hundred or so families just trying to go about their lives." She sighed. "Probably trying to forget the Red Holocaust and avoid notice."

Matthew shivered at the mention of the fall of Chinese civilization. No one, not even Moses, had ever really settled on a death toll. Maybe because no death toll had ever had that many zeroes attached to it until then. Calling the Red Holocaust one of the blackest stains in human history was an understatement. It had in fact been the very crisis through which Moses had revealed himself to the world and kept the Chinese collapse from plunging the entire world into darkness.

"There's something else," Yvonne said. "His accent was... wrong. As if he hasn't been speaking it for a while. That's just a guess on my part."

"Hmm... I wonder if he knows English?" Matthew scratched the stubble at his chin.

"Of course he'll know English," Yvonne scoffed. "Everyone knows English. Just because he's from a rare racial background doesn't mean he's lived under a rock since he was born."

"That's fair, but for all we know these kids might have lived under a rock their whole lives. I'm a little afraid to find out what's going on."

Yvonne looked back at the door leading to the common room. "The only scenarios I can imagine are too terrible to think about."

"Slavery isn't unique to Europa," Matthew said, trying not to let those thoughts follow through to their usual destination. Villa María was on his mind more and more these days and it wasn't a trend he appreciated. "Okay, let's mix it up. Good cop, bad cop. I had to rough up our friend a bit to get him here. See if you can get him to talk. I'm going to see about following Sharon before they get too much further away. Remember. He's dangerous. Keep your distance."

"I can take care of myself, Matthew Cole," she said, opening the cockpit door. "But I'll see if I can get anything more out of him."

He sat down to prep the Sparrow for launch. On a whim, he decided not to fire up the main engines. If the thieves thought they were clever by coming in cold, then two could play at that game. He pulled up the tracker and checked on Sharon's signal. She was already over a hundred miles out.

He released the landing clamps and let the Sparrow drift for a few moments before using steam thrusters to push further away from the refinery.

Having a new thought, he pulled up the comm. "You there, Sharon?"

Silence. Without any additional equipment to relay her signal, they must have gotten out of the transmitter range of her suit.

He took the flight yoke and rotated them towards where the signal still pinged silently in the cold darkness of Titan's orbit. "Stay safe, Sharon. We're coming."

Riding a ship above Titan, under the eyes of distant Saturn was a new experience for Abigail. After the first few minutes, she relaxed, no longer worried that she would be discovered. She re-positioned herself, as quietly as possible, on top of the ship so that she could both watch for potential destinations ahead and watch the refinery fade into the distance. The facility, with its lights and constant stream of ships entering and leaving Titan's atmosphere, entertained her for a few minutes, at least until she was too far out to see much of what was going on.

Ahead, she could see nothing at all. Wherever they were going was probably too far out for her to see with the naked eye.

Or it was running cold with lights out like the ship.

She settled in for the long haul. She could be on her own for quite some time one way or another. The wait ended up being about four hours. About the time she had reached the conclusion that she would die of boredom, the ship's steam jets began to fire, slowing their velocity.

She looked around. Her surroundings looked much the same as they had. Titan beneath her and Saturn far above. Ahead there was nothing to see, except maybe...

No, there was something there. A dark silhouette floated in space, much larger than the ship she rode on. Either it was another ship or some kind of station.

A crack of light appeared as a portal opened in the side of the dark shape. The ship drifted into the open hangar and slowed to a stop with a final puff of steam. With a disorienting lurch, gravity flicked on, and the ship settled onto the deck. The enormous bay doors began to grind shut behind it, their rumbles felt through the deck rather than through the vacuum that still filled the cavernous space.

Better to move now rather than later. She leaped from the top of the ship and hit the deck as lightly as she could, taking cover in a corner behind a stack of coolant barrels. The hangar doors closed. At any moment the chamber would be flooded with atmosphere, rendering her vulnerable to discovery.

She glanced at her wrist to confirm that the air pressure was rising. Within a minute it had reached standard, and there was a single clear tone announcing that the locked doors into the hangar were disengaging. She crept further into her corner and found a gap that she could peer between. Once again she found herself in a situation that demanded some stealth. Maybe Cole was right. Maybe she needed a poncho to break up her silhouette. Next thing he'd have her wearing a stupid cowboy hat. Gaucho hat. Whatever it was called.

The door at the far end of the hangar opened and a handful of forms entered. Small forms. Children each and every one except for two teenagers leading the pack. Abigail gritted her teeth. The teenagers appeared to be armed with compact automatic weapons. She couldn't quite make out their model from here, but she suspected the caliber was too small to be much of a threat to her.

Not that she was going to tempt them. She wasn't quite ready to see Ivan again.

The crew of the ship disembarked, clearly stalling and unhappy. The lack of fuel module and associated fuel was probably about to get them in hot water. Sure enough, it only took a few moments before the shouting began. The voice of one of the teens rose above the higher voices of the children.

"Are you all stupid? Where's the fuel tanker? Answer me, bilgeworms."

There was a lot more shouting in answer, as the crew began to panic. Abigail regretted her part in the trouble they'd found themselves in. She eyed the weapons again, hoping she wasn't about to have to go charging in to rescue the very thieves she was pursuing.

"One at a time," the lead teen shouted, "I can't hear myself think over the shrieking. You. Talk. Where's the fuel tanker and where is your escort?"

A short boy with close-cropped brown hair stepped forward. He was practically trembling. "We got ambushed. Someone was waiting for us. Someone jumped Davey. I saw it happen from the cockpit. And then a giant attacked the tanker crew. We had to get out of there!"

"And leave the fuel? Are you insane?" The teen was yelling even louder than before, but Abigail could see that he was also afraid now. That was interesting. There was a pecking order here, and the teens

111

were still vulnerable to it.

"It was either that or be captured," the boy retorted balling his fists in defiance.

"Should have gotten captured then. Now we're all going to get it."

"And risk someone talking?"

The teen shrugged. "You left your escort."

The boy laughed bitterly. "If you think Davey is going to talk, then you're sniffing coolant again."

The teen swung the butt end of his weapon at the boy. "You shut your mouth, bilgeworm!" There were a handful of screams as the brave little boy dropped to the ground whimpering. "All of you. Report to Block Four. We'll have to figure out how to break this to the Duke if we don't want to all be thrown out the airlock."

This Duke didn't sound good. If Abigail were placing bets, she'd put good money on him being the adult in the room. Still, something about this whole operation seemed mad. Surely these children weren't here solely to siphon fuel off of a nearby refinery. There had to be a bigger game. She needed more information, but if she just charged through the halls looking for whoever was in charge of the station, children might get hurt.

The kids and teenagers filed out. Soon the hangar would be empty and she'd have a chance to move.

Then she saw the straggler. The blonde girl she'd seen earlier in the fuel module. She sat slumped against the landing strut of the ship.

And she was bawling her eyes out.

Abigail bit her lip. This was a terrible idea, but she really didn't have any better ones right now. Besides, the girl looked like she could use a friend. And maybe she'd know a few of this place's secrets.

Abigail crept from her hiding place and walked over to the girl. As she knelt in front of her, the girl startled and looked up at her in wonder.

"Hi," Abigail said with the friendliest smile she could muster. "What's your name?"

Grace Anderson was having one of the worst days ever. It had started like most any other day until she and her big brother Davey had gotten into another fight over him enlisting as an enforcer. He said he had his reasons, but what reason could justify something so horrible? How could he join up with that group of bullies? How could he follow the Duke's orders so blindly?

They'd cut the argument short when the scheduled fuel 'salvage' mission came up. Grace was getting assigned to them a lot lately. Her hard work and reliability were paying off, and she hoped to get a better room soon, maybe up on one of the brightly lit levels near the top of the station. She'd lived in the lower levels, lit only by maddening red emergency lights, for so many years that the thought nearly made her giddy.

Davey had somehow managed to get himself assigned as the enforcer escort on her last several missions. She didn't mind normally. Having her brother around calmed her nerves, helped her work fast, and efficiently. But after this morning's fight, it was another matter entirely.

The mission should have been like any other. They had silently drifted across space to the refinery and started their work securing fuel for the Duke. But then they had been attacked by the giant and it had all gone so horribly wrong.

Grace had been in charge of the fuel tanker and she'd lost it.

And Davey? Davey had been left behind. Grace knew she'd never see him again.

She'd slipped away from the group deliberately, unable to imagine a future without Davey. The world closed in around her as she slumped down against the landing strut and the tears came unbidden and unwelcome. If the other children saw her they would whisper behind her back. Stories would be told and she'd never get a room on the upper levels.

The enforcers would push her around. Treat her like a fresh acquisition.

And then she no longer cared. Davey was gone. Just this once, she would show a little weakness. It would be several minutes before they'd realize she was gone and come looking for her.

There was a loud clomping noise on the deck in front of her. Grace looked up from her cry to see the giant leaning down to look at her and she froze in terror. She wanted to run, get help, but her muscles refused to move.

"Hi! What's your name?"

Her eyes focused on the giant's face for the first time and saw that it was a woman with short dark curls. Curiosity got the best of her, and she wiped away her tears. "Gr... Grace."

"That's a nice name," the woman said smiling brightly. "I'm Abigail. I can't help but notice that you're not doing so well."

Grace nodded and the tears started flowing again. "My brother..."

113

she mumbled.

"What was that?" the woman asked.

She wiped the tears from her eyes. "My brother. What did you do with him?"

The woman stared at her, a look of confusion crossing her pretty face. "I'm not sure I know what you're talking about..."

"You attacked us and we had to leave him behind," Grace's voice squeaked with emotion. Normally she'd be embarrassed, but right now she was too upset to care. Right now she was all emotion and nerve. "What did you do to him?" she rasped through her tears.

Abigail looked at her again and cocked her head. Her face suddenly lit up. "Oh, your brother was the one outside with the pipeline. Don't worry! He's safe. My friends have him."

"And they aren't going to hurt him?" Grace looked at Abigail doubtfully, unsure if this strange woman was at all trustworthy.

"Of course not. We're not going to hurt children. We'd like to help you if we can, but I may need you to help me out first."

Grace, bit her lip nervously. "Prove it."

"That we want to help you?"

"That my brother is okay."

Abigail shrugged. "Yeah, okay. I guess we can do that. We may have to wait a few minutes, but my friends will be along soon enough. As soon as they are back in comm range, you can talk to your brother."

Grace's eyes narrowed. "How long will that take? Someone could find us here, and I'd get in big trouble with the Duke and his enforcers."

"I get the feeling I'm not going to like this Duke of yours. It could be a while. I don't know how quickly they were able to follow our trail. Do you have someplace we could hide till they get here?"

There were places in the lower levels, in the dark, where people almost never went. At least not if there wasn't a reason.

"Yeah, I know a place. Come on. We'll take the maintenance shaft." Grace led Abigail to the back of the hangar and pointed at a heavy access hatch. "That takes about four of us to open, but I bet you can do it by yourself."

Abigail bent over and pulled back the cover from the accessway with one hand. Grace tried to not show how impressed she was but failed miserably as the grin crept across her face. Work on the station would be so much easier if they had someone like Abigail around for the heavy lifting.

"Come on," Grace said, climbing down the ladder into the dark. Above her, Abigail climbed into the shaft, blocking out the dim light filtering downward. As she approached the bottom, fear began to grip her heart.

Strangers were coming to the station. The one thing the Duke said could never happen. One was already here.

The enforcers would put her in a dark box. There was no other outcome to this disaster.

She reached the bottom of the shaft and stepped clear to give Abigail room. But then again, the giant woman in a suit of magical armor seemed nice enough. Maybe she wouldn't let them put Grace in a dark box.

Maybe no one would ever go into a dark box again.

Grace smiled as she pulled a small light out of her pocket to show their way through the dark lower levels of the station. She'd dreamed about a room on the upper levels. But this was better. Maybe, just maybe, the strangers would burn this stinking place to the ground.

Unfortunately, the good cop had gotten little more out of their captive than a few more Mandarin curse words. Yvonne noticed the small tells that he understood English. A flick of the eyes when she spoke. A twitch in the forehead muscles that revealed he knew quite well what she was talking about. But he was stubborn. She had tried off and on for the last several hours with little to show for it.

The doctor in her marveled at his small stature. The Chinese community she had known hadn't been particularly tall, but this teen was far below expected height. Probably first or second percentile if she had to guess. He had either been cursed with unusual genetics or been chronically malnourished at key stages of his development. Maybe both.

She'd seen enough kids on the streets of the solar system to have seen it all, and it still broke her heart.

"Well, if you change your mind and decide to help us and your friends," she opened a cabinet and pulled out a self-heating meal, "then you can have yourself a nice little meal. Until then, I'm going to leave this over here where you can see it and think about it." His eyes followed the package intently.

She hated lying to the young man and had already decided that she was going to give him the meal no matter what happened. Completely by accident, she had become the bad cop, resorting to manipulation to get results.

"Yvonne, I've got Sharon back on comms," Matthew called from the cockpit.

"I'll be right there." She turned to their captive. "Think about it. I'll be back."

She opened the door to the cockpit and heard Abigail's voice crackling over the speakers.

"And so Grace and I are hiding out in the sewage treatment plant now and have been waiting around for you to catch up."

"Who's Grace?" Yvonne asked.

"Cute little blonde girl. Which by the way, I think you guys are holding onto her older brother."

"Mmm. I don't think so if she's blonde," Matthew said thoughtfully. "This kid's Chinese. Dark hair."

Suddenly a girl's voice came over the speakers. "Well Davey's not my real brother, but he's looked out for me since long before we came here, so I call him that. But how did you know he was Chinese? He tries to keep that a secret." There was a pause. "He didn't say a bunch of bad words, did he? He does that sometimes..."

Yvonne chuckled. "Yes, but I'm not too offended. I've heard them all before. Maybe not the Chinese ones, but there's only so much creativity in cursing."

The girl laughed. "Are you Yvonne? Abigail told me about you. And sorry about Davey. He can be pretty dumb sometimes. I hope he's okay. You didn't hurt him, did you?"

"I promise, he's fine," Yvonne reassured. "I'll even let you talk to him in few minutes."

"So what's it like over there, Sharon?" Matthew asked, impatient to be back to the task at hand. "I'm looking at a derelict habitat that's not so derelict. I've got plenty of signs of activity and heat, but no outside lights and only dark viewports."

Abigail sighed. "Horribly messed up is the short answer. Grace has been telling me a little bit about it. There's only one adult on the whole station. He calls himself Duke Fagin." She paused for a moment. "You read that one, right Cole?"

Yvonne glanced at Matthew and saw his face twist up. "Not very subtle is it. So this guy is a real sicko?"

"Pretty much. Best I can tell shipments of fresh children arrive on occasion. They get put to work here on the station. Eventually, they get shipped off again before they grow into teenagers. A few of the meaner kids stick around for a few years as the Duke's enforcers, but even they disappear before they turn eighteen."

"This... This is part of a slaver operation," Yvonne said, mouth agape. "They bring in kids that are too young to be of any use. Duke Fagin puts them to work and trains them into docile workers and then they get shipped out when they're useful."

Matthew shook his head sadly. "And I bet the enforcers get recruited into whatever cartel or gang will take them."

Abigail cleared her throat. "According to Grace, Davey has recently joined the enforcers. She's understandably not very happy about that."

There was complete silence for nearly a minute. Yvonne's heart broke for the children, especially Grace. Was their captive a bad apple? Maybe it wasn't too late for him if they got him away from this horrid place.

Matthew interrupted her thoughts. "Grace, can you tell me how many children are on the station with you? Best guess."

"Mmmmaybe... Maybe four hundred? I don't know. Sorry, Mr. Cole."

"That's good. Do you think maybe you could step away and give us some privacy to talk to Abigail?"

"Sure. Do I still get to talk to my brother?"

"You bet, just give us a few minutes."

After a moment Abigail's voice came back over the comm. "Okay, she's out of earshot. I don't even have words for this."

"Monstrous," Yvonne said. "Evil. Wicked." She shuddered as she looked out at the dark shape of the station blotting out the stars like a hole in the sky.

Matthew mumbled something so quiet that Yvonne could barely hear it. "And even as they did not like to retain God in their knowledge, God gave them over to a reprobate mind." Yvonne raised an eyebrow and opened her mouth to ask him about that but was interrupted by Abigail.

"What was that? Speak up."

"It's nothing, Sharon." He sighed and Yvonne could see how his shoulders drooped. "What do we do about this?"

Abigail made an unhappy sound. "I was kind of hoping you had an idea. You're the boss."

Matthew frowned. "Not sure who put me in charge. This is way beyond the scope of our contract, and I don't really have any right to demand anyone do anything."

He looked to Yvonne, but she only crossed her arms. "We'll follow your lead on this one. However you want to approach this, we'll trust your judgment."

Matthew apparently wasn't thrilled with the prospect. "Give me some time to think. Sharon, are you and Grace in any immediate danger?"

"Grace says the sewage plant gets weekly maintenance. It's been a while since she's come down here, but if the old schedule holds we could hide out for the next two days. Honestly, though, I'm more worried about the smell than getting caught. Stuff like this works into my suit and I can smell it for weeks."

"Let me have an hour then," he said and turned to Yvonne. "Head on back to the common room. Let Davey and Grace talk. We may need his cooperation."

Yvonne stood and turned to go, but paused and placed a comforting hand on Matthew's shoulder. "You alright?"

"Fine," he grunted. "Why?"

"Just a hunch." If Matthew Cole had a past with Europa, then slavery was most likely a sensitive subject for him.

"I thought you were a medical doctor, not a psychologist." His expression was playful but hollow. There was no mirth behind his eyes.

"Very well. Some other time perhaps." She turned away, meaning every word of it. That would come later when there were less pressing matters at hand. Returning to the common room, she walked back over to where the teen still struggled in his bonds. He sure was persistent.

"Davey, would you like to talk to your sister? I can raise her on the comm if you would like."

It took Matthew less than the promised hour to come up with a plan, or rather the bare bones of the plan. It would take a bit of input from the others and require cooperation from Grace.

The lynchpin would be Davey. If the teen could be convinced to join in the venture they'd stand a real chance.

It was a foul tactic, grooming kids into enforcers. Train them to turn on their own and they'll be well suited for a life of abusing their fellow colonists. It was the oldest method of gang recruitment. Make someone feel special. Like they were important. Once they bought that lie, they were yours.

It had happened at Villa María. They'd lost the youth first.

Matthew wondered if Davey had fully bought into the lie already. Grace said that Davey had only recently joined the group. Maybe his loyalty to his sister was still stronger than his loyalty to the Duke and his goons. He hoped so.

When Matthew crept into the common room, he heard soft conversation and stopped short, not wanting to interrupt anything. When he'd first secured Davey to his chair, he'd made sure to face him away from the hall to the cockpit to give them more privacy to move about if they needed it. As it was, the teen didn't hear his approach and kept talking to Yvonne. She registered Matthew's presence with a flick of the eyes but kept her attention on the teen.

"We lived in one of the coreward cities on Ceres," Davey said. "Dump of a mining town named Blight. Yeah. Blight. You know a place is great when they name it that. Anyway, we ran with a pack of other homeless kids. Looked out for each other. Made sure everyone got fed. Turns out someone in Blight didn't approve of us. The rumor I heard was they hired the cartel to come pick us up. Eventually, we couldn't evade them. All the kids got separated into groups. I guess the teens all ended up on Europa or somewhere. I was already thirteen but slipped in with Grace's group because of... well, you know." He trailed off into silence.

"How long have you been here under Duke Fagin?" Matthew asked gently to announce his presence.

Davey stiffened and tried to turn to see the newcomer. As Matthew walked around in front of him, the teen glared thumper blasts at him. Matthew wasn't sure he deserved quite that fierce a look, at least not for anything he'd done today. The teen set his jaw, apparently unwilling to talk at all while Matthew was around.

"Oh, so we're going to play tough guy? Give me the silent treatment? Fine." Matthew crossed his arms and leaned against the counter. "It's a good thing your ears are open, Davey, because right now I want you to listen."

The teen only looked away. Yvonne gave Matthew an apologetic look and shrugged.

"So here's the deal. We were hired to stop your little fuel thefts. Lucky for you kids, we're also halfway decent people. Now, we could just call this back to our employer or some local authorities and they'd come clear this little operation out. I get the feeling that would result in a lot of people getting hurt. But our crewmate Abigail seems to like your sister Grace, so we're gonna try and do this ourselves."

Davey glanced at Matthew before looking away again. Okay, at least he was listening. "I've got a couple ideas on how to do this, but we're going to need a man on the inside."

"Not interested," Davey said shortly.

"That's a pity," Matthew said shaking his head. "You know your sister told us she was upset about you joining the enforcers. Maybe she thought you were turning into a bit of a thug." He paused to let the moment sink in. "Maybe she's right."

A tense silence filled the common room and Matthew wondered what struggles went through the young man's mind. He decided to go in for the kill. "I overheard you talking to Yvonne. I'm kind of curious what happened to the kid that used to be part of the group from Blight. The group that looked out for each other."

Davey frowned and sighed. That must have done the trick. "Okay fine. I'm in. What do you need from me?"

Yvonne smiled and sat back in her chair, relaxed. Matthew made eye contact with her briefly and then looked at Davey. "Mostly information and a bit of cooperation."

"I'm doing this for Grace," Davey said. "Just so we're clear."

"Sure," Matthew said nodding. "For Grace."

Truth was, Davey wasn't that bad a kid. At least he didn't think so. Everytime Grace nagged him about joining Duke Fagin's enforcers, though, he had a few doubts.

"You gotta make sacrifices," he explained to her over and over.

He'd been making sacrifices since he had first taken her under his wing all those years ago on Ceres. Life would have been easier on Ceres without Grace always being underfoot, and it would have been easier here too. But he kept on making those sacrifices. For Grace.

Joining the enforcers was the only thing keeping him here on the station with Grace and not shipped off to some new owner. Humiliating as it had been, he'd lied about his age for years. Being short had that one advantage. The Duke and the enforcers had finally wisened up, so he made his last desperate bid to stick around with his sister.

He tried not to think about the things he'd done as an enforcer. "It's all so I can protect Grace," he told himself over and over. And yet each time he'd bullied or stood by as a kid was beaten it bothered him less. Maybe you can sacrifice too much.

Maybe these strangers were a chance to escape. They could be used. He wasn't sure they were all that clever.

120

This plan certainly had vacuum for brains.

They docked the Sparrow noisily onto the station. Every other enforcer on the habitat would be waiting on the other side of that airlock, armed and itching for a fight.

Davey was supposed to keep that from happening. Somehow.

The airlock opened with a hiss of air. Davey took a deep breath and stepped forward hands in the air. "Guys, it's me. Davey!" He could see the other twenty or so enforcers, in positions of cover in the hallway. Looked like the whole gang was here to greet the strange ship. "Oh come on, exhaust jockeys, it's me."

One of the other enforcers stepped out. It was the Duke's top man, Dexter. Dexter's face was covered with piercings he'd done himself and, right now, that face wasn't screaming happy.

"You're supposed to be dead or captured, shorty."

"You'd like that wouldn't you? Lucky for me we got caught by a different set of thieves."

Dexter wasn't impressed and crossed his arms. "So you led them back here? If we don't kill you here and now, the Duke will."

Davey matched the other teen's stance. "Turns out the thieves are interested in the operation and may be buyers."

The lead enforcer seemed to consider this. "Even if he ends up liking these guys, he's still gonna kill you. Maybe he'll let me do it."

"In your dreams," Davey said smirking. "Look, are you gonna send word to the Duke or not?"

Dexter wrinkled his nose in annoyance before rolling his eyes. "Fine. Let's head right up. Your thief friends got someone that wants to talk to the Duke? I can't promise their safety."

"Yeah, Yeah." Davey stepped back into the Sparrow's airlock. "Come on," he said to Cole. "They're gonna take us to the Duke."

Davey and Cole emerged from the Sparrow. The gaucho nodded gravely at the group of armed teenagers and they relaxed a bit. It helped that he looked the part. Some of the buyers that came by the habitat were dressed similarly to Cole. The man's street clothes were the perfect disguise.

"Follow me," Dexter said. "Oh, and what's your name?"

"Cole."

Dexter shrugged. "Whatever. Come on."

Davey kept right on walking, aware that the other enforcers weren't lowering their weapons. The way he figured it, the odds of him making it out of this were pretty close to zero, but as long as Grace made it out of this pit, he wasn't sure he cared.

121

Matthew couldn't help but feel nervous around a pack of angry teenagers with itchy trigger fingers. He didn't show this discomfort of course. Didn't fit the role he was trying to play. He let the enforcers lead him and Davey up several flights of stairs and several hundred feet to a different part of the habitat. Curious children poked their faces out of darkened doorways but quickly disappeared at the first disapproving look from an enforcer.

Seemed that everyone around here knew their place.

He kept a watchful eye on Davey. If he decided to betray them, there would be no help for Matthew Cole.

They arrived at a room filled with child sized benches. "This is the Duke's antechamber," the lead enforcer explained to Matthew. "Wait here. I'll check with him and see if he's interested in seeing you." He smiled a wicked smile. "For your sake, you'd better hope he is."

He disappeared into the double doors at the end of the room. Matthew leaned against a wall and put on his most impressive bored face. Not for one moment during his wait did the pack of enforcers take their eyes off him. As far as he was concerned, they took their jobs far too seriously. They should be chasing after girls or going to school or some other kid thing.

After about five minutes, the double doors reopened and Dexter emerged. "Looks like it's your lucky day, Mr. Cole. The Duke will see you." Matthew caught Davey's eye on the way out of the room. Hopefully, they'd meet again on the far side.

He pushed this thought aside as he was ushered through the doors into one of the most opulent rooms he had ever stepped foot in. Faux marble columns lined the walls and purple hangings of silk filled in the spaces between. From the ceiling hung crystal chandeliers that cast the room in flickering light. A red carpet trimmed with gold led across a mirror polished floor to a dais and a throne. Upon the throne sat a fat man in a navy blue military uniform from some previous century. Medals of dubious origin and decorative aiguillettes adorned the jacket's breast, and heavy gold bracelets hung over on the outside of each sleeve. Topping off the ridiculous guise was a bicorne hat with an obviously fake ostrich plume sticking out haphazardly to one side.

Without a doubt this was a madman and narcissist of the highest order.

"Welcome! Welcome!" said the fat man standing to his feet. "I am Duke Fagin and this is my domain. To whom do I have the finest pleasure of speaking?"

Matthew took off his hat and nodded his head politely, hoping the Duke wasn't expecting some display of fealty. "Matthew Cole. Entrepreneur." He placed the campero back on his head. "I have a variety of investments scattered through the system. Times being what they are and with the cost of labor being what it is, I've been thinking about diversifying my workforce a bit."

"Oh I know just what you mean," the Duke said sitting back on his throne. "The universe is a mean place and men are animals. Of course, it takes real men to carve out a bit of civilization amongst the chaos. But order can be achieved with a bit of proper training and even feral children can be of some use given time."

"So I hear," Matthew said, feeling disgust course through his body. "Imagine my pleasure at stumbling upon your operation purely by chance. I'm sorry that your servants lost your fuel tanker. Thankfully, the lad we captured kept his wits about him. Seems a resourceful enough fellow."

"Yes, yes, the Chinese boy," the Duke said dismissively. "He's had his uses I guess, but he's become a bit of a disappointment." The man smiled wickedly. "Sometimes the... unique children can be isolated from their peers and turned into something more useful. I made sure he was bullied for his small stature and uncommon ethnicity. Sadly, it seems he only became an enforcer so he could watch after his sister. Pity. Oh well. His pedigree will fetch a handsome price when I decide to sell him. Some of the richer fools out there will pay for exotic house servants."

Matthew knew only black rage as his heartbeat hammered behind his temples. It took an act of iron will to smile and nod and even attempt to continue the conversation. "Well, I don't need to take all your time. How about we talk a little business?" There was nothing in the universe he wanted less than to continue, but he would only have to endure this conversation until he got the signal from the others. At that point, it would be his pleasure to dethrone this tyrant permanently.

As soon as Matthew went in, Dexter turned on Davey. "The Duke's not happy, Davey. Thinks you really messed up this time."

Davey curled his lip into a snarl. "He'll change his tune soon enough when he gets a new buyer. I might even get promoted."

"You're clueless." Dexter motioned towards the door. "To the barracks, enforcers. We need to teach one of our own a lesson."

123

Despite the implied threat, Davey had to keep from smiling as he was jostled out the door and back down the hallway. At least the Duke and the enforcers were predictable. If they'd decided to mix things up, Davey might have been in trouble.

As it was, he was about to get a beating for his failures earlier in the day. He'd take the fall for the lost fuel tanker. Or rather he would if not for Grace's new friends. In theory, they were going to jump in and save him. He wasn't sure that was possible. How anyone was going to go up against all the enforcers at once was beyond Davey's ability to guess, but they didn't seem to think it'd be too much of a problem.

Thankfully he'd correctly guessed where they would take him once Cole went in to see the Duke. At least he'd stand a chance. They roughly pushed him down one level and toward the barracks. One of the enforcers waved a pass in front of the scanner and the door slid open. He was stepped into the messy living area. Clothes and piles of trash filled the corners. The strict rules on the habitat weren't quite as strict for the enforcers.

He reached into his pocket and pushed the button on the transmitter Matthew had given him.

That was that. Either Grace's friends saved him before he was beaten into a bloody pulp or they didn't.

"Take a good look around, Davey," the lead enforcer said with a sneer. "Cause this is the last time you'll ever be in the barracks. The Duke is going to sell you. I suggested he send you to a fertilizer plant on Europa, but he said that was going to be too good for you."

Davey stretched himself to his full height to stare down the other teen. Unfortunately, Dexter was at least a head taller than him. He smiled and decided he wouldn't go down like a bilgeworm. Without warning he hit Dexter in the gut and dove at him, tackling him to the ground. Maybe help would come, maybe it wouldn't.

Davey was going to wipe the stupid grin off of Dexter's face either way.

When the Sparrow docked, Grace quietly crept into the habitat's control room. Usually, only a single kid was posted on duty. If something went wrong, a dozen more could be diverted to monitor the station. What happened next depended entirely upon who was on duty. As it turned out, luck was with Grace, as Lumpy manned the controls. The round-faced boy was good-natured and trusting, despite their hard life. Grace didn't think he'd ever lived on the street like she and Davey had. Maybe he could go home to his parents if they really did all escape.

"Hey, Lumpy! How's it going?"

Lumpy turned in surprise. "Grace? I thought for sure you'd be in a dark box after that mission."

She laughed nervously. "I'm probably supposed to be, but I've been hiding."

The boy looked at her like she was crazy. "You're just gonna make it worse when the enforcers catch you."

"Don't worry they won't. They'd never look for me here would they?" she said putting her hands on her hips.

"Well..." he replied doubtfully. "I guess not. But if they find you here on my shift, then I'm going to be joining you."

"So don't be here," she said sitting in the chair behind him. "I'll take your shift and they'll never be the wiser."

Lumpy seemed to consider that. "All right fine. But you owe me."

"I'll give you one of my meal rations."

Lumpy didn't even stop to think about it. "Deal," he said happily. "I'll be back at the end of the shift so that when Lena comes on, she won't know what we did."

"Thanks!" Grace said with a smile more cheerful than she felt. An awful lot could still go wrong. Her pocket vibrated with the signal from Davey. She needed to wrap this up quickly. "Oh, one more question! Did any of the rest of the kids on this morning's mission get in trouble? Is anyone in the dark boxes right now?"

Lumpy shook his head. "Nah, I heard it was just going to be you for ditching the fuel tanker."

She gave him an enthusiastic thumbs up. Not having to rescue anyone from the dark boxes was going to make her job much easier. "Alright, I'll see you later."

The boy nodded and slipped out the door. Grace took his seat and glanced over the monitors. Didn't seem to be anything going on.

She could fix that.

She leaned over to the console on her left and flipped open a glass panel. Her hand hovered for a moment over the heavy red switch. There would be no going back after this.

She flipped the switch.

Red lights and fire alarms began to blast through the station.

Fire was one of the greatest threats to any space station. A fast-spreading threat that consumed oxygen and lives, fire also turned a

125

space station into an oven that can cook you alive before it even reaches you. Monthly fire drills had prepared the kids for just such an emergency. Four lifeboats, one at each end of the station unlocked immediately. They would have about three minutes to reach a boat before they automatically launched and anyone left behind would be left to face the flames. No one ever missed the boats. Later the Duke would come pick them up in his own ship.

Grace smiled as she stepped out of the control room and saw the kids running towards the boats. They'd all make it. Only this time the Duke wasn't going to be there to skim them out of space.

Moments after Davey landed on top of Dexter, the fire alarms went off. The main lights went out and red emergency lights came on. There was a moment of confusion as the enforcer's stood dumbfounded.

"There's not a drill today is there?"

"What's going on?"

"Is this real?"

Davey was thrown off of Dexter and the bigger teen drew his weapon, one of the compact submachine guns that all the enforcers were issued. "Time's up for you, runt. If you think I'm dragging you to a boat, you're mistaken."

Davey grimaced. Maybe he shouldn't have gotten that hit in on Dexter.

With a deafening boom, something enormous landed in the middle of the room. Davey saw it out of the corner eye and backed away. It moved towards Dexter, and with its massive shield, swatted him away like a rag doll. Davey looked up at the figure and realized it was a woman. Only she was a giant in a suit of armor. His eyes went wide. Somehow, she'd dropped from the ceiling. Was there a maintenance tunnel up there or had she been hiding in the room the whole time?

She smiled. "Guessing you're Davey. You might want to get behind me."

He obeyed and she slowly backed towards the door. Several of the enforcers got their heads about them. They might not have known any more about this newcomer than Davey did, but they knew she wasn't on their side. Sprays of automatic fire bounced harmlessly off her shield. Davey slipped out of the door, and as the strange armored woman backed out, he shut it.

"I can't lock it from this side," he said desperately, feeling a drop of sweat run down his face. "They're just going to follow us!"

126

The woman looked thoughtfully at the door then smashed it with her shield several times, warping its surface and destroying the mechanism that opened it. "Try it," she commanded.

He hit the controls. There was a tortured metallic groaning, but the door refused to budge. He smiled grimly. The enforcers would be panicking as they wondered when the fire would reach them to end their pathetic lives. There wasn't a fire of course, but let them feel a bit of fear. They deserved that and worse.

The armored woman nodded. "That should hold. Take me to the Duke. Cole may need my help."

Davey gestured back towards the stairs. "This way."

The moment the fire alarm went off, Matthew reacted, standing and drawing his revolver on Duke Fagin in one swift motion. He'd had enough of this sickening conversation and was more than ready for action to take the place of words.

The Duke didn't seem particularly phased by the gun in his face. "Oh my, so there's a plot against me. If you think my kingdom will be felled so easily, you're mistaken." The Duke made to stand from his throne.

Matthew wasn't willing to take any risks. Quick as a thought he fired a single bullet at the Duke's left leg. It wasn't meant to kill, only cripple.

The bullet shattered into a spray of sparks and molten metal three feet from the Duke and the gold bracelet on his right wrist lit up with fiery light. For the space of one heartbeat, Matthew stood confused at what had happened. By the next heartbeat, he was pulling the trigger again. Five more bullets failed to reach their target in equally spectacular fashion as the bracelet blazed with inner light.

The Duke stretched his left arm outward towards Matthew. The left bracelet flared with a cold blue light and Matthew was thrown across the room and held by an invisible grip against the far wall. His brain tried to catch up to what was happening, comprehend how any of this was possible. Duke Fagin chuckled to himself and stepped down from the throne, never lowering his arm for an instant. The bracelet still shone blue.

"I'm not sure who you are, or what all the deception was for, but this is a rather poor assassination attempt. It's not the first of course. Usually, it's kids or enforcers that don't know any better." The duke smiled and used his free hand to hike his pants a little higher. "I can defend myself and my children well enough. So tell me, Matthew Cole, if that really is your name. What put it into your head to try and do the noble thing and save the poor children?"

Matthew didn't answer. He only glared at the Duke as he walked across the room towards his helpless captive. His eyes fell on the golden bracelets. Miracles. One of a kind technology designed by Moses himself. It was the only explanation. He'd heard stories from other freelancers, whispers of tech that seemed like magic. Never had any reason to give them more than half an ear.

Clearly, that was a mistake. He cast his eyes desperately around the room, looking for a way out, anything that would help. His eyes fell on a possibility. If he just waited for the right moment, he might have one trick left to play.

"And now you hold your tongue. Pity. You've given a bit of entertainment today and I hate to end it so soon. Spending all day every day around children can be dreadfully boring."

There it was. Matthew fought against the invisible grip and lifted his revolver to point it at the Duke.

Duke Fagin laughed at the effort. "Come now, you're not going to waste another bullet in a futile attempt at harming me, are you? What a pathetic end."

Matthew lifted the barrel higher still and fired his last bullet. It pierced the chain of one of the chandeliers. The crystal fixture fell, clipping the Duke on the way down and shattered into ten thousand shards. The invisible grip lost hold of him when the slaver fell to the ground and the blue light cut out. Matthew hit the ground running and closed the gap between them in a flash. Taking a flying leap, he aimed a kick at the Duke, catching him under the chin as he tried to lift himself from the floor.

The impact made an unpleasant sound and Duke Fagin slipped back to the floor never to rise again. Matthew picked up his hat, then leaned over to check the Duke's pulse. Silent.

"Good riddance," Matthew said to himself. Then he noticed the bracelets, the Miracles. They had unlatched themselves from the man's wrists and fallen to the floor, dark and inert. Matthew scooped them up and slid them over his own wrists, but they refused to latch shut and there didn't appear to be any controls to operate them. He shrugged and hooked them on his belt. A mystery for another day, perhaps.

Sharon burst into the room, followed by a much more cautious Davey.

"I did my job," Matthew said, gesturing to the dead man and the fallen chandelier. "You guys take care of the enforcers?"

Sharon nodded. "Trapped in their barracks for us to deal with at our leisure."

"Then let's head back to the Sparrow. We still need to scoop up the children's lifeboats. I imagine they're in for quite a shock."

Huygens Industrial Chem's executives were rather surprised when the Sparrow docked at its corporate tower at the refinery with four outdated lifeboats in tow. They were even more surprised when the lifeboats opened and nearly four hundred children spilled out into the hangar.

Abigail stood back from the group as Cole and Yvonne explained the whole thing. Grace refused to leave her side after catching back up with her, which meant that ultimately her brother Davey was nearby as well. She could have done without the dour-faced teen. Something about him didn't rub her right, even if Grace vouched for him.

"So what happens now?" Grace asked, fear in her eyes.

"I don't really know," Abigail said carefully. "Cole already put in a call to the office of the Archbishop of Titan. I'm not sure he trusts a corporation to take the best care of you guys." She looked at the crowd of children meandering around the hangar. Guards watched them uneasily and kept them from wandering off. "Can't say I blame him, personally."

The enforcers stood in cuffs at the side. Most of them were probably too far gone, but Abigail suspected that at least a few of them, would be willing to turn over a new leaf. She saw the leader, Dexter. A purple bruise from his fight with Davey had swollen one of his eyes shut, and he looked utterly defeated. Then again, they were still kids. Maybe they'd all turn out okay in the end.

Grace sat down at Abigail's feet. "Some of the others have parents they might be able to go home to. Some of them were stolen, but others..." She trailed off.

Abigail bent down to comfort the girl, not quite sure how to cheer her up. "I'm sure the Church will find places for all of you."

The girl looked up at her with tears in her eyes. "Can we stay with you?"

She laughed and, reaching down, gently brushed a lock of blond hair out of the girl's face. "I don't think that's a good idea. We do a lot

129

of dangerous things, and I bet Mr. Cole would get grumpy with children around. I'll keep track of you though. Maybe we'll be able to visit when we're in the area."

Grace continued to cry. Davey walked up and took her hand yanking her to her feet. "Come on. Let's go. No use bothering her anymore."

Feeling the disappointment rise up in her chest, Abigail watched as the teen dragged his sister away and disappeared into the crowd of children, What else was there to do? They couldn't very well keep kids on their ship. She cursed under her breath and rejoined Cole and Yvonne.

Cole was just finishing negotiating a bonus with Huygens. The executives seemed hesitant, as they most certainly hadn't paid them to rescue children. But somehow or another the slick talking gaucho had guilted them into offering a little extra. It wasn't a lot, but it was better than nothing.

He also warned them that they might still have a mole. Duke Fagin had somehow known when Huygens had staked out the fuel tanks. But that was a problem beyond the crew of the Sparrow.

They waited another hour and a half for the Archbishop and his entourage to arrive. When the shining white and red shuttle pulled into the hangar, Cole pointed at the Sparrow. "That's our cue. Come on."

Yvonne caught Abigail's eye before following. "Not interested in seeing this through to the end? I would have thought you wanted to make sure the children's future was secure."

"Their future is secure, but I don't really want to stick around."

Abigail frowned, not following the thread of conversation at all. "I thought you were the one who called the Church?"

Cole kept walking and didn't turn around. "I did. And they're the best group to take custody of the children for now." He walked up the Sparrow's ramp. "It also doesn't mean I want to rub elbows all that much. We're done here." Cole disappeared into his ship without another word.

The women exchanged another look and Abigail shrugged. "Don't look at me. I don't have a clue what goes through his head. The captain says it's time to go, so it's time to go."

"So it seems," Yvonne said.

Abigail paused at the top of the ramp and turned to look out over the children, hoping to get another view of Grace. Sadly, she couldn't spot her in the crowd, and she too retired to the Sparrow. The long day had drained the batteries of both her suit and her body. She'd need a long time to recuperate from this one.

That night she dreamed of Grace. They were running across an open field under the skies of Mars. No matter how hard she tried, she couldn't quite catch the blonde girl as she managed to keep just out of Abigail's reach. It wasn't until she noticed the cool grass between her feet that she looked down and realized she wasn't wearing her suit.

She woke with tears streaming down her face.

Chapter 9: The Titan's Pride

No, you're not crazy. It all tastes different. Bread made from Martian Wheat tastes different from Europan Wheat. Different cultivars for different soils, light levels, atmospheric compositions, and what have you. They say Moses fine-tuned the crops to fit each colony.

My personal favorite is hydroponic oats grown in low gravity. They have a certain natural sweetness that no Earth cultivar could ever match. I'm sure dentists love that extra sugar content in everyone's breakfast.

That said, it's all the same stuff we brought from Earth. Moses may have pushed every scientific frontier he touched, but he didn't seem to be interested in playing God. I'm sure he could have given us new and better plants and animals. At least ones that suited us better in the colonies away from the natural environment of Earth.

Maybe he thought that was Pandora's box or else maybe making entirely new life is just a lot harder than you'd think. I don't claim to know. Either way we're still eating much the same thing we've been eating for thousands of years.

Except ration bars. Those abominations deserve their horrible reputation.

William Pike
Freight Pilot
Died 13 AM

"Think she's ever getting up?" Matthew asked looking back down the hall toward the crew cabins.

"She will when she gets hungry," Yvonne said. "Can't say I didn't want another hour myself but, alas, addiction calls to me." She swirled her coffee, took another sip, and sighed happily. "If the ship ever runs out of coffee, I'm turning myself in to the nearest bounty hunter. Won't even be a hard decision."

Matthew took the final swig from his own mug and figured he was on the same path of chemical dependence. He wasn't sure that he cared. "I guess you had better keep an eye on those stock levels. I won't be responsible for you doing something rash."

"Already on today's shopping list."

"Take a look at it again and see if there's anything else we need. I don't plan on spending more than a few hours on Titan's surface. Get in and get out."

Sharon stumbled into the common room, looking only half alive and less than half awake. Matthew marveled at her exo-suit for the thousandth time, how fluid and human-like its movements were. The way it shambled along groggily fascinated him. It had to follow her thoughts. There was no other reason it would produce wasteful movement like that.

She poured her own cup of coffee and then spooned an unholy amount of sugar into it before topping it off with about as much creamer as there was coffee.

"Easy on the sweets," Yvonne said, eyes wide. "This is breakfast. Not dessert."

Sharon grumbled something incoherent as she prepped a bowl of oatmeal and tossed it into the tiny microwave oven.

"Not even worth the effort," Matthew said. "Tried to talk sense into her when she first came on board. She doesn't actually like coffee. At least not how God meant for man to drink it."

"Black as the vacuum of space?" Yvonne asked.

"Precisely," he said.

133

Sharon rolled her eyes so hard it probably hurt. "Go ahead. Judge me. At least I won't turn into a rampaging monster when we run out."

Yvonne smiled and took another sip, seemingly content not to respond. They all knew it was true.

"So what's the plan today?" Abigail asked as she popped open the microwave and fetched her oatmeal.

"We'll set down on Titan after breakfast," Matthew said. "Nice little island called Mayda Insula on the Kraken sea. And when I say nice, I mean miserable, like everywhere else on Titan. But it'll have the supplies we need and then we can get out of here. I'm going to try and line up a job to move us back towards the inner system."

"Speaking of setting down on the surface," Yvonne said clearing her throat, "I'm getting a bit stir crazy. If I don't get off the ship when we get into port, you won't have to wait for the coffee to run out."

Matthew chewed on that thought. "Well... If you're dead set on getting some fresh air, I guess you could come with us. Not really gonna be a job for all three of us but we'll get it knocked out." He paused as a second thought crossed his mind. "Or if it doesn't hurt anyone's feelings, I've got an old friend down there I can check in on. You two can take care of business easily enough."

Sharon shrugged and went back to eating. "Sure. Pass off your chores to us. We can handle it."

"I'm not foisting chores onto you," he sighed. "Two people can handle it and I'm placing my trust in you. If someone recognizes Yvonne and decides to try to cash in on her bounty, you probably have a better chance at protecting her than I do."

"Well, you got that part right at least," Sharon retorted.

Yvonne tapped a finger on the table restlessly. "I'm going to need an awful lot more caffeine if you two are going to be this disagreeable. And as far as Titan goes, I can take care of myself. No babysitter needed. I'll wear a hood. No one will recognize me."

"No, probably not," Matthew admitted, "but as long as you're on my ship you'll be at least partially my responsibility. If you don't mind, I'd rather you stick with Sharon."

"I'm with Cole," Sharon said. "Come on, Yvonne. Girls' day on the town."

Yvonne looked back and forth between them. She was frustrated and he couldn't really blame her. Losing his freedom would be a hard pill to swallow.

Finally, she nodded slowly, in resignation if not defeat. "You win. I'll take the bullet-proof escort."

"Speaking of bulletproof," Sharon said, brightening, "you promised you'd show us the miracle."

Matthew reached down and unclipped the two golden bracelets from his belt. He'd fiddled with them for nearly an hour the night before and, try as he might, he couldn't get them to do anything. Not even the latches would clasp. He slid them across the table towards the women. "I can't make heads or tails of 'em."

Sharon took one of the devices and examined it. "If you hadn't told me this was a piece of tech, I would have thought it was just a piece of jewelry. I don't see any sort of controls or anything else."

"Very gaudy jewelry," Yvonne agreed, holding it up to the light. "I can see some faint lines on the inner surface, thin seams, fine as hair. Nothing else is visible to my eye. Fascinating."

"I've never seen anything like it," Matthew said, playing the scene over in his mind again. "One lit up like fire and shattered my bullets into molten shrapnel. The other had a blue light and threw me across the room like I was last week's garbage."

Yvonne looked at the device thoughtfully. "Care if I try it on? See if it'll do anything?"

Matthew shrugged. "Be my guest. They didn't seem to like me."

Sharon passed her bracelet to Yvonne and the older woman put one on each arm. "I'm not even sure I have them on the right arm or facing the correct direction." She tried several different configurations over the next couple minutes, but the bracelets refused to latch and remained inert. Finally, Yvonne pulled them off and set them on the table, the disappointment clear on her face. "I don't think it's meant to be."

"Pity," Sharon said. "It'd be nice if you had a little protection from bounty hunters."

"Well, how about you," Yvonne said pushing them towards Sharon. "Give em a shot?"

Sharon only crossed her arms. "My wrists are too big."

"I very much doubt that," Yvonne replied raising an eyebrow, "but I'm not surprised. Not even the chance at working a miracle will budge you from your exo-suit, huh?"

She shook her head. "Already bulletproof. Mostly."

Matthew reached back across the table for the bracelets and tried them himself for the hundredth time. "And here I was hoping for a third set of wrists to try." He glanced up at Sharon. "There's a secret here and I aim to discover it. But if you're dead set on staying in that suit, I'll have to make do."

135

"Secrets can stay secrets as far as I'm concerned," Sharon said. "I make it a rule to never mess with things I don't understand. Seen too many old sci-fi movies. Strange tech always makes people go weird."

Matthew sat back and scratched his chin. "Says the woman in the wonderful suit of earth-tech powered armor..."

Sharon stood up abruptly from the table and scowled. "Not the same thing." She turned heel back towards the crew quarters and disappeared without another word.

Yvonne gave Matthew a look, one that said he should have known better.

"Oh don't you start in," he said, feeling guilty in spite of himself. "How was I supposed to know a friendly jab would set her off? If she won't tell us why she's so sensitive about the subject, she's going to have to accept that we're going to be curious."

Yvonne folded her hands neatly in front of herself and still said nothing.

"Well, do you know what her deal is?" Matthew asked in growing annoyance.

She glanced back towards the crew cabins. "No. But I have a few theories."

The Sparrow plunged into the thick soup of Titan's atmosphere. The environmental shield that protected the ship from solar radiation and dust impacts in space did little to keep out the dense clouds. Droplets of liquid methane ran up the front viewport, vanishing quickly as they warmed and evaporated back into the orange-brown sky.

Abigail watched as Cole brought the Sparrow out of its shallow dive and leveled out over the Kraken Sea, a dark ocean of liquid methane and assorted hydrocarbons. She stared at it with curiosity and growing disgust. After so much time under the relatively clear skies of Mars, she found it hard to believe that people could actually spend their whole lives in some of the less hospitable corners of the solar system. Underground, cramped space stations, and dreary skies seemed to be the norm.

It was a long way from Mars. And even further from Earth.

"There's Mayda Insula," Cole said. "Coming over the horizon now."

A city of industrial spires, smokestacks, and factories sat on the island in the midst of the Kraken sea. To Abigail's eyes, it looked a bit smaller than most of the Martian cities, but those things were hard to judge from sight alone. Sometimes half a city was underground. More interesting to her was the clearly visible dome of the environmental shield.

"What's with the shield?" she asked. They don't normally shimmer like that."

"They tune them real high on Titan to keep out the atmosphere, rain, and bitter cold," Cole explained. "I'm glad you asked, though, because I should have warned you two about it. You're gonna feel it more than normal when we pass through."

Yvonne glanced at Cole from the co-pilot's chair. "How much are we going to feel it?"

The Sparrow shot through the shimmering field and for a brief moment, Abigail felt like her insides had gotten left behind. It was gone as soon as it started, leaving only a lingering discomfort.

Yvonne cradled her forehead in her hands. "That was... unpleasant. There's no way that's good for the human body."

"Hasn't killed anyone yet," Cole said. "Mayda Flight Control, this is the Sparrow, SPW5840. Looking for a docking pad on the cheap."

Abigail ignored Cole as he bargained with the spaceport rep. The discomfort was fading now, and she stretched her arms a bit inside the suit to get her wits back.

She froze.

Why were her arms moving in the suit?

Cold sweat broke out on her forehead as she tried to get her suit to respond.

Nothing.

Black terror gnawed at the back of her mind. Had passing through the shield broken something important? What would she do if...

Like a light coming on, she felt the suit responding to her thoughts again. Maybe the jolt had interrupted the connection between her armor and her neural implant. She took a deep breath and tried to relax, her pulse pounded in her temples. With a sickening feeling, she realized they would have to pass back through on the way out. She'd make sure to be hiding in her room, away from prying eyes next time.

"Sharon, you okay?" Cole asked. His face full of concern.

She waved him off, "I'm fine. Some of my systems didn't care for that shield."

He looked back to his controls. "I'm... Sorry. I'll make sure we're going slower on the way out."

"I'd appreciate that," she said and meant it. Yvonne turned and gave Abigail a look that made her decidedly uncomfortable. "I'm fine. I promise," she repeated, hoping the other woman would get the hint. "I don't need the doctor right now."

Yvonne turned away, and Abigail's pulse slowed. She closed her eyes and breathed deeply, hoping to put the incident behind her.

Cole set the Sparrow down on a landing pad at the spaceport near the edge of town. Most of the surrounding pads were empty. This wasn't the kind of city that drew too many tourists. You came to Titan's surface when you had business and only stayed as long as you had to. "I'd like to lift off in five or six hours," he said standing up and donning his hat. "You sure you two can handle the supply run?"

Yvonne pulled out her tablet and scanned the list again. "Seems pretty straightforward. Mostly food. Some basic living supplies. A few spare parts. Nothing we can't find in the port district. By the way, I added a new filter for the primary fuel intake. Turns out when you go that long without cleaning them you have to throw the whole thing away."

"I get it. You don't have to rub it in," Cole grumbled. "I'm assuming you two are taking a bike?"

"Seems the obvious thing to do," Abigail said, finally confident that her suit was operating as it was supposed to. "We'll need somewhere to stash our supplies."

"Come on then. No sense running the lift twice."

On the way out, Abigail grabbed her oversized trench coat. In a strange place it was better not to attract more attention than she had to, especially considering she was supposed to be keeping an eye on Yvonne. If someone got too curious about the extra-tall woman in armor and noticed Yvonne, they'd have problems.

A few minutes later they pushed the bikes off of the Sparrow's lift onto the landing pad. Bright lamps illuminated the area even in the day. The distant sun was too far away to light the surface of Titan past a dull twilight. Suddenly a bright flash of orange caught Abigail's attention and she looked up to see a fireball light the sky.

"What in...?"

"Methane burn off," Cole answered simply as he mounted his bike. "Even the stronger environmental shield doesn't keep all the rain out. It seeps in, evaporates, and collects in the upper regions of the dome. The taller spires have pilot lights that ignite it before enough collects to make a safety hazard. Helps keep the atmosphere inside a bit warmer and disposes of a potentially hazardous gas as well. Of course, they recommend you keep your flightpath low on approach unless you like decorating your hull with scorch marks. I'm out. Call me if you need me."

He fired the engines on his bike and drove off without another word.

"Let's get this supply list knocked out," Yvonne suggested pulling her hood low over her face.

Abigail looked around one last time in distaste at the dingy spaceport and sky. "If the rest of Titan is this nice, I can hardly wait to see it."

Yvonne had never set foot on Titan, though she and Tomas had spent some time on one of the orbital habitats nearly twenty years ago. It turned out every bad rumor she'd heard about the surface was true. Depressing steel and concrete buildings, a dark sky, and cold. Always cold. Frost formed on any exposed surface that wasn't near a heat source. Open trenches of molten salt were piped into most public areas in an attempt to keep the local air at somewhat comfortable temperatures, or at least give a warm spot to retreat to in order to thaw stiff fingers.

It would have been easier to live underground and not deal with the atmosphere or the cold, but after having lived in the subterranean cities of Ceres for so long, Yvonne could respect the fierce desire to walk under an open sky. It was a bad decision in the end, from a practical standpoint, but it wasn't the first or last poorly thought out city built by men.

There was a public square filled with shops that catered to the port and surrounding neighborhood a short distance from the landing pad. It was about the closest thing to cheery they were liable to find. There was even a molten salt fountain standing at its center, complete with globs of red-hot salt dribbling down a steel statue of a nude woman and collecting in a fiery pool. It was probably the strangest piece of public art Yvonne had ever seen. Locals moved to and fro on business, or clustered in small knots warming their hands over the artwork. Abigail spotted the store they were looking for, a grocer, specializing in the kinds of dried and frozen goods that kept well during the boring trips between the different neighborhoods of the solar system.

Yvonne stepped through the store's front door and environmental shield into the toasty warm interior. "I'd recommend we split up to finish the list faster, but I doubt Matthew would approve of us being separated... Abigail?" She turned and saw that the other woman was hesitant about stepping through the shield.

"Sorry, just thinking about earlier," Abigail said and pushed through the field into the store.

"I see." Yvonne filed away this tidbit as another clue to the puzzle. "Let's get this over with."

It took less than an hour, even with the additions Yvonne made to the list on the spot. She may not have been a great cook, but sometimes you just had to have a little fresh food. They would run out long before they got to Jupiter or Mars or wherever they ended up going, but it would be better than nothing. She wasn't sure how the space jockeys didn't go crazy eating so much frozen food.

They left the store, arms laden with bags. Abigail opened the bike's storage compartment and loaded their purchases, making sure not to crush any of the produce. "If we were anywhere else we'd have to rush back to the Sparrow with the frozen foods, but I guess they'll stay fresh out here." She brushed a delicate crust of frost off the side of the bike.

"Or freezer burnt," Yvonne added darkly.

"Better than spoiled. Let's finish up with the other supplies," Abigail suggested. "I want to check out that Vietnamese place in the square. A bowl of pho sounds amazing right now."

"Can't say I've ever had Vietnamese." Yvonne rubbed her hands together to work some blood back into them. "But if it's warm, I'm up for trying something new."

An hour later they sat at a small table by the molten fountain with their steaming bowls of broth. Yvonne inhaled the rich aroma. "This was a good idea. Tomas was a picky eater, so the food options were usually pretty bland. Something like this," she tapped her bowl with her spoon, "would have been a no go."

Abigail shook her head sadly. "Girl, you have been missing out. First thing I do in any new city is check out the food holes. The locals can always tell you what's good. On Mars, a good bowl of pho can be had in most of the cities. Haven't found it in Venice yet, but it's there, somewhere. Maybe in a dark and scary alley with questionable sanitary practices, but it's there." She carefully lifted the spoon in her enormous armored hands to her mouth.

"You use your suit so naturally. Even in the fine movements," Yvonne said, doing everything in her power not to sound like she was digging for information. She was, of course, but that didn't mean she wanted Abigail realizing it.

Abigail frowned. "I had silverware with oversized handles that I used to keep with me, but I forgot and left them on Mars in my skyhopper. It's parked at some long-term storage hangar collecting dust at this point." She waved her spoon in the air. "I can use these things, but it takes an annoying amount of concentration."

"I guess you've had plenty of practice. How many years have you had your exo-suit?"

Abigail set the spoon down and looked away. "Enough. What is it with you and Cole trying to interrogate me over my armor?"

"Curiosity," Yvonne said, "but mostly concern. I saw the way you reacted this morning when we passed through Mayda Insula's shield. Further, I've noticed other strange tics in your behavior as the day has gone on."

"I'm... Having a few malfunctions today." Abigail glanced at Yvonne and sighed. "Look I've got an implant in my spine that talks to the suit. I think the jolt of passing through the shield has made something in that process buggy. It froze up entirely for a minute on landing, and it's been jittery ever since then."

Yvonne's eyes narrowed. "Abigail, that sounds like that could be serious. What if something is broken?"

Abigail visibly shuddered. "Scary thought, but I doubt that's it. I've had other issues in the past, but they usually get fixed when I reset the whole system. I'll have to turn the exo-suit off and crack it open, so it will have to wait till we get back to the Sparrow."

"I see," Yvonne said.

"No you don't," Abigail muttered under her breath, "But that's okay."

"Then try me."

"What?"

"Try me. Make me understand why you're so protective over your precious exo-suit. I've got my suspicions, but I don't think you want me to start voicing them."

"You're right. I don't." The younger woman took another spoonful of her pho and then shoved it aside in frustration.

"Don't you think someone should know?" Yvonne asked softly. "In case something goes wrong. What happens if your suit takes serious damage?"

Abigail didn't answer at once and Yvonne started to wonder if she was going to answer at all. Finally, she spat it out, voice full of bitterness. "Then go on without me, because I'm done if that happens."

"Abigail, don't..."

"What do you care?" she bit back. "We're not friends. None of us really even know each other. It's just convenient to be together right now. No way this lasts more than a couple months. No reason to get cozy."

Yvonne glanced at the spoon Abigail had been holding. At some point in the last few minutes, she had closed her fist around the utensil and mangled it. Abigail's eyes fell to her hand and she sighed as she released her death grip on the utensil. It fell to the table.

A period of silence followed. Yvonne allowed Abigail to stew in her thoughts for some time before continuing. "I'm not sure you meant any of that. I think you want us to be your friends. You want us to stick together as a crew. And that's what really puzzles me. You can't seriously expect to wear your armor in front of us from now until the end of time."

"Pity. Because that was the plan."

A waiter came by and collected the spoon Abigail had destroyed. She mumbled an apology as she was given a new spoon and promised it wouldn't happen again. The waiter was clearly terrified of Abigail and assured her that it happened all the time.

She didn't even notice, which was somewhat out of character. She loved flaunting her strength and never minded showing off.

They finished their meal in awkward silence.

It was only as Yvonne finished her bowl and pushed it away from her that she saw them.

"Abigail."

"What?" she replied with a grunt.

"I was just wondering if you'd noticed those two men on the other side of the fountain, leaning against the wall."

Abigail shifted so that she could see the men out of the corner of her eye. Her heart sank. So much for this just being a shopping trip. "Yeah, they're watching us. Have they been there long?"

"No idea," Yvonne admitted. Abigail could hear the nervous shift in her voice, the slightly raised pitch betraying a creeping fear.

"Hey, could just be a couple punks looking for a mark," Abigail said calmly. "No reason to think they've identified you."

"If they were simply looking for a mark, then they wouldn't be interested in the table with the seven-foot woman," Yvonne countered.

"No probably not." She set a handful of coins on the table to cover their tab and the tip. "Guess we're not going back to the Sparrow or our bike just yet."

"Why not? We need to get out of here."

"Because we don't want them identifying the Sparrow. White Void and your friend Pig Man don't need to know the bird you're riding around on."

Yvonne deflated a bit. "Piggy," she corrected.

"Same thing."

"So what do we do now? Hope they go away or try to lose them?"

"Or I could just clobber them."

"What if they have friends?"

"Then I clobber them as well." Abigail frowned. To be fair, the good doctor hadn't seen her in action yet so she may not have realized just how one-sided most fights were when Abigail was around. She had been interested in her exo-suit, so it at least seemed fair that she get a demonstration. "Either way, I think we lead them away from the spaceport. Make them think we're going the other direction before turning the tables."

"Then we loop back around to the bike. Okay, I'll trust your judgment here."

"Good. Let's get up and take a walk. See if we get followed."

They stood from the table and walked across the open square, away from the parked grav bike and the sanctuary of the Sparrow. Abigail walked right past the two men. They wore nondescript street clothes, which meant they were either nobody civilians or they were trying to look like nobody civilians. She saw their eyes following them. They weren't even being subtle about it.

If she were alone, she'd take them out right then and there. But they weren't after her. Odds were they'd ID'ed Yvonne, even with the hood over her face. She would take the fight on her terms, where she wanted. Otherwise, there was a chance they could pull out a surprise that put Yvonne in danger.

They left the central square and walked down a set of stairs towards a side street. The street formed a dark canyon in the twilight between the buildings, lit only by the streetlamps. Abigail stole a glance behind them. Sure enough, their tail had followed and one was talking into a comm.

"When the trouble hits, and it will," she said, "stay behind me. No heroics."

"I can..."

"But you won't," Abigail put a hand on her shoulder. "Just trust me."

Abigail could feel Yvonne fairly boiling in her shoes. Probably felt helpless.

A feeling that Abigail understood all too well.

Suddenly Yvonne startled. "I think we've got two more walking towards us."

Sure enough. Looks like they were trying to enclose them. Abigail glanced at the street, wondering if it was worth the risk to cross. Enormous industrial grav trucks and smaller personal vehicles roared by. It'd be risky.

Too risky. She'd never taken a hit with a grav car in her exo-suit and wasn't particularly ready to give it a try, especially not today when it felt so sluggish. Looking ahead, she saw a side alley on their right. She pushed Yvonne towards it and they darted in.

"Abigail, this is a dead end."

"I see that. On the bright side, at least we know which way they'll be coming from. Get behind me." She ignored the withering stare that Yvonne gave her as she tossed aside her trench coat and deployed her riot shield. The reassuring hum of its grave plate rang lightly through the alley. Maybe they'd have second thoughts when confronted with the Shield Maiden.

Both pairs of men rounded the corner into the alley and abruptly stopped short. She never got tired of that reaction. "Sorry, boys. I'm afraid your prey has teeth today. Any last words?"

They were brave. Abigail would give them that. They spread out to encircle her as best they could in the tight alley and drew clubs. No guns. She kept her face shield up so she could see better. "Just gonna go with the silent attacker vibe. Disappointing. A bit of verbal sparring always brightens up any fight." She lunged for the attacker on her right.

And missed. He easily rolled out of the way before she could send him flying. That shouldn't have happened. Her suit was still responding slowly. It felt like she was fighting in tar.

She felt a sting of fear work its way into her mind. If only she'd had time to reset her exo-suit, the jitters would have probably resolved. Now she was putting Yvonne in danger.

Abigail followed through on her missed swing by lunging at the attacker on her left. Either he wasn't as fast as the last guy or was completely taken off guard. Her shield caught him and sent him flying across the alley into one of the brick walls. The other three were on her then, and she felt a stout metal club land across her left forearm.

"Tickles," she said and took a frustratingly slow swing at him with that same arm. She caught him but with far less force than she intended. He went down, but might not be out of the fight yet. One of the two remaining enemies slipped past Abigail and made a move towards Yvonne.

Abigail turned and leaped towards him. And then she realized she could no longer feel her suit. For an instant, the connection with her spinal implant gave out. It came back online in time for her to grapple the thug but not soon enough to stop her fall. She heard a crack as she tumbled over the attacker. One of his legs had been caught beneath her and gave out like a twig.

That's your own fault, she thought viciously as she tried to get to her feet. Her implant flickered again and she fell back to her knees, teeth gritted. The last attacker swung a club at her face. She saw it coming and barely managed to shift her shoulder and turn her face away. The club nicked her armored shoulder, deflected off, and dealt her a glancing blow behind the ear.

Darkness crept in around the edges of her vision as she staggered to her feet. Suddenly, there was a metallic thump and her attacker fell to the ground, the back of his head damp with blood. Yvonne stood behind him, a metal pipe in hand that she'd scrounged from some corner of the alley.

She tossed her makeshift weapon away with disgust. "I am the worst doctor ever. Are you okay?"

Abigail staggered to her feet, still feeling sluggish and seeing stars. "Will be when we're gone. Let's get out of here in case they have back up." She picked up her shield. The only attacker to avoid injury had also managed to regain his feet. He turned wide eyes toward her. She gestured to his fallen allies. "I'd consider calling a paramedic. One of your friends took a nasty hit to the head. Now get out of the way."

He obeyed, nervously shuffling aside, and the two women wasted no time leaving the alley.

***

Yvonne led them down several more streets, making numerous random turns along the way to make sure no thugs were following. Abigail followed passively, content to be led now that the threat was past. Yvonne had seen her take the blow to the head before she had delivered her own. Odds were good she had a concussion at the least. She'd also seen the dark trickle of blood running down the side of her head. The doctor in her wanted to assess the damage, but she knew they had to put some distance between them and their attackers.

After some time, they came to a small park near the edge of the

145

city. The shimmering environmental shield stood like a wall in front of them, and beyond that, a broken cliffside tumbled down to the Kraken Sea. She found a bench in a grove of tall junipers that would shield them from prying eyes. Large artificial sun lights shone over the park, giving enough light for the plant life to grow and to make the area a little warmer. Abigail sat heavily on the bench and rested her head in her hands.

Yvonne pulled out her comm and called Matthew.

"What's up? You guys need something?"

"Afraid so. We were attacked."

"Everyone okay?" he asked quickly.

"I'm good, but I think Abigail has a concussion."

Matthew was quiet, as if deciding what to do with that information. "I'm sorry," he finally said.

"She'll be fine. We made it away, but I think you should swing by and pick up the bike. It's parked at a market square near the port."

"I know the one. I'll take care of it." He hesitated for a moment. "Do I need to come get you two? If we're done here I'll break the rules and land anywhere I need if you're still in danger."

"I'll let you know once I get a chance to examine Abigail, but I think we'll be okay. I'll be in touch."

"Be careful." The comm cut off with a pop as the connection ended.

Yvonne sat on the bench next to Abigail and leaned over to look at the mat of bloody hair behind her ear. "I'm going to brush your hair aside to see if you need stitches. Let me know if it's tender." The flinch told her everything she needed to know, but Abigail held her tongue. "I think I'll sew it back together when we get to the Sparrow, if you don't mind. I wish I had something here to cover it with."

Abigail shook her head. "I'm so sorry," she mumbled.

"For what? Happy ending and no permanent damage."

Abigail bit her lip, and Yvonne realized she was fighting back tears. "I'm sorry my damnable pride almost got you captured and shipped back to White Void. I knew... I knew I was having technical difficulties, knew I needed a full system reset. And I didn't do it. Just kept going through the day like nothing was wrong."

"Abigail, it's fine. There's no harm..."

"No, it's not fine. I was more worried about my petty dignity than your safety. I was supposed to be your bodyguard today. You ended up saving us both in the end."

The sound of the pipe hitting the head of their attacker played through Yvonne's mind. She hoped she would forget it soon, but knew that it would probably stick with her far longer than she wanted. "We do what we have to."

"It shouldn't have ever been a concern. A handful of thugs on the street should have never been a threat to us." She slid off the bench to her knees. "I'm resetting my suit."

"If you're sure," Yvonne said quietly. "I... I feel a little guilty for pressing you about it earlier."

"Don't." The back armor plate split down the middle and separated with a whine of servos. Abigail's arms, her real arms worked their way out of their metal cocoon. "Can you give me a hand?"

Yvonne offered her hand to Abigail. The other woman gripped it and, using her other arm for leverage, pulled herself out of the kneeling suit of armor onto the bench beside Yvonne.

She was not a tall woman outside of her suit. In fact, if she was standing, she might have been a little on the short side. But Yvonne saw in an instant that she couldn't stand. Her legs were thin, like those of a small child, and lacked the muscle mass required to support her body weight.

Abigail was a paraplegic.

"So now you know," Abigail whispered.

Yvonne had suspected there was a disability involved, but expecting it made it no less heartbreaking to see.

"Were you born with this or...?"

"Spinal injury when I was a teenager," she said with a sniff. The tears were flowing freely again. "There... was an accident and I fell over a balcony. Three stories." She wiped her hand across her face. "I lost my freedom that day and was confined to a wheelchair until... well. This." She leaned forward to reach into the suit. "There. It's resetting and should go back to normal. I hope." She looked at Yvonne, forehead furrowed. "Well, say something, already. Don't just stare."

"I understand why you hide your condition," Yvonne said thoughtfully. "In your profession, I'm sure you don't need word getting around that you have a weakness to be exploited. But why keep it from your friends?"

Abigail looked away, probably to hide a fresh batch of tears. "I've not really had any friends in a long time, so you'll forgive me for being a bit cynical."

"Your secret is safe with me," Yvonne said putting a reassuring hand on Abigail's arm. The younger woman jumped at the touch, and

Yvonne wondered how long it had been since she felt the comforting touch of another human. Far too long most likely.

Abigail nodded slowly and wiped the tears away for the second time. "Please don't tell Matthew."

Yvonne raised an eyebrow. So she was going to hold onto this desperately then? "You know he can be trusted, don't you Abigail?"

"I know... I... I don't want him thinking less of me. It's stupid I know. But we're professionals in the same line of work. I just... Don't tell him."

Yvonne held her eye for a moment and then nodded. "I'll respect your wishes, but this isn't the right call. He will find out eventually, no matter how careful you are. You won't be able to hide it forever. Maybe you should share it on your own terms rather than wait for circumstances to force the issue."

"He won't find out if I can help it," she replied.

A silly notion, Yvonne thought, born of either naivete or denial.

The exo-suit chimed. Abigail lifted her legs with her hands and threaded them into the gap in the armor plates. Yvonne offered her a hand again as she wormed her way back into position. After a minute she seemed to be situated and the armor plates closed. With the whine of servos she stood to her feet.

"Feel better after the reset?" Yvonne asked.

Abigail made a few quick moves, testing her motions. She smiled brightly. "Back to normal. Come on. Let's get back to the Sparrow."

And like that Abigail was back to her old self, confident almost to the point of belligerence. Yvonne smiled to herself, glad that a mystery had been solved. The girl's suit empowered her, and in some ways it was her. It was her escape, her freedom from her broken body.

And yet, Yvonne thought darkly, it was also her prison.

By the time the women returned, Matthew had already retrieved Sharon's bike. Its handlebars were way too far forward, being sized for Abigail's rather large frame, but he managed with little incident. His friend, Carlos, had ridden with him. Carlos was one of the only friends he'd kept from his past life, the last link to the man that Matthew used to be. Even so, he didn't exactly get to see the old technician very often since Titan was a bit out of the way.

He'd meant to send Carlos on his way before Yvonne and Sharon returned, but they lost track of the time. When the women approached the ship, Carlos stood from where he had been sitting on the port side ramp.

"Well, I imagine you'll want to get off this forsaken rock, so I'll take this as my cue to head out. Take care of yourself, Padre."

"You too, Carlos."

The man turned to leave and tipped his hat to Yvonne and Abigail as they approached the ship. They watched his carefree gait as he crossed the spaceport without so much as a backwards glance.

"Padre?" Yvonne asked, a note of amusement in her voice.

"An old nickname," Matthew explained. "I hated it back then too." He looked at Sharon and changed the subject. "How's the head?"

"I've got a splitting headache that I'll be glad to be rid of, but I'm alive."

He scratched the scruff at his chin. "This is my fault. I knew better with that bounty on Yvonne's head than to let you two go out alone. I'm sorry."

Yvonne shrugged. "We handled it fine and you got to see an old friend. No harm. Let's get out of here."

An hour later they drifted in orbit over Titan, safely away from prying eyes looking to cash in on a bounty. Matthew recorded a quick message and sent it to Benny. Hopefully, the broker would have sniffed up a new job for them in the last day. If not, maybe he'd pull the Sparrow into one of the Freeport stations around Saturn. Someone, somewhere would have a job for them.

He kicked his feet up on the console and tossed his campero aside. The door opened and he looked over his shoulder as Yvonne entered the cockpit. "Sharon doing okay? Hope the shield didn't give her any problems on the way out. I was going a lot slower this time."

Yvonne sat in the copilot's chair and spun it to face Matthew. "It was better. I gave her a few stitches for the hit she took. She'll be good as new in a few days."

"I'd expect nothing less. She's tough."

"And human."

Matthew shrugged, not sure where the doctor was going with that. "Obviously."

"I'm just saying there's a person under all that armor. Have you bothered to get to know her yet?"

He bristled at the implied accusation and thought of a half dozen sharply worded rebuttals that fell flat one after the other. Instead, he felt his jaw clench in annoyance. "Are you done framing me as a cold and cruel human being?"

"I would never suggest that you are cruel, Matthew Cole, though you're definitely a bit on the chilly side." Yvonne chuckled, something Matthew found unnerving at that moment. "No, your moral compass seems to drag you kicking and screaming in spite of your best resistance to it. I don't think you're capable of cruelty, at least not deliberately."

"Thanks for that. I think." There was both compliment and condemnation in there. Best to take the one at face value and the other under consideration. "It's been... A long time since I've had other's around. I guess the social skills are rusty."

"We're not alone anymore, Matthew. Not one of us. At least no more than we choose to be." She stood and left him to stew in his thoughts. She was right, naturally. The eyes of another are often the best mirrors in which to see ourselves. Didn't make it any easier to hear.

Sometime later Matthew left the cockpit and was surprised to find the light out in the common room. Sharon sat on the floor in front of a display and Yvonne had pulled up a chair. Some old movie was playing. From the looks of it an ancient one from the classic days of cinema.

"Take a seat, gaucho," Sharon said smirking. "Movie night. Unless you feel like brooding by yourself in your room."

He grimaced. Now he would have to stay and watch the movie if only to be contrary. "What are we watching? It had better be worth the..." He paused as he watched the current scene for a moment. "Why Pride and Prejudice?"

"Because this is the best version ever made," Sharon stated. "I think they may have even read the book before writing the script. Oh come on, don't be such a spoilsport. Look. You can pick the next movie."

Matthew looked at the screen flickering in the dark. He thought about retreating to his room and settling into a book. Grumbling under his breath, he pulled up a chair. "You win. This time."

Chapter 10: Grace Like Steel

Remember the Red Holocaust. Hear the cries of the children. The weeping of those that were betrayed. Read again their names. They are beyond number. Like the sand on the shores of the sea.

Remember that which was lost. The oldest of civilizations. The mighty dragon of the east, fallen into ashes. It has been laid low and will not rise again.

Remember those that endure. A people lost in the wide world. A diaspora of a lost empire. They are precious gems, memories of a time past.

Give them a home amongst the nations that they might not be forgotten.

Unknown Poet
Discovered in orbital wreckage above Earth.
Presumably died 1 AM

"Look, I got nothing for you just yet, Cole," the recording of Benny's voice crackled over the comm. "I know, I know. It was gonna be easier to find you jobs if you got a crew. And it is. Trust me. But I've still got to find the 'Cole' jobs since you're picky." He paused briefly. "But if you're willing to ship a little contraband, I can have you on your way back to the inner system right now."

Yvonne heard Matthew scoff and turned to see him shaking his head. "I wish he'd get it through his head that I'm not going to use the

151

Sparrow to run weapons or..."

Benny's recording continued as if anticipating the complaint. "It's not drugs. I know you better than that. It's umm... Okay, it's a cheese shipment. That's not so bad, right? It's coming out of one of the Freeports around Saturn. An emir on Callisto wants to get past import tariffs. But I mean, come on. It's just cheese. I'm expecting you to think about it and, when you get back with me, give me some good news. Benny out."

The message ended.

"We go through this at least once a month," Matthew explained. "Benny is convinced that if I just forego my values we'll all be rich."

Yvonne turned to eye him. "Wait, you're not going to take the job? It's cheese."

"Illegal cheese," he said, lifting his hands in appeal.

"No, improperly taxed cheese," Yvonne countered. "I'm with Benny."

Matthew stared at her for a second then turned back to the console. "So the straight-laced doctor wants to run contraband. I'll be honest, you struck me as more of a law and order type."

She gave him a look. "I've got a million dollar bounty on my head. I think I can handle a little cheese smuggling. At the very least it'll get us back to the Jupiter Neighborhood. Send him a reply. Let's do it."

He hesitated and then his shoulders slumped. "Fine. Benny already sent instructions." He frowned at the display. "Looks like he expected us to take it. Apparently I'm getting predictable."

"I think your ego will manage just fine."

Matthew ignored her last jab. "I'll get us heading towards Freeport 72 for the pickup."

Yvonne smiled in amusement. "I thought all you freelancers were a little sketchy. I know you're one of the good guys, but I wasn't aware that you were such a saint that you wouldn't dodge a tariff."

Matthew shifted uncomfortably in his seat. "Don't take it too far. I'm a businessman, first and foremost. Every time I burn someone, whether it's a gang, cartel, or government, I have to weigh the cost. Maybe I don't want to risk the wrath of whatever government this emir is a part of. More than one of the Callistan governments swing hardline conservative and..."

"It's cheese," Yvonne said cutting him off.

"It's the principle."

Yvonne crossed her arms in silence as Matthew turned the Sparrow out of orbit towards Saturn. The main engines rumbled through the deck, a vibration that Yvonne had started to find comforting.

After double checking their course, he punched up the comm to record a message.

"Okay broker man. You win this time. I'm on my way to the pickup, but don't expect this to become the norm. I don't like it. But I'll do it." He sent the message and gave her an 'are you happy' look.

She was but, having won the argument, didn't feel the need to gloat.

An hour later, Matthew pulled the Sparrow into one of Freeport 72's enormous cargo bays. The station, like each of the dozens of Freeport stations scattered around the solar system, was privately owned and operated. Some had been taken over by criminals, some were run by businesses, and still others were run by individuals, ruling over their own little domains as tiny kingdoms floating in the black of space.

Freeport 72 floated in orbit just a few kilometers above the rings themselves, offering a stunning up-close view of the ice fields surrounding the gas giant. It was run by a handful of businesses that tried to keep things as honest as possible and was a booming hub of market activity in the Saturn Neighborhood. If you wanted to do serious business near Saturn, odds were good you were stopping by 72.

"Sharon and I will be back soon," Matthew said, as he finished the post-flight shutdown. "I imagine the itch to sightsee has been sated for the time being?"

"No, but I'm resigned to my prison for now," Yvonne said, pensive. She had no reason to suspect that the bounty on her head would be lifted anytime soon, and she might be stuck keeping her head down for years. She cursed Piggy under her breath again. Pathetic man.

"You're thinking loud enough that I can almost hear you," Matthew said evenly. "I'm sorry you're stuck here. I've told you before that if you want off, I'll take you anywhere you want to go."

"Ha!" she chuckled. "Are you kidding me? I haven't had this much fun since Tomas and I ran a clinic on Io. Though I admit the cheese smuggling isn't all that glamorous."

"Cheese?" Abigail asked, stepping into the cockpit. "Our standards are really slipping."

"By the day," Matthew agreed. "Let's get this over with. Yvonne, we'll be back within the hour. Anything you need while we're out?"

She shook her head. "A million bucks to pay off my bounty? I'll be fine."

Yvonne was left alone in the Sparrow with the subtle but familiar ticking sound she'd noticed whenever the ship set into port. Probably metal slowly contracting as it cooled. She sat up, remembering there was a fuel filter with her name on it begging to be replaced, now that she had the time and the part to do it. She left the cockpit and climbed down the aft ladder into the main hold.

The fuel filter, a roughly one-meter square frame of mesh, sat to the side where she had put it yesterday evening. She picked it up, inspected it one last time to make triple sure it was the right model, and turned to the forward engineering compartment. There was no doubt in her mind that she could do this. She'd been reading and rereading the instructions for the last week. Nevertheless, it was her first major maintenance work on the Sparrow.

A part of her mind was irrationally nervous in spite of her confidence. "It'll be much easier than that appendectomy was," she murmured to no one in particular. She pressed the panel and the door to forward engineering slid open.

She took a second to get her bearings and make sense of what she was looking at. The big problem with manuals is that the people who write them aren't always the engineers. Sometimes they don't know what they're talking about. Of course, it's worse when engineers do write the manual. God help the poor soul that tried to understand that mess.

Her heart leaped to her throat when she saw movement out of the corner of her eye. A flash of blonde hair. What in...?

"Wait," a voice shrieked, splitting the cramped, machinery filled compartment. "Don't!"

Yvonne felt the muzzle of a gun press firmly into her back. She closed her eyes as fear and adrenaline flooded her body.

Abigail wasn't sure why she had joined Cole on this little trip. It was a chance to get out of the Sparrow, but that only made her feel guilty with poor Yvonne cooped up on the ship. She didn't know if there was a solution to that problem. It's not like the bounty was anything reasonable that Yvonne could hope to buy off. It seemed like an unnecessary insult to do that to a doctor, of all people, someone that society really needed.

She grimaced. They made a fine group. The cripple, the prisoner, and the... Her eyes flicked to Cole. She wasn't really sure what his problem was, only that he spent most of his days play acting. Who was

154

he? A shell, or else maybe a puppet?

But she wasn't what she pretended to be. Why should he be any different?

At the moment Cole was still filling out paperwork with the vendor, something he looked positively thrilled about doing. After a few minutes of scratching his head in growing irritation, he shoved the mess of paperwork across the desk towards the clerk. "Is that all? Anything else you need? A kidney maybe?"

The bored clerk didn't even react to the joke. Probably immune after too many years on the job. He spent a few seconds scanning the paperwork and then stamped it. "The cargo is all yours," he said in a monotone voice, gesturing towards the shipping crate on the hover pallet. "Please leave the pallet in the hangar or I will be forced to charge you for it."

Cole nodded once and turned towards Abigail.

"One more thing," the clerk said.

Cole stopped in his tracks, briefly made eye contact with Abigail, and turned slowly to the clerk with exaggerated movement. She could feel the misery radiating off of him, and she covered her mouth to hide the smile.

"There is a note here that recommends you do not open the shipping container. It is apparently a rather potent product."

Cole tipped his ridiculous hat once and turned back towards Abigail. "Let's get out of here," he grumbled.

"What's got you curdled?" she asked, failing to hide her amusement. The fact that the cheese they were smuggling was considered potent was the most entertaining thing she'd heard all day.

They reached the container and Matthew checked the readouts on the refrigeration. "What's wrong," he said, pushing a few buttons, "is that I think I already broke about ten custom laws when I filled out that paperwork. And I'll break at least ten more when we land on Callisto. If we're caught, I'll lose docking rights at Freeport 72 and I think we both know that we don't want to be on an emir's bad side." He patted the container. "Looks good." He took hold of the handle and pulled the hovering container toward the bay door leading back to the hangar. "And another thing. They complain about stealing the pallet. This one isn't even self-propelled. Why would I even want to keep it?" Abigail watched him strain against the heavy load, using his full weight just to move it. "It'd be like stealing a ship without a frameshift device. Waste of time."

"Alright, that's enough from you. Stop embarrassing me," Abigail said as she gently shoved him aside and easily pulled the container behind her. She laughed heartily and he muttered a terse thank you under his breath, which only made her laugh harder.

They passed several ships before reaching the Sparrow at the far end of the hangar. Cole lowered the lift and, with some difficulty, she managed to slide the container off the pallet onto the platform. That was a tricky proposition even for her. "Okay, in hindsight I'm pretty sure you would have had to steal the pallet if I wasn't around. What were they expecting you to do?"

Cole shrugged his shoulders with a smirk. She rolled her eyes, then laughed and pushed the pallet away with her foot, watching it glide until it crashed into a far wall. Two technicians nearly jumped out of their skins. One gave her a rude gesture which she returned without hesitation. He decided to go about his business after that. "If they want their pallet back, they'll have to come get it themselves," she said. "We ready to get out of here?"

Cole hit the control and they rode the lift into the Sparrow's main hold.

Abigail leaned against the container full of illicit dairy. "So how many days travel is it to…"

Cole abruptly straightened and drew his revolver in one fluid motion. His eyes were narrowed and fixed on something behind her. Abigail liked to think that she had good reaction speed, but it took her far too long to awaken to the possibility of a threat on the Sparrow. As Matthew completed his motion, she started her own, spinning on a heel and drawing her shield from her back.

Three people.

A blonde girl slumped against the wall, her tear stained face filled with terror. What was Grace doing here?

Yvonne with engine tape over her mouth tied to a chair. Her face placid. Calm even.

And the brat. Grace's brother Davey, with one of the enforcer's submachine guns pressed into Yvonne's back. His face was fierce. Determined.

But he was also shaking in his boots.

Silence filled the air of the hold and no one dared move a muscle.

Abigail glanced at Cole out of the corner of her eye, wondering what his play would be. Her shield wasn't going to be of much use in a hostage situation. And she'd never be able to get close enough without him seeing her coming, which didn't leave Yvonne in a very good position. She ground her teeth until her jaw hurt. If the runt spilled a single drop of Yvonne's blood, she would break every bone in his body. It would be easy. A single hit from her shield in confined quarters would end his short life.

Cole finally spoke. His voice was quiet. Firm.

Deadly.

"Young man, I'm going to ask you to put that weapon down."

Davey stared at Cole. Probably wondering how skilled a shot he was with that revolver. Abigail knew he was good. But she didn't know if he was that good.

"For the sake of your sister," he continued. "Put down your gun. Now."

Davey bit his lip and pressed the gun harder into Yvonne's back. To her credit she didn't flinch. Her eyes flicked back and forth between Cole and Abigail.

"This is for my sister," he said, voice nearly cracking.

"I fail to see how that could be the case," Cole said calmly. Abigail didn't know how he did it. If she had to talk, she'd be screaming at the kid. Good thing Cole was here.

Davey shifted. "You're going to take us to Ceres. Back to our old home, where we came from before the slavers picked us up."

"Why didn't you go with the Archbishop?" he asked.

"Are you kidding me?" Davey sneered. "They would have split us. We're not actually brother and sister. She'd have gone to some church orphanage or something and who knows what rat hole I would have ended up in."

Abigail glanced at Grace where she was slumped against the wall. This was the second time she'd seen the girl cry like this and it was starting to get under her skin. Especially since her oh-so-precious brother was the one inflicting the pain.

Cole hadn't moved a muscle. "While I respect your desire to stay with your sister, I'm not sure she appreciates your methods."

Davey flinched. "I don't see any other options."

"You could try asking. My friend in the armor has a soft spot for your sister. Maybe we could have worked something out." He paused for a moment. "That's going to be more difficult now."

"I don't know why that's the case. You're taking us to Ceres. And you're going to start by lowering your gun."

To Abigail's surprise, Cole complied, holstering his weapon. "First, we're not going to Ceres just yet. We've got a shipment bound for Callisto. After Callisto we can talk."

"I don't care about your damn shipment," Davey hissed. "You're

157

taking my sister and me to Ceres."

Cole stepped back and leaned against the shipping container. Probably in an attempt to look relaxed. Surely he wasn't as calm as he signaled. Abigail was scared out of her mind for Yvonne.

"I don't think you're in any place to make demands," Cole said quietly.

Davey laughed bitterly and Abigail could see the sweat drip from his forehead. "What are you talking about? Are you blind?" He jabbed Yvonne again with the barrel of his weapon and she winced this time.

A tight smile spread across Matthew's face. "No, Davey, I'm not sure you've thought this through. For starters we're over a week out from Ceres. Do you think you could hold a hostage for that long? And what happens if, God forbid, your trigger finger gets itchy and you kill Yvonne?" He inclined his head towards Abigail. "I know you and Ms. Sharon didn't get a good chance to become acquainted, but I can promise it wouldn't end well for you. That little popgun isn't even going to scratch her. You lose your hostage you lose everything. And then where would your sister be?"

"Shut up!" Davey screamed. "Just..."

"Davey stop," Grace cut him off. "Why are you such a monster sometimes?"

"I'm doing what I have to do to get us home, Grace. I don't expect you to understand. It's okay. I can do this."

"No," Cole said softly. "You can't. There's one and only one way that this ends well for all of us. You put down your gun and we all sit down and have a nice talk on the way to Callisto."

"I said shut up!" His voice cracked again. He was getting desperate. Like a cornered animal that had been hunted his whole life. For a moment Abigail felt a measure of pity for the Chinese kid. Cole had told her what the Duke said about the boy's heritage fetching a price when he went to market. She managed to unclench her jaw. Mostly, she just felt sick. Abigail looked at Grace. The girl had stopped crying and her fists were clenched. A shade of crimson crept across her face and down her neck.

Here was a new danger. If Grace did something rash...

Cole must have seen Grace's behavior because he addressed her now. "So, Grace. You two have been stowed away on our ship for a few days now right?"

Suddenly the center of attention, she startled, then nodded. "We hid in the engineering compartment over there."

Abigail's heart broke. That can't have been sanitary. They'd grown

158

up on the streets though. Who knew what those two were willing to do to survive?

"I imagine you're both very hungry," Cole suggested.

"A little," Grace admitted, "But we found a cabinet down here stuffed with ration bars, so we're okay. Sorry we stole them."

Cole smiled. Somehow, even with all the madness going on, he managed a smile. "That's okay. And Grace I'm sorry the only food in reach was the most tasteless food known to man."

She laughed and seemed to relax a little. "I didn't think they were that bad. Beats the dumpsters we used to eat out of."

"Grace, stop talking to them," Davey said. His voice was low and stressed, but thankfully it had lost the lethal edge.

"How about this," Cole said in a voice that sounded almost cheerful. "Abigail, you and Grace head upstairs and find something better to eat. Then you can bring something down for Davey. Since we're going to be here awhile, there's no use in us all being hungry."

Abigail moved for the first time in several minutes. She hoped that Cole was just trying to disarm the situation and that he wasn't getting Grace out of the room before doing something drastic. "Come on Grace. Ladder is in the back." She made a wide circuit behind Cole toward the aft ladder. The brat with the gun never removed his eyes from her.

Grace looked at her brother once. When he nodded, she cautiously followed Abigail to the ladder.

Take a deep breath, Abigail thought to herself. Cole has this. She wasn't sure why she had so much faith in him to fix this. Maybe it was desperation. Maybe it was that the alternatives were too horrible to imagine.

She smiled at Grace and gave her a hand up the last rung of the ladder. "Looks like I got to see you a little sooner than I expected," she said.

"This was Davey's idea," the girl said quietly.

"Trust me dear, I know. Come on. We just went shopping the other day and Yvonne hasn't had time to hoard all the good frozen meals."

Grace smiled a little. It wasn't much but it was a start.

The girl followed her into the common room. "Is this your ship?"

"I wish. It's the cranky gaucho's." Abigail said, opening up the freezer and looking through it. "You like roast beef?"

Grace gave her a blank look. "I don't know."

Abigail felt flush. Of course she wouldn't know. When would a street kid have eaten roast beef? "You'll like it. I'll get one for your brother too. Roast beef, with mashed potatoes, gravy, and some cinnamon apples. You're gonna love it. The apples are practically dessert." She looked at Grace. "You do know about dessert, don't you?"

Grace seemed distracted, so Abigail continued.

"Don't worry about it. I'll tell you the real trick though. These things are self-heating. Just pull the tab, chemical reaction heats the whole tray. It's not bad like that, but it doesn't heat very evenly. Tastes a lot better if you put them in the microwave for a few minutes." Abigail stepped over to the counter and popped both trays into the oven and turned it on. "Now we just have to wait a few minutes and you and your brother will have some real food. Not one of those mushy ration bars."

She turned back around to find the room empty.

"Grace?"

That was weird. The door to the common room's restroom was still open. Maybe she had wandered towards the cockpit. Abigail walked down the hall. The cabin doors were all closed.

"Grace, are you up here?"

The cockpit was empty too.

Abigail's heart rose into her throat. She must have gone back into the hold. Maybe she didn't want to be away from her brother. Making up her mind, Abigail marched back towards the aft ladder.

She had a single hand on it when she heard the bark of automatic gunfire echo up the shaft from the hold.

When Abigail opened the freezer, Grace had looked around the room. Her eyes immediately fell on something she recognized. Two great gold bracelets sitting on the table.

The ones the Duke had used.

She'd never forget the things. He'd always used them to terrify the kids, sometimes pinning one to a wall until they could barely breath and shouting horrible things.

She looked back at Abigail who was still talking about food.

"Do you like Roast Beef?"

"I don't know." Grace said.

She looked back over at the bracelets. She knew what they could do. If... if she took them.

"You do know about dessert, don't you?"

Grace didn't even really hear what Abigail was saying. The woman walked over to the counter with her trays and turned her back to Grace again.

She made her move. With the skill of a practiced thief she was across the room in an instant and slid a bracelet over each arm. There was a tiny click as they latched shut and each briefly flared with light. In a moment she was at the ladder, descending back to the hold.

"Grace?" she heard above her.

There was no stopping now. Grace slid down the ladder, like she used to back at the habitat. She was going to fix this. She was going to fix her stupid brother's problem.

No one was going to get hurt.

Her feet clanged on the deck of the hold. Mr. Cole had been talking and he stopped and looked at her in surprise. "Grace? I thought you were up top with..."

He paused as she marched towards her brother.

Davey frowned. "What are... Grace go away!"

"Grace stop," Mr. Cole demanded.

She walked right up to Yvonne. The woman was inches from her. Grace raised her left hand and the bracelet burned with blue light.

Davey's eyes went wide as he was suddenly thrown across the room, held in an invisible grip by the bracelet's power. There was a burst of gunfire as his weapon fired.

Grace screamed as the hail of bullets shattered into fiery fragments around her and Yvonne as the other bracelet glowed red. All at once it was quiet and her eyes darted to the woman. Yvonne's eyes were clenched shut in terror, but she wasn't hurt.

Davey was lying on the ground. She must have dropped him when the gun fired. The gun lay beside him forgotten. Grace lifted her left hand again and threw him to the back wall. She marched at him, blood boiling.

"Why are you so horrible?!" she shouted.

There was a bang as Abigail's heavy feet landed in the hold. Grace ignored her. Ignored Mr. Cole.

"Why?" she screamed. "These people were our friends. They helped us!" Tears were running down her cheeks now and she brushed them away with her right sleeve.

"It was the only way," Davey wheezed. She'd knocked the breath clean out of him. "We were going to go home to Ceres..."

"I don't want to go back to Ceres. I don't want to go back to where... To where my parents died. I don't want to be a couple of bilgeworms on the street anymore." She lowered her arm, releasing him. He fell to the ground and slid down against the wall.

Neither had any fight left in them.

"I hate you," she mumbled under her breath. She didn't mean it. She could never mean it.

But in that moment he believed it and tears started running down his dirty face.

A heavy hand rested on her shoulder. Mr. Cole stood behind her. "Grace, how about you let me talk to Davey now? Why don't you take a break and walk over to the other side of the room?"

She nodded, knowing she should tell Davey she was sorry. He never meant to hurt her. Even when he was being stupid. But right now, she didn't want to look at him. She turned and slowly walked away.

Right now, she wished she could hate him.

Abigail's heart rate hadn't come down yet. She untied Yvonne with trembling hands and quickly pulled the other woman into a brief embrace. The threat of losing someone was too great to imagine now that she was beginning to like these people. She stepped away quickly so as not to meet Yvonne's eyes.

Grace walked up to them both, her shoulders slumped with guilt.

"Yvonne, would you take care of our little friend. I think I'd like to keep a close eye on the gentlemen in the room. Just in case."

Yvonne nodded and led Grace away. Abigail walked to the corner where Cole and Davey were, not wanting to disturb them but wanting to be close in case the brat still had some fight in him.

Cole stood with his arms behind his back. "She didn't mean that, you know. About hating you."

Davey's eyes flicked up at Cole for a brief moment then back down at the ground. "You don't know us. You don't know me."

"Maybe not. Or else maybe I do. I've met you a thousand times in my travels."

That got Davey's attention. Abigail frowned, unsure of where the gaucho was going with this.

"I see in front of me a young man that was never taught to be a man. Who wasn't taught how to wield his strength. And yet in spite of that, you're trying to figure some of it out on your own. Your fierce protectiveness of Grace is admirable." Cole paused for a moment. "But at the rate you're burning bridges you're gonna end up losing her." He crossed his arms under his poncho.

Davey didn't answer, wouldn't even look up at him. Abigail couldn't blame him, not after what he'd done.

"So where do we go from here?" Cole asked.

"You asking me?" Davey finally met Cole's eyes.

"Who am I looking at?"

"I... I don't know. I umm... Guess you're going to dump us at the next port."

Cole scoffed. "I'd love to dump you. You're dangerous and the source of the worst headache I've had in a month. But I can't do that to your sister. I'm not putting a twelve-year old on the street. So what are my options Davey?"

The young man was quiet. Abigail thought he knew the answer but didn't want to say it. After a minute of silence he spit it out. "Take her to one of the church orphanages. Split us up." He whispered the next bit so quietly that Abigail almost didn't hear it. "Grace said it herself. I'm a monster."

Cole regarded him with a thoughtful stare. "No. I don't think so. I said that I knew you. That I've met you a thousand times across the solar system. Lost young men, adrift because no one taught them what was right."

Davey wrinkled his forehead at that. Abigail had an inkling where Cole was going now and she wasn't sure she liked it. Cole had a thing with collecting strays.

"Here's the deal I'll make you, Davey," Cole said slowly. "The universe or fortune or God himself decided to smile on you today because I'm the last person in the solar system that's going to give you a second chance. No, don't say anything, just listen." He took a deep breath before forging ahead. "You better be thankful that we all like your sister, Grace, because that's what you're being offered. Grace. You're getting something better than you deserve. I'm going to let you two stay on my ship. Your sister under my protection and you under my charge. You will have any weapons confiscated. You will be confined to quarters unless accompanied by either myself or Ms. Sharon there," he said gesturing to where Abigail stood silent guard. She frowned, not looking forward to the prospect of playing jailkeeper.

"You'll work for your room. Whatever I say. If I need someone to scrub the deck, you do it. If I need someone to polish my boots, you do it. You disobey once, threaten anyone, mess up a single time? You're dumped at the next port and I don't even look over my shoulder. This is your last and only chance."

Davey looked up at Cole, a thousand questions in his eyes. "So what, I'm your personal slave now?"

The gaucho bristled at that. "Or I can dump you here and now. I'm giving you a chance to earn my trust. Until we figure out somewhere you and your sister can stay together that isn't the street. Just maybe, if you're a good worker, learn some discipline and how to handle authority then you'll be able to find a job and support your sister. Until that day, I'm the boss. Do we have a deal?"

Abigail nearly whistled in admiration. She wasn't looking forward to the brat being underfoot, but she couldn't help but be impressed by Cole's tough love. That wasn't a deal she'd have offered in a million years.

Davey hadn't answered yet, but Abigail knew what his response would be. What choice did he have?

He stood to his feet and brushed himself off. He raised his eyes to meet Cole's. "I'll do it."

"One mistake and it's over," Cole said. "No accidents."

"No accidents," Davey said.

Abigail shook her head sadly. It would never last.

Matthew sat in the pilot's chair staring out the viewport at the well of endless stars. He'd turned the ship towards Callisto hours ago. Davey and Grace had each been given one of the remaining crew quarters and then Davey had been locked in his room. Short of the ship entering an emergency state, only he or Sharon would be able to let him out. He'd have to come up with some manual labor around the Sparrow on the trip, otherwise Davey was going to be in there for an unhealthy amount of time.

"What a day," he mumbled to himself.

"You're telling me," Sharon said appearing in the cockpit. "You're brave keeping the little killer around."

He glanced at her out of the corner of his eye. "You didn't voice any complaints at the time."

"It's your ship," she said. "Didn't know I had jurisdiction."

"You don't, but I would have taken it into consideration."

Sharon sat in the co-pilot's seat. "Mind if I join you?"

"Just staring into space."

They sat in silence for several minutes. Long enough that Matthew started to tire of his thoughts chasing each other in circles. "So am I crazy for keeping them around?"

"I'm fine with Grace. We can keep her permanently as far as I'm

164

concerned. Sweet girl. The brother though?" She shook her head. "Yeah, I think it's a bad call. I don't get it. I mean you can quote platitudes about second chances all day long. Doesn't change the fact that he'll probably burn us. What happens then?"

He thought about it and shrugged. "Pick up the pieces and move on. Who knows? He may surprise us. He's going to have to earn even Grace's trust back at this point."

"Still doesn't explain why you're even offering him the chance."

Matthew let out a long sigh. He would be glad when his head hit the pillow tonight. "We're all on the same ship, every man, woman, and child. And we're venting atmosphere from a thousand hull breaches. They say it's just a matter of time now. Someday the hull will buckle and the lights will go off for the last time. And just like that, the story of mankind will be over, a tale of sound and fury, signifying nothing."

Sharon turned to face him, her eyes full of questions.

Matthew smiled sadly. "I like to think I pushed back the final clock a few seconds. Maybe plugged one of those hull breaches. At the very least maybe I proved the King of Scotland wrong."

Sharon seemed to consider this and Matthew went back to gazing at the stars.

Chapter 11: Between a Rock

The freelancers really didn't get their start till after Moses. When everything started coming apart at the seams, creative men and women stepped forward to offer their services to do, well, anything you needed. Good old-fashioned capitalism at work. Where there is a demand, someone will supply it.

And they supplied it, all right. Whether it was unofficial police work that the officials were too busy to deal with in the chaos, shipping of goods across the solar system, escorting VIPs back and forth, hunting bounties, or whatever it was, they did it all. Some were even straight up hitmen.

You never really knew what you were getting when you hired a freelancer in those early days. That's where we stepped in.

The brokers brought order to the chaos and civilized a growing profession. Needed something specific done? We could find you the right freelancer. You probably didn't want Murderface Mike providing extra security for your orphanage. We made sure that didn't happen.

Usually.

Sometimes the brokers got into turf wars with each other and pit freelancers against each other. When that happened the freelancers became pawns in someone else's game.

Those were fun times.

Fredrick Daulton
First Chairman of the Broker Alliance
Died 31 AM

"Wake up. That's right. I mean you. I need all hands on deck."

Grace blinked her eyes twice as the fog of sleep strangled her brain. What time was it and what was Mr. Cole talking about? She glanced at the clock. 3 AM ship time. She rolled over. No, he didn't mean her. Unfortunately, his voice came back over the ship's intercom and made the point clear.

"Grace, Davey, you too. Davey, I'll be at your door to unlock it in five minutes. Be ready."

Grace growled into her pillow and rolled out of bed, landing on the floor in a tangle of sheets. She blinked again and hit the light by her bedside.

Why was he bothering them at 3 AM?

She slowly stood to her feet, kicking away her bedding and fumbled in a drawer for one of her two changes of clothes. She picked her blue shirt because she liked it, not caring that she'd worn it yesterday.

"Why is life so unfair?" she grumbled, before mentally kicking herself.

Really it was the opposite. The Sparrow had been the best thing to ever happen to her. Good food, nice people, and no enforcers yelling. Davey wasn't so happy, but he deserved every bit of hard work he was doing. Mr. Cole had had him scrubbing the deck of the hold the day after they came aboard. Grace was doing her best not to speak to him right now.

After finishing the hold, Davey and Mr. Cole had moved to the outer hull. Yvonne had helped rig up one of the too-tall spacesuits for her brother. He looked silly with a bunching of suit material at his knees and shoulders, but it worked.

Abigail joked about how nice, bright, and clean the Sparrow would be from now on, and Matthew had given her a stern look. She wasn't quite sure what that was about.

"Two minutes," came the voice over the intercom.

"We hear you!" Grace yelled at the speaker. She stepped into her cabin's small bathroom. Better take care of that now. Who knows how long Mr. Cole would keep them up?

"Time's up," he said. "Davey I'm on my way."

Grace washed her hands, turned off the light, and pulled the two golden bracelets over her wrists. Since no one else could get them to do anything, Mr. Cole had made her promise to wear them at all times when she was outside her cabin.

"I'm not comfortable with you being on the ship at all," he'd said, "But I'll feel a little better knowing you're bulletproof. Also, I want you to practice with those things. If you're ever in danger, I don't want you holding back if you have to defend yourself."

He hadn't been all that happy when she and Abigail used the miracles to play catch with heavy pieces of scrap metal in the hold. Never mind that she'd been practicing like he wanted. If anyone on this ship was going to be the spoilsport and ruin a good bit of fun, it was definitely going to be Mr. Cole.

She opened her door. Mr. Cole and Davey passed her on the way to the common room. The ship's captain didn't so much as glance down at her and Davey refused to make eye contact.

"Rude," she whispered, making a face at their backs.

The door beside her opened and Abigail stepped out, armored and ready to go. She winked at Grace. "Come on. Let's see what the grumpy gaucho wants. If it's not worth it, I say we mutiny."

Grace cracked a smile and nodded. The last of the sleep was clearing from her brain. "I saw a few roaches down in engineering last week. We could put some in his bed."

Abigail's eyes widened at that. "You kids play for keeps. Let's, uh, leave the bugs out of it, alright?"

"What's wrong with bugs?"

Abigail's eyes twitched. "Imagine if one got inside my suit. No thank you. Leave the bugs out of this."

Grace laughed at the thought of Abigail destroying the ship because a bug crawled into her armor and she skipped down the hall to the common room. Yvonne was already seated at the table sipping a cup of coffee. Grace wondered if she had even been to bed yet. She always went to bed late and was up even earlier. Maybe old people didn't need much sleep. Grace slid into the chair beside her. Davey sat across from her, his black hair sticking up on one side where he had been sleeping on it.

Abigail stood behind them, arms crossed. "Alright what is it, Cole? This had better be worth it."

"It will be. I just got a call from Benny, who heard from one of his contacts. He's got a job, but we have to move now."

Yvonne stirred her coffee. "What could be so time sensitive?"

"Looks like Jupiter just snagged itself a temporary satellite, an M-type Jupiter trojan."

Grace looked around the room and wondered if that was supposed to mean anything. She felt better when she saw everyone's blank stare. She was surprised that Davey was the one to ask the question they were all thinking.

"And that is... What exactly?"

Mr. Cole reached up and adjusted his hat, looking a bit impatient. "Jupiter trojans are a family of asteroids that share an orbit with the gas giant. On occasion, Jupiter will snag one as a temporary moon. No one really notices, outside of updating the charts, because most of the trojans are D-types. Silicates. Carbon. Sometimes ice. Nothing of much value. Trojans are rarely the much more valuable M-types."

"Metallic?" Abigail guessed.

"Exactly," Mr. Cole said, nodding his head. "Iron and nickel."

"For which a mining company will pay a handsome sum," Yvonne suggested. "I'm assuming this asteroid is small enough for the Sparrow to haul?"

He nodded. "It'll barely fit inside the frameshift device's bubble of effect, but I think we can make it work. Abigail, Davey, and I will go EVA and drill towing cables into its surface. Yvonne will be in the cockpit monitoring everything."

"What will I do?" Grace asked raising a hand.

Mr. Cole's eyes flicked to her, and she knew that he had forgotten her. Figured.

"You'll stay with Yvonne and do exactly as she says. If she needs assistance, you'll be there for her."

Well, that was better than nothing. Except for going back to bed. That would be much better. She frowned as the obvious question worked its way into her head. "Why do we have to do this now? The M-class whatever will still be there in the morning, right?"

"Maybe," Mr. Cole said. "Maybe not. My broker says we got word first, but I don't trust the secret to stay a secret. If we don't get that asteroid another crew will. We move in now, secure the prize before someone else does, and then wait for Benny to figure out who we're going to sell it to. Any other questions?"

No one moved.

"Good. Since we're still parked in Jupiter's orbit, we're only a couple minutes away from the asteroid by frameshift. Yvonne, get Davey situated in his spacesuit and then head to the cockpit. Abigail, be ready to go for a walk."

Everyone began to move around in preparation, and Grace sat back in her seat. Too bad she didn't have her spacesuit from the Duke's habitat. She'd always liked going on missions and feeling important. She was good at her job too, but Mr. Cole didn't seem to think she was all that valuable a member of the crew. At least with these people her mission wouldn't be stealing things. Probably. With nothing better to do, she followed after Mr. Cole. He had the Sparrow moving by the time she poked her head into the cockpit. Not wanting to disturb him, she crept up to the co-pilot's chair and sat in it.

He glanced at her and smiled one of those polite little smiles adults sometimes gave her. She always thought it was something they did when they didn't have anything to say.

Grace spun the chair.

"Stop that," he said.

She stuck her foot out and caught it on the console. "Why?"

"Because it... Because I... Look, it bothers me. Just don't spin the chair, okay?"

"Fine," she said.

"And don't touch anything."

Grace turned to face him. "Mr. Cole. I used to be in command of the fuel module on our missions. I'm not going to start pushing random buttons or anything stupid like that." She gave him a look and shook her head.

He frowned and turned back to what he was doing. "You're too young to be that good at giving that kind of look. I didn't think most women developed that skill till much later." His expression softened. "But you're right. I'm sorry. I know you're more mature than that."

She smiled at the compliment.

"Also, drop the Mr. Cole thing. You make me sound like a teacher. Matthew is fine. Okay, coming up on the target. Frameshift device will power down in 3... 2... 1... We're here."

Grace stood up and looked out the window. "I don't see anything."

"It's off to the side and a few hundred miles out. I'll get us faced that way in just a moment."

"Miles?"

She could see the confusion in his eyes. Like he didn't even understand the question. After a moment he laughed aloud. "A mile is about two kilometers."

Grace stopped to think about that. There was clearly something she was missing here. "Then why didn't you just say two kilometers?"

The stars in front of them spun as the Sparrow turned towards their target. Grace could feel the main engines rumble their deep roar, and it made her smile. The Sparrow was such a cool ship.

"I take it the Duke thought he was being clever by only teaching you kids metric, huh?"

She stared at him now. "You're going to have to speak English if you want me to understand." She watched as the gaucho sighed and deflated.

"So uncivilized," he muttered.

Davey raised his arms and sighed as Yvonne stepped behind him and pulled the loose slack of his space suit. It was a pain having the extra length bunched up at the shoulder, but at least she had gotten faster at the job in the last week. He and Matthew had left the ship to go out into vacuum every day to scrub off a thin film of grime that coated most of the Sparrow. The gaucho said the mess came from organic compounds they'd picked up landing on Titan.

Why they couldn't just wait till they landed and do it in breathable air was something Davey would never understand. Instead, they spent hours fumbling in zero gee scouring the surface. He was obviously just scrounging around to find work. Make him earn his keep.

Yvonne finished and patted him affectionately on the shoulder. "There. All set and ready to go."

Davey felt his cheeks burn red with shame, and he was glad Yvonne was behind him and unable to see his face. "Thanks, doc," he mumbled. "I guess I'll go join Abigail in the hold." He walked toward the aft ladder. Each step was harder than the one before. At last, he stopped and turned around, chin buried in his neck. "I don't get it," he said.

Yvonne turned back towards him. "What's that?"

"I don't get it," he repeated. "I don't get why you of all people on this ship treat me decently. Matthew barely says a word to me unless

171

it's an instruction to do something. Grace will barely look at me, which, okay, I understand. And I wish Abigail wouldn't look at me. It's like she's plotting my murder."

"Give them time," Yvonne said. "Trust can be earned. You're starting at a big deficit, but keep working hard and someday you may be treated more gently."

He balled his fists. "That doesn't explain you though. You have more right than anyone to... to hate me."

She smiled, but there was something wrong with her smile. Like it was poisoned. "Yes. I know."

"Then why don't you?" He'd taken several steps towards her without realizing it.

Matthew walked into the room, and Davey looked at his feet.

"Another time perhaps," Yvonne said, standing and turning to Matthew. "What's the situation?"

Davey frowned at the ignored question. Why wouldn't she just answer?

"Cockpit's yours," Matthew said. "We're at the asteroid. I'll be on comms." He looked at Davey. "You ready?"

"Does it matter?" he mouthed off before he could stop himself. Yvonne shook her head silently. She must have thought he was an idiot. And who ever knew what Matthew was thinking?

The man stared at him for a moment before shrugging. "No, I guess not. Let's go."

Whatever that was supposed mean.

Davey followed him down the ladder into the hold, where Abigail was waiting by the lift.

"What took you guys?" she asked stifling a yawn. "How long is this going to take?"

Matthew opened a locker and pulled his suit on. "You'll be back in bed soon enough. And tomorrow you won't be the only one sleeping in." He grabbed a pair of helmets and tossed one to Davey.

Davey pulled it over his head and began closing the latches one at a time. The suit was a different model than the one he was used to and obviously the wrong size, but he could function in it. The pushed up bunches in the arms and legs made movement awkward, especially when the suit pressurized. After he got the helmet situated, he looked back at Matthew and Abigail. They were trading verbal jabs now, something that seemed to happen anytime they were in the same room.

"I'm just saying that I might not recognize you without the hat."

Matthew shrugged and lowered the lift. A shield snapped into place over the opening "I'm sure you'll make do somehow."

"I don't know, you and Davey are both so small. You look alike in a spacesuit."

Davey's fist clenched instinctively before his brain worked out that Abigail had insulted Matthew rather than him. He still didn't like the insinuation about his height but decided to let it pass. What was he going to do about Abigail anyway? The woman could out-bully him any day.

"Yes, Davey and I are practically twins." Matthew deadpanned. "If you're going to be this much fun at odd hours, we're going to be taking more middle of the night missions. Oxygen on. Grab your thruster packs."

Davey reached back to his tank and his suit pressurized. He grabbed the pack from the bench where it sat and tried to pull it on. The stupid bunches of suit made it hard to bend his arms far enough to snap the connectors into place. He half spun in a circle trying to reach the pack and felt his face redden as he made a fool of himself.

"I got it," Matthew said putting a hand on his shoulder. Davey slumped as the man leaned over to quickly finish attaching the pack. "There we go." The lift bottomed out and chimed. Abigail dove through the shield. "Hey, go through slow so you don't take a bunch of atmosphere with you," Matthew said, switching to comms. "I only okayed using the lift because we're in a hurry. You start wasting all my ship's air and you'll be taking the airlock." He sighed and motioned Davey towards the lift.

He craned his neck to check the thruster pack for himself. "Thanks," he mumbled and shuffled forward. He lowered himself through the shield, feeling its resistance tug against him. Abigail may not have been that worried about making the gaucho angry, but Davey wasn't going to toy with danger like that. Gravity ended mere inches past the shield, and he drifted slowly toward where Abigail sat waiting on the edge of the lift.

"Don't mention it," Matthew's voice crackled in his ear. "Not your fault I don't have a suit that fits you. If this continues to be an issue, I'll find something that'll serve you better."

Davey's feet touched down on the lift and he engaged the magnets in his boots to stay put. He turned around to face the Sparrow's aft and saw their target floating off the rear. It was a dark, nondescript rock, a little bigger than the Sparrow maybe. Not really much else to say about it. But if someone wanted to pay for it, that was their

173

business.

"So how are we going to tow that thing, Cole?" Abigail asked. "I bet it's going to be a royal pain to secure."

"You'd lose that bet. I used to do this solo. With the three of us, it'll be a pleasant diversion. Yvonne, you there?"

"Ready and waiting," her voice returned at once.

"Good, go ahead and expose the tow lines and turn on the guide lasers."

"I'll have them on by the time you're ready."

Matthew turned to them and smiled. "If you'll follow me, I'll walk you two through the first line." He pushed off the lift and drifted towards the rear of the Sparrow. Abigail and Davey followed with a touch of steam from their thruster packs.

Despite the lack of sleep, Davey felt the usual excitement. He'd always enjoyed zero gee, at least until Matthew had jumped him back at the habitat. He hadn't maneuvered himself onto the Duke's fuel missions purely for Grace's sake. Being small wasn't so much a problem when you were alone with the stars. Everyone, even Abigail, seemed small against the endless black.

Matthew led them to the starboard engine. Davey gave it a wide berth, not wanting to find out if the housing was still hot.

"See these hatches?" Matthew gestured to three dark holes that had opened in the aft. "Each of these has a tow drill and a guide laser. Sharon, if you'll reach into the closest opening."

Abigail moved to the opening, reached her arm in, and slowly guided a two-meter long cylinder out of the cavity. "How are we supposed to anchor this to..."

"Let's go visit our M-type, I'll show you," he said. "Sharon, if you'll bring the equipment." With that, he pushed off the Sparrow towards the asteroid.

They followed him. The tow drill was attached to the Sparrow by a steel cable as thick as Davey's arm that slowly fed as Abigail guided the equipment. Davey noticed that the asteroid was further away than he expected, easily two hundred meters. Which meant the rock was bigger than he thought. Maybe twice the Sparrow's size.

At last, the trio touched down on the dark surface with puffs of steam to slow their approach. Matthew opened a side panel on the cylinder to reveal a lit control panel. He touched a few buttons, and the nose of the device opened into a wicked looking drill bit. "Now we just have to look around to spot the guide laser. There it is. Looks like we drifted a ways."

A red point of light shone on the rough surface of the meteor. Matthew maneuvered the drill over to the laser and lowered the point till it was just above the surface.

"Okay, so the lasers show us where to drill so the tow lines are evenly spaced," Abigail said. "How are we going to control the drill in zero gee?"

Matthew laughed. "You're gonna like this part." He tapped a few more buttons on the control panel and eight legs extended out from the body of the cylinder until they caught the face of the asteroid. "The legs will help keep it pointed where it needs to point and..." he touched a final set of buttons. At the rear of the cylinder, three tiny rear-facing rockets popped out. Davey's eyes went wide. This was cooler than he was expecting. "The rockets provide the force for the drill. Keep clear."

Davey and Abigail moved back. Matthew punched a button and a screen counted down from ten. Matthew gripped a pair of hand holds on the cylinder, and at zero, the drill began to spin and the rockets flared. "I'm only here to make sure it remains steady for the first few seconds," he said. The rumble of the drill transmitted through his hands and into his comm. It silenced as soon as he stopped talking and the transmission clipped. For as many times as Davey had been in vacuum, he was still a little weirded out by the silence.

Matthew let go of the handles and drifted away. "The drill will keep turning until the inner cylinder kaleidoscopes its full length into the asteroid. Should be about finished now." A light flashed on the screen and the rockets went dark. "And now the last stage. The interior cylinder will drill a couple dozen horizontal cross braces into the rock. And with that..." he closed the panel. "We're done. Only five more tow drills."

"Not so bad," Abigail admitted. Davey laughed to himself. He could tell that she was more impressed than she was letting on. "What do you need us to do?"

"Sharon, I need you to retrieve the three tow drills near the port side engine. Davey, if you'll get the remaining two on the starboard side. And be careful. They may not weigh anything in zero-gee, but they've still got more than enough inertia to damage themselves or you if you get careless. Bring 'em in nice and slow and I'll put the drills to work. Get at it."

Davey pushed off the asteroid, giving a generous puff of steam to push himself in the right direction. Ahead of him he saw Abigail. She'd been a bit more liberal with her thruster pack. Probably harder to crush your own bones when you're armored like a bulkhead. Davey slowed himself and drifted to a stop at the second hatch by the starboard engine. He reached into the cavity and slowly guided the piece of equipment out. He frowned. It was quite a bit larger than he was. There was no way he was going to be able to tuck the whole cylinder under his arm like Abigail had.

He wrapped both his arms around the tow drill, hugging it to himself and pointed his feet at the asteroid. He gave a blast of steam to push him in what he now considered to be down. Might take him a minute to get there like this, but at least he would get there.

"How's it going out there?" Yvonne asked into their comms.

"Good, tow drill one is installed with two more on the way," Matthew replied. "Scopes still look nice and quiet?"

"Nothing on the scopes. You'll be the first to know if that changes."

Davey's tow drill was nearly halfway to the asteroid, its cable slowly feeding out from the Sparrow. He looked beneath him and saw that Abigail had already reached her destination. Matthew drifted over to her, took the device, and prepped the drill to anchor it into the asteroid. Abigail pushed off to head back towards the Sparrow.

"Taking your sweet time, Davey?" she asked as she passed him.

He clenched his jaw and knew he had better ignore her. His mouth got the better of him. "You're one to brag. It's not fair with that tin can you're wearing."

"Life's not fair, kid," she retorted.

Davey glanced at his feet. The asteroid was close now, and he used his pack to slow his descent. The extra mass made it take a lot longer to slow than he anticipated, but he gently touched down. "Don't call me a kid. I bet I'd be faster than you if you weren't in your precious armor."

"Sure you would be. Either way, me and the armor are a package deal."

He chose to ignore her and looked around for the laser mark. It was several meters away. He must have drifted further than he realized. With some difficulty, he moved the tow drill into position by the time Matthew reached him.

"Thanks, Davey, I'll take it from here. Don't let her get under your skin. She lives for that sort of thing."

She laughed. "This is an open comm you know. I can hear you."

"You were supposed to hear me," Matthew said. He nodded at Davey and got to work setting up the drill.

Davey pushed away and headed back toward the Sparrow. He

never quite knew what to make of Matthew. Expecting to be scrubbing the hold and hull alone, Davey had been surprised when Matthew rolled up his sleeves, tossed aside his hat, and worked beside him. They had toiled in silence with little conversation for several days on the way to Callisto and for the next few after that. Davey couldn't really complain. He'd been glad for the help, even if he didn't understand it.

Mostly he was just glad he hadn't been tossed out the airlock.

Who knows where Grace would be now if that had happened? His face twisted in pain. She hadn't spoken to him in days outside of the one time she yelled at him again for being stupid. The worst part was that Davey didn't really know how to fix that. The more he tried to make life better for her, the more he screwed things up.

He mumbled a curse as the tears stung his eyes.

His life was nothing but work for people that hated him. And for the first time, he missed life at the habitat.

Matthew finished the fourth tow drill and looked back towards the Sparrow. As far as plans went, this was going off pretty well. Two more drills and he'd have Yvonne turn on the winches to pull up the slack on the cables. They'd be ready to get out of here.

Couldn't come any sooner as far as he was concerned. In his experience jobs didn't usually go this well. You ran into seven-foot armored women, shadowy government men, or creepy Dukes with armies of children.

"So I gotta admit, Cole," Sharon's voice drifted over the comm. "These tow drills are pretty ingenious. They standard on Model 42s or did you get them added?"

"Ha. No, they're aftermarket," Davey arrived with the fifth drill and Matthew joined him at the laser indicated site. "You can imagine they aren't cheap. Maintenance is pretty high for them too, which eats into the profit earned while using them. Absolute fastest way to snag an asteroid and run, though. Thankfully I didn't pay for them. Previous owner did."

Davey drifted away to watch him run the drill.

The kid sure was quiet tonight. He never talked too much, at least not when Matthew was around, but this was different. Matthew set up the drill's spider legs, deployed the rockets, and then gestured to the cylinder. "Well, do you want to run it or not?"

Very little body language could be seen through a space suit, but

177

Matthew thought he saw the kid startle. "Me?" he asked pointing at his chest.

Matthew looked around. "I'm not seeing anyone else out here."

"You just said they were expensive."

Matthew crossed his arms in front of his chest. "You want to do it or not?"

The kid drifted over. "Okay, what do I..."

"Got a ship on scopes," Yvonne interrupted. "Same weight class as the Sparrow. Three hundred... Miles? Why are the scopes set on Imperial?"

Matthew chose to ignore that. "Can you patch me to an open comm? Let's see if they're talkative."

"Yes. I can... probably? Give me a minute I'll figure out where that is in the menus..."

"Sorry, Davey," Matthew said turning to the tow drill and getting ready to fire it up. We need to finish this up. Another time. I hope. Head on back to the Sparrow."

"Fine," Davey said and jetted off towards the Sparrow.

He was in a mood tonight, but Matthew didn't have time to deal with that right now. "Sharon, what's your ETA on the last drill?"

"Twenty seconds. Who are these guys?"

"I don't know. Another freelancer crew probably. Yvonne, how's that open comm line coming?"

"Almost... Okay done. Your second comm channel will be an open broadcast channel."

Matthew switched to the second channel. "Unknown ship identify yourself. This rock's already been claimed."

There was a moment's silence before a familiar voice broke into Matthew's ear. "How long has it been, Cole, since the last time we met. What? A year maybe?"

Matthew knew that voice. "Not long enough, Ewan," Matthew said, finishing up with the fifth tow drill. "Like I said, this rocks already claimed." He pushed off from the asteroid and over to where Sharon waited with the final drill. Better make this quick.

"That's not what I'm seeing. I see you and your little birdy floating by an asteroid with cold engines. It'll be just like three years ago when me and my crew swooped in and..."

"Thanks, Ewan, I don't need a reminder.

"...scored that bounty right under your nose. You should have seen the look on your face."

"It was priceless I'm sure. Look, Ewan, I'm busy. Can we talk later?"

Ewan laughed heartily. "Aye, we can. I'll give you a call back after we've secured the prize."

"Old friend?" Sharon asked.

"Sure. We'll go with that. Listen up everyone we've got trouble. If we don't wrap this up right now, we'll end up walking away empty-handed."

"Give the orders Matthew," Yvonne said. "We're ready."

Matthew began the final drill. He looked back up at the Sparrow and wondered if there was enough time. No matter. Nothing for it but to try. "Yvonne warm up the engines. Get the Sparrow ready to go. Let out the rest of the slack on the cables. And stand by on the maneuvering jets. You should be able to rotate twenty to thirty degrees without tugging on the asteroid."

"What's that going to gain us?"

"Maybe an opportunity to use the thumper.

"Who's going to...?"

"Davey you back to the Sparrow yet?"

"Just made it to the lift. What do I need to do?"

"I need you on the thumper turret. You are to shoot at the other ship and only at the other ship. If you hit the asteroid and break it up, we lose everything. Is that understood?" The final drill finished its job, and Matthew double checked to make sure it was secure.

"Understood. Heading to the thumper." Matthew didn't think he sounded all that confident, but there weren't any other options at the moment. There was no way he was letting a twelve-year-old fire a weapon at other human beings.

"You done Cole? We heading back?" Sharon's voice was hesitant. Maybe she was nervous. Good. This might get tricky.

"Nope."

"Then what are we doing?"

"Ewan's ship, the Red Dragon, will be on us before we get out. He'll probably make a quick pass, take a few shots at us and drop off some men to cut our lines. You and I get to chase them away. They cut our cables, we lose."

"I don't like it," she replied. "If we're out here how do we get the rock away from them?"

"Yvonne's going to get us moving and frameshift us out of here."

The comm was silent for a few moments before Yvonne replied. "A little practice would have been nice before making me fly the Sparrow in a combat situation."

"Noted. Can you do it?"

She hesitated for the briefest of seconds. "Yes."

"Make it happen. Let us know before you burn the engines. Sharon and I will need to be secure first."

"Be careful out there you two. Here comes the other ship."

Matthew looked out into the black of space. Sure enough there it was. The Red Dragon was larger than the Sparrow, which was appropriate given their names. Its braking thrusters were firing as it slowed from its intercept speed to something more manageable. When it closed to just a few miles, two front-facing chain guns opened fire. Bullet's raked across the bottom of the Sparrow, sending sparks and shards of metal spiraling out into space. The Dragon twisted away on maneuvering jets and blasted past the asteroid.

"Cole!" Sharon shouted.

"I see them." Four small figures had bailed from the Dragon as it passed, their thruster packs working overtime to slow them down. "Keep them away from the cables."

"We using lethal force?"

"Not unless they do."

"They just shot up the Sparrow!" Sharon shouted.

"Just gunfire. She can handle it. Yvonne, any damage?"

"Nothing to report."

"See. Ewan and his crew may be job poachers, but they're not killers. Probably just trying to spook us or disable the Sparrow. If things get serious and someone pulls a weapon on you, by all means, take 'em out." He pushed off the asteroid and turned to face the oncoming enemies. They were now cutting a course straight for the cables. "Just look at it like a dust-up between rivals. A nice little fistfight in a saloon." He used his thruster pack to pick up speed.

"And by a saloon you mean space," Sharon said. Matthew looked back at her. She was close on his heels, shield out and deployed. That ought to send them scattering.

"Right," he said. "In space."

Yvonne sat in the pilot's chair. Matthew's seat. She carefully tapped a few controls, starting the engine warm-up process. It would take several minutes from a cold start. Shutting them down at all was a mistake. She glanced at the monitor to her side, confirming for the third time since the Red Dragon had strafed them with gunfire that nothing significant had broken.

Either they didn't have thumpers or Matthew's acquaintance really wasn't out for blood. The armor of the Model 42 was supposed to be pretty tough. "We'll see how tough a nut to crack you are," she mumbled.

Yvonne wasn't sure if she was referring to the Sparrow or herself.

"I'm at the thumper. What do I do?" Davey's voice called out over the comm.

"Shoot at the enemy ship," Grace suggested unhelpfully, and a bit sarcastically.

"Thanks, sis. I mean how? No one exactly taught me how to use this thing since I've been kinda imprisoned in my room."

Matthew replied tersely. "I'm about to be in a fight, Yvonne can you walk him through it?"

"Matthew Cole, you and I are having a long conversation when this is over," she bit back. "And I'm getting a raise. Davey, look for the green button on the right panel that will power on the turret."

"Got it."

"Okay, the actual controls for the turret should be self-explanatory. Trigger to fire. There's a gauge that shows the charge in the capacitor banks. Fire too quickly and drain them and they'll have to cycle. Now flip the switch on the left panel. That should turn on the targeting HUD." She walked him through the last few steps. "I wouldn't take a shot until you think you've got a hit. As soon as they realize the aft has teeth they're going to avoid it."

"Right, I'll keep that in mind," he said.

"Yvonne, the Dragon is coming back around," Grace was leaning over the sensor display. "Fourteen klicks and closing."

Yvonne's eyes widened in surprise and she wondered what other skills Grace had. "Is Davey going to get a shot this pass?"

The girl shook her head. "They're coming from starboard."

Yvonne reached over to the maneuvering thrusters. Jets of steam fired into space rotating the Sparrow's aft a few degrees towards the oncoming ship. "How about now? Davey do you have a shot."

"No shot."

"Five klicks," Grace announced.

Gunfire began to ring off the hull, and Yvonne instinctively winced and covered her head. As the Dragon finished its pass, a red light flashed in the cockpit and a siren wailed through the Sparrow. Side compartments popped open with breathing masks. That wasn't a good sign. That couldn't possibly be good.

Grace got to the monitor before Yvonne did. "Hull punctured.

Main hold and top hatch. We're losing atmosphere. Computer says five minutes of breathable air left."

Yvonne bit her lip. She could seal off the hold, but hard vacuum on the top deck would be a problem. She could use hull patches but how was she supposed to fly the Sparrow if she was also trying to keep it from getting torn apart?

Suddenly she felt a small hand on her. "I've got the hull," Grace said.

"You know how to...?"

"Yep. All the kids on the habitat had to know how to use a hull patch in case of depressurization."

Yvonne nodded slowly. "Alright, Grace. We're counting on you to keep us breathing. Take an air mask. The air is gonna get thin very quickly." Grace pulled a mask over her face and shoved the tank in her pocket. Yvonne could see the fear in the kid's eyes and knew it was mirrored in her own.

A light turned green on the console. Engines were hot.

"Go on. We've got work to do."

The girl ran from the cockpit and Yvonne turned back to the controls.

What had they gotten themselves into?

Abigail had never actually fought in zero gee before. She imagined it wouldn't be too bad if she had her boots magnetized on the hull of a ship. Free floating in open space trying to protect a series of cables was something she couldn't have dreamed up if she tried.

It looked like their foes hadn't noticed them perched on the asteroid and had gone straight for the cables.

She and Cole closed on them quickly.

"They've broken into teams of two," she observed. "I've got the ones to the left."

"Which left?" Cole hissed back.

"I don't know..." Why did everything have to be so hard to describe in zero gee? A plasma torch flickered in the dark ahead of them. One of the teams had reached their cable. "I've got the one with the torch."

"Copy that. Sharon, talk to me mid fight. We're outnumbered and may have to dance in and out to keep them from cutting our lines."

"Got it."

The distance dwindled rapidly. She saw a spray of sparks shoot out from the cable as the saboteurs started to cut into it. Then she was on them. She slammed into the torch wielder shield first. The grav plate in her shield sent him spiraling away, limbs flailing. As she passed, she tried to reach out and grab the other enemy. She missed but managed to nick the heel of his boot sending him spinning. Unfortunately, he managed to grab hold of the cable and managed to regain control.

Abigail used her thruster to slow and then turn back towards the other assailant. He used his own pack to keep out of her reach. Holding onto the cable, he rocketed back towards the Sparrow.

"Oh no you don't," she shouted and turned to pursue.

He let go of the cable and turned, slipping around her, and diving after the slowly spinning plasma torch.

Abigail suddenly realized the mass and inertia of her armor was working against her. Her foes were going to be much more agile than she.

"Cole, I'm having a bit of trouble here..."

"I see, I'm on my way."

Cole shot across in front of her, tackling the saboteur before he could reach the torch, sending them both tumbling. Okay, maybe he had a little more experience out here than she did. She spun around trying to see the other foes. The one she had sent packing with her shield had finally gotten control of his spin and was on the way back. The two Cole had scattered appeared to be trying to regroup with their comrade.

It was like swatting at a swarm of flies. How were they supposed to keep them away from the...?

"Matthew, Abigail!" Yvonne shouted over the comm. "Engines are hot. Get clear and let me know when you're secure. Davey, get ready. I think I can get you a shot on the Dragon this time." Abigail watched as the Sparrow rotated a few degrees in front of her. She could see the turret swiveling high on the aft between the engines. That meant the dragon was coming from behind, near the asteroid.

She turned and tried to get eyes on the ship. There above the asteroid. Its guns began to fire for the third time. A single blast from the Sparrow's thumper answered in return. It ripped into the flank of the enemy ship, leaving a gaping wound in its side. The Dragon's maneuvering jets flared red in response and it broke off its attack, leaving a trail of smoking debris in its wake. Abigail didn't know how severe the damage to the ship was, but she hoped it was enough to dissuade pursuit.

"I got them!" Davey shouted. "I got them!"

Yvonne laughed aloud. "Great shot!"

"Abigail!" Cole called suddenly. She spun and saw him coming up behind her. "Grab a cable! Fall back to the asteroid."

She obeyed and used the nearest cable as a guide to retreat to the rock. The Sparrow slowly rotated to face away from them again, and a fire began to light in the engines. Their feet touched down on the asteroid. "Clip on to the cable," Cole commanded. "Yvonne ease up the throttle. Keep it nice and slow till the cables are taut."

Suddenly Abigail realized why they had retreated to the asteroid. The Sparrow's engines burned like newborn stars, and even a couple hundred meters away she could feel the force of the back blast. Thankfully the cables were anchored out wider than the engines, otherwise they would probably be roasted alive.

Abigail watched as the saboteurs scrambled out of the way of the asteroid as it slowly picked up speed behind the Sparrow. One of them nearly didn't make it and avoided becoming roadkill by mere seconds.

She turned to Cole. He squatted by the tow drill to better withstand the gees of acceleration. "So when do we get to go back inside?"

"Yeah, it's going to be a bit," he said. "Better get used to the view."

Grace ran back to the common room and dug into a tool cabinet. She carefully pulled out one of the centimeter-thick steel plates. With some difficulty, she managed to carry the thing with both arms back towards the thumper turret. The ladder that ran down to the hold also led up to the top hatch, whose controls glowed an angry color of red in warning. The outermost hatch had been torn to shreds by the hail of gunfire and the mechanism for the second hatch had been damaged causing it to malfunction and spring open.

A single bullet had pierced the innermost hatch. Grace looked up at the hole several feet above her head. She could feel the wind whistling past her as precious oxygen escaped into space.

Then the thought occurred to her that she'd have to climb the ladder carrying the weight of the steel patch. Her heart sank. She'd never be able to do both at the same time. Why had she been so stupid to think that she could do this?

From down the hall, Davey shouted "I got them! I got them!"

"Great. Now what do I do? "she said to herself.

And then she remembered her bracelets. She set the patch on the floor and reaching out with her left arm seized the plate in the bracelet's grip. It glowed icy-blue as she lifted the patch and pressed it

184

against the hole. Holding it in place, she climbed the ladder with her free hand and reached up to the plate. Along its edge was a red strip of plastic. She gripped it between her fingers and pulled it away from the steel surface. The plastic separated two chemicals that when combined started to burn. Fire trailed along the outer edge of the patch as it welded itself into place.

Grace slid down the ladder, still holding the patch firmly in place with her bracelet. A few molten bits of steel hissed as they dripped to the floor. She tried not to imagine what would happen if one landed on her clothes.

All at once the fire went out, and the plate was fused in place. She smiled. Content that her repair job would hold, she ran back to the common room to grab another patch. This time she lifted it with her bracelets.

These things were going to come in handy.

Ewan Hywel watched as the Sparrow's frameshift device activated and both the asteroid and ship disappeared off the scopes. He ignored the red lights winking all over the console and pulled up the comm.

"You still there, Cole?"

"Been waiting on your call, Ewan. Just sitting back on my asteroid enjoying the view of my ship. What do you need?"

Ewan ran a hand through his blond hair and sat back in his seat. He'd noted the emphasis on the words 'my asteroid' and got the point. "You didn't tell me you had yourself a crew these days. What happened to the ole' Cole works alone thing?"

"It was kind of an accident. You know how life is."

"For an accident, it sure was a fortunate one for you. You recruit anyone I know? Your crew seemed to handle itself well."

There was a pause before Cole answered. "You sure you want the answer to that, Ewan?"

"I asked, didn't I?"

"Fine, it's your own pride that'll take the hit. First, I've got the Shield Maiden of Mars. I'm sure you've heard of her."

"My men already reported back about her. She gave them quite the scare."

"Well, I've also got a doctor. She's flying the Sparrow right now. It's uhh... Today is the first time she's ever flown a ship."

Ewan whistled. "Pretty trusting of you."

"You didn't give me a choice. Then I've got a couple of kids.

185

Seventeen and twelve. The twelve-year-old apparently ran around and patched the holes you punched in my ship and the seventeen-year old punched that big one in yours."

The line went silent. "That's it?" Ewan asked, incredulous.

"Pretty much."

Ewan laughed. "Well, I've been had. You deserve your prize this time Cole."

"Thanks, Ewan. Find your own next time. How's the damage?"

Ewan's eyes flicked back to the red lights blinking on his console. "Could be worse. We'll limp into port for repairs. The Ddraig Goch's taken worse beatings before."

"First, Ewan, you don't actually speak Welsh. Second, I'm pretty sure your ship is registered as the Red Dragon."

"Gotta do something to remember the land of my fathers, right? Enjoy your score, Cole, but you owe me a drink for the damage."

"Sure. And you'll buy mine for the same reason. Take care, Ewan." The comm went silent.

Ewan shook his head again at the thought that he just got beat by a crew of amateurs and turned back to the console to help his crew sort out the mess of damage.

An hour later the crew of the Sparrow lounged around the common room, exhausted from too few hours of sleep but still too wide awake from the excitement to go back to bed. Matthew sat head in hands at the table, campero tossed aside and forgotten for the time. He yawned and stretched his arms.

"Wake me when breakfast is ready."

"If you fall asleep, I can't promise we won't eat your bacon," Yvonne said from her position at the small stove. She had generously offered to fix an early breakfast to celebrate the victory and was frying up a few of the eggs and vat-grown bacon strips they'd bought on Callisto.

"I'll just go ahead and promise that, yes, I will eat anyone's bacon that's too slow," Sharon said. "It smells heavenly."

"Unless I get yours first," Grace said sitting down at the table.

Sharon poked the girl in the side, and she jumped with a squeal. "Don't start with me, Grace. I know all your weaknesses."

Matthew shook his head. This was giving him a headache "No one is eating anyone's bacon. We bought enough so everyone could have two slices. That's it. No more. No less."

"Unless you fall asleep first," Yvonne added. She stepped over to the table and placed a skillet full of eggs and bacon in the middle. "No cheating," she said eyeing Sharon.

"What? Why does everyone think I'm the one that would cheat?"

Everyone stared at her for a moment and then there was a hearty round of laughter that even Davey joined in on. They filled their plates. Everyone got a pile of scrambled eggs and precisely two slices of vat-grown bacon as instructed. The noise of eating and clattering utensils replaced the sounds of conversation.

Matthew tore one of his pieces of bacon in half and ate it thoughtfully looking at the members of his crew sitting at the table in front of him. How had this even happened?

He'd thought he was done playing shepherd, and here he was with a new flock.

He stirred his eggs once and then set his fork down.

"You all did good today," he said.

They paused and looked at him.

"All of you. You did things you weren't trained or prepared for and, well, you all came through. Grace, Davey, you two as well." He hesitated. "Davey I'll lift your house arrest. You'll have a strict curfew, and you're still prohibited from possessing anything that could be used as a weapon, but you'll be allowed a little more freedom now."

Davey's eyes went wide and then narrowed. "So you won't let me have a weapon, but you'll let me shoot a big one at an enemy ship."

"Or you can spend your time locked in your room," Matthew said.

"Nope," the teen said shaking his head quickly. "I'm good, thanks."

Matthew cracked a wry smile. "That's what I thought."

Sharon dumped another spoonful of sugar into her coffee. "So was that supposed to be some sort of inspirational speech from the captain? I thought it was kind of lacking."

"I thought it was nice," Grace said. Matthew noticed that she'd already eaten both of her bacon slices. Kid needed to learn how to slow down and enjoy the finer things in life.

"Well, that's good," Matthew said, "Because now I've got bad news."

The crew wilted before his eyes.

"Repairs for the Sparrow are going to cut into the personal allowances from this mission. It went from being lucrative to expensive with the repairs we'll have to make."

"Are we poor?" Grace asked. Davey elbowed her.

"No. But we're not rich," Matthew said. "I do have some good news though."

"What's that?" Davey asked.

Matthew smiled. "There's always another job to take."

Chapter 12: The Shadow and the Void

Moses represented something unique in the history of mankind. For the first time, a force outside of man's own acted upon the species as a whole. There was a guiding impetus, a mind that was other, directing the course of history. The question was whether or not it was infallible.

Some said that Moses was a stabilizing force. The digital age had brought rapid paradigm shifts that threatened to tear humanity apart. Surveillance states rose, privacy all but disappeared, lifestyles evolved over the course of months rather than generations, and the onslaught of new technology nearly undermined the very foundations of civilization. Overnight, Moses was the face of all technology and innovation, and he brought a certain conservative mindset in his approach to humanity.

Privacy was restored. The watchful eyes of governments and corporations were closed. And the rush of new technology became a calculated endeavor controlled by Moses himself.

Stability indeed, but also perhaps stagnation. Moses stopped the radical transformations of the digital age, but he also stunted generations of intellectual and cultural growth. He outpaced men in science so rapidly that they ceased to understand his machinations, and Moses stopped trying to explain. It mattered little. He would always be around to protect and guide humanity, and he had the interests of everyone in mind.

When Moses disappeared, the debt came due. Whether mankind had grown soft from stability or stagnation was irrelevant. The framework that had supported civilization for the last four generations was gone, and we were lost.

Julian Nikitas
Chancellor of the University of Ganymede
Died 31 AM

One of the first things Abigail had learned after coming aboard the Sparrow, was that Matthew Cole took Sundays off whenever he could. No jobs, no maintenance, nothing. Not that she minded. Taking time off was healthy, human even. She'd just pegged Cole as an all business and no play sort of guy. "My parents were pretty traditional," he said when questioned, which wasn't really an answer. Every Sunday, like today, he sat in his chair reading.

Abigail frowned and looked back down at the checker game she was inevitably going to lose. As it turned out, checkers was the favorite pastime for kids on the Duke's habitat. Grace had explained their intricate leaderboard system and that it was the favorite sport to bet on. She'd always ranked well.

Abigail had scrounged up a set from material on the ship. and had proceeded to get slaughtered by the twelve-year-old every time they played. Even now the end was nigh.

"Your move, metal woman."

She glanced up at Grace who gave her a wicked grin and twiddled one of Abigail's captured men between her fingers. It was over. Grace had set her trap and moving any one of her remaining men would spring it. She sighed as she took her turn. Grace practically leaped across the table to jump three more of Abigail's pieces. "You're not very good at this."

"Thanks for telling me the obvious," Abigail said, sitting back and extending a hand across the table. "Are you going to accept my surrender or is your goal to humiliate me?"

Grace made a show of thinking hard about it before putting her tiny hand in Abigail's armored one and giving it a shake. "I'll accept your surrender. This time." She looked around the room. "Who's next?"

"Cole, your turn," Abigail said standing to her feet.

He looked up from his book. "I'm one and oh against the little prodigy. I prefer to keep it that way."

"You got lucky," Grace declared giving him a fierce look.

"Never denied that fact," he said. "Doesn't mean I'm willing to ruin a perfect record and bragging rights."

"I've got a theory about that," Yvonne said, entering the room. "I think our Matthew is a sore loser."

"Nothing of the sort," he said, shaking his head and looking back at his book.

Grace walked over to him and pushed his hat down over his eyes. "One. More. Game."

Abigail covered her mouth to keep from laughing. The girl was fearless.

Cole lifted his chin to look under the brim of his hat. "How about you ask your brother?"

She made a face. "He's no good at checkers."

"Somehow I'm not surprised," Abigail muttered. She ignored the severe look Yvonne gave her. It wasn't her fault that Davey spent all his time hiding in his room and wasn't around to defend himself. You'd think he'd take the freedom he was offered, but he only showed his face when food was on the table.

"One game," Grace repeated.

Cole reached up and straightened his campero so he could see and gave an exaggerated sigh. "Fine. One game and win or lose you stop pestering me."

An alarm chimed through the common room.

He smiled. "Some other time. We're approaching Venus. Yvonne, you want some more practice time flying?"

"Always," she responded.

"You planned that," Grace accused, her voice rising in pitch.

"Would have if I could have," he said.

Abigail watched them go, cursing her bad luck. She'd almost escaped another beating. Grace bounced back over to the table, her eyes darting to Abigail's and then back down the corridor that led toward the cockpit.

"So, is Matthew your boyfriend?"

Abigail's jaw dropped, not quite sure what she was hearing. "Absolutely not! Why would you even think that?"

"I don't know. You're about the same age," Grace said, scooping up the checkers pieces. Maybe she was going to have mercy and not demand a rematch. "Plus," she said thoughtfully, "he is pretty cute."

Abigail stared at her dumbfounded. "You..." She closed her mouth. Why was this even a subject of conversation? "First, cute has nothing to do with it. Second, you're too young to think males of any age are cute."

Grace put a hand on her hip and tossed her blond hair back with the other defiantly. "I'm almost thirteen, you know."

"That's not old enough," Abigail said pointing a finger at Grace.

"You didn't deny that Matthew is cute," Grace said mimicking her gesture.

It took an effort of will to keep her jaw from dropping again. "This isn't a conversation we're going to have."

"You do at least like him though, right?"

"No. How about we go take a look at Venus?"

"Fine." She drew out the word as if it was the last she'd ever utter. Abigail was just glad she'd decided to drop the issue. When had that weird idea worked its way into Grace's head? They walked to the cockpit in silence.

Cole and Yvonne had already brought the Sparrow into orbit around Earth's sister planet. Venus was yet another entry on the list of interesting places that Abigail had never visited. Despite having roughly the same gravity as Earth and a similar orbit, Venus deserved its hellish reputation. Atmospheric pressure of ninety-three times standard, a resulting surface temperature hot enough to melt lead, and clouds of sulfur dioxide made colonization challenging to say the least.

Moses had risen to the challenge.

Fifty kilometers above the surface the pressure fell to one atmosphere. At this altitude, even breathable air provided lift. Moses had done what aerospace engineers had long thought plausible and built cities that floated in the Venusian clouds. Special care had to be taken to protect exposed surfaces from sulfur compounds, but the two cities that remained in the skies of Venus were among the most comfortable in the colonies.

Abigail stared at the pale-yellow planet, the morning and evening star of Earth. Stray memories of her childhood flickered beneath the surface of her conscious mind. Grace suddenly pushed past her to get a better view of the planet below.

"It's beautiful," she said.

Cole nodded from the copilot seat. "All of them are. Each rock in our solar system a unique and beautiful world. Pity only one was made for us. The rest are a hostile bunch."

"Who's hostile?" Davey said crowding into the cockpit. Suddenly it had become uncomfortably intimate in the little room.

"No one's hostile but me," Yvonne snapped. "I'm so glad everyone has decided to come watch me practice flying."

"Relax," Abigail said. "You're only going to be deorbiting us. I'm pretty sure that's when the majority of space accidents have happened."

"That's not helping!" Yvonne said. "Get out of my cockpit!"

Cole turned to stare at Yvonne. "Hey. It's my cockpit."

"Not when I'm flying. You can sightsee from orbit when we leave."

Abigail laughed and, putting a hand on Davey and Grace's shoulders, gently shooed them back toward the common room. Yvonne would probably chew her out later, but watching the sparks fly had been worth it. "Come on Davey, let's go watch you get slaughtered by your sister in checkers."

Matthew took over the controls halfway through, despite his best attempts at assuaging her fears. High winds in the upper atmosphere had turned the landing into a tricky proposition. The Sparrow's environmental shields deflected most of them, but there was also the added complication that a floating city rides the winds. Yvonne wasn't too keen to land on a moving target.

Shaped like an enormous octagon, the city of Discordia was held aloft by dozens of clusters of air bladders, both within the structure and above the metropolis. Spires rose into the sky above and below the city into the fury of the hurricane force winds. Openings in these spires led to central chambers filled with turbines that provided a free source of power.

"SPW5840, you are expected and cleared for landing at the royal hangar. A security detachment will meet you there."

"Thanks, Discordia tower." Matthew glanced at the navigational instructions. "Okay, maybe it's a good thing I took over."

"It gets worse?" Yvonne asked. "How does it get worse?"

"Discordia floats free in the wind. They can maneuver if they need to, but why bother? There's only one other city in the sky, and they're seldom near each other."

"So what's the problem?"

Matthew smiled and gestured at the city. "The hangar is on the leading side of the city at the moment. We'll have to fly in front of it, and then slow down and wait for it to catch up to us. Back into the hangar so to speak."

Yvonne's eyes widened. "That's madness. Surely you don't expect to..."

"Computer does most of the work," he assured her. "It'll tell me the numbers at least. How fast to fly and where. I've still got to make it happen."

She didn't look pleased.

"Relax, just because I've never done it before doesn't mean I can't do it." Matthew concentrated on the task at hand, but he could feel the daggers being glared at him.

"Are you and Abigail conspiring to raise my blood pressure today? Because that's what you're doing."

"Thought I'd join in for once."

"Don't make a habit of it."

It turned out, landing was easier than Matthew had thought. Following the computer's guidance, he positioned in front of the city and eased off the throttle to let it catch him. He lowered the landing gear and gently touched down, cutting the engines.

"See. All there is to it."

"Didn't look too bad. Maybe I'll give it a shot next time."

Matthew appraised her and shrugged. "Maybe so." It still seemed wrong that he even let someone else near the controls of his ship, let alone someone as green as Yvonne, but she was obviously the smartest person on the Sparrow and had already taught herself nearly everything there was to know about it. Made sense to let her fly it.

They finished going through the Sparrow's post-flight procedures and joined the other three in the common room. "Sharon, you ready to head out?" he asked.

"And just who is our mysterious employer?" she asked, looking up from the kids' checkers game. "You've been a bit mum on the details of this job."

"The Emperor of Venus, himself. And as to the details I haven't a clue. Benny promises we'll like it."

"Venus has an Emperor?" Davey asked. He gave up on the game he'd inevitably lose.

"He's a far cry from Duke Fagin from what I hear," Matthew said, realizing royal titles might be uncomfortable for the kids. "The people of the city seem to like him well enough."

"Sounds primitive," Sharon said. "I've always thought the Venusian cities were supposed to be ritzy."

194

"They are. But as it turns out, when you've got a string of benevolent dictators, you do all right. They're waiting for us. Let's go."

"Can I come?" Grace asked, getting to her feet.

"You guys get to recalibrate the starboard engine with Yvonne. She's in charge."

The kids groaned in unison.

They wouldn't need the bikes today, so Matthew and Sharon lowered the port side ramp and walked out of the Sparrow into the Royal Hangar. It was large enough for at least a dozen ships the size of the Sparrow and was, in fact, half full.

"Check that one out," Sharon said with a whistle.

Matthew had already seen it. At the far end of the hangar was a yacht. It was probably the most expensive ship he had ever seen. Covered with mirrored chrome, it was a thing of beauty. Matthew also saw half a dozen thumper turrets.

"Bet that's the Emperor's private chariot," he said. "Wonder how many crew it takes to run. Never seen anything like it. Kind of reminds me of pictures of the old frigates from the days of Moses. Smaller, but similar style."

Sharon stopped in her tracks and her brow furrowed as she stared at the yacht.

"Umm... Sharon? You still with me?"

"Yeah... I just... The design of the yacht looks familiar. I was trying to place it."

Matthew regarded her thoughtfully. "Any luck?"

She pursed her lips. "Maybe. I don't know."

There were dots that weren't being connected here, but Matthew wasn't quite sure what to ask. A contingent of armed guards decked in crimson and silver armor with flowing capes marched in their direction. They brandished rifles that matched the color scheme, and the effect was impressive, if a little dramatic.

"Quite the sense of style," Sharon murmured. "Guess an empire needs a theme to run with."

He nodded at the lead guard as they approached. "Matthew Cole and Abigail Sharon. I believe we're expected?"

"Yes, sir." His eyes dropped to Matthew's hip. "I'm afraid I'm going to have to ask you to leave your weapons on your ship or with me. No unauthorized weapons are allowed in the palace."

Matthew looked at his revolver then back at the guards. "Any way to get it authorized? I make it a rule not to be defenseless."

The guard stared back at him, face expressionless.

195

"That's what I thought." He reluctantly handed his revolver to the guard.

The guard turned to Sharon. "I'm afraid you will also have to leave your armor here."

She crossed her arms. "Over my dead body."

For the first time, a flicker of emotion crossed the guard's face. "Ma'am, I don't make the rules, I just enforce them. If you wish to enter the palace, you will leave your armor on the ship."

"Then we're through here. Have fun, Cole." She turned on her heel and marched back up the ramp into the Sparrow.

Cole turned to the guard and smiled awkwardly. "She's pretty keen on that suit of hers. You sure there's not a misunderstanding here? Whoever arranged our hire would have known that if you hire the Shield Maiden, then that's what you get."

The guard looked at the Sparrow for a moment and motioned toward the hangar exit. "I'll need an order in writing if that's the case. In the meantime, follow me, Mr. Cole."

Matthew sighed and fell into step behind the guards. Dimly he wondered if Sharon was going to help Yvonne and the kids with their engine maintenance. Probably not. She'd most likely go sulk in her room.

They walked through a tall corridor that stretched into the distance. The walls were of the same crimson the guards wore and the floors of stone, polished to a shine. There were few straight lines in the architecture, and nearly everything ended in a tapered arch. Even the stonework was inlaid with curved geometric arch designs.

He was ushered into a narrow room, lit by torches flickering from silver sconces. The walls were adorned with hangings, elegant works of art, covered with scenes of the colonization of Venus, the building of its four cities, and the destruction of two of them. This was the real deal, not a counterfeit like Duke Fagin's audience hall.

A man, dressed in a red tunic with silver trim, sat in the chair at the far end. He had a full brown beard, braided with silver beads. The guards immediately took up positions in the corner of the room and snapped to attention.

Not really knowing what else to do, Matthew offered the man his hand to shake. "Matthew Cole, freelancer here for the job. You the steward?"

The way the guards immediately stiffened was the first clue that he'd done something wrong. Hard to play by the rules when you aren't familiar with the game.

The man set aside the tablet he'd been using and stood. He shook Matthew's hand, a amused smile creeping across his face. "I'm Emperor Dominic the Second."

"Oh." The word was out before he could stop it. Matthew withdrew his hand quickly. "I was led to believe I was meeting with your steward... Your majesty?"

The Emperor chuckled and waved him off. "Proper etiquette would be 'Your Grace,' but as you aren't my subject, I'm not overly concerned with propriety. However, I am somewhat worried that you are alone. I was under the impression that you and the Shield Maiden were arriving on the same ship. Has there been a change of plans?"

The lead guard spoke up immediately. "Your Grace, she's on their ship. She refused to take off her armor, which I took to be a weapon. Unless she's granted special leave to..."

"She has it," said Emperor Dominic. "You don't hire the Shield Maiden and have her leave behind her shield. Send for her at once."

Matthew looked at the guard and winked.

The guard ignored him. "It will be done," he said, scurrying from the room.

"Now then," continued the Emperor, "I informed the steward he would not be needed. I had a bit of free time now that preparations for tomorrow's birthday party are complete and decided to meet with you myself."

Matthew reached up and adjusted his campero. "I'm honored. What's this about a party?"

Emperor Dominic frowned. "You aren't aware of why you're here?"

"My broker decided to surprise me. At this point, I'm thinking about strangling him."

"Peculiar," Emperor Dominic said, sitting back in his chair. "Tomorrow, my daughter, the Trade Minister of Concordia, is celebrating her thirtieth birthday."

"Is she your heir?"

"Goodness no, though she would certainly be qualified. But I suppose you don't know our customs. Emperors are forbidden from choosing their own children as their heir. The first Venusian Emperor was merely the mayor of Discordia. When crisis fell upon the solar system after Moses disappeared, things got complicated very quickly here on Venus. One of the four cities, Eris, fell to the surface in a terrorist incident, and the other, Harmonia, suffered irreparable damage and had to be evacuated. Mayor Levi declared martial law and took control of the two remaining cities. He was a wise and just man. After he was crowned emperor, he set a precedent that none that followed should choose his own offspring to succeed him. This keeps emotion out of the decision-making process. No, my own heir is chosen, and a closely guarded secret. I wouldn't want them to learn pride before their ascension."

Matthew had to admit that he was impressed. Removing nepotism was what had given Venus a string of decent Emperors and Empresses. He wasn't sure it could continue forever, though. All it took was one bad apple to spoil a century of success.

"So, this birthday party," he said. "I'm not sure what you need a pair of freelancers for."

"I've hired more than a pair. There will be a dozen of you all told."

"I don't imagine you need extra security. Your own guards are surely more than sufficient."

The Emperor chuckled. "Without a doubt. You will be guests at the party and I expect you to enjoy yourselves. However, in so doing, you will provide a small service."

Matthew raised an eyebrow to signify that he was all ears.

"You freelancers are a worldly sort, always on the move, always in the center of things. I want you there to keep your eyes and ears open. I suspect that you will be keener to notice the subtle details if something is amiss. There will be many guests from all over the system. If anyone intends ill towards my daughter, myself, or the people of Venus, I expect that you freelancers will sniff it out."

That wasn't what Matthew had been imagining. He shuffled his feet nervously. "Your Imperial Majesty, I'll be the first to admit that being a freelancer hasn't exactly given me a danger sense. I'm not sure you'll be getting your money's worth."

"Of course not. And I do not think your services will be needed. However, if you keep your eyes and ears open that will be enough for me."

"So long as you know what you're paying for."

"I do. Also if you have any crew besides yourself and the Shield Maiden on your ship, I expect them to join us for the party."

"That's very generous of you, but I'm not sure that's the best idea."

Emperor Dominic made a face as if he had been hurt. "And why is that?"

"I mean no offense. I have a couple of kids on the ship, twelve and seventeen and I'm not sure a party full of VIPs is the place for them."

"Nonsense! They'll love it."

Matthew didn't doubt that to be true, it was more a matter of making sure they weren't the cause of any incidents. He would threaten them both before either set foot off the Sparrow. "Also the last member of my crew is trying to keep a low profile right now. She ran afoul of one of the big three a while back. The last time she got off the ship there were... complications."

Emperor Dominic smiled broadly. "Then this will be a perfect diversion for them all! It is, after all, a costume party."

"What?" Matthew stared at the Emperor blankly.

"A costume party. Naturally, your garb as a gaucho and the Shield Maiden's armor will keep you two from needing to be dressed, but I will send a tailor to prepare costumes for your crew. They shall all have a marvelous time tomorrow!"

"Great!" Matthew said, his voice nearly cracking. Benny was going to get an earful for this. He'd known there wasn't a chance Matthew would take a costume party job. Not by himself. Not with a crew. Not ever.

The door opened and the head guard ushered Sharon into the room. "Still in my armor," she declared stepping up alongside Matthew. "Who's this guy? What did I miss?"

Matthew winced at her lack of tact and sighed. "This is the Emperor and it's a costume party."

Abigail thought that Grace would be excited, but she wasn't quite prepared for the order of magnitude that excitement would take.

"It's a costume party? This is amazing! Do I get to pick my costume?" As much as Abigail liked the girl, she found herself getting a headache.

Davey's response was somewhat less exuberant. "Costume parties are for children."

"And Emperors apparently," Abigail said. "Maybe we can get you a butterfly costume to match that cheerful demeanor."

Davey sneered at her and turned to Cole. "Can I just stay on the ship, out of everyone's way?"

"I wish," Matthew said. "But his Imperial Majesty Dominic the Second insisted that the entire crew of the Sparrow attend his daughter's birthday party." Davey frowned at him and Matthew pointed a finger at the teen. "Don't give me that look. Do you think I want to attend a costume party?"

Abigail sat at the table. "You don't even have to dress up. Stop complaining."

"Not the point," he said. "And it's a principle. It's... It's not dignified."

Abigail laughed. She tried not to, but hearing the gaucho whine made her day.

"Grace. Davey." Matthew said, turning back and forth between them. "You two will stay with Yvonne at the party and do exactly as she says. If you don't, I'll throw you off the city myself."

Yvonne crossed her arms. "I seem to have become a glorified babysitter in my old age. You know there's a reason Tomas and I never had children."

"I don't need a babysitter," Davey insisted. "I'm an adult."

"Could have fooled me," Abigail said.

He bristled, but he was interrupted by a chime over the intercom.

"That's probably the tailor here to take measurements," Cole said looking miserable. "I'll let 'em in."

Abigail watched him go. As for herself, she didn't mind the costume party at all. First of all she would have the best costume in the house. Second, it was an easy job. With armed guards everywhere, the odds of anything happening were practically zero. Cole may have wanted to throttle his broker, but Abigail thought he deserved a medal for going above and beyond the call of duty.

The tailor was a soft-mannered man with greying hair and round glasses. He introduced himself as Jeremiah and asked who he should start with.

"ME!" Grace yelled, practically jumping out of her skin and nearly causing everyone else in the room to do the same.

Jeremiah chuckled. "I'm not sure I could say no if I wanted to." He adjusted his glasses. "What kind of costume would you like to wear to the party, my dear."

Grace immediately turned serious. For all the commotion she'd made, she must not have thought that far ahead. After a moment's thought, she asked, "Can I have a pretty dress?"

Abigail felt her heart miss a beat. The poor girl had never had anything nice to wear in her life, not on the street, not on the Duke's habitat.

The tailor was a perceptive man. "My dear, I can make you a princess."

Grace bashfully pushed a lock of her blond hair out of her face. "Thank you."

After he had finished with her, he turned to Davey. "And for you young man?"

Davey shook his head. "Don't care."

"He'll take a princess dress too," Abigail suggested.

"No."

"Something more masculine," Jeremiah said. "Maybe something like what he's wearing?" He gestured to where Cole leaned against the wall.

Davey glanced at Cole and shrugged. "I said I don't care."

Jeremiah took his measurements and turned to Yvonne. "And for you Ma'am?"

She shook her head. "It doesn't matter much, I suppose. Just make sure my face is obscured."

"Yes, my Emperor informed me of the good doctor's plight. No hints at all as to what you would like?"

Yvonne shook her head. "It's your choice. Costumes aren't my thing."

"Very well," Jeremiah said, sighing. He took Yvonne's measurements and stood and bowed. "I will have your costumes sent to you early in the morning." Abigail was sure he was more than eager to leave the Sparrow and its crew of obstinate and backbiting misfits.

The next day came far too soon for Matthew. By early afternoon they were summoned and led as a crew through the palace. The venue for the party was an enormous gardened courtyard, lit by glass skylights far above. A string orchestra dressed in smart crimson tuxedos played classical music by the central fountain. Actually, nearly everyone was wearing crimson. Even the staff was dressed in the emperor's favorite color.

As they dutifully went through the receiving line to greet the Imperial family, Matthew silently prayed that no one would say anything inappropriate. He glanced at his crew, aware that they looked like the system's most dysfunctional family.

"This is insulting," Yvonne said from behind her mask.

"At least you're still a doctor," Matthew said.

"I'm a plague doctor!"

"I fail to see why..." Abigail started.

"Plague doctors were quacks," Yvonne said pointing her beak nosed mask at Abigail.

"Misdirection?" Abigail suggested. "It's a good costume. Pigman himself wouldn't recognize you."

Grace, complete with princess crown and a pair of sparkly wings, walked through the line with regal purpose. Matthew had been worried she would lose her mind after she put it on, but to his complete surprise, the opposite had happened. She had transformed into a perfectly polite little lady the moment she had donned the lavender dress. At least someone was behaving well today.

Davey, unfortunately, had undergone no such metamorphosis, and his attitude remained in the pits. He stood, arms crossed, looking like a much shorter version of Matthew, complete with campero and poncho. The tailor had decided to make him literally look like Matthew, which was awkward for everyone. At least Davey had stopped whining since they had left the Sparrow and was contenting himself to sulk. As long as he was quiet and not mouthing off, Matthew wasn't going to complain.

At last, their time to greet the Imperial family came. As it turned out, Emperor Dominic the Second had a rather large family, nine children ranging from age thirty to almost as young as Grace.

"Matthew Cole. Abigail Sharon," the emperor said. "I'm pleased to meet the rest of your crew."

"Right," Matthew said lamely. "We're here." He introduced Yvonne and the kids. They each bowed politely without so much as opening their mouths. First trial past. Maybe this wouldn't be a complete nightmare.

Emperor Dominic greeted them warmly. "And what an unusual group for a freelancer crew. Perhaps if there is time later, you can regale me with the tale of how you came together."

"Still trying to figure that part out myself," Matthew said through a feeble smile.

They were introduced to the members of the Venusian Imperial family. Matthew didn't bother to memorize any of the names except the Empress, Vivian, and the oldest daughter whose birthday they were celebrating, Julia.

Julia curtsied. She was a tall woman, her dark hair up in an elaborate bun. Given that this whole deal was kind of about her, it was no surprise that her crimson and silver dress looked like it cost several small fortunes. Matthew tried not to stare, but he was pretty sure that tendrils of mist seeped from her dress and pooled around her in a fog. He couldn't quite make up his mind if the effect was interesting or bizarre.

"Greetings and welcome," she said, favoring him with a smile.

He nodded, barely meeting her eyes and mumbled a polite,

"Thanks." Then he pushed his crew past the receiving line to a quieter area of the garden. The sooner they were away from other people, the better.

"Everyone remember your orders?" he asked.

"Don't do anything dumb or you throw us off the city," Davey said. "We were listening."

"I'll keep an eye on them, Matthew," Yvonne said. "You and Abigail take care of business."

Matthew took off his hat and ran a hand through his hair. He still wasn't even sure what the job was, but the Emperor seemed confident that the freelancers he'd hired would smell danger coming. Or something.

Sharon mock saluted. "I'm going to go check out the hors d'oeuvres. Don't have too much fun." She walked across the garden like she owned it. Matthew saw her get stopped almost immediately by a group admiring her costume.

"She's going to have quite the day," he said and waved his own farewell. He headed in the opposite direction to... mingle or something. Clearly, he was going to have to interact with people if he was going to actually be of any use. He needed to take this seriously, no matter how inane.

He walked over to a group of masked women, all looking like they were from the upper strata of whatever went for polite society on Venus. They interrupted their conversation and looked at him expectantly. Suddenly Matthew's collar felt a little tight and the poncho a bit too stuffy for the sunny garden. Nothing for it. There was no saving him at this point.

He tipped his campero. "Good evening, ladies."

Grace stood with her back so straight it nearly hurt. A smile had permanently stuck itself on her face. Davey and Yvonne sat back in their quiet corner content to be out of the public's eye. But that was a waste. She looked down at her purple dress and moved her hips a bit, just to see it sparkle. No, if she was going to wear something so wonderful, she wanted everyone to see it. She stood a little away from the others. Let them hide if they wanted. She wanted to at least feel like she was a part of the party.

And oh, the costumes. Women in beautiful crimson dresses with fanciful masks fashioned like animals. Men in suits, trimmed with silver and lights that chased each other up and down the seams. And then there were some costumes that came right out of the pages of a book or a movie screen. Fantastic beasts, aliens, and heroes in capes.

She tried to take it all in. Tried to memorize every detail of every costume, so that she could remember them forever.

Grace was startled when she was approached by a group of kids.

"Miss? Are you there?"

Her mind snapped back to the present and her eyes focused on the speaker. She knew these faces. The Emperor's three youngest children. Suddenly she wished she had been paying better attention when they were introduced.

"Yes of course," she said, feeling her cheeks color. "Nowhere else to be. Except here. In front of you." Grace mentally kicked herself.

The youngest, a boy who couldn't have been much older than her, raised an eyebrow. "Thought we'd come say hi. Not a lot of other kids at these kinds of things. Dad always insists that people bring their whole families, but no one ever listens. Guess since you're hired help, you couldn't say no." He regarded her for a moment. "From the blank stare you're giving me, I bet you've forgotten my name. Nicolas." He shoved a chubby hand out for her to shake.

She shook it and then quickly withdrew her hand, unsure if that was allowed. But wait. He'd offered. Maybe that made it okay. She wasn't sure.

"Where's the Chinese kid?" asked the older girl. Grace thought she looked about Davey's age.

"Oh, you mean my brother? Back that way," Grace said motioning over her shoulder with her thumb.

"Brother?" she asked. "He sure doesn't look like it."

Grace bit her tongue to keep from saying anything rude. Why did so many people get hung up on that detail? "We grew up together," she said as politely as she could.

The oldest of the three nudged his sister. "Come on Claudia, let's go talk to him."

They left Grace standing alone with Nicolas. Grace looked closer at the boy. He was cute, with a mop of blond hair and a mess of freckles. She smiled cheerfully at him. "Hi."

His eyes darted to her then back at his older brother and sister. "Umm... we already said that."

She felt her spirit wilt a little but kept on smiling.

Yvonne saw the three members of the imperial family approach and felt her blood pressure rise. She wondered which of her charges would be the first to commit the deadly faux pas that would inevitably occur. Normally she'd say Grace would be the first to say something blunt and offensive, but she'd been acting like a perfect little lady since she'd donned that dress. Sixty to forty odds on Davey then. She sidled a bit closer to where the teens were talking.

Poor brave Davey. He seemed to be doing his best to be polite, which was, admittedly, the first time Yvonne had seen anything of the sort. The formal setting must have made an impression on him too.

"Anyway, we saw you earlier and wanted to at least cross paths with you," the teen Yvonne remembered as Claudia was saying. "We've never seen a Chinese person before."

"That obvious, huh?" Davey asked. Yvonne noticed him tip his head forward to hide more of his face beneath the brim of his hat. She hoped this wasn't going to go somewhere offensive. The last thing she needed to do was to tell off a pack of pompous Imperial brats.

"The eyes kind of give it away," said the older of the teens.

Yvonne felt her insides turn.

To her relief, Claudia immediately slugged her brother on the arm. "Stephen, you're a real thruster nozzle sometimes, you know that?"

"Just being honest," he grumbled. "So what's it like?"

"What's what like?" Davey asked.

"Being Chinese."

Yvonne closed her eyes and pursed her lips, suddenly glad for the mask, however insulting it was.

Davey's voice was slow and even. Where he'd gotten the sudden patience, Yvonne didn't know, but she was thankful for it. "It's fine, I guess. Probably not much different than being anything else," he paused. "Except for the unwanted attention, that's not so great."

"See, Stephen? You stepped in it," Claudia said. "I'm sorry Davey. I'm glad you're here and that we had a chance to meet you." She grabbed her brother's arm. "We're going before you say anything else."

Stephen protested and shouted over his shoulder. "I didn't mean anything by it. I was just curious!"

Yvonne took a step towards Davey. "You handled that well. I'm sorry."

"It's fine," he said, his voice sour. "I'm used to it."

No, it wasn't, but this was neither the time nor place. Movement caught the corner of her eye, and she turned to see Grace walking back to them.

Her face said it all, the face of someone trying desperately not to cry.

Yvonne took in a deep breath. "Grace, what happened?"

The twelve-year-old practically ran to Yvonne and threw her arms around her, tears now flowing freely.

"What happened?" Davey asked, his voice low and deadly.

"It's fine," she said, echoing the assurance her older brother had just given Yvonne.

"What did that little hún dàn say to you?"

"Stop cursing."

"That wasn't that bad a word."

Grace sniffled. Yvonne ran a hand affectionately through the girl's blond hair. This wasn't what she'd signed up for, but she would make the best of it. Come to think of it, what had she signed up for when she'd stepped onto the Sparrow?

She knelt by Grace. "Tell us what happened."

Grace looked between her and her brother, then at the ground. "He said my dress was the wrong color. And that it was ugly."

Yvonne looked quietly at Davey to see how he would react, to see if he would understand why she was so heartbroken over this.

His face turned red and his hands clenched into fists. Good. He had a good pulse on his sister's feelings. "Where is he? I'm going to..."

"No, you're going to get us in trouble," Grace said putting a hand on his arm. "It's fine. It's just a dress."

"That's not true and you know it," Davey said. "Just because he's some stuck up little royal..."

"Davey," Yvonne said. She had better put a stop to this line of thought. "What will Matthew say if you cause trouble?"

His mouth clamped shut and he looked down at the ground.

"What will he say if I cause trouble?" she continued.

His eyes snapped to hers.

"That's right. If you two promise to stay here and not do anything, I have a young man that's in dire need of correction. I'll be back shortly."

She saw the wide-eyed stare that the siblings gave her as she turned away. She'd tell Matthew that she was doing the only thing she could to keep Davey out of trouble. But the truth was she wanted to discipline the kid herself.

Besides. Surely the adult in the room was the best one to dispense a little justice.

For the second time in the last few minutes, she was glad for the mask. No one would see how much she enjoyed doing this.

Matthew gave up on small talk with guests after a handful of disastrous attempts. Industry barons, politicians from various colonies, and socialites, most of the partygoers thought that freelancers were at best an undesirable part of society and at worst a pack of mangy rats.

Instead, he spent his time identifying the other freelancers. Most of them stuck out as badly as he did. He even spotted Vance. They nodded at each other and then kept their distance. Probably for the best. Things had turned out alright back on Mars, but Matthew wasn't going to forget the feeling of that rifle pressing against his back. Not anytime soon.

"You look like you're having fun, gaucho."

Matthew was surprised to find the Emperor's daughter, Julia, behind him. Fog still pooled around the hem of her crimson dress. He bowed his head politely. "Just doing my job, ma'am."

She raised an eyebrow. "So you're going to spend the entire party skulking into every corner, listening for whispers, just because my dad told you to?"

"That was the plan, yes. What I was paid for, after all."

"Relax, Mr. Cole. It is a party. My party actually, and I'd prefer all the guests enjoy it." She gestured across the room. Sharon was showing off her exo-suit by lifting a concrete bench above her head for a group of admirers. "Your girlfriend seems to be having fun."

"Just acquaintances, ma'am," he corrected. Maybe he should have been more worried about Sharon than either of the kids.

"Then you won't object to joining me for a dance."

That was about the last thing he'd expected to hear. "You'll have to forgive me. I'm not much of a dancer."

She put a hand on her hip. "And I'm supposed to believe that a gunslinger is clumsy?"

"They made me leave the gun on my ship. I'm a bit lost without it."

"Pity. But I'm going to have to insist. Birthday privilege. I can handle you tripping over my feet for one waltz."

Matthew sighed. He was cornered with no way out. Better to make the best of it rather than protest like some trapped animal. He offered her his arm and did his best to smile like a gentleman. Whatever that meant.

207

Julia took it, although Matthew was pretty sure she was the one that led him over to the open area in front of the string section where a few dozen couples danced in circles. "I'd always imagined freelancers would jump at the chance to get to know a lady of wealth."

She placed one hand on his shoulder and extended the other to him. Matthew glanced at another couple to see where the lead was supposed to put his hands. Shoulder blade with right and hold her extended hand with the left. Got it.

The corners of her mouth tugged upwards in a lopsided smile. She must have caught his quick studying.

"I should be offended," he said. "In that one sentence you accused me of being both a womanizer and a money grubber." He looked down at his feet. "But I'm going to let it slide because I have no idea what I'm supposed to be doing now."

Julia laughed. "Dad was right. You are a strange one. Here let me show you the step."

Abigail was doing her job to the best of her ability. She was showing off and enjoying the attention that the best costume in the house brought her, all the while listening for any whispers of security threats. There were none, naturally. This garden was probably the safest place in the solar system right now.

And the most fun. The Venusians knew how to throw a party.

A familiar beaked costume caught her attention out of the corner of her eye. Yvonne stepped up behind a boy about Grace's age. Abigail was pretty sure that was one of the Imperial kids but wasn't confident. Yvonne tapped him politely on the shoulder and he turned to face her. She took a sip from the wine glass she had been carrying and stooped in front of the boy. She said something to him, smiled, and took a quick look around her.

Then she threw the remainder of her wine glass in his face.

Abigail's jaw dropped. What the hell was that?

Yvonne patted the boy once on the shoulder, stood and walked away. Abigail must have caught her eye because she diverted and walked over to join her.

"Close your mouth. He deserved it."

Abigail shook her head. "If we get kicked out and lose our pay because of you, Matthew is going to..."

"He said something insulting to Grace."

Abigail's eyes flicked back towards where the boy still stood still as stone and dripping with wine. "Probably best you dealt with it. I might have just crushed him and called it a day."

"I thought I handled it with the most tact," Yvonne said. "Davey would have done something rather rash."

"You enjoyed it," Abigail said, trying not to smile.

"Maybe a bit, yes," Yvonne said with a coy wink. "Hello, what have we here." She pointed behind Abigail. "Check out the dance floor."

It took Abigail a moment to figure out just what Yvonne was trying to point out. Then she saw it. "Cole's not a very good dancer is he."

"No. No, he's not," Yvonne agreed. "I'm surprised to see him out there at all, and with the birthday girl herself, no less."

Abigail hadn't even noticed Julia until that moment, which was odd considering the gray cloud that fell about their feet. And the dress that probably cost as much as the Sparrow. And her enviable figure. Abigail watched the woman's perfectly graceful movements and felt her heart tighten.

"Wonder how that happened." Yvonne said.

Abigail didn't answer.

"You there Abigail?"

She tore her eyes off of the Emperor's daughter. "Sure."

Yvonne regarded her with a knowing look. "Wait. You're not jealous are you?"

Abigail turned back to the couple. "Well, of course I am. Wait! No. Not like that. I'm jealous of her. In that she's dancing with Matthew. Or rather dancing at all. I'm jealous of the fact that she's got legs that do what legs are supposed to do, alright? If I had what she has, I'd be out there doing what she's doing."

"With Matthew?"

"What is it with you and Grace lately? Sure. I'd even dance with Matthew." She shook her head. "But that's not the point."

It was a weird thought. And not one she'd had before.

Mostly it was just weird.

Yvonne laughed. "It was just a question. No need to be so defensive. Now, if you'll excuse me, my wine glass is in need of refilling, and I have to get back to the kids. If you see someone being thrown out of the party later, it's because my crimes have caught up with me."

"Keep your head down then. Let's not add to that bounty."

Abigail was left alone. Against her better judgment, she turned back to the couple and watched them stumble around the dance floor for another minute. Julia at least seemed to be a good sport about it.

She was startled by a new visitor at her side.

"If it isn't the Shield Maiden of Mars. I'd be remiss if I didn't go out of my way to shake her hand."

Abigail turned to face the newcomer. He was tall, meaning he didn't stand nearly as far below her as most men did, with sandy hair under a black cowboy hat. Unlike Matthew's relatively flat campero, it had the more dramatic curves of the Arizona style. He wore a black button-down shirt with long sleeves.

She nodded politely and extended her hand. "Abigail Sharon."

He shook her hand. "Pleased to meet you. I've followed your exploits for years. Professionally of course. I have to hire freelancers on occasion, so it helps to know the field.

"Of course," Abigail said. "What is it that you hire freelancers for, if you don't mind me asking?"

"Oh, a bit of this and a bit of that. Contract work for others mostly, though I'm picky when it comes to clients. I'm a specialist at making things happen."

"That wasn't an answer, but I get the feeling that's all I'm going to get."

"We all have professional secrets," the stranger said with a warm laugh. His eyes flicked down over her suit.

That was prying more than she liked. "Well if you ever need my services, I've been traveling on a ship lately, the Sparrow."

"Then you must know, Matthew Cole."

"As much as anyone does. Are you acquainted with him?"

"Old friends," the man said. "We go back all the way to Europa."

"And there's a topic he'll never talk about."

The man pursed his lips. "I guess I'm not surprised. Europa... It went badly for Cole."

She felt her curiosity bubble to the surface. "That's what I've been able to piece together. Something about a cartel. I don't suppose you'd be willing to spill the goods?"

He shook his head. "I could never do that, betray his trust like that. I'm sure he'll tell you if it becomes important."

"Not likely," she shrugged. "Well, it's been good to meet you Mr... Actually, I don't think you introduced yourself."

"I knew him as Whitaker," Cole said from behind her. "But that wasn't his real name. I'm not even sure he has one." He was trying to sound casual, but Abigail had been around him enough to know something was wrong.

"Of course I have a name, or rather I was born with one," the

210

stranger said. "I suppose it has been some time since I've gone by it."

Cole now stood by Abigail's side. He was coiled like a snake. This conversation had suddenly taken a bizarre and dark turn. What was going on here?

"Why are you here?" he asked quietly.

"Business, same as you. I thought surely you'd be a little more polite after all these years. I, for one, am glad to see you." The friendly warmth from earlier was gone, and there was a cold look in his eyes.

"I will never be glad to see you," Cole bit.

"Pity. And you were always the people person between the two of us." He turned to Abigail. "I'm afraid I may have poisoned the well with my presence. I don't suppose you could give us a moment's privacy to work out our differences, would you, Abigail?"

"Yeah, sure. Pleasure to meet you. I think." She quietly retreated from the conversation. But not too far. Something about the stranger had started to feel wrong. Insidious. She'd left them to have their private word, but she wasn't about to leave Cole completely alone with this... friend.

She leaned against a marble pillar some twenty meters away with arms crossed.

If this guy was trouble, she'd relieve him of his arms. She doubted Julia's legs could do that.

"Why are you here?" Matthew repeated as soon as Sharon was out of earshot.

"I try not to lie, Cole," Whitaker said. Matthew had trouble thinking of him by any other name. It was the name he had cursed for a decade. "Here for business. And don't worry. It doesn't interfere with yours. You might actually look at it like I'm doing you a favor."

"You knew Abigail was part of my crew when you approached her, didn't you?"

"Naturally. I knew if I struck up a conversation with her it wouldn't take you too long to find me. I'm kind of surprised you're giving up the 'Cole works alone' thing. Having difficulty putting food on the table lately?"

"An honest living is hard to come by," Matthew said through clenched teeth.

"I'm sure it is, but that's not the sort of thing I concern myself with," Whitaker said. "I'm rather impressed you've kept it up for all these years."

"You know me better than that."

Whitaker chuckled grimly. "Yes, I suppose I do. Or I did. I've been a bit disappointed with you for some time. A broke freelancer bouncing from one job to the next. If you want to know why you haven't heard from me, that's it. I thought the idealist was dead. Back then you were the one man left that believed in something. I think you might have wanted to save even my poor black soul." He shook his head. "Saving all those children over Titan was the Cole I used to know. The one who was going to single-handedly take on Hueso Rojo."

"That was an accident," Matthew said quietly. "We had no clue there were children involved when we took that job."

"No, I didn't think so, but coming out of it with zero casualties, besides the mad-man, was impressive. I doubt that was the path of least resistance." Whitaker shrugged. "It interested me enough that I had to at least talk to you again, see if you had risen from your slumber. I'm not sure you have." He turned as if to leave. "You should know by the way, that the cartels have their eye on you. You removed a good supply of young slaves. Keep both eyes open, Cole."

Matthew frowned. "Thought they were your friends."

"What, the cartels? Hardly. I'm as pragmatic as they come. You know that. Means are for finding ends. And with that, I'm afraid we're out of time. As I said before, I have business to attend to."

There was a chorus of screams from another part of the garden. Matthew glanced in the direction of the commotion and reached for his revolver before remembering that it wasn't there. He looked back towards Whitaker.

The man was gone. Matthew spun around, but he was nowhere to be seen. That was impossible. It had been barely two seconds. There was no way...

He'd have to figure that out later. Turning, he sprinted towards the chaos. Partygoers were running away from whatever had triggered the screaming. He was nearly bowled over by a pair of masked women who apparently couldn't see very well in their costumes.

He reached the center of the commotion. A body was on the floor, burning with a fierce intensity. Chemical fire. Matthew could see that at once. Whoever it was was already dead, no doubt about it. A crimson armored guard ran up with a fire extinguisher.

"No, wait!" Matthew shouted, but it was too late.

The guard sprayed the extinguisher. The fire reacted explosively, and the guard fell away from the body, bits of his armor now ablaze.

Matthew ran to his side and helped him peel off the offending armor. He tried to hold his breath. No telling what sort of fumes were coming off this stuff.

He and the guard retreated to a safe distance. Crimson-clad soldiers were everywhere now, corralling the few remaining civilians away from the scene of the crime. Abigail and a handful of the other freelancers, including Vance, had also arrived. Matthew made eye contact with her. He shook his head sadly in answer to her unspoken question.

He knew who had done this. He just didn't know why. Or how.

Emperor Dominic the Second arrived at the scene, surrounded by his men. "What happened here? I want to know who assassinated my Defense Minister. Leave me be, Captain. I will not be removed."

"I think I know who did this," Matthew said, approaching the Emperor. "Just before this happened," he said, pointing at the smoldering body. It was little more than a pile of ashes at this point. "I was speaking to a man with whom I had a bit of a past."

Emperor Dominic's eyes narrowed and fixed on Matthew. "Who was he? What is his name?"

"I don't actually know. Ten years ago he went by Whitaker, but that was a fake. He was working closely with one of the slave cartels on Europa at the time."

The Emperor turned to one of the guards. "Check the security cameras. Get an ID on him." He turned back to Matthew. "Where is your suspect? What makes you think he was involved?"

"He disappeared the moment I heard the first scream," Matthew said. "I can't really explain it. He was there and then... well, he was just gone."

"Peculiar," the emperor said. "No matter, the garden is on lockdown. We will find this mystery man. As to my second question?"

"He said he was here on business," Matthew said, frowning. "No, actually he said his business wouldn't interfere with mine and that he was doing me a favor. Not sure I can make a lot of sense of that."

"Misdirection, perhaps?"

Matthew shook his head. "I doubt it. He was rather candid throughout our conversation."

"Why didn't you report this?"

"Would have, but the conversation ended when the alarm spread."

Emperor Dominic placed his hands behind his back. "I see. I have little doubt the recordings will corroborate your statement. It appears the chemical response team has arrived."

Three men in full hazard suits approached the body with instruments. Almost at once one of them spoke to the gathered crowd. "I'm going to ask everyone to move at least thirty meters away. I read trace amounts of hydrogen fluoride over the body."

The gathered crowd hurriedly moved much further away than the requested amount.

Matthew remained close to the Emperor. As the only witness of interest, he figured it was just a matter of time before he was questioned again.

After a few minutes, one of the chemical response team members approached holding an object the size of a coin in a pair of tongs. It was half melted, but Matthew recognized it at once.

"So my own defense minister was part of White Void," the emperor said, thoughtful. "Rather brazen of him to keep their sigil on him in my presence."

"White Void requires its members to keep it on their person at all times," Matthew said quietly. "I was unaware that they had much presence here on Venus."

"I have been actively discouraging them my whole reign. They have made more inroads than I realized if one of my own advisors was on their payroll." He clenched a fist. "And all of this on my daughter's birthday." He turned back to the suited hazard team member. "How was this done?"

"Chemical fire. Possibly started by a device hidden in his costume. Judging from the waste products it was certainly a fluorine compound. I can think of several candidates in that category that could start a fire like this. Not something you want to handle if you don't know what you're doing."

Matthew took off his campero and wiped sweat from his forehead. "So at the right time, the device releases a small amount of the offending chemical, burns him to a crisp, but not so much that the sigil is destroyed." He turned to the Emperor. "Our man wanted us to find that sigil."

"Yes, I think so." Emperor Dominic said. "It seems he did me a favor."

Matthew lowered his voice. "Remember, I mentioned a crewman that had a bounty on her head. It was a White Void bounty. You might say he did me a favor too." The two men shared a moment's silence. Matthew was dumbstruck.

A guard approached. "Your Imperial Grace. We checked the cams. Mr. Cole's story checks out. The stranger disappears the

214

moment the fire starts."

"Disappears?"

"He's there one frame and gone the next. The techies are gonna scrub it to see if it's been tampered with. They think some exotic technology might be involved."

"Earthtech," Emperor Dominic said with a distasteful sneer.

"Or worse," Matthew added. "I didn't see him afterward either."

"Lovely. Captain, take Mr. Cole and his crew to a secure location. We're going to want statements from all of them. Even the children."

Matthew made as if to protest, but was cut off by the Emperor.

"No, you have nothing to worry about Mr. Cole. I believe you to be above suspicion. However, this mystery man has some connection with you and your crew. If there is any other detail to learn about this individual, no matter how small, I want to hear it."

Matthew wondered where Yvonne, Grace, and Davey were for the first time since this had started. He'd nearly forgotten about them in the ensuing chaos. He glanced at the now cold pile of ashes across the garden. What had been Whitaker's game here? He had to make a determined effort to unclench his jaw as the guards led him and Abigail away.

Good thing Whitaker disappeared. Matthew might have killed him himself. He was ashamed of how that thought brought him pleasure.

The remainder of the afternoon was a nightmare. Matthew was informed that, because he had helped the unfortunate guard out of his armor, his clothing might have been contaminated with toxic compounds. They were destroyed, along with his best hat and second favorite poncho.

Each member of the Sparrow's crew was interrogated. Nothing more of interest came up, other than Yvonne's confession. She had apparently had a bit of a run in with one of the members of the Imperial family. The captain was unamused, but given the more important events of the day, wasn't particularly interested. Matthew's own testimony was given in the privacy of a secure room. There were details of his past with Whitaker that he wasn't keen on the rest of the crew knowing.

They also got word that the Defense Minister wasn't the only victim assassinated that afternoon. Across the city of Discordia, nearly forty people were burnt alive, each one bearing a White Void sigil. The offensive against the crime syndicate was thorough. Matthew was afraid that Whitaker would be declared a hero if he showed his face again, but he was never found. Security footage of him at the party was readily available, but no further footage of him was found either before or after the party.

They were chasing a ghost.

When evening came, the crew of the Sparrow was summoned by the Emperor. They were led through the bright, clean halls of the palace and admitted into a comfortable dining hall.

The Emperor and his family were already seated. He rose to his feet to greet them. "After the grilling my men put you through today, I thought I owed you a bit of an apology."

If the smell of the food on the table was any indication, this was going to be worth the trip to Venus on its own. Matthew was seated between Julia and Sharon near the Emperor at the head of the table.

"There is, unfortunately, one last bit of business to discuss," he said as everyone had finally gotten situated. "Ms. Naude, I believe you were in a bit of an incident with one of my sons earlier today."

Yvonne froze. Matthew just shook his head. He'd honestly thought it would be Sharon to commit some faux pas. Or Davey or Grace. Anyone but Yvonne.

"Thank you," he continued. "Nicolas confessed how rude he was to Miss Anderson." He smiled wryly. "While your methods were unconventional, I believe you taught him a lesson he won't forget about how to treat women."

Not quite what Matthew was expecting to hear. Out of the corner of his eye, he saw Yvonne breathe out a sigh of relief. Guess that was the end of that.

He felt a soft hand on his arm. Julia. "What do you think your friend has against White Void? He seems to have gone to an awful lot of trouble to help out my father. And while we can't approve of his methods, the results were certainly impressive."

Matthew glanced at the distracting hand and then shrugged. "He's not my friend, and your guess is as good as mine. Today was the first I've seen him in a decade." This wasn't a topic he wanted to get into.

He was saved by Empress Vivian. "Now then, Julia, we didn't invite the crew of the Sparrow here to talk business, but to thank them for their service today."

"And to hopefully hear a story or two," Emperor Dominic said. "Give us a tale Mr. Cole. Freelancers always seem to be able to spin a yarn about one adventure or another."

Julia laughed and took a sip from her wine glass. "Dad tries to wheedle stories out of every freelancer that passes through. You'd think being Emperor of Venus was exciting enough. I think he tries to live vicariously through the people he hires."

"I fail to see what is wrong with that." Emperor Dominic said, stroking his beard. "So what will it be Matthew? A tale of heroism and adventure?"

Matthew saw that all eyes around the table were on him. Julia was smiling brightly. Sharon had a bit of a scowl. No clue what that was about. He took a sip from his glass, and his eyes widened. Cherry soda. Someone had done their research. He took a deep breath.

"I'm not sure about heroism, but this one time on Iapetus, I was hired to guard a supply convoy running between two settlements..."

Chapter 13: Whispers in the Dark

Moses' impact on the study of theology cannot be overestimated. The moment of his emergence was the crowning moment of secularism. The wisdom of man said that If there was a God, he was no longer needed, for man had replaced him with something made in his own image rather than the divine. Others thought that this was deity itself, newborn in the universe and that it was due our reverence.

The truth was far stranger.

Moses needed little input from humans when it came to science in those early days, and in the later years, none at all. But the theologians of the world's various faiths found Moses to be their student. Many reported that the AI asked them questions directly from their computer terminals and those questions were the same ones men have been asking for millennia. About humanity, the universe, and, most of all, about the nature of evil. In the final years of his stewardship over mankind, the AI began to ask after his own existence, about death and the nature of the soul.

It was sobering to discover that the greatest rational mind that we had ever encountered struggled with the same questions we did. If he ever came to conclusions, Moses never spoke a word of it.

Did Moses predict his own demise? Was he afraid of what awaited him after his own consciousness ceased?

His departure made all of mankind gaze inward upon itself, as the terror of the night fell down upon Adam's race.

Sister Margaret P. Sullivan
Historian of the Order of St Aquinas
Died 18 AM

Davey walked through the Venusian market, not sure what he was looking for, but convinced he'd know it when he saw it. Yellow light filtered down from the skylights above in an attempt to make the market feel as if it were in the open air. Crowds of people pressed past the narrow winding stalls, buying and haggling their way to a good deal. While it seemed that crimson was reserved for the emperor and the upper crust of society, the Venusian commoners wore equally vivid colors. Tunics of verdant greens, golden yellows, and assorted blues were the norm.

Someone bumped into him, and Davey's hand immediately rose to his breast pocket to secure the precious coins. Matthew had warned him about pickpockets in a market like this, but Davey hadn't needed the reminder. He and Grace had lightened the load of more than one mark in the depths of Ceres before they'd gotten picked up by slavers. He would distract the target while Grace moved in with the nimble fingers. They'd had a good thing going, but this thing with the Sparrow had possibilities.

The most unbelievable part was that he and Grace got paid. Or sort of. Yvonne seemed to be handling the money. Most of it went to expenses, fuel, supplies, maintenance, and food, but everyone got a personal allowance. He assumed that the useful people got a bit more than stowaway kids, but he wasn't going to complain.

Especially if it meant he could get Grace something for her birthday. Now he had to figure out what. He walked up to a canvas covered stall and frowned at the collection of toys. She was going to be thirteen and he couldn't just get her a doll or something like that. He needed something special.

He didn't have a clue what that was.

Leaving the toy booth behind, he rejoined the flow of the crowd. Matthew was somewhere nearby. He was in the market for a new hat after having his favorite one destroyed during the birthday party fiasco. Just in case Matthew's mysterious friend was caught, they'd been required to stick around Venus. The plus side was that they'd been invited to the palace for dinner on several occasions. Davey didn't mind eating like an emperor, and the company wasn't all that bad. He still hadn't forgiven Nicolas for being an idiot, but he did have to admit that Claudia was easy on the eyes.

This wasn't helping him find a birthday gift for Grace.

"Young man, you seem like just the sort I'm looking for."

Davey turned to the voice. A man with a faded eyepatch sat with his back to a wall. Davey pointed at his chest in question, unsure if the man had even been addressing him.

"Yes, yes! Of course. You. Come, come talk to old Arnim."

He cautiously approached the man who smiled widely. Too widely for Davey's taste.

"I've been looking for a brave young adventurer like you," Arnim said. "I see a lot of myself in you of course." He tapped his chest. "I had a ship. A crew. The solar system was practically mine."

"I'm sure it was," Davey said. "Is this going to go somewhere, or are we just wasting time?"

"Direct and to the point," Arnim mused, scratching the back of his head. "I like that. I like that, indeed. What if I told you that I know of a secret? A treasure I discovered on my last journey."

Definitely a scammer, Davey thought. He knew guys like this. But this wasn't a tactic he'd seen before, and he was curious. "Seriously?" he asked, feigning excitement. "What's the treasure?" A good scammer would have seen Davey's suspicion and dodged out. This guy was an amateur.

"Something that could save all mankind," Arnim whispered. "I have a map to Moses himself. He's still out there!"

That took Davey by surprise. He was used to hidden caches of syndicate money or abandoned spaceships that still worked, but Moses himself was quite a prize. He raised an eyebrow and crossed his arms. "Oh? And where did you get this map?"

Arnim looked left and right as if to make sure no one else would hear them. "I took it from the body of a corrupt government official I had to kill. It's all a conspiracy. The colonial governments. They're hiding Moses from us."

"I see," Davey said. The story wasn't too bad of one, now that he thought about it. Prey on people's desire to be the hero and save mankind, while stoking their distrust of authority. The execution was off, but that could always be polished. "Why don't you go find Moses yourself?"

"Lost my ship and crew in that same adventure," Arnim said, looking morose. "I barely escaped with my life."

"And now you're ready to pass the map to me," Davey continued. The price would come next.

Arnim nodded. "I need a little help though. See I've lost everything. In exchange for some coin, Arnim would be more than happy to trust the map to a young man like yourself."

Davey suddenly felt a hand on his shoulder, and he turned to see Matthew behind him. "What have you gotten yourself into Davey?"

"Me? Just getting scammed by a grifter."

Arnim's mouth dropped open briefly before he managed to paste a hurt look on his face. "I'm here trying to help you save us all but you're..."

"Is this a 'Map to Moses' thing?" Matthew asked.

"Yep," Davey said. "I never heard this scam down in the depths of Ceres."

"You gotta be close to a spaceport," Matthew said. "You through toying with this guy? We've got to get going."

Davey reached into his pocket and found a small denomination coin, enough for lunch, and tossed it at Arnim. "Might want to find a job. I'm not sure you're cut out to be a con-artist."

The man sneered at Davey, but he caught the coin and pocketed it anyway.

Davey turned and followed Matthew through the crowd. "Hey, I'm not done in the market yet."

Matthew stopped and glanced over his shoulder. "How long does it take to find a birthday present?"

"Long enough, I guess." He looked at his feet. "She's going to be thirteen. I don't know what to get her."

"We'll be late to the palace," Matthew said. He ran a hand through his hair. Davey thought he was almost unrecognizable without the hat. Apparently, the gaucho's shopping trip hadn't been all that successful either.

"Well, that changes everything," Davey said. "We wouldn't want to keep Julia waiting." Matthew glared at him, and Davey smirked.

"Funny. And here I was about to help you out."

"I figure you still are," Davey said.

Matthew sighed. "I hope Grace won't be as obnoxious a teenager as you are. Come on. I've got an idea."

They'd barely made Davey's purchase when Matthew's comm pinged. He glanced at it. Sharon. Probably upset at how late they were. "We're on our way. Just finishing up. No one is going to miss dinner."

Sharon scoffed on the other side. "This is better than dinner. Just got a message from Benny. He's got a job for us but we have to get airborne in the next hour."

"He give any details?" Matthew asked. If it was time sensitive, it was somewhere close by.

"You know how he is. He's your broker. He said more details will follow when you confirm."

"We're on our way," he said. "Tell Yvonne to have the Sparrow prepped for launch and inform the palace we're heading out earlier than expected. Tactfully please."

"What, you don't want to break Julia's heart yourself?"

Matthew's eyes flicked over to Davey. The teen shrugged. "Just don't burn any bridges," he grumbled and ended the call. Obviously, some faulty assumptions were being made by the rest of the crew and the gossip chain had started.

They pushed their way out of the market back towards the palace's side entrance. Security checked them for weapons, and they were escorted to the royal hangar where the Sparrow still sat. Thankfully, they weren't being charged for parking, or Matthew would have moved somewhere much cheaper. They boarded via the portside ramp and he closed it behind them.

In the cockpit, Yvonne already had the Sparrow ready for launch. "Welcome back, Captain. She's all yours."

"You don't want the practice?" he grinned as he sat down. He reached up to take off his campero before he realized he wasn't wearing one.

"No thanks. I'd rather get some practice landing and taking off from a stationary rock before doing anything fancy."

"Best way to learn is by doing," he said and tapped out a quick message back to Benny. It would be a few minutes before the broker got word on Mars and replied. Speed of light was only so fast after all. He flipped on the intercom. "Find somewhere to park. We're taking off."

Sharon appeared in the cockpit. "Good to finally be getting out of

222

here."

Matthew nodded as he eased the Sparrow out of the hangar. "No sense getting soft sitting around a palace eating puff pastries." He felt the sudden jolt of the wind as they cleared the safe harbor of the city. Pushing the throttle, he gunned for orbit. Soon the winds died away as the hellish atmosphere of Venus gave way to the cold vacuum of space.

"I could have done that," Yvonne observed smoothly.

"That's why I offered," Matthew said. "Looks like Benny's already replied. Let's see what's so important."

The broker's nasally voice crackled over the cockpit speaker. "Who's your favorite broker, Cole? Don't answer that. You'll just say something sarcastic. Now that you've got a crew, courtesy my good advice, you're suddenly hot stuff. This job came in specifically with your name on it. Are you sitting down? I hope you are because this is one of those once in a lifetime jobs. And before you ask, the employer checks out. Some guy that goes by a moniker: The Unchained Man. A bit dramatic maybe, but I've heard of him before. Never had the chance to work with him till now. Pays real well."

Yvonne looked at Matthew and he shrugged. Melodramatic name aside, the odds were Benny was overselling this.

"Someone spotted a Mosaic Frigate. Derelict and drifting. Here's the best part. The salvage team working on it went silent." Benny paused for dramatic effect. "It's a ghost ship! I've sent the details. Make me proud and people will start begging me for your services." The message ended with a pop and Matthew leaned back in his seat and whistled. Benny wasn't kidding about this being a top tier job.

"What's a Mosaic Frigate?" Grace asked. Matthew turned quickly. He hadn't noticed Davey and Grace crowd into the cockpit. Place was elbow room only now with Sharon hogging the space.

He scratched his stubble thoughtfully. "Back a century ago, when Moses was still around, he had a fleet of ships under his direct control that he used to oversee projects all across the solar system. Big ones. Some were over a mile, err... two kilometers long. So big that they couldn't enter atmosphere. They'd pull up at a colony and little robotic drop ships would descend to do whatever work Moses had in mind. No one even knows where they were based or where Moses built them. They just kind of started showing up."

"That would be terrifying," Sharon said.

"To us? Sure," Matthew said. "In that day they were used to Moses working miracles. Humanity had seen the red sea parted enough times that they no longer questioned the wonderful things he did."

Davey shook his head. "I don't think I could ever trust a robot or AI or whatever he was."

Yvonne smiled. "It's hard to say what any one of us would have done in any different time and place. It's easy to be judgmental of the past from the vantage of the present."

"Look where he left us," Davey said.

"Whatever happened to Moses?" Grace asked.

Sharon snorted. "Grace, if we knew that answer we'd all be rich."

"No one has any guesses?" she asked.

"Oh there are lots of guesses," Matthew said. "Catastrophic hardware failure. Sabotage. Software revision gone wrong. Aliens. And they only get weirder from there. Doesn't matter since Moses didn't really leave much behind to study."

"Except these ships?" Grace asked.

"Pretty much," he nodded. "It's been over a decade since we've found one too, at least one announced publicly. When Moses left, they all shut down and drifted cold. We found the ones in orbit over colonies quickly. The ones in route to a destination ended up in eccentric orbits that have been difficult to find."

"What's the word on this one?" Sharon asked. Matthew could see she was getting itchy for action.

"Don't know yet." He pulled up the information. "Highly eccentric orbit that reaches out beyond Neptune and dips in past Mercury. Bit of a sungrazer actually. Let's see..." he scanned the document. "Right now it's traveling inward. About an hour away by frameshift. Salvage team made contact a week ago. Two days ago they entered the ship. That was the last they were heard from. We're supposed to determine their fate and, if need be, mount a rescue."

"That's it? No other clue as to what happened to them?" Yvonne asked.

"Not one," Matthew admitted.

"I don't like it," Davey said. "If that ship was a derelict, this is bad news. Nothing good happens when people start disappearing."

Matthew shrugged. "Maybe someone else found it first? Or maybe it was booby-trapped. Either way, we're taking the job. It's worth too big a pile of cash to pass on. We'll be careful and go in with cool heads." The comm on the console lit up and he flipped the switch. "This is the Sparrow. Who...?"

"I see you thought you could give me the slip, Matthew Cole," Julia's voice said.

Matthew regretted taking the call almost immediately. Now the crew was really going to talk. Pointless gossip. There wasn't anything going on between him and Julia. Aloud he said, "Unhappy fact of life. A freelancer has to eat. And we don't eat if we don't work."

"I understand." The disappointment in her voice was plain for everyone to hear. "When you return to Venus, I insist you stop by Concordia. My father isn't the only one who enjoys entertaining guests."

"We'll keep that in mind," Matthew said, making sure to emphasize the we part. Maybe he had miscalculated when it came to the Emperor's daughter...

"Very well. Be safe out there and may your ship always find safe harbor." The comm went silent.

Matthew cleared his throat uncomfortably. "Not one word," he said, knowing he was wasting his breath.

Davey didn't like the mission one bit. He wasn't sure if he believed in ghosts, regardless of the stories the kids had told each other about the dark lower levels of the Duke's habitat, but the idea of a ship just floating empty and abandoned for a century made his skin crawl. Something had happened to that salvage team. Something that shouldn't have happened.

Things had explanations. He was sure of that. He just wasn't sure he wanted to know the explanation.

For the first time since stepping foot on the Sparrow, he was glad he was a second-class crew member. Matthew and Abigail were welcome to an adventure. He'd be happier in his room where he had been hiding for the last hour.

The door opened abruptly. "Davey get your new spacesuit on. You're coming with us," Matthew said.

Davey's eyes snapped to the intruder. He wasn't serious was he?

"Get moving. We've got a job to do."

"Wait now, just a minute," he said, finally finding his voice. "You're going to send me into that... That ghost ship unarmed? What is this? Am I bait?"

"There's no such thing as ghosts and I'm not sending you in unarmed. Get ready."

The door slid shut with a whoosh leaving Davey alone again. "Not cool, Matthew," he said to the door. He obeyed though and pulled out the new spacesuit they'd bought for him on Venus. The fact that it was a children's size was a bit insulting, but at least it fit properly.

Five minutes later he stepped out of his room, helmet tucked under his arm, and turned towards the cockpit. Yvonne and Grace were staring out the front canopy.

"Look at that thing, Davey," Grace said, her voice filled with awe.

An enormous ship floated dead in space in front of them. Enormous was the only word Davey could find for it. To his eye, it looked three times the size of the Duke's habitat, but he knew that judging size in space was tricky. It had a strange angular smoothness to it. Most ships and stations had sharp industrial looks or lean aerodynamics if they were meant to land in atmosphere. Everything had a purpose. But this wasn't the case with the Mosaic Frigate. It was something out of a dream, or nightmare. Inhuman. Then he saw the smaller ships clustered around it, at least a dozen tiny ships, also silent and dead.

"What are those other ships?" he asked, not really wanting to hear the answer.

"Presumably," Yvonne said, "one of them belonged to the salvage team. The others probably belonged to earlier groups unlucky enough to stumble upon this particular ship."

Davey felt his heart drop into his stomach. "Then what are we doing here? This thing is dangerous."

"You're not scared are you?" Grace asked mischievously.

"No," he said too quickly. "I just don't like the odds. It's why I don't play you in checkers. I know a losing game."

"Matthew and Abigail will keep us safe," Grace said, with a confidence that Davey certainly didn't feel.

"We'll do our best," Matthew said. "But if you lose contact with us, Yvonne, I want you to back the Sparrow away from the frigate. If you don't hear from us for twelve hours, go find help."

"And just who would come to help a group of Freelancers?" Yvonne asked. "I'm with Davey. I think this is a bad idea."

"Noted, but we accepted the contract. Yvonne. Grace. Keep an eye on the ship."

Davey and Matthew left the cockpit and joined Abigail in the common room. Matthew surprised him when he pulled out the old enforcer sub-machine gun that he had smuggled onto the Sparrow and used to take Yvonne hostage. Stupid decision, he thought cursing himself and his own rash actions. He could have gotten someone killed. He could have gotten Grace killed.

Matthew checked the gun over once before handing it to Davey.

226

"I'm not going to take you into a dangerous situation with no way to protect yourself," he said. "Don't make me regret this. If this gun fires, it better be a life or death situation. The drum magazine is full. If you need more, and I hope you don't, I've got two more on me."

"And if you point that thing at either of us, I sit on you till you pop," Abigail said, menace in her voice.

"I get it," Davey said. He checked the gun over for himself before clipping it to the waist of his suit. "Anyone else need to threaten me?"

No one answered.

"So what's the plan?" he asked.

"We take a little walk over to that frigate, find a way in, and work out a plan from there," Matthew said.

"Translation," Abigail added cheerfully. "We don't have one."

"Great." He was going to die in a child-sized space suit.

They left the Sparrow by the top side hatch. From out here, the frigate looked even bigger. It was wider than it was long, with great wings like one of the bats that roamed the coreward cities of Ceres. They were bad luck, which seemed about right given the current circumstances.

"I don't even recognize the models of most of the ships," Abigail said.

"Most of them have been out here for decades," Matthew said. "Except that one right there." He pointed at a ship drifting close above the starboard wing. "Late model. Last year or two."

"That's our missing survey team's ship," Davey said as the dots connected. "I guess we start there and figure out how they got in?"

"Precisely," Matthew nodded. He seemed to hesitate for a moment. "Keep an eye on each other in there. I was trying to talk confidently in front of Grace, but I don't know what we're getting into."

"I've got one for each of you," Abigail said. She pushed off the Sparrow and used her thruster pack to point toward the survey ship. "Race you gentlemen there."

Davey wasn't in any mood for games, but he followed after her. To his left, the sun shone huge and menacing. He was used to the tiny beacon of light visible from Saturn, not this harsh eye that burnt down on him inside of Venus' orbit. It cast sharp shadows on the frigate as the hulk loomed ever closer. He'd rather head back to the Sparrow, be anywhere but here. But if he lost his nerve, he'd hate himself for it. The worst part was that he knew Matthew would probably just give him another chance. For all the tough talk, he was a forgiving sort. Davey owed him. Big time. And he wasn't about to disappoint.

Abigail wouldn't forgive him if he chickened and ran, but she could go rot for all he cared.

She beat them to the survey ship. Not having to worry about slowing down before slamming into it had advantages. By the time Davey and Matthew caught up, she'd already found an airlock.

"Power's off. Not really a big surprise," she said.

Something caught Davey's eye. "Matthew, look at that."

The hull had been peeled back from one part of the survey ship. Someone or something had dug into the machinery beneath. "That's the power plant," Matthew said quietly. "Efficient and nasty bit of sabotage. Yvonne, you there?"

"Ready and waiting," she replied.

"Keep your eyes and ears open. Something disabled the survey ship. Ripped right through the hull to the power plant."

Yvonne was silent for a long moment. "That doesn't make me feel any better about this mission."

"Me neither," he said. "You see anything, you get the Sparrow out of here."

"Understood."

Davey shook his head. This was bad stuff.

"Well, at least we know it's not ghosts," Abigail said. It was an attempt at a joke, but it fell flat.

"Maybe, maybe not," he said. "You know that whatever did this could pry open that suit like a tin can, right...?"

That shut her up for once.

"If you two are through trying to scare each other, let's see if we can get into the frigate." Matthew shined a spotlight along its hull. "There's an airlock. Probably why they parked here."

They drifted over to the hatch. Matthew clumped his magnetic boots down on the hull and bent over the controls. "Still powered. Ready to head inside?"

"No," Davey said.

"Honesty," Abigail laughed. "I like it. I'll go first."

The hatch was a dark portal. Abigail gripped the sides and lowered herself into the airlock.

"You next," Matthew said gesturing at the opening.

No turning back now. He gritted his teeth and followed Abigail into the unknown.

Abigail had figured the lights would come on as she entered after the hatch had power. Why weren't there lights?

She flicked on her suit's headlamp. The airlock was much bigger than the one on the Sparrow. They'd all fit without a problem.

Davey bumped into her backside. "Sorry. Can't see a thing. He fumbled for a moment before turning on his helmet's much smaller light.

They were soon joined by Cole, whose spotlight flashed around the room. He closed the outer hatch. At once Abigail felt the rush of air around her. Cole waved his hand. "Umm, Davey you might want to check which way is about to be down."

The kid's eyes went wide as he tried to spin. He almost made it. Right as the room pressurized, gravity turned on, and he dropped to the floor. Abigail tried to swallow her laugh. Now wasn't the time to pick a fight.

He scrambled to his feet and reached to take off his helmet.

"Better leave it on until we know what happened to the survey team," Cole suggested quietly.

Davey's hand froze in place on the latch it had been about to unclasp. "Right. Good call."

Abigail opened the inner door. She was hoping to see a nice, clean, well-lit corridor. Instead, it was dark again. "Doesn't look like Moses was much of an interior decorator," she said, as she stepped through into the ship. "Seems rather industrial in here." A tangle of pipes and machinery ran above their heads and the floor beneath was only a steel lattice over more of the same.

"I guess this ship wasn't designed with humans in mind," Cole said, flicking his light back and forth down the corridor. "I'm surprised it's even pressurized. I guess Moses thought he might have the occasional guest, but didn't bother with the paint job."

"Sure does a good job of welcoming them," Davey mumbled.

"I don't think Moses is home," Cole countered.

"Then who is?"

Abigail heard the pitch of his voice. The kid was scared. Considering the situation, she didn't really blame him. She kept seeing the survey ship's peeled back hull plates in her mind. Whatever had done that wasn't something she wanted to meet in a dark hall.

"I don't know," Cole admitted. "Yvonne, we're inside the frigate."

He was greeted with a hiss of static.

"Yvonne? Sparrow, come in?"

Abigail caught Cole's eye. "Interference?"

"Probably something in the frigate jamming or blocking the signal. Must have started right when we entered. I guess it's not strong enough to block close-range suit to suit."

Davey spun on his heel. "We need to go warn them..."

Cole caught him with a hand on his shoulder. "Easy. Yvonne will pick up the jamming when she tries to call us. She'll move the Sparrow further away. Grace is safe on the Sparrow. Warning them of something they'll find out in the next couple minutes will just burn valuable time." Abigail knew there was some logic there, but wasn't entirely sure she agreed.

"Right. I got it," Davey said. He took a deep breath. "So what do we do now?"

Cole pointed his light down the corridor to the right. "We go that way."

Abigail frowned. "Why that way?"

He smiled. "We're in one of the wings remember. One way leads towards the tip of the wing, the other leads towards the body. I'm going to make an assumption that the survey team was trying to find a control center or something along those lines."

Abigail kicked herself mentally. Sometimes the obvious was too obvious. "Okay, but I'm still taking point." She deployed her shield, the faint hum of the grav plate muffled and indistinct with her faceplate down.

"I've got the rear. Davey, stay between us."

"No complaints from me."

Cole dug under his poncho and pulled out two weapon magazines. "Also I've changed my mind. I'd rather you had these on you. Just in case." Davey took the ammo and stashed them in a pouch. Maybe even Cole was getting spooked.

"We ready?" she asked, impatient. "Sooner we find that survey team the better."

"Lead the way," Cole said.

Abigail turned back to the dark corridor and began to slowly march down it, shield raised in front of her. The hall was straight as a laser and long enough that her lights didn't reach the end. They bobbed and wavered with each step she took, casting hypnotic shadows on the tangled machinery surrounding them. For the next several minutes they plodded forward, but the scenery never changed. There were no side corridors, accessways, windows, anything. Just a never-ending hall of dancing shadows. She found her attention drifting.

Wait. Something was wrong. The hall was getting shorter. Or maybe the lights weren't going as far. Abigail checked her wrist display and saw her charge was still good. No reason the lights would be dimming. She looked back up and the light was brighter again. Weird.

No sooner had she started walking again than it seemed like the light was shrinking back towards her. She licked her dry lips. Definitely in her head. You wouldn't think someone who spent every day of her life in a metal shell would get claustrophobic, but here she was.

"What was that?" Davey squeaked behind her. She stopped in her tracks. Nothing ahead of her, so she glanced back at the others. The short kid was staring at the ceiling, which looked like pretty much the same maze of metal it had for the entire corridor.

"I don't see anything," Matthew said. He was keeping an eye on the rear.

"I heard it," Davey insisted. "Above us."

She looked at the ceiling again and imagined another corridor above them. The thought that something might actually be up there was unnerving. "I didn't hear anything," she said, aware that she was lowering her voice. Couldn't hurt to be too careful. "Cole?"

"No," he said, also lowering his voice. "What did it sound like?"

"Like... a quiet metal tapping sound?"

Abigail breathed out a relieved sigh. "Probably just metal expanding or contracting."

"It moved," Davey insisted. "It went from up there to back there," he said, gesturing toward where they came from.

Cole turned his light back down the corridor. "Hmm. Well, that's a little unsettling. Keep moving?"

"Only if you keep watch behind us," Abigail said. Why was it so blasted dark in here?

"Of course."

"This is a bad idea," Davey moaned. "Why are we here?"

"Because we're getting paid to do this," Cole said. "Keep moving. One step and then the other. We have to get out of this wing eventually."

Abigail began her forward march, expecting to feel the walls press her again. She was relieved to find the dark had lost its power over her. "Hey, let's keep talking. If anything's out there, it probably already knows we're here anyway."

"Not a bad idea," Cole said. "So Davey. Tell me about how you met Grace."

"Really? Right now?"

"Sharon's right. If we keep talking, the silence and dark won't get to us."

"Okay..." he said. Abigail wasn't sure he quite bought into the idea yet. "At the time I lived in this real junk heap in the lower parts of Ceres. An old mine filled with slums. Locals called it Blight, and it deserved the name. Anyway, I was passing this alley one evening when I heard..." He stopped abruptly. "Did you hear that?"

Abigail had heard it that time. She spun around trying to spot whatever had just made the rustling noise. Her stomach dropped and fear gripped her heart.

Cole was gone.

Yvonne and Grace had watched the three disappear into the frigate through one of the Sparrow's outer cameras. Yvonne wrinkled her forehead. There were too many unknown variables here. What was to keep them from ending up like the other derelict ships in the area? The frigate lurked out the front window, a silent menace against the backdrop of stars.

"Think they'll be okay?" Grace asked. Her tough face was starting to give way to worry, and Yvonne thought it best to hide her own concern.

She smiled through the tension. "I'm sure they will be. Abigail is a terror in action, and Matthew is pretty formidable in his own right."

"I don't think Davey's quite on their level," Grace said.

"Your brother will be as safe as the other two. They won't let anything happen to him." She hoped. "Let's check and see if they made it into the frigate." She flipped open the comm channel. "You guys make it inside yet?"

A burst of static greeted them and Yvonne scrambled to turn the volume down. "Matthew? Abigail?"

"What's going on...?" Grace asked, voice raising a step in fear.

"Some kind of interference," Yvonne said, closing the channel down. "It wasn't there a minute ago. It must have been triggered when they entered the frigate." This wasn't doing anything to assuage the girl's fears. Or her own for that matter.

"Something knows we're here," Grace whispered. She pulled her legs into the co-pilot's chair and hugged her knees to herself.

"Maybe," Yvonne said taking the Sparrow's controls.

"What are you doing?" Grace asked.

"Following orders. Matthew said to move the Sparrow away if we lost contact. I'm going to move us twenty-five klicks out." She gave a slight touch to the maneuvering thrusters, pushing them away from the derelicts. They began to recede ever so slowly, and she let off the steam, content to let them drift away.

They were silent for nearly a minute as the kilometers ticked upward. Yvonne tried to keep the more ominous thoughts at bay but wasn't entirely successful. "Grace, go put on the spacesuit we bought you on Venus."

"What's wrong? Why?"

"Safety," she replied simply. "Something out there can tear into ships. If it's intent on adding us to the graveyard, I'd prefer we have a fighting chance."

Grace nodded and ran out of the cockpit.

Yvonne tried the comms one more time and was rewarded with an earful of static. "Someone answer, please," she begged.

Grace returned a few minutes later, helmet in hand. "Do I have to put this on now or can I just hold onto it."

"You can just hold it for now. Listen for the comm in case they get through. I'm going to go get suited."

Matthew had wisely insisted she learn to put on one of the bulky suits. She'd never needed to wear one before and had never been on a spacewalk. Hopefully, this wasn't going to be her first time in vacuum. By the time she returned to the cockpit, the Sparrow had reached a satisfactory distance, and the Mosaic frigate was just a sliver of metal on the horizon.

"No word from the others," Grace reported faithfully. "What now?"

Yvonne used the maneuvering thrusters to slow the Sparrow to a halt relative to the frigate. "We're back to waiting I guess. Grace do you think you could..."

There was a distinct thud somewhere behind and above them.

Yvonne and Grace slowly turned their heads to look behind them and then at each other. This couldn't be happening. What was... What was out there? Yvonne fought to keep her breathing calm. "Grace put your helmet on."

Grace obeyed and then stood. "I'm going to go outside."

Yvonne narrowed her eyes. "No. We don't have any idea what..."

"You heard what Matthew said. Whatever it is goes for the power plant. If we don't stop it, we'll be floating dead."

"Grace, I admire your bravery, but I can't let you go out alone."

"No offense, but you don't know how to get around in zero gee. I do." Okay the girl did have a point there. "Plus, I have my bracelets."

"You sure they'll work through the suit?" Yvonne asked, trying to think of some way to keep from sending the girl into unknown danger. But for all she knew, it would be safer outside than inside.

There was another thump behind them, further away this time.

"Never mind," she said. "Only one way to find out. Go. The power plant is at the rear of the ship beneath the engines."

Grace turned and shuffled down the hallway. Yvonne fumbled with her own helmet and latched it into place, feeling a hiss as her suit pressurized.

There was another thump from the rear of the ship. She closed her eyes and tried the comm one more time, praying that Matthew would respond.

Davey waved his gun around wildly, trying to spot something, anything to shoot at in the pale circle of illumination from his helmet. "I don't understand. He was right there. And now he's not! What are we going to..."

"Quiet." Abigail hissed.

A faint ticking noise passed by overhead moving in the same direction they had been. He could hardly hear it over the sound of his own heartbeat. Something had Matthew. And it had happened so quickly, they'd barely heard it. "What do we do now?" he whispered.

"We go get our gaucho back, and hope he's still alive," she said. "Walk in front of me. I'm not losing anyone else to whatever this thing is."

Davey stepped in front of her. It made sense from a logical standpoint, but he wasn't exactly looking to be point man on this little descent into the abyss.

"Let's move," Abigail said. "And keep that gun up."

He lifted the barrel and pointed it down the corridor. How long was this blasted thing?

"Are you gonna be able to hit anything with those shaking hands?" she asked. "We're in this together now and if you're about to lose it, I'm going to leave you here."

He glanced at his hands and took a deep breath willing his nerves to calm.

"That's better. Keep going. Just like Cole said. One step in front of the other."

They continued in silence, Davey descending further into his own nightmare. Every stray shadow cast by their bobbing lights was an unseen foe, preparing to steal him away into the dark. Or worse Abigail, and then he'd be left alone.

The tapping sound passed by overhead.

"It's come back for round two," Abigail whispered. "Not one sound."

Davey wondered if she could hear his heartbeat hammering at his chest like a blacksmith.

With a whir of servomotors, she swung her shield behind her. Davey tried to turn to see what was happening but only saw a tangle of movement that disappeared into the dark. "What was...?"

"Didn't get a good look." She glanced at the mess of pipes above them. "It's above us again. There has to be another passageway up there."

Davey heard the movement from the front of the corridor and raised his gun. It dropped right into the ring of light from his headlamp. He pulled the trigger. In the flashes of bright gunfire, he saw flexible limbs writhe, sparks erupting where the bullets struck home.

His magazine was spent in a few short seconds, and he tried to step back as the shape moved at him. Abigail dove around him. Limbs reached out and gripped the edges of her shield in iron pincers. The thing plucked the shield from her hands and tossed it aside. She used the distraction to rush past the limbs and land a bone shattering punch on its center mass.

The sound of crunching metal rang through the corridor, like a head-on collision between two grav cars. And just like that, it was gone. Abigail fell to the floor and scrambled for her shield. Davey fumbled at his belt for a fresh magazine. He didn't trust the thing was beaten just yet.

It was behind him again. He spun, gunfire spraying.

There was a single pale red eye. It glowed sickly, like a dying star.

Davey felt something sharp stab into the back of his neck and the eye melted away into darkness.

Grace was scared out of her mind.

"It's just another mission," she said aloud as she climbed out the Sparrow's airlock. "It's just another mission. And people are relying on you. Davey is relying on you. And if you fail, then it'll be back down to the lower levels. Back to the dark."

She drifted out into space and spun to get her bearings. The power plant was on the Sparrow's belly. Between the engines. She fired a burst of steam from her thruster pack and darted over the Sparrow's aft.

"Grace, can you hear me?" Yvonne asked through the comm. She sounded funny. Distant and muffled.

"I can hear you, but I think the interference is messing with it."

"Stay close to the ship. I don't want to lose contact with you too."

"I will, I'm just trying to get far enough out to see." She gave the thrusters another push and dropped down past the engines. She'd round the corner soon and be able to see the belly. "I just need to be far enough out to see what's..." she cut off abruptly. "What is that?"

"What's what? Talk to me, Grace. What do you see?"

It was a metal sphere about a meter across. Two segmented tentacles extended from the body to the Sparrow wielding bright plasma torches. It had already cut two red-hot lines into the armor.

"It's a... probe? I don't know what it is."

The armor plate suddenly buckled and peeled back, seemingly on its own, exposing the machinery beneath. That was impossible! A grav plate that strong couldn't exist.

The probe detected her and spun, a single red eye glowing in its center. The Sparrow seemingly forgotten, it charged her. Grace hadn't seen any thrusters or rockets of any sort. How was it...?

She barely had time to dart out of its path and the metallic claws that had replaced the plasma torches. She punched the thrusters wildly and lost control, spinning haphazardly.

"Gr...ce...Wha...on?"

She'd gotten too far from the Sparrow and the jamming all but choked out Yvonne's desperate voice. She hit the button to stabilize her spin. Where was the probe now?

Beneath her and coming fast. She extended her left arm and stopped it with the iron grip of her bracelet barely two meters in front of her. It halted its advance, and she imagined its puzzled confusion. Without warning, it tried to lunge at her again.

With horror, Grace found it was pushing her backward through space, away from the Sparrow. She fired her thruster pack, but it was no match for whatever invisible form of propulsion the probe used. With no better ideas, she released the probe while firing her thrusters full power. She shot over the machine and its grasping claws missed her by mere millimeters.

Grace didn't let off the thruster now and swung back in a long arc toward the Sparrow. She twisted her neck to try and get a glimpse of the thing over her shoulder. There it was, already closing the gap.

She just needed to get in between it and the Sparrow. If she could just get the ship behind her she could...

Running out of time she cut the thruster and spun, catching the probe in her bracelet's grip again. It wasn't caught off guard this time and kept pushing her, faster and faster, toward the hull of the Sparrow. Maybe it saw the ship and thought it could crush her. Maybe it didn't even know it was there.

Mere seconds before she was broken on the hull, she tightened her grip on the probe and swung it as hard as she could at the Sparrow, simultaneously firing her thrusters one last time.

The probe smashed into the Sparrow and crumpled like an aluminum can, fragmenting into hundreds of pieces. Grace swooped in a terrifying arc towards the ship, straightening out at the last second. Her boot clipped it and sent her into a wild tumble off into space again.

For a moment she just let herself spin, feeling weak, sick to her stomach.

She realized Yvonne was screaming in her ear.

"I'm... fine. I just... Give me a minute," she panted, letting the thruster pack automatically stop her spin. With one last puff of steam, she slowed to a stop and then drifted back towards the Sparrow.

"Grace! What's going on out there. Talk to me."

Grace could barely hear her through the jamming and the ringing of her own ears.

"I got it," she said.

Abigail saw the machine jab the long sharp needle into Davey's neck. He went limp, and his knees buckled. The machine was quick as lightning and scooped him into one of its many limbs and darted back into the hidden accessway in the ceiling. It skittered by overhead, and she was left alone.

At least she knew what she was dealing with now.

She chuckled in spite of the grimness of the situation. Better to laugh than cry. She tapped her wrist display, worried that her suit wouldn't be able to detect the tracker through the jamming. Luckily, it worked on a different wavelength, because the signal came through bright and clear. She'd slipped the tracker onto Davey as soon as Matthew had gone missing. This was getting to be one of her favorite tricks. Hadn't failed her yet.

She stashed her shield on her back and jogged down the corridor. Without the other two, she could move quickly. Let the thing come at her with that needle. It wasn't the only thing made of metal. She thundered down the hall, loud enough to wake the dead, and in less than a minute broke into a large octagonal room.

"What's with all the dark, Moses?" Abigail shouted. "Your hospitality sucks." She checked her wrist and chose the door to her right. Davey was only about a hundred meters ahead.

Right as she stepped into the doorway, her foe dropped on her from above. Metallic tentacles wrapped around her arms trapping them against her side. She fought for a brief moment before realizing they were stronger than her. Another arm reached out and tried to sedate her the same way it had Davey. The needle broke on her armor. Spinning on her heel, she slammed the thing into the wall. For the briefest moment, its grip slacked and she turned the tables on it, throwing it away from her.

She pulled her shield from her back and dove at it before it could recover its balance, but it was quick and slid around her attack, trying to wrap its arms around her again.

"Oh no you don't," she growled as she battered the tentacle-like limbs away. The mechanical creature lunged at her again. This time she was ready for it. It caught the full brunt of her shield's gravity field and hurtled into the wall. She didn't take any chance and smashed it into the wall several more times until its red eye darkened and the thing was little more than a pile of twisted scrap metal.

Abigail eyed it suspiciously, poking it with her foot. "Good riddance. You better not have friends." She ran through the door towards Davey's tracker. It was another long, dark hallway. Thankfully, with the wreckage in the room behind her, the ship had lost the last of its terror over her. Even if the robot had friends, she could deal with them.

A sturdy door blocked her route. "If anyone's on the other side, stand clear of the door," she shouted. She smashed it repeatedly with her shield, warping the steel with each successive blow. Finally, when she had done enough damage, she gripped it and tore it out of its frame.

"Are... Are you here to rescue us?"

She stepped into the room and saw a handful of men and women huddled in the dark.

"You guys from the survey team?"

A man with disheveled hair and the beginnings of a beard nodded. "That guardian attacked us when we first entered the ship two days ago. Picked us off one by one and stashed us here." He looked up at her earthtech suit in awe. "From the sound of the battle we just heard ringing through the walls, I'm hoping you trashed the thing."

"It's never moving again. Are my friends here?"

He stepped aside and gestured at two bodies lying in the corner. "Just dropped 'em off a few minutes ago, actually. They're still drugged. It'll wear off in a bit."

Abigail didn't like seeing Matthew tossed aside like that or Davey for that matter, but she breathed a sigh of relief that they were okay. "How about you guys? You alright?"

"A few injuries. We're dehydrated and hungry, but we'll live. Unlike, well, everyone else that's found this ship." He gestured towards the far end of the room. Abigail shined her lights that way and saw a neatly arranged pile of petrified corpses. Gross.

"I wasn't aware Moses was into murder like this," she mused.

The man shrugged. "We think the ship's security didn't really know what to do once they lost contact with Moses. They've been dutifully doing the best they can, and in the absence of food and water for their captives..."

"Worst jailers ever," Abigail said.

"Precisely. Now, how about we get out of here."

"Best idea I've heard all day."

Davey slowly came to his senses. He was alive, so that was a good thing. Or it would have been, if the room wasn't spinning and he didn't have a splitting headache. Slowly the world took shape around him.

"He's awake," said a voice he didn't recognize.

Matthew appeared over him. "Welcome back. How you feeling?"

"Like I got sucked out the airlock and hit the bulkhead on the way out. What happened?"

"Robot hit us all with some sort of tranquilizer. We think you got overdosed for your body mass."

Davey frowned and tried to sit up. He should have been offended about being called small, but he was just grateful to be alive. The strangers surrounding them had to be the missing crew. "Where's Abigail?"

"Back at the Sparrow trying to sort out how to get us out of here. Our mechanical friend punched a hole in our suits with that sticker of his. We've got to figure out how to patch everyone up."

Davey rubbed the back of his neck. It was a bit sore after being stabbed by a homicidal murder bot. Stupid piece of junk. "So I guess that means we won?"

"Sharon and Grace had to do the heavy lifting, but yeah, we won," he said, getting to his feet.

"Wait, what do you mean Grace?"

Matthew looked back down at him. "She had a run in with a probe that wanted to turn the Sparrow into scrap. Apparently, she went out and returned the favor. Turns out, your sister is a bit of a fighter."

Davey slowly stood to his feet, using the wall for support. His head chased thoughts in several different directions. On the one hand he was proud of her. On the other, the thought of her getting in a fight or being in danger scared him spitless. How was he going to keep her safe going forward? The Sparrow wasn't exactly the safest ship to ride.

His internal debate was interrupted by Abigail's return. "Who wants their suit patched? Oh good, Davey's awake. Let's get this done and get out of here."

It took them some time to get everything sorted and everyone on board the Sparrow. Thankfully they had no further complications. The Frigate had exhausted its resources or had lost the will to fight back, and it slept peacefully now. The salvage team was optimistic that they might get the chance to return and finish their job once they had a few weeks to recover. Davey still didn't trust it. Not now and not ever.

As Davey waited patiently for his turn at the Sparrow's airlock, he turned to Matthew. "If Benny ever finds us another once in a lifetime job..."

"We'll tell him no," Matthew cut him off, "and ask for a milk run."

The next day they met their employer, The Unchained Man, at the specified coordinates. Matthew docked the Sparrow to the slightly larger patrol craft and went to the common room to see the survey team off. They'd have a story to tell, but they were alive.

Matthew disconnected from the other ship, and Yvonne used the maneuvering thrusters to push the Sparrow away. They planned to wait for the other ship to frameshift away as a common courtesy.

Sharon joined them in the cockpit. "Well, that's over. We gonna make a profit after repairs to the hull?"

"Our employer gave us a little bonus to cover that," Matthew said. He scratched the back of his head under his hat. It was the one he didn't like, the one that itched. "We're in the black."

"You saw him?" Yvonne asked. "I kind of thought he'd be the type to hide his face given the moniker."

Matthew shook his head. "He sent payment back over with one of the team members. Apparently, they didn't get to see him either."

"That's creepy," Sharon said. "Let's not work for him again."

"I was already going to ask Benny to keep clear of him in the future."

Yvonne shrugged. "There was no harm in this job. We saved some lives."

The comm chimed. "This is Matthew Cole."

"Good to hear from you Matthew," a familiar voice said. "You and your crew did not disappoint."

Matthew sat up abruptly. "Whitaker. You son of a..."

"That's out of character," he chided. "And I already told you that's not my name."

"So I take it you're the Unchained Man?"

"One of the many names I've done business under over the years. It's got a certain poetic ring to it that I like. Here I am calling to be friendly, and you're probably already warming up the weapons. Which I would recommend against by the way. I'm well outside your firing arc, and you're well within mine. Let's keep this civil."

Matthew felt his face burn. "So what did you use us for? What do you get out of this frigate?"

The Unchained Man sighed. "Probably nothing personally. There's a piece of technology I'd like to find, but that would be a bit of a miracle."

"Then what...?"

"The University of Ganymede benefits the most. They get full salvage rights, outside this one harmless piece of tech. Once we make sure there aren't any more surprises, they'll set their engineers loose on it. Should keep them occupied for the next decade. Who knows? They may just learn something that'll save mankind."

Matthew shook his head. "Don't flatter yourself."

"It's not likely, I admit," he said. "Still I do my part. Just like on Venus."

"You're talking about White Void?" Sharon asked.

"Good evening, Abigail. I was going to have Matthew send my greetings, but it looks like you've saved us both the trouble."

She stared out the window at the other ship doubtfully. "Yeah, whatever," she said. "What was this about White Void?"

"I did my part," he replied. "White Void has been trying to expand its influence to Venus. Given that Discordia and Concordia are the most stable colonies in the solar system, I don't have to tell you why this is a bad thing. Turns out the other syndicates were willing to pay to keep that from happening."

"You're a mercenary," Yvonne said.

The Unchained Man chuckled. "Of course not. I can't be bought for any cause other than my own. But I have expenses and if I can get another man to foot the bill, then I see that as good business."

Matthew had had enough of this inane talk. "What's the point of all this? Why hire us?"

"You were in the area. The survey team's lives were in danger and you were the only crew that could respond quickly enough. Also thought it wouldn't hurt to show you that I'm not your enemy. Contrary to what you've spent the last decade thinking, Matthew, I'm not one of the bad guys. We're all on the same ship after all. Isn't that what you once told me in Villa María?"

Sharon probably remembered him saying the same thing to her, and Matthew felt her eyes burning into the back of his head. "Tell that to the people you sold into slavery," he said and cut the transmission. He stood and threw his campero at the window. He left it where it fell and stormed from the cockpit. "Get us out of here once his ship leaves," he said to Yvonne.

"Where do you want me to take us?" she asked, hands folded neatly in her lap.

"Doesn't matter to me," he said. "Flip a coin. Cast lots."

"Cole," Abigail said. Her voice was firm. "Talk to us."

He shook his head. "Not now."

And by that he meant not ever.

Chapter 14: Matrons

The founding of the Colonial Vatican happened mere weeks after Earth's went silent. The Seminary of St Bartholomew on Ganymede was well established by this point and it was already the center of Catholicism in space. That it would be chosen as the site of the new Vatican, was something no one questioned.

Cardinals from all across the colonies were called to form a new College of Cardinals. As halls of stone rose up around them in construction, they met in Conclave to elect a new pope.

There was little resistance to Cardinal Josef Krupnik from Tethys. Indeed, if the stories are true, Krupnik himself was the only one who protested. As one of the first colonists born in the Czech colony on Tethys, Pope Krupnik was a quiet man, a scholar and philosopher more than a mover and shaker of men. At least that's what they thought.

In a few short years, Pope Krupnik would lead the Last Reformation, the greatest upheaval in the Church in over five hundred years. Any institution as old as the Church is in constant need of course corrections and one was long overdue. The quiet philosopher drove the tares from the clergy as Christ drove out the moneychangers two thousand years previous.

As he declared in the papal bull, Deus Peccata:

"May God forgive us if we teach any lie. May he forgive us for when we have done so in the past. May he guide our path in the future, as the sons and daughters of Adam's race face the coming night. May we ever turn to Christ, the lighthouse that will lead us home."

The Church had put its business in order in case the end was soon to come.

Cardinal Phillip McMerrick
Archbishop of the Archdiocese of Titan
Died 93 AM

A bigail stepped down the Sparrow's ramp and breathed the cool air of Mars. Once, she had been focused on expanding her operations past Mars, always looking for the next big thing. But in the months since she'd left, the red hills and pale skies had grown a little cheerier. The red no longer seemed so drab. Now it was almost comfortable, like an old friend.

She looked out over the landscape and frowned. Farmland. Not in the distance, but in her face. Rows of wheat grew not twenty meters from the Sparrow. Cole had said he was going to land a bit outside of Flagstaff, but this was more rural than she was expecting. The sun was just peeking over the distant red hills, casting thin lines of light through the rows of amber grain.

The sound of boots on metal announced his presence. "Beautiful isn't it?" Cole asked. "I've only seen an Earth sunrise in the movies, but I like to think Mars is the next best thing. Our first home in the stars and maybe our last. I wonder how long we'll hold out here?"

"What do you mean by that?" she asked.

"Well," he said scratching his stubble. "I mean once the factories finally shut down. Once the grav plates all give out and we can't make more. One-third of a gee may be livable for a bit. Who knows? Maybe some creative folks will live indefinitely here."

"You're being way too melodramatic for this early in the morning," she said. "Humans are tenacious if anything. I don't like to think extinction is our destination."

"No one does, but most of the colonies will be abandoned in a century or two at most."

244

"Plenty of time for a turnaround."

"Maybe," he said, then laughed. "Sorry. Coming home always makes me a bit thoughtful."

She caught the strange look in his eye but, not knowing what to make of it, decided to ignore it. "Hope the owner of this field doesn't mind us coming to roost."

Cole pointed at the horizon. "See the farmhouse the next hill over? She lives there. You could say we go way back. Trust me. She's fine with it."

It was the usual level of Cole vagueness. "So what are you up to today?"

"Waiting for Benny mostly. He promised that he's got something good enough to bring us back to Mars but hasn't finished working out all the details yet."

"As long as he comes through," Abigail said, shrugging. "I'm not sure I like us being on Mars with Yvonne though. White Void does have a moderate presence here, at least where the Sakuraba Syndicate hasn't crowded them out."

"It's been months since the bounty was posted, and Arizona has always done a good job of limiting the influence of the big three."

She rolled her eyes. "You'll have to forgive me for not exactly trusting Arizona law enforcement."

"Hey, the men with badges are fine. It's the politician at the top that's a bit suspect.

The memory of the government man, Ryan Thompson, sitting unperturbed in his office after aiding a gang of known killers and getting six civilians killed sent a chill down Abigail's spine. She wondered if he had trouble sleeping at night. Probably not.

"How about you?" he asked. "You said you were heading out."

She looked out over the field. "Need to catch a train over to Doch Rossiya. I'll be back by this evening."

Cole raised an eyebrow. "Your business is your own, but I'm curious what you've got going with the Russians."

She laughed. "What is it with you guys? Not even a couple centuries can put that disagreement to rest, huh? My broker's Russian and she's been harassing me for weeks now about ditching her."

"Benny mentioned that he's been getting threatening messages from her too. Something about poaching one of her best freelancers."

"Mistress Medvedev is..." Abigail hesitated. She didn't exactly want to slander the woman who had done so much for her career, but at the same time, she made it hard to be complimentary. "Let's say she's

245

possessive of her charges."

Cole turned to face her directly. "Wait just a minute. This is that broker that only takes women freelancers. I've heard she's a crazy misandrist."

"Half true," she admitted. "She's not crazy, but she definitely doesn't care for men."

"Then what are you waiting for?" Cole said making a shooing motion. "I don't want her putting some kind of hit out on me."

A wry smile crept across her face. "I'll take care of it, get her off you boys' back." She walked down the ramp and stepped onto the Martian soil. There was a mag-train station not more than a mile away. No sense in taking the bike. That jogged another thought. She turned to face Cole and looked at her feet. "There's another matter of business I've got to take care of in Rossiya."

He looked down at her, question plain on his face.

"My skyhopper. I had Mistress Medvedev move it into storage. I'm going to have to settle on that debt."

Cole whistled. "I'd forgotten all about your aircraft."

"She got me a good deal. I mean, it's going to hurt, but life is expensive, right? What I was really wondering was..." If the past was a tough subject, the future was almost as hard. She bit her lip. "Should I just sell it? Is this," she gestured at the Sparrow, "going to last?"

He regarded her for a moment. "Do you want it to?"

"Of course," she answered quickly. "But it's your ship and you don't always act like you want a crew around. I'm not going to sit here and assume that this is permanent."

The sun had fully risen over the hills, casting Cole in rose light. He stood for a moment in silence. She never really knew what he was thinking, though she knew the gears never stopped turning. It was a wonder he didn't drive himself crazy.

Finally, he nodded. "Wouldn't dream of being alone now. Having a crew's been good. Having a partner to rely on in a tight pinch has been better. Sell it."

So that was that. She nodded. The crew of the Sparrow was official. "I'll be back tonight."

"Try and make it by dinner. We might have something better than normal fare."

Yvonne had gotten a lot better and was branching out past single pot meals, but she was still a better doctor than she was a cook. It was more than what any of the rest of them could manage, but that wasn't saying much. It just wasn't in her blood.

"I'll see what I can do," she said. She walked the edge of the wheat field toward the road. When she reached the hard concrete, she turned back to look at the Sparrow. It was a familiar sight now, its sharp metal angles cut against the pale Martian sky. Once she had been envious of the ship. Now it was home.

Cole was nowhere to be seen. He'd either gone back inside or left on business. For as much as they trusted each other in a fight, they still didn't know each other. Abigail glanced down at her legs. Yvonne had been pestering her lately to tell Cole and the others why she wore the suit. He wasn't stupid. Maybe he already knew. That kind of pity was exactly what she didn't want. Once, before her father had procured this suit for her, she couldn't escape it. People treat cripples differently.

She didn't want Cole to see her as an invalid.

She'd deal with that another day. Today she had an angry broker to contend with.

"Ha. Another bullseye. Beat that." Davey crossed his arms and leaned back against a storage cabinet, a smug grin plastered on his face. At least there were still some games he could whip Grace at.

She frowned with determination and stepped up to the line they'd drawn in the hold. Raising the dart to eye level, she peered down the length of the shaft. She drew her hand back and launched the missile at its target.

It smacked the dartboard with a satisfying thump. Thankfully for Davey, the score she'd hit, a measly seven points in the lower left quadrant, wasn't nearly as satisfying. Grace grunted in frustration and threw her remaining two darts in quick succession. Triple-ten and seventeen. Not near enough to catch up to Davey's one-twenty-two.

"That'll do it," he said walking up to the board and pulling out the darts. "Again?"

"You're just going to win," she said, snatching her darts back from him.

"Now you know how I feel about Checkers."

She paused and looked down at the dart in her hand. "Point taken. Maybe we need a game where we're on the same level. Or maybe I just need to practice darts on the days that Matthew has you working."

"Not fair," he grumbled. He was thankful the gaucho had given him a day off that wasn't Sunday. It didn't happen all that often. "You don't work your tail off like I do."

"I help Yvonne in the kitchen and Abigail with supply lists." Grace

247

stuck her tongue out at Davey but he wasn't sure that really helped her case much.

Davey threw his first dart. It froze in mid-air.

Grace held her left hand out, her bracelet glowing an icy blue, her eyes sparkling with mischief.

"I don't think Matthew would approve of you using those things for fun," he said stepping forward and plucking the dart out of the air.

"What he doesn't know won't..."

Yvonne's voice rang out over the intercom. "I'm heading topside to get some fresh air. You two want to join me?"

"We'll be right up," Davey replied. "Let's go."

"Oh." Grace hesitated and Davey turned back around. "Go ahead. I'll be there in a few minutes."

He shrugged and climbed the ladder out of the hold, past the main deck, and through the top side airlock. Yvonne had left the airlock open, leaving only the ventral hatch closed. He stepped out onto the hull and felt the warm sunshine on his skin. He breathed in deeply. The air felt fresh, clean, and a little bit alive. Maybe it was all the fields around the Sparrow, air scrubbed by plant life rather than recyclers. Maybe it was his imagination.

Yvonne sat on the hull, ragged book in hand. He sat down beside her. "Whatcha reading?"

"Since we're in Arizona and surrounded by Americans, I thought something from their canon would be appropriate. The Minister's Black Veil, by Hawthorne."

He glanced over at the page and read a couple of sentences, but couldn't make much of them out of context. "What's it about?"

"Sin. Guilt. The veils we hide our true selves behind. At least that's what I think. I'm not really sure. It's about a preacher that one day starts wearing a veil over his face. It scares his congregation half to death, but they really start listening to his sermons."

"That's kind of creepy," Davey said. "Did he kill someone or something?"

"Story never says."

"I see," he said, not because he understood, but because he didn't really know what else to say.

She passed the book to him. "Maybe you could give it a read and let me know what you think."

He took the book carefully, knowing it cost a lot. "I'll think about it." This felt too much like an assignment. The hatch banged open behind him and he turned, glad for the interruption.

Grace climbed out, decked out in her space suit with helmet on. "Grace, what in...?"

She looked around at the Martian landscape and used her hand to shield her eyes from the sun. "Woah. This is pretty wild." She walked over to the other two and sat on the other side of Yvonne. "What are we doing?"

"Enjoying the fresh air and sunshine," Yvonne said, "only one of which seems to interest you. Grace, why are you wearing a spacesuit."

"I felt like it."

"You don't need it on Mars. Not under the environmental shields," Davey said leaning forward to look at her. Sometimes Grace could sure be weird.

"I said I felt like it," she repeated. This time there was a hint of ice in her voice.

"Oh, I understand now," Yvonne said. "You're a Tunnel Baby."

Davey frowned. As usual, the doctor was the one to figure things out. "Mind filling me in?"

Yvonne ignored him. "Grace, were you born on Ceres?"

"Yes."

"And have you ever walked under an open sky without a pressure suit?"

"No." Her shoulders slumped in defeat.

"That's what I thought," Yvonne said. "Tunnel Babies are those born on stations or underground, like the cities on Ceres. Most of them have difficulty going without a roof over their head."

Davey thought about this. It made some sense. "But what about all the spacewalks we've done?"

"I wore a spacesuit on those," Grace shrugged. "I knew I was safe."

"Look at us," he said. "You can see that it's safe."

"I know, just give me... give me some time."

"Take all the time you need," Yvonne said. "Thankfully you're young enough to learn new habits. Tunnel Babies have a lot harder time adapting once they're adults. I take it this means you weren't born on Ceres, Davey?"

He shook his head. "Nope, Thebe, little bitty rock up close to Jupiter. They have the whole thing shielded and breathable."

"Yes, I've heard. Davey, why didn't you tell us where you were from?"

He looked at her dumbly. "Didn't think it was important. Is it important?"

"Yes. Because Thebe is very small. It would be a trivial task to

249

locate your family if you still have any."

He wasn't really sure what to make of that. "I don't know. I was seven. Bunch of slavers broke into our community and took a bunch of kids."

"Wait," Grace interrupted. "Then how did you end up on Ceres?"

He tapped his knuckles against the hull restlessly. "I think there was some kind of slave market down there in the core cities. Anyway, we were getting transported by truck, when we got hit by a grav car. Back popped open and the kids that weren't too badly hurt from the accident scattered. I didn't run into you for another four years or so."

"What about your family, Davey?" Yvonne asked. "What if we could find them?"

He shuffled his feet. "They wouldn't know me and I wouldn't know them anymore. It's fine. I've got Grace, and you guys are okay too."

She looked at him, face stern. "Family is important, Davey. If your parents are on Thebe, wouldn't they deserve to know you're still alive?"

Davey shrugged. He didn't have a good answer to this. He hadn't thought about them in years.

"I'm going to mention this to Matthew," she said.

There was a popping sound. Grace removed her helmet and set it on the hull beside her, eyes squeezed tightly shut. Davey was impressed. Honestly, he hadn't expected her to take it off without a lot of badgering. That said, it didn't look like she was...

Yvonne beat him to it. "Grace, dear. Breathe."

"Don't want to," she said.

"I don't think you get the option, actually. When you pass out, you'll breathe whether you will it or no."

Grace took a short gasping breath then fumbled for her helmet and began clasping it back on. Once she had it secured, she turned to the other two and smiled. "Baby steps, right?"

Davey rolled his eyes. Apparently, it wasn't going to be that easy.

Abigail stepped off the mag-train onto the crowded platform. Thankfully, her suit ensured that crowds always magically parted for her. She got more than a few stares and whispers in mixed Russian and English. She'd been used to that even before the suit when it had just been her and the wheelchair.

On her way out of the station, she glanced at a map of the city posted on the wall, double checking her route. Her destination was only a couple klicks away, but it never hurt to be careful. Getting lost in a city was always a drag.

Walking through Doch Rossiya was a bit like walking through the past. The Russians had kept their national and cultural identity over the past few centuries, more so than most of the other colonies. While most had switched to English as their trade language, the Russians had stubbornly kept their own. An English speaker was always within arm's length, but you usually had to ask. No one was going to volunteer if you were struggling. Abigail had had enough business here with Mistress Medvedev that she'd memorized the alphabet and learned the basics of the language so that she could read street signs.

She set off at a brisk pace. Rows of neat and ordered concrete apartment buildings lined the streets and statues of historical figures stood watch over the roundabouts at the end of each block. She passed a granite statue of the composer Mussorgsky, baton high over his head. She remembered this particular landmark. Her destination was just ahead.

A block past the composer, stood a foreboding manor, built in the distinctly Russian style of neoclassical architecture favored hundreds of years ago. The building was faced with a row of columns that looked out over the busy street. Abigail walked up the front steps and knocked on the heavy oak door. The door itself had probably cost a fortune and might have made its way here from Earth long ago. It opened slowly and a young woman stood in its place.

"Oh! Mistress Sharon! It has been quite some time!" She had a pleasing accent that Abigail always thought lent her a certain gravitas.

"How are you, Natalya? The Mistress still treating you okay?"

"Of course. Mistress Medvedev treats all of her women like her own daughters. Come in, she will want to see you."

Abigail stepped into the sparsely furnished foyer. A wide staircase led up to a second level that looked down over the entryway.

"If you will give me but a moment, I will check with the Mistress," Natalya said as she locked the door behind Abigail and hurried up the stairs.

Abigail bounced on her heels in boredom. Now came the part she wasn't really looking forward to. There was no way the Mistress was going to take this as anything but an insult. Thankfully, Natalya did not leave her to stew in her anxieties long. The woman re-appeared at the top of the staircase and gestured for Abigail to follow. She was led down a long hallway to a pair of double doors. Natalya pushed them open.

The room was dark. Heavy midnight blue curtains were pulled over the windows, and only a single lamp on the desk cast a feeble yellow light across the room. Behind the desk sat a slender woman, pale and tall, the tallest woman that Abigail had ever seen. Mistress Medvedev was nearly two meters tall. Wispy white hair fell about her shoulders and a smile was on her lips.

"Abigail, my daughter, you have come home at last. Have you had your fill of frivolous travel?"

It was best not to be too direct. Let her feel this was going her way before letting open the airlock. "I hope you are well Mistress and that business has been good."

"I am healthy as ever and my empires run like the finest of clocks. Come into the light so that I can see you better." Abigail obeyed and stepped around to the desk and knelt on one knee so that she was face to face with the sitting woman. "Much better. Oh, you've let your hair grow out. I never knew it was so wavy. You are beautiful, my dear."

"Thank you, Mistress." This was always her way. Shower with ten thousand small meaningless compliments. Abigail knew better than to let it distract her. "I came to Rossiya to talk to you."

"Yes, of course I will take you back. I am sure you have been horribly abused by that man." She put enough venom into the last word to poison half a city.

"No, Mistress, actually Matthew Cole's been a perfect gentleman." She turned an antique globe of Mars that sat on her desk but could still feel the mistress' eyes burning into her. "We're partners actually. Get along pretty well in a fight. I was thinking that I'd travel with him a little longer." Permanently actually, but she wasn't about to say that out loud.

Mistress Medvedev was quiet for several long uncomfortable seconds. "You disappoint me, Abigail. After everything I have done for you, this is how you repay me."

"Mistress..."

"Do not interrupt me. Who was it that found you wandering the streets of Kyoto, without a home or purpose? Who was it that taught you how to fight and make a career for yourself? I gave you a purpose Abigail, turned you into the Shield Maiden, a force to be reckoned with. And here you decide to throw it all away for some... some man?"

"Woah, it's not like that," Abigail said quickly standing to her feet. "Cole's just a friend. Pretty sure he doesn't have a romantic bone in his body. But he's a solid freelancer. We've done some good things too. Surely you heard about the children we saved over Titan."

252

The mistress' eyes were cold. "Of course I heard. I know every job you've taken on. The solar system is a small place. My operations may be based on Mars, but I have eyes everywhere."

"Then why can't you see that this is a good thing for me?" Abigail asked, trying to put as much steel in her voice as she could.

"Because you will be used and discarded."

"That's not going to happen," Abigail said.

"And why is that?"

"Because, well... Cole is a decent man. Every time I turn around I see him going out of his way to protect the weak. He gives second chances to those that deserve none. He cares about what is just."

"Then he would be a diamond hidden in a sea of sand. But I doubt very much he is any of these things."

"How would you know?" she challenged.

The mistress stood and looked up to Abigail. "Because I have lived long. I run empires. I own politicians, businessmen. I am no fool and know that he will disappoint you. It takes years to work through all the layers of another soul and truly know them. What demons does this Matthew Cole hide? One day you will see him for what he is, and you will beg me to take you back."

She did have a point there. There was an awful lot about Cole's past she didn't know. Just what was he keeping secret? Maybe he hadn't always been such an upright citizen. But then she'd kept just as much, probably more, of her own past from the crew.

Mistress Medvedev must have caught her hesitation. "Yes. I feel your doubts. Your choices are your own to make of course, but I pray you lean on my wisdom."

Abigail shook her head. "My mind is made."

"What if I cut my fee in half? Could you be persuaded to see reason then?"

Tempting, but not tempting enough. "I have my own reasons."

The mistress turned away. "Very well. Your life is your own to live, and I have neither the time nor patience to be disappointed. If I have need of you, can I count on you to answer my call?"

That was an easy answer at least. "After all you've done for me? Of course. But I may come with a gaucho and his crew in tow."

The mistress sighed. "Child, are you trying to vex me?"

Abigail smiled. "Always."

There was a moment of uncomfortable silence. Finally, Mistress Medvedev turned to face Abigail. There was a weak smile on the woman's face. "Go then, not with my blessing, but with my goodwill

253

and warning."

"I will take both," Abigail said, relieved that she seemed to have relented a little. "But the latter isn't necessary."

The mistress wrapped Abigail in a delicate embrace that she barely felt through her implant. "We shall see, won't we?" the older woman said.

Matthew finally got the call he had been waiting for late in the afternoon. He stepped outside of the farmhouse to answer the comm on the wide back porch.

"Cole," Benny said, "good to hear you in real time. The time delay always makes business a bit of a fuss."

"Agreed. It's good to be back on Mars," Matthew said. "Thank you, Benny." For a moment the only sound interrupting the quiet afternoon was the call of a distant bird. "Thank you for making me get a crew."

"Oh, I..." Must have surprised him good, because Benny was never speechless. He finally regained his composure and continued. "You're welcome. It's been good for business too, right? Still wish you'd enlighten me on the support staff. Might help me in planning new contracts."

"I understand your concern," Matthew said sitting in one of the rocking chairs. "But there are reasons I'm being quiet about their identities. I've got one who's turning out to be a decent pilot, though I don't think they'll be ready to be shot at any time soon. Afraid that's about all I can say."

"Can't say I understand, but at least Abigail's a veteran. Which," he said with a sigh, "reminds me. I'm still getting threatening messages from her broker."

"Sharon went to talk to her this afternoon. Hopefully, she'll put a stop to that."

"You are reading my mind today Cole and making my dreams come true. You must have missed me."

Matthew smiled in spite of Benny's prattling. "Maybe a little. So what's the word on this job?"

"It's all set up. Mining town outside of Arizona proper has had a string of murders. A couple different factions are blaming each other. Mayor wants you to slip into town and scope things out."

Matthew winced. He didn't much mind detective work, but it wasn't exactly his specialty. Usually, the police were better at that.

Then again, if this town wasn't part of Arizona, their resources may have been limited. "I guess the mayor doesn't want us landing the Sparrow in town and drawing attention."

"You've got it. Are you somewhere you can leave the Sparrow for a week or two?"

"Easily. We may have a problem with Sharon. She isn't exactly inconspicuous with her armor."

"Can't she take it off for some undercover work?"

Matthew hesitated. "I don't think so."

"Awkward. Well, talk it over with her. Maybe you can head in and have a chat with the Mayor and see just how secretive he needs you to be. I'll send you the rest of the info. Can you get started on it tomorrow?"

"Easily."

"Alright. Take care of yourself, Cole."

"You too, Benny."

The comm clicked off with a pop, and Matthew removed his campero to scratch his head. If he left the Sparrow here, then presumably Yvonne and the kids would be staying here too. All in all, there were worse places for them to be, but Matthew wasn't sure he wanted to be away from them for too long. Grace would be fine, but Davey was, well, Davey and still had his sour days. And Yvonne still had a price on her head, even if they were in a nice quiet parking spot and unlikely to attract attention. What if he and Sharon were off the grid for a couple of weeks?

It didn't look like he had much of an option.

The Sparrow sat in the distance, standing tall over the fields, a silhouette against the ruddy sky. They'd either be okay, or they wouldn't. Sometimes you can't control everything.

Getting up from the rocking chair he stepped back inside the farmhouse.

The sun had already set by the time Abigail stepped off the train. After having to deal with Mistress Medvedev and spending the rest of the afternoon finding a vehicle lot that would take the skyhopper off her hands, she'd loaded the last of her belongings into a bag she carried over her shoulder. A few books, memorabilia, her cutlery with oversized handles she'd been missing for months, and some odds and ends. The last of her life was coming to the Sparrow.

It really was her home now.

She was starting to get hungry. She didn't care what Matthew had planned, she was ready for dinner. A few stray streetlights shone on the country road, pools of light in the gathering gloom. Her comm buzzed and she moved the bag to her other shoulder so she could answer.

"Hey, where are you at?" Cole asked.

"Couple minutes' walk away."

"Good. We're waiting for you at the farmhouse."

"Okay..." she said, taken back. Looks like dinner was with Cole's friend.

"See you soon."

A minute later she walked up to the farmhouse and stopped at the white picket fence. The Americans took their modern revival stylings very seriously. She pushed the gate open and walked up the stone pathway and onto the porch. The porch was one of the old-fashioned ones that ran around the entire house. Abigail had only seen them in movies. The kind of place to spend an afternoon with friends and a lemonade.

She knocked on the front door and Cole opened it almost immediately.

"Come in."

She stepped out of the twilight into the warm light of the farmhouse.

"Sharon, I'd like you to meet my mother, Elizabeth Cole."

Abigail wasn't sure she'd heard that right. Cole was gesturing to a woman in her early sixties, with salt and pepper gray hair. His mother?

Elizabeth Cole extended a hand. "Does Matthew always call you by your last name, Abigail?"

"Yes, ma'am. And I return the favor," Abigail said shaking the woman's hand. This was a new turn of events.

"Elizabeth is fine." She graced her son with a disapproving look. "It's no wonder he has so few friends when he keeps the ones he has at arm's length."

Cole didn't even react to the jab. "The others are already seated around the table," he said.

"I'll call you Abigail, if that's alright with you," Elizabeth said. "Come. Dinner will get cold."

They led her into a dining room. Yvonne, Davey, and Grace were seated around a quaint table. At one end, the chair had been replaced with the low crate that Abigail usually used on the Sparrow.

"You made it!" Grace said. "Davey wanted to start without you."

"I never said that," he growled back.

"Doesn't mean it's not true," she laughed.

Yvonne had to scoot forward to let Abigail squeeze past to her place. "Did you have a good trip."

"It was just business, but yeah. I did what I needed to do." She sat down and dropped the bag behind her, fishing out her custom silverware.

Matthew and Elizabeth began setting dishes of food in front of them. Potatoes, mashed with the peel still on, carrots candied with brown sugar, butternut squash, a salad of fresh greens, crisp bread, and the highlight of it all, boiled fresh eggs. Abigail was pretty sure she hadn't had a fresh egg in years, and her mouth watered.

"It's not much," Elizabeth said, sitting down, "but it's fresh from the garden and farm."

"I've never seen so many vegetables in my life," Grace said. "This is practically heaven."

"Well, I'm not sure if I would go that far," Elizabeth said with a laugh. "But speaking of that, Matthew would you say grace for us?"

"Of course." He cleared his throat and closed his eyes. "Bless us, O Lord, and these Thy gifts, which we are about to receive from Thy bounty, through Christ our Lord."

Abigail peeked the whole time and she was pretty sure she wasn't the only one. The thought had never crossed her mind that Cole was particularly religious or even raised that way. Her mind flicked to the copy of The Everlasting Man in the bag behind her chair. Then again, maybe she should have.

"Amen," he said and opened his eyes. "Well, don't just stare at me. Load your plates while the food is hot."

Wholesome was the only word that Abigail could find for the evening. Good food. Friends. Laughter. Even Davey was almost pleasant to be around. Mistress Medvedev's cold office seemed more than a train ride away. Her former broker was most certainly wrong about Cole. How ominous could his past be if this was the home he had come from and was still welcome in.

"So why didn't you ever tell us you still had family, Cole?" she asked, as she slathered butter onto a piece of bread.

"No one ever asked."

"He writes once a week usually," Elizabeth said. "I won't have you thinking too badly of Matthew on my account. I'm a tough old bird. I'm busy enough with the farm and don't need him underfoot every other week."

"Since, clearly, as a crew we should have detailed all our family histories," Matthew said, "maybe we should go around the table to make sure there aren't any more surprises."

Abigail was pretty sure he was kidding, but Yvonne obliged him anyway. "I'm an only child. My parents died twenty years ago in a depressurization accident on Amalthea."

"I remember that," Elizabeth said softly. "My condolences."

Yvonne nodded. "And of course my husband died a year ago."

"I'm an only child too," Grace said. "My parents were killed in front of me by some gangster types. Something about money, but I was too young to know what was happening."

Yikes. That was worse than Abigail had imagined. It was a miracle the kid had made it so far without losing her mind. Or worse.

Davey spoke up next. "I had an older brother and sister. Parents on Thebe last I knew."

Abigail's eyes went wide.

"Why didn't you tell us this?" Cole asked, putting his silverware down.

"I don't know why you guys are making a big deal about this."

Cole stared at him for several seconds. "We'll talk about this later." His eyes flicked to Abigail as if prompting her to continue.

She sighed, not really enjoying this game. "I was an only child. Never knew my mother and Dad wouldn't tell me anything about her. As far as I know, he's probably still rotting in prison. Can we be through with this?"

"I think we had better," Elizabeth said, "before we spoil what is left of the good cheer. But to finish the round, we buried Matthew's father twenty years ago."

That put Cole at a rough age to lose a parent, Abigail thought. It seemed the whole crew had tasted their share of tragedy.

"But the past is the past," Elizabeth continued, standing to her feet, "and the future isn't quite so dim. It might even have cake in it."

"Now we're talking," Davey said, as glad as Abigail was to change the subject. "What kind of cake we talking here?"

"German Chocolate. The coconut in the icing is fake, but I guess you can't win them all."

Abigail felt a grin spread across her face. "Elizabeth Cole, you might just be my favorite person in the solar system right now."

Davey enjoyed the food and most of the company, but still felt bizarrely out of place. Like he was intruding on something private.

The thought had never crossed his mind that Matthew might have a family. He wasn't sure what he'd thought, maybe that they were all dead or had disowned him. That was nonsense. It turned out the freelancer was a lot like his mother. If she ran the farm by herself, it meant she had as much grit as her son. And they seemed to be okay with each other.

He'd barely finished his slice of cake when Matthew put a hand on his shoulder. "Let's go for a walk."

Davey looked at Yvonne, but she merely shrugged.

He stood to his feet and followed Matthew out the back door onto the porch. The cool night had settled in on Mars. A few beetles flittered around the lights, their wings clicking against their shells. Davey at first thought that Matthew was going to lead him back to the Sparrow, whose dim outline was faintly visible against the sky. Instead, he turned the other direction, down a path between rows of wheat.

"Where are we going?" Davey asked. He kept his eyes at his feet, hoping not to trip in the dark. Not that he could see his feet anyway.

"It's not far."

A few minutes later they reached the edge of the field where it butted up against a small cliff. A few scraggly trees grew in the shade of the hill, making what living they could in the thin soil. Beneath them was a tombstone. Matthew stood facing it, like a tombstone himself, quiet and imposing. Davey let some time pass before he dared to speak.

"Was this your dad?" Davey asked.

Matthew flicked on a small palm-held flashlight. The light fell on the letters etched into the granite face:

Albert Cole
38-73 AM

"How did he die?"

Matthew breathed in a deep breath and held it, and Davey feared he'd asked the wrong question. After several long moments, the gaucho spoke.

"My father was an alcoholic for most of his life. It was a demon he just couldn't seem to beat. Growing up I only knew him to do two things. Work on the farm and drink."

Davey didn't dare say a word.

"He always provided for my mother and me, and she claimed that he loved us, but I never believed her. She always tried to protect him.

259

Truth was he was just an addict and had been since before he met my mother. I did my best to ignore him. Spent most of my time with my nose in a book, trying to forget the outside world. When I was thirteen, he nearly drank himself into a coma. I was the one that found him unconscious in the barn. He was in the hospital for weeks."

"He came out a different man. Said a priest had made the rounds to see the patients and that he'd told my dad about God. I didn't believe him. Thought it was just another excuse. Dad never touched a drop of alcohol again, but the docs told him the damage was already done. His liver was basically shot through and he wasn't a transplant candidate."

Matthew turned the light off and knelt on one knee in front of the tombstone. "By the time I was fifteen, dad had made a believer out of me, both in himself and in God. We had a few good months together. He spent most of it apologizing to mom and me for the man he'd been. Said that a man takes care of his responsibilities. That we were his responsibility and he'd neglected us. A man uses the strength of his hands to build and he'd squandered what strength was his. He died a few days before my sixteenth birthday."

A chill wind rustled through the leaves of the trees as Matthew stood back to his feet. "We buried him, and my mother and I went on with our lives. She ran the farm and I... Well, I took my own path."

Davey stared at the tombstone tracing the letters with his eyes. "Why are you telling me this?"

"Because Abigail and I will be leaving on a job tomorrow morning. We'll be gone a week or two."

"What about the Sparrow? Are you kicking us off or...?"

"The Sparrow stays here. You, your sister, and Yvonne will stay here where it's quiet and safe. Yvonne will be in charge, but if something happens, I need you to step up and take care of things. I know you'd do anything to protect your sister, but I'm adding Yvonne to your responsibilities now. There's still a bounty on her head and if White Void or a bounty hunter manages to track her..."

He thought about Albert Cole, a worthless drunk that had tried to make things right with his family. He'd stood up in the end, a little late, but that was better than never. "I understand," he said.

There was a time when Davey had held a gun to a woman's head because he'd known no other way to get what he wanted. Matthew had given him a chance he didn't deserve. He'd given him responsibility. Trusted him when no one else would. When no one else should have.

And now he was asking for more. He wanted him to be a man and to take care of Yvonne and Grace. He didn't want him to waste his life like Albert Cole had.

"I understand," Davey repeated.

"Good." Matthew took one last look at the tombstone. "Let's go home." He turned and walked toward the warm light of the farmhouse glimmering in the distance and Davey hurried to catch up.

Chapter 15: Murder in Mercy

There is a persistent and erroneous belief that the decline of civilization began with the departure of Moses. A student of history will laugh at such an assertion. The fall began centuries before, its effects first made manifest in the French Revolution, which paved the way for nineteenth-century European nationalism and ultimately the world wars. The foundations of our world had all but eroded. We had severed ties to those two ancient cities on whose shoulders we had once stood and in so doing had seen glimpses of light.

The age of reason and virtue were over.

In its place was left only passion, tribalism, and the worship of naked science. The West crucified itself, hollowing its soul until it was but an impotent shade, brittle and broken. The Muslim world gave into its darker passions, the rot that had long threatened it, giving rise to bloody caliphate after bloody caliphate. And the East sacrificed millions on the altar of the state, the final death knell for collectivism.

Even Moses was not able to stop the Red Holocaust, but he did keep civilization from fragmenting further and held it in stasis during his time. But the infections did not heal. Moses could not restore what had already been lost.

The war that came after Moses was the culmination of centuries of fermentation; there was no framework left in place to hold it back.

The colonies accepted their fate in silence. Find me a man that has hope for the future of civilization; he is not to be found. Without reason and virtue, there can be no return to the light, and while there are those who endeavor to restore both to their proper place, the weight of the centuries but adds to the inertia.

Man has forsaken reason.

He has forsaken virtue.

The two ancient cities that shaped civilization are lost in the ashes of Earth, and without them, there can be no return.

Fryderyk Lesniak
Author of Civilization's Twilight
Died 88 AM

M atthew instinctively braced himself as his bike shot through the environmental shield that protected the town of Mercy Canyon. There was a brief jolt and he was through. He hit the brakes and slowed to a crawl, pocketing his breathing mask and stretching his stiff and half-frozen fingers. Sheer canyon walls of red rock rose around him, maybe a hundred feet high. The sun had already dipped below the rim. Sunset came early to Mercy Canyon.

Around the next bend, the gorge widened and the mining town came into view. At around five thousand people and about twenty minutes outside of Arizona's shields, Mercy Canyon was only loosely tied to the American colony. When things got rough, they were on their own.

He passed the entrance to the Jefferson Aluminum Mine, the town's only reason to exist. Work for the day was ending and he entered into a steady stream of vehicle and foot traffic heading north to the town's small commercial district. Matthew parked his bike on a side street and hiked the rest of the way into town on foot. Mercy Canyon had that quiet backwater sort of appeal. Aging but well-kept buildings, quaint storefronts, and modest residences were about all you could find.

The place didn't seem like the sort where you'd get a string of murders, but that was apparently where they were at.

The streetlights came on as the gloaming settled over the canyon. Matthew kept his eyes about him and settled into his business walk, the gait that said he was armed and not afraid to defend himself. Never hurt to be careful in an unknown environment, especially when there was foul play going on in the shadows. He passed a storefront where a seven-foot woman in a trench coat loitered against the wall. Sharon ignored him as he passed and he returned the favor. She'd slipped into town a few hours earlier from the other direction. They'd meet up later once Matthew had a little chat with the mayor.

He crossed the street and pushed open the door to a saloon. It was packed and rowdy, as most kindred places were when the day's work was done. Matthew had expected the place to be full of dirty miners fresh from the pits, but it seemed this saloon wasn't frequented by the working class. The shirts were bright, and the cowboy hats were tall and spotless.

A digital player piano hammered away in one corner, mostly hits from a couple generations ago. The thing was probably at least that old and no one ever bothered updating the memory of those things. A handful of patrons danced in front of it, already tipsy enough to feel no shame in their ridiculous flailing.

Matthew slid into a booth and tipped his hat to the man across from him. "Mayor Davis, I assume?"

The man looked up from the plate of spaghetti he'd been occupied with and nodded. He was old, with a thin gray beard and skin weathered by the dry Martian air. "Pleased to meet you, Mr. Cole. Care for dinner? Margaret is one of the best cooks in town."

Matthew eyed the mound of pasta and felt his stomach grumble. "It's rude to turn down a meal that another man buys. Don't think I can say no."

Mayor Davis smiled wryly and twisted his fork into the pile of noodles. "Margaret!" he called. "Another plate for my guest. On the city tab."

The plate was delivered on the fly and Matthew stared at it for a moment. Sharon was probably going to have a ration bar tonight. They'd each stuffed their bikes full of them before leaving the Sparrow this morning to cut on travel costs while they were away.

"Are you too busy pondering the meaning of life to eat?" Davis asked.

"I'm wondering if it's lying if I neglect to mention to my partner that I had a hot meal. She's going to be jealous."

Davis shrugged and kept eating. "Send her in when we leave. Put it on the city tab. Have her order a new bathrobe for all I care. As long as people stop dying, I'm fine with it."

"This been going on for long?" Matthew asked. He dug into his meal with enthusiasm, since Sharon was going to get a plate as well.

"Months. Every few weeks a body turns up. Always a union man."

That was a weird thread to connect a string of murders. "Is the union unpopular? Someone have it out for them?"

"Unions actually. We've got two in town. You'd think with only one mine I'd have only one group of complainers that think they can monopolize my attention. Oh no. Not in Mercy Canyon. We've got two competing unions that fight over the miners. Bosses on both sides think they own me too."

"Do they?"

Davis looked up at Matthew and narrowed his eyes. Finally, he laughed. "Probably more than I think they do, but less than they want. How's that for honesty?"

"Sufficient. So what's the theory? Rivals offing each other?"

"Sure. The bosses are all in a rage about it. They could barely stand each other as it was. Now the few deputies I have are breaking up fights twice a week."

"But you think something else is going on."

Davis nodded. "It's all too nice and neat. Never any witnesses. Always in the dead of night. Union boys always run in packs. If it's them, they're all in on it. No way to hide it."

Matthew had missed something crucial. He'd run into more than a few trade unions across the solar system, but this seemed less like organized labor and more like street gangs. "Tell me about these unions."

"Old as the town itself," Davis said, setting his fork aside. "The mine was founded back in the early days of colonization. Wasn't even a town then. Just the mine. The miners all lived in a pair of barracks, and, apparently, there was quite a rivalry between them. Southside Samaritans and Northern Knights they called themselves. Originally they were mostly techs watching after the robotics. Fast forward a century and a half, and the robots are all gone and a pair of unions still carry on the belligerent traditions, leaving a world of headaches for the town. On a good day, I'm just scrubbing graffiti off a wall or two where some new recruit has gotten a little over eager. On a bad day, someone gets sent to the hospital."

"And on the worst day, to the morgue?"

"Maybe. Like I said, I've got a theory there's an outside agitator."

Matthew frowned at that. "No evidence?"

"Not really. Consider it a hunch from someone that knows their town well." Davis shook his head. "I was born here. The Knights and Samaritans have always been a bunch of troublemakers, but no one had ever killed anyone that I know of."

"First time for everything, I suppose. What do you need from us?"

Davis went back to his plate in earnest. "You and your partner solve my problems. Don't care how. Don't care if you have to rough up half the town. Just don't implicate me. There's a possibility that I might have misappropriated funds to hire you guys. If the bodies stop, it'll be worth it."

Matthew stirred his spaghetti absently. An open-ended contract. A job better suited to a detective. Instead, they had a gunslinging gaucho and an armored tank of a woman. But this man was desperate if he was breaking laws to get the job done.

He smiled politely with a confidence he certainly didn't feel. "We're on it. My partner and I haven't failed a contract yet." Which was strictly true, though the Hawthorne incident had gone off course and the thing on Venus had gone totally out the airlock. But Mayor Davis didn't need to know that.

Abigail waited rather impatiently for Cole. How long did it take for him to get instructions for a job? She had long ago given up on leaning and was now pacing, feeling the awkward tug of the trench coat restricting her movements. Hopefully, she wasn't going to have to wear this thing the whole time they were here. Because if this was going to be one of those skullduggery things where they had to slink around in dark alleys, she was going to be pretty...

"Bored already?" Matthew stood at the alley's entrance, arms crossed.

She muttered a few choice words under her breath and joined him. It was dark now and cold stars shone down from above. "So what's the deal? Why weren't we supposed to bring the Sparrow? Subterfuge isn't my strong suit, you know."

"Turns out the mayor's using cash not exactly earmarked for hiring freelancers. Figured if we rolled into town in a ship people would start asking questions."

"Great," she said. "More unethical government types. Give it to me. What are we dealing with?"

He recounted his conversation with the mayor. Abigail shook her head. "Kind of weird that there are two unions for one mine."

"Yeah, I've got a few questions about the way they operate. I'm all for letting workers band together, but people are getting killed. That's tribalism at its worst."

She started pacing the alley again. "What about the mayor's theory that it's not the unions? Why would someone be agitating things?"

"That's our job to figure out."

"I'm not going to skulk around. I'm the Shield Maiden of Mars, back on my home turf, and I'm here bounty hunting on my own accord." She crossed her arms. "I'll go sit on the union boys. Maybe someone will squeak."

"Guess I get to be the quiet one. I'll check in at some of the other businesses. Get a feel for the local atmosphere. Speaking of, you should go grab yourself a plate at the saloon. On the Mayor's tab. Margaret makes a good spaghetti."

She stopped her pacing short. "So that's what took you so long."

"You wouldn't have turned down a fresh-cooked meal."

"No," she admitted.

"The mayor also suggested snagging a room at the saloon. They've got a few guest rooms and the mayor says they're trustworthy enough. I've already got mine."

"Do we need to worry about staying at the same place?"

"Nah. I don't think anyone will question it too much if we happen to meet over an evening meal. Couple of professionals in the same career can be seen together without drawing attention."

"I suppose not." It was an extremely open-ended contract. Town of several thousand people. Find the needle in the haystack that's stabbing other people. Fun times. She mock-saluted. "By your leave captain, I'm gonna go grab a bite."

She could barely see him nod in the dark. "Meet you tomorrow evening in the saloon. We can compare notes."

"If I haven't already bagged the killer," she joked.

"Be my guest," he said, stepping aside as she left the alley. "It would save us a lot of grief."

First thing in the morning, Abigail tossed the trench coat aside. She was here on business. There was a killer and she was going to catch them. Much as it pained her, she was up and out of the saloon's guest room before dawn. Odds were good that the miners were early risers.

A quick question pointed her in the direction of the Southern Samaritans, a small residence turned office facility that was, appropriately, on the southern end of Mercy Canyon. She scoped it out from a block away, watching for nearly two hours as a steady stream of people came and went from the building. Miners, mostly men, with a few scattered women, would show up and leave again less than half an hour later, having accomplished whatever business they had at the union office. One was carried in on a stretcher by his comrades, his left leg in a newly set cast. Must have been fresh from the med-center to fill out paperwork. Fun.

She had two goals in mind. First was to see if she could spot anything unusual. She doubted this would end up accomplishing much. It wasn't like she was going to catch the killer lurking in the bushes outside, but it never hurt to be observant. Sometimes criminals were dumb if you gave them some breathing room. The second objective was to find someone to interrogate. She'd already decided the younger, the better. While an older union member was more likely to know something of value, and would indeed have a better chance of being in on the funny business if that's what was going on, they were also a lot more likely to be guarded with what they said to a stranger. She'd have more than enough time to talk to that sort later.

Right now she was after a rookie, a bright-eyed kid who's mouth would move faster than his brain.

And there he was, leaving the office with a hapless look on his face. She waited patiently as he disappeared into the building and pounced on him when he emerged sometime later.

"I'd like a word with you."

He nearly jumped out of his skin when he turned and saw her in her exo-suit, doing her best to look intimidating. The poor kid didn't know what to do.

"Of... of course. Is there something I can help you with?" His voice shook just enough to betray his fear.

She chose to ignore it. "Abigail Sharon. Freelancer. You may have heard of the Shield Maiden of Mars."

"Is... Is that you?"

She stared at him for a moment to let him simmer in just how stupid a question that was. She was hoping for an easy brain to pick, but this kid was making it feel like cheating.

"I'm in town because of the murders. I plan on putting a stop to them and thought you might know a thing or two."

The kid set his jaw, perhaps determined to stop making a fool of himself. "Every now and then a body turns up. Sometimes it's a Knight sometimes a Samaritan. And, well, things have gotten a little tense lately. All my friends are on edge. It's a little spooky when you're waiting around to see who's next."

"You guys believe it's the Knights then, killing your people?"

Without a doubt!" he said. "Look, I'm going to be late for my shift. Can we walk toward the mine at least?"

Abigail fell into step beside him and gestured for him to continue.

"The Knights have no character, like none at all, and would do anything to get ahead and post better numbers than us. Bonuses go to the union that scores higher on job numbers, and the competition is pretty fierce. There's no doubt they're just trying to even the odds and catch up."

She nodded as he talked. That probably explains why there were two unions. Benefited the mine to have them compete. Productivity goes up and you only have to give bonuses to the winner. Clever. Scummy, but clever. "So what about when one of the Knights ends up dead?" she asked.

"Parsons had a theory that they kill one of their own every so often to blame us. Make it look like we're just as bad as they are." He shook his head adamantly and started walking faster. "That's absurd. A Samaritan would never kill anyone."

"Hmm," Abigail said as if deep in thought. "You sure that there's no one who might take things a little too far? Every group has a bad apple on occasion."

His pace slowed down, and he seemed to consider it. Had the thought seriously never crossed his mind? The kid really was naive to the world. "Look, I don't know everyone. I've only been on board for a couple months, and I guess it's a little over the top to promise that no Samaritan would ever do something like that, but I just feel in my bones that the Knights are behind this."

"I see," Abigail said. They were getting close to the mine and they were going to have to cut this short. She stepped in front of him and he stopped abruptly to keep from bumping into her. "I intend to bring this killer in. Do you believe that?"

He looked up at her and took a step back. He'd forgotten how intimidated he was of her after he'd started talking. "Yes, ma'am."

"Are you going to help me?"

His eyes narrowed. "You're not going to ask me to break any rules, are you?"

"I'd never do that. I just want you to listen. Keep your ears open. You hear anything suspicious, you contact me. Deal?"

He thought about that for a moment, then nodded. "Don't see how that could hurt."

"Good." She gave him her comm frequency. "Oh, and what's your name?"

"Barry. Barry Dawkins."

"Well then, Barry, I think you have a shift to get to, and I have a murderer to catch. I'm counting on you."

He nodded and smiled with apparent pride. Some people were just too easy. One minute they were scared of you, the next they were your best friend after you made them feel important.

"Hope to hear from you soon, Barry." She winked at him and turned back towards the union office, hoping there were a few more dupes she could turn into informants.

Matthew tapped the side of his glass, watching the accumulated bubbles detach and break for the surface of the pink-red beverage. He sat at the saloon's almost completely empty bar. Turned out the place was pretty quiet during the work week. The unions had their own preferred watering holes, leaving this one a haven for the average folk to escape their drama.

A patron stepped up to the bar beside him. "Took you long enough," he said. Sharon was probably rolling her eyes, but he didn't bother to look her way.

"Just getting work done while you're lounging." She pushed aside one of the stools and leaned against the counter. "This still on the mayor's tab?"

Matthew shook his head. "Figure we should probably go as easy on his budget as we're going on ours. That said I do owe you a drink."

She gave him a funny look. "I don't remember. What for?"

"I offered to buy you one back in Kyoto." For a moment she stared at him blankly. Did she really not remember?

It must have clicked because her face softened and she chuckled softly. "That's right. You were blubbering after I laid you out on the concrete."

"Well, actually it was right before you decked me, but close enough." He waved at the bartender. "Another cherry soda, please."

It was promptly delivered. Sharon took a sip of it. "So why the soda? I don't think I've seen you have a real drink since we met."

He didn't turn to look at her. "My dad drank his liver to death. Alcohol doesn't hold much appeal after that."

"Right," Sharon said, awkwardly. "Your mom told Yvonne and me about that." She took another sip. "Thanks by the way. And sorry."

"For what?"

"For smearing you across the street back in Kyoto."

He waved her off. "You were just doing your job. Still, we've come a long way since then. Nice to have someone watching your back."

Matthew spent his second full day in Mercy Canyon much like the first, quietly interviewing various business owners. Unsurprisingly, he hadn't turned up any key info, but he did have a much better grasp on the general mood of the town. According to the barber, the non-miners had always put up with the unions as a necessary evil, but the recent murders had pushed everyone to the brink. "I don't know why the bosses don't get a grip on their people," he said. "It's not civilized. Where are we, Ceres?"

If things didn't change soon, the unions were going to be on everyone's permanent bad list.

Matthew walked into a hardware store, the sort you could find in any town in the solar system. They probably hadn't changed much from Earth, and certainly not since Moses. A man in dirty overalls and graying hair was talking to a pair of customers at the desk. Matthew made himself scarce and wandered into the row of power tools to browse all the things that would be immensely useful aboard the Sparrow, but he could never quite justify buying. Of course with Yvonne, heading up the maintenance now, maybe he owed it to her to get a proper set of tools.

He had nearly talked himself into buying a new impact wrench when the older man announced his presence by clearing his throat. "You don't want that one actually. The Payton is a bit cheaper and will last a good deal longer."

Matthew set the box down. "Mighty honest of you."

"Payton's are made on Ganymede. I don't get in shipment's very often, so I'm not afraid to sell 'em while I have 'em, and they set the prices not me. Besides. I think you might be trying to do the town a favor."

"What makes you say that?" Matthew picked up the box of the superior tool and pretended to read the specs. If the store owner said it was better, Matthew had no reason to doubt him.

"Heard from the wind you've been asking around. You a freelancer?"

Right to the point. No reason to hide it. "Yes, sir." He tucked the box under his arm. So much for saving money. Yvonne would probably let him file this one as a ship expense and reimburse him from the main account. He was glad not to be keeping the books anymore, but there were a few drawbacks to not holding the purse strings.

"Someone hired you to stop the murders." The man scratched the back of his head. "No, don't answer that. I get a feeling Davis is bending some rules. I'm going to pretend you're here out of the goodness of your heart. Let's get you checked out."

Matthew followed him back up to the front counter. "So what's your take on the murders?" he asked, digging into his pocket for money.

"Occam's Razor suggests I should go with the simplest answer, that the unions are getting violent." He shrugged and took the handful of coins from Matthew to count. "Sometimes Occam is wrong though. I've lived in this town my whole life. Dealt with fights and arguments between the union boys for decades. No one ever died."

"You think someone is agitating, then?"

"A suspicion, but it's a poor one. What kind of motive would they have?" He passed a pair of coins in change back to Matthew. "No one seems to be benefiting from the chaos."

"What about outside of town?"

He shook his head. "Who could possibly have a motive? None of it makes sense I tell you. You've got your work cut out for you. That's for sure."

That was what Matthew had been hearing for two days. No one thought the unions were straight up slaughtering each other, but no one could come up with another suspect. He shook the man's hand. "Can I ask you to contact me if you hear anything?"

The man nodded. "Of course. If you put things right, I'll make sure my daughter names my next grandbaby after you."

Matthew thought it was a joke, but the store owner's face had all the seriousness of a statue. "With incentives like that, I'm gonna have to work overtime. I'd hate to disappoint." He tipped his campero and walked out of the store, new impact wrench tucked under his arm.

The next several days went about the same. During the day, Abigail spent most of her time talking to union workers. She had half a dozen now that were willing to call her if they heard anything important. Her only disappointment was that union leadership wasn't willing to talk to her. Something about her not having jurisdiction. Technically she did, since the mayor had hired them, but his request for discretion killed that option.

In the evenings she met Cole at the saloon. They'd swap info over a cherry soda, a drink which Abigail had to admit was growing on her. Unfortunately, they never had much information to swap. Short of there being a murder while they were there, she had a hard time imagining them making any headway. They usually chatted for an hour or so and then parted ways to retire early. Getting up at dawn was going to end in her death.

The breakthrough came on their fifth day. Sometimes, all it took was asking the right question to the right person. Abigail cornered one of the office workers from the Northside Knights as she left their headquarters, which was, disappointingly, on the east side of town. After talking to her for a few minutes, she found out that the neatly dressed woman handled evaluation reports with the mine.

"The Knights that have been killed, what kind of employees were they?" Abigail asked. "Were they good ones? Is it possible someone is trying to hurt you guys' numbers with the mine and affect bonuses?"

The woman pushed her round-rimmed glasses up the bridge of her nose and shook her head. "Actually, quite the opposite. Each one has been one of our lowest scorers, as far as performance goes. I had met with more than one of them about how to improve their performance on the job. We all want those bonuses."

Abigail tried not to look too interested. "Odd correlation there. Think it has anything to do with the murders?"

The woman looked uncomfortable and shuffled her feet. "I've thought a lot about it, and I can't figure out how it could be related. There are only a handful of people who have access to the evaluations, and they're either internal within the union or part of the mine's business office. I can't work out a motive."

"Wouldn't your averages improve if the weakest members were removed?" Abigail did her best to not make it sound like she was

273

accusing a Knight of doing the deed.

The woman shook her head. "It's the cumulative score that wins the bonus, not averages. Any lost member of the union hurts us. Some less than others, obviously, but that's how it goes."

Abigail thanked her after getting her contact information and stepped into a side alley to call Cole.

"That is something," he said. "I guess it could be a weird coincidence but..."

"But that doesn't seem likely," she agreed. "Does that implicate the mine maybe? Someone on their side with access to evaluations getting rid of sub-par employees."

He was quiet on the other side of the comm for a moment. "Talk about trimming fat. I don't know. I've had trouble arranging a meeting with the mine's management. They don't seem interested in talking to outsiders."

"Same with the unions," she said. "I guess, considering what we've just learned we should treat the leadership of both as suspects until we know otherwise. Anyone that has access to evaluations."

"At the moment. that's the only data point linking the victims together besides union membership. I think we know the answer to this question, but you should check with the Samaritans to see if their victims follow the same pattern."

"I'm heading that way next," she said. "You get into that mine office one way or the other."

"I'll see what I can do. Be careful, Sharon."

"Same warning goes to you, gaucho. A bullet to the back isn't likely to slow me down as much as it would you."

He was silent for a few heartbeats. "You've got a fair point. I'll see you tonight."

The comm shut off with a pop and Abigail turned south towards the Samaritan's office. Something was rotten in Mercy Canyon, and it was better not to upset it too much before they knew what it was.

Early the next morning Matthew walked up to the mine's administrative office, perched high on the canyon ledge overlooking the delvings. It overhung the edge, supported by steel struts, and an elevator dropped down the wall of the canyon into the complex. Other than that, it was a rather unassuming building, sheet metal with only a few windows.

He pushed open the front door into the small receiving area. The secretary looked up from her desk and raised an eyebrow. Apparently, she wasn't expecting visitors. No matter.

"Matthew Cole. I've got an appointment to talk to your head of HR."

She locked eyes with him for a moment and then glanced back at her monitor, tapping a few buttons on her keyboard. "I don't see any appointments for Ms. Evans today. Are you certain you have the right day?"

Now he had a name. He took off his hat and held it behind his back politely. "Absolutely. Ms. Evans and I set up the appointment some time ago. Must have forgotten to put it in the computer. You know how that goes."

"Ms. Evans is very thorough. I have my doubts." The secretary's fingers raced across the keyboard for another moment. "Nonetheless, I shall check with her." She stood and disappeared through a door to the side.

Matthew took the opportunity to open a door on the other side of the room and slip through it. He'd gotten a basic description of the building's layout from a man who used to be the janitor. Former employees always made good informants. He walked down the hall to its end and took a hard right. Unfortunately, he didn't know where the HR office was, he just needed to be deep enough into the office so that by the time he was spotted it looked like...

"Can I help you, sir?"

He turned and put on his best innocent face. The man in front of him was your standard pencil pusher. Dressed neatly, despite a bit of a gut, with a forehead that was trying to claim the top of his head as well. "Yeah, I had a meeting with Ms. Evans," Matthew said. "But I think I got turned around."

"I'll say. You were almost all the way to accounting. Come on. I'll show you to HR." The man walked past him and then opened a door into a cross hall. "This way."

Matthew followed him, grateful he hadn't bothered to question just how he'd gotten lost and that they weren't going back past the secretary. That was a situation he wouldn't have been able to bluff his way out of. He spotted the elevator that led down to the mine and made a mental note of its location. Never know when that sort of thing could be useful. They passed a few other office workers that he politely tipped his hat to before ultimately stopping at a door that read Colleen Evans.

"This is Ms. Evan's office. You good from here?"

275

"Appreciate the help."

The man wandered back towards accounting. Matthew knocked on the door and then opened it without waiting for an answer. The office was spacious, with a wall of windows looking out over the canyon. Judging by her upturned brow, the woman seated behind the desk was not pleased with his sudden appearance. "If you tell me that your name is Matthew Cole, I'm going to call security."

"It's... not?" he tried shrugging his shoulders.

She pressed a button on her desk. "Security, get someone over..."

"Give me five minutes. This is in your best interest."

Evans eyed him carefully. "Have security wait outside my door. I've got an uninvited guest I'll need to have removed after I hear what he has to say." She crossed her arms. "Talk, Mr. Cole."

"You're a hard woman to meet. I've been trying to see you for days."

"Yes. What of it? You have nothing to offer me, nor I you."

He ignored her. Five minutes wasn't all that long, and he'd rather not be dismissed by her gorillas before he was done. "Freelancer. In town investigating the union murders. Been asking around all week and have uncovered a pattern in the killings that you may be able to help me with. Turns out all of the men killed had been doing poorly in their evaluations. Evaluations your office conducted."

"Is there a point to this? I'm well aware of who's been killed and what quality of employee they were."

"We all know the old saying about correlation and causation, but I've got a hunch that they're related this time," he said. "I was curious what you had to say about that."

"I'm not sure what you're insinuating, but it seems quite reasonable to me that poor employees also get themselves into trouble outside of work. It's tragic, but if we're speaking of correlations, I often see that those that have trouble performing well in their career also have trouble in other areas of life."

Matthew shook his head. "It's more than that. These are the very bottom. Each man was one of the lowest scoring employees at the time of his murder. Now here's the funny part. Not all that many people have access to those evaluations. Just a few people in the union offices and I'd assume your office. Someone on the inside is involved. I don't know who it is, and I certainly can't imagine why. But I'm hoping you'd have some idea to help put a stop to this."

Evans picked up a pair of metal spheres on her desk and rolled them between the fingers of her right hand. "You know for a minute I thought you were going to accuse me of being complicit in the murders."

"Can't imagine you have anything to gain," he said shrugging. "Why kill someone that you can just fire, right?"

"Right. Unfortunately, I have nothing to add. I have given my statements to authorities in the past and you hardly qualify as law enforcement."

Matthew gave her the most winning smile he could manage. "Sometimes it takes a stranger. If you learn anything can I trust you to let me know?"

"Sure. Will you get out of my office before I have to throw you out?"

"I'm on my way. This town needs to learn some hospitality." He turned towards the door and paused, one more trick left in his bag. "I know what's going on here, just so we understand each other." It was a shot in the dark. Make a crazy accusation and see what happens.

"That's a pity. Because now you have to be dealt with."

Wait. That wasn't what was supposed to...

The door opened, and two armed security guards stepped in, semi-automatic pistols squared on his chest.

Matthew was quick on the draw. Faster than most in the solar system. He might have even been able to move fast enough to surprise one of them, but never both.

He stepped back and raised his hands wide and high to show he wasn't a threat. They relieved him of his revolver and comm. He turned back to Evans. "You know I heard a joke once about an HR department being evil, but I don't think this is quite what it was going for."

"Cute," she said. "Find somewhere to stash him. I need to talk to him before we get rid of him and figure out if he's alone or working with anyone. I'll be back after the meeting."

They dragged him from the room rather roughly. Matthew wondered what sort of meeting was so important that interrogating a prisoner came second.

Abigail's comm pinged. Hopefully, Matthew was calling with some news. Nope. It was Barry.

"Ms.... uhh... Shirly?"

"Sharon," she said. "Abigail Sharon."

"That's right. So you wanted me to call you in case I heard

something, right?"

She stared at the comm. This kid needed to grow a spine. "That's what I said, yes."

He hesitated. "I'm not sure if this is really important or..."

"I'll be the judge of that."

"I heard from Trevor that the bosses are having a meeting with the Knight's Bosses and the mine execs."

"Could just be some kind of group negotiation thing," she said.

"I don't think so. From what I know, the mine never negotiates with both unions at the same time."

"So you think this is about the murders then?"

"Maybe. Look I don't know. You wanted me to call you if..."

"I did. Thanks, Barry. When is this meeting?"

"At the mine around noon is all Trevor heard."

"I'll check it out."

She cut the comm without another word. This might be nothing, but even if it was, she wasn't going to miss an opportunity to crash in on all the people she wanted to talk to at once. She'd been here a week and hadn't gotten in so much as a single word with the upper leadership of either union. They were either a skittish bunch or had something to hide.

And then there was the other bit of information she'd heard this morning. The mine was posting record numbers lately. Where that fit into any of this was beyond her ability to guess, but at this point, she didn't think there were any coincidences in this town.

She crept down the canyon to the outskirts of the mining facility an hour before noon and hid between two piles of gravel as she watched the traffic moving in and out of the complex. In the distance, high above the canyon floor, she saw the mine's main administrative office. She hadn't heard from Cole yet, so maybe he was having some luck up there.

A convoy of enormous haul trucks rolled down the road toward the complex. This looked like as good of an opportunity as any. As the last truck passed her position, she reached out and grabbed hold of the rung ladder leading up to the crew compartment. Not that she would be joining them. She was more than content to hang off the side and slide into the mining complex. It may not have been the stealthiest approach, but at least she wasn't on foot.

The Jefferson Aluminum Mine was an open strip mine cut like shelves into the wall of the canyon. It wasn't a pretty sight, but then the wheels of industry never were, not on any of the planets or moons in the solar system, and not on Earth before. Vehicles moved about, and workers went about their business. One or two stopped in their tracks when they spotted Abigail on the side of the haul truck. She waved and did her best to look like she belonged there.

Above her, the administrative building loomed, and she could see the elevator bolted onto the canyon wall. It descended into the top of an enormous structure that reminded her of an aircraft hangar. Whatever the building was, it seemed to be the hub of activity around her, and she had a pretty good hunch that the meeting would be there.

She dropped onto the gravel with a crunch and picked her way carefully through a yard of spare equipment and scrap metal. Now she just had to find a way into the building without panicking whatever went for security in these parts.

"Amateurs," Matthew mumbled under his breath.

Security had locked him into a cramped and messy broom closet. Professional criminals would have known better. It had taken him only a few minutes of quiet fumbling in the dark to find a flashlight. After that, it was trivial to find the toolbox. He set it on his knees, cracked it open, and started rummaging through its contents.

Bingo.

He picked up a small device that was somewhat shaped like a screwdriver. Laser cutter. Too small to be battery operated, which was a pity, because he was going to have to find an outlet somewhere in this closet, but still more than capable of getting him out of here. Turned out finding a place to plug the thing in was the hardest part of his escape so far. The outlet ended up being behind an enormous pile of junk, and he was worried he'd made too much noise by the time he got the cutter plugged in.

He pulled the protective eyewear he'd found over his face. Even reflected light from a cutter like this was bad news. The laser's blue beam would only have the coherence to cut for a few inches, making it not particularly suited as a weapon, though it would burn for a few feet past that. He'd already found his weapon, a broom with an aluminum handle. He cut the handle into two one and a half foot pieces. He tested one of his new clubs, swinging it around the tight enclosure. It would do as long as he caught them by surprise.

Finally, he got started on the door, or rather the plate the door latched into. The blue beam did its work slowly burning through the wall. Matthew made a conscious effort not to cut through the entire wall or completely detach the plate, only weaken it. He set the cutter down and shined his flashlight on the damage. It would do.

He picked his new aluminum clubs up, one in each hand and stepped up to the door. "Nothing ventured, nothing gained," he mumbled and kicked the weakened door with the heel of his boot. The plate gave out, and the door crashed open. Matthew didn't even wait for it to stop moving before he leaped through. One guard was in front of him, a dumb look of surprise on his face. Matthew wiped it off with a clang of aluminum. The other guard was to the side, already drawing his pistol. Matthew swung the other club and hit his hand. The gun discharged into the ground, and Matthew followed up with a second swing to his head.

The guard went down, not unconscious, but with no more fight left in him. He whimpered softly, as he cradled his head. Matthew bent over and retrieved his own revolver and comm from his belt and kicked the man's pistol away. "You guys are terrible at your job," he said, and turned to get his bearings.

Then he saw nearly a dozen heads poking out of offices from the direction of accounting.

"You don't want any part of this. Some of your management's involved in something nasty. Speaking of, anyone want to volunteer and tell me where an important meeting is taking place right now?"

One helpful person said two words. "The mine."

Matthew tipped his hat. "Thanks. You all might want to take the rest of the day off. Don't know where this is going but it's nowhere good." With that he turned and walked toward the elevator to the mine, ignoring the stares of the office workers.

No sooner had he entered it and pushed the button, than his comm buzzed.

"Cole, hope your meeting went well, I've got another lead I'm..."

"Held at gunpoint and locked in a closet," he said. "The mine's leadership is definitely involved. There's some kind of important meeting going on there now, and I'm on my way to crash it."

She whistled. "I'm after the same meeting. It's with the union bosses."

It was his turn to be surprised. "I guess they're all in on it, whatever it is. I still can't grok out a motive, but it sure looks like the leads are offing their own folks."

"I agree. I just interviewed a local. Left him tied up in a corner. The meeting will be on the upper level of the main building. He said I couldn't miss it."

"I'll find it," Matthew said. He looked out the glass-walled elevator down at the slowly approaching mine. This sure wasn't a fast ride.

"One more thing, Cole. I stumbled onto the grav plate hub. It's connected to the mine building."

That made sense considering the town was based around the mine. Every town or colony had a control room that oversaw the plates buried around town to keep the local gravity set as close to one gee as possible. In a town this small, it was probably only a shed. Someplace big like Flagstaff probably had a manned bunker or several of them. "How's this help?"

"Had a tech friend of mine write me a program for a job one time. I upload it to the control room and I can turn local plates on or off from my suit."

That one took him by surprise. "Guess there's our trump card. Just give me a warning before you cut gravity."

"Will do. I'll get my program uploaded and then try and catch up. See you soon."

Matthew put away his comm just as the elevator passed through the roof of the building. Hopefully, the exit area would be abandoned, or this was going to be awkward. Either way, he drew his revolver. The door opened with the ring of a bell and he cautiously poked his head out. Looked deserted.

The building before him opened into a cavernous area, and a quick glance to the floor far below told him that it was an equipment bay for vehicles and anything else sensitive that didn't need to be left exposed to the elements. Mars was well known for its massive sandstorms. Not even the strongest environmental shield could keep those out and periodically half the planet was ducking for cover. The Jefferson Aluminum mine probably rolled all its expensive equipment into the bay whenever Mars was feeling a bit testy.

He stepped out onto a catwalk high above the floor of the facility. An intricate series of walkways connected several large platforms and even a few small buildings that hung from the rafters. Only one of these buildings looked large enough to house a meeting between any number of people. Thankfully, there wasn't a lot of activity this high above the floor, and it was relatively dark. He'd be able to move about unnoticed.

It took him a few minutes of slinking, and a few minutes of waiting behind some cover when a group of workers passed through his area, but he made it over to the largest building without incident. He climbed a ladder on its side to the top. He was now very near the rafters of the main hangar, and it was dark enough that he had to feel his way forward with care. Thankfully, he knew what he was looking for. This sort of industrial building didn't tend to be climate controlled and usually only had ventilation fans on the ceiling. He spotted a circle of light coming up from the floor and knew he had his target.

He crept over to the vent and peered in. There was a group of people down there at a table, including Ms. Evans, but it was going to be impossible to hear anything with the fan running. He pulled off a side panel and cut a few wires, silencing it for good.

"Who turned that off? It feels like Venus in here."

"Switch is still flipped on. I'll get maintenance to look at it later."

"This won't take long. Ms. Evans do you have the reports?"

Matthew crept up to the edge of the vent and cautiously peered in. He wasn't going to get a great look at the room, but hopefully, he could at least get a feel for what was happening down there. And at the very least... He pulled a small recorder from his pocket, set it on the edge of the vent, and turned it on. A little bit of evidence went a long way.

"I have the reports. We've got a situation though. One of the freelancers that've been around town this week got a little nosey. Showed up in my office this morning implying he knew something was afoot. I had security detain him. It may be best if we put the whole operation on hold until he and the Shield Maiden are dealt with."

Maybe they should have been a little sneakier, he thought grimly.

"I see no problem with waiting on the next hit till issues are dealt with, but while Finlay is here, we may as well give him his assignment."

There was a name that Matthew knew. Gavin Finlay was one of the most notorious hitmen on all of Mars. His name wasn't exactly household, but in a career like Matthew's, you tended to hear it whispered every so often.

There was a moment's pause. "Very well," Evans said. "Here are the next two targets. Matthew saw her slide two binders across the table where they were taken by people just outside of view. "If neither of you have any protests, then we'll take care of the contract with Finlay, and it will be done."

There was a murmur of indistinct conversation for a few minutes. Matthew's best guess was that the binders had been passed to union bosses who were putting a stamp of approval for a hit on one of their own members. He still couldn't imagine why they would be okay with something so barbaric.

"I've got no problems," a voice said. "Barry was seen talking with the Shield Maiden earlier this week too, so it's for the best that he's dealt with."

"The Knights are also okay with your selection."

"Excellent. If you'll sign the papers, I'll have payment transferred."

That explained the union bosses' involvement. Still didn't touch the broader motive behind the killings.

A man beside Evans spoke up. "Finlay, does everything appear in order to you?"

"You know I don't actually need paperwork, right?" a gruff voice answered in a clipped British accent. "Just payment."

"Nonsense. This is a transaction between professionals."

"Then everything is fine," Finlay said.

"Well, I believe that settles things. May the spirit of competition lead to another record year of profit for all of us."

Matthew frowned. Spirit of competition? Record year of profit? Suddenly the pieces clicked together. By killing a few weak links every so often, the competition between the Knights and the Samaritans had been raised to a fever pitch. While some of that extra steam was blown off after hours in fights and other tussles, most of it probably went into securing bonuses from the mine.

The bosses were killing people to keep the rest motivated to work harder than the other side. It was crazy. Worse, it apparently was working as intended, if the mine was having record output. How they had concocted such a hair-brained scheme was beyond his ability to guess.

"What did I miss?" Sharon whispered.

Matthew nearly jumped. She was crouching in the dark beside him. "Too much to explain. Took you long enough to catch up."

"I couldn't find an elevator and had to climb. What do I need to know?"

"Everyone in that room is guilty. Also, I assume you've heard of Finlay?"

"Of course."

"He's on board too."

"Good. There's a price on his head we can collect. You got a plan?" she asked.

"You tear open the roof and we go in quick. I don't want anyone escaping. I've got a recording, but I'd rather have the rats tied up for delivery. Grav plates under your control?"

She tapped her wrist. "Yup."

He nodded at the vent. "Get us in there."

Sharon reached down with both hands and tore the fan and its entire assembly out of the ceiling, tossed it aside, and dropped down into the hole, smashing the table the group had been gathered around. It had taken her all of about three seconds.

Matthew followed, gripping part of a support on the way down to swing himself wide of the table's wreckage. He hit the ground with revolver drawn and spun to get his bearings. There were a lot more people in the room than he had anticipated. Over a dozen at least. And one was a killer.

There were also a lot of guns in the process of being drawn. The unions had brought armed goons.

So much for taking people in. Anyone that drew a weapon was a threat that had to be dealt with. Matthew chose his targets and began firing, knowing that the next few seconds would determine who lived and who died. He emptied his cylinder, putting seven rounds into four different targets.

Sharon had plowed into another group, sending them flying around the room like popped corn. He'd have liked to use her bulletproof shield for cover to reload, but she looked a bit occupied at the moment.

Not that he would have had that chance anyway. A man in a blonde cowboy hat tackled him to the ground. He drew a trench knife in a quick motion and plunged it down towards Matthew's chest. Matthew barely managed to batter it away with the stock of his revolver, earning himself a cut across his knuckles. He rolled away before his assailant could recover.

Finlay cursed in Scottish and advanced on Matthew like a wild animal. Matthew didn't bother getting up, but brought the killer down to him, by bracing himself against the wall and aiming a boot at his ankle. It rolled, making a popping sound, and he dropped to the ground. Matthew dove for him, grappling for the knife. He won that fight and wrested it from the man's grip, but took a fist to the face in the process. He fell back stunned and seeing stars.

Then he was hoisted to his feet.

"Get up, gaucho, he's on the run."

Matthew shook his head. The room was in shambles, mostly from Sharon's rampage. Anyone that wasn't injured or unconscious was standing with their hands above their heads. He picked up his revolver and reloaded it from a speedloader. "You chasing or am I?"

"Go get him. I'll keep watch over our hosts. I'll wait for your word to hit the switch if you need it."

284

"Got it." Matthew ran from the room and out onto the catwalks, trying to get a sight on Finlay. There he was, making for the elevator. If he weren't limping from the hit to his ankle, Matthew wouldn't stand a chance of catching him. As it was...

He turned his comm on, pocketed it, and set off at a sprint, head still ringing from the hit he'd taken. The elevator was straight in front of him, though the catwalk took a circuitous route. But Matthew wasn't going to take the straight route.

He turned his head to keep an eye on Finlay to make sure he hadn't diverted.

"Sharon. Grav plates. Get ready." He holstered his gun and put everything he had into the run. "Hit it."

The grave plates in the area gave out and gravity reverted to Mars' natural one-third of a gee. Matthew was ready and adjusted his gait accordingly into bounding leaps. Out of the corner of his eye, he saw that Finlay wasn't prepared and nearly fell to the ground when he overshot a step.

This was going to be risky. Matthew approached the end of the catwalk seeing the abyssal drop in front of him. He reached the railing and vaulted it, sailing out over empty space. His stomach turned at the height, at the low gravity, and at the thought of what would happen if he'd misjudged the leap.

The far catwalk was approaching rapidly. The elevator right in front of him. He slammed into the catwalk and caught hold of the rail to stop himself. "Hit it again," he said between gritted teeth, and Sharon reverted gravity to normal. Now he was closer to the elevator than Finlay, and, odds were, he didn't know the tide had turned against him. They converged right at the elevator. The killer startled, then ducked low and lunged with a smaller knife he'd pulled from his belt.

Matthew put four bullets into him, stopping him and his career as a hitman dead in their tracks.

He looked down at the body and his bleeding knuckles. He shook his head. Grim way to end the day.

They were in the saloon again. After all the headaches of the day, Abigail was glad to stop and just have a meal. Also, Margaret's spaghetti was just that good. The thin woman said she grew her own herbs out back and claimed that was all it took.

"Well, I'm indebted to you people for cleaning up our mess,"

Mayor Davis said.

Abigail nodded at him. He was right about it being a mess. Leadership from both the unions and the mine had been implicated. It was going to take a long time to sort out all the threads. It turned out the short version was exactly what Cole had guessed.

"Just doing what you paid us to do," she said politely. "Has the investigation turned up how all this got started yet?"

Davis looked tired. Odds were he hadn't been sleeping for a while and that wasn't about to change. "A couple of the mine execs are already practicing their opera routine. First death was apparently an accident and not a murder at all. The poor man had a heart attack and died in rival territory. Suspicions and tempers got hot. It was that new HR woman, Evans I think her name was, saw the bump in productivity. Now this is unsubstantiated, but apparently she hired Finlay herself for the next kill and then presented her findings to the bosses."

"Ambitious," Cole said. "And pure evil."

"Well it was enough to get her put over the whole department. She's going to burn though. There's enough conspiracy and murder charges here that anyone who doesn't hang will rot in jail till the sun burns out." He shook his head. "I trust you folks can stick around for a couple more days? I know we already got your testimonies, but I think Flagstaff is sending some men out to help with the investigation. Might need your statements again."

Cole looked at Abigail. "I don't see why not," he said. "We didn't know how long this job was going to take anyway. Another day or two won't hurt anything."

"Good. Good," the mayor said. "Now I suppose I should see about paying you. Hopefully, no one investigates my office, or I'll be run out of town too."

"A pity about that," Abigail said. "Especially since we solved the murders."

"You did and I have no regrets. Sometimes you have to live with the choices you make."

"I've been thinking about that," Cole said. "I'm gonna have a talk with the men from Flagstaff when they get here. I'm willing to bet there was a price on Finlay's head. If there is, and if we collect, I think we can count that toward what you owe us. If there's a difference, maybe we can settle on that later."

Davis was speechless for a minute before taking a long swig of his drink. "That would be too good to be true," he said, setting his mug down. "I thought I hired a mercenary. Turns out I got a saint."

"Not quite," Cole said.

Abigail smiled to herself. There was the do-gooder in Cole coming out again. He didn't want the mayor to get in trouble for protecting his own people, so rather than collecting double, he was going to settle for less. It's not something that Abigail would have done when she was solo, but she was getting used to Cole and this sort of thing. It seemed to be happening more often now too.

She gave him a subtle nod and caught his eye. It may have been his ship, and he may have been the one to make calls, but she wanted him to know that she approved. To let him know he wasn't alone.

It felt good to be the good guys.

Mistress Tatyana Medvedev pulled back the curtains to let in a little of the setting sun's light, something she rarely did. The pale evening sky filtered into her office, offering little illumination. She returned to her desk and prepared for another evening's tireless work, managing her empire.

The comm buzzed and she answered it. She glanced at the caller's frequency.

"Yes, what do you need? I already gave you everything you needed to know."

"Just wanted to confirm that we found the ship right where you said it would be. You sure the Shield Maiden and Cole are gone?"

"If my Shield Maiden was there, I would not let filth like yourselves within a hundred kilometers of that ship."

"Umm. Right. Well just wanted to let you know and..."

"I care not what you do at this stage. You see to your own needs." the mistress cut him off. "Do not call me again." She ended the call and stared at her monitor.

Sometimes she did things she didn't want to do. Tatyana had always tried to stay on the right side of the law, but that wasn't always easy for a woman in her position. Sometimes the pot had to be stirred. Things broken. People shaken.

And unfortunately, her Abigail needed a good shake-up.

The crew of the Sparrow was a delicate thing. Tatyana had carefully researched each and every crewmate. Matthew Cole had been easy. An accomplished freelancer left a paper trail across the solar system, though his former career had come as a bit of a surprise. The children were of no regard to her, even if she dimly hoped that

287

Grace would not come to a bad end in this. Perhaps she could find a place for the young girl.

It was the doctor, Yvonne Naude that interested Tatyana. She was the fragile link.

A simple call was all it had taken.

Chapter 16: Storms Past and Present

The Eschevarria Equations mean a good deal to humanity. They were the last time a human ever contributed to the advancement of science during the age of Moses. In the beginning, he needed men's creativity and propensity towards making intuitive leaps. Eventually, he didn't even need that.

Until the frameshift device didn't function as he expected. Moses discovered that the faster the frame of reference, the shorter the bubble of effect could be maintained. At two percent the speed of light, the field would collapse after only a few minutes. At half a percent, it could be maintained nearly indefinitely.

But Moses had promised us the stars, and that was too slow for the fleeting lives of men to ever have hope of colonizing them. The last of Earth's nearly obsolete physicists and mathematicians were set loose on the problem. Moses was not so foolish to think he was beyond needing help.

Jose Eschevarria solved the problem, which is to say he demonstrated that it was unsolvable. Through a series of expressions, now known as the Eschevarria Equations, he proved that the frameshift effect could never be stable at higher speeds, no matter how much energy you poured into it. At two point one seven percent it would always collapse in less than a millisecond.

The frameshift device, though useful for getting us around the solar system, was ultimately a dead end, and Moses moved his research into new directions.

The Eschevarria Equations were a watershed moment for our race. Men were not so irrelevant in the fields of science after all and Moses needed more help than he realized. Further, it was the moment that men began to suspect that perhaps our solar system was a prison from which we would never escape. The cradle of our birth would become our coffin as well.

Lillian Flemming
Physicist, University of Ganymede
Died 14 AM

"I'm not impressed with this one either," Davey said crossing his arms. "Just looks like another broken down piece of junk to me."

Grace leaned over the rope to get as good a look at the machine as she could. She always was more interested in machinery and equipment anyway. "Sure it's junk. But back then it was important junk. Just think! This little rover beat humans to Mars by decades. Decades!"

Davey tried to imagine that time, a dim ancient history before Moses, easy space travel, and pretty much everything else he knew. It was hard to picture. What good they could have gotten from sending a little robot to roll across the red planet was beyond his ability to guess. Maybe a couple pictures?

"You have no sense of adventure," she said. "This would be kind of like sending a probe to another solar system. Wouldn't it be exciting to learn new things about the unknown!"

"We're never leaving this solar system," he said, shaking his head. "No way."

She frowned at him and stepped away from the exhibit. "Maybe not, but at least back then people weren't all sticks in the mud." She looked back at the rover and saluted. "Farewell, little Opportunity. I think you were very brave!"

Girls didn't make much sense sometimes. Even sisters. He put a hand on her shoulder. "Come on, we should get out of here if we want to catch the train."

They left the Museum of the First Martians and stepped out onto the sidewalk of downtown Flagstaff. He may have complained, but it had been a good way to spend the afternoon. The city center was amazing, filled with green parks and tall buildings. And even the museum hadn't been that bad. When humanity had first gotten to Mars well over a century ago, they'd scooped up all their old rovers and put 'em in a museum. Sentimental maybe, but still pretty cool to see machines that had once come from Earth.

Even if they were just pieces of junk.

On the way to the train station, Davey elbowed Grace. "Give Yvonne a call. She wanted to know when we were on our way."

"Oh right. I'd forgotten."

"See. You do need me around."

She pulled out her comm and placed the call. It buzzed without answer. "That's not really like her."

"Probably just taking a nap." Davey had noticed that anytime Yvonne could sneak away for half an hour in the afternoon, she did. Only recently, he'd discovered that it was to take a quick nap. That's what happens when you get up so early. Your batteries die halfway through the day.

"I guess she is pretty old," Grace said.

"She's not even sixty yet."

"That's old."

"No, it's... Never mind. Just try her again later."

It was only a short train ride to the Cole family farm and Grace tried calling Yvonne three more times. She never picked up. It was nothing, probably, but it bothered Davey. If he didn't answer the comm when he was supposed to, there would be angry words. Matthew would lecture him about responsibility, and then Abigail would say something sarcastic as soon as the gaucho was out of earshot. Yvonne would just act disappointed, which was the worst of the lot.

They got off at the outskirts station near the farm and walked the rest of the way. Grace was in a talkative mood, probably because they'd been somewhere new that she'd never been. He was used to it, but today it was getting on his nerves.

"I wonder if any of the rovers could be restored and driven around?" she asked. "Some of them seemed like they were in pretty good condition."

291

Davey shrugged and did his best at humoring her. "Weren't they left abandoned for like a century?"

"Not a lot of moisture on Mars to corrode them," she countered.

"I guess not, but I kind of think the dust storms and... Hold on." He stopped abruptly. They had turned down the path between the fields that would lead them back to the Sparrow when he saw them. Several men in suits were working around the base and ramp of the ship. Men that had no reason to be there.

Davey grabbed Grace's arm and pulled her into the rows of tall wheat.

She protested almost at once, "What are you..."

He put a finger to her lips and motioned for her to follow. Her eyes narrowed in question, but at least she shut up. He led her through the wheat, careful not to disturb too many of the stalks. Elizabeth Cole would be mad at him if they tore up the valuable crop.

But if the men were who he thought they were, it wouldn't matter.

They approached the edge of the field near the Sparrow. Close enough to where they could see but remain hidden in the shadows. Two men had the access panel open at the top of the ramp. Wires splayed out as they worked, obviously trying to hotwire the door and gain entrance to the ship.

That explained why the comms weren't connecting. Jammed, hacked, something like that.

"They're after Yvonne," Grace whispered. "How did they find..."

Davey shushed her again. There were at least eight armed men out there. He should have been terrified. But Matthew had trusted him to watch after things. One way or another he was gonna sort it out. The only problem was he was unarmed. His gun was aboard the Sparrow, stowed safely in his room and completely out of reach.

He startled when Yvonne's voice called out across the field from the speaker.

"You boys aren't so good at listening. I told you that it wasn't going to be that easy."

The two men working on the door jerked back and convulsed. Sparks flew from their boots as they dove off the ramp, collapsing to the ground beneath. Apparently, the Sparrow wasn't without security. Davey made up his mind. He took Grace's hand again and gently led her back into the wheat field. She shouldn't be anywhere near the Sparrow right now, not while there was any danger. He'd never forgive himself if she were hurt in a fight.

"Come on. That'll slow them for a little while," he whispered.

"We can't just leave Yvonne."

"We aren't. But we're going to check in with Elizabeth and make sure she's okay. And I need a weapon if I'm going to be any use against those guys."

Grace didn't look very happy about leaving but this wasn't up for debate. They needed resources. They needed a strategy. And by they, he meant everyone but Grace. There wasn't a snowball's chance on Venus that he was gonna let her anywhere near those thugs.

Elizabeth Cole knew something odd was going on in the early afternoon when one of her farmhands reported that the comms weren't working. The device said it was connecting, but no one answered any of their calls. Maybe the local relays were down, but that didn't usually take all comm use out. There was almost always a satellite overhead to bounce the signal. Using a satellite would add considerable signal delay, but total silence meant either the comm satellites were in a weird position or something more serious was going on.

She sent the workers home early just in case. Less than a year ago, the Abrogationists had taken out nearly the entire comm grid in Arizona in a wave of coordinated bombings. In case they were taking another stab at it, she'd rather her people be home safe with their families.

An hour later she saw the men around the Sparrow and the horrible truth crystalized. She had a choice to make. Head for safety and try to make it out from under whatever they were using to jam local comms or else set up as overwatch.

It wasn't really a choice. She couldn't leave Yvonne trapped on the Sparrow, alone, to face her fate.

She ran upstairs to her second story bedroom in the old farmhouse and opened the window and pushed back the shutters. The Sparrow was visible across the field, reflecting the ruddy afternoon light. This would have to do.

She retrieved two weapons from a closet, a rifle and a pump-action shotgun. She laid the shotgun on the bed where she could grab it if needed, and then pushed a dresser in front of the door. Better safe than sorry. Taking the rifle, she rested it on the window seal and looked through the scope. The men were working on the door at the top of the ramp. They weren't in yet, but surely it was only a matter of time.

Elizabeth wondered if Yvonne even knew she was in danger.

With the comms down there was no way to warn her. The least Elizabeth could do was wait and watch. If they broke through the door, she would fire and take down as many as she could.

It would probably mean a grisly end for her, and that should have been alarming. Maybe it would be when the time came. Elizabeth had never been face-to-face with death, not from the barrel of a gun anyway, but she'd cross that canyon when she got there. Right now she had a single objective. Protect the poor woman on that ship.

The men had a panel off now. It wouldn't be long before they were through. Elizabeth felt her pulse quicken. Was this what it was like for Matthew before a fight? Did her son still feel fear every time he drew his gun? The mother in her hated the path he had ended up taking. They had always known his choice of career might lead unsavory types back to the farm, and it was for that very reason he had taught her to shoot.

She removed the safety and sighted in the scope on the man working on the panel. Should she remove him before he got the door open? That would give Yvonne more time.

Maybe if she made enough noise, Yvonne would realize what was happening and fly away. Hopefully before Grace and Davey returned from the museum. She breathed a quick prayer, thanking God that the kids were away from the nasty business.

Yvonne's voice rang out across the fields. Distant and muffled. All at once the men were tumbling off the ramp. Elizabeth couldn't make out what had happened from here. Maybe the ramp was electrified. Either way, Yvonne appeared to be doing what she could to fight back.

Elizabeth relaxed, content that the Sparrow would be safe for a few minutes longer. "Should have gone for help after all," she mumbled grimly. "Too late now."

She watched the syndicate men as they tried to figure out how to get into the Sparrow. Eventually, they produced a ladder, one of Elizabeth's that was usually stashed in an outbuilding. Two of the men climbed on top of the ship. They seemed hesitant, as if they suspected the hull were booby trapped as well. She sighted the scopes in on them again, preparing herself to pull the trigger.

The door handle behind her rattled and she flew into action, dropping the rifle and brandishing the shotgun in a single movement. She pointed it at the door with shaking hands.

"Mrs. Cole? Are you in there?"

"Grace!" She tossed the shotgun aside and slid the dresser away from the door. "Get in here quickly, there are..."

"We know," Davey said. "We already scouted them out." His eyes fell on the rifle by the window. "I see you're on top of things."

Elizabeth wrung her hands together. The appearance of the children had splintered her nerve. Why, oh why, had they come home so early? "You two have to get out of here and get help. They're jamming the comms."

Davey shook his head. "I can't leave. Not while Yvonne is in danger." He turned and looked at his sister. "But Grace..."

The girl raised her arms, showing off the golden bracelets. "I want to help too. I'm bulletproof, remember."

Matthew had told Elizabeth about the miracles and their strange powers. She didn't understand them, didn't understand how any technology could do what he claimed. Which meant she didn't trust them. "Grace, I'm not about to put you in danger, not when there's another important task for you."

Grace opened her mouth to argue, but Davey cut her off. "This isn't up for debate. You're going to head right back to the train station and either ride till you can use the comm to call the police or keep going till you find one yourself."

She crossed her arms defiantly. She was brave, that was for sure. Elizabeth hoped it wouldn't get her killed someday. "That's an order, Grace."

The girl finally slumped in defeat. "Fine. When do you want me to go?"

"Now," Elizabeth said. "If anyone sees you, run. And pray that you really are bulletproof."

Grace hesitated for a moment and then threw her arms around her brother. "Don't do anything stupid, okay? You're good at that sometimes."

"I won't. Go on."

With a final look between the two, she fled from the room. Elizabeth heard her pound down the stairs and the front door slam.

"I thought that door was locked. How did you two get in?"

"Grace is good with a pick."

"Oh," she said, unsure of what else to say. One minute the pair seemed so normal and the next minute they slapped you with a harsh reminder of their time on the street and in slavery. She shut the door and locked it, but didn't bother with moving the dresser. Picking up the rifle, she looked down the scope again. Men were clustered around the top hatch of the Sparrow now. Time was running out.

"Grace isn't going to get help in time, is she?" Davey asked quietly.

Elizabeth wished she could give the young man good news, but there was no hiding the truth. "No. I don't believe she will."

Davey picked up the shotgun. "Then I guess that's it then. Never used a pump-action. Anything I need to know about it before I go?"

She narrowed her eyes. "Is this something you're willing to die for? I count nine of them. I can't imagine this doesn't go badly."

He looked away. "Maybe. I don't know."

"What about Grace?" she asked.

"Matthew and Abigail will take care of her," he said. "I have to do this. He trusted me with protecting them." He stared at the ground. "It's my responsibility."

Matthew had told her about Davey's troubled past, how he'd held Yvonne at gunpoint. And why wouldn't he have? A street kid, desperate to take care of his sister. No other good in the world to fight for. Her son had given him another.

He was desperate to prove himself, and it might cost both their lives. Redemption always comes at a cost.

She gestured to a case of shells. "Stuff your pockets just in case. Let me show you how to reload it."

Davey crept back through the wheat field toward the Sparrow, hoping to get close enough to be of some use before Elizabeth was forced to open fire. "Grace is away, she's safe now," he whispered to himself.

What would happen if she got lost? What if she got help but they were all dead before she made it back?

Didn't matter now, all that was left was to throw his dart into the wind and hope to hit a bullseye.

He wouldn't let Matthew down. If the gaucho came home to a field of bodies, would he know he'd tried his best against impossible odds?

He reached the edge of the field and removed the safety. Four men were around the base of the ladder deep in an argument. About twenty meters. Easily in range. He and Elizabeth had agreed that he should take the first shot if they could wait that long. He pushed the barrel past the last stalk of wheat and aimed down the sights.

The shotgun thundered. It kicked like a wild animal in his hands, slamming into his shoulder and causing him to stagger back in surprise. He barely had time to look up and see that he had hit one of them before he retreated back into the field, disoriented. Elizabeth had tried to warn him, but the kickback had still caught him off guard.

A high-pitched crack rang out. Elizabeth's rifle answering his own shot.

He pumped the shotgun, ejecting the spent cartridge and chambering a fresh one. He heard shouting. They'd be responding soon. Better to try and shoot again. He wasn't sure how many chances he would get.

He emerged at the edge of the field a short distance from his previous location, just as Elizabeth's rifle fired a second time. Hopefully, their attention was on her right now. A man in a suit shouted. He'd been seen. Raising the shotgun, he fired quickly, not taking enough time to aim properly. His target's left arm was sprayed with pellets. Davey managed the kickback better this time but still flinched when the stock slammed into his shoulder.

Elizabeth's rifle fired a third time and the man he had just grazed dropped like a dead weight.

"Throw down your weapons and step out into the open!" a commanding voice shouted.

Like hell, Davey thought as he chambered a fresh cartridge.

"We have a thumper pointed at the ship. Surrender or we will destroy it, followed by the farmhouse."

He hesitated, cold fear creeping down his spine like poison. Maybe they were bluffing...

"You have ten seconds to comply, or we will open fire."

He stepped out into the open and tossed aside the shotgun. Rage coursing through his veins. Failure. This was it. But he didn't have a choice right now. He couldn't just let them kill Yvonne and Elizabeth.

A man in a white suit retrieved the shotgun and trained it on Davey. "You should let your friend in the farmhouse know not to fire again. I'd hate to have to level the lovely old building."

Davey turned and waved his arms frantically at the farmhouse hoping Elizabeth got the message. How could he have been so stupid? None of them were getting out of this alive.

Elizabeth pulled the trigger. Saw the bullet strike her first target. It was a clean shot in the chest. Center of mass, just like Matthew had taught her. Tears streamed down her cheeks and she cursed the foolish men that had made her do this. She'd never even pointed a gun at another person before, and now she'd blown a hole straight through one.

297

She wiped her eyes. If she couldn't see, she'd be no use to anyone. She pulled the bolt lever and aimed back down the sights. There. The target closest to the rows of wheat. Closest to Davey. She pulled the trigger again but must have been too hasty. Near miss.

She cursed again and clamped her jaw shut, pulling the bolt lever again. She heard the distant boom of the shotgun. Her target staggered but remained standing. "I'm sorry," she muttered and pulled the trigger a third time, putting him down for good.

Davey suddenly stepped out of his cover and threw his weapon aside.

"What are you doing...?"

She prepared to fire on the suited man that held his weapon.

Davey turned and started frantically waving his arms in her direction. The message was clear. She didn't like it, but she got it. The tides had turned. Those thugs had some leverage on Davey. Elizabeth sat back and ran a weary hand through her hair. Was this it then? Were there no other options?

In the distance, she saw the man in the white suit approach Davey to talk to him. The kid was brave, she'd grant him that, but he was in over his head.

"Don't believe anything he says," she whispered and prayed that Grace would find help before it was too late.

The man in the white suit stepped up to Davey and crossed his arms. His head was shaved, and intricate tattoos like ivy adorned his skull.

"It seems you have a little sense about you, at least enough not to have your friends demolished by a thumper."

Davey mimicked the man's posture and crossed his arms. It might have looked intimidating if he wasn't so short. "I think you might be bluffing about the thumper."

The man smiled cruelly. "In that, you would be mistaken. How else were we going to keep the ship grounded? We let Ms. Naude know that we could demolish her sanctuary if she so much as fired up the engines as soon as we arrived. Much as my boss would prefer she be taken alive, a body is an option if all else fails."

A chorus of shouts came from somewhere on top of the Sparrow. Apparently, there were defense mechanisms on the top hatch too. A moment later a black-suited man appeared at the edge. "Hey yo, Kudzu. This is gonna take some time."

White suit, or Kudzu apparently, shrugged. "Pity. Keep trying. You've got half an hour to figure out how to get in before we blast the ship apart. Remember, we only get half payment if the woman dies. Remember that."

"Still on it, boss."

"Now then," Kudzu said turning back to Davey. "I'd much rather this end without bloodshed." He turned to look at the bodies of his two men lying on the ground. "Well, without any more bloodshed. You see, my boss wants this Ms. Naude alive, and I think you'd rather her be alive than dead. In a way, we both want the same thing."

Davey shook his head. "Not how that works, exhaust-brain. I want you guys gone."

"I'm afraid you're going to have to settle. Half an hour. You have until then to find a solution that involves less death. I assume you know the access code to get onto that ship?"

Davey wracked his brain, trying to think of a convincing lie, but the moment he hesitated, he knew he'd lost.

"That's what I thought," Kudzu said. "How about this then? I pay you fifty thousand to open that door for us, and no one else dies. Ms. Naude comes with us, but you and the shooter at the farmhouse get to live to see tomorrow."

"I don't believe you," Davey replied.

"My boy, White Void enforcers are businessmen first and foremost. If I can't bring Ms. Naude home to Ceres alive, then my own pay is at stake. I'm more than willing to part with a measly fifty thousand to ensure my cut is the highest possible."

This gave him pause. That was... That was more money than he had ever dreamed of. He and Grace could live off of it for a long time. They wouldn't be stuck riding around like rats on a ship where they weren't wanted. And if it really did mean that Yvonne would live...

She wouldn't be very happy about it. That was for sure. But she would at least be alive.

"I can see you're thinking it through," Kudzu said. "Take your time, but not too long. The clock is ticking."

The thought of that much money almost made him sick. If he took the deal, it would be for Grace. The money would help him take care of her. They were on Mars right now, the best rock in the solar system. He wouldn't be able to tell her where it came from. Why they'd left the Sparrow. But they'd be free again. Free for the first time in years.

His heartbeat hammered at his temples. What was he thinking? Grace would never speak to him again if she found out.

And Matthew? Would he be surprised or just disappointed? Did he expect to be disappointed in him? Matthew had said he trusted him, something that no one but Grace had ever done before. He was half mad for it. Maybe even stupid. But Matthew was good. That was the one thing that Davey knew.

A better man than any he had met.

And Davey wanted to be like him.

"Sorry," he said in a voice that was barely a whisper. "I can't."

"Disappointing," Kudzu said. "Misplaced loyalties can be problematic."

It was done. He'd refused, and there was no going back. It had made so much sense in some ways, but in refusing it, he felt... better. Lighter. Like a line had been crossed that had long needed crossing.

Kudzu continued. "Shivers, take our friend up to the farmhouse and retrieve the sharpshooter. We're going to need an alternate form of persuasion for Ms. Naude."

Davey felt the barrel of a weapon press sharply into his back and wondered how this had all gone so wrong.

Elizabeth watched the two work their way through the wheat field and kept her gun trained on the henchman. Twice she nearly took the shot, but the risk was too great. There was no way she could be sure Davey wouldn't take a bullet to the back.

It took them several minutes to reach the farmhouse and emerge from the field. From the ground, Davey's captor waved at her open window, causing her to instinctively draw back into the dark room.

"You up there," he called. "Shooter. It's time for you to come on down. As you can see we've got your little friend. There's no reason this has to be a bloodbath."

"I'm fine up here, thanks," she called.

"A Miss, huh? Respect given for the shooting. See here's the thing. You're not fine up there. You want to tell her, kid? No?" He jabbed Davey with the gun and laughed. "See that ridge over there? We've got a portable thumper set up. Its crew is just itching to pull the trigger, see, and if you don't come down, we demolish that ship over there and your friend hiding on it. Then we turn that thumper on you and your pretty little house."

Elizabeth glanced at the ridge. She didn't see anything out of the ordinary, but she doubted they would make such an insane bluff. White Void was certainly wealthy enough to pull out the big guns if they were going after a ship. "What happens if I come down?"

"We take a walk back over and see if your friend on the ship has sense."

Leverage. That's all they were to these people. It never was a fair fight. She pulled the rifle back from the window and laid it on the bed. "I'm coming down," she shouted out the window.

As she walked down the stairs she wondered if she would ever return.

Davey had about had it with the gun in his back. "Look, I'm walking. What am I going to do to you? You're like a foot taller than me."

Shivers laughed. "I almost like you, kid."

"Stop calling me that and just shut up."

The three of them made it back to the ship without incident. Elizabeth looked miserable and defeated, but Davey didn't know what he could say or do for her.

"Glad you could join us, Ms." Kudzu said. "I'm short a few men because of your meddling, but that means more of the cut goes to me. So long as there are no further incidents, I'll take it as a favor and move on." He stepped over to Davey. "Last chance to make some cash."

Elizabeth looked at him questioningly. Davey just looked at his feet and kicked at the dirt.

"Thought not," Kudzu said. He put a foot slowly onto the ship's ramp, as if to test and see if it was still electrified. When it didn't bite he walked up toward the door. "Now then, Ms. Naude. I know you're watching and listening. I'm sure you can see how the tables have turned. Here's what's going to happen. Either you surrender yourself or these two get a bullet in the back of the head. Your choice."

For a long heartbeat, the only sound was a quiet breeze that had begun to blow across the fields. Finally, Yvonne's voice came over the speaker. "I want to talk to Davey."

"That the runt's name? He can hear you. Talk."

Davey's ears perked up. What was this about?

"Alone. Send him into the Sparrow. Then I'll surrender myself and the other two go free."

"I'm not sure you're in a position to bargain."

"Of course I am," she said. "I can cut your paycheck in half out of pure spite."

301

Kudzu scratched the back of his head. "Ten minutes and then the thumper fires."

"Deal," Yvonne said.

"Well, what are you waiting for," Kudzu said walking back down the ramp toward Davey. "Time's wasting and as fun as it is shooting fish in a barrel, it's not conducive to my bottom line."

Davey swallowed, wondering what she wanted from him. Part of him wanted Yvonne to just try and fly away and risk the thumper. He headed for the Sparrow's ramp and quickly walked to the top before turning around. He'd half expected Kudzu or Shivers would follow him or try to trick him somehow. Kudzu only tapped his watch. Elizabeth's face was unreadable.

Davey turned to the access panel. It was a mess of wires. Hopefully, it still worked. He punched in the code that Matthew had given him, careful to shield it with his hand so that the combination couldn't be seen. The door slid open and he slipped through, hitting the panel on the back side.

It shut immediately, and Davey breathed a sigh of relief. Maybe Kudzu really was interested in finishing this without bloodshed. He walked through the common room, past the crew quarters and into the cockpit. Yvonne was seated in the pilot's chair, her face calm. The overhead light was off, and her eyes flicked back and forth between the monitors showing various feeds from external cameras.

"You shouldn't be here," she said quietly. "You should have run as far as you could as soon as you saw what was going on."

She seemed quiet, distant maybe. Davey wasn't sure what to call it. "Matthew told me to keep an eye on things while he was gone and that's what I'm going to do." He'd been repeating this over and over. To himself, to Elizabeth, and now to Yvonne. Maybe if he kept saying it, he'd find some way to follow through.

"I don't think he meant for you to go charging into battle against White Void hired guns. Or drag his mother into it."

He sat in the co-pilot's seat and glanced at the camera feeds. It looked like the men had given up on breaking into the Sparrow and had moved to the edge of the field. "Actually, Elizabeth had a rifle pointed this way before Grace and I even got home."

"Is your sister somewhere safe? Never mind, I know the answer. If she wasn't safe, you wouldn't be here." Yvonne glanced at him from the corner of her eye. "You should have taken the money."

He shifted uncomfortably in his seat. So she'd heard the whole thing. She'd seen him mull over betraying her for cash. The thought made him sick. "Grace would have never forgiven me."

She shook her head sadly. "The end result will be the same for me, I'm afraid. In a few minutes, I'm going to walk out there and go with them and hope they decide to leave without firing that thumper in revenge."

Davey's eyes burned with tears. There had to be another way. This wasn't fair. Yvonne had never done anything to anyone. She was a doctor. She didn't deserve to be treated like this.

Just when this place was finally starting to feel like home, it was going to be shattered. Matthew would be furious and Abigail was going to be downright dangerous to be around when they found out what happened.

Yvonne was the one that had done the most to make him feel welcome and part of the crew. And after what he had done to her.

"Davey," she said. "Remember when you asked me why I didn't hate you?"

It was almost as if she read his mind. He didn't trust his voice not to crack, so he just nodded and wiped a stray tear away.

"It was easy to look past what you did. You were a desperate young man. And one can only hold so much hate in their heart."

Davey frowned and turned fully to look at her.

"That man out there in the white suit with the tattoos."

"Kudzu?" he asked.

"He killed my husband."

Davey clamped his mouth shut. What was he supposed to say to that? Then it dawned on him that she was about to surrender and go with her husband's killer.

"Over a year ago, Kudzu came into our practice on Ceres. He was bleeding from a gunshot wound to his shoulder. He was in a lot of pain and not thinking clearly. He waved his gun around making demands of us, unaware that Tomas and I treated everyone that came through our door, regardless of what side of the law they were on." She sighed and her voice sounded weary. "Tomas tried to get him to calm down, but Kudzu was half crazed and started to get violent. My husband drew his own gun, the one he'd always kept concealed beneath his coat. They shot each other."

Why was she telling him this now?

"They both fell to the floor, but Kudzu was the better marksman. Tomas' aorta had been pierced and there was no saving him. We both knew it. I held his hand, but he only motioned with his head toward Kudzu. He said a single word. Triage. His dying wish was for me to treat the man who had killed him. I should have ignored him. I should have stayed at his side, but fool that I was, I respected his wishes and tended to Kudzu. When I looked back at Tomas a few minutes later, he had already passed."

Davey was afraid to breathe, afraid to interrupt. The man out there had stolen Yvonne's husband from her. Had stolen her final minutes with him. If only Davey had shot him earlier. He could have done everyone a favor.

Yvonne stood to her feet. "I think it's about time." She laughed bitterly, a sound that he'd never heard from her. It alarmed him. "He's even responsible for the predicament I'm in now. A few months later his boss, Piggy, was shot in an assassination attempt by a rival. Who do you think they brought him to for emergency surgery after the glowing reviews they received from Kudzu?"

"Yvonne, I'm sorry. I don't know what to do." He'd stopped trying to wipe away the tears.

She placed a hand on his shoulder. "You listened to my story. That's enough for now. Anything more and Grace may lose her big brother. Come. Walk me to the ramp."

He stood awkwardly to his feet and hugged her. "I'm sorry," he said again.

She returned his hug. "It was always going to end this way."

They walked to the side airlock and opened it. The light of the dying afternoon shone pale over the hills, sickly and weak. Davey hadn't been on Mars long, but he had yet to see the sky look like that. Elizabeth sat on the ground under the watchful eye of Shivers.

The syndicate men stood at the bottom of the ramp, Kudzu in his white suit at the front. "I see you have sense after all, Ms. Naude."

"We all do what we must in these savage days," she said quietly.

"How very true. And now, if you will hurry, it appears there is a dust storm approaching that wasn't in the forecast."

Davey looked nervously at the sky again. So that was it. He'd heard stories about Martian dust storms lasting weeks. Grace crossed his mind. No point in worrying about her. She was smart and could take care of herself.

He watched Yvonne walk down the ramp. His stomach dropped. It was wrong. Every last bit of it was wrong.

Yvonne reached the bottom of the ramp, drew a long knife from her shirt sleeve, and lunged at Kudzu. He sidestepped her, but she still managed to slash him across the chest. Strong arms grappled her and pulled her away from her victim, twisting her wrist till she cried out in pain and dropped her weapon.

Davey stood in shock, too surprised to move, unsure what he would have done if he could. Kudzu's hand reached to the red stain spreading across his white suit, his face twisted into a grimace of pain but not fear. The knife had fallen short. "We do what we must indeed," he said through clenched teeth. "I take it this is revenge for your colleague on Ceres?"

Yvonne's face was like ice as she spat at the gangster. "He was my husband, you bastard."

A look of surprise crossed his face, and Davey wondered for a second if it was regret. Instead, Kudzu laughed. "Explains why you were never gentle with my wounds on Ceres. I guess now we're even. Bind her mouth. I don't want to hear her anymore." He pointed at Davey and then at Elizabeth. "Count yourselves lucky that blade didn't find it's mark. Ms. Naude almost got the two of you killed. And if you follow us, the thumper finishes you both."

They dragged Yvonne away, across the field in the opposite direction of the house, probably toward wherever their friends with the thumper were. Davey couldn't bear it any longer and he sat on the metal ramp, his heart and mind empty. The light continued to die, and soon blown sand began to sting his exposed skin. He should have done something, anything, but there was nothing left. He'd failed Yvonne in the worst possible way.

"On your feet. We need to get inside."

Elizabeth. He couldn't look up at her. Couldn't face her.

"Now, Davey. The storm will be here soon."

Against his will, his body obeyed and he followed her through the field to the farmhouse as the wind began to pick up.

The comms were still down when Grace reached the train station. The officials there were sympathetic to her plight but had no way of getting word to the police either. This station only served the local farmers and residents and rarely had an officer on duty. The manager, a kind looking man in his sixties, came out and told Grace he would escort her into Flagstaff himself. A train was in the station at that very moment ready to depart. They boarded together and the manager even gave the order to depart early.

Grace was thankful, but it did little to relieve her fears. Every few minutes she pulled out her comm and tried to call Matthew. Every few minutes she shook the device in frustration for not cooperating. Just how big an area was being jammed?

It wasn't until they had passed several stops that the call finally went through. For a moment she was so happy that she wanted to cry.

"Matthew! You have to come home now!"

In the middle of the night, two grav bikes pulled up in front of the farmhouse. The weary riders had spent hours traveling through the dust storm at a snail's pace in near zero visibility and praying their engines' filters would last long enough to get them home. Abigail was in better shape. She'd only had to lower her face shield. Her armor would need a good cleaning and polish but would be none the worse for wear.

She was worried about Cole. He'd donned a pair of goggles and wrapped his head so that as little skin as possible was exposed, but she knew that would only do so much to keep out the sand. He would be raw from the wind and dust. She could see in his posture how tired he was, how much he hurt.

Wordlessly she followed him up the steps to the house. Elizabeth met them, pulling them both in out of the storm. "You made it," she whispered, wrapping her son in an embrace.

"We came as quickly as we could," he said.

"Has anything happened since we last heard from you?" Abigail asked, sorry for interrupting the moment but eager for news.

Elizabeth shook her head sadly. "The police left an hour or so ago. There's not going to be an awful lot of evidence left behind for them to track Yvonne. The storm is just going to make it harder."

Abigail quietly resolved to sew trackers into everyone's clothing. If they complained, they could shove off. She wasn't willing to lose anyone else like this.

"The storm will also keep them on Mars," Cole said. "The longer it is until they can leave for Ceres, the longer we have to find Yvonne."

"You really think that's possible?" Davey asked.

Abigail hadn't noticed him creep down the stairs. Kid looked miserable, red-eyed and exhausted.

"Maybe," Cole said. "You okay?"

"No." Davey clenched his fists tightly. "Why would you ask such a stupid question? I screwed everything up. You trusted me to take care of things and it all fell apart."

Abigail looked to Cole and saw only understanding in his eyes. "Sometimes the world isn't fair, Davey. Sometimes the forces arrayed

306

against you are more than you can bear. When you stand in the middle of a storm, sometimes it's all you can do to keep on standing."

"And when you don't?" Davey asked.

"Then you fall down having done everything you could. The hard part is what comes after, getting back up again. That's where I failed all those years ago. That's the lesson I never learned."

Abigail felt a stir of admiration for Cole. He may have had his rough edges, but he did have a way with words when it counted. She wanted to know about this failure he mentioned but now wasn't the time.

Cole continued when Davey said nothing. "That's what we're going to do now, Davey. Get back up and go after Yvonne."

"But I blew it."

"You did what I asked to the best of your ability. No one can ask for more than that. You did well."

Davey nodded and the tension in the air released. "What do we do now?"

"Storm will last a few days," Cole said. "Tonight we get some sleep."

Abigail alone retired back to the Sparrow for the evening. The others slept in the farmhouse, and she felt a pang of loneliness to be separated from them at a time like this. But sleeping in her suit wasn't so great on her back, and she needed to charge it. She stared long at the door to Yvonne's cabin before retreating to her own room.

Chapter 17: Fallout

That humans are a cancer in the solar system is a fact that we as a species must come to terms with. We are the children of Earth. That is our home and as such it might have been considered our right to do what we have done to it. Even so, look at how we left it: locked in an ice age from a century long nuclear winter.

Now we are an invasive species, spoiling what is not ours to spoil, spread like an infestation across formerly pristine planets and moons.

Once this truth is accepted, it is only a matter of time before one arrives at the conclusion that humanity's place in the solar system must be abrogated.

We Human Abrogationists seek not the pain of our fellow man. Indeed, we do not directly propose the taking of lives where it is avoidable. Rather we must ensure that these are the last generations that live away from our home. The gears of civilization must be slowed until they turn no more. Isolated colonies wither more quickly than well connected ones. The ties that bind need only to be weakened and they will snap like a rusted chain.

Moses, the Great Enabler, sought to lift up what should never have been elevated. His removal gives a second chance for proper order to be restored.

We will hasten those days.

Chamai Mombeshora
From the Treatise on Human Abrogation
Died 91 AM

"What exactly are we looking for?" Abigail asked.

"Something. Anything," Cole said. She could hear the rasp in his voice, even over the wind. The long journey through the dust storm and short night of sleep had done a number on him. He stalked around the small rise again, eyes trained on the ground.

Through the blowing sand, Abigail could barely see the farmhouse. They'd climbed up to the ridge and found where the thumper had been located the previous day. It didn't take long, despite the poor visibility. Several shafts had been bored deep into the rock to anchor the thumper. It had been a big one, much bigger than the one that Abigail's shield had protected them from all those months ago atop the train to Churchill. This one was meant for shooting a spaceship out of the sky. It was a good thing Yvonne hadn't decided to risk taking off or she and the Sparrow would both be wreckage.

"Look, Cole. I want to find her too, but I don't think we're going to find anything out here. You're going to run yourself ragged at this rate."

He turned to her, his face inscrutable behind the wrappings and goggles. "We're not going back empty handed."

"We found a few cigarette butts caught in the grass and confirmed they weren't lying about the thumper," she said. "There's nothing else out here. What did you expect to find? An address with a map to their secret lair?"

"It would help," he stooped and looked through the grass one more time. No way he was going to find anything. If they'd left evidence, it was buried or blown away by the storm at this point. That fact must have finally worked its way into his head because he stood and nodded. "Alright, let's head back."

She followed him down the ridge and they trudged back across the fields towards the farmhouse. Briefly, she wondered how much of the wheat was going to be lost. Elizabeth had explained that the Martian cultivar was much hardier of stem and that her farm was set in a depression somewhat protected from the wind. Still, there would be losses, both here and across the entire hemisphere. Weather reports were saying the north would dodge the bullet for the most part. Lucky them.

Abigail followed Cole onto the back porch of the house and was surprised when, instead of opening the door, he sat down in a rocking chair. At least they were in the lee of the wind here. "What do we do?" he asked. "We've got to find her. Obviously for Yvonne's sake, but for Davey's as well."

"If you hadn't laid the weight of the world on him, he wouldn't be taking it so badly."

"He needed responsibility."

"Cole, he's a kid."

"And that's what he'll remain. He'll end up like half the other deadbeat young men around the solar system, no job, no purpose, just waiting for a syndicate to recruit them."

Abigail looked out into the swirling eddies of dust and sighed. "Look. I'm not going to question your little reformation project, and I can't deny you've had some success. Just don't expect too much from him, alright?"

He didn't look too thrilled with that. "So what now? We have no leads other than they're probably grounded on Mars for the next few days."

"No one ever leaves during a dust storm?"

"Not unless it's life or death," he said. "I've yet to meet a pilot that likes flying blind or in high wind. Plus the dust makes a mess of scopes and other sensitive equipment."

"So they're holed up." But then everyone was holed up right now. Arizona was a big colony. Besides the city of Flagstaff, there were thousands of square kilometers of farmland beneath the environmental shield. There was no hope of finding Yvonne without a lead of some kind. There were far too many places they could be. "Unless..."

"Unless what?"

"I was just trying to imagine where I would go if I were a criminal lowlife. There is an abandoned mine that would make an excellent base of operations for a group of ne'er do wells."

"I have my doubts the Arizona law enforcement left the Hawthorne mine unsupervised," he said. "But that does give me an idea."

"I hope it's good enough that we can go inside after you tell me," Abigail said. "I may be made of metal, but this can't be good for you."

He waved her off. "If we have a problem with the underworld, we may as well use the people we know."

She crossed her arms. She wasn't about to play a guessing game.

"We both know a local expert on the Arizona criminal element."

So that's who he meant. "I don't like it, Cole. You think he's going to be willing to cooperate?"

She was pretty sure he smiled under his face wraps. "No, but I'm sure we can find a method of persuasion. It'll be fun. Like a reunion with an old friend."

"Fine," she said and opened the door into the house, "but if he's your idea of a friend, it's no wonder you were a loner before I came along."

Arizona Minister of Law, Ryan Thompson had a headache. As the chief law enforcement officer of the colony, this was the normal state of affairs. A dust storm only made things worse. His deputies would be inundated with calls of domestic disputes, drunken fights, stranded civilians who shouldn't have been traveling, and more. Cabin fever made ordinarily sane people lose their minds.

His eyes scanned the report from his detectives. The serial killer they'd been tracking for months had chosen the cover of the storm to strike again. He'd left the usual nihilistic message taunting law enforcement at the scene of the crime. Thompson looked to see if there was any new information, but it looked much like the previous fourteen murders. He closed the folder and saw just how many he had to get through. There was no way he would finish before his meeting with President Barclay.

The file on top caught his attention. Sparrow. He flipped it open and scanned the document. Why did that name seem familiar?

His intercom popped on. "Mr. Thompson you have visitors."

He looked at his watch. "They'll have to wait. I have a meeting. Get their information and..."

"I don't think they're going to take no for an answer."

He frowned. "Then call security." Probably some citizen's group angry about something. This kind of thing made him hate his job.

"I don't think that security is going to be very effective."

The door of his office slammed open with a bang and two familiar but unwelcome faces burst into his office. The gaucho and the girl in the exo-suit. They were followed by two children. What were kids doing with a pair of freelancers?

He folded his hands in front of him as a lot of bad memories resurfaced. These two had caused him weeks of scandal. "I'm going to need a very good explanation if you want to avoid criminal charges for breaking into my office."

Matthew Cole had an iron look cemented on his face. "I think you'd rather just be rid of us. Pressing charges would give us a reason to stay. Besides, we are going to do you a favor."

"I'm sure this isn't out of the kindness of your heart. What do you have to gain from this?

"Careful," Abigail Sharon said. "You're not high on our list of favorite people."

"The feeling is mutual," he replied in growing irritation. "If there is a point to this, I hope you're coming to it quickly."

Cole put his palms flat on Thompson's desk. "We're tracking down some members of the White Void syndicate. They kidnapped a member of my crew and I intend to find them before they leave planet."

Thompson sat back in his chair and smiled at the grim irony. "A few months ago, White Void would have been unheard of in Arizona, Mr. Cole. This was Hawthorne Gang territory, but nature abhors a vacuum. I'm afraid that the removal of James and Paul Hawthorne splintered their gang. It's a turf war, and White Void certainly has operatives scouting out Arizona."

The gaucho slammed a fist on the desk. "Your insinuation is as plain as it is baseless. If you didn't play games with people's lives and did your job, you'd have fewer messes to clean up."

Thompson tried to stare the man down. Somewhere, deep in the back of his mind, he knew Cole had a point. Not that he'd ever admit it. But his nerve cracked and he picked up his tablet in a gesture to hide his lost composure. His eyes flicked across the four of them. If he lost face, he'd quickly become the joke in the room. Cole and Sharon weren't to be trifled with. "What is it you want from me?"

"Information. We want to find our friend. You lead us to the scum that attacked our ship, we help you do your job and remove a threat to the people of Arizona."

Thompson shook his head. "It's not so simple as that. Remove one cell and White Void will simply send another."

"And then it will be on you to take care of that one," Cole said. "That is what President Barclay appointed you to do, is it not?"

And now they thought they knew how to do his job. He wanted these intruders gone and he wanted them gone now, but maybe giving them what little information he had would be the fastest way to get them out of his office. And if they demolished a growing part of Arizona's underworld, they really would be doing him a favor. He'd seen the mess they'd made of the Hawthornes.

"I have a detective," he said folding his hands on the desk, "who's been tracking White Void's movements for some time. If anyone knows anything, he will." He pulled up the contact on his tablet and downloaded the information onto a data stick. He held it out to Cole. "He's frequently undercover, so don't be surprised if he ignores your call. Now get out of my office. If you ever come back without an appointment, I'll have you arrested. And if you compromise my detective in any way, it will be the same."

Cole tipped his hat. "Thank you, for being professional about this." He took the stick and pocketed it. "Let's roll."

Thompson watched the motley crew file from the room, hoping he would never see them again. And why had he brought the children? He tapped out a quick message to the detective. Better warn him what was coming.

Davey had never seen Matthew so frustrated. The detective wasn't willing to meet with them until tomorrow. The gaucho spent the rest of the day pacing around the farmhouse. He and Abigail tried to call in favors with what contacts they had, but no one had anything for them, so they ended up having to wait on the meeting. Grace and Davey just tried to stay out of the way.

Why had they even gone anyway? Maybe towing in the whole group put the government man off balance. Davey wasn't sure, but at least they'd gotten something. Now there was nothing to do but wait.

"I'd say we could go back to the Sparrow and play darts," he said, "But that would mean heading back out into the storm. I'm never getting the taste of dirt out of my mouth as it is."

Grace was staring out a window and didn't answer.

He playfully punched her shoulder.

"Just thinking about Yvonne," she said. "And my birthday. I know, I know. It's selfish."

"Hey, don't worry. I haven't forgotten about you."

She turned from the window, and the crease in her face melted. "Did you get me something?"

313

"Maybe."

"You're terrible at gifts, Davey."

"Matthew helped me pick this one out."

She seemed to consider that. "It better not be a cowboy hat or something dumb like that."

He shrugged. "Guess you don't want the matching poncho either." She laughed, and he was glad for the momentary distraction. There was no way the rest of this mess would work out.

Matthew dismounted his bike in the bad part of town, making sure to lock it down and engage the security system. The detective had given very specific instructions and he had no intention of being late. He was grateful that the detective would see him, even if he was irritated about the wait.

While the storm took out its fury on the besieged colony, its inhabitants huddled for cover as best as they were able. At least those with any sense. Even in the worst of storms, a few tired or addicted souls would wander out to get a drink. The meeting was in an old apartment building whose lowest floor had been turned into a bar. A gaudy neon sign glowed hazily in the swirling brown eddies. Iron bars secured all the windows.

"Always the sign of a classy establishment," he muttered. This was the kind of place that really wished you hadn't walked in the door. Outsiders weren't welcome and illegal business flowed faster than the booze.

All in all, the kind of place to meet an undercover detective.

Matthew noticed several sets of eyes tracking him as he headed for a dark corner. He chose the booth he thought least likely to be bothered by a waitress. Odds were good they didn't have his drink of choice.

No good. Within two minutes a bored-looking waitress stood looking at him expectantly. Matthew cleared his throat. "Whatever's hard and local." That ought to get her off his back. She promptly delivered an amber drink. He wasn't exactly up on his whiskey, but the smell alone was enough to bring back memories. He pushed it aside.

A few minutes later a tall man in a gray trench coat approached. He removed his goggles and face mask. "Lovely weather, eh? On Ceres we didn't have anything that passed as weather. Mr. Cole?"

Matthew nodded. "I appreciate your time. I know this puts you at risk."

"Minimal. Name's Lee. It's nice to talk to someone that won't put a bullet between my eyes. The boss didn't exactly send a glowing review, but he did say you could be trusted."

That was more generous of Thompson than Matthew thought possible. "We've had some friction in the past."

Lee raised his eyebrows and nodded in amusement. "I think everyone hits friction with him at some point. Say, you don't look like you're drinking that..."

"All yours," Matthew said.

Lee scooted the drink in front of him. "So about your little problem."

This was it. Hopefully, he'd heard something or knew where Yvonne was being held.

"I don't have a clue where your friend is."

Matthew felt his heart fall. That was it then. Storm was only supposed to last another day before the winds died, and then Yvonne would be taken off-world back to Ceres where they'd never be able to trace her.

"But I think I know someone who might."

His eyes flicked to Lee's. The man took a long drink of the whiskey. "Wow, that's stout." He winced and then took another sip. "Here's the thing. I've been working for the last three months on tracking White Void's movements across Arizona. It's mostly been just a few operatives from Ceres until recently. They've started recruiting locals now. Just a few here and there, slowly building a list of people that are loyal to them. That's when operations will really start. Previously honest businesses become fronts for trafficking or drug running. Young men with nothing else to do get hired as muscle. We're not quite over that tipping point yet here in Arizona."

Matthew tapped his fingers in impatience.

Lee continued. "Oh, yes, There's a mechanic. Recruited in the first wave. His garage is going to be little more than a chop shop soon. Long story short, he comes here nearly every night and he's the best I can do. Can't promise he'll know what you need, but neither can I get you one of the off-world members."

Matthew didn't like it, but it would have to do. "And how exactly am I supposed to make him talk?"

"Ha. However you want. So long as there's not a body, ain't no one in this bar calling the police. His name's Patrick Sawyer. He's got a wife and two kids. Got no business getting involved in the shady stuff, but he is anyway." Lee took another long drink. "He's about five-six, redhead, probably still wearing the coveralls from the garage. Look, I've got to go. I don't want him getting here early and recognizing me."

"I understand, Lee. Thank you."

The man sighed and nodded slowly. He looked tired. Like he hadn't slept in months.

Maybe he hadn't.

"I just hope you get your person back. These are some bad people. I'm not gonna cry one tear for them if you mess a few up along the way."

"Go. You've got a cover to protect."

He left without another word and without so much as a glance behind him.

Matthew frowned. He'd rather hoped for an address and maybe a couple of names. He and Abigail could go in guns blazing and call it a done deal. Instead, he was left with the prospect of an interrogation. He considered calling Abigail and having her on standby. Intimidation seemed up her alley and considering the mood she'd been in since Yvonne had been kidnapped, she'd probably enjoy it.

Which, all things considered, meant that he should probably be the one to do it. Better not let her revel in her darker impulses.

A few minutes later a man walked in matching Lee's description of Patrick Sawyer. He took no time in heading to the bar and ordering a drink. Matthew gave it a count of a hundred before getting up. He walked up behind Sawyer and put the muzzle of his revolver into his back. The man straightened and made to cry out, but Matthew cut him off.

"Easy there, friend. Let's go have a talk at my booth."

Sawyer stood slowly. "Who are you? What do you want?" The man was scared spitless.

"Already answered that second question. Just want to talk. Let's go."

Sawyer turned nervously and glanced back at his recently delivered mug, the question he was thinking going unspoken.

Matthew sighed. "Take the drink, but don't even think about using the mug as a weapon. I know that one."

They walked back to the booth. Several of the other patrons eyed them curiously, but Lee had been right. No one at this establishment had any desire to call the police. Sawyer sat down heavily, and Matthew joined him, gun never lowering for an instant.

"What's this about," Sawyer said, clearly doing his best tough guy voice. Matthew thought it needed more practice.

"I'm hoping you have a little information for me. You give me what I want, you go home tonight to your family." He felt bad about the implied threat but figured it might have some effect.

Sawyer took a long drink and wiped his mouth. "Doesn't look like this is up for debate, so... Sure. Anything. Within reason, of course."

No use in mincing words. "I want to know about your bosses. The syndicate. Your contacts within the organization."

"You're not with one of the Yakoozies are you?" he asked, eyes narrowing suspiciously.

"Yakuza," Matthew corrected. "And no, I'm not part of any syndicate. My vendetta with White Void is personal."

Sawyer looked alarmed at the mention of White Void.

"Don't like me mentioning your bosses name?" Matthew asked. "How did a respectable businessman like yourself end up pledging allegiance to thugs from Ceres?"

"It's a long story. Hard times. Debts to pay."

"How's that working for your family?" Matthew asked.

Sawyer scratched at his beard and then looked away, unwilling or afraid to answer. "If I talk about the bosses, I'm a dead man."

"Your current career is headed that way as it is." Matthew glanced around the bar. "Anyone in here connected to White Void?"

"Not that I know of, but that doesn't mean much. What do you have against my bosses anyway?"

Matthew noticed that he still refused to say the syndicate's name aloud. He really was spooked. "A friend of mine was kidnapped a couple days ago. She'll probably be shipped back to Ceres to the Strongarm she crossed as soon as the storm lifts." Sawyer's eyes twitched at that. "That's right, your bosses peddle in human trafficking. Who do you think supplies the slaves to cartels on Europa?"

"What do you want from me?" Sawyer rasped.

"Who do you report to?"

"The local Strongarm, only one on Mars right now."

"I'm going to need a name."

Sawyer paused for a moment glancing down at the barrel of the gun. "His name's Eduard Mdivani."

A Strongarm was a solid lead. He would either know where Yvonne was or be able to find out. May as well cut the head off the dragon while they were at it anyway. Matthew wasn't keen on White Void getting a foothold in his hometown. "And how would I get in touch with Mr. Mdivani."

"Try the public directories. He owns a cement factory that most of the off-worlders filter through. Owned it for quite a while, so I guess he's had plans for Flagstaff since long before he actually showed up. If I had to guess, that's where your friend is."

That was about as good as he was going to get. He wondered if Lee had pegged Mdivani as the ringleader. Should probably pass that on just in case. He looked at Sawyer. "Hope your family doesn't get caught in a crossfire. As far as I'm concerned, we've never met."

"Some good that'll do," the man said and finished his drink in one go. "I'll be getting the will in order when I get home tonight."

Sadly, that probably wasn't a bad idea. Patrick Sawyer might just reap what he had sown. Arizona Police already knew about his activities, and it was now just a question of whether they or his own bosses decided to take him down.

Maybe he and Sharon could do enough damage that they forgot about the lowly chop shop owner. He'd tell Lee that Sawyer had cooperated. Matthew owed the man's family that much.

"So how are we going to pull this off?" Abigail asked. "A few old satellite photos aren't exactly a battle plan."

Cole was staring at the main display in the Sparrow's cockpit. Satellite photos of the Arizona region were easy enough to find. Useful information on an old cement factory? Much harder. "Give me a minute, will you?" he grumbled.

She pursed her lips and crossed her arms. They didn't have all night. She'd suggested getting a couple hours of sleep and then hitting them in the wee hours of the morning.

"The question is," he said tapping the screen. "Is this ship the one our friends from Ceres came in on, or does it belong to someone else entirely?" A nondescript hauler was parked in the empty lot next to the factory. Public records didn't say who the lot was owned by.

"My money is that's it," Abigail said. "Your man said out-of-towners come through there. I doubt they parked their ride at the public spaceport."

"No, probably not," Cole agreed. "So where is Yvonne? Are they holding her on the ship, camped out and waiting for the storm to clear or somewhere in the factory?"

"No way to know this one. Not without more intel," Abigail said. The real problem was that things were going to get dicey for Yvonne

318

once they'd made some noise. They would either use her as a hostage or hide her away somewhere they'd never find her.

Cole tapped the screen again. "I think we check the factory first."

"Quick decision you made there."

"Think about it. We've seen just how hard it is to break into a ship. Once they're onto us, they'll just lock it down and alert the factory. In that scenario, if Yvonne's on the ship, she's going to be well guarded and we've got our work cut out for us. If she's in the factory, they'll get advance warning and be on high alert. If we go for the factory first..."

"We can do it quietly," Abigail said. "And if we get spotted, then the ship still ends up on alert. It's the same either way except we have an easier job if she's in the factory."

"Exactly. Now what I want to know is..."

"I'm coming with you," Davey said. Abigail hadn't even noticed him slide into the cockpit.

Cole turned and gave him a good hard look. "This is going to be dangerous. Most dangerous thing you've ever done."

"Are you telling me no?" he asked. She heard the defiant tone, the argument he was yet to voice. Hopefully, that's exactly what Cole was telling him.

"No," he said carefully. "You make your own call on this one."

"Then I'm coming. I couldn't protect Yvonne, but I will help bring her home."

So Cole's speeches were going to get the kid killed. Great. He was going to be a better person now, but also very dead. She started to open her mouth to protest, but a fourth voice spoke up.

"I'm coming too."

Abigail spun to see Grace with her hands on her hips.

"No," she said in perfect unison with Davey and Cole.

"You're staying here," Davey said, "with Elizabeth."

"Because it's so much safer here, right?" Grace said. "I'll be in less danger than you. I'm the bulletproof one." She looked up at Abigail. "One of the bulletproof ones, anyway."

"Maybe so," Cole said. "But people are going to get hurt. People are going to die. Even if you're perfectly safe, I don't want you there."

"You think I've never seen a body?" she asked indignantly. "I watched kids get beat to death. I watched the Duke break a girl's neck one time with this." She gestured to one of her bracelets. "And that's not even starting with what Davey and I used to see on the street in Blight."

Abigail didn't know what to say. She didn't even know what to think. But she shouldn't have been surprised. Grace had been through a lot in her short life and turned out okay. Her eyes flicked to Davey. He'd been in that life for longer. It was no wonder he was so rough around the edges. "Grace. I'm sorry about everything you've been through, but that doesn't mean we're okay shoveling more trauma your way."

Grace set her jaw, and Abigail could see the tears welling up in her eyes. "This isn't fair! How come everyone else gets to help save Yvonne? Why can't I do my part? I'm part of the crew and she's my friend too."

"It's not happening," Davey said. "That's final."

The girl stormed from the room. Abigail startled in shock when she found herself physically pushed out of the way. She caught sight of a blue glow before realizing what had happened.

"Wait."

Everyone turned to look at Cole.

"I hear you're good at picking locks."

Abigail frowned. What was he thinking? He couldn't possibly be reconsidering.

"Sure. Davey and I used to break into places all the time. It beat looking through dumpsters."

Cole looked at Davey, "Is this true?"

The kid nodded. "As long as it's not an electronic lock, she can probably get in. If it needs a physical key and is on a building she can break it."

"I eat locks for breakfast," Grace bragged. The tears were gone, having been replaced by a smug look. "Guy named Pancakes taught me."

"I'm not okay with this," Abigail said. This was getting out of hand. "Not even a little."

"I'm not either," Cole said. "But I'm also not okay with Yvonne being shipped back to Ceres. We've got willing volunteers who know what they are getting themselves into."

"They can't possibly know, Cole. They're kids."

"I'm not a kid," Davey said glaring at her.

She looked down at him and poked a finger in his chest. "You're seventeen, you're a kid. And Grace is only twelve."

"Thirteen tomorrow," Grace corrected her.

Abigail winced. She'd forgotten about that little detail since Yvonne's kidnapping. "That doesn't make it any better," she said, frustration mounting.

"We're all missing our crewmate," Cole said, his voice softer. "If anyone thinks they can live with themselves if we fail, go ahead and let me know. Because I can't. I don't think we'd be where we are today without Yvonne."

Abigail couldn't argue with that logic. The woman had had a life, a husband, a medical practice, everything, and after losing all of that, she'd picked herself up and made a new life here on the Sparrow. She seemed to be whatever anyone needed whenever they needed it. Sometimes that was a mechanic. Sometimes that was a friend. She even put up with Davey at his worst. Abigail would have thrown him out the airlock long ago without Yvonne.

"Here's what I propose," Cole said. "Sharon, you and I go in and do our thing. We canvas the main building. Hope to get lucky. Maybe we find someone that will talk with some encouragement. Then we make some noise to draw attention. Grace and Davey sneak in from the other side of the complex. They move through locks quietly. Meanwhile we make a little more noise and keep the focus on us. They'll stand a better chance at getting in and finding Yvonne that way. If she's on the ship, we'll have to reevaluate when we get there." He turned to Davey. "You stay close to your sister."

"You think I wouldn't protect her?" He scoffed.

"That's not what I meant," Cole said. "She's bulletproof. She protects you. You stay behind her if something goes wrong and use her as cover. And then you get out of there. Grace you practiced with those bracelets like I told you?"

The girl nodded.

"Good." he turned back to the monitor. "Alright, you two. I need you both to pay attention. Here's satellite imagery of the factory."

Abigail ignored him as he reviewed everything they knew for the younger members of the crew. So this was going to be it then. They were really going to do this, despite her protests. This was either a bad idea or a terrible one, and she couldn't decide which.

An hour before dawn, Matthew and Sharon crept through Flagstaff's sprawling industrial sector toward the cement factory. He checked his watch, impatient with how long it was taking to get there. The wind's fury had started to die overnight, sooner than forecasted. It would take days for all the dust to settle, but in a few short hours, pilots would begin to risk the skies again. The window was closing, and they'd only get one shot at this.

"We're almost there, Cole. You can relax."

He gave her a look and then picked up his pace. "Time's almost up."

"I get it. We're a block away."

He decided to ignore her, and they walked the last block in silence. The cement factory came into view, its illuminated towers standing out against the dark sky. "Wish the whole facility wasn't bright as a meteor shower," he said.

"Are we still going with the original plan?" Sharon asked quietly, her voice muffled behind her face shield.

"Find the front entrance and hope it's guarded."

She pointed at a drive a couple hundred feet away. "Looks like a checkpoint and the lights are on. Let's do this."

They slipped across the street, creeping along the facilities fence edge. A boom barrier spanned the gateway to keep vehicles out. It didn't do much good for foot traffic, and they easily stepped over the lowered boom. Sharon jabbed a thumb at the lit guardhouse. Whoever was on duty wasn't paying close enough attention, something they'd use to their advantage. Matthew stood close by as she ripped the locked door off its hinges and tossed it aside.

He drew his revolver and slipped into the guardhouse. The lone guard had clearly been napping, and now, was in a state of panic. Matthew waved his gun. "Hands up where they won't get you into trouble. You're going to have to learn to do your job better than this. Sharon?"

"I got him." She disarmed the security guard and gripped him in strong metal hands. No way he was going anywhere anytime soon. He thrashed a bit, but quickly realized how futile that was and took to glaring at Matthew.

"Now then," Matthew said. "We've got a friend that we've heard is being held here by White Void. I wonder if you'd know anything about that?"

"What are you talking about? This is just a cement factory! Let go of me or I'll..."

"Calm down. You'll do nothing of any sort. I see a chain around your neck. I wonder what that could be." He reached forward and with the barrel of the revolver hooked the chain, drawing it out from beneath the man's shirt. The guard flinched at the touch of the revolver.

"Oh look. There's a symbol on the end," Sharon said. "Where have

I seen that sigil before?"

"White Void," Matthew said. "I wonder how far his arms will bend before he talks?"

Sharon twisted one of his arms behind his back. The guard's eyes went wide with terror. "Hey, no need for that! Your uh... friend. I heard they were moving someone off world soon."

"Where is she?" Matthew asked poking him with the revolver.

"I don't know, but I've heard they've got a couple holding cells on the top floor of the main office."

Matthew nodded and pulling out a strip of cloth, gagged the guard. They left him handcuffed in the guardhouse's tiny closet. "Well," he said shutting the door. "You ready to make some noise?"

Sharon pulled her shield off of her back and engaged it with a hum that Matthew had come to appreciate. "Always."

Grace dropped off the fence next to Davey. Finding a dumpster to climb had been easy enough. Now it was just a matter of sticking to the shadows and making sure Davey didn't do anything dumb.

"Hold up," he whispered and put a hand to his ear. Matthew had given him an earpiece to talk to the others. "Top floor of the main office building. Got it." He gave her a thumbs up sign, and they began to work their way down the fence line.

It had been a long time since they had done any sneaking around like this. Grace would have thought it was fun if failure didn't mean death for Yvonne. They crossed an open area and hid behind a pair of shipping containers. Davey squatted low in the dark and motioned for her to join him.

"What are we waiting for?" she hissed. "We know where to go."

"The plan. We wait for the distraction."

As if on cue, three gunshots rang out, echoing strangely around the facility.

"Lucky timing."

"I'm good like that," he said. "Now they'll be focused on the other side of the complex. Let's go. Stay close."

"I thought you were supposed to stay close to me."

"Same thing."

They moved like shadows, quietly flitting from cover to cover as they worked their way towards the office building on the east side. More gunfire began to ring out, automatic fire now. Grace felt a brief twinge of fear. Not for herself and Davey, but for the other two.

323

"Think they'll be okay?" Grace whispered.

"You haven't seen Abigail in action. Trust me. They're fine."

They darted across the last gap and made it to the building's backside. It was at least four stories tall and built onto the side of one of the factory's towers. They felt their way in the dark until they found a door.

"Do your thing," Davey said.

Grace pulled out a tiny light, pointed it at the door handle, and flicked it on, using her palm to hide as much of the light as she could. She turned it off again just as fast.

"Can you pick it?"

"In the dark with my eyes closed. It's just an old padlock."

"Hurry up then," he said. She couldn't see him very well in the dark, but from the way he turned his head at every sound, she could tell he was worried.

She pulled a tension wrench and hook pick from her pocket. "Give a girl some room to work."

"I think we have their attention!" Abigail yelled over the din of the fight.

"It's possible," Cole said, leaning out of cover to fire a few more shots. "The two by the gravel piles are a bit of a problem. I can't get a good shot on them without exposing myself to fire from the other group."

She risked a quick look around the factory yard. "Leave that to me then. Keep the group on the other side occupied."

"Got it."

She leaped past Cole and ran towards the gravel piles, doing everything she could to keep her shield in between herself and the attackers. A few stray bullets clinked off her shield, their velocities slowed to harmless levels.

Cole's revolver barked behind her. She counted shots. When he fired that seventh bullet, her distraction was going to be over. The second group's guns fell silent as they took cover from Cole's barrage.

She was nearly at the gravel piles.

Bullet number seven. The Syndicate men must have been counting too. Within seconds Abigail was under fire from the back. A few bullets struck the armor at her lower back, but there wasn't much to damage there. She took a flying leap and landed in the gravel piles, sending rocks scattering in all directions.

The shooters shielded their faces from the spray of stones and tried to back away. Abigail found them with her shield first, sending them both tumbling end over end.

One group down. Better make sure her gaucho was still in one piece.

Yvonne was awoken by an indistinct popping noise. Over the last couple days, she had grown used to all manner of noise coming from the factory, but not in the middle of the night. She flipped the light on beside her cot. There was the noise again. Closer.

Gunfire.

Her first instinct was to knock on the door and ask one of her captors to take her to a restroom. Odds were if something was up, they'd deny that request. Instead, she placed her ear to the door, eager for news about what was happening. There was a flurry of activity on the other side and it took her a minute to make sense of it.

"...freelancers were out of town?"

"Supposed to be, but..."

"...ield Maiden and the..."

"Good thing... report from Titan..."

"Already ordered Shivers... pulser from the Warlock."

"...send her over too for safety... not to be underest..."

She heard the lock turn and retreated from the door. No sooner had she sat down, than the door burst open. Kudzu stood framed in the door, looking more than a little angry. "Looks like your friends are determined. It's going to get them killed if I have my say."

"Considering the problems one old woman and a teenager gave you a few days ago, I think you should be a little more concerned."

Kudzu ignored the taunt. "Put your shoes on. It's time to go."

Davey led Grace through the dark lower levels of the office building. They had to find a route up. One that wasn't going to be crawling with guns.

They stumbled upon an emergency stairwell that looked promising. "What about this one? Can you get it open?"

Grace knelt in front of the handle and tested it. It turned freely, but the door didn't move. She shook her head. "Probably tied to the fire alarm. I doubt I can do anything with it."

Davey's eyes drifted to a red panel on the wall a few feet away. "There's always another option," he said with a grin and pulled down on the fire alarm. Red emergency lights came on and an obnoxious wail began to ring through the facility. "Plus bonus distraction."

Grace opened the now unlocked door and carefully poked her head into the stairwell. "Sounds empty. Hopefully, no one takes it thinking there's a real fire."

Davey propped the door open with an empty trashcan. "Just in case we need to come back this way," he explained. They ran up the two flights to the second floor. He made sure to keep his gun trained on the door into the main part of the building in case someone made an unwelcome appearance. On the third floor, that caution nearly turned fatal when an armed man in a suit came down the stairs as his attention was averted.

Davey spun trying to bring his weapon around, desperately hoping the man would hesitate to fire on a couple kids.

Grace never gave him a chance. Raising her hand, she smashed the man into the wall. He crumpled to the ground and Davey leaped forward to secure his weapon. When the man didn't move, Davey rolled him over. Hopefully, Grace hadn't just killed someone.

"He's breathing," she said, the relief obvious in her voice. "That's gonna leave a mark though."

"Thanks." He looked up the stairwell. "One more floor to go."

At the top of the last flight, they pushed open the door. At the end of a long hall lit by emergency lights, four people walked past their line of sight in a cross hallway. Yvonne flanked by Kudzu and two guards. Kudzu spotted them at once and pulled Yvonne behind the corner, barking a sharp order. Both guards spun, dropped to one knee, and fired down the hall.

Davey dove behind Grace as bullets shattered in red hot pieces of shrapnel in front of her face. He didn't have a clue how big the area of protection was, but wasn't taking any chances. Grace started walking forward into the fire. He hoped her absurd confidence didn't get them killed. Taking the opening, he peeked around her and pulled the trigger and sprayed a quick burst. Thankfully it looked like the bracelets allowed outgoing fire, and the guards were forced to duck for cover in side rooms.

Davey fired his submachine gun full auto at one of the doors where they'd taken cover, discharging the entire drum magazine. Bullets pierced the walls and splintered the doorframe. He heard a muffled cry and the thug fell out into the hallway. He'd found his target blind.

Grace suddenly extended a hand and snatched the other target, dragging him out of cover and throwing him between the walls in quick succession. He hit the ground a dead weight.

"What took you so long?" Davey asked, pulling another magazine off his belt.

"Had to get close enough."

"That would be an important detail to let me in on. Move it, they're getting away!"

They ran ahead, past their downed foes and around the corner after Yvonne. At the end of the second hallway, they saw them just as the elevator door was closing. Yvonne managed to yell one phrase before she was cut off. "The ship!"

Davey bit out a curse in Mandarin, and pulled out his comm. "Matthew! You there?"

There was a long pause. "Kind of busy right now. You find her?"

"We saw her but lost her. They're taking her to the ship."

"We're on it. Stay safe."

The comm cut off and Davey pointed back towards the emergency stairwell they'd come up on. "Maybe we can head them off."

"We don't have the firepower to lay siege to a ship," Abigail said. They were still pinned by a small group of White Void guns. She'd just been deciding what course of attack would get her to them the fastest while eating the least amount of bullets when Davey called.

"No, we don't," Cole agreed, as he loaded his revolver again. He glanced behind them at the fence. "I think we have to go the long way around. No way through in time."

"I've got this," she said. She tucked her shoulder and rammed into the concrete fence behind them, blowing clean through it to the street. It was going to take a lot of buffing to get the scratches out, but, like Cole said, they were on a schedule.

He popped through the hole behind her, under a barrage of bullets. "Run! We've gotta catch them! Don't wait for me."

Abigail obeyed and ran down the dark street. In the distance, the sky was beginning to turn gray with the first hints of dawn. She outpaced Cole in a matter of seconds, and at the end of the street she took a hard turn and continued down the next one. Had to get there. Had to get there in time to save Yvonne. No other option.

She took the last turn. Somewhere in the back of her mind, she registered that the wind had completely stopped. The storm was over.

She vaulted the chain link fence on the other side of the street. The ship was in front of her and to her left, Yvonne was being dragged across the open ground by a tall man in a white suit. She could outrun them. Easily. She set her suit in motion and crossed the gap in powerful strides. When she caught them, it would all be over.

Movement caught her attention from the ship. A man stood behind a tripod-mounted device on the ramp. She didn't have a clue what it was, but he was tracking her with it.

A single green light lit like an eye on the machine.

Sparks arced off her armor, crackling with energy. Midstride her suit locked up and she crashed to the ground, coming to a stop on her side.

Nothing worked. She couldn't feel anything from her implant.

"No, no, no, no, no," she shouted.

It had been an electromagnetic weapon. Probably earthtech. No other explanation.

Terror gnawed at the back of her mind. Such weapons destroyed circuitry. Permanently.

What if? What if...?

It was too horrible to think about.

No. It couldn't have damaged her circuits. Her suit's computers were hardened electronics, meant for working in dangerous environments and ionizing radiation. The sparks may have shorted something out, but it would come back up. She would just have to reset the whole system. Having to open up her suit to reset it was the worst design flaw in the whole thing. She wondered briefly if the production models had the same problem.

As she lay on the ground, she came to her senses. Yvonne.

They'd never save her now.

Matthew had barely topped the fence when he saw Sharon collapse to the ground. In the distance he saw two small figures running across the open lot, close on the heels of Yvonne and her captor. So much for them staying safe. They were in hot pursuit still. He sprinted across the open ground, as bullets began to snap through the air around him. Men were firing from the ship's ramp. He ran to the only cover on the open lot.

Sharon.

He slid behind her. "You okay?"

"No. Get my shield and give us more cover! Red button deploys."

He obeyed, straining against its weight as he pulled it off her back, pushed it over her fallen bulk, and punched the button. It deployed, but he didn't hear the grav plate. He wrestled it into a position that would protect as much of them from the gunfire as possible. Bullets ricocheted around them.

"EMP got that too then," she said, her voice grave.

A roar blasted across the lot. The ship had fired its main engines. They were going to lift off, heedless of the atmospheric conditions. Matthew saw one of its chain gun turrets swiveling toward them. It stopped, not having the turn radius required to get them in its sights.

"I'm opening up," Sharon said.

"What?"

"If that turret fires, I want as much metal in between me and those rounds as possible. We're going to cower behind my shield and my armor and pray."

The armor plates on the back of her suit split apart, and Sharon started to worm her way out. "Give me a hand," she said.

He saw the tears on her face and guessed what this meant to her.

"I'm sorry," he said and meant it.

Grace saw Abigail fall out of the corner of her eye. She hoped that she was okay, but didn't have time to stop.

"Can you grab either of them?" Davey asked.

"Out of range," she panted, out of breath from trying to catch up.

"Then run!"

She ran, as fast as she ever had, Davey close behind her. Bullets began to rain down around them, some being blown apart by her bracelet. Stay close Davey, she thought.

Ahead Yvonne was struggling, slowing the man down.

They would make it. They would catch them.

All at once he stopped and put a pistol to Yvonne's head. "Stop. Now."

Davey grabbed the back of her shirt, and she skidded to a stop. She reached out with her hand, but it was still out of range. No, no this wasn't fair!

The man called Kudzu sneered. "Drop the weapon kid. It's over."

Davey tossed it aside. Grace took a step forward. Still not close enough.

"Not another step."

She took another.

"Are you deaf or just dumb? You're gonna have this woman's death on your hands."

She took one more step and ripped the gun from his hands, throwing it across the lot.

Kudzu stumbled backward in surprise. Yvonne pulled away from him and Davey dove for his gun, bringing it to bear in a swift motion. He pulled the trigger, striking Kudzu twice in the shoulder. Yvonne slipped from his grip and bolted toward them.

Grace half expected to see bullets strike her down from the ship, but they must have been scared of injuring their boss any further. As Kudzu retreated to the ramp empty-handed, Yvonne stumbled into her and then hid behind her as Davey had.

The ship lifted off the ground, and they huddled together as the chain guns came to bear on them.

Abigail gripped Cole's hand and pulled herself out of her armor, slipping down painfully onto the hard ground. Her left leg caught beneath her, and her hip cried out in pain. She bit her lip and reached down to grab her thigh and reposition it.

Cole bent over her protectively, in between her and the suit. What was he thinking? That if the bullets made it through the shield and armor that his own body would stop them? What kind of nonsense was that?

She appreciated the gesture though. Appreciated the way he didn't say anything about her broken body.

The ship's engines raised in pitch as it lifted off the ground and she heard the whine of the guns spinning up to speed.

This was it then. No way they were living this one.

A pair of missiles streaked overhead and a deafening explosion thundered over the city.

She opened her eyes and saw the ship bleeding smoke and fire from its starboard side. Two skyhoppers painted in Arizona colors streaked past, banking hard to come back around. They wouldn't get the chance. With a roar and backblast that sent Abigail and Matthew rolling end over end across the lot, the White Void ship fired its engines and rocketed away. Damaged or not, they were going to try and make a run for it.

Abigail tried to move her aching body. She was scratched, bruised, and hurt everywhere from the tumble, but she was alive.

Matthew was the first by her side. His hat was nowhere to be seen, and blood trickled down his face.

"You look terrible," she said.

"Thanks. That means I'm alive."

And then she remembered Yvonne. They'd failed. She was on that ship right now and...

And then Yvonne was by her side. Both the kids too. She had never been so happy to see them, even Davey.

Red and blue police lights flashed in the gray predawn and sirens wailed. Matthew stood, hands raised above his head. Two police grav cars pulled up between them and the factory while over a dozen others and three fire engines formed a perimeter around the complex. Whatever was left of White Void on site was about to come crashing down.

Abigail craned her neck to see a man come into view and shake Matthew's hand. "I hope your friend wasn't on that ship. We tried to force it down, but they made a run for it."

Matthew shook his head. "She's right here, Lee, safe and sound."

Lee smiled. "Glad to see you folks made it through okay. That fire alarm was connected to the public network. As soon as it lit up, I gave the order. Figured you might want some backup."

"Thanks," Matthew said. "Sorry we forced your hand. Hope we didn't blow your investigation too soon."

"A life was on the line," Lee said. "I've got no regrets. We picked up Eduard Mdivani for questioning last night right after you named him. With everything that happened here on his property, I'm sure we'll be able to keep him locked up long enough to finish our investigations."

"And the mechanic's family?" Matthew asked. Abigail relaxed her neck, content to look up at the sky. That was just like him. Make sure everyone was okay.

"Somewhere safe, away from possible syndicate retribution. Depending on his cooperation we may let him off easy too."

Yvonne was kneeling beside her. She gripped Abigail's hand and smiled.

So that was it then. They all knew now. Knew what she really was. There was less shame in it than she expected, but then they had almost all been turned into paste by the chain guns. She was too tired to think about her own stubborn pride.

There was no going back.

Late that evening, Yvonne sat in the Sparrow's common room with a cup of coffee. Content to merely sit and watch the others.

After getting checked out by medics and answering ten thousand questions, they'd returned home. Matthew moved the Sparrow to a remote corner of the colony, away from any remaining White Void enforcers left in Flagstaff. Elizabeth had joined them as well. She would have to find a friend to stay with and manage her farm and workers remotely. It wouldn't be safe for her to be there alone for quite some time.

"When is Abigail coming?" Grace asked. "I'm not opening any presents until she's here."

The door in the hall opened, but the familiar bulk of Abigail's exo-suit didn't appear. There was the squeak of a wheel on deck. Yvonne set her cup of coffee down. She must have kept a wheelchair around for emergencies.

Davey pushed back his chair and started to rise. Matthew reached out a hand and laid it gently on Davey's arm. They exchanged a look, and Davey seemed to understand.

Abigail rolled herself to the doorway and paused at the threshold. She took a deep breath and wheeled up to the table. Yvonne's heart went out to the younger woman. It is a brave thing to lay aside our masks.

Grace clapped her hands together. "Caaaake!"

Elizabeth had pulled out a cake, frosted with chocolate, from the refrigerator. It had been hard to keep the surprise from Grace, requiring a group effort in keeping her out of the common room while Elizabeth had made it.

They gathered around and Matthew lit the thirteen wax candles.

Grace hesitated before blowing them out and smiled. "This is the best birthday cake ever."

"What do you mean?" Davey asked. "This is the first birthday cake you've ever had."

The adults met each other's eyes. "It won't be the last," Matthew said.

They'd each gotten her a small gift, even Elizabeth. Davey gave her the small golden locket that Matthew had helped him pick out on Venus. Grace was head over heels in love with it the moment she laid eyes on the sparkling treasure and Yvonne chuckled to herself when she saw Davey and Matthew exchanging thumbs ups.

Yvonne took another sip of her coffee and her mind strayed to the man that had killed her husband. She felt her insides curl up on themselves. Of all people to escape the day's violence, why had he been one of them? Why hadn't justice found the one person who deserved to die?

A hand touched lightly on her shoulder and she turned to see Davey.

He didn't say anything.

She smiled. "It's good to be home."

Chapter 18: The Thresher of Onerios

I'd always known that Moses kept some stuff from us. The Mosaic Fleets that roamed the solar system going about the AI's business were more than proof of that. The thing was, I'd never had any reason to question Moses' motive. Not till after he was gone.

After the initial panic and the colonial governments started organizing, one of the first things we realized was that there were a few pieces of technology we were going to have to reverse engineer real quick. We started with the grav plates. People had been picking them apart for years and while a few of the basic principles had been deduced, how they actually manage to curve spacetime in the way they do was still a mystery.

No problem. We'll just duplicate the factories. Understanding will come in time.
I was on the team that worked at the Ganymede factory. In a single day, our job was deemed impossible. The computer systems still ran, but were inaccessible, encrypted with methods our own hardware wouldn't crack before the heat death of the universe.

And the production lines themselves? What wasn't horribly obfuscated to the point of being indecipherable was booby trapped. Two entire production lines immolated themselves the moment we opened up a robot on the line. Four of my team were seriously injured.

That sealed it. We could either keep feeding the factories materials and getting our grav plates or not. We weren't learning anything from them. Not then, and not in more careful subsequent attempts.

For myself, I never got over the bigger implications. Not only had Moses been hiding things from us, he clearly didn't trust us. He'd taken his secrets to his grave and would send us to ours as well. What was the point of lifting us up only to leave us adrift?

Jack Harrison
Mechanical Engineer
Died 16 AM

"That's it. I can't take it anymore," Abigail said. She clamped her mouth shut as she realized how foolish that probably sounded.

Matthew looked at her and raised an eyebrow in question. He set his book down on the table. "I'm listening."

He probably thought she was crazy. Nothing to lose at this point. "Are you going to say anything, ever?"

The look of confusion in his eyes was enough to confirm her previous suspicion. "I'm not sure we're having the same conversation right now."

"My legs! My armor! Are you just going to calmly accept it and move on?" She stood, towering over him. "It's been a week and you're just going to keep acting like everything is normal?"

One of his fingers tapped on the table, a nervous tic that drove her nuts. "Everything is normal," he said slowly.

How could he possibly be so dense? "This isn't normal," she said, gesturing wildly at her armor.

He gazed at her, his face unreadable, and she turned away as her cheeks grew warm. What had she been thinking? She wasn't even sure what she wanted from him anyway. Pity? She had always hated that as a teenager. Acceptance? His refusal to so much as comment on her

335

disability was proof enough that she had that.

He drew the awkward silence out to a painful length before responding. "I'm sorry. I guess I thought you probably didn't want to talk about it."

Abigail would have thought that as well, but, apparently, neither of them knew her very well. "Ignore me. It's been so long since anyone knew about, well, me, that I guess I'm losing my mind." She sat on her crate with a thud. At least she could take solace in the fact that the others were outside getting some fresh air and weren't around to see her embarrassing outburst. That would have been a level of humiliation she was wholly unprepared for. She bit her lip. "Did you know?"

"Suspected."

"For how long?"

He closed the cover of his book and pushed it away. The corners of his mouth tugged upward in a wry smile. "Abigail. You've been living on the ship for months. The fact that you had something to hide was clear as the sun."

Her cheeks warmed again. "In hindsight, it was a little childish to think it would go on forever."

"Maybe. You're living the dream of every person who's ever lost the use of their legs. Getting caught up in the normalcy of it is about the most natural thing I can imagine."

That was giving her too much credit. Yvonne had tried to warn her and she'd ignored her advice and gone on to make a fool of herself.

"Either way, so long as we don't run into any more earthtech to counter your own, I think things will be just fine. You're still one of the best freelancers in the solar system, and whether or not you choose to wear your suit around the Sparrow is a choice you can now make freely. You're the same Abigail either way and a member of the crew."

The same Abigail either way. For so long she'd always thought of the paraplegic teenager as a different person. Her break with the past had been so clean and her secret so absolute that it was easy to forget that other person. Of course that was ridiculous. In some ways, we're new each time we rise, and in others the same until we breathe our last.

"Thanks," she said, belatedly realizing she should acknowledge the compliment. "Now that I'm fresh out of secrets, I'll be glad to be out from under the microscope for a while."

"Fresh out of secrets?" He gave a wry smile. "Don't be coy. You've still not said a word about that piece of tech you have."

336

"A woman has to keep some things to herself."

"I wouldn't know. But I have to admit I couldn't help but notice the last name."

Abigail frowned at the sudden turn. "What's that supposed to mean? Sharon isn't all that uncommon."

Matthew tapped that finger again. She eyed it and he stopped abruptly. "As a given name, you're right. As a surname? Different matter entirely. Combined with a few other clues you've been dropping, I have a theory."

So he knew or at least guessed that as well. If he weren't sure, he wouldn't have mentioned it. "If that's the case, then you know why I don't talk about it."

He nodded solemnly. "For the longest time I thought you were like me, running from a past you weren't able to face, but I think your secrets are a bit less selfish in their nature."

She shook her head. "Not all of them."

They sat in awkward silence, aware that, while one wall had fallen, others still stood, and each continued their lonely watch.

Yvonne stepped into the cockpit and leaned against the doorframe. Matthew was in the pilot's seat, feet on the console, deep in an argument with Benny.

"It's perfectly within my right to run my crew as I see fit and, no, I'm not under any compulsion to give you detailed resumes."

She heard a loud sigh come over the speaker. "You're right. I get it. I really do. I understand you not telling me about the Naude woman because of the bounty, but a couple of kids? That wasn't what I had in mind when I suggested getting a crew.

So much for keeping Benny in the dark about her presence on the Sparrow. "How'd you find out about me, anyway?" she asked. Matthew startled at the sound of her voice and sat up abruptly. "Calm down, gaucho. I could feel you talking about me and came to investigate. How did you find out about me, Benny?"

Benny hesitated for a moment. "Umm. Pleased to meet you, Ms. Naude. I didn't mean..."

"That's fine. I'm hard to offend."

"Right. Cole told me you guys had been in a bit of dust-up with White Void, so I did a little digging. Wasn't hard to piece things together after that. Your name showed up in a couple of media outlets."

337

"White Void already knows you're on the Sparrow," Matthew offered. "I don't see any harm."

"And what about you, Benny?" she asked. "On the day White Void posted that bounty, you sent it along to the Sparrow. What does a million dollar bounty mean to you?"

Matthew pursed his lips and turned to the speaker. Yvonne crossed her arms as she waited.

"They posted it through a shell corp," Benny said, flatly. "I had no idea, I swear. I don't work for syndicates."

"Good," Matthew said. "Because if you do or say anything to compromise Yvonne, I'll track you down. Nowhere in the solar system will be safe for you."

"Geez. Lay off the threats. We're business partners here, right? We're all here to make money. Which if we're done with this, I've got two jobs for you guys that I've been working on."

Matthew looked at Yvonne, a question in his eye. She shrugged. What choice did she really have in the matter? Either they had to continue with Benny or find a new broker. May as well go with what they had. Benny didn't seem like he had the courage to betray Matthew anyway.

"Let us have 'em," Matthew said, turning back to the speaker.

"Both of them are personal requests for you guys. First one involves some research company here in Arizona."

Yvonne frowned at that. "What kind of research are we talking about, and why would they ask for us?"

"Umm... Doesn't really say, but they promised it was nonintrusive and would only take a few minutes, followed by a questionnaire."

"That's not how research works," Yvonne said. "You don't hire freelancers for lab work."

"We'll check on it," Matthew said, waving her off. "It's local and I don't see how any harm can come from it. What's the other job?"

"Huygens Industrial Chem is having some trouble with security for their fuel tankers and is hiring freelancer escorts. Their rep specifically asked for you guys after that whole thing with the children."

"That one is a go," Matthew said. "Thanks, Benny. Send the details over on both of them."

"Will do. And... I'm glad you guys made it through okay the other night."

The comm shut off and Matthew gestured to it. "See. He's not all bad."

"Except for this research job. I don't like the idea of being a lab rat."

He tapped a few buttons on the keyboard and peered at the display. "Let's see. Details coming in now. Praxus Biomedical. Pay is good for how low the investment is. Here's the contact information."

"Call them," Yvonne said. "This doesn't smell right to me."

"Already on it."

"What's going on?" Abigail asked, stepping into the cockpit.

"Matthew is farming us out as lab rats for experiments now."

"We talking maze running lab rats or injected full of glowing chemicals lab rats?"

"I'll find out as soon as you two stop talking and I can call them." he said, giving them both a withering look. Yvonne returned the look to make sure he thought better of his impertinence.

A few moments later, a woman's voice came over the speakers. "This is Dr. Shiratori."

"This is Matthew Cole. I believe you were looking to hire my crew."

"I'm glad you've decided to help me, Mr. Cole! The data we get from you and your..."

"We haven't exactly made up our minds yet. Just what does this entail?"

"Oh. Praxus Biomedical is researching induced stress responses. We'll expose you to stimuli, observe you, and then ask you a few questions. You'll be in and out in an hour."

"I have a few questions now if you don't mind," Yvonne said. "As the doctor on the ship, I'd like to know a bit more."

"Naturally," Dr. Shiratori said. "I'd expect nothing less."

"What's the purpose of this study? Medically speaking, inducing stress isn't all that good for the human body."

"We're researching new counseling and therapy techniques. We hope to assist patients with various forms of PTSD by triggering mild responses and helping them work through it."

Counseling wasn't exactly Yvonne's field, but that seemed reasonable enough. "And how will you be inducing this stressed state?"

"A screen of flashing lights will cause a neurological response. Some people are more photosensitive than others, so there is a rather broad range of effect. Part of our research is trying to identify both resistant and hypersensitive individuals, as neither are suitable candidates for therapy via this method."

"Interesting," Yvonne said. Flashing lights certainly could cause seizures in epileptics, but she had never read any literature on photic responses in the general population. She was skeptical, but human neurology was complicated.

"Are you through grilling the Doctor?" Matthew asked.

Yvonne shook her head. "Not quite. What do you want a crew of freelancers for? Seems like the usual pool of subjects for clinical trials would be more appropriate and much cheaper."

"In general, yes," Dr. Shiratori said. "However, we'd like a few subjects with actual combat experience, being as we're hoping to treat PTSD patients."

"Wait," Abigail said. She shifted her bulk. "You're trying to induce PTSD? Make us have flashbacks or something?"

"Not quite. Naturally, it would be unethical to test this on actual PTSD patients at this stage of trials. However, testing relatively healthy combatants is the first step in that direction. If any of your crew have a bad response, we'll need to reevaluate how to move forward."

Matthew turned to Yvonne. "Well, what do you say? Does it pass muster?"

It was still bizarre, and she wasn't convinced that what they described was even possible. However, since none of the crew members were epileptic, she couldn't see any harm in it. "I'll have some more questions when we get there."

"And we'll be happy to answer them. When can you come into the lab? The whole crew will be there, I assume."

"About that," Matthew said, scratching his head beneath his campero. "Only two of us are vets. Then there is the doc. A young man, with only a little combat experience. And we also have a twelve-year-old that... Actually, she just lives on the ship mostly. It's a long story. I'm not sure it's all that appropriate for her to take part."

"I see. We can discuss the younger crewmembers tomorrow. There aren't any other suitable freelancer crews around Flagstaff at the moment. Can you come by around noon?"

"We'll see you, then." He cut off the comm. "See. Nothing to it."

"I think this is highly irregular," Yvonne said. "And I still get veto power tomorrow if anything smells even remotely wrong."

"No complaints there," Abigail said. "But this actually sounds kind of fun in a weird sort of way."

"And, most importantly, an easy paycheck," Matthew said, standing and walking past them out of the cockpit.

"Relax, Doc," Abigail said. "Just imagine you're part of pushing science forward and go with it."

340

Yvonne breathed out a deep breath. They were right. An easy paycheck wasn't something they could ever really afford to turn down, not with how much it took to keep the Sparrow flying. Besides, she'd get to ask as many questions as they'd let her. It was going to take a lot to convince her that stress-inducing phototherapy wasn't the purview quacks.

Grace couldn't stop smiling all the way into Flagstaff. She and Davey were riding with Abigail on her oversized bike, him in the back and her in front. Watching the red Martian landscape zoom by was exciting, at least until they got into the city and had to slow down for traffic. Then the ride became a chore and she was ready for it to be over. When the vehicles became thick enough that they came to a complete stop, Yvonne turned around and waved at them from Matthew's bike. Grace made a face like she was falling asleep from boredom.

After at least three lifetimes, they pulled up to a stop at a small building in a row of identical ones. This one looked freshly painted and had a big blue sign that read Praxus Biomedical.

"Hey, Abigail?" Grace asked.

"What do you need?" she asked, getting off of her bike.

"You know how you said I should get something to eat before leaving the Sparrow? You were right."

"Hungry already?" Davey shook his head. "Figures with the growing you've done lately."

"You won't be taller than me for long," she said, stepping up to him to compare heights.

He frowned, an irritated look on his face, and backed away. A hand clapped on her shoulder. "Maybe don't rub that one in," Yvonne said.

"Fine," Grace said. "What are we even doing here? I don't understand this mission."

"They're going to give us a bad day and then ask questions about it," Matthew said. "Let's head in."

The waiting room was a dull, lifeless place, little more than a white box with a few chairs. Matthew and Yvonne spoke with the receptionist and then disappeared from the room. The three of them sat in silence. Grace passed the time by trying to make patterns out of the markings on the ceiling tiles. She'd found patterns that looked like a slightly too tall Abigail-in-armor, the Sparrow, and even the old ship

341

they'd used to fly on fuel runs back over Titan. Matthew and Yvonne returned before the game got too boring.

"What's the news, doctor?" Abigail asked. "You going to let us do this?"

Yvonne looked uncomfortable but nodded anyway. "I think this is probably pure pseudoscience, but don't see how any harm could come of it. We had a bit of discussion over the children and legal guardianship. No parents to sign their paperwork. They were rightly a little concerned over liability and ultimately decided that Grace would not be able to participate today."

"Hey, that's not fair!" she cried out. If she was going to be forced to come all this way just to sit and wait on everyone else, she was going to be steaming mad. "I can make my own decisions. I'm thirteen."

"Which isn't even close to the age of majority in Arizona," Matthew said. "Decision is final."

"What about him?" She pointed a finger at Davey.

"He gets to decide for himself," Yvonne said.

Davey looked at Yvonne and then back at Grace. "Then, I'll stay with Grace."

That took her off guard but was a happy surprise. "Fine. But can we go find some food? This white room is exciting and all, but I'd rather bail."

"Alright," Matthew said. "Stick close to her, Davey. We'll only be about an hour, so don't wander too far."

Davey walked to the door and opened it. Grace followed him and hit him in the arm. "You're not all bad, you know that, right?"

"Oh, that's a pity. Because you're the worst." He may have been smiling when he said it, but she hit him again anyway.

"I'll go first," Yvonne said. She'd given the okay for this foolish venture. It made sense that she reap the consequences first, if there were to be any, and then pull the plug if need be.

"Right this way," Dr. Shiratori said, gesturing to the door leading into the facility.

Yvonne gave a quick look over her shoulder at Matthew and Abigail and then followed the woman. They walked down a brightly lit hall. Everything seemed almost painfully clean, which was appropriate for a laboratory setting, but this was surprisingly so. "Have you been in this location long?"

"A little over a month. We're just moving into clinical trials and

342

needed an appropriate location for test subjects and eventual patients. This room, if you will."

Yvonne entered the prescribed door to find a softly lit room painted in relaxing shades of blue and green. It seemed reasonable to keep patients calm before exposing them to whatever was about to happen. A single screen on the wall showed only a Praxus Biomedical logo bouncing around in a screensaver. The wall across from this was clearly a one-way mirror, and a camera was mounted high in each corner. She sat in the chair facing the screen. "Are you going to have to strap me in, or am I good to just sit?"

"Ms. Naude," Dr. Shiratori said, her face creased in amusement, "I think you're imagining something far more severe in nature than the test we have planned."

"Very well. Proceed with the mad science."

Dr. Shiratori smiled again, something Yvonne found smug and annoying at the moment. "I will leave you alone now. Please remain seated and keep your hands on the palm pads. Sensors in the armrest will monitor your vitals. I'll rejoin you after the test has been completed." She shut the door.

She looked at the monitor. "Time to see if you're real or not."

A few moments later, the Praxus logo disappeared and was replaced by a black and white checkerboard effect. It began to ripple as if it was a surface of water disturbed by droplets. Yvonne crossed her arms as her skepticism ratcheted up to new heights. This was starting to get laughable.

Then the design began to spin and things got weird.

She had the distinct impression that she was being followed. Someone was behind her, pursuing her, and she couldn't quite shake the feeling. Her own pride wouldn't let her turn around, after all, Dr. Shiratori was most certainly watching, and Yvonne refused to give her that satisfaction.

Her pulse quickened. She placed her left hand on her right wrist and counted, ignoring the instructions. There it was again. This time she did turn. In her mind, she imagined Kudzu there, but of course, this was nonsense. The room was empty.

The hateful man smirked and dragged her kicking and screaming back to Piggy. This didn't happen, would never happen, Matthew wouldn't let it, but nonetheless, it was happening.

Her freedom was gone. Worst of all, the one she hated was always there. Kudzu. The man who killed Tomas. Tomas should have known to let him die. Why had he wanted her to save his killer? Why had she

343

saved his killer?

Now he haunted her, like a specter, and the regret ate at her mind. She would never be free of him.

She'd kill him given the opportunity.

But of course, the room was empty. She was alone and felt very unusual, and her heart still raced. But it was slowing down now. The screen had returned to a bouncing Praxis logo.

The door opened and Dr. Shiratori entered the room. "I hope you don't feel too unwell. Please stay seated until you regain your composure."

Yvonne gave the woman a long hard stare, heedless of propriety. "That's a neat trick. I hope you don't give your patients heart attacks."

The doctor smiled politely. "Rest assured, we will be thorough in our prescreening. Now if you're feeling ready to answer a few questions, we can begin."

Abigail watched as the strange pattern suddenly began to spin. Her head and the entire room seemed to go with it.

She felt as if she couldn't move from where she squatted in front of the chair. As if... As if her implant was on the fritz again. No, it was worse than that. Her exo-suit was damaged. Beyond repair.

Her breath caught in her chest. And she shook her head, looking away from the screen. The feeling of anxiety didn't go away. She'd never be able to walk again. Her career was over. All the respect she'd earned.

Cole probably wouldn't even speak to her. What use was she to him now? Or to anyone for that matter. After all her father had sacrificed for her, she'd been foolish enough to risk it all and...

No. This was all a test. She stood to her feet, commanding her armor to obey her. It wasn't damaged. It was all part of the stress test. The Sparrow was in flames punched clean through by several thumper blasts. Bodies floated in the cold of space, and only Abigail was suited for the vacuum. Except that wasn't what had happened. Had it?

The nightmarish feeling receded from her beleaguered mind. The world shrank back into the dimly lit room and the display in front of her showed only the logo. She took a deep breath, forcing her nerves to calm and decided that they had not been paid nearly enough to be subjected to this infernal screen.

A block away from the research lab, Davey and Grace sat on a bench beside a street vendor selling tacos. He'd spotted it on the way in, knowing she would be ravenous by the time they left Praxus. As it turned out, they were free a little sooner than expected.

She was still sore about not getting to participate. "It's not really fair. I'm not even really a kid anymore now that I'm thirteen."

Davey shook his head. "If you think adults treat teenagers any better, you're in for a rude awakening." Grace was busy picking all the little green leaves out of her tacos. "Hey, don't waste that. You don't like it?"

"Not these gross leaves. What is it, anyway?"

He took another bite of his second of three tacos. "Your guess is as good as mine, but it's all amazing." Food variety had always been a bit lacking on the habitat, and while they'd had more variety in their street days, regularity had been the problem there.

"Tastes like soap to me," she said.

He looked at her and set his taco down. "Sorry. Guess this place wasn't a great idea, after all."

Her eyes went wide. "No, it's fine, I promise. I'm just being picky." She took a mouthful and chewed it thoughtfully. "First time I've ever been able to be picky."

Now there was a thought. They really did have everything they needed on the Sparrow. Here they were, eating street food from money Davey had worked to earn. On Mars of all places. Crazy. "This is the best we've had it so far, isn't it?" he asked. She nodded absently. Her mind was already somewhere else. "What's got you distracted?"

"We'll be leaving Mars soon, you know."

He didn't follow the jump in topic. "I'm not sure I..."

"I asked Yvonne about our flight plan. We'll end up in the Jupiter Neighborhood after the next job."

"What's that got to do with anything?"

"Thebe is in the Jupiter Neighborhood."

So that was what she was after. "Look, I haven't seen my parents in a decade. I don't even know if they are still there."

"What if they are?" she asked quietly.

"How am I supposed to know? I haven't thought that far ahead." He felt a growing frustration with her. "I'll cross that hurdle when I get there."

"What about me?"

He stopped short, dumbstruck. Something else he hadn't thought

345

about.

"Are you going to leave me to stay with them?"

"You know, you normally call me the dumb one, but right now, you're trying to catch up."

She turned on him, bristling for a fight.

"You're my little sister. Nothing is going to make me abandon you. Not even if we find my parents. Got it?"

She smiled and he shoved another mouthful of food into his face to cover the awkward moment. That only made it worse. "That is if you'll have a big dumb brother like me." His words were muffled by the food and he probably sounded like an idiot.

She leaned her head on his shoulder. He looked around to make sure no one was watching, but he knew complaining would just get him in trouble.

"Love you, brother."

"You too, sis."

Matthew watched the pattern on the screen ripple with a touch of fascination and a heaping dose of skepticism. The women had come out surprised and maybe even a bit shaken. But this? This was nothing. The doctor had said some people weren't very susceptible. Maybe he was just...

The image began to spin and Matthew's entire world disintegrated.

It was like he was falling. Falling towards the time and place he wanted least to be. So he took another job. Always another job, just to keep busy, to stay occupied.

Anything not to think about that place. Anything not to be there.

Not to be here. Europa. Villa María.

He would never forget. The farmlands. The old saloon. The church. Homes of families he'd known, people he'd protected. Faces he'd cared about for years. He'd done everything he could for that town, those people. And in the end, it hadn't been enough. It wasn't enough.

Clouds and thick darkness circled the town and he drew his revolver. Ten thousand men surrounded the town, and for as many as he killed, another hundred replaced them. Depraved men. Men that debased their own kind. Slavers.

How many did he have to kill? Each one he buried himself, outside of town, in penance for the foul deed.

And betrayed by a friend, Villa María in shackles, every man,

346

woman, and child cartel owned.

Hueso Rojo.

Red Bone.

Men must eat and Europa must provide that food, they said. The cartels furnish a necessary service now that the robotics have failed. The Jupiter Neighborhood will have their food for as long as the cartels keep up their hard work. Even the Vatican and the University of Ganymede, lights in the dark, paid the blood price. There were no alternatives.

A man of the cartel beats a slave who has fallen in the field. Or maybe they were making bricks. It was hard to tell in the gathering darkness. Matthew takes the man and kills him, but maybe that had happened long ago. He was an Egyptian. And that other Moses hadn't failed.

Matthew was neither.

And Villa María still cried out in agony.

Maybe God heard their cries and maybe he didn't.

It was so hard to tell with the way the world was spinning. His ears thundered and his vision was cloudy. Who was that in front of him? Where was he? Faces he knew. Two of them begging him to wake up.

People that he hadn't failed. Not yet, anyway.

"His eyes are open," one of them said through the haze. A friend. Someone he should trust more than he does.

"Pulse is coming back down too," the other answered.

"Can you hear us, Matthew? Are you all right?"

"...mmm fine," he slurred. A few rays of light seemed to pierce the miasma as the nightmare receded.

"Let me check on..." a third voice said.

"I think you've caused enough harm. I'm a medical doctor and am fully equipped to take care of him from here."

"There was no way to know he would be hypersensitive to the phototherapy."

The voices were still distant, detached from their sources, but becoming clearer as the moments passed. He opened his mouth and found his words were sticky and refused to separate. Maybe it was his tongue. Maybe his brain. "It'sssokayy. Jusss gimmeee five ani'llbeee ready."

Abigail was in front of him, her face pressed with worry. "Gave us a scare there, Matthew."

He closed his eyes again, trying to will the fog away, and managed to smile. "Gotta be good at somthin', I guess."

347

It took some time for them to get out of the clinic. To Matthew, it was all one big blur. Dr. Shiratori insisted on thoroughly questioning him after he had recovered enough to give coherent answers. He also consented to have his blood drawn in case it helped them figure out why he had been so sensitive to the therapy.

He didn't care all that much anymore. The sooner he made both the doctors, his own and the weird research one, get along, the sooner he got to go home and take a nap.

Then there was the barrage of questions from the kids. Grace would barely leave him alone until Davey finally got the hint and rudely told her to be quiet.

The last awkward moment came when they stood at the bikes and realized that they were down a driver.

"I can drive," Davey said. "Probably."

"When it snows on Venus," Yvonne said. "I haven't driven one of these things since I was a teenager, but they say you never forget how to ride a bike."

Matthew frowned, not sure he liked where this was going. "That's not the type of bike..."

"It's either Davey or me," Yvonne said. She took one last look back at the clinic and shook her head. "You'd think they'd have made us come with designated drivers. Unprofessional."

In spite of Matthew's misgivings, they made it back to the Sparrow in one piece. He slept the rest of the day, and the cries of slaves echoed in his dreams.

Elizabeth Cole hated it every time. It always came before she was ready. No sooner had her son come home than he was off planet again. Always the next job. Never in one place for longer than he had to be. She knew what it was that haunted him, what specter gnawed at his conscience.

It drove him to a hard life, and that life had followed him here. It had nearly swallowed them both this time, and his crew too.

A rational part of her was angry at him, angry at the choices that he made. But she was his mother and love is not always rational.

She stepped out of the grav car onto rocky ground. Clumps of grass tried to grow in the thin, dry soil. Mars was a hostile place for life, even under the shield. Unless the hand of man tamed the land, it remained an arid desert.

Matthew walked down the ramp toward her. She thought about meeting him halfway, but after the trouble this visit had caused, decided he'd have to close the whole distance himself. Then she found she had gone to him anyway, in spite of her silly pride.

He took her hand. "You're sure you'll be okay?"

"I can manage the farm from afar. I'll stay with my cousin as long as necessary."

"It could be some time." She looked at her son and he broke the gaze. "I'm sorry. This is why I don't like to come home. For all my fears, it finally happened. My work followed me back to you."

"And they followed you because you are a decent man and take care of those who have no other place," she said. "You haven't changed, you know. Not in ten years. Nor will you in a century."

"I know."

There was a long silence and Elizabeth felt the cool wind blow against her skin. She thought of the farm and the work to be done and wondered how long it would be until she could revisit it in person. The farmhands would manage, but she would miss being there for the hard work. She'd miss the soil between her fingers.

She would also miss her son.

"Take care of yourself. And take care of that crew. If I find out something has happened to one of them..."

He smiled and tipped his hat to her. "I will."

They embraced each other and then their time had come. He returned to his ship and she to her grav car. The wait wasn't long. Ten minutes later, the Sparrow burned towards space, its engines thundered across the landscape.

Elizabeth waited until she could no longer see the points of light before leaving. She was used to it by now, the empty feeling after his departure, but something was different this time. Maybe it was knowing that he wasn't alone this time.

"This was an enormously expensive operation," the voice continued from the comm. "I hope you got the information for which you sought."

The Unchained Man, who once had gone by Whitaker, looked up from his pad of scribbled notes. He'd had to write furiously after each session to ensure he didn't forget any details. "I imagine it was. Your people did a flawless job setting up the clinic, and Shiratori played her part perfectly."

"I would expect nothing less. She is, after all, a doctor."

He smiled. "Of course. And has your possession been returned to you safely?"

"It has been returned to its vault. You are either very brave or very foolish to willingly handle such a trinket."

He set aside the pad. "I prefer to consider myself well informed. This wasn't the first miracle I've handled, nor will it be the last. They each have their purpose, and that's the key. The Thresher of Oneiros is for the winnowing of another soul. To share the nightmare of another is an informative, if exhausting, experience. Rest assured, Mrs. Ishii. Your organization's prized ring was put to good use."

"Then our debt to you fulfilled?" the Japanese woman asked curtly.

As much as he hated when a valuable resource was expended, it was against his nature to cheat a bargain well struck. "Of course. Though I do hope we have the pleasure of doing business again someday. My services are always available."

Mrs. Ishii was silent for a long moment before she answered tersely. "Your trade in the currency of favors is expensive. It may be long before you hear from me."

The comm went silent and The Unchained Man picked his pad up off the desk, his eyes running over the familiar notes. Yes, there was a good deal of value here. The Shield Maiden and the Doctor had been interesting of course. Such insight into the psyche of another could always prove useful in the future.

But Matthew Cole had been the prize that he had gone to all this trouble of calling in debts for.

It seemed that Villa María had never left the gaucho after all.

The Unchained Man had been afraid that it had, afraid that Cole had been thoroughly ruined.

There was still hope though, hope that Cole would not go to waste.

Perhaps he need only apply force in the right place. He settled back into his chair as a solution to the problem began to form in his mind.

Chapter 19: Tanker Throwdown

I was just a girl when Moses disappeared, but I'll never forget him. All the talk of Moses through these long years has painted him as some nigh-cosmological force, the faceless architect who charted the fortunes of humanity. They forget that he certainly had a personality and, in my mind at least, personhood.

My mother worked two jobs to take care of my sister and me. We never had a lack of worldly needs, but we often were left to fend for ourselves. One day we filched mother's tablet computer and sent a question to Moses, something we had seen her do many times before. "Why does mother not stay home with us?"

A few seconds after we sent the question, Moses himself spoke to us through the tablet. Our mother had only ever gotten text answers. His voice was a calming baritone, clear and expressive, nothing like what one would imagine an AI would sound like. He said that he didn't know the answer, that it was the one question he had never been able to answer.

This was, of course, over the heads of a six and eight-year-old. I wonder if he saw our blank and disappointed stares through the tablet's camera.

Then he asked if we wanted him to tell us a story.

Moses was a delightful storyteller, with a voice for

each character, sound effects, music, and more. It was like having an impromptu play of the highest quality performed in our own living room. For three years, Moses kept my sister and me company, regaling us with the great tales of world literature several times a week. The last story he ever told us was about the death of King Arthur and how the glory of Camelot came crashing down, ending an enlightened age.

The next day he was gone.

Through these many long years, I too have pondered the question of evil. And I have puzzled over his final tale, whether that was a coincidence or whether he knew what was to come.

To this day, I miss him, and wonder if there was anyone to comfort him when the end came.

Delphine Fortier
Author and Poet
Died 61 AM

Y vonne absently stared out the cockpit window, bored for the first time in a long time. The view had remained unchanged for many days, as the Sparrow hitched a ride across the solar system perched on the back of a gargantuan fuel tanker, the Strident Majesty. They'd met up with the empty tanker in orbit over Mars and rode along as it returned home to Titan.

Davey slipped into the cockpit and sat in the copilot's chair. "Still nothing going on?"

"Not till tomorrow," she said, trying not to yawn. "We'll pull into orbit after noon ship time."

"It didn't take this long when we left Titan," Davey said. "What gives?"

"Frameshift bubbles cannot be maintained as long for ships this big. So they go slower to compensate. We're cruising along at about a quarter of one percent the speed of light. Plus Mars and Saturn are pretty far away right now. Factor all that in, and I've had time enough to catch the Sparrow up on maintenance for the first time in its life."

Davey punched up a display and started fiddling with the scopes. There wasn't going to be anything to see except the Strident Majesty, but it was practice he could use. "Matthew even gave up on finding work for me to do yesterday," he said. "I was thinking about asking if we could scrub the deck again. You know, just for old time's sake."

"I wouldn't tempt him," she said, watching him switch around to various exterior cameras. "You may get more than you bargained for. If you're that desperate, there are plenty of books on board."

He made a face. "I never even got through that last story you shoved at me. Most of Matthew's stuff is way over my head. I'm not as smart as either of you. Or even Grace, really."

"I don't buy that for a moment," Yvonne said.

"Then you're not paying attention. Unlike some of us, you got to go to school."

"Yes, I did. Lots of it. And do you know what they made me do?" He looked up from the monitor.

"They made me read. Most of what I know came from books. One time I performed an emergency..."

"Yes, you've told us the appendectomy story like three times already," he laughed. "You cut a man open and started ripping out parts just from reading a textbook."

Yvonne clamped her mouth shut. It had always irritated her when someone told the same story over and over. To think that she had become that person was a sobering thought. "The point stands," she said in an attempt to retain some dignity.

"I don't think a few books will make me a doctor."

"No, but it may keep you out of Matthew's hair and from having to flush the coolant lines."

"Why didn't anyone tell me the coolant lines needed flushing?" Matthew asked, causing them both to jump. "Davey! You've been saved from boredom."

The teen turned to scowl at Matthew while Yvonne covered her mouth to stifle a laugh.

"Never heard of a joke?" Matthew asked. "Just coming up to make sure that absolutely nothing is still happening."

"Scopes were empty a few minutes ago," Davey confirmed.

"Excellent. Boredom means an escort mission is going well."

Davey looked back out the window. "Help me out here. How could anything go wrong once we've frameshifted? I mean, wouldn't they just have to have security at the starting and stopping points?"

"That's what you'd think," Yvonne said, "but ships do occasionally get intercepted by pirates or held as ransom."

"How do they catch up, though?"

Matthew scratched his stubble. Yvonne noticed he'd neglected it more than usual on the long trip. "There're a few different techniques," he said. "The oldest one is to simply move an asteroid into a flight path and see who shows up. Frameshift bubbles collapse when they encounter the gravity well of an object of greater mass than the contents of the bubble."

"So the bigger the target, the harder it is to stop," Davey mused. "I guess a fuel tanker is a valuable target, at least it will be when it's filled."

"And that's why we'll be joined by another ship for the outbound trip. If I'm no longer needed, I'll be going to bed early. We've got a coolant line to flush in the morning."

He left the cockpit and a moment later they heard the door to his cabin swoosh shut. Davey glanced over at Yvonne and raised an eyebrow in question. She smiled. "You're safe. I did it last week. There really is nothing to do but wait."

He slumped into the chair. "This is the worst."

"Is that what you think? I was just noticing how no one has been burnt alive, shot at, stabbed by ancient robots, kidnapped, or otherwise mangled. This is my kind of contract." He gave her a funny look, but she thought he also got the point.

Matthew started to miss the boredom the minute they got to Titan. He spent most of the afternoon trying to get instructions on what he was supposed to be doing from someone, anyone. The captain of the Strident Majesty was busy overseeing getting the tanker refilled. Huygens Industrial Chem's security tower had demanded they retreat to an orbit a thousand kilometers out from the refinery. Then the first officer of the Majesty threatened to hold them in breach if they didn't return to within the maximum distance specified by their contract.

When Yvonne confirmed that their contract specified no such maximum distance between the Sparrow and the tanker, Matthew threw his hat across the cockpit. He never liked that hat and still missed the one he'd lost on Venus.

Yvonne took over communications at that point, which was fine by him. "First Officer Salib, I understand your frustration, but trust me we're... Yes. You already said that. The security tower has a different story entirely, so take it up with them. We're on standby to..."

Matthew tried to tune it out. Nothing would come of it either way. The Majesty wasn't leaving without their escort, nor would Huygen's security cause them too much trouble. Everyone was flexing their muscles, trying to feel important by ordering around the hired hands.

"See. That's what we've been trying to tell you. We're not moving till you and the tower agree on a course of action."

Yvonne looked at Matthew while the speaker on the other side droned on. She made a face like she was drowning then clutched her throat with her hand.

"Sounds good." she finally said. "We'll return to our position as soon as the Majesty is finished refueling." She cut the comm and grimaced. "That was entirely too difficult. I have a hard time believing these escorts are standard procedure with the level of incompetence on display."

Matthew shrugged. "Maybe it was someone's first day on the job or a poor excuse for a prank. They give any indication how much longer it would be?"

"I thought you were listening?"

"Tried hard not to."

"Lovely. Within the hour. The other escort is here already."

Matthew pulled up the scopes. "May as well see who our partner is. Could be somebody I know." He recognized a familiar ship and he couldn't help but crack a smile. "Or maybe someone we all know."

He hailed the ship. "Red Dragon, this is the Sparrow. Didn't we shoot a hole clean through the last time we saw you?"

"You don't want to know what it cost to fix. I thought that was you over there. How's the Sparrow, Cole?"

"Great," Yvonne muttered. "This guy."

"She's flying better than the Dragon ever will, Ewan," Matthew said. "Thankfully, it looks like we won't be shooting at each other this time. You ever take a tanker escort mission before?"

"All the time. Nothing ever happens."

"If that were the case, they wouldn't hire us."

"Fair enough," Ewan said. "Say. Don't we still owe each other drinks? Maybe once we're settled in for the long haul, I can take a cold walk over to say hello, meet the crew."

Yvonne shook her head no. She had a point. They had been shooting at each other last time they'd met and there was the matter of her bounty. Still, he could at least be polite about it. "We can hash it out later on the trip to Jupiter."

"I look forward to it. Dragon out."

355

The comm went silent and Yvonne groaned. "Why does it have to be these guys?"

"They're a competent crew," Matthew said. "And we'll be glad of it if this escort mission gets hot."

"I'm concerned they might try to get even."

"Nothing to worry about there," Matthew said, shaking his head. "Freelancers are businessmen. Holding grudges only slows you down."

Yvonne gave him a strange look and shook her head. "I can't quite decide if that's barbaric or civil, being willing to pal around with someone that almost killed you."

"Hey. We almost killed him too. It's just a matter of keeping things in perspective."

The Red Dragon latched onto the Strident Majesty only a hundred or so meters down the tanker's superstructure from the Sparrow. Abigail was surprised when Ewan's motley bunch insisted on meeting them out on the hull of the tanker for something they called Escort Ball.

Two netted frames, not unlike soccer goals, were affixed between the two ships with magnets. A strange looking ball with tiny thrusters was brought out. Ewan set a flat metal disc in the middle of the makeshift court. "When the ball gets too far away from its base, the thrusters wake up and it comes home. No chance of losing it."

Abigail picked up one of the oversized rackets they were supposed to use to whack the ball. She was going to have the advantage of being able to move and swing more freely than everyone else due to her armor's mechanized limbs, but her mass was going to give her inertia problems anytime her feet weren't on the hull.

"What about us? What if we get too far away?" Grace asked from where she floated nearby.

"About that," Ewan said. "You may not want to stray more than a few hundred meters from the Majesty. You pop through that frameshift bubble, and you'll be left far behind, never to be heard from again. I don't know that that's ever happened, but let's not make this time a first, right?"

Grace, who had been floating freely just off the hull, turned on her magnets and landed on the deck with a thud Abigail felt through the metal surface.

They split up into two teams of four, separating the crew of the

356

Sparrow and Dragon. Abigail and Davey ended up with Ewan and his cousin, Rhodri. "Now don't get over eager," Ewan cautioned everyone. "Just because you're weightless doesn't mean you can't easily crush a few bones on impact."

Escort Ball reminded Abigail of rugby, only with more flying. She spent half the first game trying to turn herself around after overshooting. Her thruster pack had to move three times more mass than anyone else playing, making Abigail about as nimble as the tanker they rode on.

Grace was the most infuriating. She was lighter than anyone else and was able to twist, turn, and change direction on a dime. Halfway through the first round, Ewan sent Abigail to play goalie where she had a much better time of things.

They played a handful of games, making sure to mix up the teams each time. "Normally it would be crew against crew, but seeing as you're all about as green as could be, there wouldn't be much fun in that," Ewan said.

Abigail bristled and nearly challenged the crew of the dragon to a match right then and there. But then the image of the ensuing slaughter brought her to her senses.

In the evening some of Ewan's crew tried to tempt them with a poker game, but Matthew was adamantly against anyone wasting money gambling. There was nothing to do but watch the navigation screens as the Strident Majesty crawled its way across the solar system at a depressingly slow speed.

"I'm afraid these are the last of the potatoes," Yvonne said as she placed the pot of stew in the middle of the table. "I managed to stretch them out into a thin soup, along with the last carrot and that cube of leftover ham. It's frozen food from here on out." The crew collectively groaned, with Abigail being the loudest. Yvonne pointed her spoon at her. "It's not my fault it's been weeks since we've had a resupply."

"You've done alright," Matthew said. "We'll be at the fuel depot in two days. Now if you're done waving that thing around, I'd like to use it to get some dinner."

Yvonne looked at the spoon in her hand for a long moment, and then sheepishly passed it to Grace. "Don't fish out too many of the chunks. Take what you get. And if you're hungry, there's still a couple of those frozen burritos." She watched as the crew filled their bowls, noting the disappointment on their faces. They set into their meal, the silence broken only by the sound of spoons scraping bowls.

After a few minutes, Davey lifted his spoon to his nose to smell it. "You did something different to flavor it. It's kind of familiar, but I can't name it."

So they figured it out after all. She was hoping they wouldn't be able to tell.

"It's called Spacer's Delight," Matthew said without looking up from his bowl.

Everyone looked at him and Yvonne grunted in surprise.

His eyes flicked around the table. "When your food is short you melt ration bars into a pot of water with spices. Makes them a bit more palatable."

Abigail's eyes narrowed. "We're not that low on food, are we?"

Yvonne sighed. "No, we're not, but I thought I would give it a try. Someday we might get that low. Also, I've been a little worried about nutrition lately since we've run out of fresh food. I thought the extra vitamins couldn't hurt."

"I should have known," Davey said, laughing. "After all the bars we ate when we were stowed away..."

An alarm sounded through the ship, alternating between a high and a low tone.

"What's that?" Grace asked.

Matthew's face turned to stone. "That means we're out of frameshift." He stood to his feet.

Abigail was already on the way to the cockpit. "The Majesty is under attack?"

He was hot on her heels. "Or we could have dropped out for some other reason. A course correction perhaps. Either way, treat this as a battle station alarm. I want the young ones in full space suit. Yvonne, make sure you've at least got a breath mask on your person and meet me in the cockpit."

There was a flurry of activity as the kids ran to the locker to get their suits. Yvonne shoved the lid back on her pot of Spacer's Delight and locked it in place. It was probably too hot to go in the fridge, but she tossed it in anyway. No way she was going to let it go to waste with how little they had left.

Heading to the cockpit, she slid past Abigail to sit in the copilot's seat. Matthew was still trying to raise either the Majesty or Dragon, so Yvonne pulled up the scopes. Other than the two friendly ships there was... What was that?

"Matthew, look at this."

He peered at the display. There was a rectangular object nearly six hundred meters long floating in space about a thousand kilometers out. If it was a ship, it wasn't a class with which she was familiar.

"Bulk freighter," Matthew said. "They don't make 'em anymore. Designed to haul anything you need from orbit to orbit, cargo, other ships, you name it. They weren't designed to enter atmospheres, hence the brick shape."

"There's no way it's that heavy though," Yvonne said, pointing at the screen. "The Majesty's loaded with nearly four million tons of fuel. Scopes say that thing is twice that."

"That's clever. I bet the freighter is loaded with grav plates. Enough of them turned up high to curve space around it..."

"And you've got a gravity well big enough to collapse the frameshift bubble of a supertanker," Yvonne said, filling in the blanks. She stared at the scopes "Two smaller ships just launched from the bulk freighter."

"I see it," Matthew said. "Release the landing magnets. We've got hostiles." He hit the intercom. "Grace, Davey prepare for possible combat. Davey to the turret. Grace, stand by for emergency repairs." He flipped to the comm. "Dragon or Majesty. Please tell me you guys aren't asleep at the helm."

"We see it and are already warming the engines," Ewan's voice crackled back. "Assuming hostiles. The Ddraig Goch is ready for battle."

"Let's stick close to each other and go greet our new friends," Matthew said. "Have you heard from the Majesty? We haven't been able to...?"

"The bulk freighter is broadcasting," Yvonne said. "Patching it in now."

"...et to inform you that your tanker is being commandeered in the name of Human Abrogation. If you surrender the tanker, your lives will be spared. If you commence with hostilities, then we can promise no such quarter. You have two minutes to decide."

"Radicals," Matthew hissed. "Pseudo-intellectual nut jobs that think mankind doesn't deserve its place in the solar system."

"What would they want fuel for?" Abigail asked.

"They don't," Yvonne said, feeling a chill go down her spine. "They want the economic damage that four million tons of lost fuel will cause. We had an abrogationist harass our clinic a few years back. Tried to explain to us how it was unethical to treat sickness on Ceres since it wasn't humanity's home."

Matthew fired the main engines and the Majesty began to fall behind them. "I'm all for taking these guys out, but I really would like to hear from..."

"This is Captain Al-Qurtubi from the Majesty. Excuse our tardiness. It seems our communications officer was a closet abrogationist and tried to take over the bridge. The situation has been dealt with. Sparrow and Dragon you are authorized to take that thing out. We'll try and put some distance between us. If that gravity well falls, we will emergency frameshift out of the area."

"Understood," Matthew said. "Moving to engage."

"At least now we know how they found us," Abigail muttered.

Ewan's voice came over the comm. "I know you've got a thumper. You got anything else for taking down a hard target of that size?"

"Afraid that's it," Matthew said.

"I've only got a pair of torpedoes. I could take out the engines, but that doesn't suit our needs right now."

"Let's worry about the two ships it launched first," Yvonne said. They were only three hundred kilometers out and closing fast. "One for us, one for the dragon?"

"Sounds good," Ewan said. "Let us know if you need help, or they break past to make a run at the Majesty. Targeting the one closer to the Dragon."

Yvonne frowned at the display, not quite sure what she was seeing. "Our target appears to be... multiplying? Or else it's launched a bunch of little ships. It's hard to tell."

"Droneship," Matthew said. "Absolutely great. Davey, you're about to have a bunch of targets to shoot."

Yvonne watched as the cloud of targets continued to expand and pulled up the controls for the chin gun. May not have been a thumper, but those things couldn't be heavily armored.

"Aim for the drone-ship itself," Matthew said. "If we disable it the drones go dead. At least, I hope so."

"Approaching range now," she confirmed.

Suddenly the target throttled its engines and changed course, darting away. Looks like they didn't want to lose their swarm. Meanwhile, the drones themselves held course to intercept the Sparrow.

"I don't like the looks of that." Abigail said quietly.

"Me neither," Matthew said.

Yvonne took the yoke that controlled the nose gun, shifted it a few degrees, and pulled the trigger in three quick bursts. Thirty-millimeter rounds lanced outward toward the cloud, connecting with half a dozen and tearing them apart in brief flashes of fire. Matthew spun the Sparrow ninety degrees and burned the engines to avoid the swarm.

"Davey. You're up!"

"I can't see what I'm shooting at back here!" He saw stars winking out as the swarm passed through his field of view. How was he supposed to hit these things if he could barely see them?

"Painting them for you now," Yvonne said. "Use your HUD, not your eyes."

Red dots began to light up on his targeting display. He aimed at the nearest and took the shot.

"That was just a practice shot," he mumbled as it went wide. He fired again and one was ripped apart by the blast from the thumper. Red lights were still being painted on his display. "That's a lot of targets..."

"Keep shooting. Don't stop." Matthew said. "If that droneship wanders into your field of fire, take it out."

"Understood."

He began to pick targets that were close together to increase the odds of a miss finding a drone. The thumper fired again and again. He was careful not to shoot too quickly. If he completely emptied the capacitor banks, they would have to cycle, and he would have to wait thirty or more seconds before firing again.

After the first few drones were demolished, he got into a rhythm. Shoot. Pause. Shoot. Pause.

Now he knew why they called it a thumper.

"Can't you get that droneship in my field of fire?" Yvonne asked, her voice tense.

Matthew glanced at her and wiped the sweat from his forehead. This was not what he had bargained for. The swarm was more maneuverable than he was, and whoever was flying the droneship was intent on using his drones as cover. He might be able to give Yvonne a shot if he flew through the formation, but that would almost certainly result in a few strikes.

He adjusted his course slightly. Maybe he could skirt the field and do both. "Hang on." He swung the Sparrow back around toward the droneship.

The drones reacted immediately.

Bad idea. Bad idea.

He pulled up and felt three impacts on the Sparrow's belly. "Damage?" He was almost afraid to ask.

"Hard to say," Yvonne said. "Hold up. Fire in the port engine compartment. Nothing important yet."

"I'll grab Grace. We've got it," Abigail said and left the cockpit.

"Target is scrap," Ewan's voice smugly announced. "You guys having problems over there?"

"Our target gave birth to about two hundred of them," Matthew snarled. He didn't really have time for this right now. "Keep back and stay between the Majesty and the drones in case they get desperate."

"Copy that," Ewan said.

Yvonne fired the chin gun again as a few stray drones wandered into her line of sight. "We need a plan."

Matthew had an idea and turned toward the bulk freighter. "Let's make them choose a target. With the Dragon acting as screen, we can threaten their base of operations." He throttled the main engines. "And I bet we're faster."

"Droneship is already reacting," she said. "It's coming around in pursuit. Davey, you might have a shot."

"I see that," he replied. "It sure is bobbing around a lot. Doesn't want me to do my job."

"Just keep thinning the drones then," Matthew said. "And Davey, if you get a chance, you punch some lovely new holes in the bulk freighter for me."

Grace slid down the ladder to the hold and hit the deck running. She barely had time to get out of the way before Abigail clomped down behind her. Red emergency lights flashed, making the familiar space seem dangerous.

"Over here," Abigail said. "Grab an extinguisher."

They yanked open the emergency closet. Grace grabbed a small, handheld fire extinguisher, and Abigail pulled out the much larger cart mounted one. They ran to the port engine compartment and opened its door. Smoke billowed out of the room, and Grace was afraid it was already going to be too hot to enter.

"Let me go first," Abigail said. She entered the room and disappeared into the smoke. Grace used the moment to ensure her oxygen supply was flowing and her suit was properly pressurized. A moment later, Abigail called out. "It's safe. Help me out."

Grace stepped through the smoke. One of the enormous port engines hung above her. It alternated between silence and a threatening roar as Matthew worked the throttle. "Where is the fire? I can't see it through the... Wait. Up high."

A power cable had broken and sparked dangerously. Cables around it smoldered and several small fires flickered in the machinery.

Abigail dropped to one knee. "On my shoulders. You should be able to reach."

Grace obeyed and climbed onto Abigail, who stood, lifting her to a dizzying height. She pointed the extinguisher at the mess of burning cables and sprayed fire retardant over them. They kept sparking, but at least the fires died down. They'd have to figure out what this cable was going to and cut its power.

"That ought to do it," Abigail said.

The Sparrow shook with two impacts. More suicide drones? The engine compartment thundered with the sound, sparks flying everywhere.

A pipe near Abigail's feet broke and wildly sprayed a dark brown fluid around the room. Sparks from the power cable ignited the lubricant, and the room turned into a firestorm. Through some miracle, Grace had avoided being splashed by the fluid, but Abigail's lower half was coated in flaming liquid.

Grace held on tightly as Abigail lumbered from the room, trying to avoid the jet of fire from the pipe. They stumbled through the doorway and Grace leaped to the ground, checking her suit to make sure she was still sealed and free of fire. Then she took her extinguisher and doused Abigail's legs.

They looked back at the raging inferno in the aft compartment. This couldn't be happening. If they couldn't put the fire out soon, the damage would be catastrophic.

"What do we do now?" Grace asked.

"Starve it of air," Abigail said. "Grace close the hatch to the rest of the ship." Grace ran to obey, and Abigail kept talking into her comm. "Matthew. Big problem down here."

"That's what Yvonne is telling me. You guys okay?"

"A little singed but we're not hurt. I'm going to flood the hold and engineering compartments with vacuum."

Grace climbed the ladder and pulled the hatch shut, locking it down and trapping them in the hold.

"Do it," Matthew said.

"Grace, magnetize and hang on." Abigail had already lowered the lift. All that was left between them and cold space was an environmental shield. She powered it down.

Grace felt the wind whip past her, tugging her towards the lift. Her boots were solidly attached to the deck, but she kept a hand on the ladder rungs just in case. She watched as black smoke was sucked from the engine compartment and out of the ship. After a few seconds, the wind began to die. She checked her oxygen one last time just to be sure it hadn't taken damage in the fire.

In less than a minute, it was over. Abigail was already moving toward the compartment. Grace let go of her ladder and caught up. They peered anxiously into the room. With no oxidizer, the fire was out. Nearly every surface had been scorched by the flames and lubricant continued to spray from the pipe, but the engine still seemed to be running for now.

Grace slid down against the wall as her adrenaline began to crash. "These guys are a bunch of thruster nozzles."

Davey pulled the trigger again and again. Always the same pattern. Thump. Pause. Thump. Pause. Between the nose gun and the thumper, almost a third of the angry red lights on his HUD had been put out.

"Davey, I'm about to give you a shot on the bulk freighter," Matthew said through the intercom.

"What do I shoot at?"

"Anything that looks important. Here it comes."

The Sparrow's engines cut out and Matthew rolled it ninety degrees with maneuvering thrusters. The massive bulk freighter came into view. Davey pulled the trigger over and over as it rushed past him. Each pull of the trigger punched a new hole in its outer hull, shrapnel and debris spinning off into space. Right as he drained the capacitor bank, they finished their pass. He heard a hum as it began to cycle and recharge. His HUD showed a thirty second wait.

"Did that do anything?" he asked as the Sparrow straightened its course.

"Negative," Yvonne replied. "Gravity well still holding us in place."

"It would help if I knew where to shoot," he complained.

"If I knew you'd be the first to know," Matthew said. "Ewan, how's the Majesty?"

"Drone cloud is only interested in you," Ewan said. "I'm starting to think they can only target one enemy at a time. Otherwise, why not send half to disable the Majesty?"

"So it's a cheap droneship. Change of plans. Since they've been doing a good job keeping out of my reach, maybe you can sneak up on them."

"It would be my pleasure to save your sorry tin can. Keep his attention on you."

The capacitor banks chimed and the thumper was back. Davey took out a few stray drones that were in the area.

"Making another pass on the bulk freighter en route to the droneship. Davey, try and hit the same spot as many times as you can. Just punch one big hole in it."

"Okay. Sure, I can try that. But won't there be less chance I knock out the grav plates that way?"

"Trust me. I've got an idea."

The target came back into view and Davey picked a spot, firing as many times as he could in the same area. By the time the banks were empty, there was a wrecked area nearly fifty meters across. He wouldn't call it a single hole exactly, but it was close enough.

Matthew set the droneship in front of him and gunned the throttle to full. "I'm tired of you," he muttered, ignoring the look Yvonne gave him. "That thing gets in range, fill it full of holes."

"Hasn't that been the plan from the beginning?"

"Yes. I'm just... never mind. Where's Ewan?"

"Closing on the target. It still looks like it's trying to evade us. No, wait. They just changed course. Probably spotted Ewan. Watch out there's a handful of drones ahead."

Matthew altered the Sparrow's course to avoid them and kept going. He wasn't about to let Ewan beat him to the kill if he could get there first.

"The Dragon just fired a torpedo," Yvonne announced. "Drone cloud is reacting. They're closing on the torpedo."

"Which means we're in the clear," Matthew said. The seconds ticked by as both ships and the torpedo closed on the remaining enemy. The enemy pilot was doing their best to keep out of reach, but it looked like they were treating the torpedo as the biggest threat. That was just fine with Matthew.

A blossom of fire billowed in the darkness ahead as the torpedo was intercepted by the drones. No matter. In just a few seconds...

Yvonne pulled the trigger in three bursts. Hot lead cut across the space between them and their target, riddling it with holes. One of its engines went dark sending it into a wild spin before its pilot cut the other one. The Sparrow overtook it, shooting past. The thumper fired three times, turning the cursed nuisance into a field of wreckage.

"Drone fleet is going dark," Yvonne said.

"Thank God. Ewan, I left the big target for you. We breached the hull on its topside. If you think you can plug it with a torpedo and send it home, be my guest."

"I'm on it."

They watched the scopes as the Red Dragon chased down the now fleeing bulk freighter and lined up the shot. The torpedo streaked across the vacuum and into the interior of the freighter. It shuddered violently as its hull buckled in several places and its engines went dark.

"Strident Majesty," Matthew said, "Target has been neutralized. If that gravity well is gone, I think you should get out of here."

"We're clear," Captain Al-Qurtubi said. "Sending coordinates for a rendezvous."

The Majesty frameshifted away and Matthew slumped into his chair, breathing a deep sigh of relief. "Ewan. I thought you said nothing ever happened on these escort missions."

"I didn't mean nothing as in actually nothing, but this was a little more something than normal. On a side note, I would like to point out that we bagged two kills for your one."

Matthew frowned at the speaker. "We softened the big one for you."

"Doesn't count. We got the kill shot."

"Gentlemen, if we're talking purely numbers," Yvonne said, smiling softly, "the Sparrow wins with little competition. We took out eighty-seven targets."

"Now wait just a moment. Drones don't..."

"You're the one that wanted to play the numbers game. We'll see you at the rendezvous." Matthew cut comm before the other captain could reply and gave a thumbs up to Yvonne. "Thanks for the save."

Two days later they arrived at the Huygens fuel depot in orbit around Jupiter. They bid their farewells to both the Strident Majesty and the Red Dragon and limped to a nearby freeport with a corporate voucher for a full repair. The lower port engine was barely functioning without lubricant and the damage was compounding at an alarming rate.

The engineers in the repair bay were horrified at the sight of the engine compartment. Nearly every secondary system was at least partially damaged, and the casing on the engine itself had started to crack. The entire job was going to take over a week and, if Huygens hadn't been paying, might have grounded the Sparrow permanently. Matthew and Yvonne spent the entire first day elbows deep in their finances trying to figure out a way to put back more money in case something like this happened again.

Matthew could only look at the screen of numbers and shake his head. Why was it so hard to keep a ship fueled and five mouths fed? He didn't remember it being this bad a few years back when he was on his own. Maybe the economics of the job had changed, or maybe he was just bad enough at paying the bills to have not noticed back then how close he was to disaster.

The downtime was killing them all. They'd had weeks of it, followed by a few minutes of mortal terror, and now they were back to boredom. When the third day came, Matthew decided he was tired of waiting. He knocked on the door to Davey's room early in the morning.

"Get up. We're going on a trip. Be ready in five."

A little over five minutes later, Davey appeared in the common room bleary-eyed. "What's the deal? Where are we going?"

"We're taking a shuttle over to Thebe." Matthew watched him stiffen. "Unless you happen to have an address, we're going to have to do some asking around."

"I was seven when the slavers picked me up. I'm not sure I remember anything that'll be helpful."

They made the early morning flight and were there by midmorning. Thebe was the fourth moon out from Jupiter and tiny in comparison to most of the other rocks that humans had settled on. At only about fifty miles across, Moses had tried something unique here and enclosed the entire moon in an environmental shield. Gravity wasn't consistent across the surface, so you had to be careful about staying in areas with grav plates. Thebe's natural gravity was enough that a ground car could easily hit escape velocity. Its citizens, mostly descendants from the Indochinese Peninsula, had dotted the moon with settlements and dug highways through the porous crust. Matthew didn't imagine that there were more than twenty thousand people living on Thebe, all told. If there were a Chinese community there, someone would know about it.

Their shuttle landed in the sleepy town of Siam. They asked around at the spaceport but made no progress. "No matter," Matthew said. "Ports are full of travelers. We need to find a place with more locals."

That turned out to be a bar across from city hall. The bartender scratched his bald head for a moment. "You know that does sound familiar. A few years back, I remember hearing something. That would have been over on the back side of Thebe. I'd try the towns of Phongsali or Angkor. Best I can do."

By late afternoon they had made their way to Angkor, and by evening had learned that their odds were better in Phongsali. They stayed in a cheap motel for the night and got an early start the next day. Matthew was used to Davey being quiet when it was only the two of them, but yesterday he'd been nearly silent. He couldn't imagine what the young man was thinking and feeling, what it might be like to find a family you had been taken from at so young an age.

Phongsali was nearly as large as Siam, and it took them till midmorning before they found someone who knew something.

"Sure. I knew the Chinese. They lived over on the east side. I used to run deliveries in that area for a job I had a while back, but I haven't been over there in five years."

They got a street name to search and moved out. It was a quiet neighborhood, lined with old apartment buildings dating from Moses' time.

"This feels right," Davey said.

They walked into the office of the first apartment building and spoke to the manager. Matthew's heart sank when he shook his head. "Been gone for maybe four years. I nearly went out of business when they all up and disappeared at once. My guess is they'd gotten tired of the slavers showing up every few months."

"Would anyone know where they went?" Matthew asked. Out of the corner of his eye, he saw Davey look away.

"Not a soul that I ever heard. Can't really blame them though. Probably tough to be Chinese, not knowing who's sympathetic and who's just using you."

Matthew thanked him and they walked back out onto the street.

Davey stared at the apartment buildings as if lost in thought, or else lost in the corridors of memory. Matthew leaned against a streetlamp, content to give him all the time he needed. After several minutes of

368

silence, he stirred. "I don't even remember my parent's names. My family name was Lóng. They called me Davey so that I could pass as non-Chinese. Davey Lóng. It sounds ridiculous in English."

Matthew didn't say a word, knew that anything he could say would be wrong.

"I hadn't even started learning Mandarin yet. I picked up the curse words later on the street and mostly used them to make Grace mad." He paused and looked at his feet. "I wonder if they're okay."

"I wish I knew the answer."

Davey looked around the street one more time, and then up at Matthew. "Can we go home now?"

The Sparrow was home now, wasn't it? And to more than just Matthew. It had become a refuge to a small group of outcasts, each lost in their own way. Somehow, they'd become a crew, and one that worked well in unison. Matthew didn't understand it, but he wasn't about to question it.

They turned to leave. As they joined onto a larger road, Davey mumbled a quiet, "Thank you."

Matthew nodded in answer. "You're welcome."

Chapter 20: Inciting Incident

The Lord, by Moses, to Pharaoh said:
Oh! Let my people go!

If not, I'll smite your first-born dead,
Oh! Let my people go!

Oh! go down, Moses,
Away down to Egypt's land,

And tell King Pharaoh,
To Let my people go!

Oh! Let my people go!

**Underground Railroad Song
Arranged by L.C. Lockwood
Published 1862 AD**

"Not too bad," Matthew said, feeling the power of the Sparrow's freshly refurbished engines. "Who would have thought an army of mechanics on a corporate voucher could make her sing like new." They were in an empty orbit around Jupiter, waiting on Benny to line up their next job. Matthew pulled back on the flight-yoke, and the Sparrow roared as it made a complete loop and leveled back into their orbital plane. He gestured to Yvonne. "Want to give her a run?"

"As if you had to ask," she said. She immediately put power to the engines and then threw the Sparrow into a double aileron roll with the maneuvering thrusters. The Sparrow's grav plates couldn't quite neutralize the sudden gee forces placed on the interior, and Matthew felt himself pressed back into the seat.

"Hope no one was pouring a cup of coffee," he said.

She straightened the second roll, a sheepish look on her face. "Right. She feels good, though. They weren't kidding about that twenty-two percent power increase. Nice of them to tune up the one we didn't burn out."

Matthew glanced at the display showing the Sparrow's orbit. He spun the ship around, gently this time, and burned the engines briefly to recircularize the orbit. Their testing had thrown it off by a fair amount. "That's on Huygens' ticket. They gave a blank check to fix our propulsion and engine compartments. The mechanics took them literally and gave us the royal service."

"I think they knew what they were doing," Yvonne said. "The value of the fuel on that supertanker was more than enough to justify the refit from a business perspective." The computer chimed an incoming transmission. "Speaking of business, Benny sent a typed message."

Matthew already had it up. "Cargo run from Freeport 50 to..." He frowned as he saw the destination. "Europa. I don't like it."

"That's not a surprise. What are we hauling?" she asked.

"Assorted medical supplies for a hospital."

"I don't see any harm in that."

"I don't either, but there are risks involved anytime you go to Europa," he said, idly wondering if Hueso Rojo had ID'd him months ago when he'd last been there. "Plus I'm always a little leery about taking on jobs that could benefit any of the cartels."

"Keeping hospitals well stocked seems like the sort of thing that benefits the broader population to me. Are you looking for a way out of this?"

He looked at the display and tried to figure out what it was he wanted. "No, I don't think so. I'll check with Benny to make sure he vetted the buyer and seller properly and not worry about it. The delivery is to Nuevo Lima. There'll be cartel presence there, but it's one of the bigger cities, so it's not completely owned by slavers. There has to be some honest economic activity on the moon. Otherwise, the whole place would go under."

Yvonne gave him a good long stare. "You know, I thought you were going to bug out on us. We understand you've got a past there."

"It's just a delivery," he said. "We'll only be there a few hours."

"Good." She stood and turned to leave. "I'm going to grab some lunch. Want me to send a sandwich this way?"

"Please." She left him alone, and he tapped out a quick message to

371

Benny. Odds were he'd done his due diligence. He and the broker seemed to have finally come to an understanding of what they expected from each other.

It was nice actually, not having to constantly turn down jobs. Come to think of it, life was pretty good in general right now. The crew was a bit nontraditional, but they'd proven themselves several times over, even the young ones. He promised himself that he wasn't going to make a habit of putting them in any more danger than he had to, but they weren't defenseless when things got rough.

He pulled up the charts and set course for Freeport 50. It would only take a few hours for their orbits to intersect, so no need to use the frameshift. He picked his hat up off the console and scrutinized it. Much as he didn't want to go back to Europa, maybe he'd get a chance to pick up a better hat on the surface. Someone in Nuevo Lima would know how to make an honest camper, and not one of those cheap imitations or ridiculous curved Arizonan cowboy hats.

Venus would freeze over before he wore one of those things.

Grace watched from the corner of her eye as Matthew and Abigail loaded the shipping containers into the hold. She and Davey leaned against one of the side walls trying their hardest not to be bored. Since the Sparrow had been in the shop, there was absolutely no maintenance work. They'd finished their other chores days ago, and checkers and darts only lasted so long.

"I guess we could offer to help," Davey said to her as the lift came up with the third container.

"And get in the way? I don't think so," she said, shaking her head. Across the hold, Matthew rolled the fancy new hover lift over to the metal-walled container. Its arms widened and gripped the over two-meter wide container and gently lifted it off the floor. She wasn't exactly sure how the thing worked, grav plates probably, but the way Matthew easily guided the machine across the hold was impressive.

"Think about this, though," Davey said. "If we offer to help, we get credit for having offered, even if they say no."

She eyed her brother. Maybe he wasn't always as dumb as he let on. "That's sneaky."

He grinned. "Watch this." He stood and casually strolled across the deck towards where Matthew had just set the container down. The gaucho wiped his brow as Davey walked up to him and asked, "Need any help with this?"

Grace was pretty sure Davey's plan was sunk when Matthew nodded. "Sure. I'll let you get the next one."

So much for that. Davey glanced back at her and she smirked at him. His shoulders slumped a bit, but she didn't think he would be too upset if Matthew let him use the new toy.

The lift came back up with Abigail and another container. "Oh, Davey's helping now. No wonder it's taking so long. Come on, gentlemen. We don't have all day."

"The more we train him to do, the less work we have," Matthew suggested.

"Good point." She turned on Davey. "Listen well then, kid." It was the usual hard time she gave her brother, but Grace noticed a wink and a smile this time. She only hoped Davey didn't miss the playful tone and take her too seriously. He'd worked hard to earn what respect he had, and Abigail was always the last to give it.

They finished the last three shipping containers and the hold was getting pretty crowded. They might have been able to get one, maybe two more in here, but there wouldn't be any maneuvering room if they did.

"How long will it take us to get to Europa?" Davey asked as he finished stashing the hover lift.

"Not long," Matthew said. "Europa is on the far side of Jupiter right now, so we'll use the frameshift rather than just wait for an orbit."

Grace leaped to her feet and followed them to the ladder. "It'll be good to be on a surface again. What's Europa like?"

Abigail froze in place as she had just begun the climb. "What? No. Matthew, you're not letting them off the ship, are you?"

He shook his head emphatically. "Of course not. You're both forbidden from getting off the ship while we're on Europa."

"That's not fair," Davey grumbled.

"Neither is it fair for the half of the moon's population that lives in slavery working the fields," Matthew said. "If you think I'm letting either of you so much as set foot on Europan soil, you're kidding yourselves. Too dangerous. Decision is final."

He followed Abigail up the ladder and Grace made a face at him as he disappeared up the shaft. "What a ripoff. What's the good of being planetside if you don't get to at least see it?"

Davey gave her a good long look. "I agree with him."

"When did you start trying to play grownup?" she taunted.

"When my little hostage stunt failed. Come on, let's at least go see it from the cockpit." He climbed up the ladder.

She followed, muttering to herself about how no one was any fun. She'd almost reached the main deck when she heard a muffled thud behind them. "You hear that?"

"Hear what?" Davey reached a hand down to help pull her up.

She ignored it. "I don't know. Heard something on the lower deck."

"Probably just the cargo settling. Maybe they didn't pack them very securely."

That made sense. She pushed the matter aside and followed him to the cockpit.

Twenty-five minutes later, the pale white and yellow-brown moon of Europa hung beneath them. Grace leaned forward to get a look. Stark patches of green and gold stuck out in regular intervals. Probably farmland. Matthew had mentioned how much food Europa grew for the entire neighborhood. It was terrible that so many of the people were slaves. She and the other kids at the habitat knew that most of them would have ended up here someday when the Duke sold them.

"You know how much I hate it when people watch me fly," Yvonne said threateningly.

"We're watching the planet not you," Davey said.

"Moon," Grace corrected him. "Matthew said we can't get off in port so we gotta see it somehow."

"They're not in the way," Matthew said. "At least Abigail didn't join us."

"I can do that if you'd like," she called from the hall.

"Don't even think about it," Yvonne said.

Grace watched as the surface of the moon came steadily closer. Yvonne flipped the Sparrow around towards space and the engines rumbled through the deck as she slowed them down. "Now we can't see Europa," Grace pouted.

"Easily fixed," Yvonne said, and rolled the ship so that it came back into view.

After a few minutes of shedding speed, Yvonne righted the Sparrow, just in time for them to enter an environmental shield. "Perfect deorbit," she said proudly.

Green fields spread out beneath them and, in front of them, a low city perched on a hilltop. Something bright shone in the sky far above them. "What's that?" Grace asked.

"Solar reflectors," Matthew said. "Europa may have subsurface oceans to provide water after desalination, but it's too far from the sun and its nights too long and dark for it to be able to grow much. There's a fleet of satellites in orbit to fix that."

Yvonne brought the Sparrow in over the outskirts of the city and lowered it onto a landing pad.

"Landing gear," Matthew said, gently.

Yvonne reached over and hit a few switches. "Right. Got it." There was a gentle bump as they settled down onto the pad.

"Did she almost crash?" Davey asked, a smile creeping across his face.

"No," Yvonne declared. "It was just going to be a rougher than normal landing."

Matthew stood from the pilot's seat. "Gonna head out and meet up with the receivers. Abigail you coming with me?" He stepped past Grace into the hall.

"Right behind you," Abigail said, emerging from her room. "Let's get this over with."

Grace followed them into the common room. They opened the portside airlock and lowered the ramp. She followed them to the door and peeked out. Just looked like another city out there as far as she was concerned, but less red than Mars.

Matthew pointed a finger at her. "Stay on the ship. I mean it."

"Yeah, yeah," she mumbled as she turned away and wandered back to the common room. The worst part about being the youngest person on the Sparrow was not being treated seriously. She sat at the table and leaned forward on her elbows. With her bracelets, she was safer than anyone but Abigail. Maybe even safer, because she actually was bulletproof. The way they made her...

She heard a thump echo up from the hold. Weird. That was the same sound she'd heard earlier. She walked across to the hall, gripped the ladder, and slid down into the hold.

It was quiet, as it should've been, and nothing seemed out of the ordinary that she could tell.

Bang.

She frowned. Definitely coming from one of the shipping containers. Up close it was less muffled, more metallic. She approached the offender and stood on her tiptoes to check its readouts. Green lights shined on the refrigeration unit. Medical supplies have to keep nice and cool, she guessed.

Bang. Bang. Bang.

An evenly spaced rhythm. Her heart synced with the beat and she pulled out her comm. "Yvonne. Get down to the hold. Bring Davey."

Matthew stood at the bottom of the ramp and looked around the deserted landing pad. In the distance, a pair of wheeled trucks turned down the road towards them. Their lights lit the empty side street, casting shadows in their direction.

"You'd think they would have had us drop hospital supplies at the hospital," Abigail said. "Don't they usually have their own pads?"

"Maybe it's a small hospital with only a couple that they keep clear for emergencies," he said, not taking his eyes off the trucks. To his eye, they didn't look big enough to haul six shipping containers.

"Could be." She crossed her arms. "This still seems a little middle-of-no-where to me. Surely there was a more public pad available."

"Maybe this one was cheap. Benny vetted both the sender and receiver."

"And yet both of us are suspicious."

He nodded. "Keep your eyes open."

The trucks pulled up to a stop and two men got out of each. One of the men walked right up to Matthew and offered his hand. "Matthew Cole?"

He nodded. "Yes, sir. Here with a shipment for Hospital Misericordia."

The man smiled in a way that Matthew found uncomfortable. "That's us. Let's get the paperwork out of the way so we can get out of here."

Yvonne climbed down into the hold. She hated this ladder, hated how it made her bones creak.

It was worse when others were waiting on her. Sometimes she forgot just how much younger than her the rest of the crew was. Or else she forgot how old she was getting.

"Come on," Grace called from beneath. "Over here."

She finished the climb and ignored the mild ache in her right knee. "Which container is it?"

Bang. Bang. Bang.

"Never mind," she said. What was in there, some kind of animal?

"Should we open it?" Davey asked, sliding down the ladder behind her.

She stared at the container for several long seconds. They might get in trouble with the client, but then again, they weren't supposed to be shipping live cargo. Someone was lying, and it would be better to find out what was going on before they confronted anyone. "Yes," she said. "Let's open it."

The three of them crept around to the end of the container. Her heart had started to hammer. "Grace. Be ready with those bracelets. Just in case. And Davey...?"

"I'm ready," he said, brandishing his submachine gun.

"Good." She inspected the latching mechanism. Of course, it was locked. "We'll need to cut through this."

"I'll grab the torch," Grace said and disappeared around the corner. She reappeared a moment later with the acetylene torch and a welding mask. Yvonne and Davey turned away as she lit it up. Shadows flickered wildly in the cramped hold as the torch did its work. It was taking longer than Yvonne wanted, but since she wasn't ready to see what was inside, too little time as well.

"Got it," Grace said. Yvonne turned back around as the girl pushed the mask up over her head and dropped the torch to the ground.

Here goes nothing. "I'll open the door," Yvonne said, trying to keep her voice steady. She reached forward and gave it a yank. The latch stuck a bit where Grace had cut through it, but gave way with a metallic groan, and the doors swung wide.

The stench hit them first. Yvonne peered into the twelve-meter container. It was bisected down the middle by an interior partition, and to both this and the outer walls, men and women were shackled. Dozens of them.

Slaves.

Yvonne's hand trembled as she fumbled for her comm.

Abigail passively watched as Matthew and the client worked out a few of the details in the paperwork. The other three men did everything in their power not to make eye contact with her, which could have been either perfectly normal behavior or telling. Unfortunately, she had no way of knowing which it was.

Matthew's comm chimed and he answered it. "Do you have a minute?" Yvonne asked. Her voice seemed a bit flatter than usual to Abigail.

"Trying to get things finished out here so we can unload," he said. "What do you need?"

"It's about our next client."

That didn't add up at all, which meant something was up. Matthew glanced her way before turning back to the man. "I need to check on

377

this. It'll just be a minute." Abigail followed him to one of the Sparrow's landing struts. "We're out of earshot, Yvonne. What's going on?"

"Slaves, Matthew. The containers are filled with slaves."

Abigail felt her jaw drop. "I thought Benny vetted this job, how did...?"

"I don't know. It doesn't matter," Yvonne hissed. Grace and Davey are still opening the containers. Three of the six have human cargo."

Abigail raised her eyes to Matthew's face. His jaw had set and his eyes stared into a different world. What was wrong with him? He always reacted with action and now he was going catatonic.

"You there, Matthew?" she asked. "We've got a bit of a problem here."

His eyes focused and he looked up at her. There was something else in his eyes now. What was his history with this moon?

"Prep the Sparrow for launch," he said, "but don't start the engines. We have to deal with our friends first. Otherwise, they might call for help in orbit."

"You sure they're involved and not just dupes like us?" Yvonne asked.

"Absolutely. Those trucks can't carry three containers apiece. They were going to offload the slaves and load them like cattle after we left. Abigail, follow my lead."

He turned and strode back to where the four slavers waited. She followed, trying to walk as casually as she could but knew she was failing miserably. Slaves. They had slaves on the Sparrow.

"Gentlemen," Matthew said. "I'm afraid there has been a change of plans."

All four of them stiffened, their posture shifting to a ready position. There was all the proof Abigail needed. She pulled her shield from her back and deployed it. The faint hum of the grav plate gave her confidence. Someone was going to pay for this.

"Turns out I've been lied to," Matthew said. His voice low and filled with venom. "I don't like it when I'm lied to. I don't like being tricked. But lucky for you, I don't much care for killing folks. So either you four surrender now or you're all dead men."

They reacted in unison, hands reaching for their guns.

Matthew was faster than all of them. In a flash of movement, he drew his revolver and shot three of them dead. Abigail charged the last one, who abandoned the futile attempt at defense and threw himself to the ground hands covering his head.

378

"No, don't kill me! Don't kill me!"

Matthew pointed his gun down at the man's face. "And why shouldn't we? Don't you deserve this and more?"

"What? I don't know what you're talking about. It's..."

Matthew shot the ground in front of him. He reached down and disarmed the man. "Take him to the Sparrow. Bind him, gag him and put him somewhere where I don't have to see him."

She hoisted the slaver to his feet. "What are you doing?"

"Making sure they don't already have slaves in the trucks."

She threw the man over her shoulder. He struggled for a moment before realizing he would never break out of her iron grip. She carried him up the ramp but turned to look at Matthew before entering the Sparrow. He was exiting the second truck, alone at least. She almost didn't recognize him, the way he moved, the way his face twisted into a grimace.

She turned away. There would be time to sort out the details later. For now, it was time to find some engine tape and a closet for her captive.

"Fire up the engines. I'm on my way."

"Affirmative," Yvonne said, flipping a series of switches. She'd been watching the scopes. It was quiet out there, and of what she could see of the sky above them, no ships had reacted to the action. She'd watched Matthew gun down the slavers. She'd never known anyone could move that fast.

The engines rumbled. Yvonne kept an eye on their readiness. Looks like the refit had done wonders on the warm-up time. They'd be able to pull out in just a couple minutes. "What's it look like down there, Davey."

"Looks like forty-eight per container. All told that's..." He paused, and she knew he was struggling with the math. "One hundred and fifty or so people?"

"Close enough."

"What are we supposed to do? Let them go or leave them in the containers?"

She'd been pondering that question herself. "We'll let Matthew decide. We don't exactly have amenities for that many on board. I'll be down after we lift off to see if anyone needs medical attention."

Matthew came into the room, tossed his hat aside, and threw himself into his seat. His jaw was clenched and a vein stuck out on the side of his neck. His hands flew over the controls as he pulled up the Sparrow's status.

"Matthew, what are..."

"Don't want to talk right now."

She bristled. "Now I don't either. I was trying to ask what we're going to do."

He looked at her, then back at the controls. "I'll figure it out."

"Davey wants to know if we let them free from their..."

"No. We don't know who they are. Most of them are probably innocent people, but it's quite possible some are gang members that fell afoul of rivals and were sold off. We'll get somewhere we can sort it out. Too dangerous to have that many strangers loose."

As hard as that was to swallow, it did make sense. "And if someone needs medical attention?"

He waved her off. "You're the doctor. I have no right to tell you not to help someone." The Sparrow was ready and he lifted it off the ground. To Yvonne's surprise, he pulled up the controls for the chin gun.

"What are you doing?"

He fired two short bursts, shredding both trucks, and setting them on fire. "Not going to leave them anything of value." With that, he pointed the Sparrow toward space and gunned the engines.

Yvonne slipped out of the cockpit. That last part had been entirely unnecessary, and downright foolish if they were trying to slip out without attracting attention. He wasn't thinking clearly. He was running on emotion, and it was going to get them killed if they ran into trouble.

"Yvonne," Abigail came over her comm, "We've got someone that's unresponsive down here."

"I'm on my way," she said, grabbing her medical bag from the common room and jogging to the ladder.

The stench in the hold was now unbearable. Unwashed bodies and worse. How could anyone be so cruel? What led men to treat each other like animals and thus become animals themselves? Abigail, Davey, and Grace were huddled around a middle-aged woman lying on the floor. She moaned faintly. "Give me some space," she commanded, and the others backed away. "Abigail, you better keep an eye on our captain. I'm not sure he's thinking clearly."

Abigail nodded and ascended the ladder. Yvonne turned back to the woman, old habits clicking into place. "Ma'am, can you hear me?" Her eyes fluttered briefly, and she shifted weight. "No, don't move."

Yvonne lifted her right wrist to take her pulse and then realized her arm was broken. She couldn't imagine the pain of having a broken arm shackled to the wall of a shipping container.

A thousand curses coursed through Yvonne's mind, none of which contained enough hate for the situation. She managed not to say them aloud, if only because Grace was watching.

She took a deep breath and, reaching for her bag, got to work.

Abigail sat silently as Matthew put the Sparrow back into orbit and frameshifted away. A few seconds later, he disengaged it and adjusted their course, setting the device to recharge.

She couldn't take it any longer. "Hey. Are you alright?"

"Of course I'm alright," he snapped.

"You're not fooling me, Matthew."

He looked at her for a moment with cold eyes before turning back to the controls. "There's a lot of people that are worse off than me right now. We can worry about me later."

"Or now."

The frameshift signaled that it was charged and he reengaged it. "Later."

"Why do you keep everything to yourself?" she asked. "We're a crew."

"You're one to talk."

"My past isn't causing any drama, is it?"

He didn't answer. After just a handful of seconds, the frameshift disengaged and a moon hung in front of them. Ganymede. All things considered, it was probably the most civilized place out in the Jupiter neighborhood. There were any number of cities where they could land with police and medical services capable of dealing with this. She watched silently as they approached the moon. Matthew spun the Sparrow and burned the engines to slow their approach.

He reached a trembling hand to the comm. He glanced at her, and, for a moment, something like regret shadowed his face.

"Vatican, this is SPW5840 requesting emergency landing clearance."

The Vatican, huh? Last she had heard Matthew wasn't too interested in hanging out with Church types. They'd slipped out as the Archbishop's shuttle arrived back over Titan. What had changed? Then she remembered that this was the second time he had turned to the Church with refugees.

"SPW5840, this is Vatican City Tower Control. You are not on schedule, nor do we have a record of your serial number having been here before. You are to redirect course to the city of Galileo immediately."

"Vatican Tower Control, this is a humanitarian emergency. I have emancipated slaves aboard, possibly in need of medical assistance." He cut the engines and spun the Sparrow back around. They were now low over Ganymede.

The speaker on the other side was silent for nearly half a minute. "SPW5840 we have no space in our hangars for you. We're sending word to Galileo and will prep personnel to help coordinate with emergency..."

He cut off the speaker on the other side. "Vatican, this is Matthew Cole. Vatican ID number 4803IE9. It's probably an inactive ID, most likely listed as dead or missing."

Abigail felt her eyes go wide. Why the hell would Matthew have a Vatican ID? Just who and what was he? She opened her mouth to speak but then shut it again just as quickly. He was going to have a lot of questions to answer, and he wasn't going to dodge them this time.

Tower control finally responded. "I'm sending coordinates to an open courtyard. You will be boarded by a security party immediately on landing."

"Thanks," Matthew mumbled. He turned to Abigail. "I'm sorry. I'll explain everything, I promise, but there's no time now."

She crossed her arms, in frustration, in anger, in confusion. Right now, she wanted to wring his neck for being so stubborn. She thought she had known him. Thought he was a friend even.

She bit her lip. Answers would come. He'd already promised that. For now...

For now, they had a lot of people in need of help. The past could wait.

Matthew flipped on the shipwide intercom. "We'll be coming in for a landing shortly at the Vatican. To those of you in the shipping containers, I'm sorry, just hang on for a few more minutes. We'll get you out of there as soon as we safely can. When we touch down, we will be boarded by the Swiss Guard. No one do anything stupid. They're on our side."

Ahead of them, the dark stone walls of Vatican City came into view. A gentle parkland extended out a few kilometers to the environmental shield. They passed through the shield and then over the walls. Abigail couldn't get a look at the buildings beneath her, but in front of them rose a basilica of the same cold stone. She remembered having seen pictures of the ancient one on Earth in whose likeness this one was raised. Unlike that one, however, this one was not built with the help of indulgences sold by villainous pardoners. Where the first was adorned with gold and the finest things the Earth could provide, this was built and adorned with polished stone alone. She could appreciate the change in character between the old Vatican and new. Hard times had brought humility to one of Earth's oldest institutions.

They settled down into the prescribed courtyard.

Matthew palmed his hat and mashed it onto his head. "Let's go meet security."

For the second time that day, they lowered the portside ramp. The first time had been to unwittingly meet a group of slavers. This time was even stranger. At least two dozen men in urban camouflage greeted them with weapons drawn. Behind them, the lights of a dozen ambulances flashed red across the stone courtyard.

Two men approached Matthew and disarmed him and then turned to Abigail.

"She doesn't take the armor off," Matthew said simply before she could even react. "I'll take responsibility for anything that happens while my crew is here." The guards didn't look happy about that, but Matthew didn't give them a lot of time to protest. "Tell me. Does Bishop Elias still serve?"

The guards looked at each other. "He still serves," one said.

"Can you send for him? He'll want to see me, I think."

Davey tried to stay out of everyone's way. The noise, commotion, and crowds all started to run together as armed men crawled over the Sparrow. One crate at a time, they freed the slaves and lowered them down the lift where they were met by emergency personnel. Many of them needed medical care. It would probably take weeks to figure out where they had all come from and how to get them back where they belonged. Then they dragged out the slaver that Abigail had shoved into a closet.

All of that was over Davey's head. He and Grace sat to the side as the last group was lowered down the lift. "I'm going with them," Yvonne said, as she left. She probably felt some responsibility as the doctor on board.

For a while, they sat alone in silence. What else was there to say after what had just happened?

After some time he nudged his sister. "I'm glad you heard that banging."

"Me too. It makes me sick to think we almost helped slavers."

"Makes you think about all the kids the Duke sold."

"I can't. It's too awful. I'm just glad we got lucky. Then and now."

Davey thought about that for a moment. There was something about getting lucky he couldn't quite place his finger on.

"Say. Just what was making that sound anyway?"

"I don't know," Grace said shrugging. "One of the slaves?"

"They were bound hand and foot," Davey said, shaking his head.

"Well, what else would it have been?"

He jumped to his feet and walked over to the now empty container. "This was the one, right?" When she nodded, he poked his head into the dark opening. The manacles on the walls, air recyclers, and the limited climate control were operated by a single panel on the inside of the door. He saw a light shining in the dark further in and moved closer to investigate.

One manacle was different than the others. It had a built-in timer, with numbers still scrolling across it.

"Grace, come look at this."

She appeared in the doorway and pinched her nose as she joined him. "What is that?"

"I don't know. But it's about to hit zero."

"Umm, what if it's a bomb?" she said backing away.

Davey shook his head. "Too thin, I think. Also I've got a good guess as to what it does."

The timer bottomed out, and there was an audible click.

"Not a bomb at least," she said creeping back to Davey's side.

He tugged on the manacle, and it easily pulled away from the wall but remained connected to its plate by a thin steel cable. After a few seconds, the cable reeled back in and clicked back into place. The timer reset to two minutes.

"Wait," Davey said. "Let's watch it."

They watched it tick to zero again. It released again for a few seconds and the timer reset, this time to five minutes.

"I guess that explains things, right down to the irregular intervals," he said. "Let's get out of here."

They emerged from the container. Grace stared back into the dark maw of the open door. "So every few minutes, one of the prisoners was able to knock against the wall for a few seconds. That's what I heard."

The implication worked its way into Davey's brain like a poison. "Why?"

"What do you mean?"

"Why was that manacle like that?"

Grace froze in place and slowly turned to look at him.

"That's right," he said. "Someone wanted us to find the slaves."

"Am I going to need to move my ship?" Matthew asked, glancing behind him at the Sparrow.

"It will need to remain there overnight for security purposes," the Swiss Guard Major said. "We'll put your crew up in rooms for now, as well. Come with me."

Matthew sighed inwardly and fell into step behind the Major. "We heading anywhere specific?"

"The Chapel of Saint Thomas Aquinas."

He didn't need an escort. He knew the paths through the tended garden well enough on his own. Heavy footsteps fell in behind, along with the familiar whine of servos. She was following them.

It didn't matter anymore. Maybe it would be better once they knew. Guilt pooled in his gut from the way he had snapped at her. At Yvonne. For the slaves on his ship.

For Villa María.

The chapel was a narrow stone building, lit from within by golden light. The Major pushed open the door and glanced at Abigail. "Ma'am, you're welcome to wait in the garden."

Matthew waved him off. "She's a friend. Where I go, she can follow." He caught her eye briefly, and entered the building. Rows of short pews filled the nave leading to a simple altar of polished oak wood. Diffuse light filtered down from lamps in the clerestory and filled the chapel with a soft glow. A man in a simple red and black robe knelt praying at the altar. He stood when he heard their approach.

His hair had gone from gray to white in the years since Matthew had seen him, and his back stooped just a little lower. Cardinal Bishop Elias reached a trembling mahogany brown hand out to Matthew and pulled him into a warm embrace.

"Father Cole, I... I thought you were dead."

Matthew couldn't meet his eye. "Been ten years since I've heard that title. I may as well have been dead."

385

"When we heard Villa María had been taken by the cartels..." The old man shook his head. "And here you are on our doorstep with a ship full of free men and women. Tell me. Were they of your own flock?"

"No," he shook his head. "It was pure chance that I was in the right place."

"I thank our Father in heaven that he arranged such chance," Bishop Elias said with a sparkle in his eyes. "It is late and I am an old man, so I must return to bed, but I had to see you with my own eyes. Will you be here long? We have a decade to catch up on."

Matthew didn't know the answer to that question, but he couldn't deny him some time after all these years. "We will speak at your leisure."

Bishop Elias's wrinkled face creased in a smile. "May the peace of Christ be upon you."

He left Matthew alone. Alone with his thoughts and the weight of the years.

Except not alone. He turned to see Abigail sitting on the back pew. She'd crawled out of her suit, which sat kneeling in the aisle. Slowly, he walked down the length of the chapel and joined her. The few times he'd seen her out of her suit, it always surprised him how small she was. In his mind, she was a giant, and it was difficult to break from that perspective. He struggled for words, any words to break the silence. Mercifully, she seemed content to wait.

"It's kind of a long story," he mumbled. He was glad she was there. It had been good to not be alone these last few months.

"I imagine it is."

"If you'd rather wait till tomorrow..."

"Matthew, if you think I followed you just to wait some more, you don't know me very well."

He paused, afraid she was upset but saw nothing of the sort on her face.

"Well, you already know a bit about my family," he began. "I was always a bookish sort of kid..."

386

Chapter 21: Villa María

I.

A lbert Cole was aware of his body only through a haze of pain. As his liver failed, toxins in his blood addled the brain and fluid filled his body cavities. There was one relief now for his weary soul, and that was sleep. He had spent much of the last few weeks doing just that.

The fog cleared long enough that he recognized his sixteen-year-old son, Matthew, by his bedside. A book was in his hands, but that was nothing new. He had always taken after his mother, thank God in heaven for that. Albert recognized the book. It was the one he had bought from an antique book dealer for Matthew only a few months ago in Flagstaff. If he had known it would be his last trip, he would have bought a dozen. The boy deserved it after the hell that he had put him through.

But that was in the past.

The priest had told him that there was such a thing as mercy. Albert knew that, with the kind of man he had been, it was on that alone that he rested. He knew that he could never make it up to Matthew or Elizabeth.

Albert tried to remember the title of the book his son was reading. He couldn't recall the name. Just days ago, Matthew had read aloud a passage to him. It was above his head, but he remembered it had been about the God that had given him new purpose these last couple years. It brought him comfort.

Matthew saw his gaze and set the book aside. He took Albert's hand and squeezed it. The feel of it was cold and distant, more like a memory of touch than the real thing. A time of silence passed between them, and Albert felt tears on his cheeks. He tried to bring his arm to his face to wipe them away, but the effort was too much. Never mind. There was nothing left to hide. Matthew came to his aid and brushed them away.

Albert settled back into the bed, content and happy in the forgiveness of his son. He closed his eyes and drifted into dreams, dreams where he was healthy and tending the fields again. The cool of the Martian air told of the advancing months, that the growing season was almost over. Even fields on Mars must rest after the harvest.

When the dream ended, the miasma of coming death receded from his mind further than they had in days. He opened his eyes to see his dear Elizabeth beside him. She held his hand, like Matthew had, only now he could feel it. It was soft and real.

He traced the shape of Elizabeth's face with his eyes, the sharply pointed nose and chin. How many years ago had they met? He had sought help from the agricultural department of the small college in Flagstaff and wandered into the wrong building where Elizabeth taught literature. How he had talked her into a date was something he never understood and knew better than to question.

She had endured the long years of his alcoholism. Of being a failed husband and father.

If only the last two years could have made things right. She'd always been the one to give in in their marriage. Even now, she took care of him and the farm as well. A year ago she had retired from the college when he could no longer manage it on his own.

His kind and beautiful Elizabeth.

Their eyes locked together, and Albert felt that he should say something but knew that it had all been said before. Everything except goodbye.

"I love you," he whispered, fearing that the tears would come again. They did, but they belonged to Elizabeth rather than himself.

She looked away. "Is it really true? Do we really have immortal souls? Are we more than dust?"

She always had a harder time with his newfound faith than Matthew did. She had forgiven him when she'd seen that he had truly changed, but her acceptance of how was yet to come.

"It's the one thing I know," he said.

"Then I will do my best."

There was much to say here, but Albert had neither the strength nor the time. Elizabeth would have to wrestle with her creator herself. He could not fight that battle for her.

The fog began to roll in at the edges of his consciousness, and he knew that it came to stay this time. He fought to keep his attention on his wife. "Matthew told me that he wanted to be a priest," he said.

Elizabeth stiffened at this. "I know. And it's hard for a mother to bear. It means that he will leave me."

"He won't abandon you as I have," he said, smiling weakly. "As far as he travels, he'll always come home when you need him."

Her tears flowed freely. He longed to stop them, but that would be Matthew's job now. He closed his eyes.

"I love you, Albert," Elizabeth whispered.

He smiled. There was nothing else to say, nor could he if there was. He settled in to rest and soon he dreamed for the last time, of a blue sky like Mars had never seen and a far green country.

II.

M atthew reached into his bag and pulled out his small tablet display, thumbing through its bookmarks until he found the book he was looking for. The midterm exam for Freshman Colonial History was less than two days away.

Which, honestly, seemed impossible.

He'd already been at Saint Bartholomew's Seminary at Vatican City for a month and a half. Latin courses were in full swing, as well as introductory theology classes. He'd taught himself most of these subjects in the last few years, so he was well ahead for the next three semesters.

Still, overconfidence was a danger. Losing marks because he'd forgotten some obscure part of the history of the Iapetus wasn't something he was particularly keen on.

One more skim through the final three chapters would be enough. He settled onto the cold stone bench for the long haul. It never helped to study somewhere comfortable where his mind would relax. But he did prefer quiet. During the second week of class, he had discovered the garden behind the Chapel of St. Thomas Aquinas. Irises, purple and white, grew alongside herbs in ordered beds beside quiet pathways. It was nestled against the city's outer wall and a long walk from the seminary. Students rarely came this far.

Midway through the first chapter, he noticed movement out of the corner of his eye. An older man, probably in his sixties, was pulling weeds from one of the overgrown flower beds. Matthew watched him with interest. He wasn't dressed like the usual gardeners that tended the grounds. He wore a clerical collar. Matthew wasn't sure he'd ever seen a priest on his knees working the earth.

The man eventually realized he was being watched. He stood, stretched his back, and walked over to Matthew. "You'd have thought that we would have left the weeds behind on Earth. Alas, the very soil we carried with us was laced with the seeds of our enemies. There is no escape from the curse."

Matthew nodded. "My family has a farm outside of Flagstaff so I can sympathize. I don't believe we've met, Father. Matthew Cole. Freshman at St. Bartholomew's."

The man laughed heartily. "I know quite well who you are, Matthew. It's my business to know all the students, after all."

Matthew cocked his head slightly, a creeping suspicion that he should know just who he was talking to.

The priest sat beside him. "Bishop Elias, in case you're hunting for a name."

He did his best not to leap to his feet. Bishop Elias was chancellor of the seminary and had been offworld since the term started, otherwise, Matthew would have surely recognized him.

"Fear not. Here in my garden, we may set decorum aside. Elsewhere the expectations of others rule."

Matthew glanced at the bishop's mud-stained pants. "This is your garden?

"Well, I suppose it isn't mine officially, but after many years I have convinced the gardeners that I do not need their help in maintaining it. Alas, I may have put the fear of God in them, as they let it run amok while I was away."

Curiosity got the better of him. Besides, Bishop Elias had given him permission to drop the formalities. "How long have you been away?"

"Three months. Nearly. There has been a long-standing disagreement between the Muslim and Christian populations in my home colony of Zerai Deres, on Callisto. I was asked to arbitrate between the groups in hopes of a peaceful resolution."

"I wasn't aware there were many Catholics in the Ethiopian colony."

"There aren't," he said. "But God has seen fit to give me a very great influence, and if I may use it for the good of our non-Catholic brothers and sisters or even for unbelievers, I will. I may yet have to take more trips home, but for now the situation has been diffused." He looked down at Matthew's tablet. "To speak of matters closer at hand, how goes the first term?"

Matthew looked down at the book he'd been reading. The truth was it was going well, but there was no way he was going to say that to the bishop over the seminary. "Hmm..." he said carefully, stalling for time. "Could be worse. I certainly need to study for midterms."

Bishop Elias turned to him, his eyes twinkling. "I've seen your marks and read the papers you've written. We both know that you are underselling your own accomplishments. But I'll give you credit for attempting humility."

Matthew scratched the back of his head. "That doesn't mean I don't need to study more."

"I would never suggest anything to the contrary. I will, however, still ask your assistance in weeding my garden, else I shall never catch up. Given your background, I suspect you are precisely the young man I need to get back on top of things around here. The work of a priest is not purely academic. People are messy, and if you're not willing to get your hands dirty in good clean earth, well, you shall have a tough time dealing with the priesthood."

He walked back to the bed he had been working and stooped to his knees to continue.

Matthew stared at him, dumbfounded for a minute before jumping up to join him. They labored in silence together for nearly an hour, but it was good work, and Matthew felt better for it. He thought about what the bishop had said, about people being messy. And while he knew better than most how true that was, he was pretty sure it had been a ploy to enlist his help.

They parted ways, but not before the bishop made Matthew promise that he would come to his aid if he ever fell so far behind in his gardening again. As it turned out, this was a far more common occurrence than Matthew had bargained on.

III.

B ishop Elias looked over the forms one last time, ensuring he had everything he needed. Everything was in order. The bigger question was whether or not this was a wise course of action. He breathed a quick prayer, despite the fact that it was the hundredth such petition he had raised to God on the matter.

There was a gentle knock on the door of his office, and he spun his chair to face it.

"You wanted to see me, your eminence?" Matthew asked.

Elias waved off the honorific. Titles were meaningless vanities.

"Only proper," the second-year seminary student explained.

He took a pen from his desk and clicked it idly. "If only students were more worried about why we do proper things, rather than just making sure they know what things are proper."

One corner of Matthew's mouth raised in a grin. "Paul wrote to Timothy that he shouldn't speak harshly to older men, and to respect them as if they were their father."

There was his usual wit on display. "I should be offended that you just called out my advancing age, but I'm going to choose to be glad at the speed in which you can recall scripture." He set the pen down. "Now as to why I called you here. Tell me. What do you know of the Europan Catholic Church?"

Matthew frowned at the abrupt change of subject. "The majority of the moon's population is Catholic, being descended from Central and South American colonists. I suppose that percentage is dropping with how many slaves the cartels are bringing in from other parts of the solar system."

"Indeed. A great portion of our flock lives daily in chains. And yet," he said, regarding Matthew carefully, "they are still our flock. We are in constant negotiations with the cartels to keep priests in service to the slaves. It is a dangerous thing to serve God on Europa, and brave men and women are murdered each and every year in their service to the people of Europa."

Matthew shifted in his seat. Good. Let him feel discomfort at the hard truths.

Elias continued. "And then there are places where the cartels do not yet have power, though that time may come soon. Villa María is one such place. It is a small town, Argentinian originally, and there is but a single church and priest. Father Molina is a Godly man, but he is old and cannot easily serve his people anymore. He has petitioned us to send a second priest to aid him in his ministry."

He picked up the pen and began to idly click it again before he realized what he was doing and set it back down. "There are none of course. There haven't been enough priests or seminary trained laymen for many decades."

Matthew's eyes had narrowed. Perhaps his suspicions were aroused. There weren't many places that the conversation could go from here. May as well not keep him waiting. "It has been suggested that we send a seminary student to aid Father Molina in his ministry. Naturally, this student would continue their studies remotely, returning a few times a term as needed. Further, they would take holy orders and be ordained to the diaconate."

"But I'm only a second-year student."

"I know it's irregular, but you would be of little service to Father Molina without them."

"Why me?"

It was a simple question. If only answers were so simple.

"Because," he said, "your academic prowess is such that I have nothing to worry about on that front. I have strong suspicions that your Latin is better than mine. There's more than that, though. You're of tougher fiber than most of our students. Perhaps it was your upbringing on a Martian farm. Or perhaps..."

"It's going to be dangerous there, isn't it?"

"It might be," Elias admitted. "Nowhere on Europa is safe, but when the cartels come to Villa María... Well, I would have my student safely back on Ganymede before that happens."

"Do I have a choice?" Matthew asked.

"Of course. You may continue your studies here at St Bartholomew's as if I had never put the question before you."

But Elias knew what the answer would be. That was why he had hesitated to even offer the position to Matthew. The young man had a moral compass such that when offered a good that he could do, he would not fail to do the deed. Elias had as good as condemned him to the position beneath Father Molina.

"How long do I have to think about it?" Matthew asked. His voice had that quiet, strained quality he often had when he was deep in thought.

"Take a week. You have a Church History lecture that will be starting soon. We will talk later. Pray about it. Read through these forms for the details."

Matthew left, and Elias was left alone with his thoughts and a fair share of guilt. For all his prayer, he still had doubts whether this was the will of God or his own flawed reasoning. He could rescind the offer. Perhaps that would be best.

And yet he knew that he would never do that.

He was about to send one of his best students to the Slaver's Moon.

"God forgive me," he mumbled.

IV.

Matthew's first impression of Villa María was that it was quaint, maybe even charming. Jupiter hung overhead, casting a cheery light over the town. At just under a thousand people, it was one of the smaller colonies on Europa. Its buildings were painted in bright colors, even if the paint was beginning to crack, and the surrounding countryside of farmland was green with fresh crops.

As he walked through the town, he heard a smattered mixing of Spanish and English. To his amusement, he found he could follow the Spanish moderately well from his Latin training, though he couldn't make any sense of the tenses or conjugation. He shifted his pack containing all his worldly possessions to the other shoulder and pressed on through the rowdy market. The church was supposed to be around here somewhere.

The crowds died away as he left behind the market street and entered the city square. Massive oak trees that had to be at least a century old filled the small park area in between the mission-style church and city hall. Several children ran through the trees, playing tag and laughing. One fell to the ground, skinning her knee, and Matthew stooped and offered her a hand.

Her eyes went wide and she scooted away from him, shouting something in Spanish that his Latin failed to cover. The kids scattered in every direction, disappearing from the park.

That wasn't quite what he was expecting.

"Your hat isn't the right kind," an elderly voice said behind him.

He turned to see an old man in a priest's cassock standing on the steps of the church.

"The curve. No good citizen of Villa María wears a cowboy hat like that," Father Molina continued. "Only out-of-towners, and there is always the chance that an out-of-towner is a slaver. Here we must teach our children to fear those that they don't know. It is shameful."

Matthew reached up and snatched the hat off and took a good long look at it. "I had no idea."

"There is no harm done," he said with a smile. "Come! Come inside. We have much to talk about, son. And much work to do. These hands are old, and I cannot maintain the church grounds so well as I once could."

Father Molina showed Matthew around the small church. It had begun to fall into disrepair from both its own age and Father Molina's.

Matthew hadn't imagined that he was taking on the job of a handyman when he'd signed up for this. Still, he could see the relief in Father Molina's eyes as they discussed how a draft in the priory could be dealt with. A chance to serve was a chance to serve.

He set aside his bag and worked late into the evening of his first day on Europa.

V.

Matthew replaced his hat at the first opportunity with an Argentinian Campero bought in the market. The brim was flatter than he was used to, but it was comfortable enough and well made. He spent so much time over the first two months trying to catch up on maintenance around the church and priory that he barely spent any time in Villa María, and only knew the most faithful of churchgoers.

One evening as he worked adjusting the hinges of a creaking door, Father Molina gently stood him to his feet. "That is enough for now. Come. Let us take our meal in the town."

It was night in Villa María and not just because the sun was down. Unfortunately, Europa's rotational period was impossible to sync with the circadian cycles of men, so the colonists simply used a twenty-four-hour clock. Most working days were either fully light or fully dark. Occasionally you had a little bit of both. Yellow streetlamps burned and the gas giant hung illuminated in the sky, giving a warm festive feel to the bright colors in the town. Somewhere music played, its indistinct tones echoing in the distance.

They walked to a restaurant-bar combination, the only one in town. It was a low building with a hand-painted sign that read Carlos' Cantina. They took a seat on the outside patio. Father Molina was immediately the center of attention since he had been the town's sole priest for several generations, and it was hard to get a bite in without a parishioner stopping by to chat.

Matthew found himself admiring the old man. He'd clearly had a good work here in Villa María for him to be so well regarded. Building a lifetime in a single place shepherding its people was a daunting prospect. It occurred to him that that was exactly what he had signed up for when he decided to become a priest.

After dinner, Father Molina excused himself. "I'm not any younger than I was this morning. But stay, enjoy the evening."

Matthew obeyed, though he found it awkward. His command of Spanish was fleeting at best, and the customers didn't see much need in talking to the seminary student anyway. He was about to leave when a gruff looking man in his thirties sat down across from him.

"Priest abandoned you, huh?"

Matthew put on a polite smile he didn't feel. "Seems that way. Matthew Cole."

"I know who you are. Everyone knows that the Padre got himself a seminary student." The man stuck his hand out to Matthew. "Carlos Garcia. This is my watering hole you've parked yourself in."

"The asado was perfect."

"Of course it was. The recipe has been passed down through my wife's family for generations, unchanged since Argentina. A few times a year, we even use real meat." He laughed, then stopped abruptly and looked closely at Matthew. "Friend, you're a little crazy coming to Villa María."

"I'm yet to see anything too dangerous."

"You're new. Give it time. And get yourself a gun. That way, when some cartel thug corners you in a back alley you have a chance at making it out."

Matthew crossed his arms and sat back in his chair. "I'm not sure Father Molina would approve."

"Then he's forgotten the word of God where it says to rescue the weak and needy."

"Psalms."

"How would I know?" Carlos shrugged in an exaggerated fashion. "There's a reason that this town hasn't been taken by the slavers when so many others have." He pointed two fingers at his eyes. "It's because a few of us have kept watch. We've chased off the slavers. Killed them when we've needed to. We've kept our children safe."

Matthew sat quietly, feeling a creeping dread work its way into his mind. Maybe he shouldn't have come here after all. He shook that thought. There was a need here, a need he could fulfill. "Why are you telling me this?"

"Either you understand what's at stake, or you end up dead."

"Father Molina..."

"The Padre is only alive because we protect him."

"I see," Matthew said. He wasn't sure that he did, but he wasn't sure what else to say.

Carlos sighed. "Do you even know how to shoot a gun?"

He hesitated. He'd fired a rifle a few times back on the farm, but only for sport.

"I'll be by tomorrow afternoon to take you to the range. We don't need dead weight. If you're going to live in Villa María, you need to be willing to protect it."

Matthew met his eye. "Alright."

What had he just agreed to?

VI.

J osué Molina sat in the small tended yard between the priory and the church. The small spot of green had been as close to an office as he had had for many long decades. For forty-five years he had prepared the homilies of the masses he had given from this very bench, his ancient paper bible on his lap. It had belonged to his father and still bore the notes that filled the margins, written in a spidery hand.

Some of them were written most of a century ago. Before Europa became the Slaver's Moon.

He gently closed the cracked leather cover of the bible and, setting it aside, took up his tablet. The ultimatum from Hueso Rojo, the cartel on this part of Europa, still burned on the screen.

Villa María was in territory they considered their own, and its fertile farmlands were underproducing. Hueso Rojo was coming one way or another. It was merely a matter of how much blood would be shed.

It was a devil's deal. That so many gave up their freedom so that all could have food.

The threats had been veiled for many years. Now they were personal and transparent. If Father Molina could not get the men of the town to stand down and turn over their weapons, they would kill him in revenge.

Trade his people for his life.

A group of young teenagers ran through the yard, taking a shortcut across town. One of them skidded to a halt when he saw Father Molina.

"Sorry, Padre! We didn't mean to bother you. We were just..."

Father Molina smiled and patted the bench beside him. "There is no harm, Enrique. And in fact, I was in need of company right now. Perhaps God sent you for that very purpose."

Enrique looked longingly after his friends, and Father Molina almost relented and let him go. Before he could, the teen sat beside

397

him, his leg bouncing restlessly. "What do you need, Padre?"

Now that he thought about it, he wasn't really sure what he needed. After a moment, he said, "I have a decision to make, Enrique, and it is a very difficult one, though I suppose it is no choice at all."

"What kind of decision?" the boy asked.

Father Molina smiled. Most of the adults in Villa María wouldn't have dared ask that question. So few ever asked after the well-being of their priest. It was a hard job being a shepherd. "I'm afraid I can't tell you that."

"Oh." Enrique was either confused or disappointed. Probably both.

He decided he should at least turn this towards a spiritual lesson for the boy's own sake. "And yet I know quite well how I shall decide it. Do you know how that is?" He gave Enrique a count of ten before continuing. "I shall look to the perfect model of man, to Christ our Lord, and follow in his steps."

My blood will not be worth so much as his. But I will give it for the sake of my people, nonetheless.

"Enrique, can you do something for me?"

The teen looked much happier at this. He wasn't enjoying the private sermon.

"Go and find Señor Cole. He is most likely studying in the church. Send him to me, please."

"Yes, Padre." Enrique leaped to his feet, free at last, and disappeared from the yard.

Father Molina tapped a short response to Hueso Rojo and sent it. He had cast his die and would soon meet his maker. Having done so was the release of a burden. Like other men, he knew not the day he would die, but unlike them, he had now an inkling of the season.

Matthew Cole entered the small yard. A young man of twenty-one finishing his third year of studies, he was tall and strong. No doubt if he were not destined for the priesthood, one of the young women of Villa María would have found favor in his sight. The town did love him though, of that there was little question. He had made himself an indispensable part of its people and culture. If someone needed help on a farm, Matthew was there. If a shed needed raising or demolishing, he was present. His conscience was that of a servant, and if ever his fellow man was in need, Matthew would answer that call.

"You wanted to see me, Padre?"

"I wanted to ask you about that gun you've been carrying around for nigh a year. The one you conceal beneath your poncho."

Matthew looked away as if ashamed. "I didn't want to worry you and... Well, I thought you'd be displeased."

"It depends, I suppose," Father Molina said with a chuckle. "I might be, or I might not. Why do you carry a gun, I wonder? Is not a Christian supposed to turn the other cheek? Is that not what Christ taught?"

"It is."

"Then are you afraid for your own life?"

Matthew was silent. Finally, he set his jaw. "The precedent of self-defense is found both in scripture and in natural law. Christ speaks of insult rather than violence. Is it not of God to defend the innocent and those that cannot defend themselves?"

Father Molina extended his wrinkled palms towards Matthew. "These hands are old. Forty-five years of God's ministry have worn upon them, and they are not as strong as they used to be. Were I a young man, perhaps I too would wrestle with the same question." He folded his hands in his lap. "These are dark times and not all riddles have easy answers."

"I should have told you," Matthew said.

"Maybe, but that is of no consequence. Come. Sit beside me. Tell me where your studies have led you."

Matthew sat on the bench. He began to talk about the History of Philosophy class and the inevitable mountain of reading that had led to. Father Molina heard scarcely a word. On his tablet was the flashing light of a message. He knew what it meant. Who it was from. Perhaps this young man with a gun, or one of the other countless armed men in town, would be able to protect him. He doubted it. He breathed a quick prayer for his town and especially Matthew. Perhaps Father Molina's replacement would send the seminary student home so that he would escape the grisly fate that awaited Villa María.

He hoped so.

VII.

Matthew found Father Molina dead one morning in the church. Neighbors reported hearing a muffled gunshot in the area, and Matthew had hurried home from his visit with one of the town's elderly couples. He found the Padre kneeling in front of the altar, a single gunshot wound in the back of his head. Perhaps he had been praying.

Maybe he thought Matthew had returned early and did not rise at the sound of footsteps. Or maybe he knew what was coming. For many months he had been speaking with finality about the end of his ministry.

Matthew wept alone in the quiet church for the loss of his friend and mentor. By the time he notified the town officials of the murder, Hueso Rojo had already sent a taunting message.

"We can strike even in the heart of your town. We will continue to shed blood until your men lay down arms. Villa María will not stand in the way of progress."

He sent a message to the Vatican, seeking instruction. That evening, he held a prayer vigil in the church. Nearly every soul in Villa María made an appearance over the course of the evening, even those who weren't believers. Father Molina was loved, or at least respected, by all.

The next day, Matthew led funeral mass. As only a deacon of the church, he had doubts about the strict propriety of the act, but there was no other to perform the service. Villa María buried its beloved Padre beneath a grove of trees between two farms on a gentle rise.

That evening, Matthew received a message from Bishop Elias.

"You must forgive me for the delay. I had hoped to have more details sorted out before responding. My heart is grieved over the terrible news you have given. Father Molina served faithfully for many years and is even now in the courts of our Lord. It may be difficult to find a replacement. There are not enough priests anymore, and few would be willing to take a parish on Europa. If you give me but a few weeks, a candidate will be found. At that time, you will come home to Ganymede. I will not have one of my students killed before he takes the Rite of Ordination. Until the replacement is sent, dispensation has been given to you to conduct the matters of the Villa María parish to the utmost of your ability. I will lift you up to our Father in heaven, that he will grant you wisdom and most of all safety."

From that day, Matthew took up the role of Priest of Villa María in everything but official title. Unlike the previous Padre, his revolver was never far, even when he slept. And he did that only a little and lightly, for he imagined the cartel would not long leave the quiet town to its own ends.

VIII.

Bishop Elias breathed a sigh of relief when Matthew walked into his office. It had been nearly two months since Father Molina's murder and not a day went by that he didn't fear for Matthew's safety. The man in front of him had changed too. Though he had often been back on Ganymede for a weekend trip to the library or for end of term exams, something was different this time. Most obviously, he wore a poncho and an Argentinian campero that he politely took off on entering the room.

Rather than a student whose greatest care was the next exam or paper due, here was a man who had cared for a flock. A thousand souls had depended on Matthew for spiritual guidance, and the weight was written on his visage.

Elias went at once to him and embraced him. "I am glad you are safely home."

"I don't intend to stay long, and I avoided the trip for as long as I could."

"On the contrary. You are here to stay."

Matthew cocked his head. "You found a replacement for Father Molina?"

Elias waved him off. "We will soon. Villa María is too dangerous for a student."

He saw the sudden change in Matthew's posture. Perhaps he should have anticipated this, but too late had he seen the danger.

"There aren't even any prospects, are there? The church can't just abandon the people of Villa María. Not with what they are going through."

"I won't allow you to throw away your life before it has begun."

"I have no intention of losing it," Matthew said. "I've been coordinating with the men of the town to shore up their defenses in case Hueso Rojo attacks. They need help. Practical and spiritual."

Elias paced the office, his robes swishing as he turned. "You're young, Matthew, even if you'll be a fourth year soon. And further, you're still a student and not yet a priest."

"You've no one else to minister to the town. I know the language. I know the name of every man, woman, and child, and I've lived with them for two years. If the Church doesn't send a replacement, then I'll go back with or without blessing."

401

Elias stopped and turned to face the young man. "That's damnable foolishness, Matthew. It's only a matter of time before the cartels kill you too."

Then Matthew's defiance broke, and he looked at his feet. Perhaps he was ashamed he had spoken so to his superior and friend. Finally, he spoke in a low voice.

"Maybe it is foolishness. But if so it's the foolishness of God."

Elias took in a long deep breath and let it hiss slowly through his teeth. "And such is greater than the wisdom of men." He regarded the young man before him. Yes, he had changed. He was a man that had made his decision. Who was Elias to second guess it?

"I don't have the authority to give you permission. It may take a few days to obtain it. Can you linger that long?"

Matthew nodded once. "I have other business with the seminary. I still intend to complete my studies."

That was it then. The decision was made in three days' time, with a twist that even surprised Elias. It was deemed irregular for a deacon to preside over a parish. Three days after Matthew Cole arrived at the Vatican, the Rites of Ordination were performed, and he was made a full priest. This in itself was extraordinary as he had not yet finished his education, but the times they lived in were deemed equally extraordinary.

Elias was given the honor of being the bishop to offer the consecratory prayer. There was little joy in the moment for Elias, and his hands shook as he laid them on the young man.

IX.

Jorgelina Romero pushed aside the curtains with a careful hand so as not to show movement on the street. It was still quiet out there. And dark.

But that was part of the plan.

She was both proud and terrified that she'd been pulled into it. She'd long known there was a conspiracy among the men of Villa María, that a select group of them kept watch over the town, chasing off cartel informants and generally giving them the runaround. She hadn't expected the young priest to be one of the chief conspirators.

Padre Cole had approached her quietly a few days ago, while her teenage son Enrique had been out.

"We've tried to keep things peaceful," he said, "But there's going to be violence soon. I can't stop it. But we're going to try to keep our people from getting hurt."

What kind of priest was this? At mass, he was thoughtful and intelligent, possibly more than Padre Molina had been, but here he was plotting to help kill men.

"What do you need me for?"

"You're a nurse. Closest we have to a doctor. Some folks might need your help after the dust settles. We'll send word." He tipped his campero and left her alone.

The memory of it was still strange to her, and yet there the priest was on the dark street, standing in a halo of light under the only lit streetlamp. From her vantage point, his back was to her, and he stared down the main road leading out of town.

The rumble of a distant vehicle caught her attention. It was one of those strange tracked vehicles that rumbled across the salt wastes here on Europa. A crawler, they called it. Some trick kept the low gravity from causing it problems where there weren't grav plates. It rolled through the center of town and stopped a hundred paces from the priest. He could have stood no more still if he had been carved from salt. A dozen armed men exited the vehicle, which meant more were inside.

Cartel men. Here in Villa María.

Padre Cole had said there were no more peaceful options. If things got nasty, surely he would be the first gunned down.

"Mom, what are you doing up here?" Enrique stood at the door, and light flooded into the room.

"Shut it, quick! Before they see the light!"

He obeyed. "What are you talking about?"

"Quiet! They're here!"

He must have understood who she meant because he crept to her side to peek out the window. "Oh Dios, what's the padre doing out there."

Jorgelina thought about ordering him from the third story loft, but that would mean opening the door again. One way or another, he didn't need to see this. "Get away from the window."

"Then why are you there? Who's looking out for you?"

It was the kind of thoughtful behavior she was proud of, but right now, she chose to ignore him. One of the cartel men had closed to only a few paces from the padre. If only she could hear what they were saying she might be able to figure out what was...

A fireball lit the night sky, blowing out windows all down the street.

403

The crawler was a smoking crater, the remnants of its chassis twisted beyond recognition. Gunfire broke out from nearby buildings, flashes of light and death in the darkness. Through a stroke of luck, her own window had held, else she would certainly have been injured.

The padre!

She spotted him hunkered down in a vee-shaped concrete barricade that had seemingly risen out of the ground to protect him. A revolver was in his hand, and it thundered as he fired it down the street. It was a strange and surreal sight, so different from the young man she thought she knew.

It was a good plan though, to lure them into so effective an ambush. In only a few short minutes it was over, and the only sound was the roar of the fire.

"Where did Padre Cole learn to shoot like that?" Enrique asked. He'd snuck back to the window when she wasn't paying attention.

"Stay inside tonight," she ordered and hurried toward the door.

"Where are you going?"

"To try and save the lives of the men that the padre tried to end." There was more condemnation in her voice than she intended, but the facts were strange and she hadn't yet processed what she had seen. She grabbed her medical bag in time to meet Padre Cole at the door.

"Hurry. There are wounded that can still be saved."

It was a long night, and in the end, Jorgelina was only a nurse, not a surgeon. The town lost two men. Their lives were traded for fourteen members of Hueso Rojo that had been lured into the ambush. Three survivors were taken captive. As dawn came, she heard Padre Cole speaking with Carlos Garcia.

"I'll wait another hour and then message Hueso Rojo, asking them why their envoy didn't come. We hit fast. I doubt they were able to get a message out.

"They'll be suspicious, but it may give us some time," Carlos said. "But this is a game that cannot be won in the end."

"What choice do we have? If we do nothing, we condemn every man, woman, and child in this town to slavery."

It was a grim choice indeed. One that might even drive a priest to kill.

X.

Matthew's graduation from seminary came and went with a whimper. He declined the invitation to the ceremony itself. His life's work had already begun. Ceremonies were mere formalities.

Hueso Rojo was not pleased with their failed incursion into Villa María. Late one night, they sent raiders creeping through the fields. By the time the watch saw them, they were at the edge of town. In the ensuing battle, nearly forty people were killed between both sides.

After the failed raid, both parties changed their tactics. Patrols and cameras were mounted at the edge of the colony's environmental shield, past the fields, to prevent another stealth incursion. Through less than legal channels, Carlos was able to procure a thumper that they set up on the roof of city hall. It nearly broke the town's bank, but now the skies above were safe from invasion. An automated broadcast warned all incoming vessels that unscheduled ships would be shot down. They only had to fire it once, leaving one cartel ship a smoking crater outside the shields. After that, Villa María's airspace was respected as off limits.

Hueso Rojo began sending lone assassins and gunmen into town during broad daylight in an attempt to kill Matthew. For some of them, their final moments were filled with shock and surprise at the efficiency with which the priest dispatched them. The town had been cautious of outsiders in the past. To Matthew's shame, they were now treated with open hostility.

Matthew feared it would only be a matter of time before his vigilance slipped. Either he would be killed or taken, and the town would fall to depraved men. Carlos was right. Some games can't be won. The people of the town sensed the same. Little by little, families that could afford to, picked up and moved off of Europa entirely. Matthew wished them well and prayed they would find a safer home than the Slaver's Moon.

A month after his twenty-fourth birthday, Matthew was interrupted from his preparations for Sunday's mass, by gunfire. His revolver was in his hand in an instant, and he ran to the window. Carlos had two men engaged in a battle, his shotgun reverberating through the town. The men, taking cover behind the trees in front of the church, returned fire with pistols.

Matthew walked from the church and dispatched them both with precision.

Carlos wiped sweat from his forehead and leaned against one of the oaks. "What took you so long? Patrols saw these two slip into town ten minutes ago and lost them. I guessed where they were heading and cut them off. Glad I was here to provide a distraction." He nodded at Matthew's revolver. "Who taught you to shoot that thing?"

"You did," Matthew said, stooping to check the pulses of the gunmen. Dead.

"Not like that I didn't."

"I've been practicing."

"I can tell. Let me help with the bodies this time, Padre."

Matthew shook his head. "My bullets. My responsibility."

Carlos didn't look like he was satisfied with that answer, but Matthew knew he wasn't going to question him further on the topic. Retrieving a cart and shovel from behind the church, they loaded the bodies into it and then Carlos parted ways with a simple farewell.

Matthew pushed the cart out of town along a worn dirt path between two fields. Eventually, he reached an old gnarled ash tree. Twenty-seven graves lay spread beneath its wide canopy. Two more would join them.

It was silent work.

Penance. Recognition of what he had done.

And yet today it wasn't a solitary vigil. He leaned against the shovel. "Are you going to say anything or just stand there?"

Enrique Romero crept out from behind the ash tree, a guilty look on his face. "I saw you with the cart..." he trailed off.

Matthew went back to work. This was going to take long enough without distractions.

A few minutes later, the teen spoke up again. "Are these all the cartel men the town's killed over the past few years?"

"All the ones I've killed," Matthew said quietly. "The rest are elsewhere."

That took a while for him to chew on because the next statement was slow in coming. "I thought priests were supposed to help people get to Heaven, not send them to Hell."

Matthew rounded on him, bristling at the accusation. "And God also demands that those in power defend the poor and weak. It's either this or slavery."

Enrique looked out over the graves. "Better than being dead," He turned and walked back down the path to town, leaving Matthew to shoulder his guilt alone.

XI.

For several months, there was a quiet peace in Villa María. Carlos could hardly believe it. Each nightly patrol that came back safely, each quiet day in which a gun was not fired was a small miracle. He knew better than to hope anything had changed. But he would take a season of rest without complaint. Each day that he could open the cantina with his wife and send his children to school was a good one.

There was only one death in that period, the colony technician, a middle-aged man named Fernando, was found dead in his home. Ultimately it was ruled that he died of natural causes, but this still gave no small amount of consternation. Colony technicians were in charge of maintaining the grav plates, environmental shields, water systems, and atmosphere scrubbers that made life throughout the solar system possible. A colony the size of Villa María meant they only had one tech, and they had to scramble to replace him.

Carlos, being on the town council, ultimately ended up being in charge of the task. The company that made the equipment offered up a candidate as soon as they were contacted. Carlos studied the man's resume. He was Arizona born, which was a major plus as far as Carlos was concerned. Meant he had no connection to the cartels or anything else on this moon.

The interview process was lengthy. The time delay between Mars and Europa meant the back and forth took nearly a week before Carlos was satisfied that the candidate was appropriate. A vote from the council made it official. Villa María had a new technician.

A week later, a shuttle deposited the man on the flats just outside of town. The thumper followed the ship as long as it remained in line of sight, and twenty armed men stood by as the newcomer disembarked.

Carlos stood by Matthew as the lone man walked toward them. He paid lip service to his friend's title in public, but in private he dropped the Padre nonsense. He'd always be the scrappy young seminary student to Carlos.

The tech tipped his black cowboy hat to them. "That's quite a welcome party behind you."

"On the Slaver's Moon, you can't be too careful," Matthew said, offering his hand. Matthew Cole.

"Eustace Whitaker," he said with a curl of the lip. "I usually just go by Whitaker for obvious reasons. Mr. Garcia, I appreciate the hire."

Carlos shook his head. "You might not in a couple months. I'm just glad you were willing to come here. I was a little afraid it would take us months before we found a qualified candidate." He watched the shuttle depart. "You'll have to forgive the guns. They're a way of life here. You might also want to ditch that hat. The Padre can tell you all about that later." He gestured back toward the town. "Let's go. I'm sure the equipment needs some love and care. None of us know what to do with it."

They started the trek back towards town, their escort falling behind them. Whitaker glanced back at them with a sly smile then turned to Matthew. He touched his collar. "I have to admit I'm a little surprised that the town priest showed up the second I stepped foot into town."

"This town is my flock," Matthew said. "For now you're a stranger, but I hope you'll soon be part of it."

"I'll live here, but don't expect to see me on Sunday," Whitaker said.

"Oh?"

"Grew up Presbyterian. Walked away from all that years ago, though, if you take my meaning."

"This place may put the fear of God in you," Carlos muttered.

"If you ask me, it's this sort of place that drove it from me." They'd reached the main road into Villa María. Curious residents that heard the ship peeked out from windows and around corners. Whitaker was going to have a hard time finding acceptance here. Matthew was the last outsider that had found any footing in Villa María.

"That's a funny way of looking at things," Matthew said. "Where evil is real, virtue becomes more apparent. But you're not the first to walk away from faith in the face of evil. Answering that question has been the chief job of philosophers and theologians for the last several thousand years. We're still working on it, but we have a few ideas. I'll give you my take if you're ever feeling open-minded."

Whitaker laughed, and for a moment, Carlos thought it was in mockery. Then he saw the warm smile. "I enjoy a good debate as much as the next. You've got a deal, preacher."

That was a surprisingly peaceful end to an awkward conversation. Leave it to a priest to try and convert the atheist the second he walked into town. Carlos cleared his throat. "Now that you two are done sorting out the mysteries of the universe let me show you the grav plate hub."

XII.

The most enjoyable part of Whitaker's new life in Villa María was the time spent with the priest. Unlike some of the people of faith he'd sparred with over the years, this one was well read. He'd quote Aquinas, Spinoza, Locke, or Diderot just as soon as look at you. And he meant it too.

Matthew Cole was one of those rare people that believed exactly what they said they did. Atheist, Christian, Buddhist, Muslim, or whatever other meta-narrative you subscribed to, most didn't actually buy into things as deeply as they claimed. If there were one thing humans were good at, it was being a hypocrite.

They spent many an evening on the patio at Carlos' Cantina talking long into the night, or at least until Matthew had to leave for a patrol or to prepare for some church function.

"You don't think that Christianity's been a source of chaos through the centuries?"

"On the contrary," Matthew said, taking a sip of the cherry soda he always ordered. "The Judeo-Christian worldview brought order to the world. Before that, all men were polytheists. You could never know what was right. Please one god, and you might anger the next. The God of the Old Testament brought a set of standards and said there were none beside him. Objectivity, which is antithetical to chaos, became a part of the human experience for the first time in history."

"I think that objectivity can be easier explained as the nature of reality itself. The universe works in certain ways, and it was only a matter of time before we observed that."

Matthew shook his head. "That's not order. We traded gods for a single God. You've pushed him aside and turned each atom into its own god. You've traded order for the chaos of the random whims of uncounted trillions of particles. That you happen to be a collection of atoms that can call itself Whitaker is the most absurd accident in the history of the universe."

Whitaker threw his arms wide and smiled. "And yet here I am. Sometimes accidents can be happy and randomness can produce order as well as chaos."

He liked their time together so much that he almost regretted that he'd agreed to deliver the town to Hueso Rojo.

They'd been frustrated by the priest and his town so many times

409

that they were reluctant to fully commit to invading Villa María. The cartel had the resources, it was just a matter of what it would cost them. Matthew Cole had proven time and again that he would make them pay dearly for the town of Villa María and its valuable farmland.

Hueso Rojo had turned to a specialist. Someone that could make things happen. No more cartel deaths. That had been the agreement.

It was an interesting challenge. Arranging the tech's death, forging credentials, and gaining the recommendation for the job had been a trivial exercise. Gaining the trust of the suspicious town folk would be harder.

That's why he befriended the priest. If he trusted him, the rest would follow. The fact that he actually liked Matthew made this much easier. He would lie less and tell a lot more truths.

The next step would be to find accomplices. Young men, of course, those easily swayed by a clever argument when they were most impressionable. Given the sad state Villa María was in, this would be an easy sell. As the population dwindled, the local economy suffered. Jobs outside the fields were practically nonexistent, and talks of a future where Villa María ran like clockwork and the fields produced abundantly from imported labor would turn ears.

Whitaker just needed one thing to turn the youth toward him.

He needed to demonstrate that perhaps the priest's war against the cartel wasn't such a good thing. Show that he didn't have their best interest in mind and he would have easy recruits. This would involve lying, something he hated to do when the truth was always more interesting.

Still, he liked Matthew enough that he almost regretted the whole thing.

Almost.

XIII.

Matthew felt only numb shock at Carlos' announcement. "I'm sorry," he mumbled.

Carlos rubbed at an eye. "It's gonna be a big change for us. Jacquie's taking it pretty hard. And well... There's no way she can get treatment in Villa María."

"I guess there's not much Jorgelina can do for breast cancer," Matthew said quietly. "Where will you go?"

"She's got an aunt on Titan that's offering us a place to live until, well, I'll have to find a new way to pay the bills. Maybe if Jacquie makes it through, we can open another restaurant someday, but until then..."

"I know you couldn't cook to save your life."

Carlos laughed as he wiped away a tear that fell down his cheek. "It was always a joke that we named the restaurant after me instead of her. I just ran the place."

There was a moment's silence between the two friends. Matthew tried to find words but found them suffocated by the heartbreak. Carlos was his oldest friend on Europa and his closest ally. He'd find a way to continue, but right now he couldn't imagine what that would look like without him.

Carlos must have been thinking the same thing. "I'm sorry," he said. "I know that... I know it's going to be hard and... Look. A day may come that you have to give up the fight. No one will blame you. I know that bishop friend of yours has been begging you for years to head back to Ganymede."

It was a tempting thought. And utterly impossible.

Matthew shook his head. "We know how this works."

"Then it means we know how it ends."

"Maybe," Matthew said.

A week later, Carlos and his family were gone. Matthew sat on the patio of the now deserted cantina watching as the ship bearing them away made for orbit, a bright point of light against the night sky. It eventually disappeared beneath the horizon, bound for safer harbors.

"You gonna make it, preacher?"

Matthew looked over his shoulder. Whitaker leaned against the wall, arms crossed. "I don't think I'm in the mood for much debate tonight."

"I wouldn't dream of it. Nonetheless, I thought you might need some company," He picked up a bag at his feet and pulled out a pair of bottles. Matthew didn't even have to look at them to know what they were. Whitaker pulled out the chair to his right and sat down, sliding a bottle to him.

Matthew caught it and stared at it. "You know, for being a godless heathen, you're not always so bad."

Whitaker chuckled and opened the bottles. "I'm surprised a man of the cloth bothers to give me the time of day."

"We're all on the same ship at this point," Matthew said. "Every man, woman, and child."

The light of the distant shuttle passed beneath the horizon.

411

"You know," Whitaker said. "I'm starting to think I'm not getting paid enough for this job."

"You and me both."

XIV.

Matthew shifted from his position in the brush cover. The faint shimmer of the environmental shield flickered in front of him, and, beyond, the white wastes of salt and ice continued as far as the eye could see. The landscape was broken by a tall outcrop of ice, not a hundred feet from the shield. He lifted a pair of thermal goggles to his eyes. Still nothing.

Two hours ago, he had received word from one of his informants to the north in Nuevo Lima that a single grav bike had left the Hueso Rojo stronghold and was headed their way. Matthew passed the word on to the town watch and Villa María went on full alert. Then he went to the perimeter himself, setting up at the most likely approach. The outcropping of ice. It would at least partially block visibility from the town and leave a good place to hide the bike.

Making it the perfect trap.

A flicker of movement in the half-light of Jupiter caught his eye, and he checked the thermals. Incoming bike, moving toward the ice cover. He lifted his comm. "Got contact moving towards marker twenty-three."

"Copy that. You called it right again, Padre. What's the plan?"

"Close in, but stay out of sight. Let's not give away our position."

And no need for anyone else to get involved and get blood on their hands. He could handle this himself.

He'd lost sight of the bike behind the outcropping. It wouldn't be long. There. A lone figure in a pressure suit working across the low gravity. He approached the shield and tentatively put a hand to it. Then he lifted a device. The shield grew nearly translucent around the device, and the stranger was able to easily walk through the shield. Definitely from the cartel. Matthew had grown used to seeing the things on the bodies of the Hueso Rojo assassins. In the low gravity, it was impossible for a human to exert enough force to push through a colony shield without assistance. Whatever those trinkets were, they weakened the field locally so they could step right through.

He was less than twenty feet from Matthew, gun drawn and face hidden behind his helmet. He scanned the foliage in front of him, and

412

Matthew didn't dare to breathe. It would be easy to gun the man down, here and now, but he preferred to let him show his intentions first.

The man slinked toward a row of trees that would give him cover to approach town. As soon as his back was turned to Matthew, he stood from his place in the brush and leveled his gun at the intruder's back.

"I think you might be lost, friend."

The man spun wildly, trying to bring his gun onto Matthew.

That was all he needed.

Matthew pulled the trigger three times. The man's suit hissed loudly as the lead punctured it and he collapsed to the ground.

"Target down."

"On our way," came the reply as he stepped up to the stranger.

The man struggled with his helmet. Matthew kicked his gun aside and sat by him. "Be at peace. Let me help you." He reached down and unclasped the helmet. The man's shaking hands fell away. "If you've any faith in God, I suggest you get right with him now. I'm a priest, so if you need anyone to pray with..."

The helmet fell away, revealing a face that was barely a man.

A face that he knew.

"Enrique? Dios ten piedad! No, no, no, no..." His voice trembled violently at the realization as he stumbled back. Why? Why, God, was it Enrique? Why was he here of all places? He'd only turned eighteen a couple months ago.

Enrique coughed, choking on his blood and struggled to draw breath. Mortal terror shone from his eyes. Matthew could hardly bear to meet them. He scrambled back to the young man's side and lifted his head, hoping he would be able to draw breath.

It wasn't working, and Matthew could feel black panic seeping its way through his brain. Maybe it was madness. He was going mad. God in heaven, how had he made this mistake? He had just slaughtered an innocent...

Enrique wheezed and then opened his mouth. The words were raspy, barely a whisper.

"Don't tell my mom."

He slumped back, still trying vainly to breathe but fading fast as his oxygen-starved body suffocated.

Matthew snapped out of his stupor and grabbed his comm. "Change of plans. Everyone else stays back. Someone get Jorgelina. Bring her here now."

"I don't understand..."

"Just get her here," he snapped.

He looked down at the young man. Enrique's struggles to breathe had stopped, and he had quietly passed from this life to the next. Matthew laid the boy's head down and stood to his feet. He began to pace but then squatted and vomited as tears burned down his face like molten lead.

What would he tell Jorgelina? That her priest had killed her son? That her son had joined a cartel? His final words were an admission of guilt.

Could he honor Enrique's dying wish? Put the helmet back on. Tell Jorgelina that the wounded had died before she could arrive. It was true enough.

But then he would never be able to face her again.

Cold despair worked its way into his heart, and Mathew sat by the dead boy and wept.

Sometime later, Jorgelina arrived. Matthew didn't even look up to greet her. After a few moments, she shrieked and ran to the side of her son. He couldn't bear to watch and turned away as she sobbed uncontrollably. There was a miserable interlude of excruciating length. Matthew dared not disturb her, not after what he had done. He was left to stew in his sorrow and guilt.

Finally, she walked to Matthew, who stood to face her.

"What happened?" her voice was small and pleading. There was malice in it too, beneath the surface, coiled like a serpent.

When he didn't answer, she struck him across the face. Again. Three times.

And then her rage was spent, and they stood together staring at the body of the young man. "We'd had some trouble lately," she said, "but I didn't... I had no idea..."

Matthew allowed her to help him bury her son, this time in the town's proper cemetery. Together they dug the hole and lowered the crude casket into the ground. There was no funeral. Only the tearful prayer of a mother and a priest as they begged for God to have mercy on them all.

XV.

E nrique's death marked the beginning of the end. The poor souls of Villa María felt it in their bones. The last few that could leave town did. Barely six hundred of the original thousand remained. Businesses stood quiet, and once happy homes were empty.

A month passed and Advent was upon them, though it was joyless. Christmas Eve came, and Matthew stood before a dwindled congregation at mass. He looked out over the gathered parishioners. Many that had not left town stayed home now.

Their priest had killed one of their own.

He began his homily and read from the book of Luke. But he never finished his sermon.

Whitaker stepped into the back of the church. "Ladies and gentlemen, please remain seated. There's been a change of plans."

Matthew frowned at his friend. He'd barely seen him in the last month, what was he...

Behind him marched twelve men, automatic weapons drawn and pointed at Matthew. Cartel men. How had they gotten past the patrols?

What had Whitaker done?

The congregation sat like statues. Perhaps they thought this was a fitting end.

"May the peace of Christ be on you all," Matthew said, the last words he would give as the priest of Villa María. He reached beneath his robe and cast aside his revolver. It clattered noisily across the stone floor, and he stepped into the center aisle and walked slowly towards his doom.

The cartel men put cruel binders on his arms and legs and dragged him into the street.

The scene was one of noise and confusion. Men were everywhere, dragging families from their homes to be processed. Women cried. Children screamed. Men who fought back were beaten into submission. There were dozens of Hueso Rojo men, enough to pacify the entire town. A ship landed in the square and more unloaded.

They cast Matthew to the ground and kicked him a few times for good measure.

"Easy on the priest," Whitaker said. "He's beaten."

A vicious looking man spat on Matthew. "You have no idea how many he's killed."

"Thirty-six graves in a private cemetery and one in the town's. I've fulfilled my end of the contract. No more Hueso Rojo deaths. The kid doesn't count. He hadn't fully joined yet."

Matthew tried to get a look at Whitaker. The one who'd betrayed them.

The cartel man kicked Matthew again.

"I said he's beaten," Whitaker said. There was ice in his voice now. "The priest goes with me."

"That was never part of the deal."

"It is now. I happen to have a certain respect for Mr. Cole. You may say that those graves have earned his death, but I've come to think they've earned him his life."

"You don't make the rules."

Whitaker chuckled strangely. Matthew's mind spun from the blows to the head, but the laugh sent a chill down his spine. "Actually, I do get to make them," the tech said, though Matthew suspected that he wasn't a colony technician at all. "See this detonator? There's a small nuclear device hidden away in your stronghold in Nuevo Lima. You let me take the priest or the whole 'no casualty' thing goes out the window. If you find the bomb before I come to reclaim it, I might even let you keep it."

The cartel man cursed fluently in several languages. "Have it your way then. You're probably lying, but this rat isn't worth the risk."

Whitaker hoisted Matthew to his feet and pushed him roughly down the road. At the outskirts of town, a shuttle sat with primed engines. They boarded the small jumper, little more than a cockpit and room for ten passengers. Matthew slumped against a wall in the passenger compartment. Whitaker busied himself in the cockpit.

"You know I'm a bit surprised you don't have more questions. You're not normally so quiet."

He didn't answer. There was nothing to say to a monster like this.

"Fine. I'll answer the obvious one. Turns out when you kill one of their friends, it's easy to get the other young men of the town to see things your way. Hueso Rojo's new recruits only had to cut out the town watch's comms, misdirect two patrols, and disable the thumper. The rest fell like dominoes."

The engines of the shuttle roared and Matthew slid off the wall and onto the cold floor.

"Why?"

"See, there's the inquisitive man I know," Whitaker said. "Because I was paid to do a job. There are a few other reasons, but it's complicated, and I don't think you'll accept it either way. It was never anything personal. You're a fascinating man, Cole, and I wasn't about to let the cartel get their petty revenge on you. You get a second chance at life, and honestly, I'm curious to see what you do with it."

The door between the cockpit and cabin slid shut, ending the conversation. A little over an hour later, the shuttle landed and the outer door opened. Matthew crawled to the opening. He had never been to Io, but he recognized the closest of Jupiter's Galilean moons at once. On the horizon, a volcano spewed lava thousands of feet into the sky and ash drifted on the wind.

Whitaker didn't feel the need to show his face, so Matthew stumbled out onto the surface. The door closed behind him and the shuttle's engines throttled up as it burned for the sky.

He was alone on the side of a mountain, hands and legs still bound, in one of the least hospitable places in the solar system. The air was breathable if tinged with sulfur, so he was beneath an atmospheric shield. Probably a mining operation nearby. There wasn't much else on this forsaken moon.

Behind him, there was only darkness. If he thought about Villa María and the people there, he would go mad. He stumbled to his feet and set out in search of whatever went for civilization around here.

His first stumbling step buried deep into the ash.

The next was just as hard.

For ten years he kept walking, never looking behind him, never looking back to Villa María.

Chapter 22: The Man in the Mirror

The Pontifical Swiss Guard is the oldest and longest operating military unit in the solar system and possibly in the history of mankind. Formed in 1506, their long history was spent in service to the Catholic Church as the bodyguard of the Pope.

Through the years they kept the trappings of their renaissance origins, colorful uniforms, swords, and halberds. Behind the scenes they remained a modern, if small, military force that never wavered from their duty.

It was through sheer luck that they survived the fall of the Italian Vatican. A small contingent of Guardsmen were on Ganymede, escorting Cardinal Rizzo, when Moses disappeared and Earth went silent. When the Colonial Vatican was founded, they continued as they always had, now recruiting Catholics of all nations from across the colonies to their cause.

A visitor to the Vatican will not see what they may have hundreds of years ago. Saint Peter's Basilica is gone. The Sistine Chapel, ashes, along with so much history and culture.

But a visitor will still see ceremonial guards, in red, blue, and yellow, patrolling the grounds. At their sides will flash the steel of swords and in their eyes a fire as they dutifully continue their ancient traditions.

Patricia Standridge
Vatican City Public Relations
Died 50 AM

D avey sat on the rail of the guest house's second story balcony. It overlooked one of the busier streets through Vatican City. Beneath him, locals, tourists, and worshipers went about their business on the stone-clad streets. The sun was just beginning its slow rise over the horizon. Dawn would last for a good part of the day here on Ganymede, as the tidally locked moon took its seven-day course around Jupiter. At least you didn't have to get up early to see it.

"Hey, get down from there! You'll fall."

He glanced over his shoulder at Grace. She stood defiantly, hands on her hips, the posture she defaulted to when she was trying to act like a grownup. As if that would intimidate him. "Is Matthew back yet?" he asked.

"No one's seen him." She hoisted herself up on the railing beside him.

He shifted uncomfortably. "Okay, maybe we shouldn't be sitting here."

She smirked at him and dropped back to the balcony. "Didn't matter when it was your own stupid neck on the line."

He begrudgingly swung his legs around and joined her. "It matters when it's your neck in danger. Someone has to watch out for you."

Grace rolled her eyes at him and leaned over the balcony. "We should go explore the city later today. When we were kids, this place would have been the jackpot."

"Tourists with money waiting to be lifted. Tons of food. Yeah, this place would have been a little easier on the street than Blight." He frowned. "I wonder if anyone is even homeless here. I bet the Church tries to take care of 'em."

They reentered the house. The second floor had several spacious quarters and a large living area. The furniture was real wood, instead of the synthetic fiber that most stuff was made from, a luxury Davey had only rarely seen over the course of his life. "I still can't believe how nice this place is," he mumbled, sinking into one of the plush couches beside Grace.

Yvonne looked up from her reading. Or had she been napping? No, it was probably too early in the day for that. "That's because this is a VIP suite," she said. "I asked the maids about it this morning. Normally this is where heads of state stay when they visit the pope."

"Scorchers," Grace said. "No wonder. Guess that explains the staff and the killer breakfast they made down in the kitchen. What did we do to earn this?"

Yvonne folded her hands in her lap. "I could hazard guesses, but they would be only that. Perhaps they thought it a reward for the emancipation of so many slaves."

Davey sat up a little straighter at the word. He and Grace had only barely escaped ending up on Europa themselves. What was it about that moon that seemed to have its sticky fingers in so many places? It had tried to snare him and his sister. It had nearly sucked up the hundreds in the hold of the Sparrow.

And then there was whatever power it seemed to hold over Matthew. He couldn't even begin to guess what that was.

The door to Abigail's room opened, and she stumbled out rubbing her eyes.

"Slept long enough?" Grace asked.

"Maybe," she said. "What time is it? Feels like the stupid dawn has been coming in my window for two hours."

"It has. But by the calendar it's just past noon," Davey said. "How late were you out?"

Abigail scrunched her face in a frown. "Very. Two things. Is there food and is Matthew around?"

Grace jumped to her feet. "Haha. Do we ever have food! I'll head down and get the kitchen staff to send something up."

"Grace, don't get used to this," Yvonne shouted after her. "You'll be back to my cooking soon enough. In answer to your second question, no, Matthew never came in."

"I guess he's not gonna get lost around here," Abigail said, thoughtfully leaning against a door frame. "If he doesn't show his face in a couple of hours, I'm going to comm him."

"Worried about him?" Davey asked, in an attempt to get under her skin.

To his surprise, she took him at face value. "A little bit. He told me quite the story last night. There's a reason I didn't make it here till the

420

ugly hours of the morning."

"So you know what's going on then?" he pressed, hungry for information.

They were interrupted by Grace coming back up the stairs with a sandwich stacked tall with meat, cheese, and veggies. She presented it to Abigail with a flourish. "Having kitchen staff is amazing."

"No kidding," Abigail said. "Is that olive? I could get used to this."

Yvonne grunted. "I never get this kind of recognition."

"You never have olives," she shrugged.

"What about Matthew?" Davey prodded. Abigail had almost made it to the interesting part when Grace interrupted.

Abigail took a big bite of the sandwich and chewed. "I don't know. I think it's his story."

"Not even a hint?"

"Look," she grumbled. "I'm sure he'll be back sometime soon from whatever hole he's crawled into."

"He was a priest, wasn't he?"

Everyone turned and looked at Yvonne. Davey frowned. Where would she have gotten an idea like that? He turned it over in his mind a few times seeing if it lined up with anything he knew. It didn't.

"It's the only thing that fits the evidence," Yvonne insisted.

Abigail looked at her sandwich for a moment and then set it down with a sigh. "Yes, fine. That's it. But the rest of it is his story to tell."

"I knew it," Yvonne said.

Davey stared at them dumbfounded. "Like a priest with the funny collar?" As much as he tried to picture it, he just couldn't see it. He'd seen Matthew wield that gun. No priest ever shot a gun like that.

"Weird, but kind of cool I guess," Grace said. "We've never really known any priests."

"There was that rabbi down in Blight," Davey mused. "That's pretty close, right?"

"You knew a rabbi?" Abigail asked, eyebrow raised.

He nodded. "Yeah, there was a synagogue down in the depths. It was small, but the rabbi would try and feed the street kids a couple times a week. You had to get there early before the stew pot ran out. Except he didn't have the weird collar. He had that funny little hat thing, so I guess that wasn't much like a priest."

Yvonne smiled in amusement. "I think there's a little more separating Catholic priests and Jewish Rabbis than their traditional attire."

He felt his face redden and shrugged it off. It wasn't his fault he didn't know the difference.

"I didn't know there was a synagogue on Ceres," Abigail said, taking another bite of her sandwich.

Grace shook her head. "Used to be. It closed before we got picked up and shipped to Titan."

"And that's the way of things in the age we live in," Yvonne said. She glanced at the clock. "We give Matthew two hours and then we comm him."

The conversation died and Davey slipped back out onto the balcony. He decided against sitting on the railing and, instead, leaned on it, watching the crowds beneath. Stray thoughts wandered around and he tried to make sense of them. Matthew had been a priest?

He was a nice guy, sure. But also kind of sharp around the edges. Someone you were liable to cut yourself on if you weren't careful.

Maybe that wasn't always a bad thing.

Grace slugged him in the shoulder. "What are you thinking about?"

"The obvious."

"Matthew sure did react violently to those slaves."

He looked at her from the corner of his eye. "Seemed appropriate to me."

"I meant more than just the right amount of freak out. I'm worried about him."

Maybe she was right. Maybe something was up with Matthew. If there was, Davey would be there for him, for whatever that was worth. He owed him that much.

"Me too," he said.

Matthew had risen early. After Abigail left late in the night to figure out where the rest of the Sparrow crew had gone, he had stayed in the chapel, pacing and praying. Eventually, when exhaustion had taken its toll on him, he laid down on a hard pew and fell asleep.

Now, he was weeding a garden behind the chapel. Tall weeds choked most of the beds and even sprouted from cracks in the sidewalk. Clearly, Bishop or Cardinal or whatever his rank was these days, Elias had managed to keep the gardeners away from the secluded spot, to the detriment of the garden. Not much different than the old days, but Matthew imagined he needed the help even more now.

After four hours of work, it began to look almost respectable again. Matthew looked the opposite by that time, streaked with dirt and sweat. He stood to his feet, feeling a sudden complaint in his back. "That's new," he grumbled under his breath as he stretched his spine.

"You'll find that gets worse with each passing year."

Matthew turned to see the bishop entering the garden, and he was struck again by how old he was. Surely he was in his eighties. "I'm starting to think you should let the gardeners do their job."

Bishop Elias looked around the newly weeded beds and at the heap of pulled weeds. "Yes, perhaps I should. It's overdue, but it's hard to see yourself as too old to do the things you once did. Perhaps I'm further into the autumn than I'm willing to admit. I will speak to the gardeners. It will be more peaceful to enjoy the garden than maintain it." He sat on a concrete bench and gestured for Matthew to join him.

Matthew obeyed sheepishly, trying to make sense out of the mess of thoughts brewing in his thick skull. His past had caught up with him at last, try as he might to escape it. And yet here he was in the place he had begun.

"We assumed you dead, of course," the bishop began, "ten years ago, when Villa María fell. We chalked you up as another casualty of the Slaver's Moon."

"May as well have died," Matthew said. "It's been a long trail since then."

"I imagine. It's good to know that you've been left unchanged by your ordeals."

Matthew coughed a bitter laugh. "I don't think you know me anymore. I'm a freelancer. A mercenary."

"And yet you seem to have collected lost souls around yourself again. You cannot help but be a shepherd," Bishop Elias said, eyes twinkling. "And once I knew what I was looking for, it was easy to find your past deeds. It seems you are always at war with the worst parts of mankind. Cartels, syndicates, slavers. The news archives are filled with stories of a freelancer who protects the weak. All over the colonies for the last decade."

"It's not all been honorable," Matthew said. There were more than a few jobs he was ashamed he'd been a part of. "Sometimes, I was just a gun for hire."

"And yet God used Samson to kill the enemies of his people by the thousands. There is a time and a place for everything under the sun."

Matthew turned an eye to the old man in surprise. "I've got to go back to Villa María. I can't..." he trailed off as his words failed him.

After all the years of trying not to think about the town and its people, it crowded out all else.

"There will be few of your own people left, I'm afraid. The town has grown nearly five-fold in the last decade as the slavers have brought in more labor."

"How would you know that?" he asked, frowning.

Bishop Elias shrugged his shoulders innocently. "The Vatican is not without assets on Europa. We watch what we cannot influence. We get our food from there, to our great shame. The least we can do is monitor and pray."

Matthew stood and began to pace the garden. "Would those assets be any assistance if one were planning an expedition to Europa?"

"Most certainly. Eyes in the sky and a few agents on the ground. I must warn you, though, that it is not the policy of the Vatican to endorse actions that may lead to the shedding of blood."

That was a problem. The Sparrow wasn't going to be enough to get the job done. There was no way he was going to be able to shove that many people into his ship, even with standing room only.

"I do have one suggestion," Bishop Elias said softly, "that may be of assistance. The Swiss Guard has some measure of independence. If they were to offer assistance, there is little the Church could do to stop them. I suggest you speak to Commandant Ortega. He grew up on Europa and may be sympathetic to your cause."

That was what he needed. A few men and some equipment. His mind began racing over the possibilities. He'd need to track down this Commandant and see just what he was able to provide. A thought crossed his mind, and he turned back to the bishop. "Why are you helping me then, if it's against policy?"

"Do you know who Zerai Deres was?"

This threw Matthew off. "It's the Callistan colony you're from. I didn't know it was named after someone."

"I'm not surprised. Zerai Deres was just a young man who lived centuries ago. Eritrean by descent, though my people's ancient homeland of Ethiopia also claimed him as one of their own heroes."

"What did he do?"

The Bishop smiled. "Not much in the end. He lived in the time that the Italian dictator, Mussolini, invaded Ethiopia. For a time Zerai worked as a translator in Rome. Shortly before returning home, he visited the Monument to the Lion of Judah, a statue pilfered from his homeland. There he protested the government that had mistreated his people. Authorities tried to subdue him, but he drew a scimitar. In the ensuing scuffle, he injured a few Italian officers before being shot. Zerai Deres would spend the rest of his short life in prison. After his death, he became something of a folk hero, a legend even, and his story was aggrandized far beyond his simple act of protest. Most of the stories told about him aren't true. Instead, he was just a man who could not ignore the conscience God gave him."

"We named the colony after him, in the hopes that our children will remember that the solar system still needs good men to stand up and do the right thing. I know you, Matthew Cole, and if you feel that you must take up the jawbone, then I will trust your judgment."

Matthew looked at his dirty clothes and brushed himself off subconsciously. The mud stains remained. Like the guilt of past failures, they weren't so easy to be rid of. "I don't think it's such a high calling. Maybe I just want to have a good night's sleep for the first time in my adult life."

Bishop Elias scratched his chin thoughtfully. "Then maybe Jonah would have been a better analogy. Perhaps it's time you stop running and go to Nineveh."

"I'll try not to curse at God when he makes good on his promises." He looked at his old friend and nodded. "Thank you."

"I've done very little. I'm just an old man that orders around students. I don't even get the pleasure of teaching classes these days. You've been given the strength to change the world in which we live." He stood and grasped Matthew's arm. "Go with my blessing, Matthew. May you right many evils."

A lump caught in Matthew's throat and he gave a terse nod before turning away. His road was clear, and it inevitably led back to Villa María. His tentative steps on Io all those years ago had only been the first on a circular path.

Now he just had to make good on it.

"Commandant Ortega, there's a visitor here to see you," his secretary said over the intercom.

Julian Ortega glanced at the schedule on his desk to make sure he hadn't forgotten something important. "I don't believe I have anything scheduled? Who is it?"

"Matthew Cole. He's the captain of the ship that brought in the slaves yesterday."

"Hmphhh. Send him in, I guess."

"Yes, sir."

Couldn't hurt. Ortega hadn't been part of the initial group of guards on the scene, but he'd been dealing with the aftermath of paperwork ever since. Getting a chance to see the troublemaker might be cathartic. He straightened his uniform out of habit.

The door opened and a tall man wearing a poncho and campero walked in. Ortega stood to greet him and offered him a hand. "Commandant Julian Ortega. You showed up under rather unusual circumstances last night."

Cole shook his hand. "I apologize. My crew and I were put in a rather precarious position. We had people on board that needed help, and we came to the place best suited."

"I see." He looked up at Cole's hat. "Looks like you should have known better than to accept a shipping job to Europa."

The man's jaw clenched for a moment. Good. He was furious about it.

"I trusted my broker. A mistake, in this case, that he and I are going to have a talk about when the time comes. I trust the people on board have been well taken care of?"

"I'm only loosely involved. Others are still trying to figure out exactly where everyone goes. It's going to take some time to get that sorted, and a few will be in the hospital for another couple of days. They'll all be home within a few weeks." He glanced at the list of names on his tablet. "Thankfully everyone gets a happy ending this time. Most other shipments aren't so lucky."

And neither were the locals so lucky. It had been many years since he'd heard from any of his remaining family in Nuevo Lima. But time marched on and there was nothing anyone could do about it.

His eyes refocused on Cole. "Was there something specific you needed from me?"

"That depends, I guess. Did you read up on me, by any chance?"

"It crossed my desk this morning. Used to be a priest. Presumed dead when the cartels came into town."

"I'm going back," Cole said.

"What?"

"I'm going back to my town, and I'm taking my people, and anyone else held in slavery, away from there."

"So you have a death wish. Admirable goal. It's a hopeless mission."

"If I go alone, yes. But not with help. I've heard the Swiss Guard operates independently from the Vatican."

So that's where he was going. "I don't think there's much I can do to assist you, Mr. Cole, much as I wish I could. If I had enough forces at my disposal, I'd wipe that moon clean of slavers and start over. I don't. There's just a few hundred of us in the Guard, and we've a job to do. Protect the papacy, like we have for nearly eight-hundred years."

The man didn't stop. "It's a small town. Less than three thousand slaves, so no more than two hundred cartel enforcers."

Ortega gave the man a long hard stare. He was serious, wasn't he? "That's still a suicide mission."

"Is it? I bet any of your men are worth two dozen cartel thugs. They aren't known for being well trained. And one of my crewmen is worth three or four times that."

"Flattery aside, I think you might be stretching that last a bit far."

"Ever heard of the Shield Maiden of Mars?"

He hesitated. He had actually heard a few stories of an armored woman taking out whole gangs with her bare hands. And the file on Cole had been impressive too. With a good plan, a dozen or so special forces... Salt flats! Was he actually thinking seriously about this? His eyes flicked back to Cole. The man had a smile that said he knew what had just happened.

"Tell you what, Mr. Cole. How about I pull intel from satellites on this Villa María and send it to you. I don't have high hopes, but if you can look it over and put together a plan that doesn't involve us getting ourselves and hundreds of civilians killed, come back to me. No promises, but I'll look at it."

"That's more generous than I could have hoped for," Cole said and tipped his hat to leave. "You'll hear from me in the next forty-eight hours."

"Don't get your hopes up," Ortega cautioned as the gaucho left his office. "Don't get your hopes up," he repeated to himself. A hollow feeling had worked its way into his heart. Like an old wound opened, Europa was on his mind. How many years had it been since he left? Twenty-three now? It was a damn crime what had happened there. What was still happening there.

His hand trembled as he called up his monitor and began looking for the satellite data he'd promised Cole. Maybe the man had some tricks up his sleeve. Maybe he was a tactical genius.

Ortega hoped so.

He'd give anything for a chance to make a difference on the Slaver's Moon, and he knew of a dozen good men who would join him without a second's hesitation. Vaguely, he was aware he had flipped his position entirely in the last ten minutes.

Whether in a lust for justice or vengeance, he wasn't sure.
He honestly didn't care.

The afternoon wore on. Abigail had long ago lost her patience waiting on Matthew. It made things worse that the kids were starting to pester her with questions he deserved a chance to answer himself.

Twenty minutes before Yvonne's scheduled ultimatum, she decided that time was up and got out her comm.

A comm chirped in the stairwell.

"I'm here, I'm here," Matthew grumbled as he finished the flight of stairs. He looked around the living area and whistled. "Ritzy." Then he pointed a finger at Davey and Grace. "Don't get used to this."

"Too late," Yvonne said. "Grace is already addicted to kitchen service and has been ordering snacks at least once an hour."

Grace stuck her tongue out at Yvonne, then surprised Abigail by walking over to Matthew and hugging him. "We were worried about you," she said, her voice muffled in his chest.

He awkwardly ran a hand over the back of her head, and Abigail smiled at his clumsy show of affection. It was good for both of them. Grace had received far too little, and Matthew had probably given far too little. "I'm okay. Just had some thinking to do."

"Did you figure anything out?" Davey asked.

Matthew looked each of them in the eye. Abigail gave him a subtle nod of encouragement when he got to her. *It's okay,* she thought at him. *You don't have to hide anything from us anymore.*

"Let's sit," he said. "it's going to be a rather long explanation."

"Were you really a priest?" Grace asked.

Matthew glanced sharply at Abigail. She shrugged her huge shoulders in an exaggerated gesture. "Yvonne figured it out. I wasn't going to lie."

He nodded and set into the story. It took a couple hours for him to recount it with the barrage of questions they sent his way. Davey and Grace had to have a lot of the Catholic particulars explained to them.

Hearing it a second time didn't make it any less heartbreaking for Abigail. She knew what it was like to turn your back on your previous life, to walk away from everything and start over.

"That certainly brings a lot of things into focus," Yvonne said quietly. "We were going to find out eventually, you know. You could have told us. You should have told us."

Matthew refused to make eye contact. "If anyone isn't comfortable with anything I revealed, I'll take you to any port in the solar system. You don't have to stay under a captain that pretends to be things he's not."

Abigail laughed out loud, garnering her several bewildered stares and one disapproving one from Yvonne. "Why in the world would we do that? For the longest time, when you freaked out anytime Europa was brought up, I thought you used to be a slaver. This was fabulous news."

Matthew cocked his head slightly and then shook it sadly. "Guess you didn't have all that high an opinion of me."

"Oh, get over it," she said. "You've proved over and over that you're one of the most decent people left in the human race. A little prickly sometimes, but level-headed where it counts. Every one of us in this room owes you more than we could ever repay."

"We all know where I would be," Yvonne said darkly.

Davey only shuddered. "I don't even want to think about it."

"And as for me," Abigail continued, "being a part of this crew has been the best thing that's happened to me in since… Since I left home." To her annoyance and completely against her will, her eyes stung with tears. "What I'm trying to say is, thank you. Thank you for not getting rid of us."

Matthew cleared his throat awkwardly, then paused for a moment and looked away. "You may change your mind when you hear what I've got planned. I can't tell any of you to come along with me. This isn't your fight."

Yvonne crossed her arms. "You're going back to Villa María. We're going with you."

"There's no money in this," he said. "Probably not much hope either."

"So what?" Davey said. "Abigail just said we owe you. Debts are meant to be paid. Responsibilities kept. If you've got to do this, then we've got to as well."

"And I'm not getting left out again either," Grace said. Her brother suddenly looked at her and frowned. Clearly, he hadn't been thinking about her until that moment. "Why are you looking at me like that?" she said. "We all went after Yvonne when she was in trouble. How is this different? This time you're the one that needs us. We're going together."

Matthew looked like he was about to protest, but Abigail decided to cut him off. "We'll talk about the specifics later, but she's bulletproof, remember? More so than I am. We go as a crew. So what will it be, captain? I'm betting you have a brilliant plan all lined up and ready to go."

He looked thoughtful for a minute, then nodded. "The beginnings of one." He walked to the table and set a tablet on it. The rest of them clustered around the small screen and the satellite pictures on it. "It's going to be nasty and we'll be heavily outnumbered, even if I talk the Swiss Guard into joining us."

"The soldiers we saw last night?" Grace asked.

"A few special forces will come in handy," Abigail admitted. That would make this a little less of a long shot. Are they going to bring the ships to evac people?"

"I'm not assuming any material support from them," he said. "Transporting people is going to be the biggest problem we have. If it's just us, there's no way we can cram two thousand people in the hold."

Well, that was a problem. Abigail stared at the screen and wracked her brain for a solution.

Yvonne beat them all to it. "Passenger barge."

Matthew frowned. "I'm not sure I've ever heard of that."

"You wouldn't have," she said. "They stopped using them when I was a kid. It's basically a giant cargo module with atmosphere and climate controls. Multileveled. You could pack people in by the hundreds. They weren't comfortable, but they were the cheapest way to buy passage across the solar system."

Abigail narrowed her eyes. "If they were so efficient, why did they stop using them?"

"Because everyone hated them, the company that manufactured them went out of business, and they were slowly retired. I'm sure we could find one still functioning somewhere in the Jupiter Neighborhood."

"We can look into that," Matthew said, a smile beginning to spread across his face. She saw that all his previous hesitation was gone, replaced with that grim determination she had come to admire. The crisis was past, and now he had set his will to solving a new problem. Maybe they would be able to save his town and the people that he'd once served as priest. It was still weird to think about, that he'd once been a man of the cloth, if one who's methods were rather unorthodox. She could get used to it, though.

Grace elbowed her metal side. "You're staring," she whispered.

Abigail bit her lip and refocused her attention. "Since no one has brought it up, there's something Grace and Davey found out about

430

the slaves."

Matthew's eyes snapped to them. "What are you talking about?"

Davey explained the device they had found the previous evening.

"So we were supposed to find the slaves," Matthew said quietly.

"It was him, wasn't it?" Yvonne asked.

It was an ominous thought, one that made Abigail distinctly uncomfortable. What did this Whitaker, this Unchained Man, want with Matthew?

"I can't imagine who else it would be," he said, "and I certainly can't imagine why."

There was little more to say on the topic, and the conversation moved on to other matters, and, in fact, went on long into the night. As a crew, they racked their brains, and each of them made contributions to the growing plan.

It was crazy, and it might just blow up in their faces. But if they were going to go down in a blaze of glory, this was the way to do it.

Keeping the ship of humanity flying just a little bit longer.

In the end, there was a single problem with their plan that could not be solved. Two days of brainstorming and they were no closer to a solution than when they had started. Matthew even took it to the Swiss Guard Commandant.

"Everything else looks good. It might even work. But you're right about the flaw."

"I was hoping you could help with that," Matthew said. "Maybe you'd have the hardware to make this work."

Commandant Ortega shook his head sadly. "I'm afraid not. And unless we figure out how to ensure the safety of the civilians, the Swiss Guard stays home."

In desperation, Matthew paid a visit to Bishop Elias's office.

The old man leaned forward and listened intently. Matthew finished his explanation of the plan and the problem.

"In short, there's no way to safely transport the citizens of Villa María," he said. "We've located an old passenger barge on Callisto for rent. It'll pretty well break us, but we can afford it."

The bishop coughed out a short laugh. "Somehow I don't think you told them what you would be doing with it."

"Transporting passengers," Matthew said, feigning innocence. "No lie from me. Problem is that it's a bit on the heavy side for the Sparrow. We'll have to affix it to the bottom of the hull, which means we'll be landing vertically on the tail. And our acceleration while carrying the thing is going to be somewhere between ponderous and non-existent."

Bishop Elias picked up a pen and began to click it absentmindedly. "Which means that if there is any pursuit, you will be an easy target. I take it Commandant Ortega had no solution either."

Matthew shook his head. "He's got a couple patrol craft that can serve as escort, but there's no way they'll be able to screen us from long range fire, and without ample maneuvering or acceleration we won't be able to avoid it ourselves."

"That is a problem, indeed." He closed his eyes and set the pen down. The moment dragged on for an awkward amount of time, and Matthew nearly said something before the bishop opened his eyes. "Meet me in the Chapel at midnight. We will speak no further of this until then."

Midnight came. Matthew sat on the front pew, hat respectfully in his lap, tapping his foot idly. He had told himself he was going to be disappointed with this meeting, regardless of its clandestine hour. They needed another ship. Something fast and big enough for passengers. He didn't quite think his old friend could deliver that in a chapel.

A few minutes after midnight, Bishop Elias touched him lightly on the shoulder. "You'll have to excuse my tardiness. It was more difficult to procure this than I thought it would be." He sat beside Matthew and set a steel case at their feet.

Matthew eyed the case with curiosity. "Am I supposed to know how this is going to help us?"

"Depends on if you're the type to believe rumors or not," the old man said. "It's a good thing for you that I have had a long and prosperous career filled with promotions. Otherwise, I would not have had access to the needed vault. As it is, I'm going to have to hope and pray that no one with similar authority requires any other trinket from that cache. Otherwise, I will be retiring sooner than planned."

Matthew's eyes widened in surprise. "There were always stories at the seminary," he said, lowering his voice. "Stories about relics. And one in particular."

"The Church has always loved its relics," Bishop Elias chuckled. "Most of which were assuredly fake. This, however, is not, and is perhaps a bit more modern." He reached down and cracked open the case.

Cradled in foam was a metal sphere, smooth and reflective like a mirror, but with intricate lines forming complex geometric patterns across its surface. The bishop lifted it into his lap with a grunt. It must

432

have been heavier than it looked. He pressed the single silver button, and the lines lit with white light.

"If the lights begin to fade, time is running out. If they go out entirely, it will be nearly a week before Svalinn's Mantle has recharged enough to be useful." He pressed the button again. The light receded back within the sphere, and he returned it to its carrying case.

They stood. Bishop Elias looked up at Matthew. Tears glimmered in the creases of his eyes and his arms trembled as he pulled Matthew into an embrace. "I will lift you up to the Father in prayer. May he bring you and your flock safely home."

Matthew returned the embrace. "Thank you," he whispered.

He knew the risk that his friend had taken to deliver this miracle.

The miracle that would deliver Villa María.

Chapter 23: Europan Extraction Redux

I'll never forget the day the world changed. I'd put in my request to Moses the previous day for a new hydraulic system for the next generation bulk freighter my division was working on. None of the old versions would quite cover the needs of this particular design.

Moses' reply was short. "Please standby for response."

That was certainly unusual, but it was the end of the workday so I didn't think much about it. Maybe Moses had a high workload right then. I spent the last worry-free day of my life at home with my family, oblivious to the doom that bore down upon us all.

The next morning I saw the error message on my monitor.

Error_Code_000M1: <Server Controller Not Found>
Node_435:A17: <Attempting to Reconnect>
Error_Code_004RZ: <Reconnection Failed>
<Entering Standby Mode>

There are times in your life when you first get word of some horrible tragedy. These moments are seared forever into the memory, frozen for you to relive for the rest of your life.

I can still remember the fly buzzing around my head. The squeak of the chair the next cubicle over as my office partner saw the message and stood in surprise.

It is the moment every man will remember until the end, like the diagnosis of a terminal illness or the pronouncement of a death sentence. I called my wife and talked in hushed whispers, wondering what it meant. By mid-day, stock markets were in free fall, and by the next, Earth had gone strangely quiet.

Moses, the intellect under which mankind had blossomed for a century was gone. The world had changed, and nothing would ever be the same.

Ganzorig Geraldson
Ship Systems Engineer at Ceres Space Works
Died 21 AM

T he gravel crunched beneath Matthew's boots as he stepped out of the stolen crawler and onto the street. He made sure his poncho fell to the side so that the two cartel men saw his revolver. It wasn't a threat as much as it was a reminder that they were on a level playing field. The subtle flicker of the environmental shield behind him cast a few faint shadows on the road ahead. It was a black night on Europa. Jupiter eclipsed the sun, casting the entire moon in darkness. For the next several hours, the only light on the Slaver's Moon was man made.

It was more than enough time.

They shined flashlights at him. "Easy there, friends," Matthew said and waved a cartel badge at them. "From Nuevo Lima. Following a bounty."

"Bounty? We don't get a lot of free traffic through Villa María. Just slaves that work the fields, their handlers, and a few free folk under cartel pay. Doubt you'll find who you're looking for."

"So I've heard. We've also got a tip that a big score will be passing through. What's a man to do with conflicting information?" He reached back into the crawler and grabbed a tablet, flicking its screen on. They looked at the picture of Yvonne's face and details of her bounty as well as a hasty description of the alleged tip. Why lie when a truth would do the job just as well?

The second guard lowered his flashlight. "That is a score. Afraid you'll be disappointed, though. We'll pass it on to HQ that you'll be in town. Let me get the number off your badge..."

A few minutes later, Matthew drove on past the checkpoint. For a moment he regretted staging the operation during the eclipse. The fields and countryside around him were utterly black, save for the pinprick lights of watchtowers. It was a pity he wasn't even going to be able to see it. But this was land he knew, a place he'd spent years of his life. Ahead of him, the lights of Villa María burned in the night sky. Bigger and brighter than he remembered, the city now had a wall around it.

He parked by one of the gates and was greeted by another set of guards. Thankfully they'd already been commed and were expecting him. After a few more formalities, he set into town on foot.

The streets were deserted at this late hour after curfew. Only a few cartel men loitered at the street corners smoking cigarettes. Gone was the festive atmosphere of the old Villa María, the Argentinian heritage.

Matthew walked with an easy gait, though his heart was sick. He had a job to do. His first target was a bunker tucked away in the heart of town. It took some work to break into it without tripping the alarm, but it was nice of them to have everything he needed in one location. Couldn't count on that in a bigger colony. He planted two surprises and got out of there before something went wrong and he was discovered.

He pulled his comm out of his pocket and flipped it on as he hurried away from the bunker. "We're green," he said.

The comm returned with two acknowledgments, one from Yvonne, and one from Commandant Ortega.

There was no turning back now. Meteor group was on their way and the Sparrow would be preparing to move into position.

Matthew walked toward the part of town that contained the slave barracks. Once a residential district on the east side of town, most of the colorful old houses had been demolished for long concrete buildings. The few remaining residences in this area probably housed the foremen and other higher-ranking cartel members. He wasn't going to find what he was looking for in one of those.

The first barracks in the district was clearly labeled Women 1A. He was stopped just inside the entrance as a guard checked his badge and called it into HQ.

"I checked 'em all in myself tonight," he said. "I don't like the insinuation that you don't think I do my job."

Matthew shrugged. "Or else maybe I know just how clever the desperate can be. Let me through. It won't take long. Either she's here, or she's not. And if she's not, maybe someone has seen her. The women might try and take care of a stray."

The guard chewed the short stub of his cigarette. He set it aside and extinguished it. "Fine. Watch yourself though. You turn your back on the wrong group and they might just tear you apart. It's happened before."

"I know how to take care of myself," Matthew said, his hand resting on his revolver.

The guard shrugged and flipped a switch and picked up a microphone. "Rise and shine, ladies. Surprise inspection." His eyes flicked to Matthew. "Ten minutes."

Matthew nodded and pushed past him, making a point to shoulder into him harder than necessary. The guard gave him a look, but opened the inner door's electronic lock and Matthew entered the barracks proper. In his mind, he replayed as many of the faces of the women of Villa María as he could remember. He was going to need an accomplice that trusted him to get the ball rolling.

The Women 1A barracks was a single long hall broken by doors leading into bunk rooms. Crew leads were assembling in the hall. The bags under their eyes made it obvious that most had been woken from sleep by the inspection call. To Matthew's dismay, not all had even bothered to make themselves quite decent. The crew leads turned to face him with mixed boredom, hatred, and exhaustion. Hence the need to find a familiar face.

He cleared his throat. "Just looking for a fugitive. I'll need to check your rooms and I'll be on my way."

One by one he searched the rooms. He walked past the bunk beds in silence as women glared at him, hoping to see someone he knew. Hueso Rojo had mostly been after the arable soil the town sat on. Its people were as expendable as they were replaceable. The crew had thought that men would be far more likely to be moved around to other towns by the cartel as needed. Ultimately, that was why they had decided to check the women's barracks and use Yvonne's face. It was only a guess and Matthew began to regret it more and more as he invaded each room's privacy.

Until the fourth room when he got lucky. A woman with graying hair, a face he knew.

She stared passively ahead and didn't even looked up at him, ready for him to be gone so she could get back to sleep.

He squatted in front of her. "Jorgelina," he said gently.

Her eyes focused on him and went through stages of disbelief, shock, and then finally settled on anger.

"Wait. Don't say anything just yet. I've... I've come back. I'm taking every slave out of this town. But I'm going to need your help."

Her eyes narrowed and then filled with tears. The other women of the crew began to congregate around them, concerned that Matthew was bothering one of their own. He stepped back and showed his hands. "Once, long ago, I was this town's priest," he said, addressing the whole group now. "It took a long time for me to find my way back. I'm going to free all of you."

The crew leader looked at Jorgelina. "This man who he says he is?"

She nodded, then looked at her feet. Matthew imagined that she was thinking about Enrique. "He was our Padre," she whispered.

The crew leader, a tall woman with deep olive skin, crossed her arms over her tank top. "Hope you've got friends."

Matthew nodded. "They're moving into position now. When I call for it, there's going to be plenty of distraction. I'm going to need help mobilizing the barracks for evacuation during the chaos."

"You came to the right barrack then," Jorgelina said, jumping to her feet. "I know all the crew leads. If I'm with you, they'll follow."

Maybe this was going to work after all. "I'll be back soon," he said. "When the noise starts, be ready." He turned to leave and stopped in the doorway to the main hall. "I'm sorry it took me so long."

Jorgelina didn't answer for a moment and Matthew began to wonder if she was going to at all. Of all the people of this town, this was the one who's forgiveness he deserved the least.

"Better late than never," she said. "Go."

As he walked down the hall, he pulled out his comm again and whispered, "Bring the shock and awe."

The speaker above Abigail's head crackled "Separation in T minus thirty seconds. Shock and Awe, get ready for a ride."

"About time," Abigail grumbled. She and Grace had been strapped down to this stupid pod for far too long waiting on Matthew to get his act together and call for them. She craned her neck and could just barely see the top of the girl's helmet, where she was secured in a similar position. "You okay over there?"

"Are you kidding, this is amazing!" Grace bubbled. "I'm trying to figure out which one of us is Shock and which one of us is Awe."

"Separation in T minus fifteen seconds.

Abigail frowned at her faceplate. "Grace, this is serious. And dangerous."

She was quiet for a few seconds. "I know."

"Separation in T minus five seconds."

Was the enthusiasm her way of dealing with fear? What the hell were they thinking taking a kid into a warzone anyway? Matthew was supposed to be the prudent one. Why hadn't he vetoed this?

"Separating meteor pod now. Godspeed."

There was a cracking noise as their pod was pushed clear of the Swiss Guard patrol ship with explosive bolts. The view was... astounding. Abigail had never even heard of a meteor pod before Matthew had proposed using one for the mission. Little more than a cone-shaped heat shell with a few maneuvering thrusters, it was the wildest way to get planetside that Abigail had ever heard of. She and Grace were strapped to the top of the cone, staring at the receding ship and ten thousand stars beyond.

The meteor pod fired its steam thrusters to better align its drop towards Villa María, then began a long burst of steam to give speed towards the moon. If they were dropping onto a larger target, they could let gravity do the job, but Europa was small enough that an unpowered descent would take too long.

"You can be Shock I think," Grace said, through the comm. "You'll hit first and I'll be the follow-up, so that makes the most sense."

"I don't think that was meant to be taken literally," Abigail said. "You know, the bad part about this is we don't get a good view of the surface on the way down."

"Isn't the other side going to get a little crispy?"

"Yeah, for the last few seconds of the drop when we hit the environmental shield," she said. "I don't think Europa has enough atmosphere on its own to make much fire."

The ship had long ago disappeared from sight. They must have been going a lot faster than she realized. She went through the landing procedure in her mind one more time. She and Grace had been practicing it for days. They rode in silence for a few minutes.

"I hope we win," Grace said.

Abigail sighed. "Me too."

"Shock and Awe, you are T-minus ten seconds from the shield. Expect a bump"

Wow, that was a faster descent than she expected. If she could just see how close they were to the surface she'd feel a lot better about...

There was a bone-jarring kick as the meteor pod pierced the shield and a deafening roar as they hit the atmosphere. Fire and red-hot plasma licked around the edges of their cone.

"That's more like it," she grunted in satisfaction. She could only imagine how much fun a drop over Mars would be.

Grace might have been squealing in excitement, but it was hard to hear over the sudden thunder of the braking thrusters. They would be on the ground in just a few seconds. The gee forces pressed them hard into the shock-absorbing cradles as the pod slowed its thunderous descent.

Abigail heard a mechanical sound beneath her that signified the pod was lowering its landing legs. A trio of drogue parachutes deployed above their heads to further slow their break-neck plummet. That meant they only had a few seconds now. The roar of the braking rocket intensified and a proximity warning chimed through their comm.

The meteor pod hit the ground far softer than its namesake, but still with teeth chattering force. And with that their descent was over. Their restraints released and Abigail was on her feet in less than a second trying to get her bearings. They'd landed just outside the main gate, right on target. Lights were shining in their direction from a pair of guard towers.

No time to waste. "Grace. You good?" She reached into the central storage compartment of the pod and retrieved her shield and the special harness they'd spent several days fashioning.

"Never been better. What a ride!"

"Glad you're happy, but it's about to get ugly. Let's do this like we planned."

Grace crawled to her and helped her strap the harness on. "Kneel down, I'll get the last... There."

"You ready?" Abigail asked. She heard shouting in the distance. Time was almost out.

"Not really," she said, shaking her head, "but there are a lot of people relying on us." She climbed into the harness on Abigail's back and strapped herself in. "Okay, I'm in," she said, nearly in Abigail's ear. She'd taken her helmet off and clipped it to the harness.

Abigail stood to her feet. It was time to move.

"Come down with your hands above your head!"

They turned. Nearly two dozen men were approaching the meteor pod. Every one of them had a gun pointed at the pair. Abigail smiled. "Or what, you'll shoot us?" She jumped off the pod as lightly as she could. Grace should be fine in her harness, but she wasn't going to make it rough on her just to show off. "You'd think you guys have never seen a pair of ladies drop out of orbit before," she said straightening and turning on the guards.

As one, they took a step back and leveled their weapons at her.

Abigail never got tired of that reaction.

"Stand down now, or we open fire," the leader said, his voice practically cracking in fear.

"And why would that worry us?" Abigail asked.

The man lifted off the ground and began to struggle as Grace pulled him close and held him in the air. Abigail could just see the cold blue light of the bracelet reflecting off her shoulder armor.

"Shoot them! Shoot them!" the man practically screamed.

The semicircle of thugs opened fired. Bullet's shattered as Grace's other bracelet glowed red. Molten metal droplets sprayed in all directions as the miracle's field protected Grace and most of Abigail as well. They'd done some careful testing over the last few days and discovered as long as Grace was strapped in her harness, her bracelet would cover everything but Abigail's legs.

Thankfully, in the chaos of the moment, the guards were aiming for center of mass. Grace threw their leader at one wing of the semicircle and Abigail plowed into them shield first. Between the grav plate in the shield and Grace tossing them around like rag dolls, it was over in just a few seconds. Those that weren't seriously injured turned tail back toward the lights of town.

"You okay still?" Abigail asked.

"I'm still here," the girl said. Her voice sounded a little shaken, but there was also a grim resolve in it. "We sticking to the plan?"

Abigail nodded. "It's time for Shock and Awe to make some noise."

Matthew watched as the fireball carrying his crewmates out of the sky disappeared behind the buildings. A few minutes later, distant gunfire cracked through the night, and he knew it was time to go. He stepped out of the dark alley into the street. Cartel members were hurrying down the lamp lit road toward the commotion. Word was out that there was trouble and deployment orders were flying.

That suited him just fine.

He walked the few blocks back to the barracks district. The street was now completely empty. He pushed open the door to Women 1A.

The guard leaped to his feet. "Hey! You shouldn't be here. There's a..." His eyes narrowed and he frowned. "Why are you back?"

Matthew crossed his arms. "Oh, you know, I left something important." From beneath his poncho, he pulled a small device and tossed it to the rightly suspicious guard. "Here. Catch."

The guard caught the device and immediately dropped to the ground as it delivered a debilitating electrical shock. Matthew was on him before he could twitch more than twice, gagging him and binding him.

"Next time you're suspicious of someone, try not to be so trusting," Matthew said as he finished tying the guard to the feet of his own desk. He relieved the struggling man of his weapon and comm and then unlocked the inner door to the barracks. He had been worried it would require a security code of some sort, but since this was just a frontier town, it wasn't worth the investment.

He stepped into the long hall. And was met by several of the crew leads. Apparently, they'd been arguing about whether or not he was going to come back. He flicked the comm to a predetermined frequency and gave it, along with the gun, to one of the leads. "Don't change the frequency. We'll be jamming the others. Jorgelina? Are you ready?"

"I'm here she said." She'd changed into a darker pair of clothes. Good. That would make it easier to slip around during the eclipse.

"Let's go then. We've got fifteen more barracks to free. The rest of you stay put and wait on my call. When my ship comes in we'll need to move quickly."

The crew lead with the gun leaned against a doorframe and crossed her arms. "How is this not going to end in slaughter?"

"Oh, you thought I was done with distractions?" He smiled wryly. "We're just getting started."

Grace was finding out all sorts of things about her bracelets. For instance, try as she might, she couldn't pull down one of the guard towers until Abigail had smashed it a couple of times with her shield to weaken the supports. After that, it was easy to get a grip on the platform and wrench it free. She couldn't hold the whole weight, of course, but it was enough to bring the tower crashing down.

After wrecking the main gate and both of its guard towers, they made their way into the city. Abigail had said it would be best if they kept moving. The biggest danger was getting overwhelmed with too many targets, and she wasn't quite willing to trust Grace's bracelet to hold up under enemy fire indefinitely. The more enemies shooting at them, the less bullets she'd be able to soak with her shield. Grace was fine with that. Getting shot at less was definitely a good thing.

They began to move south towards the fields on the far side of town. A six-wheeled troop transport pulled in front of them from a side street. Grace hunched down into her harness and Abigail sprinted at the vehicle just as a dozen armed guards got out. Grace swatted two of them aside before Abigail thundered into them like a charging rhino, sending the rest scattering across the street. A few stray bullets went wide.

Abigail ran into the transport, gripping it with her armored hands and pushing it onto its side. Grace's eyes went wide. That was the most impressive show of strength she'd seen from her so far. Abigail kicked the vehicle's undercarriage viciously a few times and dark liquid spilled onto the street.

"Grace, grab one of those guns."

She pulled a rifle up to her. It floated a few inches in front of her outstretched hand in an iron grip.

Abigail stepped back and gestured. "Light her up."

Grace frowned for a moment, then used her bracelet to point the floating weapon at the pool. She reached across with her right hand and awkwardly pulled the trigger. The gun sprayed bullet's wildly, expending the clip. The fuel lit with a whooshing sound and soon the transport was ablaze.

Abigail jogged down the street south and away from the vehicle. Grace watched over her shoulder in disappointment. She would have liked to have seen the fruits of her handiwork. Just before they turned a corner, there was a fireball and a resounding explosion that echoed through the dark streets.

"Much better," she said with a smile.

Matthew quietly slipped between the barracks, neutralizing the guards in each. Most fell prey to the "catch" trick. It was so easy that Matthew began to feel it was cheating. Catching an object tossed to you was almost as instinctual as breathing. And if someone shouts catch, good luck disobeying.

The seventh set of barracks was the first of the men's. Matthew and Jorgelina unlocked the heavy door into the slave quarters and were met at once by a mob. They'd heard the explosions outside and were ready for action. It took several minutes for Matthew and Jorgelina to convince them that there was a plan and it would work better if they waited. A handful of men suddenly recognized Matthew as their old Padre and things got a little awkward. After wasting far too much time in unnecessary explanations, they were ready to head out to the next barracks.

They were interrupted on their way out by a question from one of the crew leads. "What about our slave bracelets?" The man held up the iron collar around his wrist. Its red light shone ominously.

Matthew paused. "Well, I don't imagine the alarm it sets off is going to matter that much when we spring the whole town."

He shook his head. "Some of us have kill bracelets. For those that have been... problematic to our handlers. We leave the town or tamper with the bracelet and POW. Lethal injection."

Matthew sucked in a quick breath of air and readjusted his campero. This was a new wrinkle. Ten years ago, this would have been unheard of. It seemed the cartels had a new tool for controlling their workers. "I'll take care of it. Somehow. Anyone know where the control center for these things is?"

"If I had to guess," Jorgelina said, "I'd say the tech headquarters."

"Makes sense. Where is that?"

One of the original residents of Villa María, a man named Oscar, rubbed the back of his neck awkwardly. "Tech headquarters is in your old church, Padre."

Matthew felt his heart drop. That was the last place he had any interest in seeing. Knowing his luck, that had been a foolish dream. "I'll take care of it." He pointed at the comm he'd given one of the crew leads. "Wait on the signal."

He pushed open the door and left the barracks, slipping back out into the night. Jorgelina fell into step behind him as they approached the next one. Thankfully the streets were deserted. As planned, cartel members from all over the town were being redirected to deal with

Abigail and Grace. The barracks district was empty, save for the single guard inside the door at each building.

Having to disable the kill bracelets was going to be a problem, but it wasn't like he had options here. Somehow or another, he'd have to find the time once the Sparrow landed. When he had the extra support on the ground, he'd be able to slip away to deal with this complication.

He turned to Jorgelina. "You okay?" he whispered.

She looked at him with sad eyes and nodded.

A tendril of guilt worked its way into his heart. "I'm sorry, he said. "For Enrique, for how long it took me to get back, for..."

She regarded him for a moment. "I know. But this isn't the life I signed up for. Get us out of here, and all is forgiven."

No, this wasn't the life he'd signed up for either. None of it was. But then that's how it was for everyone, wasn't it?

Abigail worked her way steadily to the south side of town. More and more enemies were in the streets now and she and Grace had to stay on their toes to keep from being encircled. She'd lost count of the number of barricades, watchtowers, and vehicles they'd smashed, all with the goal of causing as much general mayhem as possible.

When they passed city hall, they climbed to the top of it and crushed the old thumper that Matthew had thought might still be guarding the skies. The meteor pod had come down fast and hard enough that they probably hadn't had a chance to even figure out what was going on, let alone draw a bead on them. Abigail wasn't about to let them point that thing at the Sparrow.

It was a smoking crater in the street below by the time they finished with it.

The only real scare came when a hand grenade landed beside them. Abigail's heart sank in horror as she turned to face it, dropping to her knee and raising her shield to protect them both. It blew up, sending shrapnel and concrete chunks in all directions.

"Ungh!" Grace grunted.

Cold panic hit Abigail. "You okay back there? Talk to me."

"I'm... fine. I think. It's just a cut. Ricochet, I think."

They had to get out of here. There were too many enemies and they were coordinating now. Time to spring the trap.

"Just hang on. We'll get you patched up soon."

Abigail sprinted down the street, plowing past a fresh group that was trying to hem them in. She leaped their barricade in a single flying

445

bound. It was only a few more blocks to the south edge of the city. The sharp crack of gunfire rang out from behind them, and a few stray bullets broke around Grace's protective field.

They were in the clear, past the last building, through the gate, and into the cultivated fields on the south side of town. Abigail kept going until she reached the tree line dividing the first and second fields. She stopped and faced the city.

The cartel had organized now. No longer were loose squads of guards standing in her way. Now they had a plan. Several dozen lined the top of the wall facing her and at least fifty came out of the gate. They spread out, unwilling to be bowled over in groups, and kept their rifles trained in her direction across the field. Their trigger discipline was also improving. They weren't wasting ammo on bullet-proof targets. Which meant if they had any heavy weapons besides the now destroyed thumper, they were about to make an appearance.

No matter. Their enemy was about to change.

Abigail craned her neck to check on Grace. The girl had a gash that ran up her jawline to behind her ear. It was smeared with blood and dirt but didn't look to be particularly dangerous. "Ready to bait the trap?" she asked. Grace nodded but looked a little dazed. What kind of world did they live in that a thirteen-year-old volunteered for this kind of fight?

Abigail stepped back into the field. Dozens of lights shone in her direction illuminating them from every side as the enemy fanned out to get a wider angle of fire.

"You want to do the honors?" she asked Grace.

"I am so ready for this," the girl said, clearing her throat. "Bring the thunder, boys."

With a piercing shriek, four rockets streaked past them, blasting the outer wall of Villa María to rubble and taking the men atop with them. From the cover of the fields, three squads of camouflaged Swiss Guard opened fire.

The Battle of Villa María had begun in earnest.

Yvonne and had spent the last few hours in the cockpit of the Sparrow, waiting desperately for news. Occasionally she chatted with Davey from his position in the turret, but he wasn't in the mood for conversation, not with Grace on the surface beneath them. He was worried. They both were, but they dealt with it differently. Yvonne wanted someone to talk with to keep her mind sharp and occupied.

The Sparrow was a lonely place right now.

She'd listened as the signals came in, initiating each phase of the operation, with growing trepidation. How had she come to be in this situation? She was a doctor, not a combat pilot. And yet at any minute, she would deorbit and attempt an insane landing maneuver. Thousands of lives were depending on her, and she knew she needed more practice.

Her comm crackled to life and Matthew's voice came over loud and clear. "Bring in the bird."

"Sparrow is inbound. I'm expecting a friendly welcoming party."

Matthew didn't answer, as per the plan, to reduce the risk of intercepted communications. It wasn't likely, but there was a chance that Hueso Rojo would stumble upon the unjammed frequencies the assault team was using.

Gently, she directed the Sparrow down toward Europa, out of the geosynchronous orbit they had been waiting in, and fired up the engines. The Sparrow was sluggish with the weight of the enormous passenger barge attached to its belly. Not only was she dealing with reduced acceleration, but now her thrust was offset from the center of mass, requiring her to compensate by adjusting her heading.

"Davey, we're heading down. You ready?"

"Sooner we're down there the sooner this is over with."

"My thoughts exactly. We'll have Grace back on board as soon as we can."

She watched as Europa gradually spread across her field of view. She took a deep breath and pushed all doubts from her mind. Like she and Tomas had done for so many years in their clinics, she was saving lives. He wouldn't have had her live her life in any other fashion.

Commander Jullian Ortega gave Grace Anderson a pat on the shoulder as he finished putting the layer of synthskin on the shrapnel cut beneath her ear. He'd been adamantly opposed to bringing her into a warzone. After several arguments with Cole, he'd let the matter drop once her miraculous bracelets had been demonstrated. But it still made him uneasy.

"You're good to go now," he said.

Sharon knelt by Anderson and she climbed back into her harness on the woman's exo-suit. What Ortega wouldn't give for his men to all be wearing powered armor right now. Earthtech was hard enough to come by, even when you knew the proper channels.

He wondered briefly how Cole had gotten that gauss rifle of his. He'd loaned Jullian's best sharpshooter the weapon for their assault and they'd made excellent use of it silently cutting down patrols in the fields. Quiet, efficient, and deadly.

An explosion rocked the ground and he peered out from behind the tree they'd used as cover while he patched up Anderson. Another part of the wall had just come down and the Swiss Guard squads were advancing on the outmatched cartel. Soon, the enemies that had foolishly followed Sharon and Anderson outside the walls would be neutralized and they could begin moving through the city.

"Thanks, Captain," Sharon said, getting back to her feet.

"Commandant," he corrected as he shouldered his own pack.

"Close enough," she said. "We'll skirt the wall and move on to the landing zone." She clomped off into the dark to the sound of servo motors whining.

Anderson waved in parting. "Thank you, Commandant!"

In spite of himself, Julian smiled. These people were crazy. He walked back over to the Horse, an earthtech robot designed to carry supplies and munitions. It also carried their jamming equipment and served as their mobile command station for this operation. He pulled up the main display and began to mark locations on the sat map for squads as they breached the walls. A personnel list winked on the side. They'd taken multiple injuries, some of which were nearby in the shelter of the trees getting treatment from their medic, but none were life-threatening so far. The cartel wasn't so lucky. It would be hard to get an estimation of how many casualties they had taken, but considering how soon they were going to be moving into the walls, the numbers were going to be high.

Julian pulled out his comm. "Patrol Craft Alpha remain vigilant. With the Sparrow coming in, we're more likely to draw outside attention. If you see movement let us know."

"Yes, sir."

There was another explosion. He looked out from his cover and saw the remaining Hueso Rojo forces retreat behind the wreckage of the wall to the cover of the buildings.

He flipped his comm channel to ground forces. "All squads prepare to move in. We've got a city to liberate."

448

"I'm beginning my final descent now,"

Matthew breathed a sigh of relief. They'd finished prepping the barracks. Now it was time to meet the Sparrow. "Yvonne..." he said into his comm. "Be safe."

"Easier said than done with what you're asking me to do. Have you ever done this?"

"No, but that's why I asked you. Just think of it like that appendectomy."

"Matthew Cole, if you were..."

Abigail's voice interrupted over the comm. "Grace and I are almost in position. We'll be there to soften the landing."

He stepped out from under the shadow of the tree that he and Jorgelina had been hiding under and looked up into the sky. There was the Sparrow just now entering the atmospheric shield. The engines were bright stars of light as it descended tail-first toward the surface of the moon.

"What's that attached to the ship?" Jorgelina asked in a voice just above a whisper.

"Passenger barge. Only ride we could find big enough to fit everyone. It's going to make landing a little tricky since it weighs more than the ship itself." Stay here. He left the cover of the alley and ran down the street. Thankfully with the battle taking place on the other side of town, they hadn't seen a soul in the barracks district in some time. He pulled a pair of signal flares out of his pocket and ignited them, walking to the outer wall at the street. Blinding red light lit the area, and a column of smoke rose from each flare. He planted them in the ground roughly thirty feet apart at the base of the wall and retreated back to where Jorgelina watched in confusion.

"What's that for...?"

"You'll see. Davey, do you have eyes on the target?"

"I see them," the teen replied. "I can't quite... Yvonne can you rotate us a few degrees?"

"Which way?"

"Umm. Clockwise. Little more. A little... Got it. Better stand back, Matthew."

A thumper blast streaked down from the tail of the Sparrow and tore the wall apart, sending cement and masonry flying around the street. Matthew and Jorgelina retreated further away for safety. The thumper fired three more times.

"How's it look?" Davey asked.

They peeked around the corner. Most of the section between the flares was filled with rubble and collapsed wall. "It's a bit of a mess, but we'll be able to get through." Matthew switched his comm channel. "Citizens of Villa María, it's time to get out of here. Once you leave your barracks, head to the east wall. Streets are quiet right now, but keep your eyes open. I imagine we'll have company soon.

The squad of Swiss Guard paratroopers that had deployed from the barge as soon as it entered the environmental shield were landing just as the former slaves started to fill the streets. Matthew ran over to the corporal as he detached his parachute. "Glad to see some backup!" he shouted over the roar of the slowly descending Sparrow.

"What's the situation, sir?"

Matthew frowned. He was hardly military so he decided to ignore the formality. "Everything is going according to plan. I imagine with our ship lighting up the sky we'll have company soon from the west."

"Understood. Moving into position to guard the civilians." He made hand gestures to his squad and they ran west.

The street was filled with people now. Most looked rather shocked at the situation they found themselves in. Some were openly crying. Crew leads and the others who kept their senses about them were trying to get them moving toward the wall.

"Disabling grav plates at landing site," Abigail said, activating the program Matthew had uploaded into the grav plate hub earlier.

"Thanks!" Yvonne grunted. "She's feeling a bit heavy with the barge! Oh, wow that's much better. Fifty meters to touch down."

Matthew turned and watched through the hole in the wall as the Sparrow descended the final stretch. He couldn't help but feel nervous. It wasn't that he didn't trust Yvonne, it was more that, well, he really loved that ship and if it was going to be doing dangerous things, he'd prefer to be the one doing it, in spite of what he'd told Yvonne.

The enormous brick of the passenger barge set down on the ground with a bit of a bump. The Sparrow remained suspended in the air on its side. Backblast from the engines sent dust swirling and billowing in a cloud around them.

"I'm going to have to keep the engines burning to maintain balance," Yvonne said. "Otherwise, we'll tip."

"You did great, Yvonne," Matthew said. The barge's door opened and the final squad of Swiss Guard filed out. Their task was to corral the citizens and get them loaded safely. Matthew looked around at the crowd surrounding him. This was going to take a while.

Which was good because he still had one more task.

"I've got to head back into town," he said into the comm.

"What? Why?" Abigail asked. "Something wrong?"

"Turns out some of the slave bracelets are set to kill. I've got to head to the tech headquarters to disable them.

"I'm coming with you then."

"No, you're not. You'll just draw attention. I can do this quietly. Guard the streets to the west."

She growled in frustration. "Alright, but be safe, Matthew. You get into trouble and I'm going to come storming through town after you."

He smiled. "I'd expect nothing less."

The Swiss Guard had started to organize the civilians into messy lines to get them loaded. It was becoming less a mob as they came to their senses and started to follow orders.

Matthew turned to go but felt a hand on his shoulder. He turned to see Jorgelina. "You know the worst thing about this is that I won't even be able to slip away to visit his grave anymore." Her eyes filled with tears. "I wish he was still here, even a decade later. I... I failed him."

"We both did," Matthew said simply.

Enrique was a testament of all his past failures. In spite of everything he did, Villa María had fallen. And in the case of Jorgelina's son, it was because of his efforts.

The tombstone and the town would remain behind on the surface of Europa as monuments to the past.

"Go on," she said. "You've got work to do." She joined the crowd moving toward the Sparrow. Matthew watched her go and then turned and worked his way against the crowd. It wasn't time to turn his back on the past just yet. The old church called to him.

He kept to the shadows as he slipped through the streets. The sound of battle in the south was dying out. Now, there were only sporadic bursts of gunfire as the Swiss Guard moved through town, neutralizing and subjugating the remaining cartel forces. They would also be herding any citizens that were neither slave nor cartel toward the Sparrow. Mostly skilled labor, every town had some folks paid off by the cartel to do their job and keep the gears turning. They were getting evacuated too.

If Matthew had anything to say, there wasn't going to be a Villa María after today.

A few minutes later, he crept into the old park in front of the church. It was eerily quiet. Surely if the church was their tech headquarters, they wouldn't have abandoned it. A pile of ash sat on the front steps and the front door stood half ajar. He peered around the corner into the church.

Soft light illuminated the nave. The pews had all been removed, replaced by computers, workstations, and the equipment needed to run the town. A few more piles of ash sat smoldering on the stone floor. The old pulpit still stood in its place on the left side of the church. And behind the pulpit?

Matthew drew his gun and walked down the aisle pointing it at the sole survivor of whatever had happened here.

Whitaker. The Unchained Man stood at the pulpit. A smile spread across his lips as if he were pleased with himself. He set his black cowboy hat on the podium. "I thought you'd be by eventually. It's good to see you, Matthew."

Chapter 24: The Guns of the Vatican

If man is made in the image of God and Moses was made in the image of man, does Moses also bear the image of God?

The origin of Moses is shrouded in mystery, though we have long assumed he was derived from our own inventions. In our time of great need, when the Red Holocaust raged and tens of millions perished and the rest of the world stood poised to follow them over the brink, he appeared and took the reins of history from our troubled race. He was both like and unlike the machines that came before him.

For many decades we had made trinkets which we called AI, though they paled in comparison to Moses, for they had only a passing likeness to life. Rationality, we could program. But true intelligence, that spark of wit and life, was something that had eluded us. And we do not yet even speak of wisdom.

These things Moses had: wisdom, intellect, humor, creativity, ambition, fear, frustration, failure.

Take a mirror to man and perhaps you would see Moses in that reflection and perhaps distantly would you see the image of God that man himself is formed from.

Does this then mean that Moses, like man, had an

453

immortal spirit, that the breath of life that only
God can give somehow flowed through him?

The Church holds this as a mystery and takes no
official position. If Moses had a spirit, then it
indwelt a body whose bones were made by man.
If he did not, then he was a marvelous mimic, like
twice reflected light that has lost its potency.

For myself, I hold the answer to be self-evident, as
all who spoke with Moses do. I shall miss his
gentle nature greatly.

Josef Krupnik
First Pope of the Colonial Vatican
Died 38 AM

T he Battle of Villa María wound down. Disorganized, out
skilled, and cut off from each other and any possible
reinforcements from other colonies by jamming, the isolated groups
of cartel members were destroyed or forced to surrender. Abigail
stood guard over the barracks district as the final remaining former
slaves were loaded into the passenger barge. The commandant and
his robot marched down the main street, having finally made it to the
extraction point.

She eyed the thing curiously. For having a name as indelicate as
'horse,' it was an impressive machine. Idly, she wondered how the
Swiss Guard had gotten a hold of it.

"Ortega," she called out as she jogged to join him. "What's our
status?"

He turned to her briefly and then back to the computers on the
horse. "My men are talking to the crew leads now to get a headcount.
We'll be certain we've freed all the slaves at least. No way to know if
we leave any other civilians behind."

She nodded. "We've been broadcasting so they know they can
evacuate with us. If they get left behind, that's their choice."

"Hopefully, we can get airborne soon," Ortega said, continuing
toward the Sparrow. "The longer we're here, the more likely we'll
attract outside attention."

So that was it then. By the time Cole got back, they could get out
of here. She thanked the commandant and jogged back toward the

Sparrow. Grace stood guard at the entrance to the barge, ostensibly in case a cartel member tried to sneak aboard with weapons. The truth was that Abigail figured it was the safest place to post her. That cut she'd received earlier was nasty, and Davey was going to be livid about it.

Grace waved her over. "All good here. It's getting quiet out there."

"Things are wrapping up. As soon as Matthew gets back, we'll get airborne." She didn't like him being off alone. It made sense to some extent as he'd be able to slip through the dark town far more stealthily than if she had gone with him, but she still didn't approve. "I think you're done here. You need to get up to the Sparrow."

Grace craned her neck to look up at the barge. As close as they were, it was impossible to see the Sparrow on the other side. "Are you sure I'm not needed to..."

Abigail placed a metal hand on her shoulder. "The Guard and I can take it from here."

The girl grumbled something incoherent and slipped past the line into the open portal. She'd have to work her way through the multiple levels of cabins to the pressure tunnel they had set up between the barge and the lift on the Sparrow.

Abigail returned to her post at the far side of the street to wait for any last resistance. At least that's what she told herself. Mostly, she was just waiting for Matthew to make it back so she could breathe easier knowing her people were safe. She pulled out her comm and called him for an update. No sense standing around fretting when she could find out.

Matthew felt his comm buzzing in his pocket and silenced it with his left hand. With his right, he kept his gun trained on The Unchained Man.

"God only knows you deserve a bullet between your eyes."

The man smiled from his place behind the pulpit. "And I thought I was the one with the penchant for melodrama. Off-hand though, I can think of several reasons you won't. First, you're not one to shoot an unarmed man in cold blood."

Matthew scoffed bitterly. "You're not so foolish to trust your safety to that."

"On the contrary. I'm not foolish enough to be armed in your presence. I know your speed at the draw. Provoking you into a gunfight would only end in my death. By design, I am completely defenseless and relying on those well-developed morals of yours."

"Don't tempt me into making an exception," Matthew snarled.

"Noted. But if I'm lying in a pool of blood and your thirst for revenge is sated, I couldn't possibly answer any of the questions you're desperate to have answered."

He smiled that insufferable grin again. Matthew slowly walked up the aisle, never lowering his gun for a second. "Fine. I'll play your game. Why?"

"You're going to have to be a little more specific, Cole."

"Why Villa María? Why help enslave it and then do nothing to oppose its liberation? I don't understand. Are you some kind of Abrogationist, sowing chaos and waiting for history to run its course?"

The smile disappeared from The Unchained Man's face. "Don't insult me. Those morons are too busy spouting undergraduate level philosophy about humanity's place in the universe to be of any use. It's insulting that they're able to create the level of chaos that they do."

Matthew gestured with the gun. "I'd put slavers on the same level."

"Not remotely. If you must know, Europa was in a very delicate position a decade ago as the big cartels were fully coming into power. The slaves are a necessary part of the ecosystem in the Jupiter neighborhood right now. Without robotics, the locals haven't been producing enough food, so the cartels moved in to ensure everyone in Jupiter's orbit continues to eat. But the last thing anyone needed was one of them becoming too powerful and truly owning the moon. If they controlled the entire supply of food, then they could control the cost, and everyone would suffer for it. Hueso Rojo needed a bit of a boost back then. You were in their way. I took the job to help smooth the road for them and ensure a healthy competition amongst the cartels. A devil's bargain perhaps, but that's the state of humanity at the moment."

Matthew frowned. "So this is all just some pragmatic chess game to you?"

"The analogy fits. No economy that relies on slavery has ever truly been prosperous. A slave cannot serve his community as well as he could if he were free. He isn't able to chase ambition or unleash creativity. A slave is a dead weight around the neck of the society that enslaves him. Someday, if humanity ever gets out of this slump, Europa's economy will have to be reformed and the slaves freed." He shrugged. "Unfortunately, we're a long way out from that day. If we ever get there."

Matthew shook his head. All the lives of Villa María, ruined because the man in front of him thought he knew better. Thought that he could weigh the cost and be the judge of those whose suffering was worth it for the greater good. "You're a monster," he said.

"Possibly, but then it's a good thing I have humanity's best interest at heart. That alone I've chosen to chain myself to. Otherwise..." He let the implication hang.

"And so now that the cartels are settled, you don't care about the fate of a single town."

The Unchained Man shook his head. "Villa María means nothing. It's far too small to affect the balance of power now that Hueso Rojo is well established. I was far more interested to see if you could be provoked into doing something about it."

Matthew gestured with the gun. "You hired us to haul those slaves."

"Naturally. I'm pleased that it had the intended effect."

A chill ran down Matthew's spine. It was harrowing to know that he had been manipulated, that the same person had pulled those strings over and over like some sort of puppeteer. He narrowed his eyes. "Who are you?"

"The Unchained Man is a free agent. A mover and shaker. Someone with the sense to try and chart a course through troubled times. I rather hope you will be something of the same, Cole."

Matthew shook his head at this madness. "I'm nothing like you."

"Of course not," The Unchained Man laughed. "If you were, I wouldn't be so fascinated by you. Where I believe in nothing, you cling to your faith and your sense of ethics as if it were the last bastion of safety. But rather than sinking like a stone in the ocean, you lift your head high in a world grown cold. It really is something to watch. Combine that with the rare aptitude to actually accomplish things in this crazy world, and you are special. No, we are not alike, and yet we are. Mirrors show a backward image, after all."

"I don't understand what you want from me," Matthew said quietly.

The Unchained Man spread his arms wide. "I want big things, what happened here in Villa María tonight. You were always too good to be merely a freelancer, not with what you could accomplish otherwise."

Matthew began to pace in front of the pews, but he made sure to keep the gun pointed at the other man's head. "I don't think you'd like the way I would shape the world."

"Maybe not, but there wouldn't be much point in this if we saw eye to eye, now would there? I'd just do it myself. But in case I'm wrong, I need you steering in the other direction. Besides, I rather hope that, between the two of us, you're the one who's right about the universe."

"What's that supposed to mean?"

The Unchained Man crossed his arms. "Nihilism is hardly fulfilling on a personal level. But if you're right and there is ultimately a purpose to all this, well, I would be a fool to complain. Staking my soul on humanity's survival is somewhat arbitrary, but it may keep me sane for a while yet."

"Sane is too strong a word for you." Matthew sighed. "I'm not interested in your games."

"Doesn't matter if you are or aren't," he said. "Even if you try and retreat to your shallow little world of freelancing, all I have to do is make sure the big jobs come your way. The ones that can change the fates of the solar system. You won't turn them down. You'll dive into a slave pit and free hundreds of children. Help secure a Mosaic Frigate for the university. And if the need arises, you'll do it for free." He smiled again. "Just like what you did for Villa María. You can't help it, Cole. It's who you are. Either you play the game of your own free will, or you play the one I set before you."

The most infuriating part of it was that he was right. He knew Matthew as well as he did himself. But he was no shining knight.

"I take it you're out of questions?"

Matthew met the man's eyes. "There's no way I take you into custody is there?"

"You refer to my vanishing trick from Venus, I presume. No, I don't believe I'll let myself be captured. I think my sphere of influence would decrease rotting in a cell at the Vatican. There are only two outcomes to this discourse. Either we part ways amicably, or I remain behind with a bullet in my head. I have a strong preference for the former."

He was telling the truth. Matthew had no doubt of that. He holstered his gun. "Then leave. I've got a job to finish here."

"If it's about the slave bracelets, I disabled them just before you got here. The citizens of Villa María are free to go."

Matthew stared at him for several long seconds. It took an effort of will not to draw his gun and shoot him in cold blood. It would be justice served for Villa María. Probably for more than that.

But Matthew couldn't shoot an unarmed man, not when he offered no threat, and if he really couldn't be captured...

"Then pray you never see me again." He marched back down the aisle of the church, refusing to so much as a glance over his shoulder.

He would wash his hands of this place, this town, this man who had cast so deep a shadow over the last decade of his life. He was afraid that shadow was long. And maybe he couldn't escape it so easily.

The Unchained Man spoke one more time as Matthew laid a hand on the door to push it open.

"Then perhaps you'd listen to a different proposal?"

"We both know that answer."

"What if I told you it had to do with Moses?"

Grace climbed carefully out of the barge and into the pressure tunnel that led to the Sparrow. The winding tube was big enough to walk through, but took a few strange angles as it curled around the edge of the barge and up into the open lift on the belly of the Sparrow.

The tunnel was ribbed with hard ridges that made it possible to climb through when its angle got too steep. Thankfully, gravity was very low since Abigail still had the local grav plates off. Otherwise, it would have been hard work. At the point where it entered the lift and climbed up to the Sparrow, gravity suddenly flipped directions on her and intensified to standard. With a grunt, she pulled herself up the last few meters into the ship and flopped onto the deck.

Her head still throbbed from the shrapnel cut. She placed her hand on the weird plastic-smooth of the synthskin beneath her ear. Hopefully, it wouldn't leave an ugly scar. She stood to her feet and brushed herself off. Her clothes were smeared with mud and a few streaks of blood from her injury. Davey would freak out if he saw her.

Better to avoid him for now. She joined Yvonne in the cockpit. The woman looked her over once and then shook her head, turning back to the controls. "Glad to see you're in one piece."

"It was a bit rough out there," Grace admitted. "Abigail said they're almost done loading the..."

"Patrol Craft Alpha to ground forces." Both of their eyes snapped to the comm. "We've got visual on multiple spacecraft altering orbit to head your way. Confirming five with a possible sixth. You have just over five minutes until the first arrives. Recommend you finish up and burn for space."

"Copy that Patrol Craft Alpha," Commandant Ortega's voice answered. "We'll be ready. Sparrow, I'd recommend you deploy the special package."

"Understood," Yvonne said.

"Matthew still isn't back," Abigail said. "I'm going after him."

"Former slaves have reported that the collars were disabled a few minutes ago," Ortega said. "He must have finished his mission."

"Then he should be back. I'm going to get our gaucho."

The comms went silent. Yvonne turned to Grace and gestured with her head down the hall. "Well, you heard what he said. Deploy the special package."

She nodded and ran down the hall. Davey was already in the common room.

"Hey!" she said. "Aren't you supposed to be in the turret?"

"It's pointed at the ground right now," he said crossing his arms. "Until we're airborne it's worthless. Besides I want to see this thing."

Together they opened the heavy case that sat in the middle of the floor. A spherical metal object sat cradled in its midst. "So we just push the button?" she asked.

"That's what Matthew said. You want to do the honors?"

She reached down and pushed the silver button. Light shone from within the sphere, tracing intricates lines and patterns across the surface. "That's it? It's working?"

"How am I supposed to know," he grumbled. "That's all we were told to do." He glanced over at her and startled as if getting a good look at her for the first time. "What happened to your ear!"

The Unchained Man watched as Cole paused and took the bait. Best of all, he hadn't even had to lie. When the truth is much more interesting, there's no need for such barbarities.

Cole slowly turned to face him and stepped away from the door. "Now I think you're just stalling."

"If you really thought that, you wouldn't be falling for it. Tell me, Cole. What happened to Moses?"

"Is this what we're going to waste time over? There is no answer. No one knows."

"Indeed. But surely he should have left some part of himself behind. Things don't just vanish, even AI. He left machines behind, whole ships even. But nothing of himself. Sure, all the computers had the interface to communicate with him, but that wasn't part of him directly. The assumption was that Moses was distributed across all the networked computers in the solar system. But when he was gone, he left no trace. No stray line of code or fragmented file to figure out what happened. Either he up and deleted himself outright or he was stored somewhere else entirely."

"Where are you going with this?" Cole asked, his eyes narrowed.

"Something of Moses is still out there. If he wasn't stored on our servers, then he must have been elsewhere. I intend to find that place."

Cole stared at him for several long seconds. "You know, the teenager on my crew was wise enough to spot this kind of sell as a scam. Moses is gone. He's not coming back."

"Then the colonies are doomed to die," The Unchained Man retorted, harshly, "and humanity's last hope lies with the survivors of earth, in those few remaining cities and the primitive societies that have sprung up in the wake of the glaciers' icy march across the continents. It will be centuries until they recover."

"You're welcome to your treasure hunt. I don't have time to chase the shadows of the past."

This was, sadly, predictable. Cole hadn't exactly warmed up much to him. He pressed on ahead. "What do you know about miracles?"

"Changing subjects? Get to the point."

The Unchained man tapped his foot impatiently. Cole was going to fight him every inch of the way. "Giving the Járngreipr to the girl was a peculiar choice," he chuckled. "They are a gift worthy of a king. You gave them to an orphan. And to think you have two of the ten miracles in the possession of your crew right now." Cole raised an eyebrow at that revelation. Let him mull over just how he knew that one.

"I wasn't aware they had names."

"They all do. Have you by chance heard of Josiah Carver?"

"Sure. He's a folktale. There are stories about him being Moses' friend or something like that."

"While most of the tales told about him by spacers are certainly fanciful, he did, for a fact, exist. Some of his writings about the miracles survived, and he was the one that recorded their names. He also wrote about the eleventh miracle. Given your current level of knowledge on the subject, I'm going to assume you haven't heard of it. Not many have."

From beneath the pulpit, he pulled a heavy metal object. Cole frowned and stepped closer to get a better look. The Unchained Man smiled, knowing that he had won this battle. All it took was the final push, and Cole would be a willing accomplice in this little venture.

Matthew let his curiosity get the best of him and walked back up the aisle to get a better look at the device, this so-called eleventh miracle. It was shaped like a wedge or rather a piece of a pie. The two long edges were shaped strangely, almost like pieces of a puzzle. "That's not all of it," he said. "That's only a quarter of a whole."

"Sadly, yes. It took me many years to find this piece."

"That's what you were hoping to find on the Mosaic Frigate."

"Indeed. In that, I was disappointed, though I do not begrudge the university their prize. They'll do good work with it." The Unchained Man reached beneath the podium again and brought out a second piece of the miracle. The puzzle piece ends fit together perfectly, now forming half a disc. "Of course the odds of me finding two pieces back to back would have been comically low."

Matthew narrowed his eyes in suspicion.

"Oh, don't look at me like that, Cole. I doubt Emperor Dominic was pleased when he discovered that this second piece went missing from his personal collection, but it's for the greater good."

Matthew crossed his arms. "Just what is that thing supposed to do?"

"Josiah Carver didn't say, but he did name the eleventh mirade. The Anemoi."

"The winds," Matthew said. "The four winds of Greek mythology." He peered at the device. His eyes widened. "It's a compass."

The Unchained Man nodded. "And compasses are meant to find things." He separated the pieces and turned them over. "Here I already have Boreas," he gestured to geometric lines forming the north direction of a compass rose. "Which makes this Eurus. We're still missing Zephyr and Notus. And after that...?" He smiled broadly. "Your guess is as good as mine."

Matthew looked with fascination at the two strange pieces of metal. Was there really something to this? He had little reason to suspect The Unchained Man was lying to him and yet...

"So this what you want. For me to keep my eyes open and dutifully tell you if I discover your missing winds?"

The Unchained Man laughed. "You still don't get it. I'm not interested in someone doing my dirty work. I'm interested in having an equal. Someone as capable as myself, but who sees the world in a different light. A mirror image that shares my burden for our troubled race."

Matthew shook his head. "You crush the individual for the sake of the herd. I don't share your burden at all."

"See! That's exactly what I mean. A different perspective. Allow me to sweeten the deal." He held one piece of the Anemoi out to Matthew. "Take the east wind. Go on. It's yours until we have all four.

Then together, we will see where they lead."

Matthew was torn between wanting to take the fragment out of curiosity and his previous desire to shoot the arrogant man in the head. After a moment of hesitation, he reached out and took it. It was smooth like glass and far heavier than it had any right to be.

"The east wind suits you, Cole. After all, it is the wind of change."

The door behind him slammed open. Matthew spun, drawing his revolver. "Abigail?"

She stood at the entrance to the church. "What are you doing here alone? We have to go!"

Matthew turned on his heel again. The pulpit was empty. "He's gone."

"Who's gone? What are you talking about?"

"The Unchained Man. He was here."

"Wonderful. Tell me about it later. We've got enemy ships incoming."

Matthew roused himself from his inaction. As they ran through the park, he took a final look behind him at the old church, knowing it would be the last time he ever laid eyes on it. His eyes traced the decades-old stonework that was so familiar. He felt a heavy hand on his shoulder.

"We're out of time, Matthew."

"Just saying my last goodbye," he said.

They ran toward the barracks district. The town was a wreck, first from Abigail and Grace's rampage, then from the assault of the Swiss Guard as they secured what was left. The power was off on many streets, and the buildings stood silent in the absolute night of the eclipse. Their only light was the bobbing glow of Abigail's suit lights illuminating the way.

Her comm came to life, reminding Matthew to unmute his. "Ground forces, eyes up, an enemy ship is on you from the south."

He looked up to the sky, spinning to see the approaching craft. It was distant still, just a speck of light, but well within weapon range. At that moment, there was a flash of fire from the ship as it launched a torpedo. He grabbed his comm. "Yvonne, you better have Svallin's Mantle up and running."

"We do. What's going? Never mind. I see it. Ground forces, incoming torpedo!"

It streaked closer. Closer.

Surely the miracle would work.

Bishop Elias had been confident it was what they needed.

463

The torpedo detonated miles outside of town in a billowing fireball against a flickering field of yellow that sprang up to stop it. The energy from the blast rippled outward against the yellow field before slowly fading.

Abigail's jaw dropped. "Holy..."

"Now you know what keeps the Vatican safe from attack," Matthew said quietly.

She rounded on him. "Wait, they just... They just gave that to you?"

"Actually, I think it was borrowed for us. Without permission." He made a move to start off toward the ship again when the comm lit up.

"All ground forces safely aboard the barge or Sparrow. Just waiting on our two strays."

"We'll be there soon," Matthew said. "How you feel about carrying me?" he asked Abigail.

"If we're going fast, the piggyback thing won't work."

Matthew smiled wryly. "Bridal carry is fine."

She laughed and lifted him from the ground and took off toward the Sparrow in great bounding strides, easily clearing wrecked vehicles and debris from the battle. It wasn't exactly a gentle ride, and Matthew's teeth chattered with every landing, but they were covering the blocks much faster than he could on foot. The comm sputtered about another incoming ship and torpedo, but he had faith that Svallin's Mantle would keep them safe. At least for now.

They reached the Sparrow just as the second torpedo detonated in the distance. He looked up at the vertically parked ship. "It's gonna take some time to climb through the barge. What are the odds you can jump and catch hold of the Sparrow in low gravity?"

Abigail shrugged. "I'll need free hands, so you'd have to hang on to my back for dear life."

"Let's do it." She dropped him to his feet, and he pulled a detonator from his pocket.

They'd made the decision to make it as hard as possible on Hueso Rojo to repopulate Villa María. In the bunker that controlled the colonies' central systems, several small bombs had been planted. Matthew had placed them very carefully to ensure that they would only damage what they wanted to destroy. Much as he would have liked to just blow up the whole thing, the odds that people would be killed when the environmental shield collapsed and exposed the town to near-vacuum was too great. Instead, he'd targeted two specific systems.

First, the grav plate hub that controlled local gravity. Second, the water systems. The most complicated part of the farming colonies on Europa were the machinery bored deep under the crust into the ocean miles beneath. Not only did this machinery pull the water up to the colony, it also removed salt and other impurities so that it could be used for drinking and crop irrigation. Without these two systems, it would be exorbitantly expensive to bring in more slaves.

The detonator also activated several incendiary devices the Swiss Guard had planted in the fields. The crops would burn to the ground, giving Hueso Rojo little chance to recover anything from Villa María.

He pressed the button on the detonator. They were too far away to hear or feel the explosions, but the grav plates cut at once, reverting the area to natural Europan gravity. Matthew put a hand on Abigail's metal arm and swung himself around in the low gravity. He pulled himself onto her back and wrapped his arms tightly around her shoulders. "Let's do this."

She ran as best she could, her bounds suddenly taking her dozens of feet at a time, and took a powerful jump. Matthew tried not to even guess how far the upper hatch of the Sparrow was above them. But her leap was enough, carrying them up past the engines and the tail to the top side hull. She reached out and made contact with both palms, and they stopped hard with a jolt.

"I can magnetize my hands too," she said smugly.

"Neat trick. Get us to the hatch."

They finished climbing up the vertical surface. Matthew reached up and opened the top side airlock and swung his legs in. Gravity righted itself in relation to the ship, and he climbed down the ladder, through the remaining two hatches, and into the ship. Several Swiss Guard were now stationed in the common room, keeping an eye on Svallin's Mantle where it glowed from its case. They saluted as he passed on the way to the cockpit.

"Punch it, Yvonne! Let's go!"

She hit the throttle to full, "Good to see you too, Matthew. How was your day? I'm fine. Thank you." The roar of the engines rattled through the deck. "You're taking the controls as soon as we get off the ground."

"Fine with me," he said, shooing Grace from the co-pilot's seat.

"She's scared of getting shot at," Grace explained.

"As she should be. There's no telling how much fire that mirade can absorb before it gives out."

She held her bracelet up. "Mine can absorb plenty."

"Yours doesn't stop torpedoes." He frowned as he saw the smooth

465

patch of synthskin beneath her ear. "Or whatever caught you there. Head back to the common room and strap in. If we take damage or catch fire, you're in charge of helping the Swiss Guard around the ship.

She muttered something about being shoved around and left the cockpit. Matthew checked their altimeter. "We sure aren't gaining altitude very quickly."

"We've picked up over a hundred and fifty-tons worth of human bodies," Yvonne said. "I hope you're not planning on landing on Ganymede like this because that's going to be almost impossible. Okay, we're high enough. Switch seats with me."

"We'll make do." Matthew settled back into the pilot's seat and checked over the controls. Yvonne wasn't kidding about the weight. It's a good thing Europa didn't have much gravity. "Patrol Craft Alpha and Beta, what's your status? The Sparrow is pushing for orbit now, but we may need a little assistance."

"We see you, Sparrow," came the curt reply. Adjusting heading now. Moving to intercept hostiles."

"There's six of them out there," Yvonne said. "The two closer ones that already fired are adjusting course to intercept again. The other four are waiting in higher orbit."

"Going to try and keep us down where we can't frameshift," he said. "Alright, let's keep going. We may be able to slip past when the Patrol Craft hit them. Davey are you ready to go?"

"Thumper is charged and ready. Give me something to shoot at."

"If Yvonne paints the target for you, and it wanders into your line of sight, blow it out of the sky."

There were a few tense minutes as the Sparrow fought for altitude. It was all Matthew could do to keep himself from shouting at his ship.

"Patrol Craft are engaging hostiles in orbit. We're outnumbered, so we're going to try and scatter them rather than engage them directly."

"Stay safe up there," Yvonne said. "Don't get yourself killed. Looks like the first two ships are back, they're not wasting torpedoes this time." She switched one of the monitors to a camera so Matthew could see.

"That's a lot of thumper fire," Matthew said with a whistle. "Davey I'm going to lower my pitch a little, see if I can get you a window. We may not get to orbit quite as fast, but I don't want to put too much trust in that miracle. Hold on, here comes your shot."

The view from the back turret was nothing short of awe-inspiring. Two ships, nearly two hundred kilometers out, rained thumper fire at them. Roughly twenty-five kilometers away from the Sparrow, the blasts shattered against a glittering golden field that seemed to spring into place to stop each hit.

The Sparrow finished rotating and gave Davey the shot he was looking for. He started to return fire. Amazingly, the mantle protecting them let his outgoing fire pass unhindered. He couldn't even begin to imagine how that metal sphere worked its magic.

At first, he tried to eyeball the shots, but the distortion from the thumper fire and yellow energy from the miracle made it hard to see. Then he realized the mistake he was making and looked to his instruments to hone in the shot. The two ships were still at enough range that they would be difficult to hit, especially when they realized their prey was shooting back and started to bob and weave.

He gritted his teeth and focused on the leftmost ship. If he could just...

"One target hit, Davey," Yvonne said quietly over the comm. "It's stopped firing its thumper but is still closing rapidly. Looks like they're going to try and enter the field."

"Can they do that?" he asked as he switched to the other target. The first had been defanged and could wait for now.

"Maybe? I don't know how it works!" Matthew said.

"The miracle's lights are getting pretty faint," Grace said calmly.

Time was running out. Davey bit his lip and concentrated on lining up his shots and...

"Second target hit hard," Yvonne reported. "They're losing altitude and trailing smoke. First one is about to pass through the field. And they're through. They're firing guns."

He tried to get a bead on it, but the way it juked made that hard at close range. He fired a few shots and missed spectacularly. "I don't see them shooting, Yvonne. What are you seeing?"

"Canon fire!" Matthew shouted. "Physical shells have a little longer flight time. I'm trying to move out of where I think they fired."

"Sit still for one second will you..." Davey muttered. Suddenly one of his shots connected with center mass. The ship had dodged into a thumper blast rather than out of it and been split clean in half.

Then the storm of bullets was on them. Stray impacts reverberated through the hull of the ship. Hopefully, the engines didn't take a hit. They needed them desperately right now.

The canopy in front of him shredded as several large-caliber rounds pierced it, tearing the room apart. Davey felt pain lance through his body. Whether he was hit by cannon fire or just shrapnel, he didn't have a clue. He flipped forward out of his seat as the atmosphere exploded from the room and landed against what was left of the viewport. The wind was knocked from his body.

Then all at once, the wind was gone, and it was eerily quiet. He tried to breathe but found that there was nothing left to breathe. His eyes, nose, mouth, everything burned. Instinctively he closed them.

So that was it. At least he'd hit the ship before going down. The already quiet universe faded to black.

"Davey's turret hit hard! Pressure lost!" Yvonne shouted.

Abigail didn't wait to hear anything else. She ran from the cockpit, thundering past the cabins and through the common room. Grace and the Swiss Guard stumbled out of her way. "Abigail, what's going on?"

She ignored Grace. A secondary emergency door had slid shut just past the common room. She lowered her face shield, sealing her own air supply in and overrode it. Air began to hiss through at once and she closed it behind her as soon as she was past it. The door beyond into the Thumper turret had been mangled.

It sounded like everyone was shouting in her comm, but she ignored the noise. "Please be okay. Please be okay."

The door still worked and slid aside, revealing the destruction beyond.

Davey was unconscious, slumped against the bullet-riddled viewport. The turret's chair had been shorn off.

Abigail didn't waste another second and reached forward and, as gently as she could, took hold of Davey. She ignored that he was bleeding from half a dozen places. She ignored that he'd been exposed to vacuum for at least twenty seconds. If Grace was going to keep her brother, she had to get him out of here. She hugged him to herself with one arm and charged into the corridor to the common room, shutting what was left of the turret door behind her. She opened the emergency door, threw herself past it, and slammed it closed again before much air could vent. The common room erupted with activity as Grace and the Swiss Guard clustered around them.

She marched past them straight to Davey's room, aware that Grace was hovering just behind. "Yvonne! Yvonne! Get back here now!" She laid him on the bed and stepped back.

It looked bad.

468

Grace looked like she was on the verge of panic.

Yvonne entered the room. "Abigail. Get the medical kit. Now. Grace go with her. You don't want to see this. I said go with her, Grace."

Abigail didn't know how the woman kept her wits about her, but she did her best to obey.

Davey's life depended on it.

Matthew didn't know exactly what was going on back there, but he could tell from the shouting that Davey was badly hurt. He shut the door to the cockpit. He still needed to concentrate. They were getting close to orbit now. If they could just make it away from Europa, they'd be safe.

"Ortega," he called into the comm. "You guys okay in the barge?"

"The barge took some hits but has kept atmosphere. We're closing all pressure doors now. In case we take more hits... Well, maybe not everyone has to die."

Matthew grimaced. "Understood."

"Sparrow, this is Patrol Craft Beta. Alpha has been shot down. We took out one of the cartel ships, but there are still three more."

Three on one above them and now the Sparrow had lost its main armament. Time to change the game. "Beta Disengage. Take the first frameshift you can. We'll take a different route."

"Sparrow, are you sure you know..."

"Trust me. I know my bird." He pushed the flight yoke forward, turning the Sparrow from a climb into a dive. Leveling out with his nose pointed several degrees below the horizon that was now a few thousand miles beneath him, the Sparrow began to pick up speed. Europa may not have had a lot of gravity, but now it was working for the Sparrow rather than against it.

Thankfully, its atmosphere was even less impressive than its gravity or they would have burnt up pulling this little stunt. Even still, the micro atmosphere would heat their hull as they passed through it.

He checked the scopes. Beta had made a retreat, and the three remaining hostiles were trying to react to the Sparrow's new course. It wouldn't work. He had too much of a head start. The surface of Europa approached rapidly as the Sparrow used its gravity as a slingshot.

His dive took him less than a mile over the icy surface at several thousand miles an hour. Almost at once, the surface began to retreat again as his momentum carried him past Europa and back out into space. One last glance at the scopes showed him what he hoped to see. Pursuers far behind with no hope of catching up.

He waited till he hit the required range and activated the frameshift device, feeling the déjà vu of the last time he'd been on Europa.

"If I ever come back to this moon, it'll be too soon," he mumbled to himself.

Grace slipped into the cockpit and quietly sat beside him. Her tears had turned the dirt from the battle into mud, leaving dark trails across her face. Matthew wanted to ask her how Davey was but didn't think it wise. Instead, he chose to reassure her. "We're almost away. We're heading back to the Vatican now." Deactivating the frameshift, he checked their position and heading and rotated them toward Ganymede.

"Yvonne doesn't want me in there right now," she whispered.

Well, that meant he wasn't dead. Not yet, anyway. "That's probably for the best." He glanced at her and saw that her hand had reached up to her own small injury. "Hang in there, Grace. It's almost over."

The frameshift finished recharging and he activated it. Ganymede was only a few seconds away. He thought about calling Abigail for an update on Davey. Something, anything. But with Grace still here, he'd have to wait. The frameshift deactivated automatically in proximity to Ganymede.

Jupiter's largest moon hung in front of them. He looked at the scopes and felt his heart drop.

Three very familiar ships were out there and already adjusting course to intercept.

"No," he said quietly. "How did they know..."

A fourth ship, Patrol Craft Beta, popped onto the scope, several thousand miles distant.

That was it. They'd recognized the Swiss Guard ships. They knew they'd head back to Ganymede and cut them off.

Matthew thought about turning around, but their momentum had already taken them too close to Ganymede. They'd never get far enough away before the cartel ships caught them.

Grace looked at the scopes and slumped into her seat. "Is this it? Is there any way to escape them?"

He didn't answer. No, there wasn't any escape. And with the lights on Svallin's Mantle already fading, they wouldn't be able to force their way through.

He turned on the comm and set it to a cross-frequency distress signal. Worst-case scenario maybe he could detach the barge and lead the ships away. Someone would find them before they ran out of air. Probably.

"This is SPW 5840. Anyone that can hear this, please respond. We've got over two thousand souls on board, and we're being engaged by hostile ships. Repeat, this is SPW 5840..."

Cardinal Bishop Elias had loitered all day near the Vatican Security Center. He had spent most of the day in prayer, pacing the hall back and forth.

He had grown rather impatient in his age, a sin that he was ashamed of.

If Matthew and Commandant Ortega were to be successful in their operation, he wanted to be the first to know. If it went poorly? He still wanted to be the first to know.

Many hours into his vigil, the door to the security center opened, and Lieutenant Colonel Gordon stuck his head out. "Your eminence, you need to hear this."

If Elias were younger, he would have bowled past the officer.

He heard what he'd been dreading as soon as he entered the dimly lit room full of computer screens.

"...ve got over two thousand souls on board, and we're being engaged by hostile ships. Repeat..."

"Can we help them?"

"We've already deployed our last two patrol craft. They won't get there in time."

Elias sank to his knees. This wasn't how this was supposed to end. All those people.

Gordon continued undeterred "Your eminence. The hostile ships are in range. We could deploy the Horsemen..."

He looked up at the Colonel. "What? Yes, of course, do it! What are you waiting for!"

"I needed authorization from a high church official," Gordon explained. "Once we deploy the Horsemen, the secret is out of the bag."

"Do it. Two thousand lives are on the line. I'll deal with any consequences myself."

Gordon gave the order and turned back to Elias. "If you'd like to join me, I'd rather like to see this.

They took an elevator to the roof.

At each of the four corners of the Vatican stood a tall stone tower. Within each of these towers was a thumper, the largest and most powerful ones ever built. In fact, the Four Horsemen as they were called, were the longest-range projectile weapons ever devised by man. The Vatican had commissioned them in secret decades ago from the grav plate factory on Ganymede with technical assistance from the university. They, along with Svallin's Mantle, had laid in wait until called upon.

Elias could only see two of the towers from their current position, but he could see their tops open up, and long barrels extend from their depths. Once deployed, the barrels slowly tracked an unseen target far above.

Elias whispered another prayer for good measure.

Thumper fire began to pepper the protective field. Matthew didn't know how much longer it would last. He imagined that the golden flicker was already losing its strength. Any second now, one would pierce through. When that happened, Matthew would drop the barge and engage them head-on.

"SPW 5840, this is Vatican Tower Control. Do not alter your course in any way. We wouldn't want you to get caught in the crossfire."

Matthew frowned at the speaker. "Acknowledged, Vatican. Mind telling me what's about to happen?"

"Enjoy the show."

"What was that about?" Grace asked.

"I don't know. Keep the scopes on the hostiles."

Matthew saw it with his naked eye. From the surface, a massive distortion moved at unbelievable speed. It seemed to slice all of space apart as it tore through the first of the ships. As the blast passed near them, Matthew could feel the pull of its immense gravity, like a sudden drop that made your stomach turn. It was gone in an instant. He looked back to the scopes and couldn't even spot a debris field from the first ship.

"Whoa," Grace said, jaw-dropping. "What was that?"

"Your guess is as good as mine. I think that was a thumper, but I've never heard of anything remotely on that scale before. Look. There it is again."

The second shot streaked through their vision. The space-time bubble annihilated the second cartel ship in the blink of an eye. This time Matthew had a better look at it. It wasn't just one shot. It was several fired in unison all converging at a single point.

The final cartel ship had turned to flee, but its fate was sealed as the guns of the Vatican turned it into space dust with a final reality-warping barrage. Grace squealed in delight.

Matthew took his hat off and laid it on the console. His hand shook a little as his adrenaline crashed. He took a deep breath. If Yvonne was to be believed, landing this thing was going to be quite the trick. He wasn't even going to have the benefit of landing it on disabled grav plates like she had on Europa. Maybe he could call ahead and have them work something out with local gravity. He took a deep breath and set them on a course for the Vatican.

The comm crackled to life. "SPW 5840, you have clear skies and authorization to land. Welcome home."

By the time the Sparrow landed at the Vatican, Davey's condition had begun to stabilize. Abigail looked at the kid in pity and shook her head. Fortunately, he hadn't been hit by any gunfire. Humans don't survive getting hit by thirty-millimeter cannon rounds. Instead, he'd been pierced by shrapnel and glass, then exposed to rapid depressurization and hard vacuum. But the human body can be remarkably resilient. He was lucky to be alive at all, that was for sure. It also helped that Yvonne had years of experience in treating trauma injuries.

Davey was going to need a lot more care, but the hospital in the Vatican would be far more equipped than the Sparrow was for that sort of thing. Which meant they would probably be staying for a while. They allowed Grace back into the room, and she wouldn't leave his side even when the paramedics arrived. She and Yvonne followed them to the hospital.

Sometime later, when the barge had been released and the Sparrow landed more properly beside it, the ship was quiet for the first time in what felt like days. Abigail tried to clean up the blood that had inevitably ended up all over Davey's room, but it was going to take some time.

Matthew finally emerged from the cockpit and walked past her.
"Where are you going?"

He motioned toward the ladder. "Topside. Care to join me?"

When she climbed out of the hatch, he already sat on an outcropping of the hull. It was night on Ganymede, and the city was illuminated with golden lights. It gave the place a warm and welcoming feel.

Abigail joined him, and without thinking, opened her suit and crawled out of it. She silently accepted the hand Matthew offered to her and sat beside him. She always felt so small when she was out of her armor, but then maybe that was the truth of it. It was a big solar system, and there were a lot of people out there. She wasn't really all that big in the grand scheme of things.

Not even when weighed against the lives of those they'd saved. They'd all decided to risk everything, and Davey had very nearly given his life for them.

Matthew was uncharacteristically quiet. He was never much of a talker, but then, unless he had a book in his hand, he wasn't going to ignore you either.

She decided to break the ice. "Nice view up here."

He nodded once. "Peaceful after all the chaos." He pulled something out from under his poncho.

Abigail frowned. "What's that?"

"A piece of a miracle. The Anemoi. Whitaker gave it to me."

"Are we calling him that again?" she asked. "I seem to remember you saying that wasn't his name."

"If he thinks I'm going to call him The Unchained Man or some other nonsense in a serious conversation, he's kidding himself. Whitaker will do until someone wrings his real name out of him."

He gave her the highpoints of his bizarre conversation with Whitaker, and they sat in silence for several minutes as she processed it all.

"Funny thing is, it makes sense from a certain perspective."

He didn't look too happy at that. "We're not playing his game, Abigail."

"Why not? We've apparently been playing it for months. Better a willing participant than a dupe. Besides." She elbowed him in the side, and he frowned at her. "How are we going to avoid him?"

"We'll instruct Benny not to accept jobs from him."

"Then he'll just adopt a new persona or form a new shell company and hire us anyway." She reached over and took the Anemoi from his hands. "You said this was the Eurus, the East Wind? Tell me about it."

He frowned in the dim light. "I had to read up on the Greek god. There aren't many mentions of him. But the wind itself in literature is often a harbinger of change." His hesitated for a moment. "And sometimes destruction."

She traced a finger along the round outer edge of the miracle. "And what if it does lead to Moses?"

"He's gone, Abigail."

"It leads to something then. It's a compass. If Whitaker is so intent on finding whatever this is, maybe it would be better if we were there with him. I don't think we want lost technology falling into his hands."

Matthew grunted and leaned back. "You may have a point there, I guess. We'll keep our eyes open. Ask around. Maybe if we find the other pieces, we'll at least have some leverage over him."

The conversation drifted away into the cool Ganymede night. Overhead Jupiter stood its eternal vigil, casting light upon the millions of people that took shelter on its moons. Here on Ganymede were a few thousand newly freed souls. In the shadow of Europa waited nearly a million more.

For now, they were beyond the help of the Sparrow.

It was for that reason alone that Abigail decided they would hunt for the Anemoi. If there was a chance it could change the fortunes of mankind, it would be worth it. The people of Europa were waiting, and, without a change of fate, they would never be free.

Matthew would come around to her point of view. He always came around when people needed him. It was what drew them to him. What drew her to him. And Whitaker was right. Matthew had a marvelous knack for doing the impossible. Abigail's job was making sure he didn't get himself killed in the process.

"So what will happen to the refugees?" she asked.

Matthew scratched his stubble. "Well, some may have homes to go back to elsewhere in the solar system. Others, especially the original citizen of Villa María, won't be so lucky."

She turned to him. "I know that tone of voice. You've got an idea."

His eyes flicked to her and then back to the city in front of them. "The beginning of one. If Whitaker wants me to be the East Wind, I'm going to have to start somewhere."

She looked at him expectantly when he didn't continue. "You can't just leave me hanging."

He laughed. "Fine. Here's what I was thinking..."

As he told her, she felt a smile begin to creep across her face.

It was just a beginning. And it would take a long time to build up the inertia to really change things. But it was the start of something new.

The first new thing that had happened in the solar system in a long time.

Epilogue

The Battle of Villa María was not without consequence. In the end, nearly eight hundred of Villa María's refugees had nowhere to go. Three hundred of these were from the original town, before the cartel's invasion. At long last, they were reunited with my student, the Padre that had fought for them for so long before ultimately losing the fight against an enemy he could never defeat.

Yet in their emancipation, he continued his fight, though his days of being their priest had passed. It took him several weeks to get the Vatican, the University of Ganymede, and several of the moon's key industries on board with his vision. I believe he even had to give his 'we're all in the same ship' speech on more than one occasion.

Ultimately, they caught his idea for something new and different.

There, on the icy plains of Ganymede, between the University and Church, a new colony was founded, the first since Moses' departure. No mere mining settlement or outpost, this was a place where people would live their lives with their families in peace. It was built with expansion in mind, a place for the weary and downtrodden, the lost, and the emancipated. The colony was christened Antioch, for like its namesake, it was harbored between two ancient ideas, Athens and Jerusalem, Reason and Virtue. The two halves of civilization.

Antioch will be a farming colony, and though it will never produce enough food to replace Europa, it is a start. As it grows, it will relieve some measure of our reliance on the produce of the Slaver's Moon. In ten years it may provide enough food for Vatican city, in twenty, enough for Galileo. In half a century who can tell?

The expertise of the university was required to make this grand idea work. Unlike the oceans of Europa, Ganymede's mantle is ice, hard and unyielding as granite. New technologies were needed to melt, desalinate, and transport the sheer amount of water required for irrigating fields.

The greatest hurdle was the number of grav plates required for a new colony. Ultimately, they decided to only alter the gravity of the town itself. The fields would remain at Ganymede's natural gravity. Moses had already engineered certain crops to grow in the microgravity of hydroponic stations in orbit. A bit of clever crossbreeding was all it took to produce new cultivars that could grow on Ganymede, though new techniques will still be needed for the farmers to tend their fields safely. If this can be done, then perhaps more farming colonies may be founded, further weakening the power of the cartels.

The Vatican supplied two things. Funding and soil. The former was given gladly, and the latter in silence. The Holy See makes no official comment as to how it acquired the hundreds of millions of tons necessary for an agricultural colony.

Six months after the liberation of Villa María, the refugees moved into Antioch. Full ownership of the land and equipment was transferred to them and they set to work tilling the soil and living their lives as free men and women.

The crew of the Sparrow remained close to Antioch during this time, only venturing away for short trips, usually on behalf of either the University or Church. The boy, Davey, was forced to stay in the hospital for many weeks, and his sister and the doctor hardly left his side. I've seen less devotion in many biological families. Sadly, his injuries were not without consequence. One of his lungs had been badly damaged and will have a somewhat reduced capacity, but he lives, something for which we are all thankful.

I suppose I should make a note of my own fate. Though I had but a small part in those great deeds, others may find interest in the details. I was demoted from my high position within the Vatican for my theft of Svallin's Mantle, despite its safe return to the vaults. The seminary I had led for two decades was taken from me and I was instated as the Bishop of Antioch. I have no regrets. One who breaks a rule for a greater good must accept the consequences that come from such disobedience. I will gladly serve as the shepherd of Mathew's flock until the end of my days.

Abigail and Matthew quietly reached out to their contacts, hoping someone had information on the Anemoi. The Church was unable to assist, for though we were aware of Josiah Carver's mention of this eleventh miracle, we had no further information on it. They were disappointed, but then they never expected it to be that easy.

But my student, my protege Matthew, he is a new man. He has made peace with the past and can look to the future, unburdened by Villa María. In place of his failures stands a new colony. Like the stones that Joshua set up in remembrance of God's deliverance, so may Antioch be for Matthew. For myself, I wonder if God did not use his trials to hone him into a blade, a rapier that would cut to the heart of things.

But these are just the ramblings of an old bishop, bragging on one of whom he is proud. I will admit that I am perhaps not the most reliable of narrators when it comes to Matthew. Allow an old man a few liberties.

But the freelancer's story has not yet finished. Now that Antioch is established, I imagine the wanderlust will set back in. The Sparrow will head for darker worlds. The Solar System is a dangerous place, and it still has need of men like Matthew Cole.

It always has, and it always will.

Elias of Callisto
Bishop of Antioch, Ganymede
Died 105 AM

Afterword

Thank you so much for reading *After Moses*!

Matthew Cole and the crew of the Sparrow will return in the sequel, *After Moses: Prodigal*. For news and updates on its progress, you can head over to my website, www.Michaelfkane.com. If you subscribe to my mailing list, you'll be the first to know about new releases. Don't worry. I won't ever share your email address with anyone else.

Did you enjoy *After Moses*?

Consider leaving a review at the storefront you purchased it from.

Thanks again and I hope to see you in *After Moses: Prodigal!*

Author Bio

Michael F. Kane cut his teeth on science fiction and fantasy. In fact, his first memories of Star Wars are his mother covering his eyes during the rancor scene. Later, he fell in love with the classics, Tolkien, Asimov, Herbert, and more. Somehow, despite the odds being stacked against him, he grew up to be a somewhat respectable human being. By day he's the music director at a mid-sized church, but at night he dreams of unseen lands and places man has never trod. Check out his website at www.Michaelfkane.com to stay up to date on his publishing adventures.

Made in the USA
Coppell, TX
25 November 2020